THE ETERNAL QUEEN

The Chronicle of Maud - Volume III

Amy Mantravadi

ISBN: 978-0-9994325-2-5 (paperback)

PRIMARY CHARACTERS

The Party of the Empress

- Empress Mathilda, countess of Anjou, chosen heir of King Henry I
- Geoffrey, count of Anjou, the empress' husband, chief captain in Normandy
- Robert of Gloucester, earl of Gloucester, half-brother of the empress, chief captain in England
- Brian fitz Count, lord of Wallingford
- Miles of Gloucester, castellan of Gloucester, later earl of Hereford
- Reginald de Dunstanville, earl of Cornwall, half-brother of the empress
- Baldwin de Redvers, earl of Devon
- Mathilda D'Oyly, wife of Brian fitz Count, lady of Wallingford
- Drogo, chief knight in the empress' household
- Adela, lady-in-waiting to the empress
- Philip of Honfleur, knight in Earl Robert's household
- Henry, eldest son of the empress
- Geoffrey, middle son of the empress
- William, youngest son of the empress

- Adeliza of Louvain, lady of Arundel, former queen of England
- Mabel, wife of Earl Robert, countess of Gloucester

The Party of the Usurper

- Stephen of Blois, king of England, count of Mortain
- Mathilda of Boulogne, queen of England, countess of Boulogne
- William of Ypres, leader of the Flemish mercenaries
- Waleran Beaumont, earl of Meulan
- Geoffrey de Mandeville, earl of Essex
- Henry of Blois, bishop of Winchester, papal legate, brother of the king

Others

- Grimbald, former royal physician
- Theobald, archbishop of Canterbury

NORMANDY

Dover

Canterbury

Rochester

London

Thames

St Albans

Westminster

Ely

Windsor

Arundel

Lincoln

Nottingham

Trent

Oxford

Wallingford

Winchester

Warwick

ENGLAND

Cirencester

Ludgershall

Itchen

Gloucester

Malmesbury

Devizes

Salisbury

Test

Worcester

Avon

Wilton

Avon

Hereford

Wye

Severn

Bristol

Wareham

WALES

Exeter

For Thomas Jaideep
Rise to eternity.

"The sorrow that I have, by right is yours;
And all the pleasures you usurp are mine."

William Shakespeare, <u>Richard III</u>

I

The afternoon sun was low in the sky and the fishers were setting out from the small village of Hanton to fill their nets with the sea's harvest. It must have seemed to them a day like any other. While much of England had descended into war, this town upon the southern shore had played no role in that disturbance, though it rested in the shadow of the great castle of Arundel. How could they have foreseen that when they returned, it would be in the company of ships whose landing would alter the course of history?

Poor men! They could not have known what was about to befall them, and as such, we dearly hoped they had not set a watch, for our arrival was to remain secret as long as possible. We were come to England to make an end of the usurper's rebellion—to see justice done and restore the inheritance of my sons, the very boys whom I had kissed on their brows not long before. The warmth of their skin seemed to linger on my lips, but it would fade with each new day, and I feared that ere I saw them again there would be no warmth left in my world.

I stood upon the bow of our chief vessel, my gaze still cast toward the north, longing for the shore. I could hear the great sail flapping in the wind, even as the hull cut through the waves as a knife through butter, and all about the gulls were calling to one another. The smell of the sea, unlike anything else on earth, lingered in the air: to draw in that odor was to see the white cliffs rising and feel the call of home. Leaning upon the rail beside me was the faithful knight who had been by my side through every danger. I needed him then more than ever.

"There is a darkness over the land now, Drogo," I said. "The reign of error has brought it low."

"The reign of error will soon be at an end. Stephen of Blois is a false king and has shown himself as such. These fools are bound to destroy themselves. It has already begun," he boldly replied.

I could not help but laugh. "You sing the same tune as brother Robert. Oh, how I wish I had your confidence! The very earth seems to groan beneath the weight of this absurdity. What must the common man think?"

"The common man cares not for the travails of those so far above him. He desires naught but warm sun, hard rain, a merciful priest, and a sense of pride."

I turned to look him in his dark eyes, which reflected the light of the sun. "Do I not also desire those things?"

A sudden noise interrupted us: the voice of my brother, Earl Robert of Gloucester, chief captain of our forces.

"Less than an hour now, and we will be within sight of the coast!" Robert called as he bounded across the deck. "Have your wits about you, men! We must deliver the empress and escape under cover of night!"

When he had finished, Drogo leaned in closer and appealed to me, "Have faith, my lady! The usurper will soon feel the swift hand of judgment."

"Yes, but whose judgment? The Lord has seen fit to let Stephen rule. Are we to put them all to the sword—to cover the land with blood? Will that cure England's disease?"

He shook his head. "England cannot be cured until the rule of law is upheld—until the rightful heir sits upon the throne."

We stood for a moment without speaking. In the distance, a flock of dolphins passed by, making for the warmer waters of the south. Magnificent creatures! Yet even such beauty could not still the tremors of my soul.

"The false king surrounds himself with men of poor judgment," I whispered. "He makes a mockery of our traditions. Not even the Church is sacred to him."

"The false king shall meet his end at our hands," Robert said, as I turned to see that he had snuck up behind us. "All our devices are drawn up against him. We cannot fail."

"He will meet his end when God declares it," I argued.

"Then let us hope that day is soon!" Drogo concluded, forcing a smile.

"Yes," I agreed, "and that we do not perish in the attempt! I fear for my boys if they are left with Count Geoffrey. Oh, how I miss them already! I return to England with empty arms! At least Adela is there to watch over them."

"You place great faith in that woman," Robert said with a smile. "I admit I thought it a bit odd when you told me you had one of common blood so close to your person, but she does seem to be made of something strong. Perhaps she had some noble forbears lost to history."

"Mmm ..." I grunted, not truly paying attention. My thoughts still belonged to my three young sons, especially the two I had just left. I saw their faces like twin angels sleeping side by side, the bed beneath them a cloud of heaven. *Blow now, wind!* I prayed. *Speed my angels back to me and me to my angels.*

Another few minutes passed in which we were all deep in contemplation. Strange as it may seem, I began thinking of those lectures with Archbishop Bruno in the monastery of Trier, the tutor of my youth. I was transported back to that small stone chamber, him seated on one side of his great wood desk and I on the other, the writings of Caesar laid open before me, dimly lit in the dark of eve. I might have been ten years old.

"Archbishop, it is getting late," I moaned, rubbing my eyes. "Can we not be done for the day?"

"Ten more minutes and then we shall sup. Now, translate that sentence."

I let out a loud groan. "Oh, why must it always be Latin, sir?! I much prefer the speech of the Germans."

"Read!" Bruno ordered, signifying the chosen text with a determined poke of the finger.

Lucky Romans to be dead and spared from this! I thought, but decided it was best not to speak the words. Archbishop Bruno was more apt to forgive than my first tutor—Master Godfrey— had been, but it seemed unwise to test the limits of his patience.

"Very well," I said, then began to read. "'He himself reached Britain with the first squadron of ships, about the fourth hour of the day, and there saw the forces of the enemy drawn up in arms on all the hills. The nature of the place was this: the sea was confined by mountains so close to it that a dart could be thrown from their summit upon the shore.'[1] Oh, he must have been near Dover! The cliffs are ever so large there."

"Continuing ..." the archbishop said firmly, rising to his feet and beginning to pace around the desk with his hands folded behind his back. I remember that along with the great golden cross he wore over his black and red robes, he would always

---

[1] Caesar, Julius. *The Gallic Wars*, Translated by W.A. McDevitte and W.S. Bohn, 4.23. http://classics.mit.edu/Caesar/gallic.html. Accessed June 4, 2021.

carry several keys on his belt that would clink with each step taken by his fine leather shoes, a gift from the Doge of Venice.

"Yes, forgive me," I said, my eyes returning to the parchment. "Ah, look here! 'Our ships, on account of their great size, could be stationed only in deep water; and our soldiers, in places unknown to them, with their hands embarrassed, oppressed with a large and heavy weight of armor, had at the same time to leap from the ships, stand amid the waves, and encounter the enemy; whereas they, either on dry ground, or advancing a little way into the water, free in all their limbs in places thoroughly known to them, could confidently throw their weapons and spur on their horses, which were accustomed to this kind of service.'"[2]

"Excellent!" he declared, clapping his hands and causing the keys to clink all the louder. "We will make a scholar of you yet, though I did note one or two small errors."

"I know what happened to the Romans," I said, hoping to avoid his reproof.

"What do you mean?"

I turned in my chair to face him better. "That is, I know why they had trouble fighting. The shore in that part of Britain: it is not made of sand, but rocks. That is why they could not gain their footing. The natives must have been accustomed to it. You see, in England the land itself rises up to fight the enemy!"

"Very good!" he said with a laugh. "Though your grandfather William was able to conquer it." Here he took a seat beside me on the desk.

"He had God on his side and the cause of right!" I declared. My beliefs were firmer in those days.

"Yet the Romans were pagans, and they conquered the island as well. What say you to that?"

---

2   Caesar, 4.24.

I had not considered this piece of information. Like all young ladies of the royal class, I had been raised to believe that kings were appointed by God and the Almighty granted victory to those who were most righteous. Archbishop Bruno did enjoy poking holes in my childhood beliefs: he was a sly one that way. I had no idea how to answer him, so I told him what I suspected he wished to hear.

"I am not sure, my lord bishop, but I am certain you will tell me what I ought to believe."

"Never let someone tell you what to believe, unless it be the Holy Church!" he declared, his brow wrinkled in concern. "You must search out the truth for yourself. Here, give it to me. I think I know the page."

He lifted the volume, flipped through the brown leaves, and quickly found what he was seeking. "I have it! 'The immortal gods are wont to allow those persons whom they wish to punish for their guilt some times a greater prosperity and longer impunity, in order that they may suffer the more severely from a reverse of circumstances.'[3] Even so, does the Almighty work upon unrighteous men, for though they may be raised up, he brings them crashing back to earth. Their end is most assured. Remember that, young empress!"

"Look, my lady!"

This last voice was not that of Bruno, but rather Drogo, who called me back from my memories to the present time. He was pointing forward to a gray line that had appeared at the meeting of sea and sky.

"Land at last! Soon we shall enjoy the hospitality of the former queen."

"I dare say she is not ready for our arrival," I replied, looking out into the distance. "It may come as quite a surprise."

---

3   Caesar, 1.14.

"Let's hope she is not the only one who is surprised," Drogo concluded with a wink.

We made for the mouth of the River Arun even as the sun was setting. The fishers were returning to the village of Hanton and saw the odd ships filled with a rather more martial company, but we held ourselves with such confidence that they raised not a word of protest. As we moved up river and the forest closed in on either side, there was no sound but that of the birds. All was still, and it was hard to believe that we should be delivered so easily. Then there was a noise amid the trees, and I whipped my head around to see that some of the low brush had been disturbed.

"What was that, Robert?" I cried, the fear quickly building inside me. "Did you see?"

"Probably just a deer," he replied.

"No, it was a man!" one of the knights declared from across the deck. "He saw us and ran off into the forest."

We all turned to look at the knight, whose name I knew to be Philip. He belonged to the household of my brother, Earl Robert. I had met him in Caen shortly before our departure but spoken with him only a little.

"Are you certain?" Robert asked Philip, walking toward him.

"I'd swear it by the Virgin Mary," he declared solemnly, crossing himself.

"We have been sighted then," I concluded. "Stephen must have spared one man to keep a watch here just in case."

"It could be one of Adeliza's men, keeping watch for the same reason, but to a better purpose," said Drogo.

"Either way, if it is only one man, we have little to fear," Robert assured me, walking over and placing a hand on my shoulder. "Besides Arundel, the nearest castle is in Chichester, which is ten miles away. That should give us enough time."

I prayed to God that he was right, for if by ill chance Stephen was traversing that part of the country with his army, we would fall into his hands or simply be fallen. Earl Robert was a man among men, his skill in battle not to be matched, and his knights were as fierce as any that walked the earth, but only Hercules or perhaps Samson could have taken down ten men at once. It was at most three miles before we came to Arundel Castle, but it might as well have been three hundred. I would feel no peace until I sat within that fortress.

The rest of the journey passed with no sign of danger. As we arrived, we saw the stone keep sitting high upon the motte. What a fine construction! It was a proper castle with thick walls, buttressed on every side and ready for battle, with a few buildings below it closer to the river bank. In those days, Arundel Castle had few equals in England, though the masons have lately made great advances. We laid anchor and I set foot upon that most sacred shore: the very rocks of England! I bent down and took some of those gray pebbles in hand, as if by doing so I could gain possession of the isle.

"This is my home, the land of my birth," I said. "I know you will not let me fall as you did the ancient Romans."

"Enough idle talk!" Robert called. "We must get you safe within the keep. Stephen's men could be here soon, and we are losing the light."

He did not need to tell me twice. We mounted the few horses that had made the journey over the Channel, leaving the lesser men to climb the hill on foot. My brother's wife, Lady Mabel, had been on one of the other ships, but was able to join me at this point. The two of us rode behind Earl Robert up the winding path through the trees. I was still looking this way and that every time I heard a twig snap.

When we came to the gate, we were about to knock or at the very least cry out, when it suddenly opened before us. For the space of a few breaths, I was afraid that we had been led into a trap and Stephen's men had already seized the castle. I imagined arrows flying at me and the cries of men ready to charge. But it was not to be: Lady Adeliza was standing there to welcome us, along with all the members of her household. She was a vision of beauty in a green silk gown, her white veil blowing slightly in the wind. For their part, the servants looked very clean and their clothes showed few signs of wear. The war had clearly had no effect on Arundel. I sighed in great relief as Robert reached up and helped me alight.

"Empress Mathilda! Earl Robert! And Lady Mabel as well!" Lady Adeliza called, moving to embrace each of us in turn. "I knew it must be you when we saw the boats below!"

So, you did not learn of our coming from that messenger, I thought. *That bodes ill.*

"Queen Adeliza!" I said, using her old title, for she had been the second wife of my late father. "This is a kindness beyond words. I fear we have brought trouble upon your threshold."

She reached up to hold my face in her hands, for she was several inches shorter than me. "Oh, my dear! Trouble was already upon my threshold, and it will be as long as England remains in this state of disorder. The days are evil, but we women are strong! That is what you taught me, and I have endeavored to live by it. Now, who have you brought with you?"

"Some hundred and forty knights, including the empress' man, Drogo," Robert replied, pointing to the knight in question.

"Sir Drogo!" Adeliza cried, as he walked up to join us. "I scarcely recognized you behind that beard, but I might have known you by your height."

"I've been letting it grow out just for you, my lady. What do you think?" he asked, stroking it in a rather vain manner.

"Oh, yes. Very nice indeed," she replied, laughing.

"Honestly, Drogo, quit your jests," I scolded, though I could not help smiling as well. "As if she did not have enough things to put up with already!"

"I am not offended. Here, let us shut the gate behind you and move into the yard," Adeliza concluded, beckoning with her hand.

We did as she requested, leaving the rest of the knights to gain their entrance one by one, then resumed our conversation.

"Is Lord William at home?" I asked softly, meaning William d'Aubigny, the lord of Arundel.

"My husband is with the king, laying siege to Corfe Castle and Lord Baldwin last I heard," she answered, her tone more serious.

"Does he know that you welcomed us here?"

"I did not see why I should trouble him with such information."

"You are likely to bring great trouble upon your marriage," I said with some concern.

"Let me worry about that. Just tell me, how long do you intend to stay here?"

"I will depart as soon as I can gain fresh horses," Robert replied.

"You are welcome to anything we have," said Adeliza, pointing in the direction of a few out buildings from which the whining of beasts could be heard. "Is your goal to march on London?"

Robert directed Drogo toward the stables, then continued. "Yes, but I must first join forces with my men in the West. They are gathering in Bristol, and I have it on good authority that Miles of Gloucester has had enough of the false king and will march beside us. We also have Lord Brian of Wallingford on our side. I hope to meet with him soon enough. Yet if you permit it, my lady, I would have the empress stay here for the present. There is no need to place her in greater danger upon the road when we intend to come back in this direction."

"Very well. Off you go!" she declared. "We have a room made ready for you, Empress Mathilda. If you just follow me …"

"Wait! I must speak with my brother before he leaves," I pleaded.

"Of course, I will just accompany Lady Mabel," she replied, then left the two of us alone.

Robert moved closer to me, his arms folded. When I was certain that no one could hear us, I whispered, "You will do what we discussed, then? You will meet with Bishop Henry?" Here I referred to the man who was both bishop of Winchester and abbot of Glastonbury—the brother of the usurper who had invited me in secret to restore justice to England.

"Yes, provided that he honors his promise. I have to pass near Winchester in any case," Earl Robert told me.

"Then I must warn you, brother: that man is out for his own gain and not ours. You must never feel at ease with him. Be on your guard!"

"I will be. Have no fear!"

He said this as if it were a mere trifle, but I could not still my heart.

"If I lose you, then our cause is well-nigh dead," I said, grabbing his arm lightly. "I am well-nigh dead."

"You are not going to lose me. I give you my word."

The sky was growing dark, but I could still make out his face. There I saw the scars of many battles, soon to be joined by new ones. What would the people I loved have to sacrifice, and what indeed would I have to sacrifice, to ensure that my sons inherited England's throne? I shuddered to think of it. Already I could see great mounds of the dead. Already I mourned the passing of much that was good. I reached out and held my brother fast, as if by doing so I might place some charm upon him to safeguard his person.

"Is there anything you wish me to tell Lord Brian?" he asked.

I pulled back, and sure enough there was a rather mischievous look in his eye, as of a man who knew too much.

"You may tell him that I value his loyalty and will reward him as soon as I am able," I responded.

"Oh, lucky man!" he jested.

"You know perfectly well what I mean!" I protested, but alas, my brother was already making his way to the stables.

Yes, Lord Brian. The man I had once loved before either of us was married, and he had returned that love. Alas, I still loved him, but we were both tied by the bonds of wedlock. I had thought for a time that he betrayed me, but then I learned the truth: he never abandoned me. He had been true all along. It was my father who had forced us to part and left us in such a terrible state. I longed to see Brian, but what would I say? What could one say in such a situation? I tried to push these thoughts out of my mind, for they always drove me to guilt and pain.

I glanced up at the stars that were beginning to appear. Somewhere far off, those very stars looked down upon my sons. Somewhere nearer, they looked down upon the man who had made my life a living hell: the man who had stolen the crown of England for himself. Beyond those stars, the Lord of Heaven sat in judgment upon us all. It was to him that I prayed.

"Let the reign of error end. Let the children sing again. Let the pestilence be done. Let the battle now be won."

Having ensured the safety of both myself and his wife, Earl Robert of Gloucester left under cover of darkness and began his ride to the north. Wallingford was his aim and then the town of Bristol, but there were so many dangers along the way that his path seemed less than certain. I begged him to take more of our knights, but he would be content with only a dozen. "You have more need of them than me, for your presence here can no longer be secret," he declared. So it was that we sent him out among the wolves, there to meet his doom.

Now, the best rider in the kingdom would have taken two days to reach Stephen's position, which we guessed to be at least a hundred miles away. A large company travels none so fast. Therefore, more than a week passed before we received any visitors. How strange were those hours of waiting, and how desperate was my desire for news! There was little with which to distract myself, for those of Adeliza's household preferred not to speak with me, afraid they too might be seen as traitors, and as the lady of the castle was no great reader, I did not even have that consolation for my soul. Thus, I spent most of my time with either Lady Mabel or Drogo. I missed dearly the conversation of my maid and good friend Adela, who remained across the Channel with the princes, though I was glad at least that my sons were in her care.

I have often felt that when some stroke of doom is to fall, I would prefer it sooner rather than later, the better to suffer through and have done with it. Yet when the usurper finally did arrive, I was forced to question my choices, for the phantom of death was drawn up before me, and I found not for the first time that my desire for life was strong.

I remember it was a clear morning and I was lying on my bed in the small chamber that had been assigned to me. Adeliza had offered her own room, which was far grander, but I would not throw her out of her bed in addition to everything else. The chamber I ended up choosing had a window that faced west, allowing me to view bits of the road that were not hidden by the trees. It was there that Stephen made his approach on that autumn morn. I had been leaning back on the feather pillows upon the tall, four post bed, reading Boethius's

Consolations for the fourth or fifth time in my life, when I heard shouts from the guards upon the wall.

I raced over to the window and looked out past the castle wall to the opening in the trees, where I could see a host approaching. They must have been a thousand strong and armed, as they say, to the teeth. There were knights on horseback, a few men carrying large axes, and scores of archers, with carts full of more weapons coming up behind them. The cover of the trees had hidden their arrival until the last moment. Here and there beneath those branches, I could see them making ready to besiege us, yet I noted the absence of ladders, towers, or trebuchets, so it seemed they would make no attempt to break through the walls: if anything, they would hope to starve us out.

This is the hour. He is here. Lord, grant me strength, I prayed.

There was a knock at the door, and for a brief moment I imagined that it was the usurper himself, come to perform some bloody deed. But that was foolish, surely: he was still outside the walls. I took a deep breath to calm myself. When I walked over and opened it, I found Lady Adeliza standing there. Her eyes were wide, her hands were clenched at her sides, and she was biting her lower lip.

"Queen Adeliza," I said, "please come in."

I stepped back and she entered the room quickly, the skirt of her robe trailing behind her. I shut the door and leaned back against it, waiting to hear her words. Whatever she was about to tell me was likely to be of the utmost import. I took another deep breath as her lips parted.

"Stephen has spoken with my men at the gate," she said meekly. "He wishes to come in and speak with me that we might arrive at some agreement. Should I admit him?"

What a question! On the one hand, it seemed foolish to grant such a request: almost as foolish as the Trojans accepting that odd present from the Greeks. Yet I could see the fear in Adeliza's eyes, and she had already sacrificed a great deal on my behalf. If there was any chance that we might avoid the shedding of blood, it was to be preferred. Before I could reply, there was a knock on the door just behind me, pounding me in the back.

"Please excuse me …" I said to Adeliza, raising a finger.

I spun around and opened the door again. This time, it was Drogo waiting to speak with me, along with Philip de Honfleur, one of the young knights left behind by my brother.

"Sir Drogo! Sir Philip!" I cried. "Please, come in at once!"

I stepped back and allowed them both to enter, the younger and shorter Philip trailing behind. Even in that urgent moment, I observed that they could hardly have been less alike. Drogo was wearing quite a beard in those days, the usual remedy for men with less hair on their heads. Combined with the growing wrinkles on his face and the gray in what remained of his hair, he appeared somewhat worn but fierce. Philip, on the other hand, had long and perfectly raven locks, while his face was free of hair and his features aligned so perfectly that I could not help but suspect he must attract the attention of every young woman in whatever county he set foot. He also had twenty years of youth on his superior.

I noted all of this in the space of a breath and turned my inquiry to Drogo. The idea of letting the usurper within the castle walls caused the fear to rise within me and protest his admission. Yet seeing him face to face would give me the chance to do something I had long desired: set him in his place. Might he slit my throat in the process? Truly, it was a difficult decision, and I craved Drogo's advice.

"I have just been speaking with Lady Adeliza," I told him. "Counsel me: should we grant Stephen a hostage and allow him to enter with one or two fellows?"

Drogo nodded. "I think so, my lady. The rules of warfare require that he treats you with civility."

"The rules of warfare are often broken," I argued, attempting not to scoff in Adeliza's presence.

"Yes, but consider his position, which is very weak. He knows that any harm he does to you is likely to inflame the rebellion. We should stall for time."

"Time for what?"

He tipped his head slightly to the side and wrinkled his brow, as if my question made no sense. "For Earl Robert to arrive with an army."

"Drogo, Stephen will cut down the whole forest and raise towers before Earl Robert returns!" I cried, my efforts to remain calm failing miserably.

"With all due respect, my lady, you cannot know that," he said quietly, no doubt attempting to keep my anger in check.

I had a few choice words I wished to throw at him, but I endeavored to keep my mind on the enemy at the gate. That was the true source of my discontent.

"What say you?" I asked Adeliza, looking back at her. "This castle is yours. Are you content to admit delegates?"

"With all my heart, yes!" she replied. "King Stephen is a man of reason. I am certain we can work something out."

I doubted very much her assertion that my cousin was a man of reason, but nevertheless, I said, "Then all that is left is to decide on a hostage. He will want someone of great import, but neither I nor you can go outside the walls."

"I will go!" a voice called, and I saw that it was Lady Mabel, walking through the door the knights had left open, through which she must have heard the latter part of our conversation. The lady of Gloucester was clothed in a gown the color of wine and a silk veil held in place by a gold fillet, looking more fit for a Christmas feast than a war.

I was loath to permit her to offer herself as a hostage without the consent of Earl Robert, for she was his wife. I therefore told her, "I fear I cannot allow you to take that chance."

"Please! I have seen far worse than this," she argued, taking hold of my arm. "I know we are not familiar, Empress Mathilda, but I assure you I am made of flint. I do not fear them, and were Earl Robert here, he would advise the same thing."

Her grip on my arm was so firm that I did not doubt her claim to be made of flint. I glanced at the faces of the other persons in the room. Lady Adeliza looked very afraid indeed, her hands pressed together and her breath quick and shallow. Drogo's gaze was firm and his arms crossed: he was ready to take on the world as ever, and wanted me to get out of the way. Then there was young Philip, who had remained mute throughout this deliberation, standing at attention with his hands behind his back.

"What say you, Sir Philip?" I asked. "You are new here, but I might as well have your opinion."

This clearly took him by surprise. For a moment, his mouth hung open slightly as he grasped for the right words. "Far be it from me to stand against three such lofty ladies, not to mention the captain of the guard," he answered.

I nodded. "Very wise. It's settled, then. God be with you, Lady Mabel, and with us all!" I concluded, touching both Mabel and Adeliza on the shoulders to comfort them. I then looked at my brother's wife quite directly and said, "If anyone so much as lays a finger on you while you are over there, I will make him rue the day he was born!"

So, we gave Lady Mabel into the hands of the enemy that we might welcome the beast into the fold: a fearful choice if ever there was one, but my brother's wife was one of those women who makes one proud to be a woman, for she had within her the strength of ten men while still maintaining the gentility that is so valued in our sex.

When we received word that the exchange was complete and the usurper and his men had made their way through the castle gate, I followed Adeliza down the narrow, winding stair, with Drogo directly behind me—so close that I had to scold him for stepping on the hem of my gown. As we reached the bottom and Adeliza placed her tiny hand on the great iron handle of the door, she turned back to face us.

"There is really no need for either of you to accompany me. It will only make matters worse."

I was taken aback by her words. "But my dear lady, he has come here for me and me alone. It is my crown that he has stolen. Surely you did not imagine that I would cower in a corner rather than facing my enemy? I have several choice words I wish to throw his way!"

"But think of the danger to your person, empress!" she pleaded. "Truly, it is better that I speak to him alone and reason with him."

If he had any regard for reason, this affair would have been over long ago, I seethed, but I glanced over and saw the look in Drogo's eye as he shook his head softly from side to side.

"What?!" I spat. "You have something to say?"

Perhaps I imagined it, but I believe he stepped back a few inches before replying.

"Only that Lady Adeliza has shown us great loyalty and kindness thus far in offering her home as a refuge, and it seems proper that we should follow her counsel in this. She has only your best interests in mind."

I scowled at him for daring to question my judgment, but Adeliza attempted to spare the knight from whatever invective I was devising.

"Perhaps you could conceal yourselves in the chamber next to the entry, that you might hear what takes place but not be seen."

"Oh, very well," I agreed, telling myself, *This may be for the best. What if I should falter?* But then I thought of Lady Mabel in the hands of the enemy, the weapons pointed at us from all sides, and a voice rose up to counter: *I will not falter.*

The three of us entered the main room just beyond the door, where a dozen or so knights of Arundel stood in silver mail, waiting to receive the usurper. A large metal structure bearing at least a hundred candles hung from the rafters above, its light shining upon the images painted on the walls. As we rushed across the stone floor, I took my chance to shove Drogo ever so slightly, causing him to make a low groan only I could hear.

"Do not come between the she-wolf and her prey!" I whispered.

"Just over here!" Adeliza called, pointing toward a small door in the opposite corner.

When she opened it, I saw that the chamber was merely a garderobe. There was only enough room for one or two persons to stand and a third to piss. I was about to object when we all heard voices just outside the main door and Adeliza pushed me inside, followed quickly by Drogo.

"Wait here and do not make a sound!" she commanded.

The next thing I knew, the door had been shut and we were in almost complete darkness, with little space between me, Drogo, and the hole that was letting off a most disagreeable smell.

"Well, I hope you're happy!" I chided.

"How was I to know she was going to force us in here?" he spoke out of the darkness.

"I've hardly set foot in this part of the castle. You come through every day on your way to the stables!"

"Yes, but I've never come in here. I thought it was a broom closet."

"A broom closet?!" I objected. "Who stores their brooms where their guests are meant to enter?"

"Who puts a garderobe where their guests are meant to enter?"

Suddenly, we both heard footsteps in the hall beyond. Almost immediately, I heard a voice I knew all too well.

"Where is she?!" the usurper growled.

At the sound of his voice, I felt a twinge run down my spine. After years of plotting from afar, hearing the voice of my enemy once again made everything seem far more real. I struggled to believe that the moment could truly be happening, though I had known well enough it was nigh the moment I set foot on shore. I was in no mere game, but a battle to the death. Every action I took and word I spoke might turn things one way or the other.

"King Stephen!" Adeliza cried, and I imagine she must have prostrated herself. "Your coming is most unforeseen!"

"You know perfectly well why I've come! Now, where is she? Where is that Jezebel?!"

I placed my hand on the door knob, but Drogo did the same.

"My lady, no! It is not safe!"

I was not about to let anyone stop me—even Drogo. I stamped on something I assumed was his foot, and he once again groaned, his grip letting up just a bit. I was able to push the door open and stumble out into the entry way.

Immediately, every eye in the room was fixed upon me. Men at arms on both sides stood at attention, and between them I saw the former queen of England bowing before the false king. Oh, Stephen! He was clad all in green, the royal crown upon his head. Kings did not normally wear such things to sieges unless they were striving to prove their kingship to men by outward show, and in this case he was laboring to little purpose, for there was nothing in his features that showed me he was worthy of the crown of Saint Edward. That was the property of me and my sons. I would not let him have it.

"I have a proper name, or have you forgotten it?" I asked him.

My cousin the traitor stood with hands on his hips, his displeasure clearly evident. Even as Adeliza reached out her arms as if to stop him, he took a step closer to me and glared with all his might.

"Any number of names I could give you, and you would deserve them all!"

"Ha! Do your worst!"

"The Shrew of Anjou: that is what we call you." Here he smiled, delighted in the pain he imagined this name would cause me.

I merely laughed. "What? Not the Bitch of Anjou? Or perhaps the Whore of Anjou?"

His smile disappeared. "A whore may be pleasant enough, and a bitch may produce a fine brood, but we find no such use for you. No, you are good for nothing but the vilest treason! How dare you set foot in our realm?!"

"Your realm? Your subjects beg to differ. The news of your decline spreads far and wide."

"Yes, no thanks to you and your friends, if indeed we can call them that, for I am certain they flock to Earl Robert's banner and not yours!" he cried, moving even closer. "How could they? A female king?! The very thought repulses! It goes against the created order."

Within my mind, I was falling in the dark, desperate and reaching. I blindly grasped the first thought that arose.

"There you are wrong, cousin, for the good Lord created man on the sixth day, and woman some time after that, but I think you will find that idiots came after the Fall, and it is to that class that you belong. Therefore, the natural order of things requires that woman should be exalted over such villainy!"

I felt fortunate that my knowledge of the scriptures had led me to that reply, but it did not impress the usurper. He turned again to speak to Adeliza, who looked quite desperate, as if she would either scream or vomit at any moment.

"How can you harbor this traitor?! Your husband refuses to vouch for your actions, and I do not blame him! You have broken faith with me, lady—truly, you have!"

She bowed once again and made her reply, almost squeaking as her words grew quicker and her tone ever higher. "My lord king, I never meant any dishonor to your person, nor to my esteemed husband, but custom itself requires that when a near relative arrives at the gate, one must show them hospitality."

"Not when they are an infamous traitor!" he protested, bending down to yell in her ear.

"Please, my lord!" she cried, tears pouring from her eyes. "I am indebted to the empress on account of my time as consort to her father, when she performed many deeds on my behalf. How could I refuse her when she came in such great need, desiring to see once again the land of her fathers?"

"The land of her fathers is across the Channel where she belongs," he said, glaring at me again.

Here I took my chance to reply. "Maybe so, but this is the land of my mother and of my nearest father, the late king! Do you remember, Stephen, how you swore upon the Holy Rood that you would be my faithful servant upon his death? I watched you bow and kiss my hand. Even so, Judas kissed the Lord he sought to betray!"

"King Henry never wanted you for his heir!" he charged, standing upright again. "He saw as I did that you were an obstinate woman, rebellious in spirit and unable to command the loyalty of men! You did not even wait for him to die before you began seizing his land—you and that ruinous husband of yours. The late king was a great man, and he loved me like a son. He saw in the end that the Angevins are devils, released us all from our oaths, and appointed me as heir. We have the testimony of Hugh Bigod!"

"That testimony is worth nothing, for he was never at the king's death bed. You have peddled that lie to the very halls of power in Rome, but I will not be taken in by it! Long before the king met his end, you were making ready to invade: to set yourself up in his place. I am sure we have your wife to thank for this, for like her mother before her, she would never be content until she was made queen of England. Well, that she shall never truly be, for you hold the throne not by God's appointment, but by deceit! Everything you are is built upon lies! You—"

"No! No more! You know not that of which you speak!" Stephen bellowed so loud that I imagine the candles high above must have shaken. "You have your story from Earl Robert, who has every reason to seek my demise, as he cannot stand to take second place to any man. The conceit of that bastard!" Here he actually turned his head and spat on the floor. "Now tell me, empress, why should I not seize you this instant and make an end of all my pain?"

His scorn of my brother threatened to push my anger into absolute rage. "I might as well ask you that question! Here you stand, spinning fables and tiring us all with your incessant whining. If you intended to make an end of me, you would have done so already. You have an army: as you can plainly see, we do not. Therefore, I say again, do your worst! Burn the place to the ground!"

"Empress Mathilda!" Adeliza interrupted, evidently fearing for her castle. "Perhaps we can come to a truce with the king. There is no need for all that."

To my surprise, Stephen extended his hand and raised her to her feet. "Fear not, Lady Arundel. I have no desire to destroy your home," he assured her. "You two are now pawns in my game, and I shall make the best use of you that I can. But I leave all things until the arrival of my brother, Bishop Henry. He shall know how to advise me."

I could not help but laugh. "From what I hear, you have forsaken his counsel for that of lesser men."

"The least of my men is head and shoulders above any of yours!" he charged.

"Really? When was the last time you looked? I think you may find there are more men on our side than you suppose. But in any case, no one stands head and shoulders above Sir Drogo!"

Stephen scoffed. "Poor man to be saddled with you! Fare you well, Lady Adeliza! I offer no such blessing to this shrew. I shall go enjoy the rest of my day and await the arrival of the bishop of Winchester. He will know what to do with you."

With this final threat, he gave me one last glare worthy of the devil. He then departed as suddenly as he had come, although his stench remained in our nostrils. As soon as the door slammed shut, I clutched at the front of my gown with one hand and pressed the other over my mouth as I bent forward, the tension seeming to depart my body. The first test was over, but we were by no means safe.

"What a fearful visit!" Adeliza cried. "He will reduce this fortress to rubble!"

"I think not," I replied once I had recovered. "These walls are strong. They can withstand a siege. Before long, Earl Robert will come and do battle with him. Then we will both be the happier." This was a rather hopeful statement, but I had no choice but to offer it.

"I cannot ask my men to endure that! They are not ready to give their lives for a ruler they do not recognize."

"What is this?!" I asked, placing my hands on my hips. "You are not turning coward on me, are you?"

That was perhaps a bit unfair, but the heat of the moment compelled me.

"It is no cowardice to flee certain defeat when you might live to fight another day," she argued, stepping closer. "We must find some way to escape!"

There is no way of escape. We are committed, come ruin or damnation, I thought, but decided that it would be better to draw her attention to the positive.

"Lady Adeliza, I have reason to believe that things could still work out in our favor. As you heard Stephen say, Bishop Henry is soon to arrive, and when he does, he will induce the king to let me go without a fight."

"What?! How?"

"The king cannot afford to anger him now, having already set the Church on edge. He will do anything to keep his brother happy."

"But why should Bishop Henry help you?"

I smiled as I took my chance to reveal a great secret. "Because he seeks to punish his brother for his actions—even to remove him from the throne. He told me so in a letter. That is half the reason I am here."

"Truly?" she asked, the doubt seeming to melt from her face. "Well, that does make a difference, I suppose. But can you trust the bishop?"

"I can trust him to do what all men do: to seek his own. In this case, that may well mean helping me, yes."

"I hope you are right. We are not well stocked for a siege. I suppose if it came to it, we could eat the dogs."

I smiled and patted her on the shoulder. "If you are hoping to startle me, Lady Adeliza, I can assure you it wouldn't be the worst thing I've ever eaten."

This finally drew a laugh from the younger woman. She commanded her guards to disperse, and as they did so, I heard a voice ask, "My ladies, may I come out now!"

"Oh, Drogo!" I cried. "I completely forgot."

I rushed over and opened the door to the garderobe. There stood Drogo, pinching his fingers on either side of his nose.

"I am sorry, truly," I offered.

"You stepped on my foot!" he complained.

"Yes, well, I had no choice. You had become an annoyance."

He stepped out and breathed in the air as if he had never enjoyed such a luxury before. He then leaned down and whispered in my ear.

"I'm not sure if there was more you know what in there or out here. That man does anger me exceedingly."

"You and me both," I agreed. "Let us hope that Bishop Henry makes good on his word."

We remained in this state of suspended hostility for another three days, and had any of our friends sent word to us, it would not have made it past Stephen's guards, who set a watch throughout the surrounding country. It was on Bishop Henry of Winchester that everything depended. You may find it odd indeed that an alleged king should wait upon a bishop to determine how to conduct a siege, but it was in Stephen's nature to behave in such a manner at that time, always looking to some other man to tell him how to proceed. His willingness to rely on his brother had revealed to me that he did not suspect any treachery from that corner. Yet I knew Bishop Henry was no longer a faithful servant, having lost trust in his brother's rule. Thus, it was with great interest that I observed the coming of the bishop's party from my chamber window the following day.

Bishop Henry was a smaller man than his brother, but finely attired as befit the greatest ecclesiastic in the land. Indeed, he set such great store by his appearance that I suspected his vanity exceeded that of his brother. He had a large company with him, all on horseback and ready for battle. From my perch, I watched him enter the false king's tent, then was left to guess at their conversation.

They had been in discussion for more than an hour when Drogo entered my room. I was gazing out the window so fiercely that his presence took me by surprise. Once I had recovered, I inquired of him, "What have you heard?"

"Bishop Henry is in the midst of discussion with his brother, as is Earl Waleran of Meulan."

"He had Waleran with him?" I asked, turning back to look through the window as if he might suddenly appear from behind a shrub. "I could not see him, but the view is poor. There are too many trees in the way, and the glass leaves something to be desired. How odd that the bishop and the earl should ride together, for there is no love lost between them."

Drogo sat on the edge of the bed just to my right. "Yes, well, he is there, and between the three of them I imagine they will decide what to do with us."

"Do you suppose they will besiege us? Assail us night and day?"

"They wouldn't dare! I have it on good authority that Stephen is merciful to women. Just last year, he declined to seize Ludlow Castle for that very reason."

I scoffed. "That is little comfort! I am not just some fainting woman. I am the heir to the throne and his greatest threat."

"And a member of the royal house, and thus worthy of proper honor—"

"And a thorn in his flesh for as long as we both live, and since when does anyone offer mercy to the thorn in their flesh? Oh, it's no use! We must wait for their decision. I just hope that Lady Adeliza does not hand us over. Her courage seems to fade by the day. Apparently, she is saying now that we took the castle by force, but that is just a ploy to save herself."

"We have many knights here as well. We are not solely dependent on Adeliza."

"Wait!" I cried, raising my hand. "I thought I saw someone leaving. Yes, they are all coming out of the tent, or at least the bishop and his men are."

"Ah! The moment of truth has arrived."

By the time we made our way down to the lower level, joined Adeliza, and moved into the outer bailey, the gate had been opened for Bishop Henry, who now served as ambassador. He walked up the slight hill toward our position slowly and in great state. Even from afar, I had observed that his robes were fine, but they improved upon closer inspection. Was that damask? Such a thing was not common in the lands of Christendom. I had only seen it in Italy. I reasoned he must have bought it off a pilgrim or perhaps some visiting Byzantine. And as for the bishop's crucifix—well, it was a wonder he could keep his neck upright with such a wealth of gold and jewels upon that chain! I had no such thing in my own collection. As he was a rather small man, it seemed to overwhelm him.

He was moving across the wide yard flanked by a pair of knights, his eyes locked upon me even as he clasped his hands together. He moved right or left to avoid the refuse of the horses without ever breaking his gaze. How he did this, I can only guess. Finally, he made it within a few paces of us and bowed.

"Empress Mathilda!" he greeted me. "I have come to conduct you with all haste to Bristol, there to be delivered into the keeping of Earl Robert of Gloucester."

Here was a pleasant surprise! Of course, I had hoped this would happen, but I had very much feared one of a hundred other foul results.

"She is granted safe passage, then?" asked Adeliza, hugging my arm. "She is free to leave?"

"Yes, Lady Arundel, and have no fear for your possessions," the bishop said with a smile. "The king knows you were hard pressed in this case and that you are still his most faithful subject."

"Oh, thank you, my lord bishop!" she said, bowing before him, which I thought was a bit needless.

"So, you are to take me to the West, then? Has Earl Robert agreed to this?" I inquired of the bishop, entering the conversation for the first time.

"I have spoken with him, yes. When he heard that you were besieged, he thought it best to proceed in this manner. You will be safe with your friends there."

I moved a step closer and looked at him doubtfully. "How do I know that some evil will not befall me along the way?"

"You have my word of honor, dear cousin," he assured me, placing hand to heart, "and you are of course welcome to bring all your knights. Surely you do not think we are able to overcome so many brave warriors!"

"I suspect you are able to do a great deal, Bishop Henry," I said with a smile, "but it seems I have no choice but to trust you. I have trespassed long enough on Lady Adeliza's hospitality. However, I do have one request: that Lady Mabel be safely returned to her husband as well."

"Of course! That is one of the points of our agreement. I should have mentioned it earlier."

I nodded. "Then let it be to me even as you have said. I shall gather my things, and we will be far from this place ere the sun sets. Thank you, Lady Adeliza, for the patience you have shown at such a difficult time."

So it was that I came into the keeping of Bishop Henry of Winchester along with all my knights. I was not to feel at ease in his hands, but I did prefer him over the usurper. As ill fate would have it, they sent Earl Waleran along as well, he the first of the Beaumont family. I am certain this was against the bishop's wishes, for he had even less reason to favor Waleran than I did, but he could not go against the will of the usurper. As for me, I was in no mood to quarrel. I longed to reach Bristol and be out of Stephen's reach, even if it would delay our push to the east.

We set out that very day and made it to Chichester by dark. Our progress after that was rather slow, for the weather was not to be desired and such a great number of horsemen required frequent rest. At length, we came to Winchester and were housed in Bishop Henry's palace along the river. The castle in which I had spent a portion of my youth was just down the road, but that was in the keeping of the false king, whereas Lady Mabel and I were the special guests of the bishop. I could only hope and pray that the bishop was not in the habit of eating his guests.

After two days' rest, we kept our path south of the downs, moving through Wiltonshire until we arrived at Devizes Castle. That was the old fortress of Bishop Roger of Salisbury until it was taken from him so cruelly earlier that year. This occasioned one of the few meaningful conversations between myself and Bishop Henry up to that point. While the rest of the company was feasting loudly in the great hall, I found my cousin in a small side room, seated by the hearth with a goblet in his hand. Oddly for a castle, the walls were made of dark wood panels, suggesting that this was an addition after the main construction. It gave the place a somber feel, and it was a fine place for quiet reflection ... or plotting.

"May I?" I asked, catching his eye and pointing to the chair opposite.

"Of course!" he replied, making to stand but never rising all the way as I took my seat quickly.

"Tell me," I began, adjusting my skirt so it would fall properly, "how goes it with Bishop Roger? It pained me to hear of his ordeal."

The look on the bishop's face changed in an instant. The corners of his lips pushed into a frown, and he glared as his eyes watched the dancing flames.

"He lies now upon his sick bed, never likely to rise again," he replied, lowering his voice. He cast his eyes around in all directions to ensure that no one was listening, then continued, "I dare say it is the wrath of the king that has brought him low. I do not mind telling you: I am exceedingly troubled by what has taken place. I cannot remember a king of England acting against the Lord's anointed in such a manner—certainly not since the days of Æthelstan.[4] It was all I could do to have Bishop Roger restored to his see, but he was removed from all his other offices, condemned to live out the rest of his days in humiliation. 'Tis no wonder he longs to depart this earth!"

"Have you and the bishop been on good terms, then?"

He leaned back in his chair and took a long drink from his goblet, then let out a sigh. "I suppose there has always been a natural strain between us, for he is a man of great ambition, but though we may not be the best of friends, we have a common interest: namely, the advancement of our Holy Church and the sanctity of the clergy."

Sanctity was not the word that came to mind when I thought of Bishop Roger of Salisbury, and I believed my cousin to be a man of equal personal ambition to any who walked the earth, but I accepted his words. I leaned in closer to him and he did likewise.

---

4 Æthelstan is typically recognized as the first sovereign ruler of England in something like its modern form. He was King of the English from 927-939 A.D./C.E.

"In your letter, you bid me restore the kingdom to true religion," I whispered. "I will have you know that I intend to do so once things are returned to their proper order. I have always desired to promote Christianity, even in my time as empress of the Romans. It was quite wrong of Stephen to act against the bishops in such a manner."

"Precisely! He does not see it. He cannot understand how he has been led astray by ... well, you know ..."

As luck would have it, Waleran happened to pass the open door at that very moment, not stopping to look in. Bishop Henry moved his eyes to show that this was the man to whom he was referring.

"Why did he come with us? The two of you despise one another, no?" I asked.

"It is because he does not trust me that he rides with us, for he fears we may have secret confidences with one another."

A wonder then that he did not stop to listen, I thought.

"Does he know you met with Earl Robert?" I asked, speaking a question that had long been on my mind.

"No. Only you and me, my men, and Lord Brian know that."

"Lord Brian!" I said in wonder, allowing my voice to get a bit too loud. "He was at your meeting?"

"Yes, from what I understand, Earl Robert meant to ride up to Wallingford—"

"That was what he told me, yes."

"—but when Lord Brian heard a rumor that you had landed, he came down and joined the party along the way."

"And then they all went to Bristol?"

"No, Lord Brian returned to Wallingford, the better to defend it."

I nodded my head, but I had one more question. "And how did you prevail upon Stephen to let us go? What did you say?"

He laughed, or rather snorted. "That it would be easier to catch the two of you together and keep you farther away from London. He fears Earl Robert, so it worked."

"I see. You are an excellent source of information, cousin. However, I think Earl Waleran may be correct to suspect you of secret confidences."

"Alas for Bishop Roger!" he said solemnly. "He leaves me to fight for the Church alone."

"Not alone, surely!"

"Yes," he replied, seeming to gain his courage, "it is my firm hope that my foolish brother will soon recognize just how many of us are ready to stand against him in defense of the cause of Christ."

That Bishop Henry saw himself as the defender of Christianity, I do not doubt, but I think it safe to say that he was no angel and could compete with the poets when it came to excessive lamentation.

As it so happened, Earl Waleran abandoned us one day's march past Devizes, which seemed rather odd if his purpose was to keep a watch upon Bishop Henry. Perhaps he sensed his services were needed to the east, where Stephen was assembling his forces for the battle we all knew was coming. We were well rid of his company.

When we were within a mile of Bristol, Lady Mabel and I were greeted by the one thing we hoped most to see: Earl Robert on his horse, come to receive us. Such a happy meeting that was, and all the better as my brother was not alone. Indeed, he was joined by Miles of Gloucester, who had come to inform both the bishop and myself of his change of allegiance. I was only too glad to receive another ally and one so venerable.

We soon left Bishop Henry to return the way he had come and entered the city, where we were greeted by joyful crowds. I had enjoyed many a pleasant reception in my day, but I could not remember having so many people express such joy at my own presence rather than that of some lord. I suppose they hoped I had come to bestow blessings upon them all and grant them eternal favor. For my own part, I was simply happy to see their smiling faces, for in the back of my mind I knew that the departure of the bishop's party meant the brief peace was over. They had moved me to the West only to make war upon me.

Bristol Castle sits between the rivers Frome and Avon, using the former as its moat. In the years since he became earl, my brother had strengthened it considerably, to the point that the usurper had been too fearful to test its walls a year earlier. On my first night there, I not only met Miles of Gloucester but also saw my brother's children. William, the eldest, I already knew. He was a full man by that time. Roger was next oldest, and then Hamon, followed by Richard. Robert's daughter Mathilda was to wed the earl of Chester, and after her came another daughter, Mabel, and a son, Philip. All of them were quite lively and not unlike their parents. It was William who was set to succeed his father as earl, whereas Mathilda would achieve a comparable title through marriage.

The stone keep of the castle was similar to that of London, if a little smaller. The hall on the lower level was divided from the solar by a thin wall. In this more private chamber was something between a chair and a bed, a most unusual object wrapped in blue fabric with flowers stitched into it. I was able to sit, or rather lay, on this chair with my feet resting on the end, a great pleasure after many long miles of travel. Robert sat near me in what the ancient Romans called a *curulis* but the common people in England simply call an X chair. The sun was sinking low in the western sky, and its rays had turned the room a shade of orange.

"What do you call this thing I'm sitting on?" I asked my brother, as the two of us enjoyed our drinks. "I cannot think where I have seen something like this except maybe in Italy all those years ago."

He shrugged. "I do not know. Mabel asked the carpenter to make it some years ago when she was often with child. She would become so ill that she could do little but lay in bed. However, she quickly grew tired of seeing naught but her own chamber, so we had this brought in to allow her to enjoy the main level."

"What a wonderful idea! I wish I had such a thing when I was pregnant with my boys. I would some times walk out into the garden, lay down a blanket, and rest against one of the trees, just to breathe the outside air." This brief memory of a much happier hour warmed my heart even as it pained me, for I could no longer hold my sons so close to myself nor safeguard them with my own flesh.

"I know nothing about these women's matters," he said, "but if the wife is bearing me a child, and she says she needs money for something, who am I to refuse?"

"Very wisely spoken," I replied, raising my goblet to him. "Ah, what a kingdom you have built for yourself here, brother! It seems a pity that I am only seeing it now."

"Every man here is your servant. We shall mount an effort the like of which England has never seen and take back the throne that is rightfully yours."

"We shall see ..." I muttered, letting out a sigh.

"Oh, you of little faith! You doubt me so!"

"I do not doubt you, Robert, but as for the rest of England, I am not so sure. That they hate Stephen is plain enough, but will they accept a woman? Such a thing has never happened before."

"Any choice might be better than Stephen, but your advantage is that you have three sons already born, each of them descended from the kings of old. As long as Count Geoffrey keeps himself out of the way—"

"Count Geoffrey? Oh …" The name seemed odd to my ears, for I had not given the man a thought in some time! I had been far too busy attempting to survive, or perhaps I had merely seized the opportunity to avoid an unhappy subject.

"What?" my brother asked, a look of confusion on his face.

"Forgive me. With everything that has taken place, I had quite forgotten about him. Is that strange that I should fail to think about my own husband?"

He shook his head and leaned back in his seat. "I've met the man. It isn't strange."

"Well, before this is over, he will have something to say about all this."

"He can say whatever he likes, but it is the lords of England and Normandy who will decide."

For a moment, neither of us spoke, and I could hear the distant sound of the men playing some sport in the outer ward. It would not be long before they would have to give up the game and come inside to feast the night away. I thought I heard my nephew's voice among that crowd, and I smiled.

"William is a fine lad. You have done well in raising him."

Here the light seemed to flicker in my brother's eyes and he too smiled broadly. "Yes, he does us all proud. I find it rather hard to believe that I shall soon have a daughter married and bearing children of her own. Surely I'm not that old, am I?"

"Ha! I don't know. You are older than I am, and I feel positively ancient."

"That is because you have seen too many cares. But will be fifty this year—fifty! You must be shy of forty still, but halfway in the grave am I!"

I did not think Robert looked quite decrepit, so I chose to change the subject.

"Halfway in the grave is England if we fail to save it. So, what now? What do we do next?"

He nodded and set his empty goblet on the floor. "Make ready for war, make such grants as are necessary to ensure men's loyalty, and get you up to Gloucester."

"Gloucester? I am not to stay here, then?"

"No, Bristol is a merchant town, but Gloucester is a royal seat. It is better that you should make your home there."

"See, that is why I need you, Robert. You know the West so much better," I admitted, though part of me would have rather stayed in Bristol after seeing the strength of that fortress.

"And I place you in the hands of one who knows it even better than I: Lord Miles. What think you of him?"

The truth was that I was most happy to accept Lord Miles' change of allegiance, but I had reached the point where I found it difficult to trust anyone completely. Thus, I remained suspicious.

"I am wondering why he should support us when you and he have often been at odds in this part of the world," I replied, giving voice to my concern.

"He is a friend of Bishop Roger, whose fate has lately become the scandal of the realm."

I laughed and shook my head. "It's always something, isn't it?"

"Indeed."

"Very well, then. To Gloucester I shall go, even if it be full of liars and thieves!"

"This time of year, it is full of nothing but rain. Have Mabel give you a cloak."

"Ah, rain! A true English welcome."

II

I t was lovely for once to pass the night in a bed owned by someone who liked me. Safe within Earl Robert's castle, there were few dangers to my person. I was therefore able to gain some rest that I had sorely lacked. However, when I awoke the following morning, my mind turned immediately to my three boys still in Normandy. Oh, how I missed them! What was my Henry writing? What was my Geoffrey reading? What was my William saying? Were they still safe and healthy? It had been less than a month since I last beheld them, and already I longed for the war to be over so I might see those faces once again.

I arose and made my way to the small desk on the other side of the chamber, where a few pieces of parchment sat waiting. In a whirl, I wrote first to the archbishop of Canterbury, then to Count Geoffrey of Anjou, then to my uncle the king of Scotland. My hand already in a state of pain, I composed one more letter to be shared with my sons, then after dressing myself, I traveled below to meet with Miles of Gloucester.

Now, it should be noted that the two of us had never been in one another's presence before that time, so my aim as much as anything was to search out the man's character and determine whether I could depend on him. The day before we arrived, Drogo had asked me, "My lady, do you suppose we can trust Lord Miles? After all, he did spend the past few years fighting for the usurper."

"I have learned not to trust anyone," I replied.

"What? Not even yourself?" he asked, plainly amazed.

"Oh no, that least of all!"

Therefore, I was most eager to discover if the men of Gloucester really were liars and thieves. After all, though my brother Robert was earl of Gloucester, it was not his true home. No, that was the realm of Lord Miles. Sadly, I did not think it right to use the wonderful bed chair for a formal meeting, so I had two of the X chairs set out instead. I sat there feeling ill at ease, hoping very much that the conversation I was about to have would go well.

At length, Lord Miles entered the room and made his obeisance. The most notable aspect of his appearance was his hair, which was so light in color I might have called it yellow. His nose was long, his lips thin, and his brow high. I imagined that had I seen the Northmen of old sailing across the sea, making for new worlds with the wind at their backs, they would have looked much like Earl Miles, for such was his countenance. He could have been a great lord standing tall above the dragon's head, a fur draped over his shoulders and a helm of silver and gold upon his head, his locks of gold blowing in the wind.

I bid him sit across from me and said, "I must take this opportunity to thank you, Lord Miles, for your courtesy in receiving us here in the West. I am only too glad to accept your offer of fealty, and I shall grant to you the castle of Saint Briavel and the right of the Forest of Dean."

"May God preserve Your Highness," he replied, bowing his head, "but you must know it was not for glory that I offered you my allegiance."

"Wasn't it? Are you not a man, then?"

I had taken the opportunity to test him with this small barb. It has been my experience over the years that not all persons like to receive the type of wit that tends to proceed from my lips. I therefore said this to draw him out and see if our communication was bound to be interesting or utterly dull.

"Oh no! That is, I am a man, but if one is to go off to war, it must be for something more than vainglory, for what good is that when one is dead?"

He did not seem to have taken offense, which I decided was a good thing.

"Do you intend to die in my service?" I jested

"Not if I can help it," he assured me. "I have survived this long, but the greatest skill is only so good in battle. One arrow hits the wrong place, and that's it—just like what happened to the late king."

"You mean my uncle William?" Here I referred to the late William II, also called Rufus.

"Yes. Forgive me, should I not have mentioned him? I would hate to think I had offended you."

His tone was so earnest that I laughed and said, "It takes a bit more than that to offend me at this point. What can you tell me of the usurper? Did he make his intentions known to you? I understand you were often in his company."

Here was a subject of great interest. If Lord Miles could reveal some intelligence, I would be doubly glad for his presence among us. Sadly, he shook his head and looked rather forlorn.

"I doubt there is anything I could tell you that you do not already know or couldn't guess with ease. The more time one spends with him, the more he tends to annoy. Becoming king has not been good for his character, nor has his alliance with the Beaumonts and the Flemings."

This much was well known to all, but I pressed on in hope of something new.

"Do you think he can mount a sufficient force to besiege us here?"

"I am not certain, but I should think he will first attempt to block our lines of communication. The one who must worry most is Lord Brian fitz Count, sitting there by himself at Wallingford. I am sure Stephen will come calling any day now. He is quite alone on the eastern flank."

This news filled me with a sense of dread. I gripped the arms of my chair with a bit more force than usual but swore to myself that I would not to be overwhelmed—not in front of Lord Miles. I simply asked, "What can we do for him? Is there no way we can help?"

"Have no fear, my lady!" he answered. "Wallingford is well defended. Lord Brian is no fool."

"I never thought him a fool … I just … I should hate to lose Wallingford."

"I do not believe that will happen. Stephen will do what he always does. He will show up, take a look around, put the place under siege, then ride off and leave a small company behind. That has been his pattern since this all began, for he lacks the necessary strength to bring down a castle quickly. I will wait for the main force to leave, then while the usurper is busy elsewhere, I will strike with my men and make a bloody mess of the thing."

"Must we really wait so long?" I asked, feeling rather desperate. Truly, I had little knowledge of the ways of war, never having been taught such things, but the idea of doing nothing immediately appalled me. Would Stephen really act in such a casual manner after I had set foot on the island?

"With all due respect, Empress Mathilda, we do not have enough men to face Stephen directly: not at this time. It makes more sense to do as I have said," Miles maintained.

"Yes, I can see that. I just hate to use them all as bait."

"Better them than you!"

"I suppose," I agreed, "but I cannot stand the thought of just sitting here and allowing you all to face your doom. Not that I do not feel the threat to myself, for I know little ground separates me from the enemy, and should Wallingford fall I will see quickly enough how fast their horses can move. But I cannot ride forth into battle beside you all, and while that choice was made by God and not myself, it feels rather obscene … even cowardly."

"And yet the hour may come when you will be forced to prove how very full of courage you are," he said. "Fear not for us, good lady! We know what the game is about."

I decided it was best for me to change the subject before I grew more upset. "Now, speaking of cousins, am I to meet your relative, Abbot Gilbert?" Here I meant Gilbert Foliot, abbot of Gloucester.

"Oh, he is most eager to make your acquaintance!" Lord Miles replied. "He would have been here, but his duties keep him in that city."

"I understand he supported me at first, then experienced a conversion when the abbacy of Gloucester was vacant. Perhaps you can explain this to me?"

He paused for a moment, and I marked in his eyes a sudden discomfort, as if it pained him to meet my gaze. At length, he summoned the courage to say, "It was a difficult time, madam. We have all done things we regret. Abbot Gilbert has no love for King Stephen—"

"The usurper," I said firmly.

"Yes ... quite. As I was saying, he spares no love in that direction, but in the present situation…"

"It was necessary—yes. Well, let us hope that he knows well enough which side he is on now. If he remains faithful to me, I shall make sure he stays in his position."

"Very good, my lady!" he said with a sense of relief. "Is there anything else you need from me, then? Otherwise, I shall begin making preparations."

"Nothing at all. Be about your preparations."

"Thank you. God save you, Empress Mathilda!"

As soon as he had gone, my mind returned at once to the fate of poor Brian, stranded out at Wallingford with nothing between him and the usurper. I had not wanted to make too much of it in Lord Miles' presence for fear of raising questions I had no wish to answer, but upon ascending the stair and reaching my private chamber, I spoke my thoughts.

"Oh, Lord God, please defend him!" I whispered into the air, leaning back against the closed door and sinking lower and lower toward the floor. "I know I am worthy of nothing and deserve nothing. I am a sinner and always will be. Just let me see him again and in one piece, I beg you! In your mercy preserve his life. Let him not be cast from this world on my account!"

I walked over to the small table where one more piece of parchment remained. Without pausing to sit down, I wrote a final letter, this one to be sent to the east.

"To Brian of Wallingford, lord of Abergavenny, the Empress Mathilda sends her greeting and prays that you and yours are safe and in good health. We have received from Earl Robert your promises of fealty to our person, and it brings us more joy than you can know to have you on our side. For the love you bear us, we bid you make strong your defenses and send throughout

the nearby country for such men as are worthy to the task, for the false king is coming to you without delay. We are sending Lord Miles of Gloucester to your aid, but know that he shall not appear until after the usurper departs, the better to avoid open battle. We believe this to be the wisest course of action, though it pains our heart to think that you should be placed in danger. Therefore, we offer our earnest prayers for you both day and night, that the Lord will see fit to bless our efforts and be for you the refuge and fortress of which the Psalmist speaks ..."

I paused in my efforts for just a moment, debating what I should write next. Would it do to make some personal note? In truth, I wished to tell him all those things I had desired to say for so long, but it hardly seemed the proper time or place. My conscience pricked me at the core, bidding me not to share my thoughts. At length, I hastily scratched out the following: "*I need not tell you all my thoughts, but you are most assuredly in them.*" There was that word: 'I,' more personal than 'we.' That would have to do.

I passed all my letters to a messenger, taking care to kiss the one intended for my dear sons, and he rode off immediately to see them to their proper destinations. Whether they would arrive intact was far from certain. I could only hope and pray that both the bearer and the receivers would be spared from the violence that was about to unfold. It was to be a moment of reckoning, not only for myself, but for us all.

As Lord Miles made off on his secret errand, taking half our knights with him, I remembered something my father once said to me: "The man who stands on the front line of battle must be the most steadfast in the service of his king."

I was no king, to be sure, but I saw clearly enough that Wallingford was the key to our fortunes. Seated as it was in the vale of the Thames, south of Oxford and west of Windsor, where the rolling downs give way to the plain, its position was certainly one to be favored. It also happened to be one of the strongest fortresses in the kingdom, the linchpin of our defense through which all communication was bound to flow. Was it any wonder that Stephen should seek to claim it for himself? There with his men stood Lord Brian, ready to take on the world on my behalf. My father was right: that was no place for a man who wavers.

It was not even a day after Miles departed that I began to have serious doubts. Everything depended on the usurper acting as he always had, leaving behind a few men and heading for the hills. Were he to stay and prosecute the siege himself, retaining the greater part of his force, then Lord Miles would be quite overmatched. It was essential that the false king and the wolf of Ypres—that is, William of Ypres—should not remain at Wallingford. I therefore decided to ask my brother whom we might send to frustrate the usurper's efforts by means of distraction.

Soon after my arrival in Bristol, the rain brother Robert had prophesied for me in Gloucester descended on us there instead. For most of a week, the sky let forth its sorrow, and there was no going out of doors. Then one morning I awoke to the feeling of the sun on my face as it streamed through the eastern window, and I knew my chance had come. I asked Robert to show me the priory he had endowed. It was only about half a mile north of the castle, just across the River Frome, and our walk there was pleasant. He had told me of the fine grounds and with great joy we made our way through them step by step, passing clusters of great oak trees. When we had already made two circuits round the property, I asked Earl Robert how we might distract Stephen away from Wallingford.

"I know just the man!" he replied. "I have here among the Flemings I was able to hire away from Stephen one Robert fitz Hubert, a man without any sense of conscience or propriety, but he'll do the thing sure enough. I will send him off to Malmesbury Castle, which is lightly defended. He and the lads will make easy work of it: have no doubt. Then when Stephen has planted his siege in Wallingford, he will be drawn off to the west, and that will be our chance to strike."

My mind immediately made the connection: Malmesbury was home to the famous and beloved abbey! Bishop Roger of Salisbury had built the castle next to the abbey to defend it, but like everything else the bishop owned, it had been stolen by the usurper. It seemed highly unlikely that an action against the castle would be able to exempt the nearby abbey. No, Malmesbury did not seem like a good place for an assault of any type.

"But what of the poor monks?" I asked. "They are friends of yours. They will not thank us for sending such a man among them and bringing war upon their town. I will be cursed from here to Durham!"

Alas, in my concern, I had turned to face my brother rather than keeping my eyes on the path, and I almost fell over a tree root. Happily, my brother pretended not to see my momentary lack of dignity.

"He will not hurt the monks," he said calmly. "His aim will be the castle."

"I thought you just said he lacked a conscience. He may well burn the books and rape the women … or the men!"

He shrugged. "War is an ugly business."

"Robert!" I scolded, beginning to take on the tone I normally reserved for my boys. "You must command him not to harm the monks. I will not have that! How are we to win over the Church if we are seen to be its enemy?"

"Oh, very well," he replied, shaking his head. "William ought to send you a gift of thanks."

"Who?"

"Brother William, the chronicler of Malmesbury. I can only imagine what he will scribble when he looks out his window and sees the Flemings!"

"He may well conclude that his is no life of solitude. Now, let me ask you something, brother: what are the true intentions of Miles of Gloucester?"

Here my brother slowed his pace and looked at me in confusion. "What do you mean? He hates Stephen even as we do."

"Yes, but if I am not wrong, you and he are great rivals here in the West. I do not believe he fights for us merely out of concern for his friend, Bishop Roger of Salisbury. What am I missing, Robert? What does he really want?"

At this point, he stopped walking altogether, and I did likewise.

"Does it matter?" he asked, hands clasped behind his back.

"One must always know a man's intentions if one is to foresee his actions. What does he desire most on this earth?"

Robert looked back toward the priory church, which could be seen just between the trees. He was clearly taking a moment to consider, and at length he spoke.

"If I were to guess, I would say he desires the county of Hereford."

Again, my mind quickly made the connection.

"Which is in the earldom of Worcester, which is in the keeping of Waleran Beaumont ..."

"Yes, Earl Waleran of Worcester."

I sighed and threw up my hands. "That's it, then. That is why he comes to us. Well, it is no easy thing he desires. First there is the matter of seizing the land, which I can only assume will be an infernal task. But then, consider, brother:

if I were to make him earl of Hereford, he would be your equal in the West! He would be the greatest of the Marcher Lords, controlling the whole of the Severn, the approaches into Wales—"

"We need him, Maud. I cannot fight Stephen alone."

"I know that, and I would gladly give him that and more if I felt him truly worthy. But it is a question of honor, Robert. Just look what a mess the usurper has made raising up men left and right! Am I to do the same with Lord Miles?"

"One earl is not the problem. Stephen has made enough earls to fill an ark, and he cannot say 'no' to any of them. As long as you can say 'no' to Miles when the hour requires it, you are still in control."

"I suppose you are right, though perhaps I ought to be worried about him saying 'no' to me."

I paused for a moment to breathe. I could hear the birds speaking to one another high up in the trees. It was a glorious day, truly, but I was not of good cheer. Robert reached out and took my hand in his own, with that firm gaze of his looking straight into my eyes.

"What is really troubling you, my sister? It is not the monks and it is not Lord Miles."

"What do you know of my feelings?" I objected, pulling my hand back.

"I think you are missing your sons, and I think that you fear for Lord Brian."

The annoying thing about Earl Robert was that I had known him for so long and informed him of so many of my personal affairs that he was often able to read my mind in this way, even if I did not wish him to do so.

"I fear for all those who place themselves in harm's way on my behalf," I said, hoping to avoid the subject.

Robert smiled and patted me on the shoulder. "He is not going to die. He will live—I promise you that—and with not a scratch on his gray head."

"What? Has his hair gone gray now?" I asked, recognizing for the first time that whenever I had pictured Brian, I had done so as he was when we last saw each other. Of course he would have changed. Not that I cared if his hair was gray, or anyone else's for that matter, but I felt a sense of loss that so many years had gone by without seeing many of my friends.

"We have all of us gone gray, and the few that haven't soon will, for war does that to a man. Even you have some gray hairs, sister," Robert said, helpfully pointing.

"No, no!" I objected. "That is a vicious rumor! If you speak it again, I shall be forced to place you in the stocks. You leave me no choice!" Here I pounded a finger into his chest to prove the depth of my objection.

"Fear not!" he assured me, throwing up his hands. "I will cover them up with a crown, and then all men will declare you a symbol of youth—the greatest beauty that has ever lived."

At this, I scoffed. "I doubt that! My own husband would never say such a thing. I think he believes me to be a hag of sorts."

"What does it matter what men think if you wear the crown?"

"It matters to a woman, Robert. It always matters." Truly, I did not see how any man could fail to understand this, and not for the first time, I began to despair of that sex. "I do hope you make a point to praise your own wife from time to time, for where would any of you men be without your women?"

"In my case, far poorer."

"And without all your lovely sons and daughters, so give thanks for the bounty with which God has blessed you, and with which you continue to bless the world."

It was at that moment that we heard the pounding of hooves upon the nearby field and turned to see Sir Philip of Honfleur coming with a note in hand. The two of us walked out from the trees to join him in the open grass. The rider alighted and bowed to us both, then handed his parcel to Earl Robert. My brother examined it briefly, then broke the seal and unfolded the parchment. As the other two of us waited, he moved the letter to catch more light from the sun and must have read through it twice before I finally asked, "What is it? Not news from Wallingford already?"

"No, it is from the lord of Caerleon Castle, Morgan ab Owain."

"The Welsh prince? Why does he write to you?"

He squinted his eyes. "The better question is, what does he write to me? I can hardly make sense of the thing."

"Is it not in our tongue?" Philip asked.

"I think it is, only the writing is rather poor. They must not have a decent clerk."

"Your sight is not failing, brother?" I goaded.

"No, here it is," he said, pointing to a particular line. "He agrees to aid us in the coming war. He can have ten thousand men for us by the New Year."

"Really?!" I cried, attempting to take in this figure. "You astound me. I did not even know that many men lived in Wales."

"Oh, the women there are quite fruitful, I assure you."

"And they will fight for us?" I asked, the fervor rising within me.

"They will fight for you," my brother answered, his eyes still examining the letter. "It seems when Stephen was there not long ago, he made rather a lot of enemies. They would prefer someone else on the throne." Here he folded the letter and handed it back to Philip.

"Are they mostly pike men, or do they have any riders?" the knight asked.

"Some of both—as fierce as the day is long."

"And what is this going to cost us?" I inquired, cutting to the heart of the matter.

"Never you mind that."

"Robert," I said, giving him another one of my direct looks that only a younger sister can give to her older brother, "you know perfectly well that I have scarcely two coins to my name."

He sighed, clearly tiring of the conversation. "I have some gold, as does Miles. We can pay them off for now. Then when we take the spoils of battle, we will have our reward. This is the way you must think in a war, sister. Victory provides the payment." He moved his right hand back and forth as he said this, as if to represent the transfer of coin.

I stepped closer to him and crossed my arms. "Well, I suppose we had better win, then."

"Indeed. I will send this Robert off to Malmesbury. By chance, he happens to be a cousin of William of Ypres."

"Oh, that should bring the wolf running!" Philip cried.

That was how we left matters for the time being. Robert fitz Hubert was sent to Malmesbury, and I continued to fret.

When Robert fitz Hubert arrived in Malmesbury with his men, he set about destroying anything not made of stone, just as I had feared. It seemed he had a few things in common with his cousin. He did spare the abbey itself—thanks be to God! However, that did not keep him from entering the chapter house to seek out the castle's defenders, who had fled there for sanctuary. What he hoped to accomplish beyond offending the monks, I cannot imagine.

It took longer for us to receive the news from Wallingford. We heard that Stephen had arrived before the walls with Earl Waleran and William of Ypres, but seeing that they could not be breached and there was likely a store of food that would last for a year or more, the usurper chose to hastily appoint two fortresses, one of which was the local church. Oh, the priests did not love him for that! He then departed with most of his men for Malmesbury, where he found the town burnt to the ground and Robert fitz Hubert and his men holed up in the castle.

I have no doubt that the usurper would have preferred to blow the lot of them to pieces, and perhaps even rightfully so, but there were two difficulties. First, the abbey of Malmesbury was such an old and sacred institution that he would have been a greater fool than usual to take any action that might harm the monks. Second, as it turned out, even mercenaries know something of loyalty, at least to those with whom they share the bond of blood.

From this point on, I can tell you the story well enough from my own memories. One morning, I woke rather late—ah, the blessing of a good night's rest! I made myself ready and descended the stair to the lower level, where I found Lady Mabel reclined on her special chair and reading to her youngest child, Philip, who was not yet old enough to begin his formal training for the knighthood. When she heard me enter the room, she looked up and greeted me.

"Good morning, Empress Mathilda!"

"Morning? It must be almost midday," I replied.

"Mmm—perhaps. No matter. You need your rest."

What I needed rest from except worrying, I could not imagine, for I had been mostly limited to the castle on account of the war.

"You didn't happen to see any food in the hall?" I asked.

"There may be some bread left on one of the tables. I think the men will take their first meal in an hour or two. Would you like something earlier?"

"No, no. I am much obliged to you," I assured her.

I walked through the door opposite and into the hall. There I found only empty tables, one of which had the remnants of a loaf sitting on it. A single servant was on his hands and knees with a bucket of water and a cloth, wiping up the drink spilled the night before. Taking care not to step across the path he had already cleaned, I took the bread in hand and broke it in two. It did not split easily, and when I felt the edges, it was very dry indeed. Seeing nothing in which to dip it, I simply ate. The stuff did not break down easily. I had only just been able to chew the first half and swallow hard when I heard people yelling outside the keep, more so than was usual for sport.

"What on earth?" I whispered.

"Did you say something to me, my lady?" the man near my feet asked.

"No, no. Carry on," I told him.

I walked across the room to the large wood door that stood between me and the yard. When I placed my hand on the latch, I recognized that it was broken, so the door could not be properly closed. It was simply resting in place.

"Exactly what you want when the enemy might be at the gate any day," I scoffed, pushing the thing forward with one hand while I continued to clasp the poor excuse for bread in the other.

I was immediately struck by the light of the sun, which caused me to squint. As my eyes adjusted, I could see that the outer ward nearest the keep was completely empty of persons except for those who stood upon the walls. I therefore made my way toward one of the gates that led to the inner ward. As I did so, I crossed paths with a goat that had apparently escaped its pen. It looked at me oddly with its big eyes, although I suppose every glance from a goat is somewhat odd.

"You look as though you would eat anything," I said, then threw the remainder of the bread in its direction. The animal quickly ran toward the morsel and sniffed it for a moment, then began to gnaw on it. "May it bring you more joy than it brought me," I muttered.

When I reached the gate, I greeted the two knights who were standing guard, and they quickly admitted me. This was a smaller door only large enough for one man to walk through at a time. The larger gate some fifty feet to the left could not be used without raising the portcullis, the better to keep out invaders.

Once I stepped into the inner ward, I saw something entirely different. Men were running this way and that, most of them in the direction of the main gate in the southeast corner of the fortress. My curiosity raised even further, I increased my pace to join the others. I came upon the cluster of fifty or so men, most of them knights, but I could not see over their caps. Thankfully, one of them saw me and cried, "The empress is here!" Fifty heads suddenly turned in my direction and then bowed just as quickly.

"Is Earl Robert here?" I inquired.

The crowd parted and I saw Robert standing just in front of the gate. I took three or four steps and arrived next to him.

"Yes? We're in the middle of something right now," he said. "Can I help you?"

I thought this response a bit impatient and could see that he would have to be scolded in some way. I crossed my arms in frustration.

"You need to fix your door," I told him.

For a moment, he closed his eyes and shook his head slightly, as if attempting to clear his mind of such strange words.

"What are you talking about?"

"The door that leads into the great hall. It doesn't lock. Call the blacksmith and have it repaired."

"Can it wait?" he asked, a clear edge to his voice.

At once, I dropped my scolding tone and shrugged, for I had had my fun. "I suppose so. Now, who is at the gate? I do hope that this one works properly."

"Robert fitz Hubert."

"What?!" I cried. "He was supposed to be at Malmesbury."

My brother smiled a bit too keenly for my liking. "Now you grasp the problem."

Indeed, I did grasp it. If Robert fitz Hubert was not in Malmesbury but knocking on our door, he could not have met with success. I dared not ask how closely the enemy might be following behind him, but simply stepped forward to peek through the metal grate of the portcullis. Alas, I could see nothing on the other side of the moat, for the bridge was still aloft. From above came the muffled sound of guards yelling across the water to the visitors on the other side. I looked back at Robert.

"Does he come alone? Are they going to lower the bridge?"

"Yes, happily there is no sign of immediate danger, but even so, the man has just escaped here from a shameful defeat in which he was only able to hold his prize for a few days and directly violated the command of Your Highness not to enter the monastery. I thought we could let him wait a few minutes. Do you approve?"

My eyes grew wide. "I do approve. Yes, I approve most heartily."

"I thought you might," he replied with a wink.

The cries from above and beyond seemed to be growing louder and angrier with each passing moment, so I said, "I think it is time, Earl Robert. We've had our fun. Lower the bridge."

My brother stepped back so that the men above could see him, held a finger up, and then thrust it down to signal that the thing should be lowered. Immediately, the wood bridge shook and I could hear the chains moving as it was slowly lowered. I quickly moved back toward the crowd and observed Drogo standing off to the side. I walked over to join him.

"Some day we're having," he commented, as we heard the bridge falling into place.

Keeping my voice low, I told him, "Yes, I don't mind saying I am not looking forward to making this man's acquaintance. I hear he has all the bad manners of Attila the Hun but none of his victory in battle. That is not a combination to be preferred. I was afraid he would turn people against me, and now I fear it has come to pass."

"Hopefully he can at least give us some good information."

"That is the only reason he is being admitted."

We next heard the portcullis being slowly raised, then the thunder of hoof beats on wood as five riders made their way into the castle.

"Only five," I whispered. "That is a bad sign."

The men alighted and then one of them threw his helm upon the ground, as if in detestation, letting out a whirlwind of words in the Flemish tongue that I could not understand, not that I had any wish to do so.

"The man of the hour," I muttered, then summoned all the tolerance within me to approach.

The castle steward and a pair of grooms stepped forward to receive the horses and discarded bits of armor, even as Earl Robert moved to calm Robert fitz Hubert.

"What is it, man?" my brother cried, grabbing him by both shoulders. "What happened?"

I had not yet made my presence known to our new arrivals, for the closer I moved toward Robert fitz Hubert, the more I feared to do so. He was a large man, not in the sense of being simply tall or fat, but with broad shoulders and hands that seemed excessive for even his long arms. His forehead was flat and prominent, and what seemed most odd, he had two dark auburn braids: one descending from the back of his head and the other from his chin. Yes, his figure seemed to impose itself upon the very air, and his voice was deep and powerful as he cried out.

"I've only just come cross country from doing your thrall's work, and this is the welcome I receive! Being made to wait like some stinking peasant!" he shouted into Earl Robert's face, his words heavy with the Flemish accent. He then shouted something in his own language that I was fairly certain was a foul curse, spitting on the ground.

Thrall? This man has no idea what it means to be a thrall, I thought to myself, my loathing for him increasing by the minute.

Although I had great respect for my brother's strength, I was nevertheless amazed to see him stand there and receive this flood of words as if it were no more than a light sprinkle of rain. Truly, the look on his face gave no sign that he was affected at all.

"Am I to assume that the castle was lost?" he asked calmly.

Robert fitz Hubert scowled, shaking his head. "You didn't give me enough men. What did you think would happen, *Noorman*?! You reap what you sow. The king arrived with his army. There was nothing we could do. We were lucky to escape with our lives. I have passed through many dangers to come here and bring you this news!"

"For your pains, I thank you, as does the empress, the rightful sovereign," Earl Robert replied, pointing in my direction.

The mercenary captain spun around and looked at me with dark eyes that threatened to bore a pair of holes in my skull. I did my best to hold his gaze without showing any signs of fear.

"My lady," he said, or rather grunted, for his deep voice made many things sound like a grunt. He slowly dropped down to his knees and bowed his head.

I stepped toward him and extended my hand. I did not truly want him to kiss it, but it had to be done so he would know his place. After he had pressed his lips to my skin, I pulled my hand back and said, "I thank you for your efforts on my behalf, Sir Robert, but I must ask that you show more respect for the earl of Gloucester, as he is paying your wage. And do refrain from casting foul oaths in my presence. I will not abide it."

"Of course, my lady. I beg your pardon," he replied.

I was mildly relieved to see that he was more courteous to a woman, at the very least, but that did nothing to repair the damage he had caused to my own reputation at a time when I needed all the good will I could get.

"You have my pardon, Sir Robert," I assured him, telling a half truth. "Now, you have traveled far, and I suspect that you like me are hungry. Let us enter the hall. I believe they are making some food in the kitchens."

"An excellent idea," Earl Robert agreed. "Come, men! To the keep!"

For the next hour, the mouths of all were far too full with food and drink to have a proper conversation. Adding to the chaos, someone decided to let all the dogs into the hall. From that moment on, it became a game of seeing who could throw a chicken leg the farthest and have his dog retrieve it. Between that and the dogs all leaping on the tables to eat the scraps, I despaired of the occasion and instructed my brother to pull Robert fitz Hubert aside and join me in the solar, where we might have a bit of privacy and perhaps even get a few helpful words out of the man.

I walked into the adjacent chamber first and took my stand near the hearth. Lady Mabel and her son had long since abandoned the room for one of the chambers on the upper level. I could still hear much of the noise on the other side of the stone wall, but it was at least possible to think more clearly.

"All will be well," I whispered. "I know not how, but all will be well."

After a minute or two, Robert fitz Hubert burst through the door with Earl Robert just behind him.

"Good. You are here. Have a seat," I offered, pointing to the three in front of me.

I had assumed that the two men would take the chairs directly by the fire and leave Lady Mabel's special creation alone, but I was wrong. Without any degree of thought that I could observe, the Fleming allowed his immense frame to drop into the lounge chair, resting his muddy boots on the fine fabric. I immediately looked at Robert and could see in his eyes that he too was offended by this action. However, I did not think it would help matters to object, so I gestured with my hand for my brother to sit down.

"Now, Sir Robert," I began, addressing the man who lay with hands clasped behind his head, "I take it the usurper forced you out, yet neither you nor your men show signs of great struggle. What happened?"

He cleared his throat and sat up slightly in his chair. "We were holding the castle, you see, but Stephen and his men surrounded us. There was no way out."

"That much I gathered," I said, nodding my head.

"But my kinsman, William of Ypres … he spoke a good word for me, and we were allowed to leave without harm if we laid down our weapons. This we did, as we had no hope of victory against such a large force. After all, we were sent there to pull Stephen away from Wallingford, no? That is what Earl Robert said, and we accomplished it."

See how easily he ignores the fact that he disobeyed my order! I thought. *Perhaps there is no point in dragging it out, but then again* … I hesitated, uncertain which path to take. I could not afford to make another enemy.

"I thank you for your pains, though I do wish you had seen fit to abide by my instruction. Any abuse of the Church is a gift to the usurper and makes our efforts far more difficult." I sensed he was about to object, so I cut in, "But do you have any idea what the usurper intends to do next?" After all, this was the most urgent point.

Robert fitz Hubert shrugged. "Best I could tell, they were marching down toward Trowbridge. Stephen already took Cerney on his way to Malmesbury, so he'll be happy to have both in his pocket."

I turned to face my brother, who immediately helped to explain the situation.

"South Cerney and Trowbridge are both held by Humphrey de Bohun, who apart from being one of our allies is also married to the daughter of Miles of Gloucester."

"Ah, yes! I remember now," I said, though in truth it was enough of a web to confuse even a spider.

My brother nodded. "As Stephen cannot get his hands on Miles at the moment, he must be hoping to punish all his kin. In the process, he is building a ring around Bristol from which to strike at us."

"Wonderful ..." I muttered, casting my gaze down at the floor. Before my mind's eye, I could see the false king and his allies forming a circle around me like a pack of wolves, the waters dripping from their mouths, their teeth drawn up fierce and terrible, their deep growls causing my spirit to shake as a leaf tossed in the wind. They were close now—very close. I could almost feel the heat of their breath.

As I remained quiet, Earl Robert said to the other Robert, "I think you had best go back and join the feast now."

Sir Robert seemed only too happy to do so. He sprung out of his chair and made for the door without offering another word. I could only shake my head in dejection as my brother rose from his seat.

"This is awful," I said softly.

"Awful? No, no. This is good for us."

I pulled my eyes up from the floor to look into his.

"Good that Stephen is about to have us surrounded? I do not follow your meaning."

"Well, not exactly. I would prefer that he was locked in the Tower in London, as would we all. But pay close attention to what is happening, sister. Stephen is still making the same mistakes: running from one place to the next, always bent upon revenge and listening to poor advice. He let the Flemings go when he was under no requirement to do so. Now they will live to fight another day. And what did he gain for his trouble? He is back in control of the same castle he held before. It would be a shame if poor Humphrey de Bohun were to lose both his fortresses, but don't forget: Miles of Gloucester is still at large! He is marching toward Wallingford and Stephen has no idea. He has no sense of the greater game being played around him. Not long now—you will see."

"You make a fair point," I admitted. "Some times I get so alarmed by what is happening in the moment, I forget how carefully you have laid out the grander plot. I see only the wolves of hell ready to strike, and I cower before them."

"Do not be so hard on yourself!" he encouraged me, putting his arm around my shoulders. "War is a fearful thing for us all—even for me, and I have been fighting for decades. One never feels completely at ease until every enemy is defeated and dead, or at least locked in a prison from which no escape is possible."

I nodded solemnly, and I think Robert must have sensed my lack of ease, for he immediately said in a much happier manner, "Can I interest you in more wine?"

"Will I have to go back in there to get it?" I asked, pointing to the door.

He smiled. "No, you are right. That place is not fit for an empress or any great lady. You may go to your room and I will have the cupbearer bring it to you."

"Very good," I said quickly, but in my own mind I wondered if any amount of wine could banish my distress.

Even as the false king began to build his engines of war at Trowbridge, Lord Miles and his band of knights were moving across the fields of Oxfordshire, making the darkness their friend. Their coming to Wallingford was a complete surprise. Those men Stephen had left behind struggled to even take up their weapons before they were cut down one by one, their unhappy siege completely broken.

Now the situation was changed completely. Stephen was camped to the south, trying in vain to seize Trowbridge. Miles and Brian were united at Wallingford to the east. They had held our position along the Thames and were within reach of both Winchester and London. When the enemy heard of our victory, he had no choice but to abandon his efforts and ride east with all speed that he might prevent any incursion. Already, Miles of Gloucester had shown his great worth, and our efforts had resulted in much gain. Armed with almost nothing, we had been able to hold.

Yet while Stephen feared most for the city of London, that was never part of our design. We were still too few to mount such an invasion, and the false queen, Mathilda of Boulogne, had many of her own men who could withstand a siege until her husband arrived. Thus, we let the usurper make his move to the east, but even as he did so, Miles of Gloucester was riding in the opposite direction, ready to make his stand in the West. He would not be doing so alone:

with Stephen having left the region, I felt safe enough to send Earl Robert as well.

I remember the morning that Robert was readying to leave. We met in the stables and discussed what would happen in the coming days. He and Miles would work to gain all the castles surrounding Gloucester, in particular the cities of Worcester and Hereford. What they could not hold, they would burn to deny the usurper both food and aid. They would be always on the move, never stopping long enough for the enemy to catch them, for he was sure to return to the West when he heard of their actions.

"Earl Robert," I said, as he placed the saddle on his horse, "you know how utterly I depend on you. I forbid you to fall in battle—I simply forbid it! Therefore, take care not to tempt Fate. Think not of performing brave deeds, for you are no good to me dead. The usurper grows weaker by the day. With each victory, our host of allies grows, and soon we will have the Welsh. If the battle becomes too fierce, I command you to retreat: live to fight another day. If ever I see your head upon a spike, I shall have no choice but to kill you!"

I believe my brother rolled his eyes at that comment.

"This is not the playing ground, and we are not kicking a ball," he replied. "War is a different kind of beast. It is what makes us men!"

I scoffed. "What makes us mad, more like. Off with you, then! As soon as I hear of your victory, I shall ride north to Gloucester."

He mounted his steed, then as he rode off, he cried, "On then, men—on to the North! We fight for the empress, for God, and for Saint George!"

On the seventh before the Ides of November, the residents of Worcester awoke from their slumber and set about their daily work: harvesting the final crops, dyeing the wool, feeding the beasts, washing the clothes, baking the bread, churning the butter, crafting the metal, drying the skins, brewing the beer. All this they did under the shadow of war, for they had known for some time that their position upon the river, so close to the rebel strongholds, placed them in great danger. Nevertheless, they kept about their business. Certain treasures had been buried. Weapons had been forged and archers trained. There was nothing to do but wait.

Soon enough, they received the word that had kept them all in dread. The enemy was at the gate, and there would be no escape. Mothers gathered their children and fled to the cathedral, where they took cover in the chapter house. The monks quickly made to hide the precious relics of Saint Oswald. Such men as were able answered the call to battle, seizing their swords, axes, and even sickles. They took their stand street by street, but their foes had no intention of showing mercy. Many townsmen were cut down—still others taken for ransom. Part of the town was burned and the rest pillaged. When all of this had taken place, Earl Robert and Lord Miles came before the church, where a single man stood between them and the door, brandishing his weapon and refusing to move.

"You cannot have it!" he cried. "You can take the food, the animals, the pots and pans, but you will never have the church! You will not lay a finger on our women!"

It was at that moment that Miles of Gloucester alighted from his horse and walked forward, removing his helm. He moved close enough to the man to strike him, then said, "My dear fellow, we did not come for the church. We came for the crown."

There were many who heard what he said, and it was repeated for me by Earl Robert's messenger. I was glad at least that they had not profaned a church of the Lord, but for the people of Worcester there was no respite, and they complain to this day that it was on account of the town of Gloucester that they suffered so, for the merchants of those two cities were always at each other's throats, striving as they were for the same purse.

Thus, the town of Worcester was overcome, but neither Miles nor Robert was content to remain there. They set out to gain the surrounding country, taking the castles in South Cerney and Winchcombe. Wherever they went, they seized the cattle, horses, and sheep. They burned anything that might be of use to the false king. In so doing, they quickly made a name for themselves that was feared far and wide. At length, I received a letter from Robert saying it was safe for me to make my way to Gloucester.

I was only too pleased to have something to do, for I had grown quite tired of Bristol. In all my life, I have never enjoyed waiting around for news. That is the woman's lot, and I despise it. I would far rather see what is taking place, though I by no means sought death. In Gloucester, I would be under the protection of Lord Miles, so I did not fear to make that journey. I boarded a ship and traveled up river, for the knights had taken any horse fit to ride. It was a two-day journey, and I passed the time with the only book in my possession at the time: the history of Bede. One afternoon, I sat as usual leaning back against a pillow.

"Still reading?" Drogo asked, coming to sit beside me. "I should think that Bede is of little use in the middle of a war."

"The venerable fathers of our English Church are of much use to those who would seek to rule England," I replied, lowering the book, "and if ever there is a time for knowledge, it is during a war."

"Yes, but Bede … really?" Here he raised one of his brows.

"Do you have something against that holy man?"

"Nothing at all, but I thought you might look over the writings of Caesar, as you are wont to do."

I sighed. "This was all that was on offer. Now, are you to continue with this abuse, or may I be free to read?"

Drogo smiled and raised his hands in surrender.

"Which part is this?" he asked, looking down at the page.

"It is the story of Etheldreda—Æthelthryth in the English tongue."

"The virgin queen?"

"The very one. She was far holier than I shall ever be. Look what Bede writes of her:

> 'Thus Etheldreda, pure from sensual crime,
> Bright shining star! arose to bless our time
> Born of a regal race, her sire a king,
> More noble honor to her lord shall bring.
> A queen her name, her hand a scepter rears,
> But greater glories wait above the spheres.
> What man wouldst thou desire? See Christ is made
> Her spouse, her blessed Redeemer weds the maid.
> While you attend the heavenly Mother's train,
> Thou shalt be mother of a heavenly reign.
> The holy maid who twelve years sat a queen,
> A cloistered nun devote to God was seen.
> Noted for pious deeds, her spotless soul
> Left the vile world, and soared above the pole.'[5]

"See, that is the kind of queen the people love, Drogo. They desire purity, serenity, tranquility. That is the opposite of myself."

---

5   Venerable Bede. *The Ecclesiastical History of the English Nation.* Translated by J.A. Giles (London: James Bohn, 1845), 233. This quote has been edited to reflect the spelling conventions of the rest of the novel.

The knight scoffed. "I would much rather have you. Who wants a queen who goes off to a nunnery? What good does that do the kingdom?"

"Some would say it sets a godly example," I argued.

"I do not think you are less holy for giving birth to three sons."

I let out a rather wicked laugh. "No, I am less holy because I do not desire virginity."

Suddenly, Drogo's eyes grew wider. "Is that so?" he asked, laughing himself. "You are brave to admit it."

I recognized that I may have shared too much, and I quickly dropped my eyes down to my skirt, which I began tidying. "Yes, well, I cannot say I have taken much pleasure in carnal relations, but perhaps that was because the men in question were not, were not …"

"Interested in anything but themselves?"

"Something along those lines, yes," I replied, my eyes still looking firmly down at my skirt.

"Well, you are full of surprises, Empress Mathilda. Not one in a hundred women would admit to carnal desires."

"That is not quite what I said," I stressed, wishing to preserve at least a bit of my dignity.

"Have you never strayed, then?"

This time I looked him in the eye again—not only that, but I glared.

"I beg your pardon?!"

"That is, have you ever allowed yourself to wander outside the bounds?"

I lifted the book and hit him on the shoulder with it. Have no fear: any pain I caused was not enough to keep him from laughing.

"Of course not! What do you take me for?!" I cried.

"Forgive me, my lady!" he begged, raising his hands once again. "I thought I might see how far I could press the conversation. It was getting rather interesting."

"I thank you not to make assumptions, and I do not like that look in your eye!" I pointed my finger and pressed it on his forehead. "Your mind works mischief! Stop laughing!"

"I cannot help it!"

"Very well," I said, hoping to turn things around on him. "Tell me, Sir Drogo: have you ever strayed?"

"More times than I should care to admit. I am not proud of it."

I looked at him in all seriousness and declared, "Bede would be ashamed of you!"

"I am sure he would be."

"And you desire to be a priest!"

"Is such behavior not required of priests?"

"Was that in jest?! Swear it was in jest!" I commanded, lifting the book to strike.

"It was in jest. I repent! I repent!" he cried, throwing up his hands.

Placing the book aside, I sat back and crossed my arms, offended that he should be so callous, yet at the same time trying not to laugh myself. Finally, I said, "When we get to Gloucester, I shall make sure to lock you up at night, the better to keep you from bedding every woman in the county."

"Come now! I'm not that bad! I don't even have any bastards. My father always told me, 'You're not a man until you have a bastard.' But do I have any? No. Your brothers do. Stephen does. The Beaumonts do. Indeed, it seems everyone does but me! That is something."

"Not Lord Brian."

"What?"

"Lord Brian does not have any bastards."

"Ah, yes," he admitted, nodding his head. "He is a better man than the rest of us. That I freely admit."

"Right you are. We'll speak of this no more. I must return to Bede." Here I picked up the book again and searched for the page I had left.

"Very well, but know that you are just as good as Queen Etheldreda. Indeed, you are better, for you are actually doing something. Ethel-dread. They named her right."

"Thank you, Drogo, for your contribution," I concluded.

Upon the River Severn, between the hills of the shepherds and the Forest of Dean, lies the town of Gloucester, not ten miles south of Tewkesbury Abbey. Though it does not boast a cathedral, Gloucester becomes a key part of our tale for several reasons. First, it lies near some of the best fields and iron mines in England. Second, it is seated next to the chief river in the West Country. Third, it is within a day's ride of the Welsh border. Fourth, it has a fine castle, which in those days was under the control of our friend, Miles of Gloucester. Finally, it was perfectly placed in relation to Bristol, the city of Earl Robert. If this be not enough reasons to recommend a place, then I cannot think what would be.

Even though he was not the castellan of the town, my brother had spent much wealth of coin improving the fortress above the Severn, strengthening its walls and enriching the nearby church of Saint Peter. His aim was to create a chain of castles along the river: Bristol, Gloucester, Tewkesbury, Worcester. Although Earl Robert had not yet completed this work, he had still made great improvements that were to benefit us in the coming days.

As soon as we arrived, Lord Miles of Gloucester was standing there on the pier to receive us. I climbed out of the boat and he knelt before me, kissing my hand.

"All hail, Empress Mathilda, lady of England!" he proclaimed, bowing.

"Well met, Lord Miles," I replied. "We have heard of your triumph at Wallingford and are only too glad to make our stay in your beloved city. I take it my brother has been called away?"

"Yes, he is assembling our defense. It is certain that Stephen will return once he hears of the fate of Worcester."

"I suppose we shall have to make do without him, then. Am I to ride this horse?" I asked, pointing at the tall brown animal in front of me.

"Yes, my lady."

He helped me mount the steed and we rode together up the hill. Very soon, I could see the castle walls. A keep such as one might find anywhere in the West Country stood at a height of three stories, its four small towers rising up from each corner. Off to the right, an old barbican hill was visible on the other side of the ditch, though it was by that time stripped of any proper fortress.

"This is it, then," I said, nodding in the direction of the fortress. "This is the castle of Gloucester."

"Yes, Your Highness," Miles answered.

I turned to Drogo and whispered, "It is a bit smaller than I imagined."

"Not everything can be the equal of Caen, my lady," he replied.

"I suppose not."

Perhaps sensing a need to stress the castle's virtues, Miles appealed to its history.

"The Romans built walls around this city in ancient days, but they have since been pulled down in many places. This site by the river needed to be defended, and so it was that they raised the new castle here, where it can watch over the Severn. It is still a work in progress."

"I see. And what was there before?" I asked.

"I believe the monks had a garden," he told me.

I let out a sigh. "Alas, poor monks!"

"The main gate is around on the other side," Miles explained, abandoning any attempt to impress me. "Let's be on our way."

We rode along beside the ditch that surrounded the castle until we had reached the northern side. From there I could see a large spire above the roofs of the city's houses.

"Is that the abbey of Saint Peter?" I asked Miles.

"The very one," he confirmed with a smile. "Would you like to see it?"

"Not at the moment, no. My uncle lies buried there, and he was not the most favored person in the family."

"Oh. Did you know him, then?"

"No more than I know the pope, but it's the principle of the thing. He opposed my father's rule, and I choose not to set store by traitors and usurpers. I hope you would say the same."

His mood seemed to change. Indeed, it looked as if I had wounded him.

"I have repented of my support for the false king, having come to see the error of my ways," he said solemnly. "I believed that you forgave me."

"I did … I do, but you must allow me to get one barb in, or we shall all die from lack of excitement."

"Fair enough," he said, clearly relieved. "Shall I show you to your room, then?"

"Lead on!"

Once we had made it inside, Drogo made to help the grooms with the horses while I joined Lord Miles inside the keep. The lower level was much the same as that in Bristol Castle, with a hall on one side and a more private chamber on the other, although in this case there was also a small chapel tucked away in one corner.

When we had made our way into the solar and were standing near the hearth, I saw that all sign of cheer had been removed from Miles' face. He stood as one sent upon some horrid errand, his face grim. Then he said, "There is bad news from the East."

My mind flew immediately to the lands in that direction and all who resided there. It did not take long for me to make the connections.

"What?! Has Wallingford been assaulted again?" I asked in dismay, then a far darker thought entered my mind. "Is one of my sons dead?!" In the space of a breath, my spirit reached out to clutch them all close to my heart, the one place I could keep them safe, those souls that possessed my own, for whom I lived and breathed and was.

"No, nothing like that! Stephen has stripped me of my role as constable."

So powerful was the relief I felt upon hearing those words that I bent over and sighed, placing my hands on my knees. *Not today. My world does not end today,* I assured myself. However, this was swiftly followed by the recognition that something did not make sense.

"What? You were still a constable?" I asked, thoroughly confounded.

"Yes, but now I am not."

There was a silver pitcher filled with wine and two matching goblets sitting on the mantel. Lord Miles poured for each of us and handed one of the goblets to me. I drank deeply from it, for my hours out in the sun had brought me great thirst, and I was still recovering from the fright he had caused me. Upon stopping to take a breath, I continued the conversation.

"I have to tell you, Lord Miles, that on this point at least I think the false king might be in the right. You have been a rather poor constable."

He smiled as the fox. "Only if you frown on outright rebellion—"

"Which most rulers do, or so I have heard."

"—but it is a sore loss, and I hope that you will see fit to make me constable again once we have won our victory." Here he raised his goblet to me.

"Actually, I was hoping to make you earl of Hereford."

Lord Miles had been in the middle of a drink when I said this. He almost choked and finally cried, "Oh, my lady! You are too gracious. You do me such great honor!"

"Well, the earldom is what you desire, is it not?"

He smiled once again. "You know me too well, or perhaps you have made use of the knowledge of others. Either way, you know how to reward a man."

"You have done me a great service," I said, raising my own goblet. "I will depend on you to carry us forward. Earl Robert needs a second."

"Of course. I am at your command."

For a moment, I ran my fingers down the outside of the goblet, taking note of the pattern carved into the metal: to my fingers, it felt like hills and valleys, with paths running this way and that. At length, I took up the conversation again.

"So, you think Stephen will come back, then? He will invade the West?" I might as well have added, *He will come for me. He will leave none alive.*

"If I assume correctly, but we will be ready for him," Miles answered, placing his own goblet on the mantel and crossing his arms.

I attempted to place my fear aside. "Sooner or later, we will need to break out of the West."

"The winter is almost upon us, and the weather will be poor. Perhaps we can make a truce and use that time to build up our strength. Come spring, we shall make a charge across this island that will always be remembered!" he declared boldly.

"Oh, I like the sound of that! Not only the time to breathe, but the bid for action. In order to win, we must perform the kind of deeds that go down in legend. We are the weaker side."

"I would rather be weaker but wiser, and that is what we are."

"Very well, then," I said, raising my goblet again. "To the coming year—to England!"

He lifted his goblet and repeated, "To England!"

III

"Who is to give me a fountain of tears that I may weep for my country's impious deeds?"

Thus Henry of Huntingdon wrote when looking back on those treacherous years, and well might he rue the judgment they brought upon us all.

"Their flesh consumed, hunger fills those who mourn; skin and bones breathe out their wandering souls. Who is to bury these great crowds of dying? Behold! Here is a glimpse of the Styx, and its spreading corruption."[6]

Oh, have a rest, dear Henry! If those years seemed foul to you within the walls of your cathedral, how foul must they have been for those of us who suffered daily the changing fortunes of war? The common man fears that war may come for him, but the empress knows it will.

---

6   Henry of Huntingdon. *The History of the English People 1000-1154*, Oxford World's Classics Edition, Translated by Diana Greenway (Oxford: Oxford University Press, 2009), 75. This quotation has been edited to better match the spelling and language conventions of this novel.

I had not been three days in Gloucester ere I received the news that England's bane, Waleran Beaumont, had arrived within his earldom of Worcester to survey the damage it had lately sustained. When he glimpsed the signs of our victory, he became like a mad dog, wandering the fields, desperate for blood. There were no crops for him to set alight, but he slaughtered the beasts and seized the men for ransom. Most of those poor souls were no friends of ours, but simple folk about their business, hoping to earn an honest wage. As for Waleran, he had never once been honest or earned a wage, but received everything he had from the hand of the usurper.

Within two weeks, the false king himself was in Worcester. This was altogether too close for my liking, being no more than a day's ride from Gloucester! The defenses put in place by the lords Robert and Miles were excellent, and I was assured by many a person that there was nothing to fear: Stephen was not fool enough to assail us there. After all, we were surrounded by strong walls, they told me.

And no one shoots at men behind walls, I scoffed within my mind. *There are few things that my cousin is not fool enough to do.*

In order to distract myself from these things, and for the benefit of my soul, I decided to visit the abbey church of Saint Peter on the other side of town, for it seemed the only place where I was likely to find serenity. The abbot there was Gilbert Foliot, who in these later years has appeared once again in the tale of my son—a story for another time. It was on that day in early December that I was first to make his acquaintance. I intended for him to become my confessor, and believe me, there are few women who have ever needed a confessor as much as myself. In the space of a few minutes, I arrived before the western door of that awesome place, where I was surprised to see no abbot waiting for me, but rather a simple monk.

"Greetings, most gracious empress!" the man said, bowing. "My name is Hamelin. You must forgive my master. He did not think you would be here for another hour."

"That is not a very promising beginning," I replied, wondering if I might have read the dial incorrectly. "Has the good abbot taken leave of the place?"

"Oh no!" the monk assured me. "He is just in his lodging. If you follow me, I will show you the improvements we have made to the church these past few years."

"Very well," I concluded, and allowed him to lead the way into the nave.

Now, the abbey of Gloucester had a rather ancient foundation, but the present building was begun just a few years before my own birth, after its predecessor was destroyed. It was Abbot Serlo who oversaw the work and laid his stamp upon the place. The poor monks endured two fires and God only knows how many other difficulties, but by the year of our Lord 1139, it was mostly completed. I am told that the interior resembles the cathedral of Durham with its massive columns running down the nave, though having never seen the latter, I cannot comment with any degree of certainty. Indeed, I never knew any of this before it was told me by the monk Hamelin, who seemed desperate to fill the time while we awaited his master. I was grateful for anything to distract me from the very near presence of my great enemy.

After we had walked around in this manner for some time, with the monk speaking and myself merely listening, I finally asked him, "Pray tell, where is my uncle?"

"Your uncle, my lady?" The look on his face was all confusion.

"Yes, Lord Robert of Normandy. Where does he take his eternal rest?"

"Ah! He is just there," he replied, extending his finger in the general direction of the high altar.

Here was a moment I had not longed for, but which I knew I must face. I walked over to where the monk had pointed, but it still took me a good minute or so to find my uncle's grave. Had I not been told that it was the tomb of a former duke of Normandy, I would never have known: it was as plain as that of the most minor lord. A simple square of gray stone, no more than two feet across, was set among the floor tiles, reading only, "ROBERT NORMANIÆ."

Robert of Normandy: not Duke Robert of Normandy or Robert son of the king, I thought. *There's some derision and no mistake.*

"It was laid in haste, and without the proper coin. We hope to raise enough to build him something better," the monk said, evidently hoping to put off my anger. "Perhaps Your Highness would like to make a gift?"

Oh, how he mistook me! I could not help laughing softly, but I quickly covered my mouth when I saw the look on his face.

"Forgive me," I said. "I do not wish to seem unfeeling, but if I had two coins to put together, I should use them to feed my men and not to ornament this miscreant. It is a proper monument for one who proved a traitor."

"I ... see," he replied, clearly ill at ease. Poor man! I had finally robbed him of speech.

"Do you say Mass for his soul?" I asked, attempting to be more courteous.

"Three times a week," he assured me, swiftly nodding his head.

"Well, that is good. He shall need it."

As the monk Hamelin continued to stand back, I looked down at the roughly hewn slab. In that moment, so much of my life was uncertain. I feared the arrival of the enemy any day, and perhaps that stress freed me to speak as I would not have otherwise.

Staring at the grave, I whispered, "So, Uncle William, we meet at last. Have you been waiting on me? No, I suppose you have not. You are slaving away in purgatory, or perhaps you were sent all the way down. Well, here I am, perhaps at the ending of days. I have come to collect upon a debt, for if my judgment is near at hand, yours must be also.

"Do you know what they say about treachery, Uncle? It is the foulest of sins: the sin of Judas Iscariot. Many sleepless nights did my father suffer while yet you lived. Ah, but you say I did not love my father! You are correct, I did not … that is, I did at first, but when I saw that he would never return that love, mine rather died out. And that is your doing, Uncle.

"You trained up a son to oppose us. On his account, I was married to foul Geoffrey, who save for three boys has given me naught but grief. Do not think I have forgotten the part you played in all that! William Clito was but the sapling sprung from your rebellious tree. How very alike you were, never willing to accept the decree of God! Never willing to bend the knee to your rightful lord!

"My father was born in this land: he belonged to it, even as I do. You were ever a foreigner. Now has come the final foreigner, the rebel to end all rebels, the accursed Stephen! He too is sprung from your tree, for it was you who planted the seed of rebellion in them all. Do you think that I have forgotten how the evil Waleran first served your cause?

"Oh, I see it, Uncle, and were I not in a church of God, I would tell you exactly what I wish you to do and where I wish you to go. But since I stand upon hallowed ground, with one pledged to God in our midst, I shall hold my tongue, yet not for your sake. No, you have now what you always deserved. Fie, devil! I shall not sing a Mass for thee, the author of my misery."

"What is this?" a voice suddenly asked.

I turned around and saw that it was Abbot Gilbert finally come over to receive me. He was a man of medium size, clothed in black as befit a follower of Benedict, his hood pulled up over his head and a simple crucifix hanging around his neck. Other abbots were wont to dress in fine clothing, but it seemed that this one was a man of simpler tastes. I wondered how much he had heard. Perhaps it did not matter. As soon as I locked eyes with him, he bowed low to the ground. I beckoned for him to come near, and in doing so, he bowed again and kissed my hand.

"Empress Mathilda," he said, meeting my eyes.

"Abbot Gilbert."

"I must beg your forgiveness. I was not aware of the time."

A good man he was for taking the blame rather than admitting that I might have arrived early! We said farewell to the monk Hamelin, then he led me down the steps and out into the cloister, where the monks grew their herbs.

"So, how are you finding Gloucester?" the abbot asked, as we made our way around the bend.

"I might as well ask you the same question. You have been here less than a year, no?"

"Yes, ever since poor Walter de Lacy died and they fetched me from Cluny."

"And have you passed a happy few months here?"

"The town is pleasant enough," he replied, arriving at the door to the chapter house. He pulled out a great set of keys from his pocket and slipped one into the lock, then with his hand still on the latch, he turned and said, "It is not as warm as Cluny. I suppose I shall have to get used to that."

Having made this observation, he pushed open the door and we entered the chapter house, a large room that was almost empty. There was no fire made up in the lone hearth, so it was quite cold, the stone arches providing little in the way of comfort.

"Brother Nicholas!" the abbot called back to one of his fellows who was walking past the door. "We need a fire in here. The empress must not freeze."

"It's fine. I have my cloak," I offered.

"No, no! That will not do."

The abbot pointed to a pair of chairs that had been left out for us, and while I sat there, he gave orders to the poor monks, who poked at the sparks in earnest, bidding them break into flame. One of them brought in a bellows and proceeded to toil with it for several minutes. All the while, I thought to myself about my meeting with the abbot just moments earlier and whether he had heard any of the harsh things I said to my uncle's bones. *The fear of the hour has affected me,* I thought. When they had finally achieved a rather pitiful blaze, the abbot bid them depart, and at the sound of the closing door, the two of us were alone.

"Are you warm enough?" he asked, smiling with what seemed a genuine kindness in his eyes.

I did not dare say no after all the trouble the monks had already endured. Once he was assured of my comfort, he continued, "I am honored to fulfill my duty to you, Empress Mathilda. I shall serve as your confessor for as long as you reside in Gloucester, if that is your wish."

"Abbot Gilbert ..."

"Yes, my lady?"

"I'm afraid you may have caught me in a bad moment earlier. I do not usually chastise the dead," I told him earnestly.

He smiled again. "I did not assume that you do."

"You see, my uncle's connection with the family was rather ... rather ..."

"Strained?"

That was not the word I would have chosen, but I replied, "You could say that."

"He brought some great trouble on this city," the abbot concurred. "I can only imagine what he brought to you."

"Quite. Yet that does not excuse any foul speech I might have made. I am afraid this war has set me on edge, especially with the enemy so near at hand."

"Think nothing of it, madam. I consider it part of the natural process of complaint."

I sat there staring at the man sitting some two paces in front of me, whose words were to me as those of a sphinx.

"Forgive me ... what?" I stammered.

"Well, take me for example," he offered, placing his hand on his chest. "I am an abbot, so I always complain about the bishops, for they are the ones in authority over me." Here he moved his hand upward to further show his intent. "You complain about those in authority over you. It is the way of the world. I admit the part about the object of your wrath being deceased does lend it a slightly different feel, but I am not one to judge."

The abbot seemed to speak from experience, so I offered a question.

"You do not like your bishop, then?"

"No, no!" he replied with real fervor. "Bishop Simon is a fine man. He used to serve as chaplain to—"

"Queen Adeliza, yes. I fear I have gotten her in trouble these past few months."

"Hmm ..." Abbot Gilbert muttered, resting his chin on his hand.

"What?"

"You seem quite worried about getting in trouble, or perhaps getting others in trouble."

"If you knew me at all, you would know that is a constant danger," I assured him.

"Well, if you worry so much, then why put yourself through all of this?" he asked, gesturing broadly, as if the rest of the room represented the whole of my life.

"All of what? Do you mean the war?"

"Do not mistake me!" he said, raising a finger. "I know you fight, and well you should, but have you ever actually stopped to ask why you are fighting?"

"Is it not evident?" I asked, for he was beginning to annoy me.

"I know well enough my own belief, but if you came here to confess, then perhaps I should hear it from your lips."

This was not what I had come to discuss, but with a sigh I replied, "State your question again—in plain language."

"Very well. Why do you want to be queen?"

It may seem hard to believe, but this was the first time the question had ever been put to me. Indeed, I had not often been fully aware of it myself. My need to fight for the crown had arisen more as a matter of natural instinct than anything else: a response to injustice and maternal pride. Most days, I spent all my time worrying about this or that, pressing toward a goal that I could barely grasp in any sense of the word.

I leaned back in my seat and considered for a moment. The question could not be done away with easily. Was it pride that pushed me onward? Vengeance? Avarice? Faith? Love? At last, I had a moment of clarity—a feeling that gripped me. It continued to build, and soon I found myself speaking on behalf of an idea I was only beginning to understand.

"You are incorrect, sir, in assuming that I wish to be queen, or that any such thought has brought me thus far. Rather, I want to see England restored. I want the rule of law to be obeyed. I want the land to be freed from this treachery. I do not strive for myself, but for my children and my children's children. I will not see their inheritance denied—not only that my sons should sit upon the throne of England, but that the kingdom over which they rule should be one of justice and righteousness. That is the inheritance not only of me and mine, but of all Englishmen. If I do not fight, if I make no attempt to defend that which has been purchased at so high a price, then I shall deny that inheritance to all who come after me. That is what Abbot Boson once said to me: 'You must think in terms of a thousand years.' How right he was! I myself am nothing, but England is everything. Each of us has a part to play in what this kingdom will be, but by the smallest of chances or perhaps the very hand of God, it falls to me to cast my lot for its future, and while there is some vigor in my frame, I must do so or be judged ignoble."

"You speak well for a woman," the abbot observed.

"It is no strange thing that a woman should speak well," I replied, raising my brows.

"Forgive me! I meant no offense."

"No one ever does, or so they say."

He nodded. "I imagine it is difficult for you ... being a woman on a man's errand."

I laughed. "Abbot Gilbert, you have no idea."

My uncle David once told me that Advent was the time for miracles, and such was the case that year. Having been frustrated in his attempts to seize the West Country, the usurper made a truce with Lord Miles and left the fighting for the warmer months, much to my relief. As one of the chroniclers noted, the false king did receive pledges of fealty from some of the local folk, but others stated, "Although we will not swear, the king may, if he pleases, trust the truth of our words."[7] That

---

7   Quoted in *The Chronicle of Florence of Worcester: With the Two Continuations*, Translated by Thomas Forester (London: Henry G. Bohn, 1854), 272.

he was willing to accept such a promise made with only half the heart is proof of the weakness of Stephen's position. In any case, he was forced to fall back to the East not only by the winter cold, but also by the death of the bishop of Salisbury.

Yes, Bishop Roger, second in power only to the king under the reign of my father, but greatly reduced by the usurper whom he helped to raise up: he had given up his spirit, as all men must. I do not doubt that his concubine mourned him along with the few men left in his house. I had no love in my heart for the bishop, but I must acknowledge his skills of administration, which were far greater than those of the men Stephen chose to supplant him. Ever did he ensure the prosperity of his sovereign ... until that sovereign turned against him.

The departure of Stephen and his supporters to seize the treasure at Salisbury presented us with an opportunity to gather our own forces and finally meet face to face. Such a prospect excited me to no end, especially because it would allow both my brother Reginald and Brian fitz Count to travel to Gloucester, if only for a brief stay. I so longed to see them and celebrate the birth of our Lord together.

Sadly, there was little money for a great feast. I know the scriptures teach that even rulers ought to be humble, but when the cooks are forced to serve meat that is past its proper time, or to forgo meat altogether, you have crossed into the realm of humiliation. As we had no more wine to speak of, the servants produced a rather poor form of mead to take its place. How fortunate then that the company at least would be excellent!

The day they were meant to arrive, I was sitting at one of the tables in the hall with my nephew Hamon on my lap. He may have been Robert's youngest child, but he was still a large boy. Thus, after a few minutes of sitting in such a state, I was forced to ask him to move to the side. He wished me to read to him, so I had picked up the *Metamorphoses* of Ovid, which I knew almost by rote. I well remember the passage. It was from the twelfth book, and young Hamon asked me, "Who is this Caeneus, aunt? Is he from Caen like my father?"

"No, child," I answered. "He was a Greek: a great warrior."

"Like Hercules?"

"Something like that, yes. See what it says here:

'Already Caeneus, with his conquering hand,
Had slaughtered five the boldest of their band.
Pyrachmus, Helymus, Antimachus,
Bromus the brave, and stronger Stiphelus,
Their names I numbered, and remember well,
No trace remaining, by what wounds they fell.'

"You see, he was the strongest of the strong," I explained.

"What happens next?" he asked, bending over the pages.

"Well, his opponent mocks him. He declares him to be inferior."

"Why?" the child asked, looking up at me.

"You read it," I said, hoping to prompt him to excellence.

I slid the book over so it was directly in front of him. The boy would clearly rather have had me read it to him, but he nevertheless made his way ever so slowly through the poet's words. Perhaps you know them:

"And from a strumpet shall we suffer shame?
For Caenis still, not Caeneus, is thy name:
And still the native softness of thy kind
Prevails; and leaves the woman in thy mind;
Remember what thou wert; what price was paid
To change thy sex; to make thee not a maid:

And but a man in shew; go, card and spin;
And leave the business of the war to men."[8]

When he had finished reading this, young Richard looked at me, his eyes wide with concern.

"Does this mean what I think it means?" he uttered.

"Yes. Caeneus used to be a woman."

"How?" he asked, clearly perplexed.

"The woman Caenis was raped by the god Poseidon, and as recompense, he offered to grant her one wish. She wished to have the body of a man so that she might never fall prey to such villainy again. Not only did he transform her into the man, Caeneus, but he granted her skin that no weapon could pierce. That is why Caeneus was such a strong warrior. See how he defeats the centaur who chided him!" I said, pointing down at the passage.

The boy did not reply, so I finally asked him, "What is it?"

He looked up at me meekly and said, "Do you ever wish you were a man so that you could fight in a war?"

Ah, the wonder of a young mind not yet trained to be discreet! I accepted his question with a sigh, combing his brown hair with my fingers.

"There is more to life than fighting in war, nephew."

He furrowed his brow. "Yes, but you cannot do the things that men do. You cannot rule."

The natural affinity I had with my blood relatives was being sorely tested at this point. I dropped my hand, fighting to contain the anger that was rising within me.

"I can and I shall," I told him firmly.

"Yes, but if you were a man, this never would have happened: the war and all that."

8   Ovid. *Metamorphoses*, Translated by Garth, Dryden, et al, Book 12. http://classics. mit.edu/Ovid/metam.12.twelfth.html. Accessed 2 April 2022.

The boy in his innocence could not have known how deeply those words cut into my soul. Had I ever wished to be a man? To be free to do as I wished? Of course I had! Indeed, there was only one person on earth whom I suspected of preferring me as a woman. Yet how could I deny all that I was?

"I think we have read enough," I concluded, shutting the book. "Our guests will be here any moment."

No sooner had I spoken the words than I heard a trumpet sound. Young Hamon was off like a lightning bolt, but I remained in my seat a bit longer, attempting to calm myself. A few tears were able to break the bounds of my eyes and I lifted up my sleeve to dry them.

It is not good to dislike one's self, especially for something that is beyond one's power, I thought. *Breathe, just breathe.*

At length, I was able to contain my feelings and make my way out into the courtyard, where the riders had already alighted from their horses. I saw Earl Robert and Lord Miles walking toward the steps that led into the keep, with the two guests following behind: my father's son Reginald de Dunstanville and Lord Brian of Wallingford. My stomach seemed to leap when I saw these new faces ... and one in particular. The four of them were so busy talking with each other that they did not sense our presence there on the steps until Hamon yelled out, "Father!"

"Well met, my boy!" Earl Robert called. "Come and let us see you!"

This he did, stopping first to embrace his uncle Reginald. I watched as the four men played with the boy, and I could not help but remember how the king's lads had come to visit William and me at Westminster in the days of our youth. Apart from the clear difference in age, it might have been the same thing all over again, and my nephew did look rather like my brother. Of course, Stephen and Robert Beaumont had been among the king's lads, but a gulf was fixed between us. Things could never be the way they were before—not since war had come to England.

At once, Lord Brian was aware of my presence, and he broke away from the others to greet me. As he came within three steps and bowed, I could see how the years had taken their toll on him. His skin bore the signs of conflict: the skin on his hands was raw in places, and I could make out a new scar on one of them. His hair was certainly more gray than it used to be, even as Robert had told me. Yet he was still plainly Brian fitz Count through and through.

"Empress Mathilda, I am glad to have the chance to meet with you again. I didn't know if it would be possible," he said, standing to his full height and meeting my eyes.

"I too am glad to have you all here," I replied rather weakly, feeling ill at ease.

"I would have come earlier, but we were too busy holding Wallingford against those villains, Stephen and William of Ypres."

I nodded in agreement. "We have heard such tales of your bravery—that is, you and your men. You have done us a great service."

"It is Lord Miles who has done you the service," he argued, nodding his head in Miles' direction. "We would have been lost had he not ridden in to save the day! With your permission, I will transfer to him the honor of Abergavenny. I know he covets it, and it is the least I can do to thank him."

"I cannot let you do that!" I protested. "That is yours by right of marriage."

He shrugged. "I hardly need it now. I have my hands full with Wallingford. Please—let me do this."

"Well, if you are certain, but I still say it is not necessary."

He smiled. There was a sight I had not seen in many years! Into my mind suddenly came those words my brother had spoken to me two years earlier. "He loves you—you know that." Oh, how I wished to know the truth of those words! I should have liked to hear them from Brian's lips. It was the first time I had seen him since I decided to forgive him, having learned the true purpose behind his actions. I felt myself longing for him just as I had in my younger days. But that was a dangerous road that led to destruction, and I would not allow myself to tread upon it.

"How was your journey?" I asked, hoping that the question was sufficiently neutral.

"Good. The weather was pleasant for this time of year."

I did not have a chance to say anything else, for the other men joined us. Reginald was the first to greet me.

"My empress! My sister! How has the war been treating you? You look well. Does she not look well?" he asked his fellows.

They all nodded their heads, being faithful subjects, but I especially noted that Brian answered in the affirmative.

"Have you come to shoot another one of my cats?" I asked Reginald.

"Ah, I forgot about that," he replied. "Was it special to you?"

"A cat is a cat, brother, but I trust you can put your bow to a greater purpose. You are to return to your earldom of Cornwall, which the usurper lately took from you falsely."

"Yes, so I hear. Thank you, my lady," he said with a bow.

"Tell me, Miles," I asked, turning toward him, "how long will this truce last?"

"As long as it takes for them to appoint a new bishop of Salisbury, and for the weather to improve," he replied.

"We had best be on the move then," I concluded. "Come, Lady Mabel had some pies made up, so at least there is something decent to eat."

"That is why I love that woman!" Robert declared.

We passed through the entry way and into the hall, where a pair of tables sat on either side of the fire. The lot of us took our seat at one of them and attempted to make a meal of the pies, which in truth were not the sort of thing one ought to brag about, despite Lady Mabel's efforts. Our only other recourse was the mead that had been brewed in haste. Reginald took one drink of it and pulled back, looking at his cup as if it was an instrument of death.

"What is this stuff?!" he complained loudly. "Is this what passes for drink in Gloucester?"

"Take it up with Lord Miles. It's his castle," I replied.

"I refuse to take the blame for this!" said Miles, staring down into the liquid before him. "When last I was here, we still had some wine from Burgundy."

"All gone, friend," I assured him. "I gave the last bottle to Abbot Gilbert to thank him for his aid."

"Eww! What in God's name?!" Robert cried, having just taken a drink. "Who made this?"

"Have you failed to pay attention to anything we've said?" I asked.

"It's not so bad," Brian concluded, although I noted some strain in his face. "If you can get past the bitterness, it has a nice warmth to it. If you can get past the bitterness ..."

"Damn! That's awful!" Robert said, having tasted it again.

"Why are you still drinking it?!" I demanded.

"I don't know," he said with a shrug. "I thought maybe it would be better the second time."

"You are such a man! Here, I am taking this away from you all," I said, gathering the cups one by one, "and now I shall have no more complaining!"

"Do you have any beer?" Reginald asked.

"If you want beer, win the war," I concluded.

The Advent meeting was lovely, but it could not last: Stephen would soon have all he needed from Salisbury and the weather would not be cold for ever. Lord Brian returned to defend his castle of Wallingford. Lord Miles took one of Earl Robert's knights and a great lord in the area, Geoffrey Talbot, up to the city of Hereford, hoping to seize his earldom and with it control of the Welsh Marches. It was quite a change of fortune, for not half a year earlier, the two men were waging battle on opposite sides for the very same prize! They succeeded in taking the town but were unable to conquer the castle. Thus, once again, we were frustrated in our efforts.

I valued Miles, but a part of me feared him. There was always a lingering suspicion in my mind that he was not heart and soul for our cause: that he fought only for himself. Sadly, this was a condition too often present in the hearts of men at that time. Day after day, Earl Robert would make inquiries with the barons, hoping to sway them to our side or at least induce them to remain neutral. Yet even in that time of great tests, when the fate of us all hung in the balance, too many men were concerned only with their own gain. They might have let the kingdom burn for the sake of a few pounds. Such men are the vilest on all God's green earth, having not a care for their fellow man, nor an ounce of loyalty! Many such men will cross your path. Avoid them like the bloody flux!

On the other hand, there are those who possess something of true courage. Such a man was Bishop Nigel of Ely, nephew of the late Bishop Roger of Salisbury. He had seen the wheel of fortune turn against his kin. Although he was a man of the Church, he felt all too keenly the troubles of this world. He knew the false king was no servant of the Almighty, but an enemy of Christianity. Thus, when he heard the news of his uncle's death, Bishop Nigel made his move.

Now, the isle of Ely is not an isle in the truest sense. Rather, it is a hill surrounded by marshland so thick that when the rains have been falling for days on end, as they were that December, it becomes an island most truly. Upon that isle sat not only the cathedral, but also a small castle bordered all around by the fen. Bishop Nigel saw his opportunity. With the money he still possessed after the usurper seized the greater part, he was able to bring a company of knights into his service. They set out to strengthen the defenses, and in due course, word was sent to Stephen that Ely was now in the hands of the bishop, who intended to hold it for our side.

I imagine there were few things that would have caused Stephen to break away early from his court in Salisbury. How he had longed to take possession of the last of Bishop Roger's wealth! If only he had been willing to share a small portion of those spoils with the dead man's relative, he might have avoided the fight that came to his threshold. He was forced to abandon the proceedings and ride up to Ely. Though he moved with great speed, it did him little good, for when he arrived, he was unable to make any advance upon the island on account of the muddy fens.

That ought to have been the end of the false king's adventure, but it was in that hour that Ephialtes chose to show his face, or someone rather like him.[9] A monk of Ramsey Abbey, a man of no importance but for the aid he provided the usurper, approached Stephen and revealed to him a place where the men might ford the waters. This they accomplished by tipping over the boats of local fishermen and forming a bridge to the other side. Once they set foot on the isle, there was no hope for Bishop Nigel. His knights were far fewer than Stephen's. They were quickly cut down or forced to surrender. When the

---

9 Ephialtes of Trachis was, according to Herodotus, the Greek who revealed a secret trail to the Persians at the Battle of Thermopylae in 480 BC, allowing them to flank the Greeks (headed by the Spartan king Leonidas), who had up to that point held back the Persian invaders by blocking a narrow passage. Ephialtes' name became synonymous with treason in ancient Greek culture.

usurper made it into the castle, he is said to have cried out, "Nigel! Nigel! Foulest traitor! Show your face and face your doom! Wrong was I to let you live!"

Alas, Bishop Nigel was not there. He had been able to flee in a small boat, making his way to a local village, where he acquired a horse. He then rode with all haste to the West. Where he found to lay his head, I cannot tell you. All I know is that he arrived in Gloucester just after New Year's Day, looking as if he were half dead. We received him into our care, and he remained with us for many days thereafter.

There were a great many people fleeing in those days, running hither and thither in search of protection, or at least a dry place to sleep. Even as we took in lost souls from all over the island, I continued to meet with Abbot Gilbert. He always offered to come to the castle, but I preferred to speak with him in the chapter house, for I enjoyed a good walk. Nothing sets the mind at ease like a journey through town, especially when one's spirit is ill-disposed. One January day, I set out for the abbey with even more cares than usual. I craved the opportunity to speak with the abbot in confidence. Thus, when we were seated in the usual manner, each in our own chair facing the other, he asked me, "What brings you to us today, Empress Mathilda? Is something troubling you?"

"Indeed, it is," I replied. "I have just received a letter from my brother." Here I held up the opened parchment in my hand. "It seems he has made quite a mess of things."

"What has Earl Robert done?" he asked.

"Oh no! Not Earl Robert—I speak of my other brother, Reginald. You know I made him earl of Cornwall again upon his marriage to the daughter of William fitz Richard?"

"Yes, you mentioned it before."

"And he has taken up his residence in Launceston Castle and set about forcing all of Cornwall into submission."

"Indeed."

I let out a heavy sigh. "Well, I have always set great store by Earl Reginald's aim, but now it seems he has shot himself in the foot."

The abbot turned his head slightly to the side. "Do you mean that in the literal sense?"

"No, it was figurative. He has brought great harm upon his own cause, and by extension, our cause. For some reason I cannot imagine, he seized the church of Saint Stephen—the one there in Launceston—by force, had three men put to death, another ten bound in fetters, pillaged the place ... oh, it is too awful, really. The bishop of Exeter has excommunicated him. Can you imagine?! And now, as if that were not bad enough, Reginald writes to say that his wife has gone mad. She wanders about with her hair a mess, wailing all the while about her misfortune. Even this morning, I heard a report that Stephen was riding southwest, hoping to take back Cornwall and slay Earl Reginald with his sword. What in God's name must I do? They say my brother has placed a tax upon the houses of God. Do you think that could be the true cause of this calamity?"

As I had made this speech, I had been gesturing with my hands at every turn, rolling my eyes, sighing, groaning—in short, creating quite a spectacle. The good abbot's eyes were open wide by this point. I believe he was stunned.

"How could I possibly say, my lady? The strange workings of the Lord are beyond our knowledge," he offered.

"Really? That is your answer?" I objected, for I had hoped for something a bit more original, or at least something I could put to good use. "Understand that this poses a real threat to all my efforts here. Not only my person, but the inheritance of my sons is in danger. My heart trembles, and I would be comforted, or better yet advised."

"Forgive me," he said with a smile. "Can you not send Earl Robert and his knights to make short work of the situation?"

I folded up the letter and set it to the side. "I know not how many men the false king has at his side. I should hate to lose two brothers in an uneven fight, and one that may yield little advantage."

Abbot Gilbert leaned back in his chair and stroked his chin, considering the matter. "Would you like me to write to the bishop of Exeter? Ask him to reverse his judgment? I am only an abbot, but perhaps if some of the bishops who favor you were to join me in this cause—"

"No, I have less concern for Reginald's eternal soul at the moment. In any case, I know a thing or two about excommunication thanks to my time in the empire. Unless the archbishop of Canterbury should pronounce the same sentence, or worse yet the Holy Father, Earl Reginald may find a haven in some other see. Right now, I am more concerned that he should maintain his earldom that was only lately won and not bring shame upon my name."

Perhaps it is not wise to admit to your confessor that spiritual concerns are not your top priority, but given that he was my confessor, it hardly seemed proper to lie. Abbot Gilbert appeared to take no offense. Instead, he sat staring at the floor for what seemed like an hour but was surely less than a minute. At length, he looked up again and addressed me with a new degree of confidence.

"Then there is only one choice. Lord Miles, you tell me, is still in the North. You must send Earl Robert to save his brother."

I was surprised that he recommended this bold course of action and replied, "Perhaps Reginald will stand on his own two feet."

"My lady, I know nothing of war, but it seems to me that if Earl Reginald were to hold firm in Cornwall, and Earl Robert were to come at Stephen's forces from the east, you may well catch your enemy in the middle and thus make an end of things."

Well, here was a surprise! Some good advice on how to conduct a war, and from an abbot no less! I believe my mouth may have dropped open ever so slightly. *Could that work?* I wondered. *Perhaps it could. Oh, but the danger! But if it works ... oh, what to do?!*

"Do you really think so?" I stammered.

"Yes, though as I said, I am merely an abbot. You would do better to inquire about one of the sacraments."

"Even so, my thinking becomes clearer. I know now what I must do," I said, nodding my head solemnly. I then summoned all my breath and cried out, "Sir Drogo!"

My knight had been standing just on the other side of the door, and when I called for him, he entered the room as fast as a rabbit flees when caught eating the farmer's crop.

"Yes, my lady," Drogo replied, removing his cap and bowing.

"I need you to go to Bristol," I said to him.

"Bristol? Do you have some message for Earl Robert? Or do you require better wine?" He said this with a smile, as if it was very clever indeed.

"The former," I replied. "Stephen is moving against Earl Reginald. Tell Robert that if his spies deem it wise, he should ride out to meet him in battle. Take as many of my knights with you as you think we can spare: Sir Philip and all the rest."

"Very good, my lady," the knight said, turning to leave. It was a mark of his character that he made no attempt to question my judgment.

"Wait!" Abbot Gilbert called after him, raising his hand. "Since you are going anyway ... no, I shouldn't ..."

"I'm sorry?" Drogo asked.

"Fetch Abbot Gilbert some wine, and some for me as well," I offered. "That is what you meant to say, is it not, abbot?" I asked, turning to address him.

He did not reply but merely shook his head yes. When the knight had departed, the abbot said, "It is not for me, empress, but for the brothers. When the libation ceases, the jollity tends to follow, if you take my meaning. We are forced to save some of the wine for the Holy Eucharist."

Why must every conversation I have end up being about drink? I wondered.

Not three days after Drogo made his departure for Bristol, I received a note from the hand of Earl Robert declaring, "Now is the hour. The false king has set himself up to fail. We make for Cornwall. God be with us and grant us victory." Even as I read those words, my pulse quickened and I felt a shudder in my bones. For so long, we had avoided open battle, but now we rode out to seek it. All our fortunes hung in the balance, for it would be either our end or theirs. Oh, how I longed for it and feared it! The sooner the war was over, the sooner England could be restored. Yet depending on the victor, the peace might be worse than the war, and open battle was a bloody business.

I set to work organizing my thoughts, as was ever my habit in moments of stress. I wrote to Miles and bid him break from his winter camp in Hereford and make for the South. With the usurper occupied, he would have a clean shot at those castles that remained in enemy hands. Such knights as I could afford to give had already traveled along with Drogo, who I assumed would be glad to see his native Cornwall. Were I to send anyone else, I would leave Gloucester in great danger. There was naught to do but sit and wait. In that waiting, I wrote to my dear son.

"Henry, my love, keep hard at your studies. I fight every day for your inheritance, and there is nothing I would not do for you. Obey the commands of your father. Listen to the words of your tutor. One day, you shall be king. Remember the words of the Lord and say your prayers. Very soon, England shall be ours.

MATHILDA IMPERATRIX"

In truth, I was not as certain of victory as I implied, but it would not do to be filling my son's head with doubts. That is something my first husband taught me: "If you speak it, you will believe it."

When Stephen arrived in the West, he appointed Alan Penteur, the earl of Richmond, as his chosen earl of Cornwall. The false king succeeded in taking back most of that land, although he could not force Reginald from his fortress of Launceston. Even as he was celebrating this triumph, Stephen heard a rumor upon the wind: Earl Robert of Gloucester was riding out to meet him in battle. Well, that put an end to the usurper's plot straight away. He left this Alan in charge of the siege and made a mad dash across Devonshire, raising up such lords as he could. Sadly, it was none too difficult for Stephen to find allies among those men, for Reginald had made enemies of most of them. I place part of the blame for this on my brother, but part of it also on those who falsely accused him and sought his destruction at every turn.

Even as Earl Robert was making for Cornwall, he learned that Stephen had gained an army of ten thousand men, far larger than had been assumed. The situation had become perilous. Were a battle to take place, Robert would have been at a great disadvantage. He had not counted on all those nobles from Devon joining forces with the usurper. Thus, he did the only sensible thing: he fled back to Bristol.

I do not fault Robert for this. I had commanded him to retreat if he ever found himself facing certain destruction. Yet this mishap opened the way for Stephen to move into the Vale of Gloucester along with the Beaumont twins. His aim, we can safely assume, was to make Robert Beaumont the earl of Hereford instead of Miles of Gloucester. The army the false king had created was too strong for either brother Robert or Miles to face alone, and there was no time for me to unite them. Therefore, I wrote to Lord Miles and bid him come to my side at Gloucester. We would simply have to accept the consequences of Stephen's advancement and live to fight another day.

Those hours of waiting tore at my soul. Would my friends make it back to the safety of our fortresses before the usurper caught them from behind? I hoped and prayed that they would, but no news came to us. Things had gone from bad to worse since I arrived in England, and at last the tide seemed to have turned fully against me. How would I ever endure it?

What will I do if I see him again? If he breaks down the gate and finds me without defenders? I wondered. *What will I say when he sets the blade to my neck? What will I think before they lock me away, never again to feel the warmth of the sun? I must not fear. No, I must be brave.*

Although we received no news, I could sense the fiend was near and the hour would soon arrive when the die would be cast and my doom decided. However, it was not Stephen's banner that was seen from our walls in the end but that of Miles of Gloucester. When I heard that Miles had made it into the castle, I raced down to meet him in the hall, for I had been living every hour in fear and longed to see anyone who might lend me a sense of comfort. There I found him and several of his men standing about, looking very much in poor humor.

"Lord Miles!" I cried, while still a few paces away. "Thank God you've come! I was sore afraid! Where do we stand? Is the usurper at our threshold?"

"He passed within a mile of this place, but he is gone now to menace Tewkesbury along with that foul devil, Waleran," he reported, throwing his hat and gloves down on one of the tables. "I doubt Earl Robert's palace will survive that visitation, for we have no one there to defend it."

"Is that so? Well, that's just ... utterly awful!"

As I spoke these words, I felt overcome by the weight of it all: the usurper close enough to strike, my friends scattered. I sat down across the table from Lord Miles and hid my face in my hands, too upset to speak. What the men standing there must have thought of this display, I can only imagine. No doubt they attributed it to some kind of feminine weakness. When I had taken a moment to gather myself, I finally said, "I do not understand. A week ago, we were looking to end this war. Now it seems the tide has turned completely the other way, and we are running for our lives."

"The tide that goes out must soon return," Miles replied. "That is the way of nature."

I pressed on without heeding his words. "We have been working and working to win the West, then in one moment he comes and seizes it back—just like that! Are we really so weak? The false king has made enemies of half the people in this kingdom. Where is he getting the money for it all?"

"That I can answer," Miles offered. "He intends to wed his son to the king of France's sister. She comes with a large dowry."

"Oh, of course, it would be the king of France!" I cried, grinding my palms into the table. "My God, I hate the French! Honestly, do those people just sit around all day with nothing to do but think up ways to annoy me? I swear to you, this is their intention: they will make England weak through this weak king, and then they will take over Normandy. God curse them and their alliance!"

When I had finished saying this, I looked at the faces of the men standing before me, several of which seemed to be plastered with a look of dismay.

"I'm sorry. Have I offended you?" I asked in a mocking tone. "Well, forgive me, gentlemen, but I grow tired of being polite. Had you spent as much time married to a Frenchman as I have, you would understand."

"Isn't Lord Geoffrey an Angevin?" one of them asked.

"Yes," I replied, "but he might as well be French."

"I think we have rather forgotten the subject at hand," said Miles, leaning forward. "What would you have us do, my lady?"

I simply looked at him and shook my head, then took a deep breath. "Since we cannot win on the field of battle, I advise you to pray that God will grant us an opportunity: a chance to end this war."

"That we shall do, and often," he replied.

I turned and made my way back to my own chamber, aware as I did so that every eye was staring at me and none too happily. I could not even rebuke them, for I knew the doubts within my own heart.

What are you doing, Maud? What are you doing? I thought. *What good will come of this fury?*

I closed the door behind me and fell upon the bed, thankful at last to be alone. I lay on my back and stared up at the scarlet canopy.

What would mother tell me to do? When she had patted my head and held me tight, what would she advise?

I thought about the question for a moment, and suddenly I found myself reciting words I had learned in my youth: the hymn that she had taught me.

"Now we must honor the guardian of heaven

The might of the architect, and his purpose
The work of the father of glory
As he, the eternal Lord, established the beginning of wonders
He first created for the children of men
Heaven as a roof, the holy Creator
Then the guardian of mankind, the eternal Lord
Afterwards appointed the middle earth, the lands for men
The Lord almighty"[10]

Having spoken the words at least ten times, I fell at last into a frightful sleep in which my dreams were haunted by apparitions. Little different was the dream than the waking, it seemed.

---

10   This is a common English translation of "Caedmon's Hymn," which is based upon the Old English poem as it appears in the Moore Bede (Cambridge, University Library, MS Kk. 5. 16). The originator of this particular translation is unknown.

IV

January 1167
Rouen, Normandy

W hen did I last feel the sun upon my face? When did I last join in the congregation? "I rejoiced when they said to me, we will go into the house of the Lord."[11] I have not set foot in that house in two weeks but have been trapped in this bed. Indeed, that is not the worst of my state: I am trapped in a body of death. With each new day, my strength seems to lessen. My bones cry out. My soul aches. He has numbered my days aright, and I have felt their full weight. Shall I ever rise from this bed again? My only solace is the birth of my grand son, John.

I had not called for the archdeacon Lawrence during my illness, for though I am old and gray, I still possess some small measure of womanly vanity. I was loath for him to see me in

---

11   Psalm 122:1.

such condition. Yet I finally gave way and summoned him into my presence, fearing as I did that the closing of my days was nigh. It was necessary, I felt, to put an end to this chronicle, be it ever so crude and ill-formed.

I sat on the lower level of my small home by the Seine, in a room that I use for receiving guests. It has a hearth and two chairs with a small table. Against one of the walls, I keep my greatest treasures—my books—on a set of wood shelves. Opposite them are two windows, through which the sun was streaming on this particular afternoon, even as I sat in my chair wrapped in a fur.

Lawrence opened the door behind me and said, "You asked for me, my lady."

"Yes," I said, turning with some effort to greet him, and then casting my gaze back to the hearth in front of me. "Lawrence, my life ebbs from me as water slips through one's fingers. I fear we may not finish our project ere I am called to my eternal home. Think you that I am fit for heaven?"

"Of course! Why should you doubt it?" he asked, shutting the door behind him, taking the seat opposite, and casting down his satchel.

"In sin was I conceived. In sin have I lived and breathed."

"The love of Christ is more powerful even than sin," he assured me, his kind eyes doing their best to grant me cheer.

"Yes, but does God truly love me?" I asked, feeling nothing of the confidence he seemed to possess. "I am not the most lovable of persons, as men have often noted."

He reached out and patted my hand. "Dear empress, you must not vex yourself with such questions. If there is some sin needs confessing, then confess it and receive absolution. It will not do to dwell in despair."

I began to cough, and Lawrence reached into an inner pocket in his cloak, retrieving a small cloth. I accepted it gladly and used it to cover my mouth. When the coughing had ceased, I looked down and saw a few pink spots on the white linen. Rather than consider what they might mean, I set the cloth aside and returned to the conversation.

"I wish you had known my mother, Lawrence. She was one of God's saints. She never did anything but it grew and blossomed and made the world a better place. I leave the world as I found it: cold and broken."

"If the world is broken, it is not on your account."

I shook my head. "For me, a kingdom was rent in two, and the path to glory trod in blood."

"Your son is England's king, and long may he reign!"

"My son has wandered far from righteousness. I like to think that was his father's doing, but perhaps it was myself."

I looked down at the floor and breathed slowly. My throat was still very sore. Indeed, the pain reached into my lungs.

"You must have faith in your progeny, or else you would not have written this account," the archdeacon told me, calling me back to our discussion.

"You are writing it, Lawrence. I am telling."

"Yes, but no one will remember my name. It is your praises that will be sung until the ending of the world."

I laughed. "If they do not sing them now, then why should they sing them when I am gone?"

"Time is a healer of memories as well as wounds. Now the pain is fresh, but future generations will stand in awe of what you have accomplished."

I looked at him with eyes that threatened to drop tears at any moment and whispered, "I accomplished little."

"You set the standard by which others must be measured!" he declared with even more determination. "Things will not always be as they are now. Who knows but that some descendant of yours—some female descendant—may not sit upon

England's throne? Is that not why we are writing? For the benefit of your royal daughters?"

Here I gave breath to a concern that had troubled me for some time, nibbling away slowly at the certainty within me.

"I fear this account will find its way not into the hands of a queen, but a pauper. Perhaps my line will fail."

Lawrence seemed less concerned by this possibility than I. "All men are born paupers, drawn naked from their mother's womb, but they may in time rise to greatness."

I shook my head sadly. "If men are born paupers, then women doubly so. Even a queen may be a pauper in spirit. I should know."

I could see from the look on the archdeacon's face that he had passed from determination into frustration. I did not doubt that he wished to rebuke me, but he held himself mostly in check.

"My lady, I well remember the day when you first asked me to help you tell this story. Such a bold declaration you made. Will you abandon that now when we have come so far? Future generations wait expectantly, longing to hear your words!"

"Oh, Lawrence! No one desires to hear me speak any more than they enjoy the call of a goose."

"All God's creatures deserve to be heard!" he cried, leaning forward, pressing into the table with his hands.

"So say you."

"So says the Lord, who has ordained praise from the lips of infants, and makes the heavens declare his glory!"

I made no reply. For a moment, the two of us simply stared at one another, and I felt as if I could see the years that had made him, from when he ran through the fields as a boy with his curls flowing in the wind, through his many years of study and ministry, until he stood before me now with nothing to crown his head at all. He was a man of principle, and he was not about to let me surrender. Therefore, I bowed my head to signal that he had won the day, and he sank back into his seat, the crease in his brow disappearing and the kind eyes returning.

"Now, what shall we write?" he asked, reaching into his satchel and pulling out a stack of parchment. "I believe we left you in the year of the battle of Lincoln."

"Ah, yes," I murmured, my memory seeming to catch fire. "What a year that was! I remember it so clearly, though the rest of me seems to fade."

"Tell it then," he said, pulling out his ink and writing tools. "Your daughters long to hear. They too need hope."

I paused for a moment to think. His words certainly had merit, yet I was so ready to finish the thing. But how could I fail in this last duty to the women who would come after me? At last, I reached a conclusion.

"Fine—I submit! Make ready your pen and record this conversation as well."

"Why?" he asked, laughing.

"That the reader may know that it was you who forced me to continue this when I was quite ready to be done, wicked man."

"I accept your censure," he replied with a bow of the head. "Now, let us continue."

The usurper's wife exceeded him in both skill and ambition, and though she was a woman, she would have made a better king. While Stephen chased from one side of the island to the other, the false queen ensured a most handsome alliance for their son, Eustace, with the sister of King Louis VII of France. I am sure that this woman, Lady Constance of Toulouse, was hard pressed with the boy—for he truly was a boy, being no more than ten years of age and not yet a knight. He had naught to recommend him but his lofty birth. The French king hoped through this match to gain further control over Normandy. He knew well enough that he would receive no such benefit from me.

Therefore, Mathilda of Boulogne, wife of the false king, and her son traveled to Paris for the wedding, which must have been an occasion of some humor, the groom being much shorter than his bride. Lady Constance then accompanied them back to England, where she was accorded great honor: that is, such honor as one can receive from men who have none themselves.

There was some good news that spring, for I was to have more company in Gloucester. I had longed for some time to be joined by my lady, Adela, once again, not only to receive the boon of her presence, but to hear her speak of my sons, the royal princes. However, the war had made it truly difficult to transport either goods or people between Normandy and the West Country. Those traveling by boat from Normandy tended to take the shortest route and land in Kent, or perhaps in Sussex if it suited. That would have meant traveling through territory that Stephen controlled in order to reach us in Gloucester, so instead, anything we received from Normandy had to go the long way around the southwest of England, taking the turn at Land's End and entering into the bay, until at last it came to the port of Bristol. At certain times of year, this trip was impossible on account of the weather, so I was filled with joy when I heard that Adela had safely landed in Bristol and would be arriving at the castle of Gloucester within a few days.

It was indeed three days later that there was a knock on the door of my chamber and I opened it to find Philip of Honfleur standing there.

"Empress Mathilda, a party has been sighted landing at the pier and will shortly make its way up to the castle. It is thought to include the lady Adela," he reported.

"Excellent!" I said, for I was most eager to see my friend. "Do you know where Sir Drogo is? He may wish to welcome her as well."

"I am afraid he has gone off riding, my lady, and may not be back until evening."

"Oh …" I muttered. "That is too bad."

"Do you wish me to ride out after him, my lady?" the knight asked earnestly.

"No, no. That is not necessary. Perhaps you would be willing to accompany me down to the yard though. She should have with her a few chests of things from Anjou."

"Of course. After you," he said, standing back and beckoning me to lead the way.

As we began to walk down the passage toward the stair, I said, "It seems a shame that I know so little about you, Sir Philip."

"There is not much to know," he replied, walking just behind me. "I do my duty."

"That much I have observed, but what are your interests?"

We had reached the stair, and as I looked back briefly, I could see that he was considering the question carefully.

"I like many of the things that any man would like," he explained as we descended. "Good food, good drink, music, sport, friendship. I am not sure that any of these things set me apart though."

"Do you read?"

"Yes. I do not have many books here with me, but back home my family had a great library. I am afraid I was not as good a student as I should have been, but I remember the stories my mother told me of warriors performing brave deeds in service of the crown. I think that is what made me so eager to pursue knighthood, though my father was also a knight before me. He came over with the Conqueror."

As we reached the bottom of the stair and made our way into the solar, I said, "If your father came over with the Conqueror, he must have been quite old when you were born. You cannot be thirty years old."

"Correct. I am five and twenty. I was the youngest of twelve children by three different wives, though only eight of us remain among the living. Not that my father was married to three women at once, mind you! The first two were deceased."

"I assumed as much," I assured him, turning and smiling.

He began to walk beside me. "So, that is why I am here and not running the estate in Normandy. That went to my eldest half-brother. The second oldest went into the Church, and my other brother is also a knight. The rest were sisters."

We had made it to the door in the great hall that opened into the yard. I paused and he did likewise.

"Tell me, Sir Philip, when you heard those tales as a young man and imagined yourself performing great deeds, were they ever on behalf of a lovely lady?" I asked.

"What do you mean?" he inquired, looking nervous. "Do you wish to know if I think you a handsome woman?"

I laughed. "Ha! No, have no fear! It was merely my secret way of trying to discern if you had felt the pang of love at your age. Never mind it."

"Ah, I see! My family did hope for me to wed a maid once from one of the local towns, but it came to nothing. And of course, I have seen my fair share of beauties, but I suppose it is not meant to be—not yet."

"Hmmm ..."

"Yes?"

I smiled. "Forgive me for saying this, Sir Philip, but I would have imagined that you would have no trouble winning the affection of the ladies."

"You are kind," he said, bowing his head, "but I believe my position as the youngest son of a minor lord is not enough to attract most of the ladies at court."

"Fair enough," I concluded, then opened the door and entered the yard.

We only had to wait a minute or two before the cart came through the gate being pulled by a team of four horses. It carried several chests, and on one of them sat Adela, clad in a lovely brown dress and white veil. As soon as she saw me, she smiled broadly and began to wave, and I did the same. I felt so happy that she had made it to Gloucester safely, and I was eager to hear all the news of my boys.

The horses stopped just in front of us and Adela declared, "Empress Mathilda! My heart is full of joy to see you again. You have been sorely missed in Anjou."

I doubt that very much, I thought, but instead replied, "How kind of you!"

I walked over to the side of the cart and we clasped hands.

"How was your journey, dear? Was the sea rough?" I asked.

"Not too bad. The men pointed out all the sights to me. I quite enjoyed it, actually."

"Then you are far better on the sea than I am," I said, laughing. "I am never happy until such a journey is over."

There was a noise and we both turned to see that Sir Philip was removing the first of the chests from the cart with the help of one of the grooms.

"Who is that?" Adela whispered.

"Oh, that is Philip of Honfleur, one of the knights in our service here. I asked him to help carry things."

We looked at each other and I could see that Adela was uneasy. "Where is Sir Drogo?" she asked. "Is he off fighting in the war?"

"No, he went out for a ride." I then lowered my voice further and said, "You are not made sad by this, are you?"

I was surprised to hear her laugh. "Oh, my lady, you do not think I am still pining after him, do you?"

"Well, how should I know? I haven't seen you in ages!" I complained. "Now, come down here so we can talk properly. How we used to laugh together! I am in need of that now."

Adela walked to the other end of the cart, where Sir Philip stood ready to help her down. It was a rather long drop to the ground, so after saying, "Permit me, my lady," and receiving a nod, he placed his hands around her waist and set her down gently.

"Thank you, Sir Philip," Adela said, bowing her head. "Well met."

"Of course, well met yourself," he replied, bowing in return.

She then turned to face me and the two of us shared a sisterly embrace.

"Now," I began, pulling back, "tell me everything of my sons. I daily mourn this separation between us."

She placed her arm in mine and we began to walk toward the keep.

"Prince Henry is well," she assured me. "He grows in strength every day, and what is more, he is an able scholar. Prince William is the sweetest little boy. I cannot get enough of him! Such a happy child, and content either to play or to study. There is nothing on earth that worries him."

"And their brother?" I asked. "What of Prince Geoffrey?"

There was a knowing smile on her face. "He is a strong willed child, as you well know, and more likely to complain. But I think his heart is good, madam. He has the middle child's lot: always striving after the elder and lording it over the younger. He will come around in time. I remember well enough how he entered this world in great pain and anguish. Such marks stay with a person, I think, but they may one day fade."

Every word she uttered was a gift, but I found in hearing them that they only made me desire more. I wanted to hear their voices—to embrace them in my arms. Only victory would make such things possible, and it seemed an eternity away.

"Well, I thank you for your patience with them," I concluded. "I wish I could thank the others as well."

We had reached the door and passed through, making our way back into the solar and taking a pair of seats near one of the windows. The men were still walking through with chests, and Adela informed me that one of them was full of wine. Within a few minutes, we both had a cup and sat there sipping happily. At length, I began my inquiry again.

"What of my husband? Does he make any progress in this war?"

The look on her face suddenly changed and she began staring down at her cup. "Actually, there is something I have been meaning to tell you, but I wanted to wait until I saw you in person."

"Oh, dear God! What is it?"

She paused for a moment and looked at me with wide eyes, as if fearing my wrath.

"Whatever it is, you had better tell me now," I said. "I will only fear the worst."

"Very well," she replied, taking a deep breath. "Count Geoffrey is made a father again."

A great many thoughts passed through my mind at that moment, each wishing to express itself in different ways, but in the end, I simply laughed.

"Are you well, my lady?" Adela asked, taking my hand. "I thought you might be upset at this news."

When I had gained control again, I said, "Truly, I should be upset, but I come to recognize that I do not care how Count Geoffrey spends his private time or where he chooses to thrust himself. We are partners by necessity, and it is a great pity that I should be bound in life with such a fool who possesses no regard for proper morals. But at this point, if he were able to take Normandy for us, I would say he could have all the women he pleased. God knows, he'll never have me again. We are joined in our love for our sons. Let that be enough. I cannot concern myself with such things. We have a war to fight."

"You will take no action, then? He is to suffer no consequence?"

"Oh, he will suffer the consequences, but not in this life. Upon the earth, men may run rampant over the commands of the Lord. Woe unto them when they pass into the beyond! Let us be thankful we share not in their eternal doom." In truth, I felt the weakness of this statement, for I longed for justice on the earth, but I counted it a victory that my husband could no longer hurt me as he once did.

"Well spoken, my lady," she concluded. "Here, I have something for you."

She walked over to the same chest that held the wine and pulled out a small bag. Returning to her seat, she reached into it and retrieved a small figure of a man made of twigs and leaves.

"William made this for you. I may have helped him a bit."

"How perfect!" I cried, reaching out and taking it in hand. As I clutched it to my breast, I found I could not keep the tears from running down my cheeks.

I later placed this gift in the small chest where I kept also the few jewels I had brought with me, my mother's rosary, and of course, the amber moth. It was as if my very heart was in that box.

Even as I was delighting in the company of my friend, a matter of greater import was taking place in the city of Salisbury, which was without a bishop following the death of Roger the Great. As was the case with everything else in the kingdom at that time, this was to be a contest between Count Waleran de Beaumont, earl of Worcester and owner of the false king, and Bishop Henry of Winchester, papal legate and brother of the foul usurper.

Bishop Henry put forward a young man who by all rights should have been most acceptable: his own nephew, Henry de Sully. Now this lad was the son of William, the elder brother of Stephen and Bishop Henry, who had been rather cut out of the family. This was by the will of their mutual mother, Adela of Blois, on account of William's reckless behavior. Although this elder brother was no friend of the family, his son Henry was another matter. At a young age, he had joined the monastery at Cluny and dedicated himself to the study of theology. His reputation was excellent, and he possessed something also of that ambition that was common in the House of Blois—more so even with the women than the men, as I have noted.

There was no reason for the false king to scorn his own nephew, and yet he did so, much to the dismay of his younger brother, Bishop Henry. Despite the nomination of the papal legate, he was denied the crozier on the advice of Count Waleran. Yes, Waleran who made all things bad. Waleran who always led his master into error. It was Count Waleran who impelled Stephen to this action, for he had his own person in mind: Philip d'Harcourt, the archdeacon of Évreux, who had lately been serving as Stephen's chancellor. Here was a man who owed everything to Waleran, and who could thus be controlled. Therefore, the royal council, under the influence of Waleran and his puppet, Stephen, denied the nomination of Henry de Sully. Not for the first time, Bishop Henry of Winchester stormed out in a fury, his hatred of Waleran increasing all the more.

The false king must have felt his victory complete. He would install a bishop of his choosing, or at least of Waleran's choosing, and thus ensure that the Church would have no power over him as it had in the days of Bishop Roger. If he was laboring under such a misunderstanding, he was soon to be set right, for the papal legate had one or two cards left to play. First, the chapter of Salisbury refused to accept this Philip as their bishop, declaring him to be a man of poor character, which was surely true. Second, Bishop Henry used his influence with the Holy See to block the appointment. In anger, Philip d'Harcourt appealed to Rome, but was rejected when the pope learned of his theft of a relic from the cathedral of Salisbury, which was housed in much gold and jewels.

It was Drogo who told me all of this. He always had his ear to the ground, so to speak, and received news from his spies near and far. I well remember when he told me. We had been sitting on opposite sides of one of the tables in the great hall, each reading a book. He disturbed me at random to inform me of the situation. When I thought the conversation over, I returned my eyes to the page, but Drogo quickly began speaking again.

"Is it not curious, the manner of this Philip's downfall?"

"What of it?" I asked, not looking up. "Are you not always telling me that the corrupt are brought down by their own corruption?"

"Yes, but the nature of his crime—the theft of a relic ... does this not concern you?"

This time, I did look up and glared at him.

"If you are referring to that incident we promised never to speak of, then I would caution you to beware what you say. In any case, that was not a theft."

"If it was not a theft, then why did we have to hide it?"

"Drogo, you are speaking of it."

"Well, is it any wonder that my conscience is troubled, when I was the one who had to carry the thing?" he objected.

With a heavy sigh to signal my displeasure, I shut my book and dropped it on the table, then folded my hands together and looked him firmly in the eye.

"This Philip did what he did out of greed. He could sense that those men would never accept him, so he thought to make off with their treasure and reap a profit from the sale. Either that, or he wished to declare that he was the true bishop of Salisbury, and thus entitled to the relic, although he was never consecrated. It was wrong for him to take the thing, for he was not the true bishop. Even so, it was wrong for Adalbert to have the hand of Saint James, for he was not a true bishop. It was he who committed the greater theft by stealing an empire; thus, he annulled his own authority. We were setting the heavenly scales aright. Adalbert knows well enough why we took the relic, and he has never asked for it back, as he feels the guilt of his actions. Thus, it will remain at the abbey of Reading, for the benefit of pilgrims who seek to gaze on it in wonder."

"I suppose that makes sense," he admitted. "Yet I still feel the pang of guilt."

"All who aspire to power feel the pang of guilt. Those who enter the monastery may rejoice in their purity, having not been tainted by the things of this world. But someone has to lead, Drogo: someone has to set the world to right. One cannot do that without staining one's self in the process. We must simply hope that God will be forgiving, and in your case he shall, for you were following the orders of your empress. If anyone ought to feel guilt, it is me. Think nothing of it."

"Very well," he concluded, returning his eyes to the book in front of him.

I was about to take up my own book again when Adela entered the room and came to sit beside me.

"Good evening, my lady!" she said. "What are you reading?"

"Brother Hugh of the monastery of Saint Victor in Paris, but I have not been making much progress," I explained, glaring at Drogo once again.

Letting out a grunt of sorts, Drogo picked up his book and moved to one of the other tables, where he resumed his reading, though his eyes darted up once or twice to glare in return.

"What's wrong with him?" Adela asked quietly.

"He thinks I am corrupting him," I answered.

She turned to look at me directly. "And are you?"

"Oh, probably. It sounds like something I would do."

"My lady, I am sure that is not true!" she offered.

Even as she said this, Philip of Honfleur approached us, his entrance completely missed on account of our discussion about Drogo. I suddenly looked up to see him standing there, which caused my maid to turn and look in the same direction.

"Good evening, Sir Philip," Adela said in greeting.

"And a very good evening to you and you," he replied, bowing his head to each of us in turn. "My ladies, is there anything you require? Any way that I could be of service?"

"I don't think so," I told him. "Not unless Adela needs something."

His eyes turned to her and she said, "I am not in need of anything but good company. Would you like to join us in conversation? We were just talking about someone named Hugh at a monastery in Paris."

"Hugh of Saint Victor?" he asked, taking his seat opposite us.

"Yes, that's the one!" she replied with a smile. "Forgive me, I am usually more aware of such things, but Empress Mathilda is my best teacher, and we have been apart for some time."

"I confess I have not read any of his works either. It is difficult to find time to read during a war."

"It is difficult to find time to read when you are watching children!" she said, a smile on her face.

"Oh, I am certain of that," he assured her. "I am sure my brothers and I were quite a challenge for those who cared for us when we were young."

"Did your mother not care for you?" she asked, tipping her head.

"Sadly, my mother died shortly after I was born. She was the third wife my father lost," he replied solemnly.

"Oh, I am sorry! I did not know. That was a foolish thing for me to say."

"I assure you, no harm was done," he offered, smiling just a bit to encourage her. "I am sure you had quite a difficult task helping to raise three boys."

"Well, I would not want you to think I was miserable. I love the royal princes and would do anything to promote their welfare. They are sweet boys."

At this moment, they both turned and looked at me for the first time in the course of their conversation. Indeed, I suspect they may have continued without acknowledging my presence for a few more minutes had my sons not been mentioned directly.

"Forgive us, my lady. We have not been including you in our conversation," Adela said sadly.

"Do not worry about that," I replied, patting her on the shoulder. "As it so happens, I was just thinking that it might be time for me to seek out some rest. Have a good night."

With this I rose to leave, and when I was quite certain that neither of them could see me, I broke into a smile.

Perhaps you are no longer pining for Sir Drogo, but I think you will soon be pining for Sir Philip, I thought. *Oh, that I could have seen what you have seen! Those precious hours with my sons I would gladly trade for all I saw of Rome.*

Even as the words passed through my mind, I remembered that I had not left things well with Drogo. I turned back and walked toward where he was sitting.

"Drogo!" I called. "Who ended up becoming bishop of Salisbury?"

He looked up from his book, and I was happy to see that he did not appear to be angry.

"The see remains vacant," he said. "I suspect the false king concluded that the easiest bishop to control is no bishop at all."

"Thus is the flock left to the wolves. Alas for Salisbury!"

"Alas for England!"

I leaned in closer and said softly, "I do hope I have not offended you, Drogo. I understand the conflict you feel—"

He raised a hand to stop me. "My lady, we have been friends far too long to fall out over something like this. Think nothing of it. I dare say I will recover, for to serve a great lady is an honor among honors."

"Oh, don't make me start weeping!" I complained, though I was smiling as I said it.

I turned again and walked back toward the solar, noting as I did so that the two young people were still deep in discussion.

Geoffrey Talbot, knight in the company of Earl Robert of Gloucester, heir of the de Lacy family, guardian of Hereford, was not what you might call a great friend of Lord Miles of Gloucester. In truth, the two were mortal foes, having fought for control of the West in the years leading up to the war. Some said this was on account of the de Lacy inheritance, but for my part I can assure you that there were many complaints between them. Of course, I only heard Miles' side of the story.

"Have you ever met the man? The devil himself would cringe at the stench."

"The only woman that would bed him is a one legged whore, and then only because she thought him a priest and hoped for absolution."

"His own mother prefers me. At last, that's what she said last night."

Thus, on and so forth he would heap abuse upon the poor man, and if ever anyone questioned his animosity, he would merely target his comments at them instead. Such hatred presented no obstacle when Miles stood with the false king, but once they were forced to fight together, things became quite delicate. Brother Robert had a saying he would pronounce from time to time: "It would be easier to pull a camel through the eye of a needle than to force those two men to agree on anything."

Sadly, despite the best efforts of Geoffrey Talbot, we had yet to take the castle of Hereford. When I inquired as to the difficulty, I was told that our commanders in the field were unable to maintain a civil conversation with one another. You can imagine how overjoyed I was to learn that these men on whom I depended were behaving no differently than my young sons and they had nothing like the boys' merits to balance things. I sent them a message, the exact content of which is of no import. Suffice it to say, I let them know what I would do should they fail to act as grown men should. This had the desired effect. Although there was no love between them, Lord Geoffrey and Lord Miles set to work on a new stratagem: one that was to be rather more beneficial.

Early in the morning, before the first Mass was said, Geoffrey Talbot and some fifty men arrived at the cathedral and commanded all the clergy to leave. They then climbed the great bell tower and placed archers in position to fire upon the castle, which was nearby. As luck would have it, Lord Geoffrey had made efforts to fortify the church when he last had control of the town, so the situation was perfect, except that it was a house of God. In general, I preferred not to step upon the good will of the Church, but the siege had gone on long enough.

As the archers continued to rain down arrows upon the castle walls, Geoffrey directed the rest of his men to build hillocks below, the better to defend their position. This was a matter of some distress for the peasants, for the place that Geoffrey chose happened to be a burial ground, and as they threw the dirt higher and higher, they began to raise up certain family members long deceased. By the time they saw their error, it was too late, and they simply continued with the earthen wall, knowing all the while that they were making enemies of the locals.

While Stephen's men spent all their strength repelling this action from the west, they were soon surprised to find Miles of Gloucester coming at them from the opposite side with his engines. Thus were the defenders hard pressed from every which way, and within a few hours the castle fell. Oh, what joyous relief to have gained this last stronghold in the West! For most of a year, we had battled back and forth, the Welsh Marches always in doubt. I felt some times that the battle was less upon the field, and more in my very soul, so strained was I to the point of breaking. Every hour they had lain in wait for me, but it was not to be.

The very same day that I received this news, Adela burst into my quarter, struggling to breathe. She had evidently run a great distance to tell me something. After taking a moment to catch her breath, she said to me, "Empress! You must come outside! The sun … it has gone dark."

"What?!" I cried.

"Come quickly! You'll see!"

As you can imagine, I was eager to see this thing of which she spoke, for if true it would rival the actions of the Lord in ancient Egypt. We made our way out to the yard, and it was indeed darker than usual for midday.

"Look!" she cried, pointing toward the sky.

I cast my eyes upward, and there I saw a great dark sphere surrounded by a ring of light. I could only glance at it for a moment, and then was forced to look away, for it was still very bright.

"What does it mean?" Adela asked.

I rubbed my eyes, attempting to remove the green spots. "It is an eclipse. I've read about them, but never seen one."

"Yes, but what does it mean? Does it portend our doom?"

Just then, Drogo walked over and joined us, having come in from his daily ride.

"Look at this, Sir Drogo, but take care," I said.

"The sun has gone dark? That's bad news for Stephen," he concluded.

"Why only for Stephen?" Adela asked.

"Because he is the one who sits upon the throne: a throne that he stole with an abominable lie," the knight reasoned. "The Lord cannot be pleased with him. Perhaps his reign is coming to a close."

"Oh, you are just saying that to make us happy," I objected. "There's no way to know what it means."

"But maybe Sir Drogo is right!" said Adela. "Maybe he will not last the year!"

Even as she spoke, the light of the sun began to shine more brightly, and the two of them who had been staring up turned away, rubbing their eyes.

"Well, whatever it means, it is over. Let's get back to work," I declared.

As it so happened, the greater part of England seemed to agree with Drogo. That very week, I heard rumors that the usurper's rule was failing and his fall was near at hand. For myself, I was less certain, but as the eclipse had done so much to raise the spirits of our company, I could not help but thank God for it.

"The heavens declare the glory of God," I concluded, "and at times, the downfall of our enemies."

Perhaps you remember that rascal, Robert fitz Hubert, who had made a shambles of the town of Malmesbury. I met him but once and found him to be of little merit, for he loved himself so unduly that even Narcissus might have blushed. He would boast of a time when he burned a church with two dozen monks inside, the look of glee on his face causing me deep concern as I wondered whether the tale was true. Yet our position in that war was such that we could no sooner choose our friends than our enemies. Thus, we were forced to ally with Robert fitz Hubert, kinsman of the wolf of Ypres. As the immortal Cicero would say, "*O tempora! O mores!*"[12]

It was around that time that this man Robert got it in his head to break away from the company of the earl of Gloucester and attempt to seize the castle of Devizes, old stronghold of the bishop of Salisbury. Now, I have noted earlier that this was perhaps the greatest fortress in the land, made entirely out of stone, with walls so thick that three horses might stand end to end and so tall that the trees themselves were in envy. Therefore, his errand seemed most foolhardy—an act of wanton conceit.

Well, it is the way of the world that such arrogant men should at times have all the good fortune. When Robert fitz Hubert and his men arrived at Devizes, they found the garrison in a poor state of readiness. How this could be so in the middle of a war, I cannot fathom. Perhaps they thought their lair

---

12   Translation: "Oh the times! Oh the morals!" This is a quote from Cicero's first
      speech against Catiline.

so impregnable that no man would dare challenge their rule. From thongs of leather, Robert's men made ladders and threw them aloft, then scaled the walls so quickly that the defenders were helpless to stop the charge. Most of those poor souls were killed within minutes, but a few locked themselves in the tower, hoping to be saved by the false king. Alas, they had no food to speak of and were forced to surrender after just three days.

Earl Robert sent his son William, my eldest nephew, up to Gloucester to bring me the news of the castle's fall. I was as surprised as anyone to learn how easily it had been taken, for I likewise thought it impregnable. We took a walk down by the river in the cool of the morning and discussed what must be done, even as I struggled to keep up with the pace set by his long legs.

"Tell me, William my nephew," I said, as we strolled side by side, "have you heard anything from fitz Hubert himself?"

"No," he replied. "This word comes to us from a local maid, who for the price of two shillings surrendered her tale."

"And he said nothing to your father before he broke away?"

"No."

For a moment, I ceased walking and stared at the river as it followed its eternal course to the sea. My heart was deeply troubled.

"Are you well, aunt?" my nephew asked, placing a hand on my shoulder.

I roused my eyes from their stupor and looked at him again.

"These are ill tidings," I concluded. "Why all the secrecy? He either intends to hold the castle for himself, or else use this action to win something from the usurper."

"I think the latter is unlikely. Why should Stephen reward the man who has just put to death his own defenders?"

"But Stephen cannot take that castle without great cost, or he would have done so last year. It was only by surprise that it fell, and I doubt that will work a second time. Therefore, he may be forced to make a parley. But what of the poor souls who surrendered? I shudder to think what was done to them."

"There your instinct is correct," William replied, his face looking suddenly pained. "Our source tells us ... well, perhaps I should not say."

"You will not offend my sensibilities, I assure you," I told him, though in truth I was rather afraid to know what would come next.

"Very well," he replied with a nod. "The women they took for their own pleasures, and thus they are kept even now. Some of the men they stripped naked and tied to poles. They poured honey over all their parts—you take my meaning—and then let them sit out under the heat of the sun. In time, they were covered in flies and other creatures that stung them until they bled. These were perhaps the most fortunate ones, for those that remained they ... they ..."

He put his hand over his mouth and closed his eyes.

"What?" I whispered.

He opened his eyes again and they seemed to be moist.

"They cut them open and pulled out their entrails and burned them upon a fire, then they did the same with their privy parts and—"

"Oh, for heaven's sake, stop!" I ordered, feeling that I would soon be sick if he continued. "This man is the spawn of Satan! William, I want you to ride there now. Stop back in Bristol and take such men as you require, then call forth this Robert and tell him he must either surrender the castle or face our wrath. That will make clear enough where he stands."

"Of course. I shall do so immediately," he said, turning to go.

"And William," I called, "if he refuses, we will send your father after him. We will send Miles after him. We will not rest until Devizes is taken. Do you understand me?"

"I do, but it may not be possible to overcome them. You yourself said it is the strongest fortress—"

"Yes, I know what I said, but this is a matter of honor now. If we are in any way associated with such savage acts, our allies will flee before us—mark my words! And in any case, we cannot take England until we take Devizes, so we shall have to face it one of these days. Therefore, be on your way: that is my final word."

That was how we left things. William would take the southern road down to Devizes, and the rest would depend upon the decision of the madman Robert fitz Hubert. Despite the evil days, I was pleased at least to see my nephew again. My, how he had grown! I well remembered the time my brother brought him over to Normandy in those first days after my return from the empire. He had become the very image of his father, though perhaps a bit less forthright in manner. Yet there were not five in a hundred men as forthright as Earl Robert of Gloucester.

When William came to Devizes with his company of men and stood before the walls, he demanded that Robert fitz Hubert surrender the castle immediately, even as I had told him to do. This was how the traitor replied—I tell you the truth:

"Why should I do such a thing for the man who treats me like a thrall? I have done what Earl Robert was not man enough to do: I have taken Devizes, and now I shall be lord over both Winchester and London! We did not conquer this place merely to turn it over to one who thinks himself better than us. The bastard is not our better. Go back to your father, boy, and tell him he is not fit to wipe the shit from my arse!"

A charming fellow, truly, with all the manners of a boar. So wise did he think himself that he appealed to the nearby castellan, John the Marshal, lord over Marlborough and Ludgershall, and bid him make an alliance in which it would no doubt be

Robert fitz Hubert who held the first place. John Marshal agreed to receive him at Marlborough and discuss the matter. We had every reason to fear, for though he may not have been lord over Winchester and London, this alliance would surely make fitz Hubert ruler of all Wiltonshire.

Then something rather extraordinary happened. As it turned out, John Marshal had no more love in his heart for Robert fitz Hubert than we did. Although he was no true friend of ours, the castellan of Marlborough was not about to submit himself to one whose cruelty was the stuff of legend—not if he had the chance to do otherwise. Indeed, he must have feared that the traitor would attempt to seize Marlborough in the same manner he had gained Devizes. Thus, he chose to act first. As soon as Robert fitz Hubert arrived, the gates were shut behind him and he was dragged to the dungeon and placed in fetters. Those of Robert's men that could fled back to Devizes, but several others were trapped inside and forced to suffer torments along with their fool of a master. Even as King David wrote, "The wicked with pride doth persecute the poor; let them be taken in the crafts that they have imagined."[13]

Even so, the judgment fell upon Robert fitz Hubert, who himself was to know hunger and thirst, pain and suffering at the hands of his enemies. As for John the Marshal, he wrote to Earl Robert informing him of these things and declared that if he desired to lay hands on the prisoner, he might do so for five hundred marks of silver. This my brother was only too happy to pay, and he made haste to Marlborough. What happened after this was not entirely clear to me, nor was this John's true loyalty.

At length, Earl Robert and Lord Miles of Gloucester took fitz Hubert into their custody and brought him back to Devizes,

---

13   Psalm 10:2.

where they bid the garrison surrender in order to spare their master's life. Here we see what a poor lord was Robert fitz Hubert, whose men had no great love for him, but in the same manner as he did, desired nothing but gold and glory for themselves. Earl Robert's words did nothing to sway them. Instead, they demanded a sum of money that was beyond our power to give. Miles then hung two of the traitor's nephews in plain sight, but this likewise accomplished nothing. The evil men simply cried out for more gold. Well, both Miles and Earl Robert were men of their word, so they carried out the sentence of death against Robert fitz Hubert for his treason, even as they had sworn they would. They then departed that place, leaving the defenders to enjoy their lordship over the castle.

Later that year, Devizes was turned over to the usurper for a kingly sum, and thus the faithless garrison profited greatly from their treachery. The castle was granted to Hervey le Breton, who was made earl of Wiltonshire. Thus was an unhappy story brought to an end. The only good things to come out of all this were that Robert fitz Hubert was not lord of England and the false king was forced to part with much of the gold he had lately acquired. Those were small comforts when faced with such savage behavior, but I suppose one must look for good where it can be found. The whole thing left me with a knot in my stomach that did not abate for a good week.

In the month of June, I received a letter from my cousin, Bishop Henry of Winchester, requesting that we send representatives to a council at Bath. "I hope and pray," said he, "that we might arrive at a peaceable outcome in regard to this question and thus see England restored to righteousness. I know that His Holiness Pope Innocent wishes it to be so, for he informed me personally of his will and bid me carry it out. He places such faith in me. I stand in awe of his grace." Even so, was that man wont to write, always seeming to praise others, but truly praising himself.

If Stephen wished to make peace for a time, I was more than willing to consider it, for our reserves were scarce and we had received no Welsh fighters, despite their earlier pledge. From my husband, I heard nothing, and Earl Robert feared that the longer things wore on, the more our natural disadvantage would prove to be our undoing. On the other hand, if the false king desired a truce, that was surely a sign of weakness. Therefore, I sent forth Earl Robert to the council, along with Miles of Gloucester, Earl Reginald of Cornwall, and William fitz Alan. Representing the usurper were Bishop Henry, the false queen Mathilda, and the archbishop of Canterbury, Theobald.

Some three days passed and I heard nothing. Then on the fourth day, we received a messenger who informed us that the council had failed to accomplish its purpose, and Earl Robert and his fellows would be following shortly behind. I must say, I was not surprised, but I was discouraged nevertheless, for we were sorely in need of relief. Not least of all, I had hoped to be spared at least for a time from the fear that an enemy force was about to break down the gate and set fire and ax to the place. It was like an ever present whine that never ceased, setting my every fiber on edge.

When the ambassadors arrived back in Gloucester, I called brother Robert into my private chamber and allowed the rest of them to amuse themselves however they saw fit. It was a small room that could be entered from either the passage or my bed chamber, and at that time it had nothing in it but a few chairs scattered here and there and a table with a checks board on it.

"Whose room was this?" Robert asked, taking a seat near the fire.

"I believe some of the children were here before Miles sent them away to Wales with his wife, Lady Sibyl. I have my bed in her former room, and I use this one to receive guests … that is, the few guests that come," I said, taking a seat opposite him.

"It must be rather quiet around here most days."

"Oh, it's terrible, though not so bad now that Adela has come over from Normandy. I should not have minded the company of children, but they would not have been safe here. I wonder that you do not send Lady Mabel away. You have plenty of castles."

"I do not think she would be as content in any of them as she is in Bristol. We spared no expense in making it the house of her dreams. Have you been playing checks?" he asked, having seen the board left out on the table.

"I was attempting to teach it to Adela, but she showed little interest. I do not suppose you get many chances to play these days."

"No, the war has rather occupied my time."

"Pity that. You were one of the best."

"Well, you might say I'm still playing, but on a rather larger board."

"Indeed."

There was a small pile of logs sitting next to the hearth, and Robert bent down and used one to goad the flames, finally adding it to the top of the fiery pile.

"Thank you, I should have asked one of the servants to do that earlier," I told him, as he returned to his seat.

"Not a problem," he assured me.

"Now, tell me what happened at the council. Was the whole thing a farce?"

He laughed and pushed his hands back through his hair, almost as if he wished to pull it out in frustration. "Argh! Be glad you weren't there, sister. We showed up. We sat down. Bishop Henry got to talking, as he always does. Cousin Mathilda was there, and the archbishop, of course. So prideful, the pair of them. Well, after he had gone on for what seemed like an hour, spewing all kinds of legal nothings from his mouth, I finally told them what we had agreed on: that we would submit this matter to the judgment of the Church."

"Quite right," I said, providing a nod of assent. "And what did they say to that?"

"They withdrew to discuss it among themselves. For his part, I think Bishop Henry would have consented. He is in favor of anything that grants the Church more power. However, he clearly did not gain the support of the other two, for when they returned, it was the false queen who did all the talking, along with the archbishop. They said the pope has already made his judgment, and there is no need to concern the Church a second time. They then asked us to lay down our arms in exchange for a general pardon, which we naturally refused. We went on for another day or so, but everyone could see that there would be no agreement, so we ended it and went our separate ways."

I stared into the flames, shaking my head. "I am sorry you had to waste your time, brother. They plainly had no desire for peace, but simply hoped that we would surrender."

"I was able to have one rather interesting conversation with Bishop Henry."

"Oh?" I asked, suddenly interested.

"Yes, on the final day, he pulled me aside and we talked for a few minutes. He was quite open about his frustration with Stephen."

"Even so, he has been with me, but he does not act upon that frustration. He will not break with his brother."

"Let me continue … Apparently, Hugh Bigod rose up in rebellion in the East."

I leaned closer to him. "Would that be the same Hugh Bigod whose perjury doomed us all? The one who claimed my father forsook me in his final hour?!" I almost spat out the words, the man offended me so.

"The very same. He seized Bungay Castle, which used to belong to Waleran. It seems that he, like everyone else, has grown tired of the *Famille* Beaumont. Stephen had to make a truce with him, and once again Waleran is to blame. That is why the usurper called for the council. He is losing control of his own men."

"We have known this for a long time."

"Yes, but I think Stephen is only just starting to recognize how fatal the influence of the Beaumonts is upon his alleged kingship. He has sacrificed everything on behalf of Waleran, and what has he gained? I cannot think what makes him favor that man so, but it is a boon for us."

I suppose these words should have made me happy, but I did not feel so. It was not enough—none of it was. I leaned back in my chair.

"It may well be too late. Robert, we are running out of time and money. The harvest this year will not be half what it was in days of yore, for the crops are destroyed. You speak of Stephen having little control over his men, but it is no different with us. Just look what happened with Robert fitz Hubert!"

This time it was Robert's turn to lean forward and raise his voice, if only slightly. "Have you so little faith, and after everything we have achieved?"

"Every day that the false king survives—every day that he sits upon that throne and wears the crown—makes the task that much harder. And what if this war is to last for another year? Another five years? Can we bear it? Can England bear it?"

"Worry less about England and more about yourself," he advised me. "You are not the one who has brought the kingdom low."

"Even so, we must find a way to win, and fast! Otherwise, there will be nothing left of this kingdom but heaps of ash, and we will be gnawing upon our own bones for food."

We sat in that manner for a moment, neither of us saying anything. After all, what was there to say? Then, almost out of nowhere, a thought struck me. I am not sure why it came to me in that moment, but I was overwhelmed by the thought of my brother—that is, my full brother: the one whose corpse was at the bottom of the sea. This sudden memory robbed me of breath.

"What is it?" Robert asked, clearly noticing the pain on my face.

"It has been twenty years since William died," I whispered. "Twenty years since we were robbed of him."

"Really? It doesn't seem that long. I can still remember the sound of his voice."

"Can you? Oh, how I wish I could!"

"Well, you were so young when you left us all."

"If only he had lived!" I cried, shaking my head. "What a king he might have been! We would have been spared all this hardship."

Robert reached out and took my hand in his. "I miss him—truly, I do. He was a good lad: quite sure of himself, but he was a prince, after all."

"Do you hear that, William? He misses you," I told the air.

Robert looked around as if searching for an apparition. "I'm sorry … are you speaking to him now?"

"Oh, yes. My brother is with me wherever I go. He bids me carry on and fulfill his legacy."

He leaned forward and said with some concern, "Please tell me you're not hearing voices. I know this war has put us all under stress—"

"Never fear! I know well enough that my brother has gone to heaven, and yet his blood is in my veins. Our spirits are bound together eternally. One day, I will go to him again, where he waits with my dear mother. But until then, I can still feel him with me every day, and I know I am not alone."

"Maud," Robert said, clutching my hand, "you must not feel any guilt over what happened to William."

"Guilt? Why should I feel guilt?" I asked, pulling my hand away. His statement had placed me immediately on defense. Yes, there had been hours of darkness over the years when I heard the soft whisper in my head, *It should have been you. Things would be so much easier if it had been you.* But I was not about to contemplate it in that moment, for I knew from experience that there was no end to those questions and no hope of release from false guilt of which one could never repent.

"Because you live on and he does not?" Robert asked, or rather guessed. My tone had robbed him of confidence, though he struck near the mark.

"That was God's choice, not mine! I have enough to feel guilty about already without adding that to my record!" I declared. Still, not wanting to seem heartless, I admitted, "I do wish it had been the usurper's ship that went down though and not the one carrying the prince. Perhaps that is a sin, but given how things have turned out, I suspect God will forgive me."

This time, we both stared into the fire. I felt the grief welling up within me, and I suspect Earl Robert felt much the same way. After all, he spent far more time with William Ætheling than I ever did. What a loss it had been for England! And yet, it was a loss of a different kind to those who were bone of his bone and flesh of his flesh, as if a part of ourselves had been torn from us indeed and the wound left unmended.

At length, he sighed and whispered, "I wish I could take those days I spent with him and grant them to you instead."

I turned and faced him, even as he did the same in return. "Were you able to make that offer, I would accept, but consider also that I have seen Rome and you have not. I have passed over the mountains and sailed upon the Rhine. We do not choose life's gifts and curses. We must simply accept them and be thankful for what we have. I know of no other way."

"Too right you are," he concluded.

V

In any conflict, there are few who truly commend themselves to history, be they ever so praised in song and rhyme. There is little honor to be had in that deluge of blood, and the sacred word is not so much "To arms and great fame" but rather "Kill or be killed." Even as Virgil put it, "*Durate, et vosmet rebus servate secundis,*" that is, "Endure the hardship of your present state and reserve for yourselves a better fate."[14]

Yet there were a few men worth praising in the midst of that general chaos. One such was Ralph Paganel, lord of Dudley Castle. Lord Ralph was one of the first to rebel against the usurper's rule: good man, his conscience at least was intact. For this choice, he was to pay dearly. In the year of our Lord 1138, the false king brought all his strength against Dudley Castle and made a hell of the surrounding country, but Ralph Paganel was one step ahead. He had fortified the castle twice over, and the siege was not strong enough to overtake them. I

---

14   Virgil, *The Aeneid*, Translated by John Dryden, I.207. http://classics.mit.edu/
     Virgil/aeneid.html. Accessed 2 April 2022.

never forgot this first victory won by the lord of Dudley, and I instructed Earl Robert to devise some means of including him in our efforts.

The matter became more pressing when we lost Geoffrey Talbot In a skirmish that summer. One would hope that if a commander must be lost, it would at least come in some great battle that advances the general cause. Sadly, there was little honor in his death, coming as it did in the midst of a failed operation. Well, I cannot say that Lord Miles was too sad to see his old enemy depart from this life, but Earl Robert was another story. How fortunate then that he had already sought out the help of Ralph Paganel for his next task!

We had passed a rather mild summer, for which I was thankful. However, it made me fear for the winter that was to come. Already in the month of September, Adela and I decided it was time to exchange my light clothes for heavier garments that would keep me warm as the cool crept in. This was not the immense task that it might have been for the queen of a great palace with an endless supply of clothing. Nevertheless, it was a task, and we set about it.

Among the chests that Adela brought with her from Anjou were two holding furs and gowns. I was happy to wear these again for the first time in years. We were performing this work in my bed chamber. The chests were laid open on the floor, and Adela busily sorted through them as I sat on the bed and gave directions. Lest you think I was unwilling to make any move to help her, she often handed me things to sort while I sat. After we had gone on like this for half an hour or so, there were clothes lying everywhere: on the bed, on the desk, hanging over the chair, covering the floor, and even a few in the chests themselves.

"Oh, this is lovely," Adela said, as she raised up a green cloak with a fur collar. "The fur is so soft, and this material—it must come from somewhere in the South, for I have never seen its equal here. The needle work is excellent."

"Yes, my first husband purchased it for me in Tuscany, and I have kept it ever since," I explained. "If you wish to borrow it, you may."

"Oh no, my lady!" she cried, quickly returning the cloak to its chest. "This is far too fine for me. What would everyone think?"

"I suppose they would think you borrowed my cape; either that or they will accuse me of cheating them when it comes to payment." Even as I said this, I could imagine the looks of indignation on the men's faces to think that I had allowed my maid to spend their beer money on such a thing, and it made me smile.

"Well, I have no one to impress in any case," Adela said quietly, closing the chest and opening another.

"Why would you say that?"

She glanced up at me and looked as if she might start laughing. "Because it is true, my lady."

"A lady always has someone to impress, especially one like you who is young and pretty," I told her.

Adela made no reply, but simply shook her head sadly and stooped down to pick up a few pairs of shoes. I felt sad that she would think of herself so poorly. She did not seem as cheerful as in earlier years. I decided I would take a chance.

"What about Sir Philip?" I asked. "I have seen the two of you speaking at times. He seems fond of you."

"Ha!" she cried, turning and pointing at me. "I knew you would not be able to help yourself!"

"What do you mean?!" I cried in return, abandoning my comfortable perch to stand.

"I knew the first time I saw him that you would try to match the two of us. It is your way."

"I am most unjustly accused!" I declared, reaching out and lowering her pointed finger. "All I said was that he seems fond of you. I did not call for a priest!"

"You attempted to plant the idea in my head," she charged, raising her finger again.

"You mean to tell me that it wasn't there to begin with?"

"Of course not! I am through with men."

With this bold assertion, she reached down to fill her arms with shoes again and threw them into one of the chests without ceremony.

"What on earth are you talking about?" I inquired.

"Just what I said," she replied, turning to face me again. "Ever since I faced that shame with regard to …" She took a deep breath, as if the next words would pain her deeply. "In regard to you know who, I swore I would not allow my heart to get carried off like that again, longing for a man I barely knew, having dreams of marriage and children and everything else. Only a few years earlier, I thought I was going to be a nun, then all of a sudden, I was staying up all night writing mournful poems by the light of the moon."

"You wrote poems?"

"I do not pretend that they were good poems," she said softly. "I was, after all, still learning to write properly at the time. But when my heart was broken, I cast them all upon the fire! I will never allow myself to be thus possessed in the future."

"But Adela, surely you do not think that because things did not work the first time, they can never work?" Even as I said these words, I could tell from the look on her face that this was exactly what she thought. "Yes, you fell in love with a man, and he happened to desire to serve in the Church someday. That is not your fault. You did nothing wrong. I'm sure that neither Drogo nor myself—"

"Do not say his name!" she begged, the tears breaking free.

"Very well. I'm sure that no one would think there was any reason for you to feel shame over what happened, and I am equally certain that there are other men who would be interested in marrying you. I could easily make inquiries—"

"No!" she cried. "The last thing I want is for some man to marry me out of pity or obligation. I am quite content to live in your service as I do now."

"But Adela, your dream of marrying a handsome knight and living happily with your children and a table full of food—"

"Argh!" she bellowed, producing far more volume than I thought within her power. "You just don't understand me at all, do you?!"

At that very moment, there was a knock on the door. Adela and I stared at one another, her in tears, while I felt at a complete loss for any words that might help. I sensed that she was not about to answer the door, so I called out, "Who's there?"

"The archbishop of Canterbury!" came the reply.

When this comment did not produce the laugh that was likely desired, the voice instead said, "Actually, it's just me, the earl of Gloucester. I need to discuss something with you in private."

I did not want to simply abandon my conversation with Adela when she was so upset, but she said to me, "Have no fear. I was about to leave anyway."

I found myself struck dumb as my mind continued to search for something—anything—that might improve the situation. Before I could form any words, Adela had walked over to the door and pulled it open.

"Enter, Earl Robert," she said, her face still red from crying.

I read the concern on my brother's face as he entered the room and she immediately departed, shutting the door firmly behind her. No sooner had he been struck with wonder by this show of womanly feeling than he began to look around and see the clothes lying everywhere.

"What in God's name happened here?" he asked. "Were you two having some kind of fight that involved throwing clothes?"

"We were changing out my things for the winter and had a minor disagreement," I said, moving to hide some of my under things with my foot before he could observe them.

"I knew women took their clothes very seriously," he said, his eyes still wandering around the room, "but I would never have thought that shoes could cause someone to cry."

"That is because you have never been forced to wear women's shoes," I replied in annoyance. "Now, tell me what you came to say."

Earl Robert picked up the two gowns that were draped over the chair and laid them on one of the chests instead, then took the seat. For my part, I found a space on the bed that was not covered in hose.

"I have sought out the aid of Lord Ralph Paganel for a raid that I think will improve our fortunes," he told me.

"And what is to be your target?" I asked.

"Nottingham."

I furrowed my brow as my mind began to work out the riddle he had just given me. This was the first time I had heard anyone mention Nottingham, for it was in the opposite direction of most of our efforts. It sat on the River Trent, not far from the great road that stretched from Dover in the South to Berwick in the North. It might have been a helpful base from which to march against York, but that was certainly not one of our goals. It was south of the great hills at least and clear of the major forests, but it was not one of the old royal cities. It did not even have a stone castle, but a simple wood design that had been thrown up quickly on the order of the Conqueror. Yes, I finally determined that I could find no good reason to go after the place.

"Nottingham is a good two days' ride from our nearest castle," I protested. "What do you hope to accomplish by exposing yourself in the North, where we have few friends and fewer estates? If you must waste your efforts on some feat of courage, why not do so in the South where it might actually do us some good?"

"That is why it will surprise them," he argued. "We will pillage the place and then be off, with the usurper none the wiser. In any case, I foresee that the action will soon shift to the North."

"Based on what?"

"Intuition."

I shook my head. "So, we are just choosing our targets based on intuition now? That does not seem wise."

"Oh, really? Tell me, how many times have you ridden into battle?" he asked, crossing his arms.

"That is not fair! You know very well that I would if I could. But I'll have you know, I was forced to flee with the Saxons at my back, forced to spar with the company of cardinals, forced to give birth three times over—"

"Not the same," he interrupted, shaking his head.

I quickly groped for something that might sway him. "Forced to abide that knave of a husband!"

These words seemed to serve some helpful purpose, for the look on his face changed.

"Hmm … I admit, that is something, but the point is that when you have been in as many battles as I have, you get a sense of these things. You can almost see things happen before they … well, happen."

"Really?" I asked, still not fully won over. "Then tell me, brother, when will I be seated on England's throne?"

"In less than a year, I will deliver the usurper into your hands."

He said this without any pause, as if it was already a matter of record. It took me by surprise, and I shook my head in wonder at his confidence.

"There is a prophecy designed to please. I'd like to see you keep it."

"Care to place a wager?"

"With what money?"

"No money. If I can deliver Stephen into your hands by next summer, then I take into my possession every drop of wine in the cellars of Gloucester Castle. If I fail, you will gain all the wine in Bristol Castle." Here he leaned forward and whispered as if conspiring. "It is to your advantage to take my offer, as there is far more drink to be had in my castle than this one."

I too leaned forward. "Very well. One year hence!"

"One last thing," he said, rising to leave. "If we do take Nottingham, you will grant it to Ralph's cousin, William. That is the agreement."

"William who? I do not know this William from Adam."

"I met him once. He's a good man."

"So, this is what it has come to, then? I am to be ordered around like some hireling, having no say in the matter, relying only on your 'intuition'?"

"I wouldn't look at it that way," Earl Robert replied with a smile. "I would say you are being noble in every sense of the word."

"I like not your definition of nobility, but it appears I have no choice," I concluded.

Thus, I sent him off to the North, where he met with Ralph Paganel and a host of hired men, some of them knights of the earl of Warwick. How they were able to gain such support, I cannot imagine, for the earl was no friend of ours. I suppose it is better that my brother put his gold to that use than making it security for our bet.

When they arrived in Nottingham, it was certainly a surprise. The inhabitants fled to the church, while our forces seized what they could from the provisions. Some of those poor souls were cut down in the street, but most chose to seek sanctuary rather than fight. This was for the best, for we sought food and coin rather than blood.

The trouble didn't start until they came to the house of a man whose name I honestly forget: we'll say it was 'Hugh.' Some of the hired men ordered this Hugh to turn over his gold. He obediently led them down to the cellar, where he kept all his treasures. More than two dozen of them were making a careful inventory when the evil Hugh took it upon himself to lock the door and trap them all inside. He then set fire to the place and watched with devilish joy as the flames sprung higher and higher, consuming all inside.

This deed was the ending of Hugh, for when Earl Robert saw what had taken place, he had the man executed on the spot. Sadly, there was nothing he nor anyone else could do to keep the flames from spreading. It had been a very dry summer, and within minutes the whole town was burning, drowned in a sea of orange and red that rose and fell as the waves. Earl Robert and Lord Ralph pulled their men out of town as quickly as they could, but there would be no such luck for those inside the church. A few were able to flee, but they were forced to watch as the church caught fire and their fellows perished. It was not with any great joy that our party left the town of Nottingham to its doom, but what could they have done? In his lust for vengeance, the knave Hugh had brought death upon them all. I am sorry for it. Indeed, when I first heard the news, I felt suddenly ill and retired to my chamber, overcome by the tragedy of it all. I could almost hear the cries of those helpless souls as they writhed in agony, the flames devouring their flesh.

How often I saw my life proceeding differently! How often I wished to be other than what I was! There was no victory in those days that was not somehow tempered by grief. I cursed it then as I do now. I ask you, how do you judge me? Am I redeemed in your eyes, or am I all that they say and more?

What is life but a pale reflection of the beyond: an endless procession of splintered things and broken dreams and tales too long to tell? I assure myself that in the beyond there is meaning and some form of redemption. There our lives play out in the perfect sphere, and at length we are made whole, but I cannot see it. What is hidden from me is forbidden to me. This much I know: I live. I breathe. I am.

That autumn passed in relative quiet. The false king sent Bishop Henry of Winchester to meet with their eldest brother—Earl Theobald—and treat with the French king and all the clergy. The stated cause was to reach some agreement that might restore peace to the land, but we all knew well enough the true reason for Bishop Henry's departure: Stephen and Earl Waleran wished him as far away from themselves as possible. It is a wonder they did not send him all the way to Rome, or perhaps even Baghdad. Well, I for one wished him a pleasant enough visit … and that he might see the full justice of our cause.

I had a visitor of my own that season. Given the break in fighting while we all awaited news of Bishop Henry's council, Lady Mabel of Gloucester was able to make the journey north and visit us in Gloucester Castle. I was only too happy to spend time in her company and hoped it would take my mind off the flames of Nottingham.

I had the room next to my bed chamber set up especially for this occasion. The best of Lady Sibyl's tapestries were brought out and hung upon the bare walls. We spared more wood than usual for the fire and I even had one of our precious bottles of wine retrieved from the cellar. This shows you in what esteem I held my brother's wife. When the time of Mabel's arrival came,

I had Adela fetch her and lead her up to the chamber. As she entered the room, I called, "Lady Mabel!" and the two of us moved to embrace one another.

"My dear empress! Have you heard news of ... Bishop Henry's visit to the ... French king?" she said, kissing each of my cheeks in turn.

"Not yet. I assume they are forming some plot in regard to Normandy, but it will be of no avail unless Stephen can claim it, which I dearly hope he cannot."

Adela directed Mabel to one of the two chairs set by the fire, while I took the other. She then proceeded to open the bottle of wine and pour some for each of us.

"How could Stephen afford to fight in Normandy when he has his hands full here?" Mabel asked. "I should not think that he could bear to part with any of his men."

"Maybe so, but I would hardly put it past the French to meddle in our affairs. In any case, you have not met Adela, I think."

"No, I have not," Mabel replied, turning to study our subject more closely.

"It is a pleasure to meet you, my lady," said Adela with a bow, handing her a goblet of wine.

"And the same, I am certain. Do you come from the Vexin, love? I hear it in your voice."

Adela handed the other goblet to me and then turned back to face Lady Mabel. "I was born in a small village near Rouen: a lovely place, really, though no one has ever heard of it."

"Well, it makes little difference where you are from. Just look where you are!" Lady Mabel concluded.

Adela nodded in agreement. "God has blessed me most abundantly."

At this, I could not help but laugh. "Yes, so abundantly that he placed you in the middle of a war! Do pour yourself some, Adela. You deserve it."

This she did most gladly and took a seat at the small table for playing checks, which had lately been taken over by our embroidery. There she began stitching and sipping happily.

"Tell me," I asked Mabel, "how are all your relations?"

"My eldest, as you know, is married to the Beaumont girl, Hawise of Leicester."

"Right. I imagine that must make things ... difficult." I said this because the Beaumont twins, Waleran and Robert, were chief allies of the usurper.

"To say the least," Mabel replied with a roll of the eyes. "They were wed before the war broke out. It was a fine match, to be sure, but it has led to some problems with the lady's family. It is fortunate that she chooses our side, or it should have led to many quarrels between them. I must admit the Lady Hawise has been excellent in all things, but for producing a child. Then again, that is no wonder when she and her husband are scarcely ever in the same county!"

I set my goblet down on the small table between us and leaned in closer to speak. "Allow me to speak from experience, countess. The Lord at times delays such things for reasons all his own. They may yet have children."

"I dearly hope so, for her sake as much as mine. There is no honor for a barren woman. My daughter Mathilda is not yet with child either, but no wonder there! Her husband is a fool."

"You speak of Ranulf, the earl of Chester?" I asked with a frown.

"The very same."

"What has he done to offend you so?"

"Not myself, but my husband. Earl Ranulf, as you know, has denied his loyalty to either party in this affair, and that is a damnable sin to Robert. But more to the point, he has written more than once begging for money, when he knows very well we have none to offer beyond what he received upon marriage.

He is all greed, that one, and my husband swears, 'I would not lift a finger to help that man, for I gave him the dearest treasure in my keeping, and he has scorned it.'"

"He has not been mistreating your daughter?" I asked with some concern.

"Oh, he's a cumber for sure. I suspect there is not a moment in time when he thinks of anything but himself. He is still sore that he lost out on the lordship of Carlisle."

"Yes, I seem to remember that when Stephen granted that to my cousin, the evil Ranulf attempted to seize him, or perhaps I am wrong."

"No, that is entirely correct, I'm afraid. He felt it ought to be his, for it used to belong to his father, yet his claim was quite weak. I suppose a king may grant such things to anyone he chooses, no?"

"A king who hardly warrants the name," I objected.

"Yes, forgive me," she replied, bowing her head as if to acknowledge her shame. Poor woman!

"Is there nothing we can do for young Mathilda, then?" I asked, changing the subject. "No succor we can grant her?"

"What succor is there for women in such a time?" her mother answered with a sigh.

Here Adela decided to force her way into the conversation. "The Lord! The Lord is our succor."

"You speak rather forthrightly, girl," Mabel replied with a smile.

"There I must take the blame," I said. "She has spent too much time in my presence. Even so, you speak the truth, Adela. Now tell me, Lady Mabel: what of your son Roger? He is still in Normandy?"

"Yes, and he has an excellent tutor. Master Matthew has anchored his mind in the ancients. Whenever I read his letters, I stand in awe. He will be a fine bishop, my Roger."

The pride she took in her son caused me to think of my own children, whom I had not seen in two years. Oh dear—two years! What kind of mother abandons her sons for that long? I felt once again the pang of guilt, but I told myself that after all, everything I did was for them, especially Henry. He was the heir to the throne and the one whose inheritance was stolen. Even so, perhaps in my efforts to defend that inheritance, I had failed to find him a good steward for his mind.

"Perhaps I should seek out this tutor for my eldest son," I said. "He is at the age where he should be learning more."

"How old is Prince Henry?" Mabel inquired.

"Seven, soon to be eight. I can hardly believe it."

She nodded sadly. "Do you miss them all dreadfully?"

"My boys, yes. Count Geoffrey, no. He defines the word 'cumber.' Yet if he wins Normandy for us, I might even kiss him."

"Good Lord! I hope it does not come to that!" Mabel jested.

The pair of us raised our goblets to one another, rejoicing in this rare moment of peace and friendship. Even so, I was filled with concern for my sons. What would become of them? Would they even recognize me when we finally saw each other again? Or would we never see each other again?

Bishop Henry's time in Normandy was all for naught. He attempted to reach an agreement in which my son, Prince Henry, would be made heir to the usurper in both England and Normandy, in exchange for an end to the fighting. King Louis of France and Count Theobald were much in favor of this idea, for it would ensure that Count Geoffrey of Anjou would never reign over Normandy and there would be peace in their own lifetimes. However, the false king was not willing to yield one degree of power. That is some sign of how assured he was in his rule, for he certainly believed he could crush us on either side of the Channel.

Thus, we marked another Advent season amid civil war. How fortunate at least that the fighting had ceased long enough for our friends to join us in Gloucester! Even Lady Sibyl, Miles' wife, returned to celebrate the season at her own castle, and I was glad to have another female companion. We brought in such greens as we could find to decorate the hall. The feast was small and the minstrels few, but I declare to you, when I glimpsed within that hall so many blessed faces—Earl Robert and Laby Mabel, Lord Miles and Lady Sibyl, Earl Reginald, Lord Brian, Abbot Gilbert, Bishop Nigel, and all the rest—I thought it as grand as Westminster Hall in days of yore.

There is only one thing that can improve such a gathering, and that is some timely chatter. We received such a piece of news from the East. The usurper had been forced to travel up to Lincoln and grant the earldom to William of Roumare. He was the brother of Earl Ranulf of Chester, who was married to my niece, Mathilda: the very one for whom Lady Mabel had expressed such concern. As soon as Stephen departed, the brothers had taken custody of Lincoln Castle and were ruling quite happily over their new realm. This was all anyone could talk about on Christmas Day, except for Earl Robert, who avoided any subject that had to do with his son-in-law.

"That man will be even richer than you, brother!" I jested one day.

"Of course he's richer than me, for he does nothing but sit upon his wealth. He does not act as a man should!" was the response.

Soon, we had entered a new year, and much to Robert's dismay, the talk was still of the brother earls and what a fantastic trick they had played on Stephen.

"I heard they sent their men in dressed as women, then seized the castle by force!" one person claimed.

"No, no! That's all wrong! Their wives went in to meet with the constable, then a few of the knights came to collect them and overtook the garrison," another said.

"I heard that Stephen gave it to them as a gift," replied another. "You know, because he took all their lands away to appease the Scottish king."

"That cannot be right!" the first yelled, and so on they continued into the night.

If you could have seen Earl Robert's face during these discussions, you would not have known whether to laugh or pity him. One night, while everyone else was feasting and dancing, I saw him sitting alone in the corner of the hall, staring at a game of checks that had long since been abandoned. I decided that it would befit my role as a sister to join him.

"How now, brother?" I asked, as I approached the table. "You cannot hide over here for ever."

"Anything to prevent me having to talk about that Ranulf," he growled more than spoke.

"Are you attempting to play against yourself?"

"This was my game with Brian earlier. He beat me again. I hate it when he does that."

"Perhaps you should cease from playing, then."

"No, I must beat him!" Robert cried, pounding his fist on the table. "How can I lose when I am his elder?"

"Does age have anything to do with it? In any case, you are both plenty old now."

He sighed loudly. "Are you going to assault my dignity or are you going to sit down and play?"

"I suppose this once I shall attempt to please you," I agreed. "I will even let you go first."

"Oh, how kind of you!" he said, though his tone declared the opposite.

We began to move the pieces back and forth while the dancing continued on the other side of the room. The music was quite pleasant, and I might have even enjoyed myself had Robert not stopped me more than once to correct me.

"No, don't move that one. I'll take it here, see ..." he said, pointing.

"Robert, you can either beat me or scold me, but I will not let you do both."

"But how will you ever learn if you—"

"Robert!" I cried with an air of authority.

"Very well," he replied, leaning back in his chair. "Do as you please, but I don't want to see you crying when I vanquish you."

"When have you ever seen me cry?" I inquired, moving another piece.

"When you left for Germany?" he asked more than stated.

"I was eight years old!"

"Even so, I would not have cried at eight years old."

"No, I am sure you were killing a wolf with your bare hands at that age," I said, rolling my eyes.

"I may well have been!"

At just that moment, when the conversation was all but lost, we were joined by a third person: Brian fitz Count. I had not observed his approach, and having him suddenly so near startled me, though I attempted to hide it.

"Empress Mathilda," he said with a bow. "You are not dancing."

"No, for I am very poor at it," I replied softly.

"That is not what I remember."

"No one asked you!" snapped Robert. "I'm about to win. Let us play on!"

"Earl Robert is in ill humor this evening, is he not?" Brian asked me, smiling.

"He is indeed," I replied.

"Well, then, I say leave him to his misery and come dance with me."

I pretended to debate with myself for a moment, though there was really nothing to consider. Finally, I said, "Lord Brian, I shall take you up on that offer. I have had enough of this game."

"What!" my brother cried. "No, you have to finish!"

"Sorry," I concluded, and left him to curse me on his own.

I followed Brian over to the other end of the hall, and he held out his hand. I placed my hand in his, and my heart began to beat a bit faster. I was quite aware of this, and a rush of guilt followed close behind.

Maybe I shouldn't have agreed to this, I thought.

Then another voice inside my head said, *All you wanted was to join in the revels and have some fun. There is nothing odd about it unless you make it odd. Calm yourself!*

This second voice won out and we began dancing. The light of the fire shone upon our faces as we laughed and sang. Two steps toward one another, then another two back, then we were spinning and clapping, my movements at times less than smooth, but I cared not. For a moment, I forgot all the terrible things that had happened since I set foot in England: the maimings, the killings, the fires, the famines. It was as if time itself had reversed and sent us back to some happier age. After all, Brian and I had been good friends before anything else, and I missed our friendship. I was so caught up in all the mirth that I found myself feeling rather faint. The room continued to spin although I was standing still.

"Forgive me, I need to step out for a moment," I told him.

I was quite warm from dancing, and the air itself seemed hot as I made for the door and withdrew into the yard. Immediately, a chill filled my lungs and overtook my body. In the darkness, I could just see that the yard was empty but for a few guards standing on the far side. I had not foreseen that it would be quite so cold. The wind was most unkind and hit me like the icy breath of deepest hell. I pulled my arms in close to myself and shivered. I was beginning to regret my decision when Lord Brian appeared with a fur and placed it over my shoulders.

"Thank you," I said, holding it tightly. "I'm afraid things were a bit too much in there."

"No need to worry," he replied. "Do you wish to be left alone?"

"No, stay. I should like some company."

We stood there quietly for a moment, the glittering stars above our heads. But for the cold, it was a glorious night. My breath froze in the air. I looked over at Brian, but when he met my gaze, I immediately turned away. We stood awhile longer. At length, he said, "Earl Robert thinks our chances are good in the spring."

"Earl Robert is going to owe me all the wine in Bristol."

"What?"

"We made a deal. He must deliver the usurper into my hands by next summer, or I take all his wine. Of course, if he does succeed, I shall have to surrender my own, but I do not think that is likely."

He smiled. "Don't be so sure. He tells me the Welsh are almost ready to commit. They just need to be … encouraged."

"By which you mean more gold, which we do not have."

"Perhaps I should not have brought it up."

"No, forgive me. I just … It is easy to lose hope in such a situation, though that is no fault of yours. You have held Wallingford for us in spite of everything."

"I have many good men," he replied with a nod, "and then there was that time Lord Miles saved our skins."

I looked at him sadly. The light of the distant fires shone upon his face, and his eyes seemed almost to shimmer.

"I wish I could grant you an earldom," I said softly.

"Never fear! I don't want an earldom. Earls have too many enemies."

I was not sure if I should believe this answer. Brian fitz Count was not as plagued by avarice and pride as some men, but I did not doubt that he would have valued such an honor, all other things being equal. Even so, I dismissed the matter with my reply.

"Well, if you didn't want enemies, you should never have joined our cause."

"Stephen is one enemy worth having. I never did like him."

"None of us did." I shook my head and let out a sigh. "How did he end up getting himself crowned, Brian? How could God have allowed it?"

"Perhaps God laughs at us all," he said with a smile.

"Oh, I am certain of that!"

For a moment, we simply looked at each other, then off into the distance. I knew it was only right for me to inquire after his family, so I decided to do so.

"How is your wife?"

"Good, good," he replied, his face offering no sign of any deeper feeling. "She's a sweet woman. She has to put up with me, and that's a sore travail."

"I doubt that," I muttered.

"Well, I have placed her in the middle of a war."

"And that annoys her? Some women are so fastidious!"

This comment was intended to draw a laugh, and it did. Then a wave of sadness seemed to pass over his face.

"Of course, it pains her that we have no children."

I suddenly felt bad that I had raised the subject. "Yes, I am sorry about that. Truly, I am," I said quickly, offering words that I doubted would help in any way. After all, I had once known the pain of which he spoke.

"Thank you. I should have liked to be a father, but it won't happen now. We are both old."

I could not remember the last time we had spoken so openly. Once, it had always been like that. Another blast of wind hit us both, and my teeth chattered.

"Are you too cold? Should we return?"

I did not answer his question, for there was another rising up inside me. I felt myself suddenly bold. *Should I ask it?* I wondered. Almost before I had properly decided, the words escaped my mouth.

"Why did it have to be this way, Brian?"

He squinted. "What do you mean?"

I said nothing more, but as the look on his face changed—his eyes growing wide, his lips parting slightly—I could tell that he understood. He started to say something, but then stopped. My breath seemed to catch in my throat. I was certain he was about to speak some words of great import. Then, out of nowhere, there came an interruption: a sound from the direction of the gate.

Both of us looked toward the source of the noise. I could hear voices speaking but was too far away to understand. Suddenly, the gate was opened, and in came four riders. Three were clearly knights, and the other appeared to be a noble of some kind, for he wore a fine cloak. It was this man who alighted and demanded of the steward with great volume, "I must speak with Earl Robert this instant! Is he here?" I watched as the visitor was led into the hall on the other side. They had not observed us standing in the shadows.

"Who was that?" I asked Brian.

"I could not see clearly, but it looked like it might be the earl of Chester."

"Robert's son-in-law? Good God! What is he doing here?"

"Perhaps we should go inside and see?"

We walked once again into the warmth of the hall, where the music had stopped and everyone was staring at the new arrival. Earl Ranulf had taken a seat by the fire with his back to me and Brian, and Earl Robert and the rest were gathered in front of him, hanging upon his every word.

"And then, after he had made all those promises, he returned with an army fit to conquer Hades, and that damned Bishop Alexander let him in, after everything Stephen did to him. He just let him walk right in!" the earl cried, gesturing broadly.

"How did you get out?" Robert asked.

"I climbed over the wall, that's how! I had to leave Lady Mathilda behind with William, the poor—"

"You mean to say she's not in Cheshire?!" my brother asked, the anger in his voice growing with every syllable.

"No, she could not have scaled the wall, and in any case the journey might have killed her. We had to pass by the mountain way, sleeping on the bare ground, with naught to eat or drink."

"You left my daughter at a siege!" Earl Robert cried, taking no heed of the man's defense.

"Well, what was I supposed to do?!"

Now, I thought I had seen my brother angry before, but it was then that I recognized how everything else had been a mere pittance of annoyance in comparison to the wrath that consumed him at that moment. His face was so red, I thought his head might burst. It was left to Lady Mabel to run over, grab her husband, and say, "My dear, I am sure he did all he could. He has left her in the keeping of Earl William. Just breathe, dear, breathe!"

She was a woman of great skill, for she succeeded in keeping her husband from killing Earl Ranulf on the spot. Instead, with his finger pointed directly in his son-in-law's face, my brother yelled, "I have never liked you, boy! Never ... liked ... you!" I thought this a rather odd choice of words, as the earl appeared to have not been a boy for many years hence, judging by the lack of hair on the back of his head.

"I know that," he replied meekly, "but I have come here to seek your help. We must ride to Lincoln and relieve the castle!"

"Ha!" Robert laughed. "And how do you intend to do that? Thanks to men like you who refuse to commit, we are rather at a disadvantage." Hoping to drive his point home, he once again pointed at the earl's chest and repeated, "I blame you for that!"

"But I have gathered all the men of Cheshire to our cause and won the support of the Welsh kings!" he pleaded, the tone of his voice rising higher, approaching the squeak of a small child.

At this news, Robert's expression seemed to soften, and the finger that he had been pointing at Earl Ranulf's chest was withdrawn.

"How many Welsh?" he asked.

"Ten thousand, if we give them time."

"Time?! We have no time! My daughter is rotting in Lincoln Castle, you fool!"

"Then a few thousand. Gather what men you can. We must march on Lincoln!"

For the first time, my brother's eyes broke from this interrogation and looked toward me. Taking that as my sign, I walked forward to where they were all standing and had my first proper look at Earl Ranulf of Chester.

"Empress Mathilda!" he said, rising from his seat only to prostrate himself.

"Ah, so now you bow! I did not think to see that in all my days!" I replied.

"My lady, you must forgive me. Times have been difficult," he begged, casting his eyes to the ground. "King Stephen has been pressing me ever so hard!"

"Yes, so hard that he gave your brother an earldom and you lands from east to west, but that is neither here nor there. Tell me, Earl Ranulf, who does the false king have with him?"

Raising his head meekly, the earl replied, "He has sent Alan of Richmond to the North to gain the Yorkshire men for their cause. He has with him the earl of Surrey, the earl of Worcester, Hugh Bigod, Gilbert de Clare, of course William of Ypres and all his Flemish hounds … need I go on?"

"No, that is sufficient. And they are making a siege upon Lincoln Castle?"

"Yes, my lady, but I have brought together many of those who have been robbed of their lands and titles by this present conflict. They are no friends of Stephen. They will fight for you! Together, we can overcome the false king, as you call him."

"I call him that because that is what he is," I stated. I then turned to Earl Robert and said, "What do you think, brother?"

"I think this fool hopes merely to recover his own lands, and shows little concern for England or his wife," he replied, still scowling.

"Not true!" Earl Ranulf objected.

"Gentlemen!" I cried. "This will not do! Where is Lord Miles?"

"I am here, my lady!" he replied, stepping out from the crowd.

"I am in need of your counsel," I said. "Can we defeat Stephen if we ride out with all haste and meet him at Lincoln?"

"You are not thinking of coming yourself, are you?" he asked.

"No, I speak of 'we' meaning all of you. Can we do it? Can we defeat Stephen?!"

The whole room seemed to hang upon his response. Lord Miles looked first at Earl Ranulf, then at Earl Robert, then finally back at me.

"Yes," he concluded. "I believe we can defeat him, but we must act with all haste, as you say. We shall endeavor to draw him out into the open. Then we will subdue him in the field."

I felt none of Miles' confidence within myself, but I knew all too well how little coin and food remained for us. If we were to face the usurper in open battle, it was best to do so while we still had some strength left. And in any case, open battles are rare things: there would be few such chances to turn the tide quickly.

"Very well, then," I said. "Lord Miles, Earl Robert, Earl Ranulf: you are my captains. Gather every man we can spare and ride to Lincoln."

A great cheer went up, and every man at arms set off to some task or another—all but Brian, who was still standing there with that pondering look he wore at times.

"You think this is the wrong decision?" I asked.

"No, it makes sense. Perhaps we can even take them by surprise."

"But to wager everything on one battle: what if we should lose?"

"I must admit that is a possibility, but we do have two major advantages."

"Really?" I asked, suddenly interested to know what could possibly ensure our victory. "What are those?"

"First, we have right on our side, and second, we are better than they are."

I laughed. "Men with right on their side have often been slain, but your second reason I like."

"I have no intention of being slain, though it would be in defense of a good cause." He must have seen the fear in my eyes, for he added, "Don't worry. Everything will be fine."

"Will it?"

"Well, I hardly think Earl Robert would lose his chance to win all the wine in Gloucester!" he said with a wink.

"That is too small a prize for any man to die for, but if you do win, you are welcome to all the wine in England."

He smiled broadly. "Careful—I might hold you to that!"

"I didn't promise you the beer!"

"True."

With that, he too departed, and I found myself standing alone, half in hope and half in terror.

The next morning, I received the fealty of Earl Ranulf of Chester, then bid them all depart into the wild. Oh, how my heart churned within me! It was possible that I had sent them to their doom. What a siren was I![15] And yet it had to be done, for England was greater than us all. Yes, as I watched them ride off, I could not help but feel that they were fighting not for a lady in a castle, but on behalf of the kingdom. If I asked them to fight for myself, I may well have felt the pang of guilt, but England was the sacred ground on which our fathers fought and our mothers gave birth—at least, those of us with English blood—and we were duty bound to defend it against every foe … even if he wore a crown. To put down a tyrant is to do the will of God and free one's children from the stream of blood.

They moved into the vale of the Trent and marshalled their forces from all sides. It was to be a battle of battles and no mistake. You can imagine with what fear I received this intelligence.

---

15 The sirens were creatures in Greek mythology, part woman and part bird, who would lure sailors in with their song and cause their ships to wreck against the rocks.

More than once, I made my bed in the chapel, falling asleep with my beads in hand. Again and again, I prayed to the Virgin Mary and bid her make me like Athena, a goddess of war before whom even Ares would fall. Just once, I thought I might have heard her scold me, "Get up, Maud! I am no Greek!" A product of great weariness, I suppose.

I relied in those days upon Adela to keep me in good spirits, as well as my chamberlain Drogo, who had stayed behind to guard me. His new friend, Philip of Honfleur, had gone to the fighting under the command of Earl Robert, and I wondered if this might have weighed on the mind of Adela, though I had learned never to raise the subject again. It was not worth any conflict between us.

As we knew that every earl of note was in the North, there was little fear that we should be assaulted in Gloucester. Even so, my brother Reginald agreed to watch over me rather than seek the glories of battle. This must have vexed him greatly, and I hated to keep a man of sure aim away from such a fight, but he bore it with great conviction.

A week passed and then another week. Still we had no news, and my frustration grew by the hour.

"What are they waiting for?" I asked one day. "I know they need to gain support, but they will give away the game for sure."

"Have faith, my lady," said Drogo. "Your commanders are the finest in the land. They will act with wisdom."

"Yes, but I so wish they would do so quickly! I cannot take much more of this," I concluded.

We came to the Feast of the Purification without any word from the North. By chance, it was also the beginning of my fortieth year of life, but I was in no mood for jollity. As I marched forward in the abbey church and received my candle from the hands of Abbot Gilbert, my own hands were shaking ever so slightly. The good abbot wrapped his fingers around mine to still them, then said, "Have no fear, my child. The Lord is with you." Little did I know that at that very hour, the false king was carrying his own candle in the cathedral of Lincoln. It broke in half and fell to the ground.

The following night I had a strange dream. I saw a great battle taking place on the hills of England, then suddenly I was in the midst of it, fighting for my life. I hacked about wildly with a sword, attempting to keep the enemy at bay. Then I saw a face as of the devil himself: my cousin the usurper, ax in hand, running forward to kill me. I awoke with a scream and it took Adela most of an hour to calm me.

I passed the next day in an uneasy state. Apart from attending Mass, I would not leave my private chambers, but stayed there by the fire, with only my lady and my knight for company. I sat in one chair, staring down at my Book of Hours but not really reading it, while Drogo sat in the other peeling an apple with his knife. Meanwhile, Adela was almost finished with the embroidery project that had occupied her for the past week: stitching a new cushion. She set it down and approached me.

"Is there anything I can do for you?" Adela asked, touching my hand. "Anything that might bring you pleasure?"

"Yes. Run to Lincoln, come back within the hour, and tell me the news."

"But my lady ..." she began, then observed the look on my face and amended her comment. "Clearly you are not serious. Lincoln must be much farther away than I thought. This island confuses me."

"I was making an attempt at humor," I assured her. "Perhaps the times are too evil?"

"The more evil the times, the more we need humor," Drogo said, dropping the peel of his apple in the fire.

"Truly, my lady, is there nothing I can do?" Adela tried once again.

"Fine. Go pick some flowers!" I commanded.

Adela took one look out the window, observed the gray sky and the brown grass, and concluded, "I think your first request might have been easier."

I smiled. "Go out to the field by the east gate. There is a flower that blooms even this time of year. A white violet, they call it. Pick some of them and bring them back. They will fill us with good cheer."

"Certainly, I shall do so immediately!"

With that, she flew out of the room and down the stair, evidently thrilled to receive a commission of any kind.

"You might as well have sent her out to find a unicorn," Drogo commented, taking a bite of his prize.

"Hush, you! She needed something to do."

"I dare say, you need something to do. I have never seen you so restless."

I could tell that I was not likely to make much progress with my book, so I closed it and set it aside.

"It is only natural that I should feel so, given the state of things," I explained. "You know how I hate being left in the dark, and this may well be a moment of great significance, either for good or for ill."

"Just be thankful you are not waging battle in the mud, feeling a cold blade rend your flesh, falling to the ground in utter agony, willing God to take you from the earth rather than leave you to suffer," he said with far more glee than seemed warranted by his words, taking another large bite of the apple, his eyes wide.

My mouth dropped open for a moment, then I recovered enough to ask, "Is that what passes for humor in Cornwall?"

He laughed. "It has been many a year since I was in Cornwall. How should I know what goes on these days?"

"I have never been there. Is it pleasant?"

"Oh, it is a land of immense beauty, but the natives are quite strange. They do not speak like anyone else I've ever heard. I used to know a bit of it, but now I forget. They would stare at me when I was out in the street."

"That's because you are so tall."

He looked down at the floor for a moment, as if considering the matter for the first time. "Yes, I suppose I was likely the tallest person they had ever seen."

"You are almost the tallest person I have ever seen, and I've met a lot of people, Drogo."

"That you have," he said with a smile. "Remember Bishop Maurice of Braga? What happened to him?"

"He died in Salerno a few years ago. Consumption, I think."

"That's a foul way to go."

"Really?" I asked, raising my brow. "After that speech you just gave about being rent in two?"

"Well, depending on how one is rent in two, it might be over rather quickly. Drowning: now, there's a bad death."

I could see that it was going to be the grim humor or nothing, so I decided to join him.

"What about burning?" I asked. "I should think that would be far worse than drowning!"

"A flaming rod stuck up one's behind: that might be the worst," he said, tossing a rotten bit of his apple into the flames.

"Dear God!" I cried. "Who has been doing that?"

"It's how they kill the sodomites."

"Who's killing sodomites?"

"I don't know," he said with a shrug, taking another large bite. "One hears rumors. Not that there are any of them in England, of course."

"Oh yes, England is such a model of virtue!" I scoffed.

"You were the one who was born here, not me!" he countered, pointing at me helpfully. As he did so, a bit of apple slipped out of his mouth, and he caught it.

"Well, of one thing I am certain: there is one kingdom to which we are far superior."

With that, we declared as one, "France!"

What followed next was a rather sustained burst of laughter, no doubt brought on by the stress of the hour. We laughed so hard, I could see tears forming in Drogo's eyes. Then the moment passed, and we sat there out of breath, aware once again of the terror under which we labored. Before I knew what I was doing, I closed my eyes and began to petition God.

"For your mercies' sake, O Lord my God, tell me what you are to me. Say to my soul, 'I am your salvation.' So speak that I may hear, O Lord; my heart is listening, open it that it may hear you, and say to my soul, 'I am your salvation!' Let me see your face even if I die, lest I die with longing to see it."[16]

I opened my eyes again and looked at Drogo, who appeared rather perplexed.

"What is wrong, Sir Drogo?" I asked.

"Did you just make that up?"

"No, of course not! It is from Saint Augustine. Anselm taught it to me many years ago."

"Anselm … as in the archbishop of Canterbury?"

"Yes, he composed many of his own prayers as well, but he always loved that one."

"I see. I wonder if you—"

I was never to hear the end of that thought, for Adela entered the room again looking as if she had just run from the

16 From the "Act of Hope" by Augustine of Hippo. https://www1.villanova.edu/villanova/mission/campusministry/RegularSpiritualPractices/Resources/spirituality/restlesshearts/prayers.html.

battle of Marathon. She was clutching the door frame for support and gasping for air, her shoulders heaving.

"Drogo, get her a chair!" I ordered, certain she was about to faint.

Adela raised a hand and let go of the wall, having gained control.

"My lady! Empress Mathilda!" she said. "I just heard … in the yard … Stephen …"

Here she took a rather long breath again, and while I cannot speak for Drogo, I for one was ready to reach down her throat and drag the words right out of her. Nevertheless, I attempted to be patient.

"The battle is won!" she finally said. "Stephen has been taken! They are bringing him back here!"

This news hit me with the force of a whirlwind. Could it possibly be true? No, it was too good! Then I heard running in the passage, and Reginald entered the room just behind Adela, his face full of joy.

"She's told you, then?" he asked. "Has she told you?"

"It's true, then!" cried Drogo, embracing the earl.

"Of course it's true! I just told you!" Adela replied with a frown. She then walked toward me and placed her hands upon my shoulders. "My lady? Do you understand? My lady?"

Until that moment, I had been caught in a daze, but I suddenly felt the full dawning of recognition almost as the dawning of a new day, and I clung to her with all my strength, kissing her on the forehead.

"Oh, blessed are you, Adela, for bringing me this news! Bless you, bless you!"

I then looked back and saw that Earl Reginald and Drogo were kneeling down, along with a few of the knights who had come to join them, and before me Adela also bowed low.

"Hail, Empress Mathilda!" Reginald called. "Ruler of England! May God preserve you!"

I looked at each of them in turn, my heart pounding. I had some times imagined this moment, and yet it seemed less than real. Could it be true? Was I to be England's queen? Of course, I had worked for it and prayed for it, but seeing them all kneeling before me, I was overcome by it all. I struggled to breathe, but at last I found my voice.

"Stand up! Stand up, all of you!" I commanded, gesturing with my hands.

They did so, and I searched for the next words to say. Suddenly, they came to me, as if granted from above.

"The reign of error is over!" I proclaimed. "The redemption of England is at hand."

VI

I will tell you how the battle of Lincoln was won, for you are no doubt eager to hear. The usurper besieged Lincoln Castle with all his might, hoping to force Earl William from the keep. This continued until the Feast of Purification, when his candle was broken before the altar of Lincoln Cathedral, as I mentioned earlier. Thus was the Lord's judgment against Stephen pronounced before all: his reign was broken and he was not fit to sit upon the same throne as Edward the Confessor.

No sooner had the Mass ended, than the false king received the news that earls Ranulf of Chester and Robert of Gloucester were come upon them all, having taken the Fosse Way up from Leicester. All that lay between them and the city of Lincoln was a dyke just to the west, which joins the River Trent with the River Witham. On account of the rains that winter, the waters were swollen, and the ground was naught but mud. Therefore, our forces had halted when they reached that obstacle, uncertain how to pass.

"Quickly! To arms!" the usurper cried. "They must not cross the dyke!"

Now, there were among that company some older and wiser men who saw the writing upon the wall, as it were. They warned Stephen not to face Earl Robert in the field, for they had few horses with which to counter him, and victory was by no means assured. They pleaded with the false king to remain safe within the city walls.

I must ask you now to remember what I told you at the very beginning of this account about my cousin Stephen. His father, Count Stephen-Henry of Blois, was a most ignoble man. Though he took a vow to march to Jerusalem as a pilgrim of our Lord, he fled from the Siege of Antioch, too much a coward to face the Saracens in battle. That mark of shame was placed upon the entire family and haunted them eternally. Every action they took was meant to erase this dishonor from the memory of men. Therefore, the false king was of a mind to fight. In any case, he must have had little doubt that he would be victorious: he was full to the brim with false confidence.

Earl Robert knew all of this. Indeed, he knew Stephen almost as well as the man knew himself. They competed first in the castle yard with sticks instead of swords. They rode together in the forests and chases. There was a time when Stephen had looked to Robert as an elder brother, but then he grew high and mighty and gloried in his noble birth. From that moment in the Tower of London when he set himself above Earl Robert, the very son of the king, there could be no peace between them, for as much as Stephen exalted in his crown, some seed of doubt must have remained in his mind, working upon him night and day, and only victory over the earl in battle could prevent the seed from coming into full bloom.

Was it always their destiny to stand on opposite ends of the field, weapons drawn, hearts full of loathing? Who can say?

The Lord alone knows all. Whatever love they once bore for one another, it was gone with the birds of autumn, and all that remained was enmity. Thus, the mind of Earl Robert was set, and he would not fly from the fight if Beelzebub himself appeared upon the field.

"England has seen enough."

That is what Robert told me before he left, and it was the truth. He had with him Earl Ranulf and all the men of Cheshire, along with the Welshmen so long promised. They had some trouble crossing the Fosse Dyke, for they were harried by Stephen's knights, but once they seized the ford, there was no difficulty. Indeed, they pressed on so quickly that the usurper hardly had time to arrange his forces before they were caught in the conflict.

"I have never seen the use of speeches," my brother once told me. "A man may have his spirit raised for a moment by such flattering words, but no sooner does he see the point of the enemy's blade, then he forgets all of that and thinks only of what matters most to him in this world. If he was not fit to fight before receiving some oration, he will not be fit to fight afterward. It would be better for him to remain at home. What is more, if one takes the time to give a speech, one loses the advantage of speed, and that is the greatest ally in the field. Therefore, let it never be said that Earl Robert of Gloucester lost a battle because he spoke too long!"

Do not let the chroniclers fool you: there were no orations at the battle of Lincoln, at least not on our side. There was simply no time. Every one of our men knew why he was there. Either his lands had been taken, or his dignity denied, or his sense of justice repulsed, or he simply could not bear to have a man so false proclaimed to be all that is true. And so, they charged the lines of the usurper, with the very wrath of God impelling them and the angels of heaven guiding their steps.

In the center of our line were Earl Ranulf and his men, their swords meeting those of Stephen and his household. There the fighting was most fierce, and one cannot help but wonder if the false king's decision to abandon his horse was a mark of valor or foolishness. As for the Welsh, there was no question that they were men of valor. They ran into battle with far more courage than those on horseback. Sadly, they ran directly into the wolf of Ypres and his band of Flemings, who chased them back whence they came.

Ah, but Earl Robert was no fool! He knew the Welsh could not stand up to horsemen, but that was never his intent. "Advance toward them," he said. "Wait for them to spring, then run, men, run! Draw them back toward our own lines. Soon their flank will be exposed, and we will pick them off like birds in a cage." Once the Welsh understood what he meant, for they knew not the speech of the Normans, they agreed that this was an excellent idea. They charged at the Flemings with a loud cry, brandishing their weapons, but when the time came, they followed Earl Robert's instruction. They played the part of cowards for a moment, and that was all it took. Earl Ranulf and his men were soon on the heels of William of Ypres and the count of Aumale, cutting them off from the rest.

Then something happened which Stephen had not foreseen. Few men had fallen, and though our side was stronger, it was by no means certain that we would win. Yet one by one, the earls who had fought along with the usurper began to abandon the battle. First there was the duke of Brittany, then the earl of Richmond, then the earls of York and Surrey. Hugh Bigod saw his chance to leave, along with Gilbert de Clare. Well, the Flemish mercenaries were not about to stay and fight for a foreign lord who was unlikely to pay them and who had few knights to speak of, so they too ran off along with the evil wolf of Ypres.

How the false king must have cursed in that moment as he saw the treachery of those lords! Only in that hour did he come to recognize how great was the anger of his nobles. Even as our men chafed under Stephen's misrule, so the old earls began to see what kind of man they had placed upon the throne. He had rejected the laws of the land, assaulted the Church of God, and raised up the Beaumonts at the expense of everyone else. A great king never wants for followers, for he holds them in thrall by the power of his person and the excellence of his judgments. Stephen was no such king—indeed, he was not a king at all! Too late did he finally come to see the damage he had wreaked upon England. Only in that fateful hour, when he needed them the most, was the full disloyalty of the earls revealed.

But that was not the worst of it. The one man who ought to have been at Stephen's side, to whom the usurper had given everything, was no more faithful than the rest. I am told that Earl Waleran of Meulan stayed on that field scarcely ten minutes before fleeing like a wounded deer. Such ingratitude from the most fortunate of men! For myself, I was not very surprised, for I had seen Waleran's treachery even in the days of my father. When he recognized that Waleran had left him, I am sure it did Stephen's heart grief and made him question every decision he had made from the time he set foot on England's shore. Perhaps he thought himself as the Lord forsaken by his apostles. Such was the extent of his pride, but for righteousness was our Lord betrayed, whereas Stephen was the lord of iniquity.

Now Earl Robert and Lord Miles led their men against the remainder of the enemy line. Whatever sorrow he must have felt, the false king refused to surrender. I have accused my cousin of many things over the years, but never of being a poor soldier. There were few who could match his skill, and in that moment, his anger seemed to propel him to even greater heights. He fought as a man possessed, they say: like a beast trapped in a corner. Those knights who remained with him were so inspired that they too began taking on two or three of our men at once. Thus, the greater part of the battle was spent attempting to defeat this last circle of resistance.

I am told that Stephen fought first with an ax, then when that broke in his hand, he took a sword from one of his fallen companions and used it to slay at least five of our men. Had all of his earls behaved in such a manner, there would have been no way for us to win, but as you can tell, the real battle was lost before anyone took the field. In the end, one of the knights of Robert's household lifted a rock and threw it at the false king's head. He was knocked to the ground, and the knight seized him round the neck and shouted, "Here, everyone! I have the king!"

Oh, that I could have seen it happen! That I could have shared in that jubilation! The dog that had hounded England and made himself drunk on its blood, who had scoffed at its traditions and fancied himself the lord of the earth, building his throne upon injustice and falsehood—his reign was at an end, and not a moment too soon. Rightly does the Psalmist say,

"O Lord God the avenger, O God the avenger, show yourself clearly.

Exalt yourself, O Judge of the world, and render a reward to the proud.

Has the throne of iniquity fellowship with you, which frames mischief by a Law?"[17]

A few men were taken with Stephen, but none worth noting. Less than a hundred souls perished in that battle. That

---

17   Excerpts from Psalm 94.

is proof enough of my account, for had the false king's earls stayed to fight, far more blood would have been shed. I suppose it was a double mercy that we should have gained the victory and done it almost with clean hands. There would be no such mercy for those citizens of Lincoln who had welcomed Stephen within their walls and fought beside him, though he was most unworthy. Their town was stripped of its treasure and many were taken as captives, for it was on their account that so much calamity had taken place. The greatest blessing for Earl Robert was to find his daughter safe within the castle walls, no worse for wear than when he saw her last. They remained one night in Lincoln with the usurper as their prisoner, then began the long journey that would take them back to Gloucester.

That is a true reckoning of all that took place at the battle of Lincoln. May it live on in the memory of men for a thousand years!

"Stop staring out the window, Adela! They will be here soon enough," I said, patting her on the shoulder.

She turned from the lone window in my private chamber and replied, "Yes, but I want to see them as soon as they ride over that hill. I want to see the look on the false king's face. He must hate to be led in chains!"

"I am sure they gave him a horse."

"Why would they do that?" she asked, her tone and her brows both revealing great offense. "They should make him walk! God knows, he has put you through enough!"

"Yes, but that is not how things are done, dear. We must be gracious in victory. He may be a villain, but he is still a noble. Well, there is nothing noble about him, but he owns land."

"I wish that I owned land," she moaned. "Then I would not have to walk!"

"Walking is good for the soul," I assured her, once again patting her on the shoulder. "Now come, let us sit and read for a while. If we continue to watch, they will never arrive."

At that very moment, Abbot Gilbert entered through the door we had left open and declared, "My ladies, the lords are sighted not three miles away. I am sent to bid you join us below."

"Thank you," we both replied.

"What were you speaking of just now?" he asked, looking from one of us to the other.

"Adela does not like walking," I responded. "She wishes to ride on a horse like the great men."

"Oh, but walking is such a benefit to the soul! How many times did our Lord Jesus traverse the hills of Canaan on foot? And he was the greatest lord who ever lived!" he said earnestly.

"True, but did he not also walk on water?" Adela asked. "Oh, that I could walk on water! I cannot even swim."

"Yes, well, this is all very interesting, but I believe that the abbot has pointed out something of more direct import: we must head down to the yard," I said.

With that, we made the final preparations for their arrival, which is to say that I put on the finest gown I had with me and the jewels Adela brought from Normandy. That dress was the only red thing I owned, and I loved it. I felt it allowed me to make a good impression, and on that day, I would need all the help I could get. We may have been granted victory by God, but there would be many in England who still doubted that a woman could rule. Therefore, I reasoned that I must look even grander than a king.

We had but one mirror and that of poor quality. I looked upon my reflection and found that even I was not entirely certain of my ability to be a queen, but perhaps that was on account of the green tinge. I had just about contented myself that there was nothing else to be done, when Adela brought out one more item: the amber moth given to me in my youth.

"Here, my lady," she said. "It will give you good luck."

"I doubt that very much," I replied, but upon seeing the look on her face, I corrected myself. "Yes, perhaps it might. Thank you." I slid it into the pocket by my hip and patted it twice.

Ever since I heard of my cousin's defeat, I had imagined what our meeting would be like: the broad smiles on the faces of the victors and the look of dismay upon him who was defeated. Was that a tear that I would see in Stephen's eye as he bowed before me and said, "Forgive me, empress! I have sinned!"? No, surely it could not be! He would never do that. Perhaps he would say nothing, but merely stare at me with utter hate in his heart. Or would he refuse to mark me, as if I were a common flea?

Well, you see how my mind worked. I desired for him to admit his guilt, but he seemed too steeped in iniquity to turn back. Repentance is the death of pride. It is an execution. I have seen men cringe at the sight of one begging for mercy, even as they look on untroubled at the poor soul about to be hung, for the one whose body is given over to death may yet keep his dignity, but the one who puts to death his pride is the most humbled of all. No, I did not foresee that Stephen would repent.

As we walked out into the chill, I found that it hardly seemed cold, so fierce was the beating of my heart. On the steps before the castle door, we took our places: myself, Earl Reginald, Sir Drogo, Lady Sibyl, Lady Mabel, all the men of Lord Miles' household, and standing directly beside me, Abbot Gilbert. The sun appeared from behind a cloud, letting its warmth fall upon our faces. Such a welcome change after the long months of winter! It was not exactly proof of divine favor, but it would do for the present.

"They should be here any minute," Reginald said.

I closed my eyes, bowed my head, and breathed deeply. Over the past week, I had given some thought to what I might say, but no matter how hard I tried to devise a pleasing turn of phrase, nothing seemed to satisfy. How ought a woman to act upon such an occasion? For all her efforts, this was something my mother had never taught me. I breathed again and looked up, even as the gate opened before us.

The trumpets sounded and in rode Earl Robert of Gloucester, his fist held high in the air. In rode Lord Miles and Lord Brian and all the rest of our friends, accompanied by the Welsh king, Morgan ab Owain. How happy they looked despite the scratches and bruises! Then at last I saw the prisoners, made evident by their scowls. Among them was the man I hoped most to see, if only for one last time.

They had indeed given him his own horse, though it bore none of the trappings of a royal steed. If I had to say how my cousin appeared in that moment, I would have told you he looked very tired, not just in the sense of needing sleep, but as if he were weary of the world itself. He bore upon his body three bloody cloths, no doubt binding up the wounds he suffered in defeat. A cut on his face was clear enough for all to see, and he was covered in far more dirt than one is accustomed to seeing on a king ... but he was not a king.

I had been paying such close attention to Stephen that I almost missed brother Robert bowing before me and proclaiming, "Empress Mathilda! It is with great joy that we return to you, having been victorious in battle at Lincoln!"

With this, all the men cheered and held their hands high in celebration.

"Earl Robert, King Morgan, Lord Miles, Lord Brian!" I said, looking at them each in turn. "The news of your great deeds at Lincoln has certainly reached our ears. We commend you all for your valor, and not only you, but the men who have fought and bled beside you. You do us great honor, and your fame shall live on for ever!"

The four of them each came forward and kissed my hand one after the other. I felt that I really ought to be kissing them, so great a service had they done for England.

"As promised, we have also brought to you the vile usurper, Stephen of Blois," Robert continued. "He is your prisoner to do with as you wish."

I looked back to where Stephen was standing, surrounded by Robert's knights. I did not say a word but used my hands to beckon him. With that, Stephen walked forward ever so slowly to the base of the stair and stood there with his arms crossed, saying nothing. It felt as if this took an hour, but it must have been the space of a few breaths.

"Bow before your queen, traitor!" Reginald called, prompting cheers from the crowd, but I held up my hand to quiet them.

I descended the stair until I was almost face to face with my cousin. As he was a good bit taller than I, this meant that I did not make it all the way to the ground. He looked directly into my eyes, but without word or expression.

"Good day, Count Stephen," I said, not loud enough for everyone to hear. "Are you not going to bow before your queen?"

"My queen is in London with our royal sons," he replied.

"Forgive me, I was not clear. I do not mean your wife, but your sovereign, for that is what I am, cousin. You must know that."

"You are a rebel against divine authority," he said, a glare finally forming on his face. "I will not bow to you."

Robert moved forward as if to push him to the ground, but I said, "No, leave it!" After Stephen had sent an evil glance at Robert, I continued, "If you refuse to recognize my rule, Count

Stephen, which you yourself swore to uphold upon the Holy Rood of our Lord, then I warn you, I am well within my rights to hold you guilty of treason. Is that what you want?"

"It is all of you who are the traitors," he scoffed. "Lock me up, torment me, kill me—do your worst, but I will not submit to rebels."

The men around me looked ready to strangle him, but I merely sighed and said, "Oh, Stephen, take care! You must have small regard for your head that you would tempt me so to cut if off, but your words cannot shake me. Lord Miles, I commit this prisoner to your keeping here in Gloucester Castle until I decide what to do with him."

"Very good, my lady," Miles replied, taking Stephen by the arm and leading him off to the cheers of all.

When the noise had died down, I addressed them. "Men of England, Normandy, and Wales, you have done a great service to me and to this kingdom. You have held yourselves nobly in battle and cast down a tyrant. Therefore, know most surely that you have done the work of the Lord, who stands in opposition to all injustice, and to whose rule I submit myself, even as all men must. England has walked in darkness these past few years, and there is much work yet to be done, but with your help, we shall restore order and the rule of law. We shall bring peace to this island again!"

There was much clapping and then I continued.

"I am the daughter of King Henry of England, the grand-daughter of King William the Great, the descendant of the kings of old. In our rule, the houses of England and Normandy are made one. I know there are many who broke their pledge to support us. Where there is contrition, there will be forgiveness, for I know how they were led astray by evil men who sought their own benefit rather than that of the people or the Church. Yet the greatest reward will be for those who have stood with us when all hope was lost. I shall not forget how you came to our aid. Therefore, let us press on together! Thank you and may the grace of our Lord Jesus Christ be with you always."

It was the first real speech I had ever made, and judging by the looks on the men's faces, I had done well—at least, well enough for the moment. As the jubilation continued, Lord Miles beckoned them all into the hall to celebrate further. As they began walking in, or running in some cases, Brian touched my arm to gain my attention and declared, "Incredible!" He then went to join the others, and before I knew it, I was being embraced by Earl Robert.

"That was a great victory, wasn't it, Maud?"

"Yes, it really was. I admit I had my doubts when you left."

"See, that is the problem right there: you must never doubt me, sister. Never! I told you I would deliver the usurper to you within the year, and I kept my word."

"That you did."

"So, now you will empty the cellars for us?"

"What?" I asked, feigning ignorance.

"It is your turn to keep your word," he said, breaking off the embrace and pointing at me. "You swore to me I would have all the wine in Gloucester!"

"Oh … I forgot about that." I could see the look of offense swelling in his eyes, so I quickly added, "Of course, you shall have all the wine! I will just have to think of some way to make it up to Lord Miles and Lady Sibyl."

"Aren't you granting him an earldom?"

"Yes, I suppose any man should be happy with that."

As the two of us entered the hall arm in arm, I began searching the room for Miles. He would not be pleased with this news. Suddenly, Sir Philip of Honfleur stepped in front of us, still clad in armor and with his helm in hand.

"A great victory, my lady!" he said with a bow. "May I ask where the Lady Adela went? I should like to greet her."

My eyes searched the room until I found her standing in the corner next to the ladies Mabel and Sibyl.

"She is just over there," I replied helpfully. I considered a further comment, but bit my lip, as I had sworn not to meddle in that affair again.

"Thank you, Empress Mathilda, Earl Robert," Philip said, nodding to each of us in turn. He then raced off toward the object of his search.

"What on earth was that about?" Robert asked.

"I wish I could tell you, but I seem to be wrong about everything these days," I said with a sigh. "Now, there is Miles, filling his goblet."

The two of us continued arm in arm to Miles' position, and I shouted a word of greeting.

"Lord Miles, thank you for your hospitality these many months!"

"Of course, my lady. It has been an honor," he replied. "You are welcome to remain as long as necessary."

"There is just one problem," I continued. "I promised Earl Robert that if he put Stephen in fetters within the year, he would have all the wine in Gloucester, or at least here at Gloucester Castle. Now, I know this is a terrible cost to you, but given that I did promise, would you have your men bring it all up from the cellar?"

The look on Miles' face changed instantly, and I could tell that he was attempting to work out how to object without earning my censure. The truth was, there were not many bottles left, and therefore the cost to his household was not so great, but nevertheless, I decided to help him.

"I am certain this request will not be difficult to perform, will it ... Earl Miles?" I asked.

His expression changed again, this time to a broad smile, and he replied, "No, my empress! It will be the work of a moment!"

As he rushed off to retrieve the wine, Robert said to me, "You handled that quite well. You might make a good queen after all."

"I hope so, Robert," I told him. "I truly hope so."

For a day or two, I simply enjoyed our victory and did not trouble myself with thoughts of the prisoner below or the barons. Perhaps this was foolishness: after all, we had many enemies yet abroad. Even so, the war had taken a toll on us all, and while I might have been glad enough to run off to Winchester at the first opportunity, my men needed rest for both their bodies and minds. We did receive a letter from Bishop Henry of Winchester, the false king's own brother, requesting a meeting as soon as possible. I was only too happy to grant his petition, for I knew he was the key to earning the support of the Church. Therefore, I wrote back and assured him I would be willing to speak with him ere the month was out.

On the third day, I made myself ready and walked down to the lower level, where Lord Miles had his prison chambers. Not all castles have such quarters set aside for criminals, but the fortress of Gloucester was able to meet the need. The rest of the usurper's allies had already been ransomed or sent elsewhere, so I suppose it must have been rather lonely for Stephen.

I descended the stair and arrived in that dark passage lit only by a single torch. The ceiling was low and the smell not unlike that of a wet dog. I was fairly certain that if more light flooded the place, I would see vermin scrambling in all directions. The overall effect made one feel trapped indeed, even without being shackled.

I spied the warden, a Welshman named Edwin: a man short and burly, with a long beard resting on his upper chest. As soon as he was able to make out my appearance, he bowed and said, "Empress Mathilda! I did not think to enjoy this honor. Only, that is you, isn't it?"

"Yes, I am the empress, and you must be Master Edwin. Tell me, how is Count Stephen today? Any complaints?"

"No, no!" he assured me, taking the torch from its sconce and raising it up to see me better. "He's been quiet for the most part."

"And how does he pass the hours?"

"Some of the time he reads. Some he spends at prayer. The rest he spends playing checks with the men."

"You gave him a checks board?" I asked.

I was not angry, but the warden clearly assumed I would be, for he quickly said, "Lord Miles told us to give him whatever was necessary for his comfort, so when he asked, I saw no reason to deny him. Have I acted wrongly?"

"No, do not trouble yourself. I was merely curious. If that is how he chooses to pass the time, so be it."

"Honestly, my lady," he added, leaning in and whispering, "I think he would prefer a more active pursuit, but given his situation …"

"Indeed. Tell me, Master Edwin, how is his manner?"

He stepped back and shrugged. "His health seems good enough. His spirits perhaps less so, though he remains quite sure of himself."

"And how is he doing at the game?"

"The game? He has yet to lose. Why?"

"Hmm … Good for him," I concluded. "Now, Master Edwin, if you would be so kind, give me a moment to speak with him."

"Certainly, madam. I have three of my men in there now. I'll just call them."

He pulled the ring of keys from his belt, producing quite a bit of noise as they struck one another, and proceeded to undo each of the locks in turn, yelling through the small window, "Look alive, men! The empress is coming in!"

At last, he pulled the door open with no little effort, for it was rather old and became stuck more than once as he pulled it over the stone floor. I reasoned that this might be another method of preventing escape. When he finally had it all the way open, I could see Stephen sitting on a small wood bench—the only seat in the chamber—and facing in the opposite direction. Before him on the floor lay the checks board. The guard who joined him in his game was sitting on the straw that covered the floor, while the other two crouched behind him and watched. At once, they all stood up, save for Stephen, who remained in place with his eyes fixed upon the board and his back to me.

"Empress Mathilda!" one of the guards said, bowing along with his fellows. "We were just playing—"

"I know what you were doing. It is no matter," I said. "Warden, would you all please leave me to speak with the prisoner alone?"

"I do not think that is safe," Master Edwin objected. "We have not placed him in fetters."

"He has no weapon, and in any case, you will be able to listen," I replied, pointing at the small window in the door. "If you hear me scream, then by all means come in, but I doubt it will be necessary."

"Very well, my lady," he said, and with that, the four of them left.

The door was closed behind me, and I took a moment to examine the room. It was not too wet, and on account of one window to the outside, it was brighter than the passage. The cell was not more than three paces across in any direction, but it did not smell of dung, which is more than I can say for most prisons in this world. At last, I looked back at Stephen, whose eyes had now abandoned the board and looked up at me.

"You are still refusing to bow, then?" I asked.

"I only bow to my betters," he replied.

"Then you ought to be spending half your time bowing."

He scoffed. "You haven't changed at all."

"Nor have you, I am sorry to say."

"Have you come here to torment me or to talk sense?"

"I am sorry you were forced to abandon your game," I said, pointing at the board. "It looks as if you were winning."

He leaned back and crossed his arms, a look of displeasure upon his face. "There is no real honor in beating common men."

"Oh, but as you have suffered such defeat of late, I should hate to rob you of any victory, however small!"

"You are wrong," he said rather pointedly. "You have not defeated me."

"Then I wonder that you are locked up," I replied, "but before you object, tell me, am I worthy enough to merit a game?"

"Of checks?" he asked, clearly surprised.

"Yes. I play. You have just forgotten."

He lowered his brow, evidently suspicious. "Why do you wish to play against me?"

"If you know me so well, then I wonder that you need to ask. But give me your verdict: am I a worthy adversary?"

"You are not my adversary," he argued. "The earl of Gloucester is my true enemy, along with all his ilk. You are merely an annoyance. But why are you laughing?"

Indeed, I could not help but laugh. "I have not heard the word 'ilk' since last I saw my uncle David!" I told him. By this, I of course meant the king of Scotland.

"He is my enemy as well!" Stephen replied with some real anger. "Evil man!"

At this, I sighed and asked, "Will you play against me or not?"

He took a moment to consider the question, evidently trying to work out how easy it would be to beat me, for he would never wish to lose to a woman, and especially one who had caused him such grief.

"Very well," he concluded. "I suppose you require my chair? Or will you consent to kneel before me?"

"I am sure the warden can fetch another."

I walked over to the door and called out for Master Edwin through the small window. He was good enough to bring in a second bench, and soon Stephen and I were seated across from one another, with the board laid out on the floor between us. We stared at one another as if we were alone in the world.

"There, now we are equal," I said.

"Ha! We will never be equal."

"Yes, I was being kind. You are the subject and I the ruler, in which case I will give you the first move."

"I think not!" he objected, taking the first move anyway. "You have no power but that which is given you by Earl Robert. In any case, you have taken neither London nor Winchester."

"We will win them soon enough," I responded, moving my own piece. "We are already in talks with Bishop Henry."

"My brother is not about to accept you as queen. He knows that the rule of a female goes against the will of God, and in any case, he would not abandon me."

"Are you sure about that?" I asked, raising my brows.

"You forget: he was the one who made me king."

"That was before he saw you for what you are. In any case, you were never truly king, for you bought the crown with a lie. You lied to the merchants, you lied to the Church, and worst of all, you had Hugh Bigod claim that my father forsook me upon his death bed. You lied before God and the archbishop of Canterbury!"

"I am no liar!" he cried, taking one of my knights in the process. "You are lying to yourself because you cannot accept the truth."

"If you mean the alleged truth that my father chose you and not me, then you are correct that I refuse to accept it. Why should I when it is so clearly false?"

"That is not the truth I mean."

"Then what do you mean?" I asked, taking one of his pieces.

"That King Henry loved me and not you."

I admit this distracted me for a moment. I rather forgot about the game and simply stared back at him.

"See, you cannot deny it!" he chided.

Well, how could I? There was no question that my father had loved Stephen. How many times had I been angered by the favor he showed that man even when there were others more worthy? It was also true that my father had never once declared his love for myself, nor implied it by his actions. That he had loved William Ætheling more than life, I did not doubt, but my father never viewed any woman in such a way. I would have been happy simply to make him proud, and even there I failed more often than not.

Of course, Stephen knew this. That was why he threw the words in my face with such an intent to wound. Yet I was deter-mined not to reveal the pain I felt. Instead, I replied, "Whether or not my father loved me is neither here nor there. Of course, he would have wished that his son had lived. We all wanted that. But since he was robbed of Prince William, he left the kingdom to me, his legitimate daughter. I admit I was not the first choice. That would not have been right. Yet when the fate-ful hour came, he sought to pass on his inheritance to the heirs of his own flesh." Here I took another of his pieces for good measure.

"Your father loved me and not you, and you cannot stand it!" he charged.

"Now wait just—"

"He saw in me all the qualities that a man would hope for in a king, whereas you—you cannot even keep a husband happy! You cannot govern your own household! How could you hope to govern England and Normandy? No, King Henry saw you for what you are, which is why he adopted me as his heir."

"If he wanted you to be king, then why did he have all the lords swear to me?" I asked, hoping to direct the conversation to safer ground.

"That was before your evil husband rebelled," he responded.

Well, I was not about to disagree with that description of my husband's character, but I said, "He did not rebel. The king failed to uphold their agreement."

"So, you admit that you sided against your father? Against your king?"

"That is not the point. I am the heir to King Henry, both by blood and by his choice. You are the rebel!"

"You speak with such certainty about a man you barely knew," he scoffed.

"And you spent so much time with him, yet you knew him not."

"He never intended for you to be queen, but for your son to be king. Then when he saw from what a rotten tree that branch was sprung, he looked to the House of Blois for salvation."

One glance at the board told me I was behind, but I pressed on, unwilling to admit defeat.

"Many men were with the king when he died, yet none of them reported these words that you claim he spoke," I replied.

"I hardly think my enemies would own the truth," he scoffed.

"Do you honestly believe that he appointed you?"

"Of course I do!"

I shook my head. "Then you are a greater fool than I imagined."

"Fool or not, I pity England under your rule, should you succeed."

"I will succeed, and I think you should rather pity yourself."

Here he took a moment to remove another of my pieces from the board. "You have yet to deal with Queen Mathilda."

"Yes, the true power behind the throne. You speak so much against the rule of women, but are you aware how much you depend upon it?"

"Don't make me laugh!" he said, setting the piece aside. "My wife is just what a woman ought to be. She lives to serve me and this house. You, on the other hand, are a rebel. You know what it is to tear down, but not to build up. Your heart is full of hatred toward men: toward the rule that God has ordained!"

"That is not true!" I cried, losing my temper for just a moment.

"You know what my brother said to me?" Stephen asked, taking one of his own pieces and pointing it at me as one would a rod. "He said the only queen who ever ruled over Israel was Athaliah, and she was the most terrible curse that ever befell that kingdom. Even so, will England be cursed if Mathilda wields the scepter!" He then placed the piece with such force that the whole board shook.

His use of such an obscure story to bolster his failing case rather emboldened me, I must say. I could see that he was chasing after the wind. Rather than attempting to respond to his charge, I brought forward my own.

"You seem to know a great deal, cousin, but let me tell you something. Bishop Henry is not on your side. He is for us. He sent me a letter two years ago, begging me to come back and restore the Church to its former glory."

"He wouldn't dare!" he cried, forgetting the game entirely. "You are the liar now!"

By this strong response, I could tell that I had actually scared him. He must have sensed deep in his person that my words might be true.

"Ask him yourself," I concluded. "He has no reason to deny it now."

"You act as if you are already queen, when in truth my supporters still hold sway over much of this country, and they will rise up to defend my cause," he said, changing the subject. "They will not suffer the rule of a woman!"

"Why should they defend the cause of a man they hate, who sits rotting in a cell? Indeed, if they wished to defend you, they would have done so on the battle field."

"They were waiting to fight another day."

"They left you to die."

"They will rise up: you will see."

"I wonder that you could exist in such a state of delusion," I said, moving my queen for the first time.

"I might say the same of you. Have you never read scripture? Don't you know that woman was made to submit to man and not the other way around?"

That Stephen was trying yet again to oppose me according to the laws of Christianity amused me more than a little, but I consented to his pretense.

"I have submitted to every man God has placed in authority over me. My first husband, my father, popes, bishops … I have even remained faithful to my second husband, who God knows does not deserve it."

"I am your king! Yet you refuse to submit to me," he objected.

"You were never my true king."

"See even now how you deny respect to those to whom it is due! You smile at men but curse them in your heart. You deny the truth that you were made to be a subject. You were made to acknowledge the excellence of men! We were created first, we were set in power by God, and we were crowned with honor. We are as superior to women by birth as a lord is to his liege. Therefore, let the one crowned with honor wear the crown!"

"You twist the scriptures for your own ends," I replied, shaking my head.

"No, it is you who twist the scriptures with this doctrine that women ought to rule! Where is that in the writings of Saint Paul? Where is it in the teachings of Christ? Show me one bishop who agrees with you, and perhaps I will acknowledge the truth of your claim."

I could see that my cousin was not about to abandon his appeal to the scriptures, so I tried to employ a different method.

"What about Deborah?" I asked.

"Who?"

"Deborah, the judge of Israel."

"I know not this Deborah."

"Ha!" I scoffed. "How convenient! What about the Queen of Sheba?"

"Was she not a pagan?"

"No more so than you."

"Look!" Stephen said, ignoring my comment. "See how your players are taken from the board! You are going to lose."

"That's what you think."

"You are going to lose the game, and you are going to lose the war!"

"No, I will just move this piece."

I completed the move and looked up to see the exultation on my cousin's face.

"Not for the first time, you have made the wrong decision," he declared.

"Why do you say that?"

"See, now I can take your queen," he said, swooping in to claim it for himself. "Your queen is dead! Long live the king!"

Sure enough, he had taken it fairly. My poor king was left without his greatest defender. To make matters worse, I had granted him the perfect symbol: a fallen queen, with his own king standing triumphant. There was no sense denying what was perfectly plain, so I said, "A good move: I admit it."

"Of course it was, and you know why I was able to make it?" he asked, still smiling. "Because you fail to consider the consequences! You make whatever move seems right to you in the moment, but you cannot see how they affect things down the line. Even so, you behave in life. You think that by becoming queen, you will save England, but you will plunge it into darkness. You will make a mockery of its traditions. If women are allowed to rule, then who is to say that any of the laws we hold dear ought to stand? You have failed to count the cost, and you are about to reap the whirlwind."

"I see by your judgment I am the devil incarnate," I replied.

"Not a devil: a shrew. A shrew who would drive the kingdom to ruin!"

"You are very harsh toward the female sex. What does your wife have to say about that?"

"She has never liked you," he informed me, as if to shoo my comment away.

"She met me once, and that was many years ago," I said, shifting my king to the left.

"That move is not going to help you. The game is as good as over," he objected.

"I will just play out, if you don't mind."

"Have it your way."

"Thank you. You are kind. Actually, I cannot help but think that in the face of such resistance, we women ought to be supporting one another, not fighting each other for scraps from the table. It is really too bad that your wife and I could not have been friends."

"I cannot imagine you have many true friends," he said, clearly frustrated that I was dragging out my defeat.

"Perhaps you are right, but a new day is dawning, and you will have to accept it one way or another. I will be your ruler, if only until my son is old enough to take the throne, and you will have to accept that, for it is the will of God. So tell me, Stephen," I said, looking him firmly in the eye, "will you accept it?"

"And surrender my manhood?" he asked, laughing. "I think not."

"Very well, then," I replied, making my final move. "Checkmate, cousin."

"What?"

"I said … checkmate."

Where had I seen that look before? Ah yes! All those years before when he had lost to Brian in much the same manner. I had done just what Brian always taught me: I sacrificed my queen in order to take my enemy's king. Stephen continued to stare down at the board, struggling to accept the truth. Indeed, his whole life was a battle against the truth.

I rose from my bench, then bent down and whispered in his ear, "Your king is dead. Longer live my king."

With that, I left him to ponder his defeat, while I informed everyone in the castle of my triumph.

VII

There was no time to waste. We had spent two full days in mirth and relaxation. Anything more would have been slothfulness. It was necessary to call together the council and decide on a course of action, for our enemies were surely devising plots of their own. Stephen had warned me—nay, he had bragged—that his queen would not surrender without a fight. Our spies confirmed that Mathilda of Boulogne was still holding court in the Southeast, supported by the wolf, William of Ypres. From the ports of Kent and Essex they maintained their link with Flanders, which was happy to send both ships and mercenaries as necessary.

What was even worse, the defeated nobles had flown from Lincoln to every corner of the island. Waleran returned to his earldom of Worcester, there to lick his wounds. Earl Alan of Richmond made a raid upon Lincoln, only to be taken and imprisoned by the earl of Chester. Foolish man! What was he playing at? The earl of Wiltonshire, also castellan of Devizes, was forced to surrender to the local citizens, so there at least was one bright spot for us. However, we knew most assuredly that the greater earls were yet afield: Warwick, Essex, Surrey, Northampton, and Bedford.

The most pressing need was to earn the support of the Church, and there the key men would be Bishop Henry of Winchester and Archbishop Theobald of Canterbury. Between them, they carried the support of well-nigh all the English bishops who had not yet come over to our side. Therefore, it was essential that we should win over these two great magnates. The trouble was that they were not in the bonds of love, so to speak. Indeed, they hated one another.

Gilbert Foliot, the abbot of Gloucester and cousin of Lord Miles, had consented for my council to meet in the monastery's chapter house, for some fifty persons had lately made their bed on the floor of the great hall in Gloucester Castle. In attendance at that council meeting were Earl Robert of Gloucester, Lord Miles of Gloucester, Lord Brian fitz Count, my brother Reginald de Dunstanville, Lord Baldwin de Redvers, Sir Drogo, Bishop Nigel of Ely, Abbot Gilbert, and two men who came especially for this occasion: Bishop Bernard of Saint David's, an old friend of my mother, and Abbot Roger of Tewkesbury. I was, as usual, the only woman in the room, yet I was the one to lead them all. As you can imagine, I was somewhat nervous.

That morning, Adela had demanded the right to dress my hair in the new style, with two long plaits hanging down on either side. I was very much opposed to this, for I knew my tresses were hardly a thing of splendor. It was for this reason as much as any other that I always wore a covering of some kind, or at the very least kept my hair knotted against my head. The other noble ladies were blessed with such fine locks—some blonde, some black, some red—whereas I had a heap of brown. Thank God I at least was not like my father, whose head was mostly bald by thirty years of age! In any case, Adela soon discovered what I had always suspected: my tresses were not meant to hang in plaits. Nevertheless, she arrived at a solution. She took two bands of silk and wrapped them around the braids until they looked almost presentable. Within a week, all the women were wearing their hair in this manner.

I made my way to the abbey by horse, though I would have preferred to walk. Ever since Drogo had taught me to ride like a man, I disdained the awful positions forced upon women. Yet as my complaints went, that was a rather small one. We women must choose our battles. I arrived at the monastery and was led back to the chapter house, where the members of my council—yes, my own council—stood at attention around a large, round table. I observed that it was not unlike that famous table of legend around which the knights of Arthur sat: Robert Wace has written of it. Drogo helped me into my chair, and the men returned to their seats. I took a deep breath and addressed them.

"Welcome, my lords, to the city of Gloucester. I, Empress Mathilda, daughter of King Henry, call this council meeting to order on this day before the Ides of February, in the year of our Lord 1141. I pray that our discussion will be for the mutual benefit of both ourselves and this kingdom. We have won a great battle at Lincoln and seized that foul usurper, Stephen of Blois. I must now determine how to proceed, and I seek your counsel in this matter. Abbot Gilbert has graciously agreed to serve as our clerk. Have you made a note of all in attendance, abbot?"

"Yes, my lady," he replied, moving the papers before him into a perfect stack. "Would you like me to call forth the roll?"

"That will not be necessary. Unless you have gone blind and I was not aware, I trust you to count them correctly. I had hoped that the bishops of Bath and Hereford might have joined us. Did they send their excuses?"

Abbot Gilbert answered, "The bishop of Hereford, Robert de Bethune, is as we all know a friend of king … that is, Count Stephen of Blois—"

"And no friend to me—I can assure you of that!" Lord Miles called from the far side of the table.

It was true that Bishop Robert and Lord Miles had quarreled incessantly since my coming to England, and things had not improved since the bishop was pushed out of his see due to the siege of Hereford. Even so, I would not allow the council to be dominated by such interruptions.

"Thank you, Lord Miles," I replied, "but what I am most interested to find out is if he might one day become a friend of mine, so let us please refrain from personal comments."

"I have reason to believe the bishop may be inclined toward friendship," the earl of Gloucester said, ignoring the look of frustration on Miles' face. "He hopes to be left alone to rule his bishopric as he sees fit."

"You mean to say he is not hoping for more grants?" I asked.

"I think not."

"Then he should be easy enough to satisfy. But what about the bishop of Bath, Robert of Lewes?" I inquired, looking back to Abbot Gilbert.

"I have carried on a correspondence with Bishop Robert for some time," he said. "He is close to the legate." By this, he meant Bishop Henry of Winchester, my cousin.

"Ah yes, Bishop Henry," I said, sighing as I thought of the crafty fox. "We will come to him. What of the earl of Warwick? Have we heard anything about him?"

Lord Miles entered the conversation again, having recovered from his earlier scolding. "As we all know, the earl of Warwick is the most peaceable of the Beaumont family. He cares more for his prayer books than great affairs of state."

"So much the better for him! Perhaps his soul is less depraved," I declared.

"I would not know, my lady," Lord Miles said. "In any case, he is a cousin of Waleran and Robert, those twins of iniquity. Yet he is altogether more agreeable than either of them if you meet him in person, and I have no reason to believe that he is close with his relatives. He hardly raised a finger on behalf of Stephen. He should come over to our side easily enough."

"I see. Thank you," I replied, hoping to restore myself to his good favor. "Abbot Gilbert, make a note to send a letter to the earl of Warwick and assure him that we will maintain him in all his estate and welcome him at our court should he pledge fealty to me and my descendants."

The abbot scribbled some words to this effect on the paper in front of him: either that or he was making a drawing of a dog to pass the time. I suppose we shall never know for certain.

"The earl of Warwick may be willing to lend his support, but you will not see him much at court," brother Robert said. "He has no love of large feasts."

"Once again, I cannot say that I blame him. Are there any other lords who might offer us their allegiance?" I asked.

This time, it was Lord Brian who had an answer. "The castellan of Oxford, Lord Robert d'Oyly, is a good man. I have met him many times on account of our neighboring estates and his relation to my wife. He has told me in confidence that he abhors Stephen. It should not be too hard to win him to our side."

"He is married to that woman … Lady Edith, right?" Robert inquired.

With this question, I was thrown off course. Edith Forne had been one of my father's mistresses before she became a noble lady, and I had half a mind to offer up some harsh words against her person for the pain she had caused my mother.

However, recognizing that I had within that very room two brothers from different mothers, I decided it was best to simply change the subject.

"Thank you, Lord Brian," I said, ignoring Robert's question. "This is good news indeed. I hear the earl of Wiltonshire is chased from his castle and the earl of Richmond is taken prisoner due to his own folly. He has been holding your earldom of Cornwall, Reginald, but I shall return it."

"I give you thanks," Reginald stated, bowing his head, "and my wife gives you thanks." Here he bowed again.

"And the earl of Surrey?" I asked, looking to each of them in turn. "He must be getting quite old by now."

"I have heard nothing, my lady," Lord Miles replied.

"Nor I," Earl Robert added.

"I see," I told them, observing that they were not much help in this regard. "I have it on good authority that the earls of Bedford and Northampton have no intention of supporting our rule at the moment. We must deal with them another day. And I need hardly tell you all that Earl Waleran of Worcester and his brother, Earl Robert of Leicester, have sworn to oppose us until such a time as either I or they fall down dead. I have received a letter from my husband, the count of Anjou, saying he intends to treat with Count Theobald of Blois. Actually, Theobald is the count of Blois, Champagne, Brie, Chartres ... well, if you are uncertain who rules a county over there, just assume it is my cousin Theobald. What is our read on him?"

"Surely if he intended to make a claim to England and Normandy, he would have done so after the death of your father," Lord Miles replied.

"I was there. He tried to!" said the earl of Gloucester.

"Yes, but he made rather a mess of it," Lord Miles countered. "He cannot have been all that motivated—not in comparison with his brother. He is all talk, while Stephen is all action."

"This is not about the past, but the future," Lord Brian said, looking at me rather than them. "Theobald may have felt cheated by his brother, but he sees well enough which way the wind is blowing. Count Geoffrey is making gains in Normandy. Stephen is in prison. His allies are on the run. There may be some in Normandy who wish to have Theobald as their lord, but I cannot see how that is possible. The game is not in his favor at the moment. He will make a deal. You'll see."

A thought suddenly came to me. "Do you suppose the king of France may attempt to enter the fray?"

"Why would he do that?" asked Earl Robert.

"Because he wants to be sole lord of Normandy, for one thing. For another, if he cannot be sole lord of Normandy, he certainly loathes the thought of an Angevin ruler. There is a great enmity between them. That is why I was married into Anjou in the first place. King Louis of France is young and will hope to prove himself in battle. He has taken as his wife the even younger duchess of Aquitaine, and his empire now stretches to the sea. It would not surprise me if he hoped to gain the North as well. What? Why are you all looking at me like that?" I asked, noticing that several of the men had confusion written all over their faces.

There was a very odd moment where no one said a word, then Earl Robert spoke. "Brian, explain to her."

I looked over at Brian, who was leaning forward and folding his hands on the table, evidently attempting to decide how he should proceed without sounding condescending.

"What is it?" I asked him, hoping very much that I was not about to become an object of derision.

"Perhaps Your Highness has been too much consumed with news of the war in England," he began. "King Louis and Count Theobald are in the midst of their own dispute over the archbishopric of Bourges: that is, the king is in a dispute with Pope

Innocent, and Count Theobald is siding with Rome. It is rumored that the pope will soon place France under an interdict, and should that happen, the young king will have no time to worry about what is happening to the west."

How foolish I felt in that moment! Had I really been so concerned with affairs in England that I had forgotten the wider world, or was I simply so tired from the long months of warfare that my memory was failing along with my nerve? There I was, striving to appear as if I was in control, but they surely thought me helpless and ignorant. I attempted to recover.

"Forgive me. You must be right. I have spent too much time in Gloucester. I have been as much a prisoner as Stephen! Not that the hospitality has been anything but wonderful, of course, but danger has held me here. But regarding this matter, Lord Miles tells me he does not think Gloucester is a proper place for prisoners to be held for months or years on end. I have it in mind to allow ransoms for the lesser men, but Stephen must never be freed, or he will certainly organize a rebellion. What think you, lords? What must we do?"

"Move him to another castle," advised Lord Brian.

"Yes, but which one?" Lord Miles replied.

Abbot Gilbert chose this moment to join the conversation again. "Would it not be best to move him as far away from his allies as possible?"

Now it was Baldwin de Redvers who had to announce his thoughts. "I say we kill him! He is a traitor to the kingdom and the true queen. If we let him live, he'll become like the former duke of Normandy, always serving as a source of rebellion for discontents."

The earl of Gloucester pushed back against this immediately. "She is not queen yet, and if we execute one who was anointed with sacred oil, we will never hear the end of it."

"That oil is not sacred which is poured out in deceit!" Earl Baldwin charged.

"May I speak for the Church, my lady, and as a friend?"

I looked over at Bishop Bernard, who had remained quiet until that moment. I was glad to hear any voice of reason.

"Of course," I said, beckoning him to speak. "I welcome your advice."

"It is better in such cases to show mercy, especially as you are hoping to gain the support of Bishop Henry and Count Theobald, who should hate to see their brother put to death, even if they despise him in their hearts," he replied.

"I agree with you entirely, lord bishop," I said. "In any case, were we to kill him, his allies would merely put forth his son Eustace as king. No, it is better to show mercy. I will be judged by all my actions, and Earl Robert is correct: I am not queen yet. Therefore, we must exercise caution. Tell me, brother Robert, can you host the prisoner in Bristol Castle?"

"We shall send him there immediately," he assured me.

"Set a firm guard about him, or he will attempt to escape and flee to Ireland," Lord Miles advised.

"Ireland!" Earl Baldwin said with contempt. "I pity any man who has to live there!"

Not wishing to encourage any sort of long speech on that subject, I quickly turned to my knight and asked, "Sir Drogo?"

"Yes, my lady?"

"Please arrange with the earl of Gloucester to have the prisoner transported to Bristol."

"As you wish. I am yours to command," he replied, placing a hand on his heart.

With that, I continued. "This brings us to the main reason we are all gathered here: Bishop Henry of Winchester. As you all know, his allegiance will be of the greatest import. Normally, one would think it might be that of the archbishop of Canterbury, for it is he who places crowns upon heads. However, it is abundantly clear that my cousin is the one who has the ear of the pope and the affection of most of the bishops. Therefore, we must look to Bishop Henry. He controls the treasury, and we are woefully short of coin. As some of you know and the rest of you must now be made aware, Bishop Henry wrote to us back when we were fighting in Normandy and besought us to return to this island that we might restore true religion. Since then, I have met him only once, and I believe he works as much for himself as Jesus Christ. Nevertheless, he will seek in everything to appear pure of heart. I will endorse him before men and offer whatever grants he seeks for the see of Winchester. In private, I will pledge to support his desire to become archbishop of Canterbury as soon as Theobald goes the way of all flesh, should he out live him. What do you all say to this? I think it may be the price of the throne."

There was no response for a moment. I had evidently surprised them with my declaration. It was Brian who finally spoke.

"If you make such a promise to him, you will be bound by it. If you must one day go back on your word, he will never forgive you, even as he is never likely to forgive Stephen."

"What other choice do I have?" I asked.

"Promise him nothing," Abbot Gilbert offered. "He may support you without any such pledge."

"I think he will want me to prove that I am on his side," I replied. "I know it will give him a great deal of power, but we must accept that he is already the most powerful man in the kingdom, and I include those of us in this room. Only by promising him what he wants will he be willing to place me above himself."

"Are you sure you've thought this through?" Lord Miles asked.

How very like a man! I thought. *He probably thinks I spend all day dreaming of rainbows and butterflies.*

"I have had nothing to do but think these many months," I assured him. "Believe me, it is not a rash decision."

"But my lady, you hardly know him," Abbot Gilbert said. "It was Stephen's mistake to give him too much power."

"Stephen never would have gained the crown in the first place if it was not for Bishop Henry of Winchester," I argued. "Therefore, he had little choice but to make those promises to the Church."

"It will not make Archbishop Theobald happy," said Lord Miles. "He is angry enough that Bishop Henry was made papal legate when he ought to have the primacy. How do you intend to win over the archbishop of Canterbury if you make such a pledge to his greatest rival?"

"That would be the point of doing it in secret," I answered, growing rather upset.

"With all due respect, my lady," Baldwin began, thus signaling that he was likely to say something disagreeable, "I am not certain that you understand the situation. You do not know these men like we do. Let the earl of Gloucester handle this. He has your best interests at heart."

"Perhaps you would prefer for my brother to be leading this meeting," I replied, for I could not help myself.

"Well, it is most unusual for a woman to lead the council—" he began, but was quickly cut off.

"Enough of this!" the earl of Gloucester cried. "The Empress Mathilda is your rightful queen, and if she feels it is necessary to make a deal with Bishop Henry, then that is what we shall do. In any case, she is right. You say I know Bishop Henry the best. He will not be bought for anything but the highest price. My lady, your instinct serves you well. We will send a letter to Bishop Henry and arrange to meet him in Winchester."

That was how it ended. We all went our separate ways to carry out those things we had discussed. I was glad to have my brother's support, but I could see that things would be difficult. Within my own council, there was discord, and I was a bit uneasy about the level of concern that had been expressed. They would hold their tongues and do their duty for the moment, but how long would that last? I tried to put such thoughts out of my mind and simply give thanks that I had survived my first ordeal by fire.

We sent the usurper off to Bristol Castle the next day, and a happy parting it was. The air itself smelled sweeter without his presence to defile it. Messengers were sent out to Bishop Henry of Winchester, and within a week they had returned with the following word: "Consent to meet with me at the nunnery of Wherwell, which is not ten miles beyond the city gates. There we may discuss the matter in all peace and good will." I had hoped to receive his support forthwith, but my cousin was a man with respect for ceremony. He would not do with a letter what he could do with a flourish.

Our company finally departed Gloucester on the thirteenth day before the Kalends of March. Many cities have looked fair to me on arrival, but this one seemed especially fair upon leaving. How the long months of torment had given way to joy! And yet, I was not altogether joyful. For the entirety of my natural life, I had been learning. The greatest minds in Christendom had raised me to be a queen, but none of them had imagined I would be a sovereign. Their teachings were about to be put to the test. I could only hope that I would pass.

In addition to my usual companions—Earl Robert of Gloucester, Miles of Gloucester, Baldwin de Redvers, Brian fitz Count, Reginald de Dunstanville, and my own household—I was also accompanied by Bishop Nigel of Ely, Bishop Bernard of Saint David's, and Gilbert Foliot, there to represent the clergy. We were a party of about eighty in all, the only women being myself, Adela, Lady Mabel, and Lady Sibyl. It took us just one day to reach the town of Cirencester, where we made our abode at the abbey of Saint Mary.

The monks of that house were Augustinians, a favored order of my late father. He had founded their abbey for the second time and consecrated the new church. Sadly, the place was still under construction when we arrived. The only lodgings available were made of wood planks that let in far too much of the winter cold. The refectory at least was completed, and that evening a great feast was held in honor of our presence. It was a magnificent room, with high soaring arches and columns into which vines were carved, wrapping around them from floor to ceiling. I was seated at the head table next to Abbot Serlo, lord over some dozen canons in residence. He was a man short in stature, marked out most by the tonsure on his head, perhaps fifty-five or sixty years old. I suppose it was nice to feel tall for once, as most of the knights were as towers above me.

One of the monks had just placed a large fish in front of me along with a pitcher of wine, and I was about to eat when the abbot said, "How do you find our monastery, Empress Mathilda?"

I set down the knife I had taken in hand. "Very nice, I am sure. The late king took especial care of the place."

"A great man he was, the late king," he continued, leaning in rather closer than I would have preferred. "On account of him, we received a third of all the market tolls."

"How wonderful!" I agreed, then made to cut the fish again.

"He was a good friend to Bishop Roger of Salisbury. You knew him, of course."

"Yes," I said, lowering the knife again, "although I cannot claim to have known him that well. I was away those many years."

"Ah, right. Well, I served as dean under Bishop Roger until I was made a canon of Merton Priory. Then I came here eight years ... no, I suppose it must have been ten years ago! You know we were given many lands by the late chaplain of Edward the Confessor. Regenbald was his name. May he rest in peace. I said to Regenbald ... I said, God bless you for your generosity. No abbot could wish for a better patron ..."

By this point, I was beginning to wonder how long his speech would last, and whether I would ever get a chance to eat my food. When he stopped to take a breath, I quickly cut off a piece of the fish's flesh and raised it to my mouth.

"That is some of our best trout, taken from the pond out back!" Abbot Serlo proclaimed cheerfully.

"Yes, I cannot wait to try it," I said, still holding the meat halfway between the plate and my mouth.

"It is my belief that trout is the best fish God ever created. It is so plentiful, and the flavor ..."

Here he placed his hand upon his heart and closed his eyes, as if paying tribute. I seized the opportunity to place the rather large bite in my mouth just as Bishop Nigel walked over and said, "A very good evening, my lady!"

Alas, I was unable to answer back, my mouth still full of fish. I simply nodded and made my best attempt to smile. Fortunately, it was not me the bishop had come to see, but Abbot Serlo. Thus, I was freed of a most tedious conversation and allowed to eat my trout in peace. As I continued to do so, I could hear the discussion among the men seated to my left. I kept my eyes on my food, seeking to maintain my relative solitude as long as possible.

"I do not care for that fellow, Serlo," Lord Baldwin said. "Why do they worship him so? I hear he keeps a concubine."

"What do you care if he keeps a concubine?" asked Lord Miles.

"It is not right! A priest is meant to abstain from such things, even as the apostles."

"He's not a priest."

"Same difference. They are not meant to keep women."

"Saint Peter had a wife," Brian informed them.

"Before he became a priest, not after," Baldwin countered, unwilling to admit defeat.

"A priest is still a man," Miles concluded. "He has desires."

"A priest is not a man!" Baldwin cried, incensed.

Brian laughed and replied, "What madness is this?"

"No, no. You mistake my meaning," Baldwin told them. "A priest is not merely a man. He has a higher calling. He exists in another sphere, somewhere closer to God. He is not like other men."

Lord Miles was having none of that. "I say a man is a man is a man. He cannot be otherwise simply because he has fancy dress."

Earl Robert chose this moment to enter the conversation. "Are we not ignoring the real issue? A priest cannot take a wife because he cannot support a family. His entire life is given to God."

"Yes, God knows a man never wore a cope who did not desire poverty," Miles scoffed. "Look around you! The bishops live in palaces, lords of all they survey! What man could better provide for his family?"

"The priest who wears the cope might, but not he who wears a simple alb," said Robert.

"Yes, God spare the hungry peasant from the austerity of the monastery!" Miles replied.

I could bear it no longer. All I wanted was to eat my fish in peace, but I could see that would not be possible. Therefore, I set down my knife, turned to face them, and entered the fray.

"Now, now, my lords! I lived among monks, you'll remember. I witnessed the privations they endure. They would put you to shame."

For a moment, none of them dared to speak or even chew. They simply stared at me, unwilling to make a move. Then Lord Miles worked up the necessary courage.

"Forgive me, my lady, but if a man chooses to whip himself to the point of fainting, he has no one to blame but himself."

"Are you so sacrilegious?" Baldwin asked. "Is nothing holy?"

Here I spoke again. "The bishop may rejoice in his exaltation, and the monk may take pride in his sufferings, but the humble village priest, alone against the forces of the world: where is his dignity? Where are the men lining up to laud his deeds? No, he seeks only the advancement of his sheep. I see a kind of nobility in that."

"Until you catch him in bed with the village whore," Miles said.

"He cannot afford the village whore!" Robert argued, pounding the table with his fist.

"Any man can afford the village whore!" Miles countered.

"You should know!" Robert yelled.

They were all in such a fury that I doubt they saw me rise from my chair and take my leave. There would be no enjoying my meal if I had to listen to such things. I took some bread and cheese, wrapped myself in a fur, and departed through the south door.

My eyes struggled to adjust to the dark of night. At length, I saw Drogo standing by a fire along with three other knights. I called out to him, and he accompanied me to the only building where I might have some peace: the church.

"Stand here by the entrance," I said to him. "Just make sure no one tries to … tries to …"

"Kill you?" he asked.

"Your sense of humor is lively as always, Sir Drogo," I concluded.

Two torches were mounted on opposite sides of the main doors. I took one out of its sconce and made my way into the darkness of the church. It was not too large, especially since it was incomplete. Even for a room without a fire, it was bitterly cold, and I was about to complain about this to no one in particular when I recognized that the masons had not yet closed off a portion of the roof. There above me the stars looked down, as if to let me know my place.

"Such a vault no man could create," I whispered, then recited, "'He first created for the children of men heaven as a roof, the holy Creator ...'"

I laid the torch down and sat upon the stone floor about halfway up the nave. It did not take me long to finish eating the morsels I had gathered from the feast. I then brushed the crumbs off my hands and looked up toward the altar, behind which sat a wood statue of the Virgin and child. The faint light reflected on their features, giving them an almost fearful appearance. Were they standing in judgment over me, and if so, for what? There were so many possibilities, I hardly knew.

I took out my mother's rosary and began saying my prayers. My voice seemed quite loud in that empty space, even though I merely whispered. I went through several of the supplications I knew by heart: prayers of the late Anselm, prayers of Saint Augustine, the prayer of our Lord. Finally, I began to speak the creed.

"I believe in one God, the Father Almighty, Maker of heaven and earth, and of all things visible and invisible. And in one Lord Jesus Christ, the only begotten Son of God, begotten of the Father before all worlds, Light of Light, very God of very God—"

I was not able to conclude my thought, for I heard the door behind me open and close. I quickly raised up the torch and cried, "Drogo? Is that you?"

"It's only me," a familiar voice answered.

As he walked into the light, I could see clearly that it was Brian fitz Count wrapped in a cloak to guard against the chill of night, the amber glow coating his face.

"You have interrupted my prayers," I said, expressing more frustration than I felt.

"Forgive me, my lady. Have no fear. Sir Drogo did not abandon his post."

"You must have killed him then, for I told him to admit no man."

"Yes, well, it was a bit of a scrape, but he permitted me to enter when I told him they had brought out a cake. He allowed me to take his place as your guardian."

"He gave me up for a cake? Damn him!" I muttered, then felt a pang of guilt. "That is … forgive me, Lord," I offered, glancing up at the stars above me. "I should not utter such oaths in church. Nevertheless, I must remember to keep better knights in the future."

"Perhaps you are upset that he did not inform you about the cake," Brian said with a smile.

"Maybe, although I do not fancy another discussion about the pleasures of priests."

"We are men. We cannot help but have such discussions," he replied, walking a bit closer. "Surely you must have learned our ways by now."

"I have. That's why I despise them so, although I cannot say that most of the women I meet are any better company."

"You are friendly enough with Adela."

"Yes, she is one of a kind. I can speak of anything with her."

"And you like Lady Mabel, Robert's wife."

"She is the best of us."

He shrugged. "Two isn't bad. I might have difficulty finding as many honorable men."

"You may have a point," I admitted. "Now, if you do not mind, I shall return to my prayers." Here I turned to look back at the altar.

"What do you pray for?" he asked quietly.

I turned again to look back at him. "The same as always: that God will grant me the strength to persevere—to endure the hours."

"Do you feel lacking in strength?"

I walked within an arm's length of him and raised up the fire so that we could see each other's features clearly. "Between you and me," I said, "I have very little faith in myself whatsoever. I have no idea what is about to happen. I am woefully unready. Everyone seems to know more than I do. They all seek to pull me in one direction or the other. And I have yet to deal with the most fearful one of all!"

"Bishop Henry?"

"The very man. I am not looking forward to this meeting. I know he seems to have forsaken the false king, but these great men are always fickle friends."

"I hope you do not feel that I have been a fickle friend," Brian replied, "or perhaps you do not think me great."

"What? No!" I cried, perhaps too loudly. "You are the very best of friends, though I cannot imagine why."

"What do you mean?"

"Look at all the trouble I put you through! Of all the men who have flocked to my court, you are the only one who has never asked me for anything. You must be careful. People might suspect you of having a secret motive."

As I said these words, I felt a sudden strain in my insides. Had I really dared to say that? Perhaps I should not have done so. After all, I did hope that he had a secret motive—namely, that he cared for me—but I also knew it was wrong to hope so. Everything about the situation was odd and painful, and I knew that if I failed to control my feelings, it could destroy everything I had worked to build. Hearing how easily those words had escaped my lips filled me with fear. I was fortunate, then, that his reply was not equally bold.

"I want to see the rightful queen on the throne. That is my motive," he said, perhaps failing to understand my meaning, or perhaps choosing not to acknowledge it.

"Well, no one is likely to believe that, are they? Indeed, it seems the least likely reason of all in an age when honor is dead," I bemoaned, and made to return to the altar, feeling a sense of relief as I did so.

Suddenly, he touched my arm and I snapped my head back around. Looking into that face, I swallowed hard. There was a real firmness in his gaze: a kind of piercing light. As he opened his mouth to speak, I held my breath. The whole of me seemed to hang upon the words he had yet to utter. But whatever I hoped for, or whatever I feared … it was not to be. He simply said, "If there is any woman on earth who can do this, it is you. Have faith in yourself. I do."

I tried to think of something clever to say, but all I could utter was, "Thank you." I could not raise my voice above a whisper, so distracted was I by that brief moment of uncertainty.

"Now then, I will leave you to your prayers, unless you would rather return to the others," he offered.

I nodded in reply and watched as he walked back to the door, placed his hand on the latch, swung it open, and departed. I exhaled loudly and spun to look back at the statue of the Virgin and child.

"I might have a few things to confess …" I admitted.

VIII

If one lives long enough, one begins to see men in the bodies of other men: characters that tend to repeat and temperaments that follow the same pattern. There are few truly incomparable men in this world. The key is to discover which kind of man one is dealing with and heed the lessons of the past, that its errors might not be repeated. Even so, I set my mind to determining the character of Bishop Henry of Winchester.

I was in no doubt as to his import. The youngest of four brothers of the esteemed House of Blois, Henry seemed determined to defy the odds and become the greatest of them all: greater than Theobald, who controlled half of Normandy and France; greater than Stephen, who had claimed the throne of England; and certainly greater than that swine of a brother, William, who was known only for lechery and prodigality. A mother often feels the greatest affection for her youngest son. Even so, Henry of Blois was most beloved of his mother, Adela, who took great pains in ensuring his advancement.

By the time my meeting with Bishop Henry of Winchester arrived, the old circle of power had crumbled around him. He had risen upon the wings of ambition to become the most powerful lord in the kingdom even as the others had been singed like Icarus. Bishop Roger of Salisbury had fallen. Archbishop Theobald of Canterbury, Henry's rightful better, had been largely pushed aside. The usurper, Stephen, was in our custody. Earl Waleran, Bishop Henry's greatest and most deadly enemy, had fled upon the wind. The only thing that could have improved this situation for Bishop Henry was to have myself and Earl Robert of Gloucester bow at his feet. As much as I hated to do so, I could see that we had no other option. The man knew how to play a game to win.

On the first day of March, we arrived at the nunnery of Wherwell and took up residence. It was there that we received word from Winchester that Bishop Henry would be arriving the following day. The abbess, a certain Ermengarde, directed me to the guest house in all honor. It was set apart from the other buildings and contained two private chambers and a small hall for receiving guests.

"I hope these rooms please you, Empress Mathilda," the abbess said, as we stood in the hall. "They were just completed last year. Is that the proper form of address? Should I still refer to you as empress?"

"I'm afraid everything depends upon the meeting with Bishop Henry—even my name," I replied.

Adela was just on the other side of the room unpacking the chests. She responded, "Surely we must call you Queen Mathilda, for that is what you are! That is what you have always been by right."

"It is not that simple, dear," I said to her, then turning back to the abbess, I attempted to steer the conversation in another direction. "That is a magnificent tapestry over there. The life of the Virgin, right? Can you tell me about it?"

I pointed to the tapestry on the opposite wall, a work of immense size on which the chief moments of Our Lady's life danced in colors of red and white upon a sea of blue. In the upper left corner, she was presented at the Temple. In the lower right, the apostles gathered around her death bed, followed by her assumption into heaven.

"It is a great treasure of our house!" the abbess replied, smiling broadly. "It was given to us some forty years ago. I had just entered and had not yet taken my vows. Seeing it made me recognize the life to which God had called me. He even came to deliver it in person."

"Who came?" I asked, assuming that the Lord Himself had not dropped it at the front gate.

"Why, the archbishop! Anselm of Canterbury, or before that Anselm of Bec, and I suppose before that Anselm of Aosta. Such a great man he was, anointed of God, and I was able to see him with my own eyes!"

I dared not tell her that I had not only seen and spoken with Archbishop Anselm, but he had also served as my tutor for a time. I simply smiled and said, "How wonderful that he should have presented the abbey with such a gift! I would not have thought it possible for an archbishop to come up with the necessary coin."

"Yes, I am not sure how he was able to do it. He was a man of great faith. Perhaps he prayed and God rained it down."

"Perhaps."

"I will leave you and your maid in peace, then. Do let us know if there is anything you require."

"I certainly will. Thank you, Mother Ermengarde."

The good abbess departed, and with Adela busy in the next room, I was left alone to ponder the beauty of the tapestry. It must have taken the weavers a full year to complete it, or perhaps more. I approached at close range and allowed my eyes to pass over every inch. The warp was most certainly wool, possibly from the flocks of England itself, but the weft appeared to be silk.

"Good Lord! You spent more on this than I thought, Father Anselm!" I muttered.

How indeed had he acquired the money? It must have been completed in Italy. Perhaps it had originally graced the walls in Bec or even Canterbury. I knew Archbishop Anselm to be far too holy to have won it at dice. Then again, I suppose you never really know a man until you have viewed his account books.

The life of the Virgin was not a very original choice of subject matter for a nunnery. It did, however, cause my mind to dwell on the nature of the female. I knew well enough that virginity is the height of godliness for any woman. Motherhood is necessary for the preservation of life. The bonds of wedlock are therefore encouraged for those who have not the gift of restraint. Whatever her station in life, a woman is meant to support and encourage the men around her, whether they be sons, husbands, or bishops. Even so, I had striven to do for the whole of my natural life, yet no one else seemed to see it.

"If only I had been like you, Mary, who combined in yourself the roles of virgin, mother, wife—even queen!" I spoke quietly to the tapestry before me. "Yes, you who are Queen of Heaven and yet earn the wrath of no man! Would that I had one tenth of your grace—nay, one hundredth! Then perhaps I would enjoy one hundredth of the love you receive. But you and I are women of different kinds. It is your lot to achieve all that is good and godly, and mine to hold the line for someone better. Well, I do not envy you your role as Mother of God. I do not envy the tears you cried at the foot of the cross, or the ones that fell as you wrapped your only son in grave cloths. By perfection you earned your place, and by iniquity I have earned mine."

I then ceased whispering and prayed within my mind.

I am scared, Mother Mary. I am driven to fear as a beast that feels the harsh sting of the goad. The men around me: they seek to control me. I can sense it. I doubt myself, Mother Mary. I doubt it all—everything. I have never known such doubt in all my days. I arrived at this point with great intention. I was certain of the path of righteousness. I still believe this is right, but I tremble. I tremble and I fear. No one must know this. At times … At times, I imagine they can see it in my eyes … That they can hear it in my voice. No, it cannot be! They must not know. The pages of history are waiting to be written, and I will not have them say that Maud was a coward. I will have them say I did it well. Help me now, for I have been … so afraid … so afraid all my life.

"Why are you praying to her?"

The question seemed so real that I turned around to see if someone was standing behind me. There was no one there. The only sounds were Adela humming in the other room and the distant noises from outside. No, of course the voice had been inside my head, for that is where the prayer had been. Therefore, I answered within the confines of my mind.

What do you mean, "Why am I praying to her?"

You already have that which you need.

Oh, really? What is that, pray tell?

Remember what I told you in the beginning. We were sitting at the table: the two of us and young William.

Of course! The other voice in my mind belonged to Father Anselm, the tutor of my youth. I decided to keep with the conversation in the hope that it might reveal something.

Ah, yes, I remember. You were reciting scripture to us.

I was bidding you to heed the scriptures.

Oh, which verses did you recite? I cannot remember.

Yes, you can. After all, you remember me.

"God is that than which nothing greater can be conceived." I remember you said that.

It is still true.

I find the perfection of God most frightful. You always knew that. Oh, but what was the verse?

Do you lack wisdom, Mathilda?

Ah, yes! "If any of you lack wisdom, let him ask of God …"

"… which gives to all men liberally, and reproaches no man, and it shall be given him."

"But let him ask in faith and waver not, for he that wavers is like a wave on the sea …"

"… tossed of the wind, and carried away."

"Neither let that man think that he shall receive anything of the Lord."

"A double minded man is unstable in all his ways."[18]

---

18   James 1:5-8.

I am sorry, Father Anselm, but that is not very comforting.

No? I thought it would be.

What man has ever had faith that does not waver? You place upon me an impossible task.

Your faith may waver, but the Lord our God never does. It is He who goes before you.

So, are you telling me this is going to end well?

How can I tell you anything? I am merely a phantom of the mind!

Were you a phantom when you came to me upon my death bed? Was it a dream or a vision?

What do you think? You control my words.

I think it was a dream. I am not godly enough to receive a vision.

A dream, then.

It's just ... you said something to me—something I have never forgotten.

And what was that?

As everything was fading, you said to me, "Rise."

And did you?

Did I what?

Rise?

I got out of bed if that is what you wish to know.

Some days that takes more courage than riding into battle.

So, what should I do about Bishop Henry, then?

You know him to be an ambitious man from an ambitious family. You know that you need his support and that of the Church to gain the throne for yourself and your posterity.

But if I offer him everything he wants, will I not become his servant? How then can I be free?

None of us are free, child, and the greatest among us least of all.

True. It appears I have no choice. Very well, then. I will give him whatever he wants as long as he bows the knee. Of course, it will really be me bowing to him, but I shall have to live with that. One day he will die, but my progeny will live on. Payment must be made now and the reward reaped later.

Quite right. Now, was that all?

Not quite. Tell me, how were you able to pay for this tapestry?

I didn't pay for it. I won it at dice.

I am certain that is not the answer the real Anselm would have given me.

But that was just it. The voice was only in my mind. I had created it from my own memories. I awoke from this trance to find that I was still staring at the tapestry, and more to the point, Adela was staring at me, her arms filled with a pair of furs.

"Forgive me, my lady, but where did you want these?" she inquired.

"Did you ask me that earlier?"

"Yes, but it is all right. I could see you were deep in thought. Where do you want them?"

I shook my head slightly, as if to remove the last remnants of distraction. "Leave one out for tomorrow. The other we'll keep in the chest."

"Very good, my lady."

With that, she left me, and I found myself staring at the panel showing the presentation of the Christ child at the Temple. The Virgin held her son out to the priest, seeking his blessing.

"Even so, must I seek the blessing of Bishop Henry, though I think he will not give it so freely," I concluded.

The next day was the sixth before the Nones, and what a baleful day it was! There was no sign of the sun from the time it ought to have risen to when it ought to have set. Only the rumor of light behind the storm clouds told us that it was day and not night. One hates to go out of doors on such occasions, and fortunately for me, the nuns were kind enough to bring over some food from the refectory. I ate very little, for my insides were in knots. Perhaps I should not have been so afraid of the bishop of Winchester. After all, I was his rightful sovereign.

Even so, I felt that a great deal depended on our meeting, not only for myself, but for the future of our kingdom.

When Adela asked me what I wished to wear that day, I told her, "Whatever looks the most costly." Alas, I did not have any damask, but we made do with what we could find.

At about half before eleven, there was a knock on the door of the guest hall, and Adela rose from where we were both seated to open it. I looked up from the book I had been reading to see Earl Robert, Lord Miles, and Lord Brian enter the room, all dripping wet. They threw back their hoods and removed their gloves, then proceeded toward the chairs nearest the fire.

"Mind you don't sit there in your wet things!" Adela scolded them.

The three of them obediently handed her their cloaks, which were laid out to dry. They then fell into the chairs with as much force as if they had just walked all the way from Scarborough. After they had caught their breath, Miles asked, "When does His Holiness get here, then?"

"He's a bishop. He'll get here when he gets here," Robert responded, a fist pressed against his forehead and his eyes closed.

"Who will serve as clerk for our side?" I asked. "Someone needs to make a note of everything that is said. I don't want him claiming I cheated him at some later date."

All three men looked at one another, their eyes accusing.

"I thought you were going to fetch someone," Robert said to Miles.

"And I thought the same of you," he replied.

"My lords!" said Brian. "There is no need to argue. I shall go and call someone." Then as he rose, he inquired of me, "Whom do you prefer?"

"That monk from Malmesbury: William. The one who keeps their records."

"Very well," he concluded, departing to fulfill my command.

"I like that fellow," Robert mused, rubbing his eyes. "Did he get a chance to hand you his latest volume?"

"I have it here," I said, holding up the book. "I cannot remember the last time I read something that interested me to this degree."

"And here I thought my letters were rather good," my brother commented with a smile.

Ignoring him, I asked, "Did you know that King Alfred only learned to read at the age of twelve? And yet he is one of the greatest scholars in this island's history!"

"Is that so strange?" asked Miles. "Not one in a hundred men can read."

"Yes," I replied, "and even fewer set any store by the words on the page, but I do find it odd that a prince should have been thus deprived."

"The first King William never learned to read," Robert said.

"England and Normandy may have both been better off if he had," I declared.

"Poor Emperor Henry is going to be furious he had to ride here in the rain!" said Miles.

For just a moment, I thought of my first husband, but then recognized that Miles was making a jest about the bishop of Winchester.

"Would you please start referring to him by his correct title?" I asked. "It's bad enough that we have to go through this. I don't need you making it worse."

"Have you decided whether or not to offer him the archbishopric of Canterbury after Theobald's death?" Robert inquired.

I sighed deeply. "Let us see if he will agree first. We will only mention that if necessary."

There was another knock at the door and Adela once again opened it to reveal Brian fitz Count.

"By luck, Brother William happened to be passing this way," he said, directing the monk into the room, "and by even greater luck, I present to you the bishop of Winchester."

Everyone stood, including me, as Bishop Henry of Winchester entered the room. As one might have guessed, his ornate garments were thoroughly wet. I cannot think why he chose to wear such regal apparel in a rain storm if not to send a shudder of fear through the rest of us. Sadly for him, the sight before us was having the opposite effect of what he intended, so drenched was he from head to toe. A small party of men entered behind him, no doubt come to observe and report. As for William of Malmesbury, he was quite forgotten and forced to content himself with a seat by the fire.

"Bishop Henry!" I said, walking over to welcome him. "Your journey must have seemed twice as long on a day such as this. How good of you to come and join us!"

"Your Highness," he replied, removing his hat and bowing low. "I would have ridden twice as far were it necessary. Of course, I much prefer to travel by carriage, but they are no use in the mud."

"Who have you brought with you?" I asked.

"This is my archdeacon, Nigel, and two of our canons …"

"Good day," I said to each of them in turn.

"And this is Abbot Edward of Reading," Bishop Henry added, pointing to the man in question.

As I moved to greet the abbot, he clasped my hands in his own and gave me what seemed to be a true smile. "My lady, we thank you ever so much for the gift of the relic of Saint James. It has been a joy for pilgrims to behold. Many have already been healed."

"I am glad," I said, earnestly hoping that the discussion would not move to how I acquired the thing.

"And rest assured," he added, "we daily say a Mass for the soul of your late esteemed father, who is buried in our midst."

Only one per day? He'll need more than that, I mused.

"I am in your debt. Come, let us all have a seat," I concluded.

There was only the single table in the room with five chairs on each side: the one in the middle rather grand and the other four quite plain. Bishop Henry and I each sat in the middle chairs with our associates on either side. Adela perched in a seat left open near the hearth, where Brother William was busy sharpening his quill over the small lap desk he had brought with him.

"Empress Mathilda, how do you wish to proceed?" Bishop Henry asked. "I know of no exact precedent for this situation."

"Nor do I," I said. "As we have entered within your see, lord bishop, I welcome you to begin." I reasoned that deferring in such a manner was a good way to earn his favor.

"Very well. We have come here to discuss your entrance into the royal city of Winchester. Your captains have been victorious in battle, and you therefore wish to claim the royal treasury and palace of Winchester, in addition to receiving the fealty of all persons within said jurisdiction. Is that correct?"

"Yes," I replied with a swift nod.

"Moreover, you wish to be acknowledged as sovereign ruler of the kingdom of England by the lords ecclesiastical and temporal."

"Yes."

"In support of which claim you state that you are the only legitimate child of the late king, Henry, who chose you as his successor and had all the lords swear to the same. Also, you claim the crown by right of conquest, having defeated the armies of King Stephen and deposed him."

"Correct."

"And you contend that the assertions made to the effect that King Stephen was appointed successor to King Henry upon the latter's death bed were mistakes."

Here I saw the need to state my position clearly. "They were lies. Earl Robert of Gloucester can testify to it."

"Your contention is noted," the bishop said in response, which I noted was not a full assent to my words. "Now, you do understand that it is a difficult matter for the Church to anoint a new sovereign when an anointed king is yet living?"

"I am aware of the difficulty," I began, working to contain my frustration, "but surely the unlawful nature of Count Stephen's coronation, in which the archbishop of Canterbury was made to act upon false oaths, renders it void."

This was a delicate point, for Bishop Henry had been one of those who supported Stephen's ascension. Indeed, it could hardly have taken place without his influence. Like the others, he did not stop to verify the truth of Hugh Bigod's claim that my father had changed his mind. He chose not to ask questions unless the answer would suit his desire. Now he had been forced to take a stand against his elder brother, and he would have to find a way to avoid the appearance of hypocrisy. I watched as he took a deep breath, perhaps stalling for time, then spoke slowly and carefully.

"All was chaos at that time, my lady. It is not for me to say what passed through the mind of the late archbishop, who accepted the solemn oaths made in his presence. Nevertheless, you have received new pledges of fealty from the greater portion of nobles in this kingdom, or you will soon do so. I therefore see no reason to oppose your claim, which is made in good faith. As you know, I cannot speak for the current archbishop of Canterbury any more than I can for his predecessor; therefore, I cannot promise the full support of the Church upon my own authority. However, I will pledge my fealty to you if you grant me assurances that the Church will in no way be usurped during your reign and that the count of Anjou shall have no authority over our affairs here." He placed particular stress on these last words, either because the Angevins were the enemies of his own house or because he could not abide the idea of another man having more power on the island than himself.

"I understand, Bishop Henry," I said. "Should I be received as sovereign by my people, I will seek your counsel in all matters of state that are of considerable import, especially when it comes to the granting of bishoprics and abbacies. You need not fear a repeat of what happened under the last ruler. I will not raise up lesser men at the expense of the Church, nor seek the advice of evil counselors. I value your counsel in everything and will welcome you always at my court. All this I pledge to do if you grant me your fidelity henceforth."

"And the count of Anjou will have no sovereignty over this kingdom?" the bishop inquired, his hands folded before him and the muscles in his face tense.

I smiled and may have even laughed softly. "You are in error if you believe that I wish for my husband to have any part in our affairs. Count Geoffrey does not care for England. It is the duchy of Normandy he seeks, both for himself and our sons. Once I am made queen of England—should I receive the support of the nobles and the Church—we shall remove the last remnants of rebellion in both Normandy and England. I foresee that Count Geoffrey will be happy to remain in Anjou and Normandy and take no part in the governance of this kingdom."

"We are most glad to receive these tidings," the abbot of Reading suddenly declared. "You must know, my lady, that the Angevins are no more beloved here than they are in Normandy. We have heard such stories of their cruelty!"

"Please, Father, you need not make the effort," Earl Robert responded. "No one at this table liked the idea of the Angevin marriage, most especially the empress herself—"

"Thank you, Earl Robert!" I said, cutting him off at the pass. "My marriage is what it is. Count Geoffrey is a fine commander in the field, and he has given me three wonderful sons whom I hope will rule over England and Normandy someday. Let that be enough."

"My apologies," Robert replied.

"I too offer my apology," said Abbot Edward.

Bishop Henry then joined the conversation once again. "I thank you for your words, my lady. We have no wish to dishonor your noble husband: only to ensure that the throne of England is controlled by those who have the English royal blood."

This was an odd explanation from a man who didn't have a drop of English blood himself, but I let it go.

"I am quite content at the present time and will be happy to receive you as my lady in the cathedral of Winchester, declaring my fealty before the bones of Saint Swithun," the bishop continued. "I believe my friend, Bishop Bernard, can help with this matter. You have with you also Bishop Nigel of Ely. I can confirm that we have in Winchester at the present time Bishop Alexander of Lincoln, Bishop Robert of Bath, and Bishop Robert of Hereford. They will all follow my lead in swearing themselves to your service."

I thought this a rather bold conclusion, especially in light of the bishop of Hereford's well known hatred for our party, but again I said nothing.

"I have sent also for Archbishop Theobald at Canterbury," he added. "He has traveled as far as London and requests a private meeting with Your Highness to decide on a proper course of action."

I could not think of what the proper course of action would be besides agreeing to crown me queen, but I simply replied, "I would be happy to meet with him at his earliest convenience."

"Quite right," Bishop Henry said. "Now, if your party would be so good as to arrive tomorrow morning in the city of Winchester, we shall receive you with the utmost hospitality. I have in my possession the keys to the royal treasury which I will surrender to you at the ceremony in the cathedral."

"Exactly what is in the royal treasury at the present time?" Brian asked.

The bishop replied, "The royal crown which was used for the last king—that is, Stephen—currently rests in the vault, along with sundry weapons and jewels, and a pair of holy books belonging to King Edward. As for the rest, there is somewhere on the order of four hundred pounds in gold and silver coins."

This was a surprise, and not the pleasant kind. The lords Robert, Brian, and Miles all looked at me and I at them in something close to despair. Upon my father's death, there had been around ten thousand pounds in the state purse. We had all known Stephen was spending money left and right to keep his place on the throne, but none of us had guessed it was quite that bad. After what seemed like an hour, but was actually no more than a few seconds, Earl Robert finally said something.

"Do you mean to tell me that for all the wealth that King Henry acquired through his many years on the throne, and for which the men of this kingdom spilt their blood, too little remains to build a single castle?! How on earth can this be?!" he demanded, leaning forward and pressing his fore arm into the table.

"I must say, I concur with the earl," Lord Brian added, frowning in a manner that for him amounted to a glare of death. "We made accounts of King Henry's finances during his reign. How could Stephen have wasted it all in the course of a few years?!"

"My lords!" Bishop Henry cried, pressing his palms on the table. "Surely it matters not how the money was spent, for it is no longer available to us. All that matters is what the empress chooses to do going forward. Empress?"

Here the bishop looked at me, for I had not yet spoken a word. He must have hoped that I would make less of a furor over this revelation. If so, he did not know me at all. I had only remained mute because the words passing through my mind at that moment were far too foul to speak out loud. Finally, I did say something.

"My lord bishop, you must see how miserable our current state is. I had hoped upon becoming queen of England to be provided with enough gold to bring an end to rebellion and repair those things which have been broken in this present conflict. I had hoped even to endow the Church with hand-some gifts, and to build fortifications for the protection of this realm. How am I to do any of that when the foul usurper has given well-nigh everything in the state coffer to the mer-cenaries of Flanders? He bought the crown with the money that ought to have gone to myself! He allowed the merchants of London to sit upon piles of wealth while the rest of the kingdom has been laid waste! He made an end of the law and heaped scorn upon the commands of God! Never has there been a more dreadful reign in the history of England than my cousin's. On account of his sins, we must bear the wrath. The scarlet of that iniquity is the scarlet of human blood poured out upon the sacred ground, and were we to drain all the holy wells in England, it would be too little water to wash away the stain."

"Here I must beg your pardon, Empress Mathilda," the bishop replied, his deep breaths implying that he too was on the verge of anger. "It was not I who chose to act in such a manner. My brother made his own decisions, and I agree that they have been harmful to this kingdom. That is why I am able to support Your Highness."

I wanted to cry out, "Yes, but you were the one who granted him the treasury in the first place!" but I did not. Instead, I said, "I have no monies of my own: only what Earl Robert and my husband possess, and that is all going to pay for our expenses in the war. When I become queen, I will have no choice but to collect a tax, or there will be no government to speak of in this kingdom."

"A tax on what?" Lord Miles asked. "The nobles have spent all their money in the war, even as Earl Robert has, and the peasants have nothing to offer. That only leaves …" Here his voice trailed off, even as recognition dawned in his eyes.

"The merchants of London, yes," I replied. "They were the ones who first endorsed the reign of error. They must help to make amends. I have no intention of bleeding them dry. After all, we rely on their trade to place food in many mouths. Nevertheless, I can see now that I have no choice but to impose a tax of some kind. Of course, I will hear your advice on this matter, Bishop Henry."

"I thank you for that, my lady, but let us leave it for another day," the bishop concluded, his eyes quickly looking down at Earl Robert—still fuming—and then back at myself. "For now, there is only one question remaining: what shall we call you? At the present, you retain your title by marriage: Empress Mathilda. Upon your coronation in Westminster Abbey, you will naturally be referred to as Queen Mathilda of England. In the meantime, perhaps we can devise a title fit for the moment. Perhaps 'lady of the English' would be acceptable?"

"Whatever you think is best," I said. "I am happy to continue as 'Empress Mathilda,' but the new title does seem proper. Just mind you do not call me 'countess of Anjou.' That is the one title I loathe."

"It's settled, then," said Earl Robert, having apparently calmed himself a bit. "Bishop Henry, we shall meet you at noon tomorrow at the western gate of the city."

"And I shall ensure that no one hinders you along your way and that you are received with joy by all the citizens," the bishop replied. He then stood up and proclaimed, "All hail Empress Mathilda, lady of the English!"

The rest of the men stood as well and echoed, "All hail, lady of the English!"

Last of all, Adela stood up and said quietly, "The lady of the English!"

Winchester: *Venta Belgarum* of the ancient Romans, capital city of King Alfred the Great, beating heart of the old Kingdom of Wessex, and site of the royal treasury. It was once the greatest city in England, yet when my grandfather, William the Conqueror, first set eyes on it, he was by no means in awe. There is a story that he uttered the words, "What a heap of rubbish!" but no living man can verify this. Suffice it to say, neither the royal palace nor the cathedral met with his satisfaction. Naturally, he chose to spend his gold on a new palace, destroying the old one along with some sixty homes to make way for bigger and better things.

By the time of the war, the city of London exceeded Winchester in greatness. Even so, the latter was not without its merits. It was the private kingdom of Bishop Henry, who through the strength of his cunning had procured monies for his see beyond any other ecclesiastic in England. While Bishop Roger of Salisbury had seen his castles taken from him by the false king, Bishop Henry played the game much better. He had the firm support of His Holiness, having been named papal legate. This gave him authority that none of his fellows in England could match, and Stephen was far too afraid to touch him.

Out of his wealth, Bishop Henry made repairs to the cathedral, expanded the halls for the monks, and finished the city walls in stone. But his greatest achievement was the construction of a new residence just southeast of the cathedral: Wolvesey Castle, envy of bishops and earls alike. There he held court, and by the year 1141, it was clear that Henry of Blois had more actual power than his elder brother, even before Stephen was defeated at Lincoln.

We rose early at the nunnery of Wherwell and began our ride southeast toward Winchester, which ought to have been no more than a half day's journey. However, as is often the case with such things, we were oft delayed. We could not have gone more than ten furlongs before Earl Robert's horse stepped on a nail and injured itself. This seemed an ill sign, for who leaves a nail lying out in the country? Nevertheless, we found my brother a new seat and continued our progress. About an hour later, one of the carts tipped over, spilling its contents in front of the cart behind it, which then turned over as well.

"We should press on," Miles said. "They can meet us later. Any more delay and Bishop Henry will be most put out."

I was certainly not going to reject such advice. We therefore split into two parties, with those who could continue going ahead of the others. I was just reaching that point in the journey when one begins to despair of one's thighs when we finally made it round the last stretch of hills and came into the vale of the River Itchen. There I saw clearly something I had not set eyes on since I was very young indeed: the city of Winchester.

"Does it look like you remembered it?" Drogo asked, as he rode beside me.

"I hardly know," I said. "Most of my memories are of the castle: the one built by the first King William, not the old one. That was before the cathedral spire crumbled. The whole place seems greater now that Bishop Henry has put his skills to work, save for that tower."

As we crossed the final furlongs, we began to see peasants looking up from their work in the fields and calling to one another in their common tongue. A few were brave enough to approach us and cry out, waving their arms.

"What on earth do they want?" asked brother Robert. "They must know we cannot understand them."

"I think they are saying, 'Hail! Hail!'" I responded. "Or perhaps they wish me to go to hell. They sound very similar in the common tongue."

At that moment, I heard a woman saying very clearly, "Queen Maud! God save Queen Maud!"

"God save England!" I called back to her. At this, they all broke into cheers.

By the time we reached the western gate of the city, I was feeling quite assured. The conflict that had lived inside me ever since I left Gloucester finally seemed to fade away, and I began to rejoice in my situation. It was, after all, a most extraordinary tale. Despite a host of difficulties, we had prevailed against the machinations of our enemies. The dream that seemed so remote just a few months earlier was now within my grasp. Such a thing might not seem a miracle to men. After all, what man isn't born with a scepter in his hand? Yet the idea that I might hold one suddenly became so real that I would have stood in awe at what had been achieved … had I not been riding a horse.

Lord Miles made a very fine show of pounding his fist on the city gate. One of the watchmen called down to him, "Who goes there?"

"Make way for Empress Mathilda, lady of the English, rightful queen of England!" he cried.

I could not help but see the humor in this. Clearly, the watchman knew who we were, but there is no sphere of life in which the traditions must not be respected. After making a show of walking away to gain permission, he returned and called out, "By leave of Bishop Henry of Winchester, I grant you entry to the city."

No sooner had he finished speaking than the doors began to open before us. They were evidently either quite heavy or quite old, for they groaned upon their iron hinges. As they parted, I beheld the figure of Bishop Henry standing beside his white horse, a steed far greater than my own and certainly finer than the one for which Earl Robert had been forced to settle.

"All hail, lady of the English!" he said, bowing low enough that his robes trailed in the mud. "I bid you welcome to Winchester."

"Thank you, lord bishop," I replied.

"Now," he continued, "if you will follow me, we shall proceed to the town square, there to meet with the people."

He then mounted his horse with a flourish and led us down the High Street, which was lined on either side by the usual collection of houses with shops on the lower level, taverns, and inns. The stalls had all been pulled back to make way for the crowds who lined up on either side. I was pleased to see that they were cheering heartily. I had been uncertain how I would be received, but everything seemed to be going perfectly. That was a dangerous word: perfect.

"There on the left!" cried the bishop. "That house used to belong to Emma, wife of King Æthelred. Before her, there were no queens in England, but her father was most intent that she should have the title, for it was the custom of her people.

Amy Mantravadi

Thus, she became Queen Emma and was gifted this home, and England has had queens ever after."

"She didn't live at the palace?" I asked in wonder.

"No, it was also the custom for her to have a separate residence all her own."

"What an original idea!" I concluded, then thought to myself, *Would that this was the custom in Anjou!*

"And just behind those buildings is the old castle that belonged to the kings of Wessex, but it was so small even they abandoned it," he added. "It will never be used again by royalty, so we are taking it apart to strengthen the other fortifications."

Did you ask permission for that? I wondered, but chose to let it go.

When we reached the market square, we found not an open space paved with stone as much as a solid crowd of people packed between the buildings. Some held banners aloft, while others simply clapped their hands, and several of the children present seemed to be enjoying sweets of some type. Bishop Henry addressed the gathered throng.

"Good people of Winchester," he cried, "I present to you Empress Mathilda, lady of the English, daughter of the late King Henry, and your rightful sovereign! Pay her the respect that is her due!"

Immediately, in one collective motion, the crowd knelt and proclaimed, "Hail Empress Mathilda!", "Hail to the lady of the English!", and "God save the empress!"

After a few minutes of this, we turned down a side street and the great cathedral suddenly rose before us. So wonderful it appeared in the bright midday sun! Few sights have ever seemed as glorious to me as those two towers rising up into the sky, proclaiming the presence of God's Spirit on earth. Standing before the west front was a gathering of men, all looking rather official. Three of them I took to be the promised bishops, but

I was not sure about the rest. Bishop Henry alighted and then helped me as I too climbed down.

"The grooms will take the horses over to the castle," he said, pointing in the opposite direction.

I turned, and sure enough, there was the old fortress, no different from my memories. What I most certainly did not remember was the new castle to the left and the great number of buildings that had sprung up in between. These were entirely the product of Bishop Henry's industry.

One of the men standing in front of the cathedral now moved forward and bowed. "This is the sheriff of Hampshire and castellan of Winchester, William Pont de l'Arche," Bishop Henry explained.

"My lady—Empress Mathilda," he said, kissing my hand, "on behalf of the city fathers, I welcome you to Winchester with open arms. We are at your service."

"Thank you," I replied, then proceeded to shake the hands of the dozen or so men standing behind him.

There followed a long discussion about the order in which we should enter the cathedral. It was agreed that the men of the city ought to go first, followed by the abbots—Ingulf of Abingdon, Peter of Malmesbury, Gilbert of Gloucester, Edward of Reading, and Roger of Tewkesbury—and the rest of the monks, then the bishops—Alexander of Lincoln, Nigel of Ely, and the Roberts of Bath and Hereford—followed finally by myself, flanked by Bishop Henry of Winchester on my right and Bishop Bernard of Saint David's on my left, then last of all the nobles—Earl Robert, Earl Reginald, Earl Baldwin, Lord Miles, Lord Brian, and all the rest. If you find that rather tiresome to read, just imagine suffering through the whole discussion!

There was a delay at the door while we waited for those in front of us to make their way down the aisle, so I had a moment to think. This cathedral was one of the most sacred places in

England, home to the relics of Saint Swithun. In it lay the bones of the kings of old: my ancestors. The weight of history seemed to hang upon that place, and as I considered that it was there that I would be proclaimed England's rightful queen, my heart began to pound even harder. Then we started to walk.

As we crossed the threshold and the rows of columns and layers of rounded arches rose before us, the sound of a choir filled our ears. It was the monks of Winchester chanting the lines of "*Veni Creator Spiritus,*" and I could not help but think of my coronation as queen of the Romans so many years before, when Bruno had carried me into the cathedral of Mainz and the same hymn had been sung. It was Anselm who had first taught me those lines when I was just a girl, and it seemed in that moment that the whole of my life had come back round, and in returning to the place of my childhood, I had finally found the purpose of my life.

Of course, the cathedral of Winchester was far emptier that day than the German cathedrals had ever been, the chanting was not as loud, and the whole occasion was less formal. Nevertheless, I was in no mood to carp about such things. There would be ceremony enough at my coronation in Westminster. As we made our way up the nave and neared the altar, Bishop Bernard whispered to me, "Your mother would be proud, my lady. Exceedingly proud." It was one of the kindest things any man has ever said to me and it was only with great effort that I withheld tears of joy.

At last, we reached the center of the church, where a seat of honor had been set on top of a dais. I assumed they had brought it over from the palace. Perhaps it was an old possession of King William—I could not say. Bishop Henry bid me sit upon it, then gestured to those standing behind me. I could not see what they were doing, but it seemed to be of some import, for the bishop had a most serious look on his face. Finally, three canons stepped forward. The first bowed and held forth a great set of gold keys.

"To the royal treasury, Your Highness," he said.

I nodded and received the keys, which were among the largest I had ever seen. *Saint Peter himself would envy these, and yet they have nothing much to reveal these days*, I thought.

The second came forth and, bowing, held forth a silk pouch.

"Your royal seal, my lady," he said.

I accepted his offering and drew out the seal, a rather heavy thing for its size. I was almost robbed of breath when I held it up and saw my own image staring back at me, or at least a rather poor representation of it. It was a design much like the one my father had used, but the image was clearly of a woman. What would the people of England think of this? What would the world think of this? I tried to put such thoughts out of my mind as I stuffed the seal back inside the pouch.

The final canon approached, and had I possessed any remainder of confidence at that point, it was surely stolen away when I saw what he carried: the royal crown of Saint Edward, seated upon a cushion. It was a circlet of pure gold lined with pearls, four flowers rising opposite one another, each with a precious stone at the center. The first was a sapphire, the second an emerald, the third a ruby, and last and brightest of all was a diamond which adorned the flower at the front. All around the circlet were carved vines and flowers so fine that only the greatest skill could have brought them into being. On the back were carved the words in Latin: *Domine, salvum fac regem.*

That crown had belonged to Edward, the last king of the House of Wessex, and to many kings before him, Æthelstan being perhaps the first. As I looked upon it, I remembered the words the Confessor spoke with the clear vision of death: that on account of the evil of our days, the land would be handed over to the enemy for a time and become a haunt of devils, until new life would spring forth when the branch which had been severed would be united once more to the great tree and bear fruit. For it was the doom of Edward to stand as witness to the warring of kingdoms—the old House of Wessex against the men of the North—and it tore at his soul.

Having no child of his own, he knew not how England would survive but for the two to be united into one. When my parents came together, some said that the prophecy was fulfilled: that William Ætheling had the blood of both houses and he alone could repel the enemy. They never thought that death would take him before his time, that the enemy would rise from within, and that they were the devils who would welcome his coming. There was only one person in whom the prophecy could be fulfilled—only one head fit to wear Edward's crown, and through many years of suffering I had come to have it placed upon my head.

"For your coronation, my lady," the canon said, bowing so low that I feared his prize would fall to the ground.

"Thank you," I said simply. I was not to wear it that day. It would be set upon my anointed head by the archbishop of Canterbury. "You may place all these things in the possession of Earl Robert, who will serve as keeper for the present time."

Every man of rank came forward and kissed my hand, swearing to serve me as his queen. Well did I remember the lords and bishops doing this many years before, when they were forced to kneel by my father. Those oaths had proven to be vapor in the wind, but I was hopeful that would not be the case again. After all, I had one advantage the second time around: Stephen was under lock and key.

IX

April 1167
Rouen, Normandy

I write to you now in the second watch of the night, or so it must be in the great castles. Among the monks, it would be better to say we are between Matins and Lauds: those few hours when the brothers are allowed some rest from their labors. I wish I could say as much for myself, but alas, sleep has escaped my grasp once again.

It is not worry that keeps me awake this time but coughing. Yes, the cough that first appeared two weeks ago has refused to leave. This is not the same illness I had during the winter, but something new. My chest aches from the violence of it. If I could only cease coughing and gasping for a few minutes, I might enjoy an hour of slumber. Oh, that the good Lord would provide me with such a blessing! Yesterday, I raised a cloth to my mouth and saw a bit of blood on it again. This is happening more often, and it hardly seems a good sign.

I must have tried to sleep for two hours, but at length I decided to make better use of my time. That is when I lit a candle and sat down before this parchment. How fortunate that my hands are free enough to write! I have suffered great pain in my extremities. At such a time, one hopes to set one's mind to other things and thereby achieve some manner of relief. Sadly, no such luxury will be afforded to me, for the world seems to once again be crumbling around me.

I have written of my son's quarrel with Archbishop Thomas. How it brings to mind the emperor's disputes with Adalbert! There is nothing new under the sun, daughter. Truly—nothing new. I am always the first person to speak in favor of Church reform, but the bishops are fools if they think they themselves are not somehow at fault for the corruption that seems to increase by the day. The bishop who lives for the increase of his own kingdom rather than that of Jesus Christ is no better than the pagans. I am the worst of the Lord's disciples, and even I know that!

They say that Thomas Becket is a changed man now. He no longer lives for gold and the high regard of others. He is a man of penitence and austerity. I am sorry to say I might have liked him better when he was in the pocket of the devil. Now that he has affected this change, he claims to be a servant of the Almighty, and yet I think his deeds are still more pleasing to Lucifer than any Christian man of good sense. Nevertheless, I have worked to heal the breach and shall continue to do so. I only wish that my son's reign was not marked by such a struggle and such a man. Would that we could be free of it! But what am I saying? I fear the lack of sleep has put me in a foul temper.

Speaking of things that have put me in a foul temper, the king has burned the city of Chaumont upon the Loire. Why, you ask, would he do such a thing? I shall tell you. The city of Tours, under the care of Archbishop Jocius, raised monies for

Jerusalem to aid the Christians who had been cruelly betrayed by the Egyptians, or so I have heard. In truth, I am unable to follow all the news in my present state but must content myself to know what takes place in this duchy. In any case, the money was raised, but there was some disagreement as to the matter of distribution. A foolish quarrel, without a doubt.

On account of this nothing, King Henry of England and King Louis of France entered into a new dispute. As the cathedral of Tours was already burned down last year, my son evidently chose instead to disturb the town of Chamont. Now there is talk of open war. Even if I was in perfect health, I would hardly be able to sleep at night! Why must the world always be this way? Is it so much to ask that we should have one moment's peace?

But perhaps none of this interests you. What you wish to know is how things went with the succession. How did my son and your father come to be ruler of one of the greatest empires in the history of Christendom? I have been telling that story. It is a long one, and I do not know if I shall be able to finish it. It is not a thing of glory, but of pain, suffering, and perseverance. I must now return to bed and attempt to get some sleep, so in the morning I might tell you what became of me all those years ago.

Then I was young, but I was not free. I have never been free. Freedom is not a thing of this world. It belongs to heaven, a place of which I am not worthy.

The day after I was lauded in Winchester Cathedral, I received a letter from Archbishop Theobald of Canterbury informing me that he was passing through Southampton and would arrive at the abbey of Wilton in two days' time. There he hoped to meet me and discuss my elevation. Usually, the archbishop of Canterbury would have traveled to the sovereign rather than the other way around, but I was in no position to command this man before he had placed the sacred oil on my head.

I therefore gathered up three or four knights and we walked the short distance from the royal palace of Winchester to Wolvesey Castle. Upon reaching the gate, I made myself known to the warden, who led us into a room that clearly belonged to the castle guard. I then exchanged words with the steward, whose name I remember was Alfred, for his parents had named him after the city's most famous resident. When he learned of my purpose in coming, the steward called for bread and mead on behalf of my knights. Then the two of us walked to the entrance of the inner court, where Bishop Henry kept his garden.

"Here I leave you," said the steward, drifting into the darkness and leaving me to face the bishop alone.

The door was standing open. The stone arch surrounding it had the appearance of a vine with flowers shaped like stars. This much I will say for Bishop Henry of Winchester: he had an eye for beauty. I then gazed out into the sun lit court, which contained rows of beds that I assumed would be quite fruitful in the coming months. Standing in the middle was the bishop, looking rather unlike his usual self. He wore only a simple habit with no head covering, and thus for the first time I was able to see the tonsure upon his head. It was easy to forget that my cousin was a monk, for he seemed very much a man of this world, but he was indeed a son of Cluny. At length, I decided to make my presence known. Approaching him, I said, "This is a fine garden, Bishop Henry."

He looked up from the plants he had been examining. He seemed surprised to see me, but not entirely unhappy.

"You should see it in the summer, my lady," he replied. "You'd think it was another Eden."

"But one free of serpents, I hope."

He gave me a knowing smile. "The only time I had a serpent here was when Earl Waleran paid me a visit."

That was quite the declaration, and I could not help but ask, "Does your hatred of that man know no bounds?"

"I am a bishop. I love everyone."

"Then you are unlike any bishop I have ever known."

He laughed. "There is one creature for which I will admit the utmost loathing."

"Ah, a confession!" I cried in delight. "Dare I ask its name?"

"Its true name is known only to God, I should think. I have heard men call it a weevil: quite proper, for it is both wee and evil. The spawn of Satan, I name it! It has been the death of my strawberries."

"Is it a fly?"

"A beetle. I remember when I first saw them climbing upon the leaves, chewing holes here and there. I told the gardener, and he swore he would do all in his power to keep them away. I do not know what he tried, but it was all for naught, for that was not the real problem. See—here they are! My prized strawberries! See how wilted they look!"

My eyes followed his finger down to the ground before us. The plants in question did look rather sad, with far more brown leaves than green ones. Still, I attempted to bring him good cheer.

"Is it not early in the year? They have only just thawed. Perhaps they will recover."

"No, all the signs are bad," he said, nodding his head sadly. "These plants will not come back."

"And this is all because they chewed at the leaves?"

"That isn't the half of it."

He bent down and dug up a handful of earth. This surprised me exceedingly, as I would certainly have named Bishop Henry one of the cleanest men of my near acquaintance. He rose with his prize and said, "Hold out your hands."

I could not imagine what point he was attempting to make, but not wishing to upset him, I replied, "Very well …"

He placed the mess of dirt in my hands, and to my great alarm, as it sifted through my fingers, I felt something wriggling about—no, more than one something. I soon saw the yellow forms of tiny beasts with brown spots on their heads. I could not help myself: I screamed and dropped them on the ground.

"What in God's name are those?!" I cried.

"Weevils."

"But I thought you said they were beetles!"

"They will be, but they are young. They feed on the roots throughout the winter, then they rise in the summer to gnaw at the leaves. This is what I failed to recognize before, for I had dedicated all my attention to what my eyes could see. I mourned the death of those leaves, but I did not account for what was invisible. It is the grub that kills the plant, for it goes after the source of life: the roots. Now I have made it my duty to defeat these foul creatures. But do not look so perplexed, Empress Mathilda. I am not really talking about beetles."

"Are you not?" I asked, still attempting to recover from my sudden fright.

"No, I speak of my role as bishop."

"I thought bishops were meant to guard the sheep from wolves," I said with a smile, attempting to be clever.

"Wolves come in many forms," he replied, moving very close to me, the look on his face deadly serious. "The lesson is as follows. These plants are like the kingdom. Day by day, it is assailed and left with visible wounds, but these are not enough to defeat it. It can recover from such things. What we ought to concern ourselves with is the damage to the foundation: the gnawing away of what we hold dear, leaving us with neither roots nor a place to stand. The enemy without is not half as fierce as the enemy within, I say. Now, what is the foundation of a kingdom?"

A number of possible answers presented themselves, but knowing whom I was addressing, I answered, "The Church, surely."

"Right you are!" he cried, holding up a finger, a fire in his eyes. "Now, as bishop, I am sworn to uphold true religion in this kingdom, which amounts to nothing less than guarding the kingdom's foundation. When I see it under threat, tell me, how can I stand idle? Is it not my duty to defend the Lord's Church: the people whom he purchased with his own blood?"

"And for this, you are willing to forsake your brother?"

The bishop took a step backwards, as if my words had dealt him a blow. "I do not forsake him! I appeal to one nearer still: my Heavenly Father. But forgive me," he continued, becoming calmer again. "I think not of myself, but rather of my duty to the Church. It is the purpose for which I was born. I cannot remember a day that my mother did not say to me I would be a bishop. From the hour the nurse held me upon her teat, I was being raised for such a time as this." Again, he moved quite close and looked me directly in the eye. "Do you know what it is to have a purpose in life, cousin?"

"Yes," I replied quietly. "That is, I believe I do."

"Well, this is my purpose. It is a sacred calling: to be set apart for the things of God. Yet neither of us are performing the duties for which we were designed. You were meant to be a consort. I was meant to be a shepherd. Now life asks me to be a king maker and you a king."

"A queen, I hope," I said with a smile.

"That as well. I thank you again for your grant to the abbey of Glastonbury."

"Of course."

"And I shall thank you in the future for your grants to the see of Winchester."

Here I could not help but laugh. "They ought to erect a monument in your honor, Bishop Henry, such good have you done this place!"

"But none of this is the reason for your coming," he continued, turning his back to me and walking forward a few steps. "I take it you have received a missive from Archbishop Theobald."

I knew that I must take great care with my next words, so I began simply. "Indeed, I have."

"And will he be coming to visit us?" the bishop asked, fingering a branch of one of the taller plants.

"No. He has not forgiven you for the quarrels of the past."

Here he turned to face me again, hands clasped behind his back. "How very like him. Whatever you may think, my lady, I assure you I have far more foes than friends. It is the lot of anyone who hopes to do something worthy. So, where will you meet him?

"Wilton Abbey, in the see of Salisbury—"

"Which is to say, not in my see."

I sighed. "You could put it that way."

"Indeed, I would put it that way."

"Do you have any advice for me … as my counselor?" I asked, attempting to appeal to his vanity.

He turned his attention again to the plants, looking away from me. "Theobald will do everything by the book, as they say, even to a fault. If you obey the rules, you should do well."

"And would being male be one of the rules?"

He looked at me solemnly. "I do not write the rules, my lady. The Lord does. Nevertheless, these are strange times. The rules must some times be bent for the sake of peace."

"Let us hope that Archbishop Theobald sees it the same way," I concluded.

I do not know how much longer we remained in the garden. He spoke to me about all the plants—fruit trees, violets, roses, and many herbs—for far longer than I might have wished, given the winter cool. None of them had blooms yet. At length, I was released to return to the palace and the business at hand. My next obstacle would be Archbishop Theobald of Canterbury.

Having settled my affairs in Winchester for the moment, I made ready to travel to Wilton for my meeting with the archbishop. Though several persons offered to accompany me, I was content to take only a dozen or so knights, Abbot Gilbert of Gloucester, Earl Robert, and Lord Brian, the latter on account of his legal knowledge. The rest of the men I left to go stalking, which I was certain would please them far more than ecclesiastical matters. My half brother Reginald was especially eager to make use of his bow. I was in no mood to dally, so I informed my fellows before we set out, "We depart on the Kalends of March and arrive on the Kalends of March. I am the queen." That last bit I added simply for effect. It felt rather nice.

Indeed, despite Bishop Henry's wish that I be addressed as "lady of the English" until the coronation, those of my own party considered the matter already settled. They were more than happy to refer to me as queen in private, and I saw no reason not to indulge their desire. After all, I was the rightful queen. What had we fought for if not for that? This was merely the recognition of what everyone had sworn to before my father's death.

We were about to depart when Adela rushed to my side brandishing a stack of letters. "From Anjou!" she cried. "From the royal princes! And this one is from Count Geoffrey."

I turned to my companions and said, "Forgive me. I must see what this is before we do anything."

Well, they were hardly going to say no to me. After all, I was the queen. I wanted to open the letters from my sons first, as I missed them profoundly, but necessity forced me to listen to my husband. How interesting it was to read those lines … well, not exactly interesting, but something like it.

My dear wife, the news of your victory in the battle at Lincoln is spread far and wide, and it has filled us all with joy to think that the foul Stephen has been thrown down. I meet daily with Count Theobald and attempt to force him to recognize our authority here in Normandy. He is a sly beast, not unlike the other members of his family. Have no fear! I shall prevail! You must send me more men as soon as possible so I may put an end to the rebellion here. Once we have gained Normandy, nothing will be too difficult for us. Have faith in me, my wife. There is no need for you to return here. Just send me more men, and some gold as well.

The letter went on in the same manner. It seemed that my husband was not fully aware of the situation. We still had much work to do in England. I could not afford to sacrifice a single man. Even so, I took his words into consideration. Having dispensed with that duty, I moved on to the letters from my dear sons, the ones who truly held my heart in their little hands. The first was from Henry. What a clever lad he had become! He wrote in Latin, with only a few mistakes: at least, only a few that I could find. My own Latin was never as good as I desired, though I could read and speak it well enough. I then opened young Geoffrey's letter. It showed little of the skill of his elder brother's, but the difference in age surely accounted for that. Last of all, I read the note from my dear William: "Master Herman teaches me to write. I like to do this. I miss you, mother. I love you. Come back soon." Below was a drawing of a cat.

"Oh, how God has blessed me!" I proclaimed. "My sons are turning into scholars! As soon as I am crowned, I must bring them here. They must see their inheritance, and I must see their faces again. What a cruel fate to be separated for so long!"

We then began our long day's ride from Winchester to Wilton Abbey. The way is quite direct, but still difficult, for it passes through a forest, up and down hills, and over rivers. Wilton itself lies at the confluence of the rivers Nadder and Wylye, a pleasant town with a glorious history. Why glorious, you ask? Because it was there that they used to mint the coins in the old days of Wessex. It was the chief city of that kingdom until Alfred—he of the burnt cakes—decided to make his capital in Winchester. Due to its royal history, the abbey was one of the most esteemed in the kingdom.

It was only after we had ridden for at least two hours that I said to Brian, who was riding along side me at that point, "Is this the New Forest?"

"No," he replied. "The New Forest lies just south of here. That is where the men have gone to hunt."

I let out a sigh of relief and said, "Thank God! I should hate to be the latest victim of that fearful wood!"

"It was not the wood that killed the second King William, but a stray arrow."

"If you are about to say that my father fired that arrow, then I shall have you strung up for treason!"

That was a popular rumor in my day: that King Henry had won his crown by killing his own brother, or perhaps by paying someone else to do it. I would have none of it, though in truth I did not fear disloyalty from Brian and mostly wanted to see the look on his face.

"No such thing!" Brian assured me. "Every man of sense knows that William Rufus was mistaken for a deer."

"Good man," I concluded, and we both smiled.

"What I can tell you is that north of Salisbury are the ancient burial grounds of the heathen peoples," Brian continued. "Have you ever seen the stone circle?"

"Stone circle? Do you mean *Stanheng*, or rather *Stanhencg*?"

"Yes, exactly."

"No, I have not. I read about it in that book Robert gave me: *Historia Regum Britanniae*. A great deal of absurdity about giants and wizards. I did not set much store by it."

"You do not believe the island was settled by giants, then?" he asked with a wink, clearly attempting to have fun at my expense.

"Tell me, Lord Brian, have you ever seen a giant?" I asked.

"I see one right there," he answered, pointing ahead to Drogo.

I shook my head. "That is merely the result of good breeding and a constant supply of food. My own grandfather was quite tall."

"You never met him."

"I never met Julius Caesar either, but I believe certain things about him."

"I find it hard to accept that you do not believe in wizards after you spent so much time with Bishop Henry."

"If there is any real magic on this earth, it is the work of an angel or a devil. Now, why do you make my life difficult? I shall not allow such defiance once I am crowned!" I declared, holding my head high in the air.

For a moment he laughed, then catching his breath again, he said in a most serious manner, "I already count you as my queen."

"Do not say that too loudly!" I warned him, looking around nervously. "If anyone over hears …"

"Who is there to hear in the middle of the forest?"

"You know what I mean."

He smiled. "Promise me some day you will go to see the stone circle. Perhaps you can hold court there."

"This is England, Lord Brian. Nothing is done out of doors unless one is content to get wet."

After pressing on in this manner for some time, we entered the great plain that covers much of Wiltonshire. Just before the setting of the sun, we finally sighted the town of Wilton itself. Here again I found a crowd waiting to greet me, but the archbishop of Canterbury was not on hand. We therefore enjoyed a pleasant evening in the halls of Wilton Abbey and readied ourselves to meet Archbishop Theobald in the morning.

By noon the following day, there was still no sign of the archbishop, so I said to Drogo, "Send a messenger to Winchester and have the men called back from their hunt. I had better set up court here." This he did without delay, which is more than I could say for the progress of the archbishop.

That evening, I walked over to the refectory for supper feeling quite tired. Whereas most of the monasteries I visited had special beds for noble visitors, this one provided me with a bed more fit for those who have sworn off the comforts of life. Alas, it was little more than a straw pallet. Oh, how I itched all night long from that thing! I need not add that my sleep was not what it ought to have been. As I walked into that chamber with its high ceiling, the arches of wood held up by two rows of columns, I suppressed a yawn and looked down both the long tables to find my brother seated among the crowd. Finally, I saw him at the end of the one on my right, not too far from the smaller table that held the barrels of wine.

I walked down and sat in an empty space on the bench across from him. Earl Robert was bent over a wood bowl full of venison stew, pulling bits of meat out with his fingers and dropping them into his mouth.

"Good evening, brother," I said.

He grunted in response, lifting one hand slightly to signal his greeting but not wishing to break from his feast.

Before I had a chance to ask for one, another full bowl was placed in front of me by one of the nuns.

"Thank you, sister ..." I told her, waiting for her to fill in the name.

"Mildred, my lady," she said, bowing her head.

"Could I trouble you for a spoon, Sister Mildred?" I asked.

With a quick nod of the head, she went to fetch one, and I turned back to address my brother. Between bites of stew, I inquired, "So tell me, Earl Robert, do you not think it odd that Theobald wished to meet here and not at Romsey Abbey? He could have saved himself a day of travel."

"Not if he is traveling farther west," Robert answered, picking up his bowl and taking a long drink.

I suddenly grew afraid, for the archbishop could have no purpose in the West except for a meeting with the usurper.

"Why should he need to do that?" I nevertheless asked, hoping that I might have missed another possibility.

My brother set down his bowl and let out a sigh. "Archbishop Theobald always uses great caution. He will not be quick to change his allegiance."

"But surely it is not a matter of choice: Stephen cannot be seen as a legitimate king whilst he rots in our keeping."

Here Robert laughed softly. "It is not that simple. Trust me."

"What are you implying, Robert?" I asked, attempting not to give way to my growing unease. "I am the rightful sovereign. It is just a matter of waiting for everyone to accept the truth. I know it will not be easy, but surely a man who has just been defeated in battle and sits in jail is not in a strong position. He would not be there if the barons had not grown weary of him."

Robert leaned in and dropped his voice down to a whisper. "I have received intelligence that William of Ypres is returned to

Kent, where he has joined with the false queen. With the men at their command, they have brought terror to the Southeast. This has emboldened the merchants in London."

I chose to remain hopeful. "But that is only because we have been held up in our progress. We already defeated the wolf of Ypres and all the rest in battle. Surely we can set them back in their proper place when the opportunity arises. Have courage!"

"I believe I have a bit of courage," he replied, his tone of voice suggesting his frustration, "but if you think Mathilda of Boulogne is like your other enemies, you are wrong. I would sooner ride against all the mercenaries in Flanders than that woman when she has put her mind to something."

"You believe the archbishop is working on their behalf, then?"

"They need someone to visit Stephen and make sure he is in good health," he replied with a shrug.

"But surely if Bishop Henry of Winchester stands against them, there is not much that can be done in any case. Or do you really think we are in danger?"

My brother took a moment before answering this question, lifting his bowl for another drink. This did nothing to make me feel better.

"I might not use the word danger," he explained, setting it back down. "Lincoln was never going to be the end. The fight for the crown is a long march rather than a quick race. We must win over the barons one by one. I have already sent out letters to those scattered abroad requesting that they come to your court and swear fealty to you. They have received many handsome offers."

"Offers? What kind of offers?" I asked, suddenly afraid of what I might have been committed to without my knowledge.

"Grants of land and the like. Royal demesne."

"I thank you not to offer such things without my permission!" I said so loudly that he backed off a bit.

"But … this is how we have always done things," he stammered. "You never had a problem with me making such offers before."

"Yes," I replied with a nod, speaking more gently, "but you always asked my permission before."

"Not always. At times there was no chance to do so."

"Well, you have had plenty of chances over the last few weeks. We have been in each other's presence more often than not."

As I spoke these words, I thought, *He never would have treated my father this way. He never would have entered agreements in the king's name without the king's consent. I hold the same authority. Why am I denied the same respect?*

"Sister, you must understand—"

"No!" I objected. "I am not just your sister. I am your queen. I thought that was perfectly clear. If you wish, refer to me as your lady, but I will have your respect."

Robert stared at me even as his breath came deeply. He clearly thought I was out of line, had lost my mind, or both, and he was pausing to avoid saying something that would cause further trouble. Slowly, his gaze softened and he was able to speak calmly.

"Very well," he agreed. "I beg your pardon."

"Granted. Now, is there anything else I should know about?"

He nodded. "I received a letter from King David of Scotland."

"King David? Why should he write to you and not to me?" I asked.

"Because he knew that you would be busy with other matters," Robert said, shaking his head back and forth in confusion. "Not everything is a conspiracy."

"Fine," I offered, sensing that he was likely right. "What did he have to say for himself? Has he repented for refusing to ride to our aid?"

"I would not put it that way. He has done much to help us, but he was forced to abide by the terms of the agreement he made with King Steph ..."

I shot him an evil look, at which point he quickly corrected himself.

"The false king Stephen. King David is our flesh and blood, my lady. He supports your rule."

"I hope so, for his sake," I said. "He has many lands in England on account of his wife. I'm sure he would hate to lose them."

Robert laughed, a response that did not seem proper. "We are in no position to be setting the rules in the North at the present time."

His laughter pushed me fully into anger. "How right you are! 'We' will not be setting any rules. I will be setting the rules. Is that clear?"

He squinted his eyes and breathed deeply once again. "What is the matter? I have never seen you quite like this before."

"You mean you have never stopped to listen."

"I am on your side! Why are you fighting with me?"

By this point, I was almost in tears, but I refused to let it show. "Earl Robert, all I desire is your loyalty and respect. You must treat me as you would a king."

"Even so, I am doing! King Henry was willing to take my advice. I hope you do not think of me as an evil counselor—"

"No, of course not."

"—because I truly have your best interest at heart."

"Oh, enough!" I said, throwing up my hands. "Let it be enough. I have no desire to quarrel any longer. We are both suffering from weariness. I for one am sorely in need of sleep.

Let us be done for the evening. I am off to bed, though it will not bring me much comfort."

"Suit yourself. I'm having more ale ... assuming that is permitted." Here he shot something like a glare in my direction.

"Come now! I'm not Beelzebub!" I objected.

With that, I made to stand up from the table just as Sister Mildred approached holding a metal spoon.

"Forgive me, my lady, I had to walk all the way over ... not that it was any trouble. Would you like this spoon?" she asked, presenting it proudly.

"Thank you, but I am afraid I've lost my appetite," I muttered.

With that, I returned to my private chamber, my shoulders drooping with the weight of the day. However, weary as I was, I did not sleep for some time. I simply laid awake, thinking over the words that had passed between my brother and me. It was not like us to fight in such a manner, and the pressure of the moment was likely to blame. I only hoped that the conflict would pass quickly, for one thing I knew for certain: I needed Earl Robert of Gloucester on my side.

The next morning, I awoke knowing that I was wrong. No matter how much I tried to avoid it, that conclusion was the only one I could reach. Yes, Earl Robert had annoyed me, but he had committed no serious error. Therefore, I faced the question of how penitent I could be without compromising my royal authority.

I made my way into the refectory again, where I saw my brother sitting with the abbot of Gloucester and two of the knights who had accompanied us. As I approached, they ceased their laughing and stood.

"Good day, Your Highness!" Abbot Gilbert said, and the rest echoed his sentiment.

"Well met, all," I replied. "Earl Robert, may I speak with you?"

He said nothing but gestured toward a corner of the room. When we were far enough away to have a small measure of privacy, I said, "I wanted to express my apologies for any comments I made in haste last night. I was weary from travel and these terrible beds they have here—not that that is a good excuse. Please know that I hold you and your thoughts in the highest regard."

"And I am sorry for any offense I might have caused," he began, but then added, "I just assumed that, since we are brother and sister, a certain amount of familiarity of speech was permissible."

I nodded heartily. "Of course, and I would not have made you keeper of the royal seal if I did not trust your judgment. However, as I am the sovereign, there must be no confusion in men's minds as to who is making the decisions."

"I certainly never meant to cause confusion, but also keep in mind, my lady, that you are still very new to all of this. You have been a fine consort for many years, but running a kingdom is different. Now is the time to lean upon the wisdom of those who have experience with these things."

I made my best effort not to let out a sigh. "I never meant to imply that I would not do so. We know each other, Robert. Nothing much has changed. However, I did not fight for the crown only to have others make the decisions for me. It is not you I worry about, but rather Bishop Henry, Archbishop Theobald, and the rest. All the nobles and men of the Church will assume that I am weak because I am a woman. I must prove to them that I am not."

"I agree, but be careful that you do not push too hard. These are still early days."

I felt once again like he was treating me as one might a small child. *I am not as ignorant as you suppose,* I thought. Nevertheless,

I said, "Very well. You may return to your food. I simply wished to calm the waters."

"Have no fear: we are on good terms," he replied.

It was at that very moment that Drogo approached and informed us that the archbishop's party had been sighted. Once they had all arrived and their possessions were stowed in the proper places, I requested that the archbishop walk with me down by the river so we might talk person to person. I do not think this idea appealed to anyone else, but when I explained to Archbishop Theobald that I merely wished to make his acquaintance before proceeding on to legal matters, he agreed.

We began our walk without speaking, for as it turned out, the archbishop was not a talkative individual; at least, he was not talkative in my presence. He stood about the same height as myself, with bright blue eyes and a face that was only beginning to show its age. I saw little of those eyes at first, for they were mostly cast down to the ground. I did not take this to be a good sign.

We made it three or four furlongs without saying anything more than, "Pleasant day, isn't it?" Finally, as we rounded a bend that led through a small wood composed mostly of elms and the odd hazel, I said, "My lord archbishop, as you are the chief ecclesiastic in our kingdom, it seems a shame that I am only now meeting you properly. I think I did see you once when you were prior of Bec, but the years of war seem to have banished a great many things from my memory. I have heard of your magnanimity, both as abbot of Bec-Hellouin and now as archbishop of Canterbury. Truly, it is a joy to speak with you!"

"And I with you, my lady," he replied, though he did not continue any further along that line.

I had foreseen that he would begin speaking to me of whatever was on his mind, but instead he was entirely mute. I could see that I would not be able to simply defer to him.

"Whence does your family hail?" I asked with a smile, attempting to spark conversation.

"I was raised in Thierville, near the abbey where I was to enter upon my sixteenth birthday."

"Ah, so not too far from Rouen."

"It is possible to ride there in one day, though most take two."

"Forgive me, I should have known these things. I was certainly aware that you were a Norman. I can hear in your voice that you were raised south of the Seine. However, you will perhaps remember that I spent much of my life elsewhere."

"Of course. There is no offense."

Once again, the only sounds were of our footsteps upon dirt and the squirrels and birds in the trees. The archbishop had not met my eyes with any of his comments. I searched for a new subject of conversation.

"And what do you enjoy reading?" I asked.

Here he looked at me directly with what might have been a degree of interest. "Mostly I reflect upon the writings of Bernard."

"I assume you mean Bernard of Clairvaux."

"Indeed."

Quick! I ordered myself. *What's the last thing I read by Bernard that I can commend?*

"I read his *De diligendo Dei,*" I told him proudly. "It was excellent."

"Yes, everyone likes that one," he replied, as if to dismiss my choice as common. He then returned to examining the path in front of him.

This time I also looked away on the pretense of observing some plant, and I am afraid I might have mouthed something not worth repeating. I then turned back and smiled.

"What is it about Bernard that draws you to his works?" I asked cheerfully.

"He follows the teachings of Saint Augustine."

"Ah, well, there was none greater than Augustine. I suppose we all can only hope to measure up to him."

Suddenly, there was a change in the archbishop's demeanor, and he launched into a speech that displayed the passion that had up to that point been absent.

"Brother Bernard also opposes that fool, Peter Abelard, who introduces heresy into our Church. Although Abelard is of my order and Bernard is a Cistercian, I say, let the white monk clean house! Let him rid us of this cancer! Abelard's work on the Trinity is nothing less than an abomination. If a man can fail at the beginning, when he is establishing the very nature of God, then what rubbish will he promote at the end? Such errors do not take place *in vacuo*. And to think that they infect the schools of Paris! The error of Sabellius must never return! I tell you, whatever men say about Fulbert, he was right to have that libertine gelded. Heretics must not be allowed to beget children, especially when they claim to be monks! Was it not enough that he was forced to burn his *Theologia* with his own hands? And now they still flock to him for his teachings. Why has Pope Innocent not condemned this? Thank the Lord that Bernard of Clairvaux walks the earth! He is the last thing standing between us and doctrinal calamity!"

"I see you feel strongly about this," I said, though that was putting it rather mildly. I was glad to have found a subject that interested the archbishop, but I also knew that if we continued in that vein for too long, I would be lost beyond all hope of recovery. The finer aspects of that mystery we call the Trinity were not well known to me, and I feared that if I said too much, I too might fall into heresy without knowing it. Fortunately, the archbishop sensed my lack of ease and offered a question of his own.

"Do you have a theologian you most prefer, my lady?"

This was something I had rarely considered, and I was pressed to arrive at a response that sounded somewhat intelligent.

"I am rather partial toward the late Anselm, your predecessor. He was my tutor for a brief time."

This answer seemed to please the archbishop, for he smiled as he asked, "And which of his works do you favor the most?"

"I am not sure. I simply enjoyed his company."

The conversation then ceased for so long that I was forced to ask, "Forgive me, lord archbishop, but I would hate to think that there was any ill will between us. I know we are relative strangers, and we need not be friends immediately. However, the fate of the kingdom is at stake, and I seek to work with you going forward, for the good of everyone. The support of the Church is of first import to me, not only for practical reasons, but also personal ones. My mother, Queen Mathilda, was a constant servant of Jesus Christ and patron of many noble causes. I seek to follow her example, and I hope that my reign will be one in which the Lord God is honored and the rights of the Church upheld, unlike the past few years. I believe we can be allies in this endeavor. I suppose I must get right to it: do you approve of my rule? Is there anything in my actions that you find wanting?"

I had granted him a perfect opportunity to make his views known. We were coming to the end of the woodland path and circling back toward the River Nadder. Several seconds passed before Archbishop Theobald finally spoke, and I did not like the suspense.

"All that has happened these past few weeks has taken many of us by surprise," he said, "especially those of us in the Southeast. I have spoken with the queen, and she is fearful for her husband's welfare, as any wife would be. We have heard that he is in Earl Robert's keeping at Bristol. Is that correct?"

"Yes," I replied, "and you may rest assured, for no harm has been done to him. We have treated him with the dignity that is his by right of birth. As soon as I am crowned and my rule is established, I am certain that we can reach an agreement as to Stephen's standing. Perhaps he will wish to return to the land of his wife, or maybe he favors his own county—"

"Empress Mathilda, I am sorry to interrupt, but we must proceed in the proper order," the archbishop said, raising his right hand. "I swore fealty to King Stephen, and when I make a promise, I do not abandon it lightly. I could not possibly think of crowning another until I had spoken with the king on this subject."

This was a most annoying reply. I attempted to tread carefully.

"I understand, lord archbishop, and if you seek an audience with Stephen, I will certainly support your wish. I share your concern for loyalty. That is why I have referred on many occasions to the oaths of fealty made to myself before the death of King Henry, which were then abandoned most cruelly and without thought—"

"I am sorry, my lady, but there again I must stop you. My predecessor in this office, Archbishop William, would not have anointed King Stephen had he not been certain of the justice of his cause. I am not denying that the king—now your prisoner—has done some harm to the Church and the law during the course of his reign, and perhaps it was the will of the Lord that he was defeated on the field of battle, but I simply cannot proceed with this most irregular coronation while we have an anointed king yet living who has not released me from my pledge of fealty. I pray you, do not ask me to do such a thing!"

We had made it to the river and walked along its bank. I stared briefly at its surface, on which the light of day danced happily, attempting to hold back my frustration. When I felt I had gained control of myself again, I addressed him.

"But surely, Archbishop Theobald, the matter is not quite as terrible as you make it seem. Bishop Henry was one of the chief supporters of his brother's kingship, and even he has now seen that it was built upon a lie and has offered allegiance to my person. If Bishop Henry and the rest of those present in Winchester have no scruples about this, then you need not burden yourself with guilt. I would never wish you to go against conscience, but surely you can see that England is changing and the right order of things is being restored."

"I see a war that has wreaked havoc upon this island and made it a playing ground for nobles while the common man sees his crops burnt and towns destroyed," he complained, the look in his eyes fierce. "Believe me, my lady, I pray daily for the end of this conflict, but unless it is ended in a righteous manner, it will only lead to another war in the future. I am filled with worry. Queen Mathilda is a most excellent woman. She has shown such love for the Church. If you met her, I am sure you would agree."

"I did meet her once," I offered, failing to mention that she had set her mother's dress on fire.

"Then surely you know what I mean!" he continued. "To think of her, lying awake at night, uncertain of her husband's fate. I am certain you would feel the same way if the count of Anjou was in danger—"

Think again, I mused.

"—but I do see which way the wind is blowing," he continued. "You have achieved a great victory, and I acknowledge it. Do not regard this as a final decision. Let me speak with the king, and I shall return with an answer."

We had made it back to the abbey, and I felt I had achieved nothing. What else can I say for the remainder of our stay in

Wilton? The archbishop continued to sing the same tune. At length, we let him continue to Bristol, and I helped myself to a bit more wine than usual.

Having moved my court to Wilton, I remained there for two weeks and allowed the men to enjoy the four legged fruits of the forest. The weather was fine for that time of year, the nuns showed us great hospitality, and as we were waiting upon the word of the archbishop of Canterbury, I saw no reason to make haste. After all, where was I to go?

The natural path would have been to Windsor, Westminster, and London, but that land was opposed to our cause. The false queen had set the wolf of Ypres and the dogs of Flanders loose upon the people of Kent. They hoped by this show of strength to strike fear in the heart of anyone who might consider swearing fealty to me. The two of them were powerful allies, having sprung from the same Flemish root.

I hoped to take my mind off these things by visiting the cathedral of Salisbury—Sarum as it once was. I also longed to see the *Stanhencg*, which was only a bit farther away. But alas, my captains wished me to stay at court, and when I finally induced them to grant me a single day's freedom, the weather which had been so fine since our arrival turned sour, so much so that it was not fit for man or beast to walk out of doors. Having missed my opportunity, I was brought low in spirit and had nothing left to do but fear the plots of the Flemings.

Soon it was Palm Sunday, on which we celebrate the entrance of our Lord into Jerusalem, and I was still wondering when I could enter my own capital. I marked the occasion in the abbey church, with the bishop of Ely administering the sacrament. We had only just left the church when Earl Robert and Lord Brian walked over toward me, bowed, and requested an audience. As I saw that my brother was holding a sealed letter in his hand, I was even more willing than usual to speak with them. There was a stone bench sitting off to the side, beneath a large oak tree. I sat upon it and said to the men still standing, "Very well. What have you brought me?"

"From the archbishop of Canterbury," Robert said, holding out the letter.

"As I suspected," I replied, taking it from him.

I broke the seal and unrolled it, allowing my eyes to pass over the words. About halfway through, I looked up and saw four eyes all staring at me eagerly, as if I were about to announce the winner of a cock fight. I laughed and continued to read all the way to the end, at which point I set the letter aside and simply smiled.

"My queen …" Robert began.

"No," I interrupted, "it must be 'my lady' at the present, or the archbishop will have you quartered."

"My lady," he tried again, "would you be so good as to share with your humble servants what Archbishop Theobald has to say?"

"He is thinking of joining the followers of Mohammad," I said, unable to keep my face from breaking into a smile.

"If you are jesting with us, then the news must be good," Brian reasoned.

"Yes, Lord Brian, as you have so cleverly surmised, we have cause to be joyful. Here, let me read what he says." Picking the letter back up, I recited, "'I found the king in good health, although he was a bit downcast on account of having been placed in fetters. This hardly seemed necessary, but the warden assured me they were only installed after he attempted to escape. I shall therefore withhold judgment on this matter. I spoke to the king and bid him seek his succor from the Lord during this time of great tribulation, for even as Daniel was delivered from the den of lions, so he may yet live to feel the sun upon his face. I explained to him the present situation in the kingdom, his wife's urgent prayers on his behalf, and my audience with Your Highness. I told him of everything that took place in Winchester, and that you had gained the support of the other bishops. Furthermore, I told him that I myself had been torn between two objects, wishing to acknowledge your own right by virtue of victory in battle, but having earlier sworn fealty to another. I begged him ease my conscience. The king was most gracious and released me from my oath, instructing me to act in whatever manner seemed fit for the times. He only asked that I should put in a good word for him with Your Highness, and that you might grant him mercy, for he grows weary of his bonds. I am therefore willing to lead your coronation in Westminster Abbey as soon as you have gained the support of the barons and established such a peace as would be favorable for such a ceremony.'"

"That seems about as good as we could have hoped for," Brian concluded.

"I agree," said Robert. "He still doesn't like any of us, but he seems content to bend the knee. Seeing Stephen locked up forced him to face the truth. What's even better, Brian has some news of his own for you."

"What's that?" I asked.

Brian smiled, clasped his hands together, and said, "My wife's cousin, Robert D'Oyly, is, as you know, constable of Oxford."

"Even so," I noted. "What of him?"

"He has written to me saying he now feels ready to transfer his allegiance to you, and he would be more than happy to welcome you to Oxford Castle whenever you wish to visit."

"Excellent!" I said. "That's it, then. We hold the entire Thames Valley—everything west of Reading, that is. We must still gain London."

"For that, we will need the help of Geoffrey de Mandeville, lord of the Tower," Robert explained. "As he goes, so goes London."

"I know almost nothing about him," I said. "What is his character?"

"Not good, to be honest," replied Brian, "but with all the lords we have on our side, we certainly have a chance to win him over. The forces of Mathilda of Boulogne are still despoiling everything south of the river. We must cut them off from the merchants in London and Flanders: then they will be trapped and starved. It should be simple enough to finish them off at that point."

"Simple?" I asked with some incredulity. "Since when is anything in this war simple?"

"What of an Easter court?" Robert inquired, changing the subject.

I sighed. "We don't really have time to arrange anything grand. Nevertheless, I should like to make some show of authority. Perhaps we should pay Lord Robert D'Oyly a visit sooner rather than later."

Just then, one of the grooms approached us and informed Earl Robert that a horse had escaped the stable and he was needed immediately. He therefore departed but not before saying, "Very well, then: Oxford. Let me know when it's arranged."

As I watched him run, I said, "I do not think I have ever seen anyone with as much vigor as my brother, and he is fifty years of age. I think he will still be riding into battle at eighty."

"Is fifty so ancient?" Brian asked.

"Oh, that's right," I replied, looking back at him. "I suppose you are over fifty now. I beg your pardon."

"You do not have to beg my pardon. You are the queen. You grant pardons."

"No one must hear you say that!" I scolded, hitting him with the letter.

This caused him to laugh, at which point I could not keep myself from laughing. When we had both recovered, he asked, "How are you doing?"

What a simple question this was, and yet I could not remember the last time it had been asked of me. Most people either did not care enough to ask or were not familiar enough to ask. Brian was one of the few who could claim both.

"I am all right," I answered. "Not exactly at peace, I suppose, but I am enduring. That's what we hope to do in life, no? Endure."

"Are you not happy to have achieved your aim?" he asked, tipping his head slightly.

"I have achieved nothing until the crown is on my head. I cannot pass on the allegiance of half the men in the kingdom. My sons need something real."

"They mean a great deal to you," he said solemnly, nodding.

The weight of memory fell upon my heart as I spoke again. "Well, I never thought I would have sons, or at least I doubted."

"I remember."

"Now they are what I live for ... but perhaps I set too much store by sentiment."

"No! You have a right to love your sons. If I had sons, they would be my everything."

"What about you, Brian?" I asked. "Are you happy?"

"I am happy to see you finally victorious. I am happy to be your servant." Here he bowed his head.

"Will you not sit with me?" I asked, patting the space beside me on the bench. "There is room."

"I think I had better not. Someone might see and suspect me of abandoning courtesy."

"Oh, good God! Is this what my life is going to be like now?" I groaned.

"I am afraid so, but fear not! You will adjust."

I closed my eyes for just a moment and felt the wind press lightly against my face. When I opened them again, I once again saw Lord Brian's eyes staring at me.

"What is it?" I asked.

"Nothing, my lady," he answered. "Actually, I was wondering, do you wish for me to bring my wife to the court at Oxford?"

As I considered his question, a number of thoughts raced through my mind. No, I did not want the lady to come to Oxford. I did not want to see her ever again. Even if she were an angel of heaven, she would always be associated in my mind with a period of hell: Westminster Hall, my father, the filthy floor, blood, misery. No, I did not want to see the lady of Wallingford. She was the living proof that for all those years, while I had been forced into a union with a pig, she had been enjoying the company of the only man who ever loved me as something more than a means to an end.

However, I could hardly say this to Lord Brian. I could not refuse to see his wife. After all, the lady herself was not at fault. If I refused, it might be clear that I had done so for personal reasons—at least, it might be clear to Brian. No, I simply had to request her presence, even if she was the symbol of everything that had ever been stolen from me in life.

"Of course I want her there!" I said with a smile. "After all, the castle belongs to her brother, and I would never refuse your wife after you have been so faithful to me. Why ever would you ask such a question?"

"I did not wish to presume," he replied. "This is your hour, not ours."

"Well, yes, you may bring her. Actually, I command that you bring her, barring ill health. Now, I must be off, for I have things to do. Forgive me."

"Of course! Thank you, my lady."

He bowed again as I rose to leave, and I quickly put as many steps between us as I could. My eyes were pointed ahead, but my mind was in another realm entirely. Not for the first time, I mourned everything that had been stolen from me in life: my mother, my brother, my freedom, my crown, and the man I loved. Rather than making it possible for me to do what I wished, it seemed that my elevation to the throne would place me in a harsher prison than ever before: one in which I would never be able to speak my true thoughts. Since I was a girl, I had been taught not to think those thoughts. I had been taught not to add fuel to the fire within … but the flames had only grown.

Even as I ought to have been blissfully happy, I found that I was filled with anger. One theft had almost been set right, but that caused me to remember others. My mother and brother would never return from the grave. I would never live a life on my own terms. The ecstasy I once felt within the arms of a man would never be mine again. I should have been smiling, but I cried. Indeed, I wept bitterly in the confines of my room, where no one could see. I wept and I cursed. The old torments were alive inside me, and all I wanted to do was fight. I bid the demons hush, but still they cried out within me. They were with me always.

X

I remember that spring like it was yesterday. As we rode through the wood on our way north to Oxford, we saw the forest floor covered in bluebells. How sweet they smelled and how fine they appeared! I asked Adela to fetch me some, and when she returned with a handful, I said, "Perhaps I should have you fashion a diadem from these. It would certainly improve my looks."

"But you are a picture of beauty, my lady!" she proclaimed.

"Oh, don't make me laugh! I am almost forty years old, and even when I was twenty no one would have mistaken me for Cleopatra."

"Who was Cleopatra?" she asked, her brow wrinkled.

"She was pharaoh of ... Well, it hardly matters. Let's just say she was handsome."

"Like Helen of Troy?"

I laughed. "Something like that."

I passed many hours with such conversation. The weather was pleasant enough, and the early bloom of the bluebells ensured that my eyes were not starved. This was rather convenient, for had I thought too long upon the purpose of that journey, it would have been anything but pleasant. We were going to Oxford, a city associated with kings, queens, and arrogant scholars. Perhaps you think me too harsh. It is a rather nice place, all in all, but by that time it was controlled by the House of D'Oyly.

Walter D'Oyly was the first to make that name great when he came over to England with the Conqueror. You need not remember him, for he features no more in our tale. He did, however, have two sons of some import: Robert and Nigel. The former left his estate to a daughter named Mathilda, including the honor of Wallingford. The latter passed on to his son Robert control of Oxford Castle. It was this youngest generation whose destiny was connected with my own in a painful manner.

Mathilda D'Oyly was married first to Miles Crispin, and when he passed on, she became one of the wealthiest widows in England. It was for this reason that King Henry arranged for her to marry Brian fitz Count. You will perhaps remember how that union left me in misery, so that I found myself disdaining the lady of Wallingford before ever I met her. Robert D'Oyly, the castellan of Oxford, was married to Edith Forne. She was once the mistress of my own father, by whom she had two children: Robert and Adeliza fitz Edith, both older than myself. Thus, Robert D'Oyly was made a cuckold before ever he wed the good lady. Everyone knew that the elder children in his house were sprung from the king's loins.

The D'Oyly family therefore brought back to mind all the ways that my father had wronged those close to him. Were it not for the sight of the bluebells and the robin's song, I might have dwelt on that pain, but nature itself seemed to bid me set aside my anger and look ahead to better days. After all, I had finally gained a small degree of freedom for myself ... or so I hoped, though I began to have worries on that score.

After climbing what seemed to be the hundredth small hill upon those moors, we finally saw the city walls of Oxford nestled upon the banks of the River Thames. The spires of the churches rose above the rest—Saint Frideswide Priory, Saint Peter in the East, Saint Michael of the Northgate, and of course, Saint Martin. On the western edge of the city stood the castle with its moat continually filled by the mill stream.

"There is a sight for weary eyes!" said Earl Robert. "Come, let us get you to the lord of the castle ere it is dark."

We crossed the lone bridge over the Thames and entered through the Southgate. Soon we were riding up Fish Street, which I was annoyed to discover smelled just as foul as I remembered from the one time I passed through the town many years before. A woman may forget sights, but she never forgets scents. The town had been decorated for my visit, and I must admit, it was very merry indeed. The first flowers of spring had been brought in to decorate every shop window. As we took a left upon Castle Street, I saw a man in the stocks, and even he appeared not entirely miserable. These all seemed like good signs.

Finally, we made it to the castle's moat, where the bridge was lowered for us. The wood planks groaned as they bore our weight, and for just a moment I remembered that I could not swim. *That would please them all if I fell in!* I thought, but immediately banished the thought. The portcullis ascended, and I saw a host of figures standing before me in the yard. Although Drogo attempted to help me alight, I nevertheless took a bad step and almost fell to the ground, resulting in a gasp from the crowd. Only my knight's strong arms saved me from complete humiliation.

Several people said at once, "My lady! Are you all right? Empress? Help her!"

"I am quite all right!" I said, pulling back from Drogo's grip and brushing the dirt off my right arm. I was so intent on making a good show, that when Drogo put his hand on my shoulder again to support me, I pushed it off and said, "I'm fine! Please, just stop!" I then saw a look of surprise in the eyes of those around me and recognized my mistake. Indeed, the good knight's eyes betrayed his pain at this rebuke. "Forgive me …" I started to say, but it was too late. The master of the castle had made his way over to my position.

Lord Robert D'Oyly, castellan of Oxford, baron of Hocknorton, was by that time a rather old man. He was small of stature and made even more so by the bend in his spine, which I assumed was due to his time of life. What little hair still clung to the crown of his head was either gray or white, depending on how the sun caught it. I did not doubt that his bones creaked every time he moved: he had that sort of look about him.

"Empress Mathilda, lady of the English!" he proclaimed with a wide smile that revealed a few absent teeth. "I bow before you and take your hand"—here he grabbed it without asking—"kissing it and offering to you my true fealty as a servant to his mistress." He did bow with some difficulty and kissed my hand with a flourish, leading everyone to clap.

"We thank you, Lord Robert, for your love and loyalty," I replied.

He then slowly returned to his feet and said, "Here are the children of my house."

This caught my interest, as I knew two of them to be my natural siblings.

"Here is my eldest, Robert, and his wife, Mathilda," he began, stepping aside to reveal them.

I looked into the eyes of this man Robert, who must have been ten years older than me, attempting to glimpse anything of my father. However, had you not told me that he was my brother, I should not have known it. He was not at all like Earl Reginald or even Earl Robert! The three of us all had the same nose as our father, but not so with Robert fitz Edith. I assumed he must have taken after his mother. His sister, Adeliza fitz Edith, at least had the same dark hair as the late king, but that was all that implied our common parentage. Hardly any of it could be seen under her habit, for she was a sister of the abbey of Osney and had no doubt been pulled away from her prayers due to the honor of my visit. In her small, dark eyes, I saw nothing of myself and would never have thought her my sister had I not been told as much.

After wishing them both well, I was introduced to the baron's natural children, Gilbert and Henry. They were a good deal younger: so much so that they hardly deserved the title of men. I greeted them each in turn. I then met a long line of local officials and persons of note, both secular and ecclesiastic. I was becoming quite weary of this when I suddenly recognized one of the faces. Indeed, it was as familiar as my own, though it bore far more wrinkles and a beard.

"Master Grimbald!" I cried before he had a chance to say anything. "I did not think to see you here!"

"I suspect you did not think to see me anywhere, for you likely believed me to be in heaven," he answered, "or did you think me in hell? Purgatory, perhaps? Well, in any case, here I am, still among the living."

"No, I only meant that I did not know you were in Oxford," I assured him.

"Yes, my lady. I have always lived here when not in the king's service. I was raised nearby, in the village of—"

"Sudtone. Of course! How could I forget? That was where I entered this world as well."

I looked the physician over from head to toe. His robes were not as fine as those he had worn in King Henry's service.

Indeed, he seemed to have adopted a rather odd look in his old age.

"It is so good to see you again," I continued. "Do you mind if I ask how old you are?"

"Eighty years young," he replied. "I shall be eighty-one ere the year is out." This last sentence was accompanied by a rather determined shake of the finger.

"My lady, if we make our way inside, there is food and drink made ready," the baron suddenly said.

"Very good," I concluded, then to the physician, I added, "It is so good to see you again, Grimbald. We must speak further."

We made our way across the yard, passing several dwellings of wood, until we arrived at the Tower of Saint George. It was connected to the wall on one side and the newly finished chapel on the other. The older keep stood high upon the motte. There were not separate inner and outer yards, but only the one. Whether that was the case in the old wood fortress, I cannot say. By the time of my visit, it was completed in stone, and they evidently had not felt the need for a true bailey.

"There is the larger hall for feasting," Lord Robert D'Oyly said, pointing to the right. "My own house is just there, but this tower is reserved for our most honored guests, which you are. Here you will reside and hold court."

One of Lord Robert's men opened the small wood door, and we had to duck to enter. There were steps leading both up and down, and the only light came from a single torch mounted on the wall.

"That is the way down to the well," the baron said. I was forced to believe him, for I saw nothing but darkness.

I ascended the stair with great care. The stones were not perfectly even, and I was afraid of falling once again. We passed one small window, then arrived at a door crowned by an arch. Here was an open room with a high ceiling. Windows above allowed light to pour in, and though the hall was only about fifteen steps across, or twelve as Drogo took them, it seemed larger on account of its brightness. A fire was burning in the hearth, and the whole place was quite nice.

There were also two smaller chambers in the tower. I chose one of them and began instructing Adela where she should place my things. Although I had little in the way of possessions for a sovereign of England, the collection had almost doubled with all the gifts I had received. Many barons were hoping to gain my good will, but they clearly were uncertain what one ought to send to a female ruler. I had therefore acquired over the course of two months a set of four lances for use in ceremonies, a chest full of furs, a bottle of oil with the scent of lavender, a wood carving of some saint—I would have believed anything from Saint Helene to Saint Cuthbert—a brightly illuminated book of hours, a set of quills for writing, and an ivory box containing cloves. I could only assume that they thought I would use the latter for cooking. None of these gifts were remotely helpful in our effort to put down the last remnants of rebellion, but a gift is a gift.

When the unpacking was well-nigh finished, I said to Adela, "Please, let me have some time alone to rest."

"Of course, Your Highness. I will just help the others in the hall."

She closed the door, and I was finally left in relative quiet. Sitting upon the bed, I allowed myself a moment of quiet contemplation. The only sounds came from the small window that overlooked the stream. There I could see directly down to the wall below. At length, I carefully removed the veil from my head and set it aside, then walked over to the basin to wash my face. As I was about to sink my hands into its depths, I saw my own reflection: a trick produced by the light from outside. For a moment, I simply stared at it. The sight of my own face was something in which I had never taken great pleasure. The sores I bore in my youth were finally gone, but there was little beauty in my features. It was for this very reason that I usually avoided mirrors.

With a sigh, I plunged my hands into the water and threw it upon my face, then groped for a cloth. When I had dried my eyes, I suddenly had a great yearning to let my hair down, for my scalp was itching ever so much. I reached up to undo the braids pinned to my head. Not for the first time, I wondered what the point of having such long hair was if no one but Adela ever saw it in all its glory ... or lack thereof.

I suddenly remembered something that made me laugh. My father had long hair in his youth and was quite proud of it. This was before God saw fit to make most of it fall out. All the nobles favored this style. After all, the ability to keep one's hair looking halfway decent was proof that the person in question could afford to bathe, and everyone prefers a man who bathes. Naturally, certain members of the clergy objected, saying that the rich ought to join the poor in their lack of hair, the better to promote their salvation. Of course, many of those bishops and abbots were living quite nicely, but that was beside the point. Never one to set much store by religion, my father refused to let anyone command him what to do with the hair on his head or his face, and all who dwelt on the subject were not welcome in his presence.

Then one day, as the king was attending Mass along with the rest of his court, the preacher launched into a fiery sermon against the excesses of tresses. He quoted the words of Saint Paul: "Does not nature itself teach you, that if a man has long hair, it is a shame to him?"[19] He raised a great pair of scissors and exhorted the nobles, "Who among you is fool enough to

---

19   1 Corinthians 11:14.

disobey the command of the Lord?!" He then approached the king directly, looked him square in the eye, and said, "My lord the king, I beg you, for the sake of your eternal soul, allow me to cut off your hair!" Well, there were not many men who ever induced my father to do something he did not desire, but the hearts of the nobles were seized by the preacher's words, and had the king refused, he would have appeared the worst of sinners.

So it was that the king suffered a humiliation fit only for the worst of criminals: to have the hair shorn from his head before a cheering crowd. Once the men saw that the king himself had undergone this torment and survived, they began offering up their own locks to the preacher's scissors, and within the hour, they were taking pride in their humility rather than their hair. My father never forgave that man, and within the year, his tresses were mostly restored. I laughed to think that the Lord's will had surely been done—not in my father losing his hair, but in forcing him to bow to the will of another.

In the present, I continued to pick at my own hair with a comb. More than once, it became stuck, and I cursed under my breath. Having finally satisfied myself that there was nothing more that could be done, I fell upon the bed and let out a great sigh. I closed my eyes and attempted to relax every weary part of my body. It was at that point that I discovered my need. With a sigh, I rose and reached over for the pot to relieve myself. As I was doing so, my serenity was interrupted by the conversation of two guards outside. This would have been of little interest, but I soon recognized that they were speaking about me. Apparently, they did not know I could hear them through the window.

"It's strange, don't you think—a woman ruler?" asked one.

"Not only strange," said the other. "It goes against the laws of God! A kingdom ruled by a woman: that's a curse and no mistake. Did you see how she treated that knight of hers? It's true what they say. She has more pride than any man, and none of the good sense."

"That's the truth, and no mistake. I heard she forces men to call her 'queen' even though she's never had a coronation. Even when the king is still alive!"

"Ah, poor King Stephen! If only his men hadn't abandoned him."

"The worst of it is, now our wives will be getting ideas—like they can order us around too. The tyranny of the female is upon us. Ballocks! Just look at their forms, and you can see they're meant for birthing children, not ruling kingdoms."

"Let me tell you, I did look at her form, and there wasn't much to see."

"Does she even have breasts? You would think a woman like that could afford to at least stuff something where her bosom ought to be."

"I can only imagine what she had to do to get all those great lords to support her."

"Oh, she's had most of them, for sure. Why else would they be doing her bidding? That's what I always say: if there's a man who bows to a woman, she's having him and no mistake."

"I don't know. I might if she was up for it."

"Oh, take it back, man! I can find you ten whores on Cornmarket who would give you a better lay than that. Hell, you'd be better off spending the night with me!"

By this point, I was so enraged that I could listen no more. I dropped the contents of the pot out the window. There was a pair of anguished screams from below—"You might have warned us!"—and I knew I had done the thing well.

I let the pot fall to the floor and sat upon the bed. I was deeply pained by what I had heard.

"Men!" I growled. "All men are wicked! Why do I even try to please them?"

Tears ran down my face. The anger seemed to be leaking out of me: breaking out of the realm of the mind and into that of the physical world. I buried my face in the bed, beating my fist against it in vain. At some point, sleep took me.

"My lady!" Adela cried. "Empress Mathilda! Are you all right?"

I struggled to break free of my slumber, rubbing my eyes.

"Yes, it was just a dream," I assured her.

"It sounded like you were in pain."

"It was a nightmare," I replied, still attempting to adjust to my change in situation.

I sat up and saw that the sky outside had turned dark.

"How long was I asleep?" I asked.

"Never mind that! What happened? Can you tell me about your dream, or would you rather not discuss it?"

"It is nothing to trouble you."

"It seems to still be troubling you, so tell me."

She was by that point seated on the bed beside me, the look on her face most earnest. I sighed and rubbed my eyes again, trying to decide whether to tell her of what I had seen. At length, I said, "I saw … fire. Fire burning all around me, and yet I felt … cold … as if I had never known a summer day. Yes, it was snowing …"

"Snow and fire together?" she asked, raising her brows.

"I never claimed it made sense. Yes, everywhere I looked there was snow, and everywhere I looked … fire. I was in this castle! That's what I came to recognize. It was as if I had awoken into a frozen fire storm."

"But you didn't—not really," she said, as if I needed to be assured of the fact.

"No, of course not. It was a dream."

"Well, that is certainly odd. Was there anything else?"

I struggled to remember, then caught something. "Yes, actually. I heard cries ... cries rising up all around me. They were calling out in pain and torment."

"Perhaps you were dreaming about hell," she said, her tone deadly serious. "Do you fear it? They say we often dream of what we fear."

"No, it did not seem like hell. It was surely this castle, as if no time had passed."

"So, what did you do?"

"What do you mean?" I asked, growing weary of her inquisition.

"In the dream! What did you do?"

"I ran, or at least I tried to. Everything began to shift. I wanted to get as far away as possible ..."

"Naturally ..." she said with a nod, attempting to goad me further.

"But I was running here and there, unable to escape the flames. I was horribly afraid. Then I heard something else: a voice calling to me. It was as familiar as my own."

"Who, my lady?" she asked, eyes wide.

I had a sudden fear that I might have revealed too much, and so I demurred.

"No. I think I'd rather not say. In any case, the voice said, 'Come, Maud, come!'"

"And did you?" she whispered.

"I don't know," I whispered in return. "You woke me."

"Oh no!" Adela wailed, holding her head in her hands. "Now we shall never know how it ends!"

"I wouldn't worry about it. Not all dreams are prophecies."

"But some are, and perhaps the Lord hopes to warn you that the fire will escape the hearth!"

I rose and grabbed her by the hand, walking her over to the window. "Look!" I commanded. "There is no sign of snow out there. We are closer to summer than the depths of winter. There is nothing to fear."

"Then why is there concern in your eyes?" she asked, pointing as if to accuse.

"Because I am a queen, and queens are always full of concern."

There was a knock at the door. We both swung our heads round and called, "Who is it?"

"Drogo, my lady," he answered.

"I am not quite ready," I said. "Give me a moment."

Adela quickly made work of my hair and set the veil and fillet in place. She then departed and allowed the knight to enter. He was carrying a letter in his hand.

"Who?" I asked, pointing at it.

"From the bishop of Winchester. He has summoned the ecclesiastical lords to a council in a week's time. He also summoned the men of London to attend, for they shall have to give their consent as well. The earl of Gloucester already opened his copy and told us all."

"The tradesmen may believe it is their right to choose the sovereign, but such a thing is nowhere written," I scoffed.

"Be that as it may, they will make their best attempt to influence the situation, I should think. Well, I'll leave it here for whenever you wish to read it," he said, setting it on a small table in the corner. "The feast is about to start. They wished me to tell you."

"Very well. Just give me a moment alone."

"As you wish."

When he had closed the door behind him, I took a deep breath and attempted to calm myself. I was still smitten from the conversation I overheard earlier. I wondered how many of the men around me shared those beliefs. How many of them thought I was in my position against the will of God? How many of them mocked me behind my back in such a profane manner?

"Set these things aside, Maud," I whispered. "You must not let them see your pain. You must not let them exalt in your weakness. Show yourself strong."

With a confidence greater than what I truly felt, I strode out into the hall. There were about thirty noble persons in attendance, all of whom stood as the steward cried, "Her Royal Highness, the Empress Mathilda, lady of the English!" Humphrey was his name: one of the family de Bohun. The poor man had asked me earlier if I wished to be referred to as countess of Anjou in addition to everything else, and I told him, "Better not, or they shall throw me out immediately."

I made my way to the seat upon the dais, which I suppose you could call a throne, but it was just an especially nice chair. Then again, what is a throne if not that? I sat up straight and laid my arms on either side, allowing my hands to hang loosely. This was a regal pose that had the added benefit of drawing attention to the rings on my fingers. If I could not impress them with my face, perhaps they would be awed by this show of wealth. In truth, I had hardly two coins to put together, as you well know, but I still maintained some of the jewels from my time in the empire—gifts from my first husband.

The rest of them began to sup, but I was not to eat that night. Instead, I took only sips of wine while the nobles came up one by one to bow and offer assurances of loyalty. It was a rather small court, for I had not demanded that all the nobles attend. To do so would, I feared, draw attention to those who refused to answer the call. We were still very much in the realm of the practical at that point.

I believe it was at this time that I made my knight, John fitz Gilbert, keeper of the royal seal. Perhaps it was the day after— my memory begins to fade. I do remember very clearly another meeting that took place. After seeing off the matter of two locals fighting over where to place a mill, I looked and saw that the next couple approaching were the lord and lady of Wallingford. I had imagined this moment many times and considered how best to approach it. Its near arrival filled me with dread, but I took a deep breath and once again bid myself remain calm.

Lady Mathilda of Wallingford was dressed that night in a lovely green gown with gold thread. Even though she was far older than myself, I did not doubt that she was one of the more handsome women in the room. She clung to her husband's arm as they walked forward, and when he gave a short bow, she dropped all the way to her knees.

"My lady, Empress Mathilda!" she said, rising to her feet. "It has been far too long since last we met!"

"That is has. We thank you for attending our court here at Oxford," I replied, noting that as in our earlier encounters, she was quite happy to speak before her husband.

"I did hope we would welcome you at Wallingford by now, but the war being what it is, I understand why you could not come."

"Hopefully we will all be able to meet together there soon," I told her, though in truth I was not eager to visit.

"Whenever my husband is at Wallingford—which is not as often as I would like, not that I fault him for his service to Your Highness—but whenever he is with us, he so often praises you, that I almost feel you are among us even when you are not!"

"What a great pain that must be!" I said, feeling suddenly nervous. "I do hope it is not quite as bad as you say. I suppose it is only natural for a knight to praise his sovereign, but Lord Brian, I permit you to speak of me less if it grants your poor wife some peace."

Both Lord Brian and his wife clearly wished to reply to this, but it was the lady who again won the day. "No apology is necessary, my lady! We are both your most humble servants. It is right for him to praise his sovereign, as you say. I am only too glad that God has granted our kingdom a ruler so worthy of praise. Forgive me for my foolish words."

Here she bowed once again and remained with her face pointed down at the floor. This allowed me to look at Brian for a moment, and I could see that he was uneasy. He was not the type of person who would ever want you to know that he felt so, but I read it in his features. I therefore said, against every natural inclination in my person, "Lady Mathilda, please join me here on the dais and we can have a proper conversation, woman to woman. Lord Brian, I thank you once again for your loyalty to me and to England."

As Brian returned to his seat at the table, a chair was brought out for Lady Mathilda. She carefully gathered up her garment and sat down, allowing the train to drop to the floor, even as I observed that this was a conversation for which I had no desire whatsoever. Alas, there was nothing for it. I had committed myself.

"Thank you for joining me, Lady Wallingford," I began. "I find myself often starved of good female conversation."

"Oh, the honor is all mine!" she said, smiling broadly as she was wont to do. "You are, after all, the rightful sovereign of this kingdom, and thus to speak with you is a great privilege."

"I am exceedingly thankful that your cousin has hosted us here at Oxford. I hardly need inform you that yours is one of the chief families in the kingdom, and when the last allies of the usurper hear that we are gathered here, they will know what it means."

"Oh … What is that, my lady?"

"Why, that the reign of error has come to an end! That the cause of right has won the day. The rule of law will be returned to England once again. It will no longer be governed by the Beaumonts and the Flemings, but those who by their royal blood are connected to England's past, present, and future. History. Continuity. These are the things that matter to me and to all men of good sense."

She nodded her head, still smiling. "Yes, I'm sure you are right. You are so very wise, but I suppose you must have been taught by some of the greatest minds in Christendom. For myself, I can only read a little in our Norman tongue and nothing in Latin. I confess, I do not even know half of what the priest is saying during the Mass! It does not trouble me though: it gives me a sense of peace to simply let the sounds cast themselves over my ears. Perhaps that is what you mean by continuity?"

Oh dear, I thought. *Women really must be taught.*

"Yes … maybe," I muttered, then changed the subject. "I am sorry for where your castle is placed, Lady Wallingford. You have seen much hardship, being so far to the east and near the usurper's den."

"Oh, do not worry about that!" she cried, touching my arm lightly. "My husband, Lord Brian, is skilled in battle. His men look up to him in everything and would follow him anywhere. Of course, he is skilled at many things. He keeps so many books in his library: books upon books upon books. Before the war, he would read deeply. He wished to become an expert in the old Roman law. He also wished to know about the different trades so that he might understand the dealings of the London merchants. And of course, he read the scriptures daily. It is hard to be the wife of a man like that. For myself, I can only claim a real interest in music. I am not much of a singer myself, but I do love to make pilgrimage to the monasteries and hear their chants."

"Which one have you enjoyed the most?" I asked, attempting to be polite.

"I once accompanied my husband to Malmesbury Abbey. He wished to visit their library. I was able to listen to the monks singing their prayers. Such perfection I have seldom witnessed! But I must be boring you with all this."

"No, not at all. Continue."

"My first husband was not a lover of books or music. He was most happy with a weapon in his hand. He had come over with the Conqueror. I think that was how he always viewed himself: as a warrior. He sought to gain more lands and pass them on to his sons. I was young. I had never been touched by a man before, and his touch was … rough. Not cruel, exactly. Well, I suspect he knew little about women. Perhaps he thought I would behave for him like a bow and arrow. Then when he found I was barren, he wanted nothing to do with me. Of course, I mourned him, as any good wife would. I wished to join the nuns at Ramsey Abbey for the improvement of my soul. I should have been content in that life, but who would have taken my lands then? So, I lived alone for almost … well, it must have been most of twenty years! Then I heard that the king wished to marry me to Brian fitz Count. When we finally did wed, it was difficult at first. I could tell he was trying, even as I was, but he seemed sad … no, grieved. I knew it was because I was not with child. Finally, I told him that it was unlikely we would ever have children. I wept as I spoke the words. But he said to me, 'There is no need to cry. I wish that God had seen fit to grant us a child, but we are nevertheless blessed to live on this earth. Let us dedicate our lives to helping others.' Such wise advice! After that, I felt at peace, and things were much better between us. He allows me to do what I wish. My lady? Is something wrong? Oh dear, I've said too much! This is too personal!"

Indeed, my eyes had grown moist, but I quickly replied, "No, no. Forgive me. I am just weary from travel."

In truth, I had wished her to stop for a very long time. What a strange woman! She must have been the exact opposite of myself. Here I was, attempting to keep all my thoughts inside, and she was only too happy to give them to a stranger. It was clear that Brian had never spoken to her of those months we spent basking in one another's love. That was surely for the best. I could not think whether to pity the woman for her lack of sight, or to envy her ability to find the good in everything and keep no secrets from the world.

"What about you, my lady?" she asked. "Have you been happy in marriage?"

"I will be happy when we finally get to London and the kingdom can be at peace," I answered.

"Of course. Oh, look! They are starting the dancing! Will you join?"

"I think I prefer to sit and observe, but I hope you enjoy it."

"Thank you, my lady."

By the grace of God, she then departed to take part in the mirth. My eyes scanned the room and I saw Lord Brian standing off to the side with a pint of mead in his hand. A shiver of guilt ran through me, and I was about to consider it when I suddenly recognized that my brother had sat down in the abandoned chair.

"Robert, you scared me!" I cried.

"Lost in thought, eh?" he said with a smile.

"Well, there is much to think about."

"Mmm hmm ..."

"Oh, shut your mouth!"

He began to laugh so loudly that I smacked him and said, "Shut it!"

"Yes, Your Highness. Whatever you say, Your Highness."

One or two people were looking at us oddly, so I quickly changed the subject.

"Tell me about Geoffrey de Mandeville."

The smile departed from his face. "What do you wish to know?"

"What kind of man is he? What does he want? What is his weakness?"

"As a man, he is a swine. What he wants and his weakness are one and the same. His father incurred a large debt when he was constable of the Tower of London. A prisoner of some import was able to escape ... or perhaps was allowed to do so. King Henry was most displeased and levied a large fine against him. Not only that, but the king also held back the lands in Essex that ought to have been passed down from Geoffrey's grandfather. Thus, the family was deprived of its wealth and they had little honor left. It was Stephen who returned all those things to him. He made Geoffrey earl of Essex in addition to being constable of the Tower. It is because of Stephen that he is wealthy and powerful—"

"But now Stephen sits in a prison cell."

Robert nodded. "Precisely."

"So, his wealth and power are in doubt."

"He will want you to confirm the grants that Stephen made to him if he is to transfer loyalty."

I leaned back in my chair and sighed. "It is a pity that we should have to work with such villains, but we must have control of London."

"And there is no controlling London without controlling the Tower, which he has in his power."

"I hate my life!" I moaned, staring up at the distant roof.

"This is the business of governance."

"Yes, thank you," I said, looking back at him. "I know. I've been suffering through it since childhood."

"There's no need to get upset."

"I am not upset. Not really. I just ... I don't know."

For a moment, we sat just listening to the music. My feet felt sore just watching the dancers. I saw Philip of Honfleur standing alone off to the side, looking even sadder than myself. Could he have attempted to woo Adela and it went poorly? I was too afraid to ask and suffer my maid's ire once again. I looked over and saw that she was in conversation with the lady of Wallingford, happily laughing and drinking. *At least she seems joyful,* I thought.

Then I noted another young woman sitting at the same table. She was most attractive and rather merry. She was the daughter of a baron—I prefer not to speak his name—and had joined our party back in Winchester to help Adela. Her eyes continued to drift toward a certain point and she cast smile after smile in that direction. I suddenly broke out of my daze and understood that she was looking just to my left. I turned my head slowly and saw Earl Robert sitting there, smiling back. He even winked at her.

"Robert …" I said quietly.

"Yes," he answered, without breaking his gaze.

"Have you bedded that lady?"

The look on his face changed immediately and he turned to grant me his full attention.

"What?"

"The young woman over there," I said with a nod of the head in her direction. "Are you sleeping with her?"

He did not answer but looked at me very directly. His expression was not so much one of anger as of pain.

"Please …" he whispered.

"Yes or no?"

His eyes returned to the woman. She was no longer smiling but seemed to note the concern in his face and reflect it in her own. Without looking back at me, he replied, "Yes."

I immediately rose from my chair. My brother grabbed my arm, eyes wide, and said, "Are you going to tell Mabel?"

"Find a priest, Earl Robert. I cannot help you."

With that, I broke free from his grasp and made to leave. He called out to me, "Where are you going?!"

"To the chapel!" I cried. "I have an urgent need to pray."

After the Easter feast, some of the nobles dispersed, and I attempted to suppress the feelings of frustration within me. Earl Robert, Lord Miles, Earl Reginald, and Earl Baldwin all remained in Oxford, but Lord Brian and his wife returned to their nearby home, and most of the clergy departed as well. The month of April was spent sending messengers back and forth to Bristol, Winchester, and London. Bishop Henry's council was to tell the tale: if he could induce the Church and the Londoners to support me, there would be nothing to keep me from marching to Westminster and having the crown placed on my head. However, this was not such a simple matter for the bishop. Having argued for his brother's right to rule six years earlier, he would be forced to make the unhappy argument that he had been out of his mind.

I tried not to worry too much about the result of the council and instead went to visit the lodge at Woodstock with its collection of creatures. My brother Reginald begged me to let him have a shot at one or two of them, but I refused. There I spent some pleasant afternoons in conversation with Grimbald, who was still working as a teacher and physician in the city. I could not imagine how he was able to do so at such an advanced age. The man clearly had iron in his bones.

It was also at this time that I dismissed the young lady who had lately become the pet of Earl Robert and sent a letter to her father bidding him marry her off as soon as possible, or else send her to a nunnery. I had no desire to grieve Lady Mabel by reporting her husband's misdeed. After all, she knew well enough that he had children with other women. No, apart from sending the young lady away, I had no intention of doing anything in response to my brother's actions, but it did make me quite angry. I did not know why it upset me so, or perhaps I did and was unwilling to admit it.

As I sat waiting at Woodstock, the council meeting began in Winchester. I have my account from William of Malmesbury and others. On the seventh before the Ides of April, Bishop Henry called the council to order. He had wisely chosen to hold it in his official capacity as papal legate, with authority from Pope Innocent himself. Thus, he was able to include the archbishops of Canterbury and York without ceding the slightest bit of authority. How it must have pleased my cousin to have the bishops, abbots, and archdeacons in England flocking to his call! After speaking with most of the main players in private, the bishop of Winchester addressed the whole assembly in his cathedral the following day.

"My ecclesiastical lords, you know what pain it has caused me to call this council, for I desire only peace in this kingdom, and far too long has it been absent. When King Henry departed this life—May the Lord have mercy on his soul!—I was ready to honor the oath that I made to his daughter and chosen heir. However, England was without a ruler, and all was confusion. We heard many rumors about the empress. Some said she did not desire the throne, while others swore she was under the control of her husband, the count of Anjou. From the empress herself, we heard nothing, and we were made to fear the worst. Therefore, as we had waited so long for a sovereign who delayed coming to England—for she resided in Normandy—we provided for the peace of the country, and my brother was allowed to reign. And although I gave myself as surety between him and God that he would honor and advance the Holy Church and uphold good, but abolish evil laws; yet it grieves me to remember—indeed, it shames me to say—how he conducted himself in the kingdom: how justice ceased to be exerted, how peace was annihilated almost within the year, the bishops made captive and compelled to give up their possessions, the abbeys sold, the churches robbed of their treasures, the counsels of evil men respected while those of the virtuous were totally despised. You know how often I addressed him, both by myself and on behalf of the bishops, especially in the council held last year for that purpose, and that I gained nothing but hatred. Everyone who thinks rightly must be aware that I ought to love my mortal brother, but that I should still more regard the cause of my immortal Father. Therefore, since God has exercised his judgment on my brother by permitting him, without my knowledge, to fall into the hands of the powerful, I have invited you all here to assemble by virtue of my legation, lest the kingdom should fall to decay through want of a sovereign."

Well, that was a pretty speech to start things off! He attributed his decision to support Stephen not to an error of judgment, but a simple lack of information. He stressed the damage done to the Church and the laws of God, knowing that this was the very thing that would unite his audience in censure of the usurper. He abandoned any talk of what King Henry had said and when. He spoke not of birth rights, nor even the blood of the ancient kings, for almost all the men there were Normans who cared little for the sentiments of the common folk and their history. He had aimed his arrow at precisely the right spot and released it with the skill of a trained archer.

At that point, no objection was raised. I am told some even clapped. Our greatest fear was that Archbishop Theobald of Canterbury would go back on his promise of allegiance, but he said nothing, despite his hatred of the legate. No, everything was going well. Had Bishop Henry not been a son of the Church, he might have made his fortune selling wares from town to town, for such was the strength of his appeals. The council decided as one to lend its support to my rule and crown me queen of England.

Had it ended there, all would have been well ... but it was not the end. No, it was only the beginning.

It was then that the Londoners were called into the assembly to discuss the process by which my coronation would take place. So powerful were they that Bishop Henry declared them to be almost nobles despite their common blood. You will remember that it was the London merchants who first lent their support to Stephen when he turned traitor and crossed the Channel to seize the crown. These were men who valued their trade with Flanders above all else: even the will of God. When the bishop attempted to speak to them about the coronation, they avoided the matter at hand and declared their concern for the usurper who was in prison. Was he doing well? Had he been given enough food? Would a deal be made for his release?

This was all rather beside the point of the moment, which Bishop Henry tried to stress by repeating the same speech he had made the day before, adding this: that Stephen had only shown favor to the Londoners that he might drain them of money. I do not know how true this was, for it seemed to me that the merchants never paid their fair share and that Stephen was as much at their mercy as they were at his. Nevertheless, the argument was made. The Londoners did not reject the will of the council, but withheld judgment on the matter for the moment.

Then Fate delivered a mighty blow. A man arrived from the Southeast: Christian, a clerk of the false queen Mathilda. He had not been summoned, but came anyway and marched right into the assembly, taking everyone by surprise. I can imagine the gasps that must have escaped from their mouths, even as they turned their heads to witness the spectacle. This Christian walked directly up to the bishop of Winchester holding a scroll above his head.

"This is a letter from my mistress, the queen!" he cried, spinning around to look them all in the eye. When he had come full circle back to the bishop, he waved it in his face and said, "Read it!"

Well, Bishop Henry had certainly not foreseen this. He attempted to solve the problem by declaring his authority.

"Young man, you have interrupted a council of our Holy Church, called according to the will of Pope Innocent himself! I will not allow you to march in here and make demands of this assembly! Hand the note to the archdeacon, and I will examine it later. Now, get you gone!"

Such a speech from the lips of Bishop Henry of Winchester would have struck fear in the hearts of most men, but the clerk would have none of it.

"Forgive me, lord bishop, but I come here on the authority of the crowned queen of England, who writes on behalf of her husband and your king! What she has to say directly affects this council, and if you refuse to read it, then I must."

He then read out the message from his mistress, which I need not tell you was full of falsehoods. She claimed that her husband had been beaten and abused. This was plainly false. She furthermore claimed that he had been denied food, which was also false. Worst of all, she declared that Stephen was the greatest champion of Church reform. We have seen that the only way he wished to reform the Church was by forcing it to bend to his own will. He never gave anything to the bishops that he did not take back and then some.

It was a letter that made Stephen out to be suffering the tribulations of one persecuted for righteousness. Of course, his behavior was in no way righteous, but by this point, she had left the realm of reason and was treading the path of fools. Last of all, she stated that as an anointed king, no one could remove her husband from his place but God Himself, and that all those who denied this were traitors. Such an argument might have been made by the English upon the arrival of my Norman grandfather and his army, but evidently the lady paid no heed to this irony.

The princes of the Church saw through these words, for they well remembered how Stephen had moved against their brethren. However, the Londoners were stirred by that old loyalty they held to the House of Boulogne. Here I must state once again that the trade with Flanders was their chief concern, and the port city of Boulogne was the gate to that county. They thought not in terms of right and wrong, but pounds and shillings. The council therefore ended with the agreement of the bishops but no conclusion with the Londoners, who returned to their city feeling that they had been ill treated along with the king and queen. Of course, they would have thought the same thing if a raindrop happened to fall on one of their heads. Some men will seek any opportunity to be offended!

I was not at all surprised to hear this news. London and the Southeast were the home of Stephen's greatest supporters. They would not change allegiance unless those who ruled them more closely did so. The false queen and the wolf of Ypres were pressing against them from the south, and the earl of Essex watched over them from the Tower. At least one must yield in order to sway the Londoners, and it was clear which one that must be, for the Flemings would fight to the death before bowing the knee.

Thus ends my account of Bishop Henry's council as it was passed on to me from those who were in attendance.

As the month of April came to a close, Earl Robert encouraged me to move closer to London so that we could apply greater pressure. We were not yet able to enter the city itself, but we could make a show of power somewhere near enough to reduce the travel time for our messengers and put us in position to invade the Southeast if necessary. I was more than happy to do so, for as you know well enough by this point, there are few things I hate more than waiting around for things to happen. I much prefer to be in the center of the action, where I may hear all the news as soon as possible. I therefore accepted the offer of Abbot Edward of Reading to visit his monastery, which was about two days' ride from Westminster. However, I did so more out of necessity than desire, for that was the site of my father's grave, and I knew the visit would be difficult.

Why did I not long to look upon the final resting place of my father, the great and mighty king of England? Because that was not how I remembered him. Great and mighty he may have been, and my father he was most assuredly, but his life was also marked by occasions of great cruelty, as more persons than myself could testify. There had been no real affection between us. Indeed, the thing I felt most in his presence was fear—a fear that waxed and waned throughout the years but had defined our bond in the end. Even though he had been dead for years, the idea of being near him again caused my skin to tingle. But I could hardly say this to the men around me, who thought only of how such a visit might benefit our cause.

"People will remember that he appointed you as his heir," Lord Miles argued, and in the end that argument won the day.

We chose to travel by boat down the River Thames, which required us to be parted from the horses for a time. This was a danger, but it showed how bold my captains had become. I had never sailed on that portion of the river before, and it felt very much like returning home. I longed to see Westminster, for it was there that I was first sent away from the home of my youth, and I greatly desired to enter the palace once again as ruling sovereign, finally free to live out my days in the place I loved. As soon as we took control, my boys could come to my side. I imagined how their childhood would be: very different from my own, and hopefully better.

When we finally reached the confluence of the Thames and the Kennet, we turned into the smaller river and came at last to the abbey. The center tower of the church of Saint James rose up against the gray sky, and beyond a pair of towers crowned its western front.

There lie the bones of my father, I thought. *Be strong, Maud. Have no fear. What harm can he do you now?*

The entire community was surrounded by a stone wall that appeared better for maintaining quiet than keeping out invaders, for it lacked the slots for archers common in castles. Abbot Edward was there to greet us as we dropped anchor at the east gate.

"The monks of Reading welcome the lady of the English within our walls!" he said, as I set foot on land.

"I thank you for your hospitality," I replied simply. I would have spoken more words, but my mind was elsewhere.

We made our way past the dormitories and around the church until we came at last to the guest house. As we did so, I continued to think of my father. Yes, Reading Abbey was one of his foundations. He had always intended it to be his place of burial. A daughter house of the great abbey of Cluny, it had continued to flourish under the patronage of Queen Adeliza, who had since become the lady of Arundel Castle. I myself had enriched the abbey with the gift of the hand of Saint James, after which the church was named. Yet, the hand of King Henry as it landed upon me again and again was chief in my thoughts.

"Do you wish to visit the church immediately?" the abbot asked, as soon as we entered the reception hall of the house. "I am sure you wish to pray at the grave of the late king. Is that not why you have come?"

"Of course," I lied. "Just not at this moment. I will go later today. Thank you once again. You are kind."

With that, he departed, and I tried to sleep, but what rest was there to be had when my mind was so restless? Those bones seemed to cry out, taunting me.

At length, I decided to put an end to my misery by going to the church then and there. I allowed Earl Robert to come with me: after all, it was his father too. Others offered to join us, but I refused them all. The two of us made our way along the short path from the guest house. It was raining ever so slightly. Is it odd that I remember that? We passed a hawthorn tree and a company of monks in their black habits. They bowed before me, but I paid them no heed. My mind was fixed on a single point, and nothing could distract me from it. With each step, my pulse increased.

We finally arrived at the west entrance, where the doors were open wide. We passed beneath the twin towers and into the nave, which was as large as any I had seen in a monastic church. Oddly, the place was empty, save for one poor monk sweeping the floor. When he turned and saw us standing there, he had a bit of a fright and dropped his tool.

"Forgive me, Empress Mathilda, Earl Robert," he said. "I was made to believe that you would be coming this evening."

"No, it is our fault for not sending word," Robert replied.

The fellow then attempted to make conversation, but given that I was nervous, I said nothing and simply clung to my brother's arm. When it seemed that the discussion was not going to end quickly, I cleared my throat rather loudly, and Robert asked for the place to be emptied that we might worship in private.

"You do not wish to take the Eucharist, then?" the monk asked.

"No, just to pray," I said quietly, offering my first words.

"Very well," he replied, bowing three times on his way out.

I heard the doors shut behind us, and then there was nothing at all.

"Are you well?" Robert asked.

"Of course! Why wouldn't I be well?" I asked, my poor humor clearly showing.

"Oh, I don't know. You just seem to be gripping my arm rather tightly."

I immediately let go and stared forward at two objects. The first, which sat just to the right of the high altar, was the reliquary containing the hand of Saint James: the one that Drogo and I had brought back from Germany many years earlier. I might have laughed at the memory of our theft, but I was far more concerned with the object directly in front of the altar. There sat a monument of black marble.

"Is that it?" I whispered.

"Yes," he said simply.

Slowly, I began to approach the grave one step at a time. I suppose there was no other way to walk, but my steps were quite deliberate. Each one brought me closer to the last remains of the man by whom I was born and under whose rule I had lived my life. The memories began to return in a flood, from the day he shoved me in the carriage and separated me from my beloved mother for ever, to the first time he held little Henry. It was all coming back faster than I could truly think the thoughts. One memory seemed to overshadow the rest, standing out among all the unhappy ones.

Get up! I heard him shout in my memory. *I command you: get up!*

Tears began to form in my eyes. With each step, I felt the blows raining down. I saw the fury in his eyes. I could almost taste the blood.

If you will not move, then I will have to break you, he spoke again in my mind.

I shuddered. It was as if no time had passed. I could feel his spit on my face and smell his foul breath.

I own you!

Those three words spoken in anger represented everything that had passed between my father and me. Some times he treated me well and other times poorly, but always he treated me as the means to some greater end. Did he love me? No, surely he despised me! And yet he wished me to be queen, for that was the only way for his descendants to sit upon the throne. His faith was not in me, but my sons.

I was by that point standing directly before his grave, or perhaps I should say directly above it. Robert was walking over to light a candle, but I barely noted him. I knelt upon the stone floor, as unyielding as King Henry himself. I clasped my hands together and closed my eyes. I could hear Robert kneeling down next to me.

"Lord God, receive the soul of our father, King Henry, into heaven, and grant him forgiveness of all his trespasses," Robert prayed.

Trespasses: there was something my father never lacked. Yes, he had established the law and settled accounts, bringing an end to the evil days of William Rufus, but there was always a cost. No one bore that cost more than the women around him. My poor mother, whose bed he abandoned, never knew a moment's peace. She had loved him and given him all of herself. Into his arms she placed a boy who was born to rule: a boy who was so cruelly snatched from the world before his time.

"Do you have anything you wish to say?" Robert whispered. "Do you want me to go on praying?"

I opened my eyes and looked down at the marker on the floor that read "*HENRICUS REX*". That was the name by which he would be known to history. I knew him as the tyrant who controlled my every waking moment—who left me with an immense task but denied me what I needed to accomplish it. He gave me the greatest titles a woman could receive but none of the privileges of a common man. He had forced me into marriage twice but had never once spoken of me with love in his heart.

"Maud? Empress Maud? What do you wish to say?" my brother asked.

As I continued to stare down at the grave, tears running down my cheeks, I took a deep breath and said, "Damn you! Damn you to hell!" I then turned to Robert and said, "Will that suffice?"

His eyes were wide with alarm and he evidently knew not how to respond. I did not wait for him to think of something. I arose, walked over to the hand of Saint James, kissed the case, then turned and left.

XI

I often hear scholars say that women are composed of too much phlegm to truly grow angry. We are the gentle receivers of male action, our weaker bodies the subjects of honor by which we fill the world with love. Within our wombs, we carry the power of goodness, and our breasts provide salvation to men. Of all the beauties in creation, we are the greatest. Why then should the fire of anger mar that beauty? If men are warlike, then we are the guardians of all that is fair.

What rubbish! A man thinks a woman's womb makes her quiet because he has never witnessed a birth. If men have reason for anger, we have far more! We come into this world screaming, crying for release. They tell us, "Hush, child!" That is the beginning. For all our days, they tell us, "Hush! Be quiet! What good will it do?" And they are right: it does no good. This world was not made for us. Life itself dismisses us before our time when we strive to do the one thing for which they will reward us. How many scores of women have entered this world with a cry and left it listening to the cry of another? This is our curse.

The ancient Romans understood this. Mars was the god of war, but only Minerva burst forth from her father's head clad in armor and ready to do battle. Thus, all men feared her. I often felt that I had something of Minerva's spirit, but none of her ability. Even so, was I doomed to live with these thoughts inside me: this dreadful anger seeking release. Like Brünnhilda, I wished to conjure a fire. I would have perished in the flames simply to watch the world burn around me. Such was my anger, and it was all I could do to contain it, for life always bids us remain quiet. "Hush! What good will it do?"

When I knelt at my father's grave and cursed him, I can tell you what good it did: I felt strangely powerful. Though queen in all but name, I had felt impotent. I could neither speak my mind nor give a single command without someone complaining that I had overstepped the bounds. Instead, every man sought to command me. My right was not recognized for what it was. No, I had to go to each one begging, pleading for them to accord me the honor that was my due. The closer I came to my final goal, the more they seemed to close in around me, like a swarm of kites awaiting my demise.

I tell you this so you will understand what happened next. I am no saint. You have read about my mistakes, and they are many. Will you judge me kindly? Imagine what you would have done.

My whole life, I tried to please others. What did I not give for the sake of my children? What command of my father's did I break if it did not violate the will of God or simple reason? You must remember this, for what I will tell you now brings pain to my soul, and on account of it I still question myself. But perhaps I could have done no other, for life made me what I was, even as it continues to make me what I am.

After I had visited the abbey church at Reading, I returned to my guest chamber and remained there until the following day, when I made my way to the refectory to eat with the monks. I was in good spirits. It was midday, the sun was shining, and all seemed fair. When I arrived, Abbot Edward greeted me and brought to my attention the code of silence observed at that time of day, which I assured him I would respect.

There were four long tables there for all the brothers. I had come with only Drogo. Without speaking a word, I sat down at the only empty table, and he took a seat on the other side. The monks then began to come by with wine, cheese, fish, berries, and venison stew made especially for my visit. Every man, it seemed, knew it was the food I loved most. I was halfway through this feast and about to break bread with my knight when I heard the door open with some force. This caused every person in the refectory to look up at once and see the earl of Gloucester's entrance.

Just as quickly, most of the monks turned their eyes back to the food, perhaps afraid of the earl's presence. For his part, Robert looked at me directly—with force. I could see that he was in a foul mood, and when he walked in my direction, I began to envy the monks who avoided his gaze. He was within a few paces of me when the abbot happily blocked his path and whispered to him, evidently informing him of the law of silence.

"But I must speak with the empress," he said rather loudly. The abbot then whispered something else, to which Robert replied, "No, it cannot wait! It is a matter of great import."

The abbot continued to protest, but as I did not wish him to be the subject of Earl Robert's annoyance any longer, nor to cause further offense to the monks, I rose from my seat and said, "I will speak with the earl outside."

Drogo began to rise, but I held up my hand and he remained on the bench. I then made my way out the door, lowering my eyes to avoid Robert's gaze. I entered the garden in the middle of the cloister, where there was a fine oak tree. Taking my stand in its shade, I looked in all directions to make sure no one else was present, then said to my brother, "What is it, Earl Robert?"

"What do you mean, 'What is it?'" he asked with a glare. "Are you forgetting what happened yesterday?"

I did not like his tone one bit, so I decided to be difficult.

"It rained," I said simply.

"You know very well what I mean! In the church ..." he cried, stammering in his anger. "You all but spit upon the grave of King Henry!"

"I fail to see the problem."

"How could you say those things?" Robert asked, moving closer to me. "How could you curse him so?"

I continued calmly, refusing to join him in his upset. "You wanted me to speak to him, and that was the only thing I cared to say."

"Do you think this is comical?!"

"No."

"Do you have no respect for the dead?!"

"Those whom I respected in life, I continue to respect in death, but that man is not worthy of my respect."

My brother shook his head in wonder. "He was your king! He was the one who appointed you to the position you now seek to hold. Where is your gratitude?"

Those words finally provoked me to raise my own voice. "Gratitude?! Do you remember anything about him?"

"I knew him better than you did! I rode into war with him. I was every day at his side. He was my father! He was also yours, and you would do well to remember that."

"Trust me, Earl Robert, there is nothing of which I am more painfully aware than the solemn truth that King Henry was my father. However, he was also one of the foulest creatures I ever knew: a violent man who thought of nothing but himself."

"Such an unjust conclusion! Are you forgetting how he built this kingdom into a thing of greatness? Men everywhere praised his wisdom, his power, his achievements …"

I nodded and attempted to restore some calm to the situation. "I do not deny that he had a certain ability to get things done, but I think you are forgetting how he treated me."

"All kings marry their daughters off to foreigners."

"Not to spoiled brats barely out of their mothers' wombs who are so inferior as to reduce the dignity of this house! And it is not just that, Robert. You know very well that he never loved me."

"Oh, of course he loved you!"

"No!" I cried, raising a finger. "He loved you. He loved Stephen. He loved the Beaumont twins. He may even have loved Brian. He loved Prince William more than life. I was just … there. I was in his presence, but not his love. He treated me like a slave to be commanded."

"We were all his subjects to be commanded."

"Ah, but there is a difference between a subject and a slave! Subjects are not usually beaten except for cause, and even then, not within an inch of their lives."

"That happened one time," he replied in a tone of complaint.

One time? One time?! Could I be hearing him right? Was he really trying to excuse the worst thing that had ever been done to me? Did he think nothing of my bloody wounds—of the hand that grabbed my womanhood and still reached across the years to declare its possession of all that I was? I wailed from the deepest part of my soul, "Once is enough, Robert! Once is enough!"

I was hurt and confused by my brother's lack of pity given what I had suffered. He had been a source of strength for me in those dark days, but suddenly he was acting as if my wounds were nothing. It pained me even as it stoked a fire inside me. I burned.

"You are only angry because he didn't let you marry Brian, but that was never going to happen," he continued. "No king could have allowed it. If you think marrying the count of Anjou was a humiliation, that would have been far more, and I say that as his friend."

"This is not about Brian," I said, but when he scoffed, I added, "This is not only about Brian. King Henry said he wanted me as his heir, but he refused to grant me the castles that would have allowed me to rule."

"What does any of this matter?" Robert asked, crossing his arms and bending forward in his frustration. "You do not put a curse upon the dead. It is not Christian."

He may have had a point there, but I was not about to accept it.

"Yes, well, maybe I'm not a very good Christian, but neither are you," I told him.

"Wait … is this about what happened in Oxford, because you swore we would speak of it no more!"

"No, Robert. I have lived in this world for a while now. I accept that you're going to have your … recreations."

"At least I keep them in check. You must get control of your temper."

It was my temper that was the problem, not the injustice that had been done to me. Surely that was what he had said. I was utterly consumed.

"Who are you to command me?!" I cried. "Don't you know that you hold your earldom from my hand?"

By this point, Earl Robert's face was quite red, and his voice took on a new and chill tone.

"Are you … threatening me?!" he spoke slowly. "After everything I have done for you?!"

I could see that I may have gone too far and opened my mouth to explain when another voice called, "My lady!"

We both turned to see Lord Miles coming out of the refectory with Earl Reginald close behind. Both Robert and I attempted to gain control of ourselves.

"What is it?" I asked.

When he reached our position, Miles looked at each of us in turn. He seemed to sense the hostility, but as we said nothing, he offered, "There is a garrison at Windsor that fights for Queen Mathilda—that is, the false queen and her evil companions. They have control of the castle, and I am afraid they will block our passage to London if we set out now. However, we should be able to hold them in check. It does not appear that the Flemings can make a charge at our position. They are too weak in numbers to pose much of a danger. We have also received word from your husband, Count Geoffrey. He has reached an agreement with Robert Beaumont. Both brothers acknowledge Geoffrey as lord of Normandy."

"What?!" I cried. "He was supposed to have them acknowledge me, or at the very least, Prince Henry. And what of England? Did they say nothing of England?!"

"That I cannot tell you," he replied, clearly afraid of angering me further. "All I know is that Earl Robert Beaumont pledged his fealty to Count Geoffrey. Waleran has pledged the same, but he remains in Worcester. If you ask me, my lady, they are hoping to split the two of you. My spies tell me that Earl Waleran is attempting to win the earl of Chester to his cause. They may attempt to seize the North."

"That bastard!" I spat as much as said. "And as for Count Geoffrey, I have no words. Yet again, he has made this about himself. Did he say anything about Count Theobald of Blois? Is he willing to pledge fealty to anyone but his brother?"

"There they did not reach a conclusion," Miles spoke quietly.

I let out a savage laugh. "Perfect! So, the Beaumonts have bought themselves some time, and we have gained nothing, not to mention we have a garrison in Windsor blocking our approach. God, what should we do?" I asked, looking vainly at the sky.

"What do you think, Earl Robert?" Miles asked. "You are quiet."

Until that point, my brother had simply stood there with his arms crossed, listening to what Miles had to say. He was clearly still upset by our earlier conversation. Just as he was finally about to open his mouth and speak, I heard a noise and turned to see my chancellor, John fitz Gilbert, running toward us from the refectory, yelling, "I have news, my lady, my lords!"

"At this rate, the monks will never eat in peace again," I muttered.

Lord John pushed his way into our circle and said, "We have word from the North, my lady! The king of Scotland is coming!"

"King David?" I asked, as if there were more than one.

"Yes, he is coming along with hundreds of his own men. The messenger left them near Lincoln, but they must be south of there by now."

"Did Ranulf actually let them enter Lincoln?" Robert asked. "The two of them are not exactly friends."

"No, he did not try, but the good news is that this holds Earl Waleran in place for the present time," Lord John answered. "My lady, the king is most eager to see his own niece crowned. He wished to know if you were still holding court at Oxford, but of course you are not. Where should we tell him to meet you?"

I looked at Earl Robert, but he gave no response. He really was quite angry. I therefore said, "Thank you, my lords, for all this news. Please allow me to speak with Earl Robert, and then I will inform you of my decision. Where is Lord Brian?"

"He told me he was going for a ride this afternoon," said Reginald. "I did not think you would need him, so I said nothing."

"Very well," I replied. "Thank you all. Just give us a moment."

The other three then departed, leaving my brother and me alone. He was not looking at me but staring off into the distance. I attempted to set my own anger aside and begin our conversation again.

"That is good that our uncle is coming down. This must mean he seeks to add his support to our cause. Are you not happy?" When he made no sound, I said to him, "Look, I am sorry that my words yesterday offended you, but I think I have a right to speak my mind. For God's sake, I will soon be the queen of England! If I am not allowed to speak, who is?"

"Fine, speak then, but you must also listen!" Robert said, finally looking me in the eye. "You cannot keep disparaging those around you. Men will judge you for it."

"Who have I disparaged?" I objected. "All I have done is seek to please Bishop Henry and Archbishop Theobald."

"Yes, but you openly rebuke your husband. How do you think that looks?"

This caused me to smile. "Oh, come now! You don't like him any more than I do! Moreover, you never complained about this before."

"You were not this close to the throne before," he explained, lowering his voice and moving closer. "Now everyone is watching you. You must show them that you can control yourself and act as a woman should if you hope to control them."

"'As a woman should.' Do you mean I should just do whatever the men around me command? What you command?"

"Don't put words in my mouth! I am trying to help you. Please, I beg you, accept my counsel in the spirit I intend it. I know these men better than you do."

"As you are only too happy to tell me, but you forget: I have some experience with these things as well. When I was married to the emperor—"

"That is not the same!" he said with great feeling. "You were a consort then. You were not exercising power."

For a moment, I simply stared at him, breathing heavily. I then asked, "What is this really about?"

"What do you mean? It's about what I said it's about."

I took a breath and offered up a dangerous question. "Are you jealous of me, Robert?"

"What?! No!" he scoffed.

"You were father's firstborn, and yet you were never considered as a possible heir. Perhaps it pains you to see a woman in the place where you yourself wish to sit."

"That is so unfair! If I did not want to see you on the throne, I would never have spent these years fighting on your behalf."

"Maybe that is why you think you deserve more. You think you did all the work. You think this is your accomplishment, not mine."

"Ballocks!" he cried, shaking his head. "There is no truth in any of that."

"Well, what is the truth then, Robert? I don't understand why you are so angry with me all the time!"

"I might say the same of you! You abandon reason."

"Perhaps I am seeing the truth for the first time! I swear to you, I—"

"Forgive me. I have heard enough."

He then turned his back to me and began walking toward the church.

"I did not give you leave to depart!" I cried. "Earl Robert, I command you: come back this instant! I'm not finished with you!"

There was not the slightest pause in his stride. I could hardly believe it. I need not tell you that to turn one's back on one's sovereign and walk away is a crime against honor. It is a thing that must never be done, and I suspected it never would have happened if I was a man. It was necessary for me to depart either through the refectory or the church. I had no intention of following my brother, so I made for the refectory.

As I passed through, I spoke to no one, though many pairs of eyes were on me. I reached the door on the other side and was about to walk through it when someone touched me on the shoulder. I swung my head round and saw that it was Lord Brian, still dressed for riding.

"My lady," he said quietly, not wishing to rouse the remaining monks. "Is something wrong?"

There was real concern in his eyes, and had things been different, I might have told him everything. However, I did not.

"I am perfectly fine," I lied.

I then set off in search of a place where I might crush something.

My hopes for a pleasant Whitsunday having been thoroughly ruined, I had to accept that I could not at that time push toward London but must return to Oxford. This seemed like an extraordinary waste of time and effort, but I nevertheless submitted to the idea. After all, my hand had been forced. My uncle the king of Scotland had elected to come south of his own accord, and I could not receive him properly at Reading Abbey. I therefore had no choice but to return. Lord Brian offered to host us at Wallingford, if only for a day or two, but as King David was already passing through the Midlands, speed was of the essence. At the first opportunity, we packed our things and returned to the boats, making our way back up the Thames.

I should have been happy to see my uncle, but my early hopes that he would serve as a strong champion on my behalf had been belied. His defeat in the battle of the Standard made a mockery of his bold claims. As it turned out, he was more inclined to safeguard his estates in the north of England than see me on the throne. Well, I knew it would be unfair to blame him for looking to his own kingdom first and the maintenance of his own house. However, that did not stop me from feeling let down—even betrayed.

As we passed through the gap between the Chilterns and the southern downs, I could not keep my mind from frustrations. The conversation with my brother still echoed in my head. Two days had passed in which neither of us spoke to the other. I had contented myself to sail with only Adela, Drogo, and John fitz Gilbert for company, along with the crew. In the ship ahead of me, I could see Earl Robert attempting to impress the knights by shooting at some poor doe that had wandered down for a drink. He merely gave the creature a fright, and it ran back into the safety of the trees. The men continued to yell at it.

"Idiots," I muttered.

"They placed all the ale on that boat," said Drogo. "Perhaps the men got into it."

"Oh, that is a certainty," I assured him.

I continued to stare at my brother. The more he smiled, the angrier I became. Who was he to decree his will to me and then bristle at my commands?

I knew what men were saying. I had heard the rumors: Earl Robert was king in all but name. He was the one who achieved our great victories. He had the love of many and respect of all. He was the ruler England ought to have. Yes, I knew they said these things, but I had never considered it a threat, for I trusted in my brother's loyalty completely. I believed we were united in our hatred of Stephen's misrule and our desire to see order restored. I had even been happy to share the glory with my brother, for I knew how much I was in his debt.

However, in those days of change, I was beginning to wonder if I had been wrong all along: if in addition to playing with everyone else, he was also playing with me. Perhaps he only wanted me on the throne because I was easier to control. Unlike Stephen, who dismissed Robert on account of his birth, I had always adored my brother, even when we did not agree. I had desired to reward him. Were these very desires the reason he sought to help me: so that I would enrich him at the expense of myself? Might he even seek to overthrow me someday? He may have loved me, but perhaps he had no fear of me. If so, that was clearly a danger.

As I continued to dwell on these thoughts and turn them over in my mind, Adela sat down beside me. "My lady," she asked, "is all well?"

"What?" I replied. "Fine. I'm fine."

"You do not seem fine. No, you must be rather upset. Are you missing your sons?"

I was glad she had struck at this subject rather than another and replied, "Yes, I do miss them. I have not seen them in … two years now. No, more than two years! I wonder if I would recognize them if I saw them."

"Of course you would! You are their mother."

"Poor William!" I moaned, shaking my head. "He was not four years of age when I left. Perhaps I would know him, but he would not know me. What kind of mother is that, Adela, who abandons her children?" Here I spoke of the guilt that haunted me night and day.

"You did not abandon them!" she assured me, placing an arm around me. "You came here to fight for their inheritance. Everything you do, you do for them."

"I try telling myself that, but at times I wonder if I truly know my own desires. There are days where I think of them less, not because I do not care, but because I am so overwhelmed with everything happening here in England. There are so many things that want my attention. Lately, I've been so ..."

Here I stopped to consider whether I should continue. Dare I speak the secrets that I kept inside? Adela was the closest female friend I had—perhaps the only true female friend. She was an excellent listener. I was therefore tempted to tell her everything at times. However, there was a gulf between us. I was an empress, soon to be a queen, and she was a peasant plucked out of nowhere to serve me. Most of the time, I failed to consider this, for we had become so familiar that we were almost like sisters. Yet, there were certain lines that I tried not to cross in our conversation, and I was coming close to one of them. After a moment of consideration, I continued.

"It's a strange and terrible feeling. I have these dark thoughts. They haunt both my dreams and waking hours. I feel a need to promote myself, and yet I loathe myself. I strive to carry on, but I have a fire burning inside me, and it threatens to consume me."

"What are you talking about?" she asked, dropping her arm, her eyes filled with concern. "Please, help me understand! How I wish I could comfort you!"

"Anger, Adela. I am talking about anger. It has plagued me at many times in my life, and it is very bad at the present. It is as if every crime committed against me from the first days until now has come back to visit me—as if the rivers of pain have reached a confluence. The wounds I thought had healed are open once again, and I am sinking: sinking in that flood, and I cannot swim to shore."

"Oh, my lady!" she said softly. "Who has done this to you?"

Here I found myself unwilling to go into it, so I simply said, "It is a matter of little import. The point is that I carry this burden within me. There are so many things I wish to say but cannot."

"But why can't you say them? Who forbids you to speak?"

"No one … and everyone," I whispered. "It is difficult to explain."

There was a loud noise. One of the drunkards had attempted to snatch a fish out of the water and missed by a furlong. He was on the verge of falling in, and the rest of the men were struggling to pull him back.

"Idiot," I muttered.

"I think you should tell them," Adela said.

"That they are idiots? That seems like a bad idea."

"No, I mean you should tell people when you are angry."

I laughed. "That is an even worse idea."

"But my lady, it does not do to keep things in! There they will fester and grow into something ugly. If someone has offended you to the point of misery, then you must let them know! Are you not the rightful queen of England?"

"What good would that do? If I speak my true thoughts, they will think me an even greater monster than they first supposed."

"Who thinks you are a monster?!" she asked rather loudly.

I cast my eyes down toward my toes. "I … I don't know. People."

"Perhaps it is not as bad as you think."

"Perhaps," I agreed, returning my eyes to meet her gaze.

"Well, I think you should let people know your thoughts, and thus release yourself from this prison of the mind. My mother always said it wasn't good to hold things in. That's why we were never scolded for belching."

I did not reply to this odd tale but allowed my gaze to drift from the boat just in front of us to the one trailing behind, which carried Earl Baldwin de Redvers and Lord Brian of Wallingford. The two of them were standing near the front of the vessel, looking in my direction. They waved at me, and I waved in turn. Earl Baldwin then departed to speak to someone else, and for a moment Brian and I simply stared at one another. Smiling, he mouthed the words, "How are you?" I made no answer.

When we arrived in Oxford, we dropped anchor and entered through the south gate of the town, approaching the entrance of the castle from the east. No sooner had I crossed the bridge, made my way into the yard, and been greeted by the lord of the castle, Robert D'Oyly, than he led me away from the others toward a wood hovel whose purpose I could not rightly guess. The ground all about was turned to mud, and I took no joy in stepping in it, but I did as my host bid. When we were out of sight of the others, he looked around in all directions, as if he was about to tell me something in greatest confidence.

"Lord Robert, what in God's name is going on?" I asked.

"Forgive me, my lady, but I thought you should know that the archbishop of Canterbury is here in Oxford."

"What?!" I cried, offended that no one had mentioned it. "Since when?"

"Since yesterday. He arrived with a rather grand party. They are staying at Frideswide Priory."

"Did he say why he is here? Why did he not inform me?!"

Lord Robert sighed and nodded, perhaps hoping to calm me. "As for why he is here, he said he wished to speak with you about the coronation. As for why he did not inform you, he did send out a letter yesterday by land. They may have passed as you sailed by. I am sorry for pulling you aside in this manner, but I was afraid of what would happen if you were informed in the presence of others."

"What were you afraid would happen?" I asked. When he said nothing, but simply diverted his eyes, I said, "Never mind it. Tell me what you wish me to do."

"I will take you to your chamber. King David should be arriving tomorrow. I am saving the other chamber for him."

"Is Archbishop Theobald here now?"

"No, my lady."

"Good," I concluded firmly. "I have no wish to see him today. Perhaps tomorrow ... for the arrival of the king."

"He had something he needed to tell you quite urgently. He refused to share it with me but was most intent that he should speak with you the moment of your arrival."

"Oh, for God's sake!" I cried, or rather wailed. "Fine. Call him over. I will speak with him at the tower."

This news did nothing to help my mood. As I made my way to the Tower of Saint George, I could not help but wonder if this was some plot on the part of the archbishop to throw me off balance. What was he thinking coming to court without a summons? Well, he might have come without a summons, but he surely ought to have sent word so I could have readied myself! After all, his visit would clash with the arrival of King David. I would have to accord proper honor to both without offending either. To make matters worse, Archbishop Theobald and I were not the best of friends. Indeed, I found him most annoying. His heart seemed to still be with the usurper and the false queen.

"Never mind it, Maud. Think calm thoughts," I bid myself.

Even so, the words of Adela were ringing in my ears. She had told me to be more forthright, and I intended to follow her advice. Archbishop Theobald had broken one of the understood rules, and while I desperately needed his support, I also had to ensure that I had his respect.

It was so hot that day that I bid Adela pull out my only silk gown, which was far lighter than those made of wool. She was about to put on my head covering when I said, "Adela, this heat will be the death of me! Can we not leave it be for once?"

"What? You mean … wear nothing?" she asked in wonder.

"Well, I am wearing a dress. That's something."

"But you are meeting with the archbishop. I do not mean to dissent, Your Highness, but I fear if you do not wear a veil, he will see it as impertinent."

"Why, oh why, is the hair on my head impertinent? I have to look at the hair on his head … or lack thereof."

"Yes, my lady, but you are a woman."

"Oh dear!" I mocked. "They'll have my head for sure!"

Adela did not respond, but simply stood there looking sad.

"It was a jest, Adela," I said. "Fine, bind me in whatever way you see fit."

"I could just attach the veil to your braids in the back."

"Perfect. Let's do that."

Five minutes later, I was sitting in a chair out in the hall, fanning myself with vigor. Only Drogo was there with me, for I had asked the others to leave.

"How do you remain civil in that armor?" I asked him. "You must be on fire."

"I think of something cold," he replied.

"And that works?"

"No, not really."

There was a knock at the door. It was surely the archbishop. I looked at my knight and said, "Do not envy me the task ahead."

He replied, "I never have, and I never will."

The door opened and Archbishop Theobald of Canterbury entered the room. He walked toward me and bowed, I gestured with my hand, and he returned to his feet. I then pointed to the other chair and he took a seat. In all of this, neither of us spoke a word, and he looked at me nervously. He may have wished for me to speak first, but I had no intention of starting. At length, he said, "Empress Mathilda."

"Archbishop," I replied with a nod, my hands clasping the fan in my lap.

"I am glad to see that our prayers were answered and you have arrived safely. I have been staying at the priory for three days now."

"I wonder that you did not inform me of this," I said.

"I sent out my messenger yesterday," he explained.

"That is not the point. You came here, I assume, to spring something on me, or to make a study of me. I am not sure which. Either way, I have not been given a moment to rest after my journey."

The look on his face was one of surprise and even incredulity. He started to laugh, then stopped—looked at the ground, then back at me.

"My lady, I am not sure what you want from me. I am of course deeply sorry for the inconvenience, but what I have to discuss with you is a matter of great import concerning our Holy Church."

The air seemed to be getting even hotter. I could feel the sweat on my back, but I dared not lift the fan again and reveal that I was a weak woman.

"Be that as it may, Archbishop Theobald, I am your sovereign, and I must ask that you request meetings formally rather than arriving suddenly and without being summoned."

The archbishop looked as if he was scoffing internally, but said to me, "Forgive me, my lady. I will attempt to abide by this rule in the future, though I am not sure why it concerns you so." I was about to object again, but he cut me off by saying, "You are aware that the bishop of Durham has lately departed this life."

"No," I said. "I have heard nothing of the sort." Indeed, I was surprised that I had not.

"Well, he has. I am not sure why no one told you. Perhaps you were busy with other affairs. In any case, Bishop Geoffrey passed away on the sixth day of this month: a week hence. Normally, it would fall to the sovereign to appoint a successor in accordance with the wishes of the canons and monks of Durham—"

"Indeed," I interrupted, hoping to prevent any contrary understanding from gaining ground.

"—but in this case, something else has happened. King David of Scotland came down from Edinburgh, stating that he wished to meet with you, but actually he invaded the see of Durham and refused to allow the burial of the late bishop until his own chosen man was installed as the new ecclesiastical lord."

"What?!" I stammered. "What are you talking about?"

He began to speak again a bit more slowly. "Durham falls within the territory controlled by King David ..."

"Yes ..."

"... and he wished to appoint a man who would answer to him, so he pressed upon the see his chancellor, William Cumin."

I was taken aback by this news. I could not believe that my uncle would be so bold as to usurp my authority in this manner, choosing a new bishop without the consent of either myself or those in Durham. Although I had tried to contain my anger, it was rising once again.

"I am glad to hear that he did this without the consent of Your Highness," the bishop continued, "for I would hope that you would allow me to counsel you in such matters."

I laughed, drawing a frown from the archbishop, who protested, "I do not see what is comical about this."

"Do you really wish to know?" I asked.

He seemed uncertain, but quietly replied, "Yes."

"You, archbishop! Here I thought you were pained to see my authority usurped by another, but you are merely offended that you were not allowed to choose the next bishop of Durham yourself. But that see is not in your realm! It is under the authority of the archbishop of York."

This upset the archbishop greatly. "My lady, I understood that you supported the primacy of Canterbury over all of England! Do you mean to tell me you do not?"

"No, that is not what I meant. I just do not see why Durham should concern you so."

"Because I wonder that the king of Scotland did not tell you. More than that, I wonder that the earl of Gloucester did not tell you!" he prodded. "Are they serving you, or are you serving them? My lady, I know that we are not the best of friends, but I think you know very well what I desire and where I stand. I desire the maintenance of order, the promotion of the Church, and mercy for the defeated. I want what God wants. Do you know what the men around you want? It seems that even your kin wish to promote themselves at your expense."

His words tore into me like sharp claws. It was as if he had seen the doubts that burned within me and sought to provoke the fire. Actually, this may have been exactly what he wished to do, but all I knew in that moment was that the anger was about to spill out of me, and I could not sit there any longer.

"Forgive me, archbishop," I said, rising up and letting the fan drop on the seat. "The heat is getting to me. I feel rather faint. I think I need some fresh air and a chance to gather my thoughts."

"Of course," he replied.

I took my leave of him and walked toward the door, where Drogo stood guard.

"Let me through," I commanded.

"My lady," he whispered, "where do you intend to go?"

"It is none of your concern where I intend to go!" I snapped at him. "Now open this door!"

He obeyed, and I raced down the stair, through the portal, and out into the yard, where several of the knights were practicing with their weapons. As I scanned the crowd with my eyes, I was seething with bitterness.

Look at these men! I thought. *None of them respect me, and Robert ... Robert, who I thought was so true ... He has used me ill. I must teach him to fear me before it is too late!*

My eyes finally came to rest upon the form of my brother, who was locked in a battle with one of the younger knights. We may not have spoken in days, but I was about to renew the conversation. I made my way through the throng until I neared his position.

"Earl Robert!" I cried.

He looked up from his work, and when he saw the expression on my face, he stopped the fight immediately and removed his helm.

"What is it, my lady?" he asked, out of breath.

"Did you know?" I asked, boiling with anger.

"Did I know what?"

"The bishopric of Durham. Did you know? Did King David tell you what he intended to do?"

"He appointed someone, then? I told him to wait until he spoke with you."

"And you didn't think to tell me?!" I cried loud enough for everyone around to hear.

"I was going to."

"When?! When he arrived? After he left? When?!"

"Calm down," he bid me quietly, walking a step closer. "People are watching."

"No, I will not calm down!" I yelled all the louder. "That's what you would like, isn't it? For me to sit in a corner and be quiet! For me to let you make all the decisions!"

"It was our uncle who made the decision," he corrected me.

"Yes, and it was not his to make, nor was it your right to withhold information, but I see now that you do not fear me. You think me a weak willed woman: a tool by which you may achieve your own ends."

"And what do you imagine my ends are?" he scoffed.

"To rule! You want to be king yourself!" I charged, pointing a finger in his direction.

He fell back a few steps, as if my very words had pushed him. He was shaking his head in dismay. "What on earth …"

"You will seek to control me, and then my son after me. Maybe you will seek to supplant us both. Well, why not?! After all, the men love you far more than me. It is you they follow into battle. So, why not?"

"I will happily bow the knee to you, but I will not accept these false accusations!" he cried. "I will not allow you to slander me openly in front of my men!"

"Your men! See, you think this is all about you. Well, Earl Robert, you must know that I am the one who will wear the crown! I am the one who will rule! If you cannot accept that, then I shall have to cut you loose!"

His eyes grew wide. "You wouldn't dare!"

"I surely would! After all, what are you? A bastard, that's what! You are not fit to sit in my place, Robert. You are not fit to wear my crown!"

I looked into his eyes and saw deep pain there. In my state, I took it as a good sign. I was a woman possessed by my anger, and I was no longer content to remain quiet.

I turned around to address all the men there and said, "This man is not your sovereign! I am your sovereign! Remember that!" I then looked into Robert's eyes and said, "Give me your knife."

Here was the second sign that ought to have served as a warning: he did not object. He reached for the knife strapped to his belt and handed it to me without a word. I should have stopped, but I had a further point to make. I grasped the thing with my left hand, then placed my finger upon the point of the blade and allowed it to pierce my skin. There was a gasp from all the men and a great deal of murmuring, which was fortunate, for I had not accounted for the amount of pain this action would cause. I believe I might have let out a slight groan, but no one heard it. I raised my hand into the air. The blood was running down my finger.

"Do you see this?" I asked Robert. "This is the royal blood of the houses of Wessex and Normandy! This is my claim! No one else has the royal blood. Some pretend. Some make due with half. But I am the only one, Robert! You must know that no one has the right to rule this kingdom but me and my sons! I will not be usurped by anyone: not by Stephen, not by the bishops, and certainly not by you! Next time you think to go behind my back, remember this! Remember what you are and what I am!"

Suddenly, a voice behind me said, "Stop this!"

I turned and saw that it was Brian. He was looking at me as he never had before. His very face reproached me. For the first time, I felt the cold shudder of doubt.

"I was just ..."

"I know," he said. "Please, I beg you ... stop."

In that moment, it was as if a veil fell from my eyes and I saw clearly. The anger was gone, and all I knew was fear. I looked back at my brother, then down at my bloody hand, which was shaking. There was terror coursing through my veins.

"Oh, dear Lord," I whispered. "What have I done?"

Before I could say anything more, Robert announced, "If you despise me so much, then I will take my leave. Men, as you were!"

"Wait!" I cried. "Robert, wait!"

He did not reply, but continued walking. I made to follow him, but Brian caught me from behind and restrained me.

"Robert!" I called, my eyes filling with tears. "Robert, I'm sorry! I'm so sorry! Come back!"

"Let him go," Brian whispered. "Let him go."

I dropped to my knees in the dirt. Brian wrapped his arms around me.

"Please! I must speak with my brother! I must make things right!"

"Just be still. Breathe."

"He will never forgive this. I know it. I've just been so angry. So very angry."

"I know. Trust me, I know. Just breathe. It will pass."

"It hurts so much. I can't believe how much it hurts!"

"Yes ... yes, it does. Be still. Breathe."

He continued to hold me as I wept. I am sure that all the men thought I had lost my mind.

"Let's get you inside," Brian said, but I did not care whether I stayed or went. I was so ashamed, I hardly knew what to do. All I could say again and again was one phrase.

"Forgive me. Lord, forgive me. Robert, forgive me. Forgive me!"

"*Ave Maria, gratia plena, Dominus tecum ...*"

I stroked the bead with my thumb, rubbing it upon my wounded finger.

"*Pater noster, qui es in caelis, sanctificetur nomen tuum ...*"

Shifting it to the right, I moved to the next one—the next one, the next one, the next one.

"*Gloria Pat* ... Oh God! I hate myself!"

No sound, no word. I beheld the altar before me: the stone table, the wood cross. There the figure of my Savior hung and bled. It filled me with new shame.

I breathed in deeply and set about my work again. The rosary I always carried—that my mother carried before me and her mother before her—seemed in that hour to be failing in its duty. No matter how many beads I moved, I could not escape what I had done.

I had fled to the chapel, for I knew not what else to do. I could not bear to speak to others, and so I thought to speak to God. But what would that help? If man was my judge, how much more the Almighty!

It was not the forgiveness of God alone that I desired, but also that of my brother. The anger that had brewed within me for weeks—perhaps for years—had burned him, even as it had burned me. I might have joined Brünnhilda in the flames, if only to escape the guilt I felt. Have you ever known that pain? Have you ever wished to burn?

A knock at the door. I had no desire to speak to any man, or any woman for that matter. I wondered how long I could remain alone. *No*, I thought. *A queen can never hide, even within the walls of a castle. Her demons haunt her everywhere.*

"Who is it?" I called softly.

"Your servant Drogo, my lady."

The one person I was willing to admit.

"Enter, Sir Drogo, but I bid you come alone."

I heard the door open behind me, but I continued kneeling, staring at the cross before me.

"Lord, grant me strength," I whispered. "Grant me the forgiveness of Earl Robert."

"What was that?" Drogo asked.

"I am at prayer," I told him, turning my head.

"Forgive me. You said to come in."

"That I did. Why have you come? To offer censure? Very well, I accept it. I am entirely in the wrong."

I cast my eyes toward the cross again, seeking some kind of deliverance.

"I thought you should know that Earl Robert left with eight of his men," said Drogo.

I closed my eyes, holding back new tears. "Of course he did. It is all my fault."

"They are gone to hunt, my lady. They are staying at the lodge in Woodstock."

"He is running away from me, and I do not blame him."

"Lord Brian rode after him."

"Him too?" I asked in alarm, turning to face my knight.

"It's not what you think. He went to speak with Earl Robert in the hope that he might make things more … peaceable."

I turned back to face the altar. I was close to weeping again, and I had no wish to degrade myself in front of Drogo as well as everyone else. I thought he might take his leave, but instead he came and sat beside me. It took a moment for him to lower his tall frame. He did not seem entirely comfortable.

"There is no need for that," I assured him.

"It is not right that I should stand while my queen kneels," he replied. "If anything, I ought to be face down on the floor."

"I am not a queen yet, Drogo. Perhaps I never will be."

"Why would you say such a thing?!" he objected.

"I have lost the love of Earl Robert," I said, shaking my head in dismay. "God only knows what he will do."

"You have not lost his love. He is simply wounded. His pride has suffered a blow."

"What was I thinking?!" I cried, holding my head in my hands.

"You would know better than I."

"I've just been so angry. The men show so little respect for me, and Robert ... he and I have not seen eye to eye. Adela told me to speak my mind."

"Adela may not be the best authority on the matter," he said with a smile.

"I see that now. The thing is, I have a right to be angry. Everywhere I go, men slander me. My right to rule is in my blood: that cannot be denied. All men must know this."

"Do you think Earl Robert doesn't know it?"

"No, but it is difficult for me to trust anyone when all men wish me ill."

"There it is again!"

"There what is?"

"'All men.' Do you think all men are out to get you?"

"Maybe ... yes ... I hardly know."

He laughed. "Well, that clears things up!"

"You are mocking me in my distress!" I objected.

"I beg your pardon," he offered, bowing his head. "I did not intend to mock, but either all men are out to get you, or they aren't. You cannot have it both ways."

"Well, it seems they all view me as a threat to themselves. Even those who support my rule object when I do what rulers do. Maybe I should face the truth that no one can accept a woman. Perhaps I should fetch Count Geoffrey from Normandy and they can give the crown to him."

"Not that, my lady! Anything but that!" he cried.

"Henry is still too young to rule. Would they let me act simply as his regent? No, I am sure they will be begging for Stephen's release any day now."

"You are merely upset."

"Why would you say 'merely'? To me, it seems a large thing."

He nodded slowly. "Naturally, but I only mean that this hour of distress will pass, even as the ones before it. I have served you for a very long time, my lady. I have seen you grow from a scared child into a powerful woman. I have seen you speak with authority to bishops and kings. I think it does them good. No man should think himself above the reproach of a wise woman."

"I cannot afford to increase your pay, Drogo," I replied, for his words seemed clearly meant to flatter.

"I mean it truly. It has been a pleasure to live beside you these many years. We have passed through dangers together. Do you remember the time we rode in haste from Goslar with the Saxons nipping at our heels?"

"Yes, how could I forget?"

"Do you remember how we marched into Rome and faced down the cardinals?" he asked, excitement filling his voice.

"Yes. A most disagreeable business."

"Do you remember how we took the hand of Saint James from the clutches of Adalbert?"

Here I paused and stared at him for a moment before saying, "I dare not comment."

"Then when your kingdom was stolen from you, we crossed the sea together. I watched you take back what was rightfully yours."

"But now I am in danger of losing it."

"Earl Robert will forgive you. I am sure he already has. If he really intended to turn his back on you, he would have made for Worcester to join forces with Earl Waleran. We will come through this too: you'll see! However, I would recommend not speaking all your thoughts out loud."

"A painful lesson I have been forced to learn many times," I agreed, nodding sadly.

"Have you ever considered writing your thoughts down instead?" he offered.

"What? Do you wish me to craft meditations like Marcus Aurelius?"

"No, not for the public to read. This would only be for yourself. Write down your story. Tell about all our adventures! It may help you feel better."

"Yelling at someone is much quicker … but I take your point."

Suddenly, we heard the distant sound of trumpets.

"That must be King David," I said, "and half of my lords are not here to greet him."

I had no more time to weep. I ran up the stair, tearing the veil off my head, and burst into the hall.

"Adela! Adela!" I cried. "Where are you?!"

"Here, my lady!" a voice replied.

I turned to see her sitting behind me, a book in her hands.

"Did you not hear the trumpets?" I asked.

"What trumpets? Is the king here?!"

"Yes, or he will be very soon."

"Forgive me!" she said, setting the book aside and following me into the private chamber. "The story was so wonderful. I must have been deaf to the world!"

"Yes, what was I thinking teaching you to read? Here, help me with this dress!"

Unlacing a gown is a task that does not lend itself to speed, yet my maid did her best to move the process along. As soon as the dress was off, she asked, "Do you have any thought as to which gown—"

"The blue one," I interrupted.

"Very well."

Now the process was reversed. Adela struggled to thread the laces, and I am sure I made her task harder with my impatience. Even before she had finished, she asked, "Which jewels?"

At precisely that moment, the trumpets played again, and I could hear cheers out in the yard.

"Whatever you find first!" I told her.

She opened the small chest of jewels and seemed to grab several at random. However, when she revealed them to me, they matched so perfectly that I would have thought she had considered the matter at length.

"Perfect. Now help me get them on!"

She had almost finished this work and was about to place the imperial ring upon my finger when she said, "What on earth?! What happened, my lady?!"

"Oh, that …"

"It's covered with blood. What did you—"

"No time to discuss!" I cried, as I ran to the basin and thrust my hand under water, rubbing at the wound with vigor.

"Do you wish me to bind it?" she asked.

"No time!"

"Very well, then. What for your hair?"

"Fetch the German crown."

"Are you sure?"

"He's the king of Scotland! I must wear a crown! Since the English one is still denied me, that one will have to do."

All argument ceased at that point, and she applied the veil and placed the crown upon my head. I looked in the mirror and struggled to convince myself that I looked like a queen, even as shame threatened to consume me.

"My lady," Adela said. "The king …"

"Yes, I must be going."

I once again entered the hall and took my seat upon the throne. It was a finer chair than the one at my first visit. Lord Robert had graciously paid for a new one to be made. No sooner had I settled into position, than the door swung open and Lord John fitz Gilbert entered.

"Empress Mathilda, I present to you His Royal Highness David, king of the Scots!"

I had time for one deep breath, with which I attempted to suppress all the bitter feelings warring within me. One breath: that was all. As soon as I had let it go, my uncle strode into the hall and removed his hat.

How strange it was to see him again after so many years, and how different he looked! He once had long, red hair, but it had become entirely gray and there was not much of it. He had evidently given up attempting to grow it and was keeping it quite short, though he had made up for this by allowing his beard to make a conquest of both his face and neck. Indeed, he seemed to have more hair on that face than he once had on his head. He was still wearing his clothes from riding, and there was mud on his boots.

For a moment, he simply looked at me, and I at him. He then strode forward and knelt before me.

"Your Highness," he said, "I am here to offer you my fealty as your vassal, and my support as your relative by blood. That which I swear, I promise to fulfill. I shall see you given the crown of Saint Edward."

He took my hand and kissed it, then looked up at me with a smile. The light caught his eyes in such a way that I saw their hue. For just a moment, the rest of it disappeared—the beard, the scars, the wrinkles—and I saw something I never thought to look upon again: the eyes of my mother. I was robbed of speech.

"Empress Mathilda?" he asked. "Have I displeased you?"

"No," I said. "That is, I do need to speak with you about the bishopric of Durham."

Here I pulled back my hand and the expression on his face changed. He returned to his feet and I added, "While I am exceedingly happy to receive you here, King David, I have been told that you sought to impose your own man upon the see of Durham, which is my right as queen and that of the men of the Church. I wonder why you chose to do such a thing."

"The situation in Durham is most difficult at the present time," he said, turning his hat over in his hands. "Factions have formed among the monks and canons. Seldom have I seen a company of men so in need of a leader! As the local lord, I thought it only right that I should provide for them in this way, lest they continue as sheep without a shepherd."

"Perhaps your intentions were good, Uncle, but this has placed me in a most … delicate situation. It seems to others that I have no control over affairs in my own kingdom, and as a woman, you can imagine how dangerous this impression can be."

"I understand," he said, nodding, "and it was for this reason that I ensured that the man would not be consecrated until you had granted your consent."

"But I hear it is this appointment rather than anything else that has led to the greatest discord among the canons and monks. Is that not true?" I asked, not content to let the fish off the hook.

"Certainly not! I do not know who has told you these things, but rest assured, all is well in Durham! I have seen it myself. They will come around: you'll see."

These words did not fully satisfy me, but neither did I wish to become angry once more. After all, a lack of trust had led me into trouble that very day. I therefore smiled and said, "It has been too long, Uncle. Come! Let us take a walk about the grounds, you and me. There are great matters of state at hand, and I would have your counsel."

XII

I had not known how I would feel upon my uncle's arrival at Oxford Castle, in particular after I learned of his attempt to set William Cumin on the bishop's throne in Durham without my consent. However, after my foolhardiness with Earl Robert, I had begun to seriously question my own judgment. To think that I had allowed the voices of the world to poison me against my brother! What especially galled me was that it should have been Archbishop Theobald who struck the fatal blow. How could I have ceased to trust those closest to me and listened instead to a man who served my enemies as much as myself? I had seldom felt such a fool.

Therefore, when King David of Scotland came into my presence, I quickly set aside any anger I harbored against him. Here was a man who knew the world far better than I, and one whose loyalty to me was founded in our common blood. If I could not trust him, I could not trust anyone, or so I reasoned. A queen must have someone to trust.

As it turned out, my uncle had brought William Cumin along with his company so that I could have the chance to address him in person and make a proper judgment. This helped to alleviate some of my concerns. He was clearly an excellent scholar and possessed a pleasing manner. Indeed, I could find no fault in him, or at least none that would cause me to withhold my assent. There was, however, the question of whether this William could earn the loyalty of those who would be serving under him. Later that evening, I asked my uncle about this very issue while we were sitting by the fire out in the hall. The company had all gone, and only a few servants busied themselves behind us, cleaning the tables and the floor.

"Archbishop Theobald would have me believe that all the canons and monks of Durham are against this appointment. Is there any truth in that?" I inquired carefully.

"Archbishop Theobald should mind his own business," King David replied. "If anyone has a say in the matter, it is the archbishop of York."

I nodded, not wishing to frustrate him any more than necessary. "So I implied when I spoke with him, but you have not yet answered my question."

The king leaned back in his chair, cherishing a goblet of beer he had lately procured. He stared down into its dark depths, running his finger around the rim. I was beginning to lose patience, but finally he looked up and spoke.

"There is one man there—a kinsman of the late Bishop Ranulf Flambard—who has made his opposition known, but his motives are hardly pure. Ever since his uncle became lord of that see, the family feels they own the place. The imposition of an outsider threatens their power. I met with him briefly during my stay, and I have scarcely known a man so oblivious to the effects of his own argument. He claimed that the appointment was irregular, but who knows not that his dear uncle bought the bishopric for two hundred pounds, was always in the bed of his mistress, and had his relatives placed in the bishopric of Lisieux, the better to take advantage of that see as well? I will not listen to any member of the Flambard family when it comes to matters of honor. This is exactly why William Cumin should be granted the ring and scepter. There is a rot in Durham that must be removed, and he is the man to do it. He is a fine administrator."

There were few things that annoyed me as much as corrupt men of the Church, so this news did sway me a bit.

"If it is as you say, then I think you must be right," I concluded. "I would of course like to discuss the matter with the archbishop of York, but there is one problem with that."

"Well, only if you consider it a problem that the alleged archbishop of York was imposed on that see by the false king who now sits in chains, against the wishes of the archbishop of Canterbury, the monks of York, and the archdeacons of his own cathedral," he said with a smile.

"I do consider that a problem, especially when we are attempting to assess the role of the monks of Durham in selecting their own bishop. No, I will not take the advice of Archbishop William of York until we have made sense of his election. He is an archbishop only in name, and to be honest, he is hardly that. The only person who has any right to influence me at this point is the bishop of Winchester."

"Because he is papal legate?" my uncle asked, the look on his face betraying his annoyance.

"Yes, but more to the point, I made a promise to him. I said I would seek his counsel on great matters of state, especially those affecting the Church."

"Why on earth did you do that?!" he protested, and I could not help but observe in this moment how the sound of the North broke through in his voice. He leaned forward in his chair, allowing some of the beer to fall to the floor. "Don't you know if you give that man a barleycorn, he will take the whole estate?"

I nodded. "He will try to, but I remember the terms of our agreement. I need not do everything he says, but only consider his words. It may be more than he truly deserves, for he helped to place the usurper on the throne. But I am nothing if not forgiving."

King David rolled his eyes but happily chose not to make an angry reply, taking a long drink instead.

"Bishop Henry has come around to me, so I will attempt to come around to him," I explained. "I only hope that Earl Robert can find it in himself to forgive."

"Still no word from him?" the king asked, setting his now empty goblet on the floor.

"Nothing for good or ill," I said quietly.

"Do you wish me to speak with him?"

I shook my head. "No, if anyone can induce him to come back, I am sure it is Lord Brian."

"Then we will place our hope in his powers of argument," he concluded.

I passed that night without enjoying much slumber. While I would have trusted Brian to do almost anything on my behalf, this particular commission was especially fraught with difficulty. It is often easier to move a mountain than a man. I attempted to distract myself by imagining the faces of my sons, but that only filled me with concern that they were in danger, being poorly taught, or worst of all ... becoming like their father.

When I finally heard the cock crow, I despaired of these efforts and rose from my bed. Not wishing to disturb Adela, I dressed myself simply and wandered out into the lower yard, nodding at each of the guards I passed. Although the sky was growing lighter, the sun had not yet risen. The night's fire out in the main pit had turned to embers, but there was a solitary figure sitting upon a bench nearby, drinking what I could only assume was a bowl of mead by the last remnants of firelight. As I moved closer, I saw that it was my brother, Reginald. When I was very near, I called him by name.

"My lady," he said, standing quickly, "I was just—"

"Warming yourself inside and out?"

He looked down at the bowl in his hand and then back at me. "Oh, this? It's for the pain. I injured my leg when we were out—"

I raised a hand. "Please, brother, I did not come here to cast judgment on you. I do not care about such things."

"What a relief!" he replied with a smile. "But tell me: why are you walking about at such an hour?"

"I could not sleep. I fear I have lost the love of Earl Robert."

He lowered his brows. "Because of the thing you said yesterday?"

"Yes."

He nodded his head and for a moment the two of us stood there quietly, both staring at nothing in particular. Reginald clearly did not trust himself to speak further on that subject. Finally, he came to a conclusion that he was comfortable voicing.

"Well, if you desire to roam, I could accompany you. Where do you wish to go?"

"What?" I asked in confusion. "You mean … outside the walls?"

He shrugged his shoulders. "Why not?"

"But there are … people … outside the walls."

"There are people inside the walls."

I shook my head. "No, I mean I cannot know if everyone out there wishes me well."

"They probably don't, but that is why I carry weapons."

He proudly held up his crossbow, which had until then been hidden beneath the bench, and in truth, I could not imagine that anyone would wish to challenge his ability.

"I suppose that if I am not known to go out at this hour, few will foresee it."

"Very good! Come, you are in safe hands. You can wear my cloak. No one will recognize you."

As he wrapped the garment around me, I said to him, "This is mad, isn't it?"

He thought for a moment, then replied, "Probably."

"Very well. Let's go."

Departing the castle was no small feat. First, I notified the head of the guard, whose name I cannot remember. He then gave permission to open the gate and lower the bridge. By this time, the sun was beginning to rise.

Once we made it to the street, I asked Reginald, "Where are we going?"

"There's a place I know that will make you feel better."

"I doubt I will find what I'm looking for in a brothel," I said, casting a firm glance in his direction.

"No, no. Something even better than that."

"I have visited all the churches."

"Better still!"

As we neared the center of town, we saw shop keepers sweeping dust out their front doors, maid servants disposing of the night's refuse, and wares being placed out for sale. We were forced to move to the side as a boy led a flock of geese down the center of the lane. I had seldom witnessed such things, for whenever I made my way down a street in the bright light of day, people would cease what they were doing and stare. How strange it was to see what most men considered ordinary! We were very near Saint Mary's Church when my brother said, "Here it is."

The building to which he pointed was a tavern, and the best thing I could say about it is that it was eccentric. Its three levels were pressed together tightly, as if one had fallen on top of the other. One of the windows was broken, or maybe two. Outside the front door, a pig was tied up and an old man lay asleep on the ground with a bottle still in his hand. Swinging high above was a wood sign that read "THE QUILL."

"Earl Reginald," I said, "I should hate to think that you have led me to a den of filth."

"No such thing, my lady!" he assured me. "This is the finest tavern in this part of the country."

"Ha!" I scoffed. "Maybe for rats."

"Also for men."

"We have just finished the watches of the night!"

"And no one should start the day without the water of life in his veins!"

I would have further impressed upon him the depths of his folly, but I feared that if we tarried any longer in the street, we would attract attention. I therefore did as he wished and stepped inside.

Oh, the smell! The combination of spilt drink, sweaty men, and the dust of a hundred years made an assault upon my nose. Every breath was a struggle. A dog covered in mange approached and began to lick one of my hands.

"Stop it!" I cried.

"Here," Reginald said. "There's a private room above."

The tavern was crammed with tables on which men lay sleeping, no doubt too drunk to know the time of day. One or two were still attempting to imbibe. The place was so dark: the filthy windows let in hardly any of the morning light, and the candles had long since burned out. Perhaps this was a good thing, as it prevented me from noticing the cobwebs. My brother led me up the narrow set of stairs, which creaked with such violence that I seriously doubted their ability to hold me upright.

"If I die here, Reginald, I shall never forgive you," I whispered.

Upon reaching the upper level, my brother lifted two men from their stupor and sent them stumbling back down the stair. He then found a chair that appeared fairly clean and commanded, "Sit here. I'll get us some drinks."

At that point, I reasoned that I had committed myself, so I did as he said. I was somewhat afraid to remain there without company, but soon discovered I was not alone. A mouse ran to and fro across the floor, picking up crumbs from the night's feast. As I sat there watching the creature, I was taken completely by surprise as a cat leapt from the darkness and grabbed the poor thing with its paws. Rather than eating its prey, the cat—which was black either by birth or on account of the filth—simply sat down and allowed the mouse to wander a few steps before catching it again, and again, and again.

"An excellent catch," I said.

The cat turned and looked at me, its great yellow eyes reflecting the dim light.

"Do you know who I am?" I asked. "I am the queen of England." When the cat said nothing but gave its attention back to the mouse, I muttered, "Yes, that is how the archbishop of Canterbury treats me as well."

I suddenly heard what I assumed was Reginald coming up the stair. Both cat and mouse disappeared into the darkness as I turned to accept my wine. However, I saw that rather than returning with drinks, my brother had brought me King David and Earl Robert. This startled me to such a degree that my heart began beating with the speed of a deer that has just seen its stalker. I was about to stand, but my uncle gestured for me to remain seated.

"May we all sit?" Reginald asked.

"Yes, of course," I replied.

As they took their places, I looked upon the face of Earl Robert, attempting to discern which way our conversation was likely to go. He did not look very cross, or so I thought.

Lord, have mercy! I prayed, or rather begged.

"Earl Robert has returned to us," noted King David, although that was perfectly evident. "You two just missed him when you left the castle, but we knew well enough where Reginald would lead you."

"I am ever so glad to see you, Earl Robert," I said. "I did not know if you would come back."

He took a deep breath before speaking, and I swallowed hard. Then he spoke.

"I admit that your words brought deep shame upon me, and I could not think why you chose to utter them."

"I am sorry," I said quietly. "I beg you, please forgive my madness. I did not mean those awful things I said. I was only angry, and Archbishop Theobald … well, I ought not pass the blame. The fault is mine alone, and I am so very sorry for it. You deserve nothing but praise from me."

"I was not sure how to respond," he continued, as if I had not spoken at all. "No one addresses me like that."

I merely nodded and closed my eyes in an attempt to keep myself from crying. Then Robert spoke again.

"Lord Brian arrived at Woodstock shortly after I did. He assured me you were deeply penitent. Even so, I was in no mood to return. Then he began to speak to me of the terrible stress you have endured, and how he was certain that your anger was not truly directed at me. 'We have all dealt with stress. That is no excuse,' I told him. Then as I was about to walk away, he cried, 'Robert, you are family! She is your sister: the child of your own father. You are bonded for ever by blood. Do not throw that to the dogs! Forgive one another. That is the only way. Think of Prince William! The two of you share a connection to him. In you, he lives and breathes. In you, the glories of the past enter into the present. You are family.' Well, this appeal had the effect he intended. I could not remain angry. Indeed, I knew that moment of anger was not your true character. I have seen wounded beasts act in such a manner, and perhaps I did not judge your wounds aright. I therefore determined to return here before morning light. So here we are: myself, King David, and Earl Reginald. We are all your blood relations, and we have come to tell you that not only do we forgive you of these grievances, but we will do our utmost to support you in the days ahead and promote the justice of your cause. We are a family: not only that, but we are a royal family. In us is preserved the heritage of old. If England is to survive, if it is to continue to be England and Normandy is to continue to be Normandy, then it needs this family, and we all need each other. So, will you join hands with us, sister? Will we pledge to stay true to one another, come what may?"

"With all my heart, I will gladly pledge it!" I cried. Clasping his hand in mine, I said, "Oh, Robert! You cannot know how happy you have made me! Twice in my life I have thought I lost you for ever, but always you return. It is a joy beyond words!"

"You did not lose me before, and you never shall," he said. "Not while I still draw breath. Just please, try not to make a fool of me in front of my men."

"Of course," I assured him, nodding my head. "I know you are all on my side. I was a fool to forsake your counsel. I will never doubt again: I swear it!"

"Then let us bind hands together."

We all did as he said, until we had formed a circle of hands around the table.

"So be it henceforth," said King David. "We, the royal house of England and Scotland, ordained by God to rule this isle, pledge to honor, uphold, and support one another, come what may, and to see the preservation of us and our descendants upon the thrones. We pledge it this day. I, the king of Scotland ..."

He nodded and we began to go around the table.

"I, the earl of Cornwall ..."

"I, the queen of England ..."

"I, the earl of Gloucester ..."

"May the Lord have mercy on us and enable us to keep this solemn pledge," the king concluded. "So be it!"

"So be it!" we all declared.

Having reconciled with my nearest of kin, I remained in Oxford for some time, always waiting upon news from London. I am sure nothing would have pleased those merchants more than to know that I, their queen, was waiting upon their decision. All the while, I was in constant discussion with the king of Scotland. As he too had experienced the torments that come with attempting to claim a throne, I dearly valued his counsel. I most looked forward to midday, when I would make my way to the green and shoot with my uncle, my brothers, and the lords Robert D'Oyly, Brian of Wallingford, and Miles of Gloucester. I had very little skill with a bow, but they were kind enough to overlook my faults and cheered if I came anywhere near the target. Of course, Reginald was far better than any of us: he might have been an archer had he not been borne of a king.

Archbishop Theobald would join us for the evening meal, at which point I was forced to talk with him. I suppose he was a good enough man, but I never once believed I was seeing his true character. I knew he came to spy me out—indeed, to spy us all out. I endured his presence, for I coveted his influence with the Church. Those bishops and abbots who had not been swayed by the word of Bishop Henry of Winchester might be made to see reason by the archbishop of Canterbury. At times I felt fairly assured of his support, but on other occasions, I thought he still longed for the return of the usurper. Certainly, it was a bad sign that he had not yet commanded the English bishops to bow the knee to my rule.

On account of these fears, I did welcome the archbishop to shoot with us once. I doubted the man had ever held a bow in his life, so I welcomed his presence if only to make my own efforts seem less woeful by comparison. I believe the lords were rather aggrieved that they could not make the same crude jests that I would graciously pardon. Nevertheless, we made it through, and the archbishop avoided hitting any of the dogs. I considered that a victory of sorts.

As the men were all setting aside their weapons and removing their gloves, a messenger approached me bearing a letter with the seal of my husband, Count Geoffrey. Without addressing the others, I quickly opened it and learned that he had gained both Lisieux and Falaise, and continued to press toward the Seine.

"When I am recognized as duke of Normandy, I would have you beside me as my duchess," he wrote. "As soon as you have completed your business in England, I bid you return to your native home and the inheritance of your sons. Then all will see us as the family we are."

Here I could not help snorting in response, and it caught the attention of Earl Robert.

"What is it?" he asked.

I made a brief summary of the letter's contents, and he shook his head in wonder.

"Why should Count Geoffrey be duke of Normandy rather than your son? It is not his by right of birth."

"Maybe so," I agreed, "but perhaps he feels it is his by right of conquest."

"He would never have gained such a conquest had we not defeated Stephen here on the island and prevented him from sending his lords to fight in Normandy," Robert protested. "Truly, we left him the easier task."

I folded up the parchment with a sigh and told him, "I am more annoyed that he thinks I should cross the Channel rather than him. I do value Normandy highly. It is the land of my fathers, and it must go to my sons. Yet England is also the land of my fathers. It was the greatest prize for which our grandfather William fought. Across the water we will always be harried by the king of France, but here we have a home indeed. It is our destiny to defend Normandy, the land of my father Rollo, but that is precisely my point: it will always be exposed to those who wish to conquer." Here I began to gesture broadly with the paper still in hand. "This island on which we now stand has every advantage granted by God, and if we strive to defend what we have been given and do not surrender it lightly to foreigners, then we will create a fortress impregnable. Yes, by all means, let us hold Normandy! Let us press even into the fields of France! But I know my home and the place where I lay my head. I was born in England and I am not ashamed." I approached him close enough to lower my voice. "There is greatness here of which the kings on the mainland know nothing. Let Count Geoffrey make his complaints. Here I was born and here I shall die."

"So, you will not be going to Normandy?" my brother asked, looking down his nose at me.

"Not yet. Someday, certainly, but he must come here first. It would do him good to be placed in the second position for once."

I did not speak of that portion of the letter which upset me most: the idea that we were a family. Was common blood enough to make a family? I had heard a rumor that steadfast love ought to be included, though I had seldom seen it put into practice.

On the first day of June, the feast of Saint Justin, I received the news I so dearly sought: the aldermen of London, along with Earl Geoffrey de Mandeville of Essex, agreed to meet me at the abbey of Saint Alban's, just a day's ride north of London. Oh, happy news! This was our chance to gain access to the city. The coronation would take place in Westminster, but I needed to enter the walls of London and gain the good will of the citizens if I hoped for things to go smoothly. As these were the men who had first lent their support to Stephen, I knew they would not surrender that good will lightly, and though they had little love for the constable of the Tower, Earl Geoffrey, his choice was likely to determine theirs. Therefore, I made it my business to win him over, no matter the cost.

As the entire company readied to depart Oxford, I sent a message to Bishop Henry of Winchester.

I make for the city of London, there to be crowned in King Edward's abbey. I greatly desire your presence and shall have the finest room at Westminster reserved for you. Also, I desire your counsel on the matter of the bishoprics of London and Durham. They tell me Robert de Sigello is the man for London, and I see no reason to quarrel. I also have it in mind to consecrate William Cumin in the see of Durham. I made his acquaintance here and can find no flaw in his character. Do come to our court and inform us of your will. I have no reason to suspect that it is different from our own. Fare you well.
MATHILDA IMPERATRIX

Archbishop Theobald was to travel with us, along with those lords who had been always by my side. I also learned that

Earl Ranulf of Chester and his brother, William of Roumare, would finally be joining us at Saint Alban's. As they were not on good terms with the king of Scotland, I had forgiven their absence up to that point, but the time for neutrality was over. As I said within hearing of the archbishop of Canterbury, "Let every man declare himself now. Either he supports our rule or he sides with the traitor. This is no time for weak willed men."

Shortly after the Nones of June, we set out from Oxford and rode all the way to Aylesbury in a single day. After passing one night there, we made our way into the Chiltern hills. This slowed our progress considerably, and by the time we arrived at Berkhamsted Castle, we needed a more substantial rest. We therefore remained for three days: long enough to receive the news that both the earl of Chester and many of the Londoners were already in Saint Alban's and awaited our arrival. Lord Miles then commanded the company to return to their horses and press on to the east.

As we were coming upon the abbey, we passed an ancient Roman wall, and I suddenly remembered something young Henry said to me the eve before I departed Caen. I sat beside him as he laid on his bed, the last hours of sunlight having long since abandoned us.

"Mother?" he asked quietly, his keen eyes staring into mine.

"Yes, my son," I replied, pushing the hair back from his brow.

"Why do you have to go to England?"

"Because that is your inheritance, and it was stolen from you."

"But I have never seen it."

I smiled and reached down to grab his little hand. "Oh, it is a wonderful land, full of green hills and dark woods, with the waves beating against the white cliffs. You belong to that land, even if you know it not."

I could see that he was nervous, and in time a question formed upon his lips. "When you go there ... will you fight in battle like *pappa*?"

"No. I am no soldier."

"Then why must you go?" he complained. "Can't Uncle Robert fight for you?"

"Because I am the queen, Henry," I told him firmly. "A queen must be in her kingdom."

He sat up and raised his voice. "I do not want you to go! If you go, Geoffrey will torment me!"

"Surely not! I will see to it that he does nothing of the sort."

"But what if the false king kills *pappa* and Uncle Robert in battle?"

I could see the fear in his eyes and guessed that we were moving closer to his true concern.

"I do not think that will happen," I said softly. After all, I could not promise anything more.

"But it might happen," he whispered.

I breathed deeply in and out and finally admitted, "Yes, I suppose it might."

"And what if ..." he began, but then his voice trailed off and he cast his eyes down. I gently lifted his chin. Although he was not a boy given to weeping, his eyes looked rather moist.

"Go on, son," I bid him. "Ask your question."

"And what if they send you to a prison, and then they cut off your head and put it on the city wall?"

"Where did you hear such a thing?!" I asked in alarm.

He did not answer but simply looked at me. I hardly knew how to reply. At last, I said, "That is not going to happen. We will defeat the false king and restore justice to England, and then I will send for you and we will all live together in the palace of Westminster, just as I did when I was young. We will see each other again soon: I swear it!"

"You promise?"

"Yes, most assuredly. I will not return until I have won us the kingdom."

This memory passed by in a flash, and as I looked upon the ancient wall, I thought, *Should this meeting go ill, perhaps my head will rest there.* Tearing my eyes away from that sight and my mind's eye from those thoughts of doom, I returned to the moment at hand, for we were passing on to the abbey grounds, and I could see the crowd waiting to receive us.

We rode through the main gate, which in addition to being the entrance to the great yard is also right next to the stables and guest houses, a perfect situation for travelers. There in the middle of the yard I saw the man I assumed to be Abbot Geoffrey de Gorham, for the sleeves of his cowl were longer and altogether grander than those of the other monks. Beside him stood a crowd of consecrated brothers. They were joined by several lords, one of whom I knew to be Earl Ranulf of Chester on account of our earlier meeting in Gloucester, but the others I did not recognize. Standing just to the right were the aldermen of London, clearly marked by their brightly colored robes and black caps, as well as the seals they wore upon gold chains.

I was about to alight from my horse when I saw that Drogo was not there. I spun my head around looking for him, but it seemed that his own horse had been thrown into a fit at the worst possible moment. Several of the lords were attempting to help them, and there was no one left to aid me.

"Here, my lady, allow me," Lord Brian said, making his way to my side.

Relieved, I accepted his aid, and when I had made it to the ground, I whispered, "Thank you. I was worried."

"No need to be worried. I am here," he said, offering me his arm.

As we made our way forward to where the entire assembly of monks, lords, and council members knelt in respect, I could hear the rest of the lords rushing to take their places behind me.

"Empress Mathilda!" Abbot Geoffrey said, rising to his feet along with the rest. "Welcome to the Benedictine House of Saint Alban. We are so pleased that you have chosen to reside within our walls."

"Thank you for your hospitality," I replied.

I next met the sheriff of London, Osbert Huitdeniers, who was a friend of my brother, Earl Robert. He had been one of two sheriffs along with Aubrey de Vere, but a rising of the Londoners had led to the latter man's death just a few weeks earlier. As Earl Geoffrey de Mandeville was a relative of the slain lord, I avoided the subject. I shook hands with the aldermen, some of whom smiled, but others seemed to regard me with suspicion. I greeted the monks and then finally came to those men who were of first concern: Earl Ranulf of Chester, his brother Lord William of Roumare, and Earl Geoffrey, constable of the Tower of London and man of the hour. I was surprised to see the pale complexion of the latter earl. Not only his skin, but his hair was so light as to be almost bereft of color, and his eyes were as blue as the sea.

As he bowed his head, allowing his golden tresses to dip down, I said to him, "Earl Geoffrey of Essex, how glad I am to finally meet you!"

"And I you, Your Highness," he replied in a deep voice that somehow did not seem to match his appearance at all.

"I understand you have come to have the grants made by the former king confirmed."

"I seek only that which is my due," he replied, the corner of his mouth rising into something like a smile, though one that seemed entirely forced.

I feared that Earl Geoffrey's definition of what was his due might be different from my own, but I told him, "I am to meet with the aldermen of London this evening. Perhaps we can speak before then."

"Very good, my lady," he concluded simply.

With that, we all made our way to our separate lodgings, while I tried not to worry about the discussions to come. I was closer than I had ever been to achieving my goal, and yet I sensed that one false move might cause my head to be placed upon the wall, even as my son feared.

Saint Alban's was not a large monastery at that time—at least, not compared to some of the houses across the Channel—yet it was forced to play host to some 1,000 persons. First, there were the aldermen of London, each of whom represented a ward, whether it was Cripplegate, Bishopsgate, or Cornhill. Underneath them were members of the precinct assemblies. These were joined by priests and friars, members of the guild, two or three Flemish merchants very much owned by my enemies, and a collection of law worthy citizens who had simply felt the need to make the journey. Added to these were the households of earls Geoffrey and Ranulf, along with my own company, which by that point numbered about three hundred persons. There were not enough guest rooms in all the monasteries of England for so many men, nor were the two taverns within walking distance up to the task. Therefore, a city of tents sprung up north of the River Ver and continued for the entire week I remained there.

I at least was granted a chamber within the abbey walls, and another was given to Geoffrey de Mandeville at my request. We were therefore able to meet that afternoon in a small reception hall within the guest house. It was not a large room, and to tell the truth I remember little about it. I was joined by my chancellor, John fitz Gilbert, but the earl of Essex came on his own. Therefore, when we were all seated at a small table by a window, I began by asking, "Earl Geoffrey, I have asked my chancellor to make a record of what is discussed between us. Have you any objection?"

"No," he replied.

The earl had taken a position in his chair that I can only describe as open, his legs spread rather far apart with his hands resting on each of the arms. I found this somewhat distracting and wondered if it was meant to send a signal to myself, but I attempted not to think about it.

"Very good," I told him. "I suppose there is no need for me to go over the reasons for our meeting. We both know well enough what it is we have come here to accomplish. I must balance your claims against those of the citizens of London, and you must decide whether or not you will take me as your liege lady, since you swore your fealty to Stephen when he created you earl of Essex and constable of the Tower, is that correct?"

"Yes," he said, once again betraying nothing of what he felt.

"I see we understand each other. Now, I will speak to the aldermen of London this evening, and I am certain they will appeal to their rights granted in the time of the first King William and later expanded under King Henry. I am sure they will also point to what was offered them by Stephen and demand that I grant all that and more. I see no reason why this should conflict with your own position. I am aware that there have been difficulties between yourself and certain citizens of London—"

"Certain Cretans in London," he interrupted.

Ah, there was some passion! He wrinkled his nose in a sign of disdain.

"If you wish to think of it that way, yes."

"I think of it that way because that's the way it is."

I tried very hard not to sigh or roll my eyes. "Forgive me, Earl Geoffrey. I hoped to avoid denouncing anyone's character at this point."

"You know, it was King Henry who took away the rights of my family," the earl explained, now gripping the chair arms with such force that I wondered that they did not crack. "My father William—he was a fine constable. Best the Tower ever had! Even as his father before him, he served the crown, and yet he was made to feel shame."

There was a fire in those blue eyes: the anger of many years brought to bear upon a moment.

"Yet you had all your lands restored and now you are constable, same as your father and grandfather before you," I offered.

"It was a great wrong the king did my father."

Beginning to feel very annoyed, I said to him, "I am truly sorry for any pain that this caused your family, Earl Geoffrey, but I do believe the king removed him from his position because a prisoner was allowed to escape—"

"It could've happened to anyone!"

That was the second time the earl had interrupted me. Who did he think he was to treat any noble woman that way, let alone his rightful lady? I bit the inside of my lip, attempting not to give ground to the devil.[20] I breathed deeply, then replied.

"Even so, I am sure. But now you are seated in the same place! I am not my father. I cannot change his decisions. All I can do is make amends and ensure that you remain in your earldom and in authority over the Tower."

He laughed and shook his head. "You don't know the Londoners like I do. New men, right? Merchants, lawyers … the lot of them. There is little you might call good breeding."

---

20 Ephesians 4:26–7 reads in the King James Bible, "Be ye angry, and sin not: let not the sun go down upon your wrath: Neither give place to the devil."

"Well, I do not know about that," I said, hoping to avoid any more scorn along that line. "I merely seek to apply the law."

"The law says that London is in a class all its own. It answers to no lord but the king, although it would be truer to say they answer to no one. My father-in-law ... he was sheriff, and they killed him, the bastards! Now I say that his office belongs to me, for I am his heir."

Not only was Earl Geoffrey direct, but I could see that he was a man whose pride knew no bounds. The role of sheriff was not one that belonged to families. Indeed, I knew well enough that the men of London would never consent to a feudal lord being made their judge. The first King William had granted them a special honor: the Londoners were a commune unto themselves, in which they could only be judged by their fellows. I therefore proceeded carefully. I did not want to lose the good will of the earl, if indeed I had ever possessed it, but he was being quite impossible.

"Earl Geoffrey, I know the great love you must have borne for your wife's father"—here I referred to the late Aubrey de Vere—"and I mourn his death. I am more than happy to confirm to you the earldom of Essex, from which estates you will receive one hundred pounds *per annum*; to grant you fifteen more knights; and to keep you as constable of the Tower. I will even make you sheriff of Essex without question. But to make you sheriff of London ... I fear the Londoners could never accept such a thing."

"And why should they not?" he protested.

"Because Osbert Huitdeniers already holds that position."

"Don't shit me!" he cried. "There were two sheriffs last month. Why can't there be two sheriffs again?"

Here John fitz Gilbert grew brave enough to enter the conversation in my defense. "Mind your language, Earl Geoffrey! She is your queen!"

"Thank you for that, but I assure you such language is not enough to harm me at this point," I replied with a smile. I looked back at Earl Geoffrey, who was certainly not smiling. He did, however, offer an apology.

"I beg your pardon, my lady," he said, "but do see that you set the Londoners straight. It is the only way. You don't know what these men are like: they show no respect for their rightful betters. Even to speak with them is a great annoyance!"

I bowed my head and let out the heavy sigh that had been building for some time. *Mother of God, help me to hold my tongue,* I prayed.

As it so happened, things did not improve very much in the coming days. I spoke with Osbert Huitdeniers in private, and he argued that Earl Geoffrey was a horrible man who ought not be sheriff over the dogs of London, let alone the people.

"Did you know that he has the princess in his possession? Lady Constance of France, the wife of Eustace? She has been kept in the Tower ever since the battle of Lincoln, even though the former Queen Mathilda has begged for her to be released. God only knows what he's been doing with her there. That man speaks much of nobility, but he has none of its marks."

I assured him that I agreed, but my hand was being forced. The earl of Essex had many men at his command, and he controlled the Tower. There could be no hope of gaining London without his consent: not without building up our strength for months in the hope of carrying out a siege that would leave many dead and possibly end in defeat. Better to save our strength for the battle against the false queen and the wolf of Ypres. The sheriff Osbert understood, and perhaps on account of his ties to my brother, he did not raise an objection when the council of aldermen met. For my part, I made it clear to Earl

Geoffrey that Lady Constance had no part in our quarrel and must be released forthwith.

The next day, I rose early and walked across the yard to the stables, where I knew my brother would be spending some time with the horses. Although he was no groom, Robert always liked to be aware of any injuries or illnesses among the beasts used by his own knights, and thus he would walk by the stalls every morning and speak with their keepers. I came upon him as he examined a rather fine palfrey with a lovely white and gray coat.

"How is he?" I asked, as I approached my brother from behind.

Robert let go of the horse's bridle and turned to face me. "Actually, it's a mare."

"Forgive me," I said to the horse, bowing my head.

My brother reached down for a brush that lay on the ground and pulled it through the horse's mane. "She is one of the best runners we have," he explained, "for she presses on through wind and rain, light and darkness, taking little time to rest. Sadly, she has a bad hoof. The grooms keep trying to repair it, but perhaps it is infected. She seems in a great deal of pain."

"Poor thing," I whispered. Truly, I hated to see any beast suffer.

"But you did not come to speak to me about horses," Robert concluded, patting the mare on the nose.

"I may have for all you know," I objected.

He looked at me and laughed. "For you, a horse is simply a way to get from one place to another. You do not relate to them as some do. You do not know the lore of the horsemen."

"There is a lot going on up here," I said, pointing to my head. "You have no idea how many things I have to remember. I do like horses, but I have no room for them in my mind any more than I have room for the habits of fish."

"Fair enough," he concluded, dropping the brush back on the ground and leaning against one of the wood poles. "Now, what did you come here to ask?"

I gave in and made my way to the point. "Exactly how strong is your friendship with Osbert Huitdeniers?"

"Strong enough that I would come to his defense in a tavern fight. Not strong enough that I would lend him my wife," he said with a wink.

"That at least is something. I am up against it, Robert. The earl of Essex does not seem like a moral man, and yet he continues to get everything he wants. Stephen begged and pleaded before him, and now I do the same. I have the terrible feeling that if I do not bow to his demands, I will not only be denied access to London, but he will go running to the false queen and her progeny for more favors. He will play us against one another."

"Does that surprise you?"

"Surprise me? No. I merely wish there was some honor left in the nobility. 'Choose you this day whom you will serve.'[21] So says the Holy Scripture. I wish men would show faith in something! I fear the earl of Essex is no better than Robert fitz Hubert, and we all saw what became of him."

Robert sighed and put his arm around me, leading me away from the stable.

"I understand how you feel, but you must know that men are wicked and always have been. We rely upon the fairer sex to redeem us."

"Now, there's a load of rubbish!" I scoffed.

The following day, the aldermen consented to allow Geoffrey de Mandeville to be made a second sheriff of London, provided all legal rulings were still subject to the mutual decisions of both men and the will of the hustings. However, when I went

---

21   Joshua 24:15.

with Lord Miles and Earl Robert to inform Earl Geoffrey that his wish would be granted, he made a further demand. No longer was he content to be sheriff along side Osbert Huitdeniers, but he proclaimed he must be both sheriff and royal justiciar with no equal. This would place him second only to myself in terms of authority over the kingdom's most powerful city. In vain did we attempt to sway him from this demand. He even refused an offer of five hundred pounds.

I can see it now: we were standing back in the small reception hall, all four of us staring at one another in turn, Earl Geoffrey's face having moved from its normal ghostly white to a deep shade of pink.

"Do you think I am some common man that you would try to buy me?" he asked. "I am a lord among men! I seek only what is mine by right!"

"What is yours by right seems to change by the day," Earl Robert complained.

Robert was of course correct, but as ever I was forced to choose between what was truly just and what would keep the earl of Essex on my side.

"Please!" I begged. "There is no point in arguing. Earl Geoffrey, grant us time to consider your proposition. I must speak to the Londoners again."

No one was very happy when the four of us parted ways, least of all me. After Earl Geoffrey took his leave, Robert and I were forced to call in Osbert Huitdeniers, poor man. He had demonstrated far more faith than Geoffrey de Mandeville, yet he was about to be the loser. I wish you could have seen the look on his face when I told him he must give up his position as sheriff. Had I not been his queen, I suspect he might have delivered a blow to my person.

"This was not what we agreed!" he cried, his small form producing far more sound than I had thought possible. "Do you think the men of London are your property that you can barter them away to that devil?!"

"Master Osbert, please, see reason!" I begged. "I know Earl Geoffrey was no one's first choice to hold this position, but he is still subject to my rule. I will not allow him to commit injustices against you."

"Won't you?" he asked, a perverse smile on his face. "If you cannot control him now, my lady, how can you hope to control him then?"

"Because now I need his help to gain the crown, but once the rebellion has been brought to an end, I will be able to deal with the earl as he deserves." I said this out of hope and the necessity of the moment, though in truth I doubted my own assurances.

"'As he deserves …' What does any of this have to do with that?" Osbert moaned. "There is no justice in England. I see that now. There is no justice because our rulers are weak and they cannot dispense it. Earl Geoffrey plays you for a fool, so now you turn to me, hoping I will become your paschal lamb! I never—"

"How much?" Earl Robert suddenly asked, causing the other man to break off in the middle of his speech.

"What?" the sheriff scoffed.

My brother did not shrink back from his purpose but looked him directly in the eye. "Every man has his price. What is yours, Osbert?"

I held my breath, uncertain how the conversation was about to go. I trusted my brother, but it was a truly awful moment.

The sheriff looked upon us both with a glare, then turning to Robert, he inquired, "How many years have I known you, Earl Robert? We have been friends, have we not?"

"We can still be friends."

He shook his head sadly. "No, my lord. Not any more. Not since you asked me that question. I can be your friend, or I can take your bribe. Which would you prefer?"

There was a moment where my brother looked at me, I assume to see if I would oppose him. I wanted to object, but feared I could not, so I remained mute. Therefore, Robert turned back to the sheriff and asked again, "How much?"

The sheriff let out a deep sigh and said quietly, "Keep your money and give him the city, for there is no honor in either. I thought you all were better than the rest, but I was wrong."

He turned and walked toward the door, then stopped to offer a final word.

"There can be no justice in England when every man is a lord unto himself. May God deliver this kingdom before everything we hold dear is lost for ever."

XIII

The words of Osbert Huitdeniers echoed in my mind. They seemed to jeer at me for the remainder of my stay in Saint Alban's, like the last haunting tone of a church bell.

"I thought you all were better than the rest," he had said, "but I was wrong."

Was I no better than the rest? That was what I continued to wonder, even as the aldermen of London fumed and the earl of Essex schemed. Since the victory at Lincoln, I had been pushed hither and thither by every man north of the Channel. Whenever I sought to proclaim my rightful authority, I was made to pay dearly. Our Lord was a prophet without honor in his home town. The one with whom he broke bread betrayed him to the Jews. But his mother, flesh of his flesh and bone of his bone, stood beside him in the darkest hour. I was no Messiah, but I too placed my hope in the last of my relatives that God had seen fit to preserve.

I was determined not to fulfill Osbert Huitdeniers' words of woe. I would be better than the rest. And so, I set out on the final journey into London with the confidence of a conqueror, even though I did not foresee a true conqueror's welcome. I remembered the words of Archbishop Bruno: "You must walk into a room as if you own it, for only then will men believe it belongs to you."

We made our way south along Watling Street, the ancient Roman way. About midday, we stopped near the manor of Hampstead, which at that time was in the possession of Richard de Balta, though he held it in right of the abbey of Westminster. There is a hill there from which one can see for miles, and as the weather was quite fine, we sat down on the grass and enjoyed a meal of salted meat, bread left over from our stay at Saint Alban's, and a fine lot of berries that sirs Drogo and Philip found growing wild despite it being early in the summer. As Adela and I reclined to eat apart from the others, I said to her, "Take note, for this is where the river begins that will create the island."

"What island, my lady?" she asked, breaking off a piece of the dry bread and placing it in her mouth.

"The isle of Westminster, or Thorney Isle of old. It is formed by the branches of the Tyburn. The water runs from this high point down until it empties into the Thames."

"Is that why the abbey owns this place?"

"They do not own this very land, but the land near us. Yes, I suppose that might have something to do with it. It probably does not hurt that this is also an excellent hunting ground."

Adela brushed the crumbs off her hands, then looked at me directly. "My lady, is it true that Stephen's son is the abbot of Westminster?"

I nodded. "His bastard son, Gervase. I do not think he was twenty years old when he was granted that title, but you will note none of the monks protested, for his appointment assured them a portion of the treasury."

"That does seem too young for an abbot."

"It is too young for much of anything. Take it from someone who became an empress before she was in the womanly way."

"The womanly way? What's this?" a voice asked.

I turned to see that Drogo had crept up behind us.

"Nothing that concerns you," I assured him. "Thank you for the berries. They were delicious."

"Yes, the blackberries will not be ripe for another month or so, but these will do for the present," he said, sucking the last bits of juice from his fingers.

"Tell me, have we heard any word from London? Are Earl Geoffrey and the rest of them ready to receive us?"

"Yes, they arrived yesterday and will meet you at the palace of Westminster."

"Westminster …" I said, my voice trailing off.

"What is it, my lady?" Adela asked.

"Nothing. It's just that … You must pardon me. It has been so long, and we have fought so hard. It seems difficult to believe that the moment has finally arrived: that I am to be received in Westminster as England's queen. Some part of me struggles to accept it, as if I am afraid to wake from a dream and find myself deceived."

"We will be there soon enough, and you will see for yourself that it is not a dream," the knight declared.

"Drogo!" I called, as he was about to leave. "Any word from the bishop of Winchester? I sent him a letter, but I never heard back."

"Ah, yes, we have not received a message from him, but Lord Miles said he was likely having to go the long way around because of the Flemings south of the river. They say Mathilda of Boulogne and her children were at Reigate Castle for some time—"

"With the earl of Surrey—of course," I interrupted.

"—but the false queen has now taken to riding out with the wolf of Ypres and his men, and they have marched as far as Croydon."

"That is far too close for my liking," I said, my mind quickly working to determine just how quickly they could cover the few miles between there and the river. "Is anyone holding the south bank?"

"I would assume Earl Geoffrey is in charge of that, Your Highness. As you well know, there are no major fortresses there. The Tower is meant to stand for all. I believe your ancestors were more concerned with an invasion by water."

"Oh, let us talk no more of it at the present, or I shall be overwhelmed!" I moaned. "Tell the lords to make their final preparations. We depart for Westminster as soon as possible."

As Drogo departed, Adela and I rose to our feet, wiping any bits of grass from our skirts. No sooner did I look up from this business, than I saw the much younger knight, Sir Philip of Honfleur, approaching us.

"Lady Adela!" he called out, clearly holding something in his closed fist.

"Sir Philip," she replied, bowing her head.

The knight appeared quite happy to speak with my maid, and it was only after he reached our position that he looked over at me and paid his respects.

"Empress Mathilda, God save you!" he cried, bowing low.

"Enough of that," I said with a wave of my hand. "Just say whatever you came to say."

"As always, Your Highness moves straight to the point," he replied with a smile, then turned back to face Adela. "I saved you the last of the berries for later."

"There was no need," she told him, dropping her gaze.

"Hold out your hand," he commanded, unwilling to brook refusal.

She looked him in the eye and held out her palm. He emptied his fist of its treasure, then used both hands to close hers over the berries. He did not immediately let go, but remained standing there, looking at her quite sweetly.

"Thank you, sir knight," she replied, pulling her hands back.

His smile faded away, and giving a nod to each of us, he left as quickly as he had come. I watched as Adela's eyes followed him for some time.

"Are we going to discuss it, then?" I asked.

She seemed to break out of whatever charm he had cast over her and inquired, "Discuss what, my lady?"

"Why, what just happened! You and Sir Philip, the berries, the touching of hands."

"What of it?" she asked, shoving the berries into her pocket.

"I think you know very well what I mean," I replied, giving her the kind of direct look meant to put an end to absurdity.

"Perhaps I do know," she admitted, "but I do not intend to discuss it with anyone, including you!"

With that, she turned and made her way back to the carriages. I was left simply to sigh in defeat and herd the company back to the road.

It took a few minutes for all the men to be gathered, the food scraps recovered, and the horses made ready. I had been clothed in my finest gown since our departure, but now the final touches were applied: the crown of the empire set upon my head and the ring given to me at my first wedding placed upon my finger. The more men who remembered me as an empress and not the countess of Anjou, the better, or so we reasoned.

As I mounted my horse again and rode past the last few miles of trees near the bank of the Tyburn, I found myself thinking of Emperor Henry. It was he who had stood beside me when I first received the news that William Ætheling was dead, when he had declared his hopes for a dynasty that would rule over half of Christendom. How would things have been different if he had lived? He could have stood up to my father. His armies would have ensured that Stephen never seized the throne. Yes, surely they would have. We might have ruled jointly over England, Normandy, and the lands of the Holy Roman Empire stretching from the Northern to the Middle Sea. The king of France would have trembled in fear to be surrounded by such an empire, but it was not to be. Instead, I had watched my husband wither and die, leaving me with those final words: "You will be a mother of kings." I liked to think he would have been proud to see me crowned in King Edward's abbey, though he would no doubt have wished to be sitting beside me.

These thoughts continued to occupy my mind until the trees on our left ceased and we looked upon an open field. I could see the Tyburn clearly there, and after riding a mile or so farther, we came at last to the bridge that leads to Westminster isle. Such beauty! The sun was peeking through the clouds, sending showers of rays down to the ground. One of them caught the tower of the abbey church, and it shone as if to proclaim to us all, "This is the house of God. This is the gate of heaven."[22]

"Can this really be happening?" I whispered.

It was only at that point that we saw a crowd come out to greet us. They must have known we would pass over the bridge, for they were standing on both sides: men and women cheering in their native tongue, and little ones perched on shoulders or running forward to see the strange sight coming their way. My knights clustered around me for protection. As we made our way over the bridge, I smiled and waved at the crowd.

"*God þe mid sie!*" I called to them.

---

22   Reference to Genesis 28:17.

Standing in front of them all was a young girl no more than five or six years old. She was clothed in a simple brown tunic with her hair flowing free, and in her hands she clutched a bundle of flowers likely taken from a nearby field. She gazed up at me, her face the image of pure joy, or perhaps it was awe. "*Cwen Maud! Cwen Maud!*" she cried, and cast her flowers before me. I wanted to stop and embrace her, but I knew it would mean embracing every other person in the crowd as well, and we had no time for such things.

The abbey grounds were mostly walled, so we rode around the northern side of the abbey church and that of Saint Margaret until we came at last to the palace gates. We were admitted into the upper yard, where I found an altogether different crowd of nobles, clergy, and servants. It was such a grand occasion, and I laughed to think that it had once been the sporting ground for the king's lads.

Somewhere near this spot, I almost hit the usurper in the head with a ball. A pity that I did not, I thought.

I alighted from my horse and stood before the crowd of officials, all of whom bowed in respect. As they rose, I looked toward the aldermen gathered to my left. They did not look especially happy, but neither had they come armed for a fight. That at least was a good sign.

Immediately before me stood a man with a very fine cap crowned by a feather. He greeted me with the words, "Welcome to Westminster, Empress Mathilda, lady of the English! I am William, the steward of this house, and this is the chamberlain, Ralph d'Arques."

I made a study of them from head to toe, finding nothing extraordinary in their features save the steward's cap.

"A pleasure to meet you both, I am sure," I replied.

"Everything has been made ready for your stay," Ralph d'Arques told me. "Would you like us to show you around?"

Amy Mantravadi

"Is it so very different from my childhood?" I asked him.

"You must forgive my fellow!" said the steward. "Of course, you know this place almost as well as we do. There have been some improvements, but on the whole the war has brought it low."

Although I was interested in how the palace had fared since my last visit, there was another matter of more immediate import I wished to address.

"Has the bishop of Winchester arrived yet?" I inquired, changing the subject. "I thought he might be here to greet us."

"No, my lady, but he should be here in the next few days," the steward answered. "He sent a letter which I have placed in your private chamber."

"Thank you, Master William."

We spent a few minutes standing there as King David, Earl Robert, Earl Reginald, Lord Miles, and all the rest were introduced. I spoke briefly to Geoffrey de Mandeville and a few of the aldermen.

Then came the moment for which I had longed: the doors to the great hall were thrown open, their planks of oak stretching up to the heavens, and I walked inside. My mouth broke into a smile as I saw again those precious walls of stone. I stood in the middle of that huge space, gazing up at the wood beams high above. There was the upper gallery from which William and I had looked down at the glorious lords and ladies, longing to join them! I had never imagined in those days that I would sit as queen in that hall. Many years of pain had passed since that time, but they would soon be rewarded. At long last, I was home—I was free.

Suddenly, a voice seemed to echo in my mind. *I own you!* it cried. *I own you!*

I shook my head back and forth quickly as if to shake off the dust of the memory. I would not allow my father's words to ruin my moment of triumph. I continued to walk across the hall, smiling in turn at each person who stopped to bow. I held my head high and willed myself to think pleasant thoughts.

Then my eyes turned to a familiar throne on the dais at the far end of the hall, and I could not stop myself from wondering if perhaps it was the same one on which my father had been sitting all those years before—the day he had left me bloody and beaten, in agony on the floor.

I own you! I heard him shout again.

I gasped for breath. My brother Robert had been walking near me and must have seen the change in my face, for he asked me, "Is something wrong?"

I made no answer, but moved forward and climbed the steps up to the dais. I placed my hand upon an arm of the throne and pressed down slightly, as if allowing it to absorb the weight of my past. Then I took my seat upon the throne and surveyed it all. From right to left, every eye was on me. I looked back at them calmly, breathing deeply, unwilling to reveal what I felt inside.

"I am the queen," I whispered to myself. "I am the queen."

There were so many people requesting my attention that it was a few hours before I was able to get away. By happy chance, the space set aside for me was the same one that had belonged to my mother many years before. It included an audience room, a bed chamber, another chamber in which the maids could sleep, and a fourth room for the keeping of my possessions. How strange it was to inhabit that place! I felt as if I was being rather naughty sneaking into my mother's domain, but in truth it had been a long time since all of that, and the false queen had left her mark on it in between. The tapestries so cherished by my mother were gone, and nothing had been put up in their place. The whole space seemed rather empty and sad.

"They'll have taken anything of value with them down to their lands in Kent," Adela noted, and I nodded in agreement.

The crown was removed from my head and the heavy chain from my neck. I treasured the few moments I would have without such a weight. As the ladies continued to put away my things, I asked one of them, "Where is the box with my private things?"

She pointed to a table by the fire. There I found the small ivory chest that held my most prized objects. I removed the imperial ring and placed it inside, then touched each of the items: the gift young Henry had made for me, my mother's rosary, the amber stone, a lock of each of my sons' hair, and the king I had taken from Stephen in our game of checks. Smiling, I closed the box, and it was only then that I observed the parchment scroll lying beside it and remembered that it was from Bishop Henry.

I sat down in the nearest chair and broke the seal. By the light of the fire, I could see that the letter had been written in some haste by the bishop's own hand.

Empress Mathilda, lady of the English, countess of Anjou, from Henry, bishop of Winchester, abbot of Glastonbury, and legate of the Holy See.

I am exceedingly troubled by your letter, in which I find that you have forsaken the agreement reached between the Church and your father and appointed your own bishop of Durham, not conversing with myself, the archbishop of Canterbury, or even the monks and canons! At first, I believed this could not be so—that I must not have understood your words properly. But then I was paid a visit by three brothers of Durham, who told me the horrid tale: how their old master lies rotting, denied a proper burial, while a fraud is to be set in his place against all the laws of our Holy Church! They assure me that the whole of Durham is against this appointment.

I am truly astounded, my lady, that you would forsake both your word and good reason in this manner. After I vouched for you before the Church council, you have made a mockery of me! You swore to be guided by me in great matters of state, in particular when it came to the appointment of abbots and bishops. Indeed, it was for this very reason that I supported your rule: that the freedom of the Church in England would be restored, but I see you are willing to set all that aside.

You who lived through that bloody conflict of late, in which the Emperor Henry was sent to an early death for his battles against the Lord's anointed—you of all people ought to know better. I beg you to see reason and not make yourself into a tyrant, or else I will be forced to appeal to the Holy Father for relief. I shall join you in Westminster at the earliest possible moment, at which point I hope to hear your answer to these charges.

I allowed the parchment to fall into my lap, and then I sat staring into the flames, my breath heavy and my heart full of anger. I was not sure which disturbed me more: that Bishop Henry had immediately leapt to the worst possible conclusion about me, or that he had displayed his lack of respect for my person so openly, not fearing to tell it to me directly. His accusations seemed to cut into my flesh. He had not even spared my poor dead husband from his venom! Then a thought crossed my mind: *This would never have happened were it not for the foolishness of my uncle.*

When Adela saw the look on my face, she asked, "What is the matter, my lady?"

I took a few more deep breaths, then inquired, "Where did they put the king of Scotland?"

"In the former king's chambers, I believe."

"Thank you."

I departed the room that instant and marched down the passage to the other side of the palace, still holding the letter in my hand. My grip on it grew tighter with every step. I needed someone to blame, and it was my uncle who was about to reap the whirlwind. At last, I reached the door to the king's chamber and said to the guard, "Admit me. I must speak with the king." This he did without question, opening the door to reveal my uncle David seated at the desk he had been provided, studying a map. He looked up and started to smile, only for that smile to immediately disappear when he saw the look in my eyes.

"This is all your fault!" I said, waving the letter in front of him.

He signaled for the guards to depart, then asked me, "What in God's name is this about?"

"Bishop Henry. He has denounced my actions in regard to Durham, which are really your actions in regard to Durham."

"What?" he stammered, rising out of his chair. "Why?"

"You know very well why!" I cried, throwing the letter down on the desk. "Because you forced your man upon the see in an undue manner."

"Not this again!" he complained, shaking his head. "I thought we were past this."

"No, I chose to let it go for the time being because I had more urgent matters at hand, but now it has come back to bite me. Oh, how I rue it!"

"Calm down!" he begged me, raising his hands as if in surrender. "He has not been installed yet. Did you not write to Bishop Henry and ask his advice?"

I folded my arms across my chest and let out a sigh that was surely far louder than necessary. "I was to hear his advice when he came to London, but that seems to be too little for the bishop's liking. He thinks I should have refused the very idea of William Cumin. He says all of Durham is against it."

"Oh, please! He cannot know that."

I noted that he had not denied the content of the bishop's words, but only claimed that he could not have possessed such information. My concern increased.

"He has had visitors!" I cried. "Monks from Durham, Uncle. Apparently, they are all in a tumult because the late bishop has still not been buried. I thought you had taken care of that!"

"It was not my duty to take care of it."

There was much of the spirit of Cain in this reply, and I liked it not.[23]

"It was your fault that no one else took care of it," I said. "You ordered them not to bury him." Truly, this point offended me more than all the rest.

"Because I did not think it proper that he should be formally laid to rest until a successor was appointed and—"

"You denied him a Christian burial!" I interrupted. "How does that make me look?"

King David took a step back, his arms folded, and scoffed. "Why are you angry at me and not your cousin the bishop? He is the one accusing you in foul terms. But you need not worry yourself so much about it. Wait until Bishop Henry is here in Westminster. I am sure you can work this out between the two of you."

"He is never going to approve your William Cumin. He threatened to appeal to the pope."

"Then let him appeal! I have as much say in this matter as he does."

"What makes you think that?!"

"Because it is my land!"

---

23 The biblical character of Cain is famous in part for asking, "Am I my brother's keeper?"

How dare you say that! I thought, but did not speak the words. Instead, I told him, "No, the land belongs to the crown of England, and you hold it by royal grant," I assured him.

He scoffed even louder than before. "So, it's going to be like that, then?"

"How else would it be?" I asked. "Have you forgotten that you are my vassal and not the other way around?"

"Have you forgotten that you would not be here were it not for me?!" he cried, his arms dropping and his hands forming into fists.

"Ha! The only thing you accomplished was to have your son swear fealty to Stephen. I do not see how that was helpful." This was a harsh comment, but the moment seemed to demand it.

"I forced Stephen to maintain a presence in the North! Were it not for that, you never could have won in the South!"

Suddenly, there was a knock on one of the side doors so powerful that I was amazed it did not break.

"Who is it?" King David called.

"Earl Robert," came the reply.

"Come in!" we both said.

My brother entered, quickly shutting the door behind him. "What the hell is going on?!" he cried. "They can hear you all the way in Brentford!"

"Bishop Henry is in a frenzy because of William Cumin," I informed him. "He thinks I have gone to war with the Church."

"Bishop Henry is false and always has been," my uncle replied. "He is probably just giving himself an excuse to throw you overboard if things go ill the next few weeks."

Ignoring his comment, I said, "I blame both of you. I trusted you. You said the monks and canons of Durham would be happy to accept William Cumin. However, it seems they have been complaining to people left and right. Why did you not tell me this? Were you using me for your own gain?" Here I looked at my uncle.

"Such a declaration is most hurtful, Your Highness, and I bid you withhold judgment until we know everything," the king said.

"But we know enough, and I conclude that I have been badly used; yes, badly used, my lords! I bid you, counsel me better, or do not counsel me at all. Now I must face the wrath of Henry of Blois, to say nothing of the Londoners."

I turned to leave, but Robert stopped me, touching my arm lightly.

"Wait, my lady!" he said. "What about the other thing we were discussing?"

"The tax on the London merchants?"

"Yes. I have given the matter much thought, and I do not think we should levy a tax at this time, even if we are badly in need of gold. If we are attempting to gain their support, then a tax will hardly be helpful. They seek the same privileges they were granted under King Edward—"

"Which I have sworn to grant them and more!"

"But this tax … it is essentially a feudal one, and the Londoners are proud to be free of the feudal system."

I let out a sigh. "What would you have me do, Robert? The kingdom has been laid waste. All the lords have been bled dry by this conflict, and the common people are lucky just to have something to eat. Only the Londoners have escaped this plague without feeling much pain. They must do their part to restore our fortunes."

"But my lady, after what happened at Saint Alban's, I fear they may rebel—"

"I will stop you right there," I said, raising a hand. "Why should I listen to either of you, when you have just led me into this mess with the bishop of Durham that could have been easily avoided? No, I thought at least I could trust my kin, but now I see I can only trust myself. It is my own counsel I shall seek in this matter. I have been badly led, my lords—badly led! God help me! I must find some way to explain this. I take my leave of you both."

With that, I left them to sulk and returned to the other side of the palace, locking myself in my bed chamber. I was still very upset, and my thoughts were spinning.

"I can fix this," I said to myself. "Surely I can fix this. I must have patience. I am the queen."

A few days passed, and there was still no sign of Bishop Henry. For a man who claimed to be in a rush, he was certainly taking his time. Meanwhile, I received a formal pledge of fealty from Earl Geoffrey and made him all the grants we had discussed. I also met with him in private and informed him of the new tax that would be introduced following my coronation. He raised no objections but stated his concern that it might not be well received by the citizens. This was sound advice, but I explained to him that I had little choice: without more money, we would not be able to push the Flemings out of Kent. However, I assured him that to blunt the pain, I would make a further grant to the church of Saint Martin within the city walls: that house so dear to Londoners. He understood, and we parted ways in peace.

The following morning, I walked over to the abbey to speak with Abbot Gervase about the coronation. I did not know how he would act in my presence, for he was the usurper's natural son and thus unlikely to be a friend of mine. However, I was pleased to find he held no ill will toward me, or at least none that he chose to put into words.

He showed me around the church, which was little changed since my last visit. Three layers of arches rose to the sky upon columns, each smaller than the next. From the upper windows, the sun streamed down to meet us below. This space always led me to spiritual contemplation, not least because it was the burial place of my dear mother. I bent down to touch her marble tomb as we passed by, hoping to receive some strength from the one who had given me life.

The abbot and I had finished this walk and our conversation was coming to a close when the door at the eastern end of the nave opened. We both turned from our position near the high altar to see who this new visitor could be. The light behind him was so bright in comparison with the inside of the church that I saw only a dark figure with no definition.

"Who goes there?" Abbot Gervase called down to the other end of the church.

I took a few steps toward the figure even as he moved toward me. Then the door closed behind him, and I saw clearly that it was Bishop Henry of Winchester in all his state. Still a good five or six paces away from me, he made a rather poor show of bowing, then demanded, "Empress Mathilda, I must speak with you immediately!"

Here was the discussion I had been dreading. A chill ran down my spine. I turned back to Abbot Gervase and said, "Thank you very much for your time. Would you mind leaving me to speak with the bishop alone?"

"Of course not, my lady," he replied, then made his departure. He seemed to sense that there was great strain between us and apparently had no desire to involve himself in our affairs. Wise man!

There we were—Bishop Henry and I—standing in the nave of Westminster Abbey, eyes locked on one another. I had never seen him so visibly angry. His breath was coming heavier than usual and the muscles in his face seemed to twitch. *He looks just like my Master Godfrey in the old days before he was about to scold me,* I thought with some degree of dismay. My insides clenched in preparation for the deluge that was about to strike me. In my mind, I called upon the aid of the saints and bid myself be strong.

"Did you receive my letter?" he finally asked.

"Yes," I replied, keeping my tone as calm as possible. "I am sorry for any confusion that has been caused. I am happy to speak with you and resolve the matter."

"Confusion? I dare say we have gone beyond the realm of confusion and into outright obstruction," he scoffed. "What excuse can you possibly give me for what has taken place?"

I took a deep breath and told myself, *Remain calm. You have done nothing wrong. He will have to answer to logic.*

"I do not offer an excuse but an explanation: I always intended to speak with you before appointing William Cumin officially. I said so in my letter." I told him this with just a bit of a smile, hoping very much that he would see my good intent. Alas, it was not to be.

"That lacks some marks of truth, my lady," he charged, shaking his head in anger. "It has been well over a month since the late bishop went to meet his maker. You had plenty of time to seek my counsel, had you so wished. Instead, I am presented with a *fait accompli* at the final hour. You should have spoken with me before even considering this, but instead you allowed your uncle to force his own man upon the monks of Durham, who have had no say in the matter!"

"I did not allow the king of Scotland to do anything. He acted according to his own will." This was a point of great import, and I hoped very much that the bishop would understand it.

"But you approved his choice."

"I approved his choice because I was able to meet with William Cumin and found him to be acceptable."

"And did you know that the monks of Durham have raised many objections about his character?"

Here I turned to look away for just a moment, as I could sense that I was departing from my carefully maintained state of serenity. Of course, I had come to know that the monks opposed the appointment, but I had not been told that at the beginning. Yes, that would be my response.

"I had heard no such thing," I said, turning to face him once again.

"Because you did not want to hear it!" he cried, taking a few steps in my direction and pointing his finger angrily. "You closed your ears to anything that would force you to break with your uncle."

"I pray you refer to him as the king of Scots since you do not call me cousin," I ordered, attempting to take back control.

"I knew of the objections of the monks. Archbishop Theobald knew, and he told you himself!"

"You and the archbishop are friends now?"

"This is no time for jesting, my lady! I have been appointed a guardian of this Church, and I must defend it against those who would harm the sheep!"

This charge cut close to the bone. It seemed that I had become the weevil of Bishop Henry's nightmares. If so, I was about to be crushed.

"Are you calling me a wolf, Bishop Henry?" I asked him, deeply offended.

"It is your choice what you wish to be. I thought you would be a defender of the Church. That is why I placed my trust in you, but at the first test, you have betrayed it!"

"I have betrayed nothing! I have taken note of your objections, and I will consider them accordingly."

"Do you mean to say you will not attempt to have this William consecrated as bishop of Durham?" he asked, his manner for once more moderate.

"I do not know what I will do, but you can be certain that your advice will be taken into account."

"That is not what we agreed on!" he cried, the brief respite clearly over.

"That is exactly what we agreed on."

"You swore to let me handle decisions like this!"

"No, I swore that I would listen to your counsel, not that I would do everything you command."

"There was a clear implication that I would be in charge of policy concerning the Church."

"In charge of policy, or king in all but name?"

Now I too had cut close to the bone, and the bishop would have none of it.

"I am no usurper!" he protested, his face by this point grown very red. "What do you take me for?!"

"I do not take you for anything but what you are. I have attempted to show you respect."

"And yet you spit upon me like a common criminal."

"I do nothing of the sort!"

"Who are you to treat a servant of God in such a manner?!"

"Am I not also a servant of God and His anointed ruler on earth?"

Suddenly, the bishop's manner changed again. To my dismay, he let out a laugh. For some reason, that laugh caused me to fear more than his angry words. Then he said something that sent a shiver through my bones.

"Not yet."

"What?" I asked, praying that I had not understood him properly.

"You are not anointed yet."

There could be no mistaking my cousin's meaning. It seemed he had grown so angry that he was willing to play the last card in his hand: preventing me from becoming queen.

"Is that a threat?" I inquired.

"No, it is merely the truth."

I shook my head in frustration. "Bishop Henry, you have charged me with abandoning our agreement, but it is you who seem in danger of abandoning it. What do you intend to do? Run back to the usurper? Spring him from his cell?"

"Perhaps I was foolish to forsake my own flesh and blood."

"How can you say that after everything he did to the Church?! After everything he did to your brother bishops!"

I felt this was a very fair point, even if I made it at high volume. However, Bishop Henry clearly did not agree. Had we not been in a house of God and I not been higher in rank than he, I suspect he might have spat in my direction.

"Why can you not simply act as a woman should?!" he asked, or rather accused. "With gentleness and restraint? Why must you play the tyrant?"

"I do no such thing!"

"You are doing it right now."

"Because I defend myself?! Because I am passionate?!"

"Because you are stubborn and do not know what it takes to rule a kingdom! You must compromise. You must show grace. You must listen to others."

"I have done all those things!" I cried in frustration.

"And yet everywhere I go, people tell me that you are arrogant, puffed up, and arbitrary! You scorned your own brother, who has been your greatest ally!"

The bishop could not have placed his knife any better. He had hit me at my point of greatest weakness, where no armor of confidence could guard me. For he was right: I had treated my brother poorly. However, it was truly none of his business. It was a matter between me and Earl Robert, and it was a thing of the past.

"You know nothing about that!" I cried. "All is forgiven."

"It left an impression, I dare say."

"You dare far too much, Bishop Henry. Were you not papal legate …"

"What?! You would push me aside?"

"No, that is not what I meant," I said in truth.

"Perhaps you should pray that the people do not set you aside."

I placed my head in my hands. What utter ruin our conversation had wrought! I tried to remember how the argument had started—where it had gone so wrong. Ah, yes: the bishop of Durham. I wiped a stray tear from my eye and looked up at him again.

"Why do we make such a tumult? We are talking about one bishop, and I have promised you I will think about it again. I will listen to what the monks have to say."

"And I thank you for that, but you really ought to have done so in the first place."

"As you have been only too kind in telling me!"

For a moment, we ceased talking. Each of us worked to recover our breath. We stared into one another's eyes with the fervor of lovers, but no lovers were we! No, we merely sought to comprehend the opponent. At length, he spoke again.

"I beg you: heed my words, Your Highness. I have only your best interests and those of the kingdom in mind."

I very much believed that he had his own best interests in mind, but I did not challenge his words. Instead, I said, "I want us to work together, Bishop Henry. I want my rule to be a boon for the kingdom. I want to pass on to my sons not only a strong government, but a strong Church."

"I believe you," he replied, "but I bid you listen to better advice. Do not be wise in your own eyes. You are a woman and thus likely to be governed by the ebb and flow of feeling. Trust the men around you. That is the only way you can hope to be a boon for the kingdom."

I could not afford to be offended by his words, and yet I said, "How different ... yes, how very different things would be if I were of Adam's kind."

"It was God made you a woman, and that doom you must accept," he told me. "It is not for the pot to curse its maker. Neither I nor any man who lives can make you other than what you are. I take my leave."

I merely nodded and watched him leave as swiftly as he had come. I turned and looked behind me down the line of columns stretching toward the altar. The spiritual peace I craved was nowhere to be found.

"I am still the queen," I told myself. "No matter what anyone says, I am the queen."

XIV

I am afraid I was in a rather foul mood, and not only because of my encounter with Bishop Henry of Winchester. I had known that my reception and coronation would not be as glorious as those of the kings of old. For one thing, there was little money to be spared for such an occasion, and for another, the public did not love me as they did King Edward or even my father. Certainly, the Londoners had made it clear for many years that they preferred my cousin over me, but there was nothing for it. The situation was what it was, and all of us were forced to deal with it.

The discussions with Earl Geoffrey of Essex had been completed favorably, and the grudging support of the Church had been received. All that remained was to reach a final agreement with the Londoners so that I might enter the kingdom's greatest city with the honor due me. My sole aim was to have the sacred oil and the royal crown placed on my head. Once that was achieved, I hoped that everything else would fall into place. Bishop Henry and Archbishop Theobald would be forced to deal with me as long as I met their most basic demands. The added strength of the earl of Essex would make it possible to put down the last elements of rebellion. The merchants would abide me if I stayed out of their affairs.

Ah, but there was the problem! The people of London were, by what they might have considered an unhappy chance, part of the kingdom of England. It was therefore necessary for them to be subject to at least a few of the English laws and to contribute in some way to the general welfare of the kingdom. I knew well enough that they wished to be an island unto themselves, but their city was perched upon a greater island: one in which they had an interest, and which had an interest in them.

I tell you all this because I do not doubt that you, like everyone else, are about to judge me harshly. Of all the choices I have made in my life, none has earned me as much condemnation as the one I am about to describe. How the chroniclers have condemned me! What fortunate souls, to sit in their monasteries far from trouble, never having witnessed the affairs in question, and cast judgment upon my every word and deed!

I do not mean I have no regrets. I earnestly hope that this account puts that idea to death. Were I to have to do it again, I am sure I would have spoken less, listened more, and behaved in an altogether more pleasing manner. But what would it have achieved? The will of God is sovereign over all. Who can command the Almighty? Who can bend the course of history to his own will? We are all of us slaves first to our own passions, then to the will of God, and finally to death itself. No, I take no man as my judge, though I am most worthy of judgment. I take you as my judge, for you have a greater interest in this story. It is your own.

On the ninth day before the Kalends of July, I made my way to Saint Stephen's Chapel for the morning Mass. I received the holy sacrament with more eagerness than my daily bread. How

I needed the grace of God in that moment, and how I coveted even more the grace of men!

As I was making my way out of the chapel, I saw Lord Brian of Wallingford standing off to the side. I had hardly spoken with him since our arrival at Saint Alban's, and I felt myself badly in need of friendly conversation. I therefore told my ladies to continue down the passage and stopped to speak with him.

"How have you been, Lord Brian? You are wise to stay out of our affairs."

"I don't know if there is any wisdom involved. There simply was no room in the palace for a lowly lord such as myself, but I have been comfortable enough in our camp. I am more interested to hear how you are doing."

I said nothing but made a face that revealed my feelings well enough.

"That bad, eh?"

"Everyone hates me, but what else is new?"

"I heard that Bishop Henry came and went."

I sighed deeply. "Yes, I am afraid we had a less than pleasant conversation regarding the bishopric of Durham. He made a few good points, but I could hardly admit that to his face: not when he was failing to show respect."

"How so?"

"Raising his voice to me, for one thing. Attempting to command me. I do not believe he would treat a male sovereign in such a manner."

"Perhaps not, but that is likely to be the way of things. The world is not what it should be." There was a sadness in his eyes as he said this, and I could sense that he truly meant it.

"Oh? And what would you have it be?" I asked.

"I would have you smile more. I do not imagine there are many women as unhappy as you upon the eve of their coronation."

"That is in part my own fault. I hear the things people say, and I become so angry! I try to fight it, but the anger simply festers inside of me until it bursts like some foul wound. But how could it be otherwise when my life is one dispute after another?"

He placed a hand on my shoulder and said, "Everything will be fine. Just a few days more, and the time you have longed for will arrive. All our efforts will come to fruition. I know many of the men in this kingdom are pigs, and there may be nothing we can do about that at the present. If you can just endure for a few days longer, I believe things will improve. And we will get your sons here! Think of that!"

There was a happy thought that filled me with cheer! My heart felt a bit lighter.

"Oh, I miss them so much! I do not often speak of it, but I think it eats away at the back of my mind little by little. Is it wrong of me to say such things?"

"Of course not!" he assured me. "What could be more proper than a mother longing to see her children?"

"Yes, but I am not allowed to be like other women, nor am I allowed to act as a man would. I seem to belong to my own special class, where anything I say or do is judged wanting, and there is nothing I or anyone else can do to change it."

Dropping his hand and taking a step back, he said, "I think what you need is pleasant distraction: something to get your mind off all of this."

"Oh, yes! We have the nightly feasts, but those are just another opportunity for business. I have not even been able to dance since I came here."

He nodded. "Come out to the tent city tomorrow morning. We will all break the fast together, then we will have games and a merry ride through the forest. What say you to that?"

"I say yes, please! Perhaps it will lift this cloud of discontent from the court, and I know it will do my own heart good."

There was a pause and something in his eyes seemed to soften. He opened his mouth as if to speak again, but I never learned what he intended to say, for at that very moment, Earl Robert interrupted our conversation without warning and said, "I'm glad I caught you both together, for I have some news."

"The good kind or the bad kind?" I asked, then seeing the look of concern on his face, I said, "Of course, the bad kind. What else could it be?"

"Just tell us, Robert," Brian said.

With a heavy sigh, he recited his news. "Somehow the Londoners must have heard about the new tax—"

"What?! How?!" I cried.

"I do not know. All I can tell you is that they found out."

"Well, the only people who know are you and me, and King David, and I suppose Lord Miles and Lord Brian. So, who told them?!"

"Is that really the question we should be asking first?" he responded.

"It is if there is someone she cannot trust," said Brian.

I suddenly had a terrible thought and placed a hand upon my forehead. "Oh God! I am a fool! A right awful fool!"

"Who did you tell?" Robert asked. "Was it Bishop Henry?"

"No, I told Earl Geoffrey because I thought it concerned him." Here I struck the side of my head for good measure. "He is constable of the Tower, after all, and sheriff of the town, not to mention the justiciar. But it must have been him. I told him I would introduce the tax following the coronation, but perhaps he informed the Londoners just to provoke them to anger. He does hate them, after all."

"Is that really the way of things?" asked Brian. "He would betray your confidence just to stick their faces in it?"

"I don't see any other explanation," I concluded.

"That is not the worst news," said Robert.

"What now?!" I scoffed. "Something worse than that?"

"Mathilda of Boulogne and her army of Flemings have advanced all the way to the river and started burning everything in sight. Some of them even forded the river to the east and came within a furlong of the Tower, but they were driven back by Earl Geoffrey's archers."

"Well, at least he is good for something," Brian muttered.

I was so upset that for a moment, I could not speak. I simply returned my hand to my temple and closed my eyes, attempting to absorb what I had just heard. Finally, I said to my brother, "So, they would rather burn London to the ground than see it accept me as queen."

"That is the long and short of it—yes," he concluded.

"And is there any danger of them accomplishing their goal?" I asked slowly and deliberately.

"The city walls will safeguard those inside, but their lands outside the walls have no defense. There is also a danger that we could be encircled without means of escape."

After another pause in which I fumed with indignation, I finally said, "You are my best captain, Earl Robert. Tell me what to do."

"The army of the false queen is not that large. They can cause us annoyance, but they are no true threat to your person. I believe you are safe here at Westminster. If need be, we will even cross the river and face them in open warfare, but that would mean putting our own men in danger. The best thing you can do to help your cause is to get the crown placed on your head: the sooner the better! Once you have received the holy oil, there will be few who dare to challenge your rule. The false queen hopes to draw in the Londoners, claiming they are better off in her care, but I do not see how she can win their favor with this behavior."

"Perhaps she hopes not to be favored, but feared," I reasoned.

"As soon as the coronation is over and the support of the Londoners ensured, I will ride out with Earl Geoffrey and send these Flemings back whence they came," my brother assured me.

"I hope you are right, Robert ... for all of our sakes," I concluded.

That evening, I was due to meet with the alderman of the city of London in Westminster Hall. I may never have dreaded a meeting so much in all my days. As you read these words, you must remember the following things. First, Bishop Henry of Winchester had fortified himself in the episcopal palace of London very much in a mood to throw me overboard after showing such scorn to my face. Second, Earl Geoffrey of Essex had, in his avarice, forced me to anger the Londoners at full advantage to himself, in addition to revealing the tax before the proper time. Third, my uncle had given little or no thought to how it would affect me when he brought about that calamity in the see of Durham. Finally, our opponents were at that very hour doing their best to make our lives miserable from the other side of the Thames, burning and destroying everything in their path. All these things weighed upon my mind, and I felt as helpless as a chick thrown too soon from the nest.

Two thrones were placed on the dais that evening: one for myself and one for the king of Scotland. Around us stood many of the chief men in my court at the time: my chancellor John fitz Gilbert, Earl Robert, Earl Reginald, Lord Miles, Lord Brian, sirs Drogo and Philip and all the rest, the steward and chamberlain of the palace, Abbot Gervase of Westminster, and Earl Geoffrey of Essex, who was both sheriff of London and constable of the Tower. The rest of the hall was filled with at least a hundred other nobles, servants, and men of the Church, all come to witness what would be the final agreement regarding my coronation and entrance to the city of London. Great banners hung from the upper gallery in colors of red, blue, and green. Some bore the symbols of horses, others of great birds of prey, and still others of leopards or weapons of war. Everything was made ready for the great moment.

At last, the far doors were opened, and the men of London strode in as one: the aldermen and men of trade, led by Osbert Huitdeniers, the man who had so lately been deprived of his role as sheriff. There were about fifty of them in total, and they marched forward with a will, stopping just in front of the dais. This was the final obstacle that stood between me and the crown—between war and peace. I sought friendship in those eyes before me, but alas, they seemed a rather grim bunch. I could not even blame the weather for this, as it had been the most perfect summer day.

They removed their hats and bowed, then one of their number by the name of Richard Walbrook stepped forward to address me. He was a man of little height but much confidence, and it showed in his speech.

"Empress Mathilda, gracious lady of the English, we the aldermen and chiefs of the city of London come before you to make petition on behalf of ourselves and our fellow citizens. A great many changes you have proposed which go against the traditions of the past, all of which we have treasured. We are willing to discuss these matters with you but beg you to remember how faithfully we have served the kings of England throughout the years, always granting what is due to our rightful lords except in those times when we were pushed to the extreme of want. Such an hour has now arrived. This present conflict has drained the city of wealth no less than the worst famine, and indeed our little ones do at times go hungry. The glories of former days have become a mere memory. Not only this, but we are harassed by the queen and William of Ypres, who have burned our crops and fired their weapons at our eastern wall. Never in all my years have we stood in such great need of support from the crown, and you are that crown, my lady. If you would hold the scepter, you have a duty to the chief city of the kingdom, even as we have a duty to you. I therefore beg you to consider again this hasty decision to place a new tax upon our citizens, a burden far beyond what the kings of old ever thought to set on our shoulders. Just when we are most in need of royal aid, you would milk the teat of the city to the point of bleeding, leaving nothing for our own people. I beg you, my lady—if you could but wait a few months until the worst of the fighting is over and trade has improved, we may stand in a position to support the crown further. But as it is, we have nothing to give that we can afford to lose. We have never broken faith with the crown. Do not now break faith with us."

I had foreseen such an argument. Even so, it annoyed me, being built as it was upon a certain degree of falsehood, or at the very least incorrect memories. I doubted very much that these men, clothed in the finest garments and friendly with the greatest nobles, were upon the brink of poverty. I therefore gripped the arms of the throne more tightly and attempted a strong reply.

"I have heard your petition and those of your fellow aldermen," I told him. "I assure you that I of all people know the privations brought about by this conflict, and that is what you must come to see. You beg the aid of the crown, but the usurper has wasted all the stores of the royal treasury attempting to steal what was never his by right. And that brings us to a key point: you say that the Londoners have never failed to honor their rightful lord. Perhaps you think I have forgotten that it was the aldermen of London who welcomed the count of Mortain with open arms and imposed him as ruler upon the whole of this kingdom, going against the will of your former lord, King Henry. You set him up as king, for he promised you all the benefits of trade. He swore to make you rich, so you broke faith with the House of Normandy and betrayed the sacred trust that ought to have existed between yourselves and us. Now, what is done is done and I am willing to forgive, but let us not pretend that these things never happened. As for your alleged poverty, I have it on good authority that the city of London benefited more under the reign of the usurper than any other. The trade with Flanders has never been stopped, and the battles have been far from here. While the rest of the kingdom has been harassed by avaricious lords, you have been safe within your walls, enjoying your great privileges. You are a commune set apart thanks to the pledges of kings. I recognize this and intend to honor it, but in exchange you must honor me. I know you are not all as poor as you would have me believe. You ask for me to rid you of the false queen and her minions before you are taxed, but this is precisely the reason we need the tax. I cannot hope to defend you without money."

I did not see any way they could reasonably get around this final point. I was not taxing them as a means of punishment, but as the only way to put down our common enemy. Wars are expensive. Why those men failed to see this was beyond my ability to understand.

It was Osbert Huitdeniers who objected next, the very same man who had made such a negative judgment of my character during our discussions at Saint Albans. "My lady, I beg you not to take us for liars! This tax is an extraordinary demand far beyond tradition. Surely you must see that. Perhaps the earl of Essex has influenced you in this. If so, I beg you not to listen."

Earl Geoffrey was standing just behind me, and I can only imagine the look on his face when these words were spoken. In truth, they may have annoyed him less than the ones I uttered next: "It is my own business whose counsel I choose to keep, but I will have you know that the earl of Essex had nothing to do with it." You will remember that I was not favoring the earl at that particular moment.

"The earl of Gloucester, then," argued Richard Walbrook, "or perhaps the king of Scotland."

"Why would you assume that this could not have been my own idea?" I asked.

"Because, my lady, you are … a lady."

Oh, what an error! Even as he made that slight pause in his speech, I could sense that he knew he was on dangerous ground. His voice, so powerful at the beginning, had faded to a whisper by the end. Now there were looks of concern on the faces of many of the aldermen, who must have known he had stepped too far.

"Quiet, Richard!" Osbert Huitdeniers chided him. Even though he had lost all respect for me, he must have known that such words would do nothing to help their case.

I held up my hand. "No, I would like very much to hear this. Tell me, Master Walbrook, do you think it impossible that a woman can rule? That she can have thoughts of her own?"

At this point, Earl Robert leaned down near my left ear and said softly, "My lady, I think you should leave this matter alone."

"No, the aldermen of London evidently believe I am unable to think for myself, and I intend to prove otherwise," I said.

Osbert Huitdeniers made another attempt to end this line of discussion.

"My lady, I beg you to see reason—"

"Again you slight my intelligence!" I interrupted. The turn this conversation had taken seemed to require a strong response, and I gave them one. "Listen now, men of London. I have declared that there will be a tax, and that declaration is final. There is no other path. I am not blind to your ways. How many times did you lavish money upon Stephen? You were only too happy to give him everything he demanded, all to keep me from the place that rightfully belongs to me and my sons. You strengthened him at every turn in order to make me weak, conspiring with those who sought my demise. I have listened to your words and I have found them wanting. How am I supposed to travel throughout this kingdom, where the good people of the land work themselves to the bone to gather the wool you sell to Flanders, and tell them that they must continue to pay the feudal wage while your fortunes are kept safe in dark places where no one can find them? Is that justice? God forbid I should enforce such justice! There will be a tax, and that is final. No man ordered me to do this: I myself have reached this decision. A sovereign has no greater charge than to safeguard the land and administer justice, and that is what I intend to do. For I am your sovereign, gentlemen. I am your queen, as sure as there is a God in heaven, and if you honor the latter, you should also honor the former."

At that moment, a new man forced himself into the conversation: a man short in stature but as large in the waist as he was red in the face. He stepped forward to join his two companions at the base of the dais.

"This is an outrage!" he cried. "King Stephen never would have treated us like this!"

Well, the man did have a point, for Stephen was only too happy to give them everything they ever desired.

"What is your name?" I asked him.

He calmed slightly. "Walter Child, my lady, of Billingsgate."

"Well then, Master Child, Stephen was never your king, and he never will be. He sits in the jail where the Lord of us all has placed him on account of his sins."

"Is he never to be released?" Osbert Huitdeniers asked. "You know Queen Mathilda is worried sick."

I gripped the arms on the throne even harder and leaned forward, raising my voice. "She is no queen, and if she hoped to gain my favor, then she should not have set fire to the country side on the eve of my coronation! Truly, how can you all not see that she is your enemy and not me? She is the one who has brought this horde to the city walls and assails you day and night. A sensible person might conclude that her concerns ought not be your own."

Walter Child scoffed. "Does she not have good reason to protest when you have locked up her beloved husband and that villain there has locked up her daughter through marriage? He's been keeping the princess Constance in the Tower, forbidding her from joining her family, and probably using her for his own ghastly ends."

I turned to face Geoffrey de Mandeville, feeling not for the first time that his friendship was of no more use than the hatred of most of my enemies.

"Earl Geoffrey, I thought we discussed this matter and you agreed to let her go," I said quietly.

"Lady Constance is an enemy of Your Highness—a traitor to your rule!" he replied, his words pouring forth quickly but without fear. "The Tower is the proper place for such a person."

"Surely not for a woman, and especially one of such noble stock!" Osbert Huitdeniers objected. "She has done no wrong and spoken no evil."

I was dismayed that once again, the men around me had done harm to my cause through their poor decisions, in this case failing to honor my express command. Nevertheless, I was unwilling to let it become a distraction from the main point. I therefore attempted to dismiss it as quickly as possible.

"I will discuss this with the earl and come to an agreement by which Lady Constance may be released to her family, but this is all beside the point," I said firmly. "I have called you here to swear final loyalty to myself that we may proceed with the coronation at the abbey church of Saint Edward as soon as possible. This has already been too long delayed. So tell me, will you all swear or will you not?"

The conversation had proceeded at a fast pace until this moment. All speech ceased, and the aldermen and I simply stared at one another. Some appeared angry while others were clearly perplexed. A few of them whispered to one another, but it was Richard Walbrook who spoke for them all.

"You do great wrong to the chief city of this kingdom, my lady. Your demands may be cloaked in words of honey, but they prove bitter to the taste. You seek to punish us for acknowledging the rule of a man anointed by the Church and beloved of all who knew him."

"Ha!" I scoffed, for I doubted that anyone outside London truly loved Stephen, save perhaps for his own family.

"It's true!" the alderman boldly declared. "He has never done us wrong, but with this tax you have trespassed the bounds. How could any man accept such a thing?"

I sighed loudly and rolled my eyes, leaving Earl Robert to ask, "Do you mean to say you will not swear?"

"We must consider the matter further, my lord," said Osbert Huitdeniers.

This attempt at delay seemed to me to be yet another attempt to deny me the crown. "You have already considered it for months!" I complained.

"Many things have changed in those months," he argued.

"My right to rule is the same."

Again it was Richard Walbrook who was happy to proclaim what wiser men might have feared to say.

"Here this now, my brothers!" he cried, turning back to face his fellows. "You know well the story of Jezebel. Her unrighteous rule was the doom of ancient Israel." Here he turned again and pointed a finger straight at me. "Even so, has this she-wolf risen up before us, and only time will tell if the dogs about her feast upon her flesh! I doubt whether they will do so, as she has removed their manhood along with their dignity. As for us, we will never surrender the dignity of London, city of the Romans, chief jewel of England!"

A gasp went up throughout the hall. Apparently, some of them had little experience of men speaking so harshly, whereas for me it was entirely common. It was even too much for King David, who yelled, "Quiet, you fool! She should have you arrested for treason!"

I simply laughed. "Fear not, Uncle. If words could make an end of me, I would have been dead ten times over by now." In truth, I was quite angry, but I reasoned that the best way to rob the alderman's words of their power was to treat them as if they were nothing.

"Your Highness, may I request that we withdraw to consider this matter?" Osbert Huitdeniers asked.

"I request you withdraw and consider what respect is owed to those whom God has placed in authority," I concluded.

I hated to submit to another delay, but not for the first time, I was denied my wish. I watched as the aldermen departed, still talking among themselves. I had no doubt that they were cursing me under their breath. I had come so far—to the very hall of power and brink of coronation—but once again I was opposed on all sides. I was glad at least that I had stood firm, for I could not let them think I was a weak woman. I could not bend, or they would break me. However, my brother did not see things the same way.

"You were too harsh with them," he told me as the crowd began to disperse. "They will go back to their hive and stir up a fury. You best hope they do not rouse their queen."

These words annoyed me greatly and I stood up to face him. "I am their queen, Earl Robert. I am the queen!"

"Do you think by repeating it you can make it so?" he asked.

Oh, if only I could have made it so! If only my words could have called things into being, even as the Lord spoke creation into existence. But it seemed they were falling on deaf ears.

Just then, Earl Geoffrey of Essex stepped forward to join our conversation. "Well, I for one was glad to see those fools treated as they deserve. They are nothing but rebels against Your Highness, unwilling to grant you your due."

Robert and I both stared at him as if he had gone mad.

"I wonder that you are speaking, Earl Geoffrey, after you have just admitted to violating my command," I noted. "You should not have taken her prisoner to begin with."

The earl smiled, which I found a very odd choice. "My lady, it is my duty to administer justice in the city of London," he argued.

"Yes, but I dare say you locked her in the Tower before I appointed you to that position."

"But I—"

"No, enough!" I cried. "These arguments weary me. I must get some rest, then I will see you all on the morrow and we will break the fast together. King David, will you accompany me to my chamber?"

I looked over to the far side of the dais, where my uncle was conversing with the abbot of Westminster. He bowed his head and answered, "Most certainly, if you wish it."

I took his arm and we walked out the double door that led into the rest of the palace, where our private chambers waited to receive us. People on either side of us bowed in respect of our joint authority, though it seemed that mine was still very much in doubt. As we made our way to the stair, I said nothing at all. I was too much a prisoner of my own anger.

God curse the Londoners! I thought. *I never did like that city. And Bishop Henry is staying within their walls. I wonder what mischief he might devise.*

As we began climbing the stair, my uncle finally addressed me. "Gracious empress, your mother was my most beloved sister, and for you I also bear a special affection. Will you listen to a word I have to say for the sake of that love? I believe the late queen would have said the same thing I have in mind."

I was not sure I would like what he had to say, but I told him, "Speak it."

He nodded and began. "Do not impose this tax. Call them back. Tell them you will delay until a later date, or better yet make a complete end of it."

"I cannot make an end of it when I have declared it so boldly in the hearing of all!" I argued, angry that he would attempt to use my late mother's memory against me. "That will just confirm their suspicions that I am nothing but a stick carried along by the river, shifting this way and that as I am pressed."

"On the contrary, I believe it would make them see that their concerns are your concerns."

We had reached the top of the stair and turned down the passage that led to our rooms.

"Tell me, Uncle," I asked, "were this happening in your own kingdom, would you do the same? Would you go back on your word? Would you submit to rebels, or would you proclaim your authority?"

"I think that is a very different—"

"No, it is not different, save for this: you are a king and I am a queen. That is the only reason this is different. It is why they think they can run over me."

King David stopped walking and let go of my arm. I turned to face him. The look on his face was dour.

"You cannot blame everything on the matter of sex. You are a woman of reason. You know things are not that simple. If I attempted to tax the chief nobles of Scotland, it would amuse them no more than these Londoners."

I could not think of why he refused to take my side. What did he have to gain by supporting the Londoners in any small way?

"I know nothing of the sort!" I swore. "From the moment I was born even until the present day, I have been hated on account of my sex. At every turn, the marks of prejudice are apparent."

He shook his head. "You cannot overturn the will of God, who made woman subject to man." With this, my eyes opened wide in anger, and he must have understood, for he said quickly, "No, I did not mean that you should not rule. I simply meant that—"

"Spare me these protests! I will see you on the morrow."

I immediately began marching down the passage in the direction of my room, leaving him to call after me, "My lady, beware the Londoners! They have the power to break you."

"Not if I break them first," I muttered, not loud enough for him to hear.

I had almost reached the door I sought when Drogo appeared from around the corner, walking in my direction.

"Ah, here is a man of good sense!" I proclaimed. "What is your errand, friend?"

"A letter, my lady, from the countess of Boulogne," he said, holding it up for me to see.

I looked toward the ceiling, closed my eyes, and let out a groan. "Any chance she writes to surrender?"

"I very much doubt it, my lady."

"Very well," I said, opening my eyes and looking down again. "Read it."

He broke the seal with great care and examined the parchment, flipping it so the correct side was facing up. Then he began to read.

"'To the Empress Mathilda, countess of Anjou, Queen Mathilda of England writes the following: I bid you release my husband from that terrible prison in which he is held, in view of the mercies of our Savior, who bid us show love to enemies—'"

"Oh, spare me!" I cried, not so much at Drogo as at the false queen.

The knight looked up at me fearfully for a moment, at which point I gestured with my hand for him to continue.

"'I have heard that he is ill and brought very low in spirit,'" he read. "'Given that he is a noble of the highest degree and a blood relative of Your Highness, I bid you again to show mercy and release him. He has committed no crime. Should you do so, I am certain he will surrender his crown and content himself to wander abroad as a simple pilgrim, living the life of a monk—'"

"God Almighty!" I cried. "Does she take me for a fool?! My wretched cousin has nothing of the monk within him, not that he is any part a king either. And she is a liar from of old! I have not forgotten the fire!"

"I beg your pardon, my lady? What fire?"

"Oh, never mind it! Do not trouble me with her children's fables. Skip to the next part."

"Very well," he said wearily, and continued to read. "'But if you will not release him, as I suspect your heart is too hard to do, then I beg you to show mercy to my son. Grant him the lands of his father across the Channel. He is due to inherit by right. You have no foundation in law to deny him what is his by birth. Know that it is only to press his right and that of my husband that I am camped now within a mile of London town. If you consent to my requests, I will be happy to return to my home in Boulogne, but if you refuse, the consequences will be dreadful.'"

By this point, I had buried my head in my hands out of frustration. When he had come to the end of the letter, I looked up again and asked, "Why on earth should I do either of the things she requests? Stephen is a traitor and deserves his fate, and given his treason I am under no obligation to honor these requests. Besides, I have no authority to bestow lands that are within the realm of the king of France. Flanders is one such land, and within that duchy lies the county of Boulogne. How can I pass on that right to a young man when his parents are both among the living and it is not mine to grant? Surely I cannot, and even if I could, I would not do so on account of this: his father is an infamous traitor! I refuse to reward treachery."

"And you do not think there will be any ill effects from this?" he asked, concern clear on his face.

"There are ill effects from everything I do of late."

"The bishop of Winchester might object, as it is his nephew who stands to gain from the false queen's request."

"Yes, Bishop Henry—I am not in his favor at the moment. I must simply hope in his integrity: that he will not allow family loyalties to rank higher than the law of the land."

Drogo smirked. "That seems a great deal to hope for."

"We must hope in something, or else what are we?" I asked with a sigh.

It was a lovely summer morning when I went out to the tent city that had sprung up just on the other side of the River Tyburn. The birds were still singing and the last drops of dew lingered on blades of grass. There I was to share a meal with those who had fought so hard to bring me to Westminster—to place the crown within my grasp. But oh, how weak my grasp seemed in those hours and how endless the abyss that stood between me and the throne! A few days only, but it seemed an eternity to wait when the Londoners had grown so angry. I tried to place it out of my mind, along with the desperate acts of the false queen. There would be partridge and the first beans of the season served at my table, and I swore to myself that I would enjoy them. I had even heard rumor of a cake.

Underneath the largest tent a few tables had been pushed together for some fifty people. Here the feast was laid out, a most welcome gift after the long months of want. It was nothing compared to the feasts I had enjoyed of old, but Lord Brian had gone to great personal expense to ensure that no one would leave hungry. Seated there were all my captains, along with the faithful lords and ladies. The king of Scotland was given a place of honor second only to mine and was caught up in conversation with Lord Miles, while I was happily seated next to Brian fitz Count. I say happily not only because he was a pleasant person to be around, but also because I was not on the best terms with my brother and uncle at that time. Even more happily, Adela was seated just to my right, so I knew that any conversation I had would be far superior to that which had passed in the last few days. It might even have nothing to do with taxation.

Near the end of the table was the bishop of Winchester, who had finally seen fit to make an appearance at my court. I cannot say he was enjoying the experience: he sat there speaking to no one, staring off into the distance and scowling at the trees. I chose to leave him be as he seemed in no mood to speak with me.

"I hope this coronation is not going to be a disaster," I muttered so only Brian could hear. "An angry crowd seems as likely as a happy one."

"Take heart, Your Highness!" he replied. "It cannot be worse than your grandfather's coronation."

Now, the first King William's coronation started poorly when he was unable to convince the archbishop of Canterbury to crown him and was forced to settle for the archbishop of York. Then the shouts of support from the crowd during the ceremony were thought to be cries of rebellion, leading the Norman knights to slaughter them even as the priests read the rites. I very much hoped we would see nothing to equal that violence, and while Brian's comment seemed to be made in jest, I could not bring myself to laugh. He apparently sensed this, for he quickly changed the subject.

"This cheese is from Somerset," he said, pointing to the block in front of us. "It is truly the best in England. Would you care for some?"

"Certainly," I replied. "How did you come by it?"

"Robert knows someone," he explained, picking up a knife to cut me a piece. "Trade is not what it was before the war, but there is a man who stored some in a cave two years ago, before things were in short supply. He only just brought it out."

"Two-year-old cheese?" Adela asked with a clear note of concern. "Is it safe to eat?"

He smiled. "You drink wine that is two years old, do you not?"

"I suppose I do," she said, "but I have also seen cheese left out for a week that went bad. It was covered in blue spots."

"They take great care in making and storing it," he assured her, handing the piece he had cut to me.

By the look on Adela's face, I could tell she still had doubts, so I lifted the cheese to my mouth and took a great bite.

"My lady, you should have let one of us eat it first!" she cried.

I made no reply, but chewed happily, savoring the taste. After I swallowed, I said to her, "See, I am still alive!"

"Sure, you are happy enough now, but wait another hour," she muttered.

Growing rather weary of this conversation, I turned back to Lord Brian and said, "Thank you. It was wonderful. I shall have to thank Earl Robert as well for procuring it."

"Only the best for our queen," he replied, raising his goblet to me.

For a moment I fell quiet, and he looked at me with concern, sensing the change in my mood.

"What is it?" he asked, setting the goblet back down. "Should I not have mentioned the thing about your grandfather?"

"No … that is, I don't know. Ever since I arrived in Westminster, I have felt the greatest dread, as if a shadow were rising over me, threatening to consume me at any moment."

He nodded, more a show of support than one of agreement. "I cannot understand exactly what you are feeling," he replied, "but perhaps you refer to the weight of duty that lies upon any sovereign?"

"Perhaps," I said, grown quite pensive.

"Or maybe it is the wolf of Ypres who brings you low? Or the Londoners?"

"Are you hoping to calm my fears or provoke them?" I asked, smiling.

"I was attempting to help, but it seems my efforts are all for naught."

For a moment, I tore my eyes away from his and looked at the others in the tent caught up in their revels. Outside, some of the men were attempting to throw coins into a bucket, hoping to best one another. Across from me, Earl Robert sat quietly next to his wife, Lady Mabel. Did she know about his misdeeds in Oxford? Sirs Drogo and Philip were merry with wine despite the early hour. Lord Miles was still deep in discussion with the king of Scotland as they sought to finish a loaf of bread.

I looked down to where my cousin the bishop sat and was surprised to see that he was staring at me. There were no marks of friendship in his face, but rather the same cold stare with which he had attempted to subdue me at our last meeting. I was considering walking down to where he stood and addressing him, when he suddenly rose from his seat, leaving almost a full plate of food at his place, and walked off in the direction of his horse, looking very much as if he intended to depart.

"My lady?" Brian asked.

I quickly turned my head to face him again. "Forgive me. I was thinking of something … yes, something in the scriptures."

"What's that?"

"I do not remember exactly. They were eating and drinking, marrying and giving in marriage, until one day …"

I ceased speaking and looked deeply into his eyes: those eyes that had drawn me in when I was young and foolish, or perhaps wiser than in my old age.

"One day … what?" he whispered.

I do not know what I would have said next, for at that very moment I heard the distant sound of bells. First a few, and then more and more, until a rush of bell song rang out across the sky, only it seemed to me less a song and more a threat. Brian heard it as well and turned his head, staring off into the distance.

"The bells of London," he said. "Strange that they should all ring now. It is not the time for such things."

My breath caught in my throat. So sweet the sound of those bells might have been to others, but in my heart I felt they were heralds of woe.

"They are sounding the alarm," I concluded. "They are calling men to arms."

I looked across the table at my brother, who was likewise staring at me.

"Do you think it is the false queen?" I called out to him.

He did not answer, but stood up and ran out of the tent, taking off in the direction of the road.

"Perhaps it is the Flemings making another attempt at the eastern wall. They will be pushed back even as they were before," Brian offered.

I said nothing but continued to stare in the direction my brother had lately run. With every second that passed, the fear within me grew. I felt a strong yearning to escape that I could hardly explain. No longer able to keep my seat, I too rose and walked out of the tent, only to find Earl Robert running back toward me, his eyes lit as if by a fire.

"Flee!" he cried out. "All of us must flee now!"

My heart began to pound as the drums of war. I immediately began looking around, searching for Drogo. I did not see him anywhere. Then I had another thought. *Bishop Henry is gone. What did he know?* I looked back at my brother, who had reached my position.

"Is it the Flemings?" I asked.

"No, the Londoners!" he replied, gasping for air. "They have taken up arms and are heading this way. There is no time to make ready and fight. We must flee!"

In any other situation, I would have stopped to argue the merits of this rash decision, but I knew my brother would not have made such a declaration unless it was the truth. We had no choice.

"But flee where?!" I asked. "How can we gather everything up in time?"

"Do you not understand what I am saying?!" he cried. "Leave everything but your horse! We flee at once, each man where he will!"

With that, he departed to begin informing others. For my part, I ran back into the tent to see who remained. There was Lord Brian right where I had left him.

"Gather what you can and mount your horse at once! We must retreat," I called down to him from the other end of the table.

He rose immediately and asked, "Where are we going?"

I thought quickly. We could not go south, for that would take us toward the false queen. We could not go east for the same reason. Every breath brought the Londoners closer. It was west or north, so I chose both.

"Wallingford," I replied. "We make for Wallingford: you, me, Robert, Miles. The rest of the lords may return to their own castles, but we must go now!"

I then ran out of the tent in a frenzy in the direction where I knew my horse was tied up under a large oak tree. Happily, I found Drogo standing there with the reins already in hand, evidently aware of the whole predicament.

"Come, my lady! We have no time to waste!" he called.

He did not need to tell me twice. I made no attempt to mount the beast like a noble woman. Drogo simply lifted me as if I weighed nothing and I sat with one leg on either side, the way I had been taught to ride at moments such as the one in which I found myself. Immediately, Drogo mounted his own horse, even as the rest of the knights began doing the same. Lord Brian's horse had been kept on the other side of the tent, and as I looked, he came riding around the bend, making to join us.

"Where is Earl Robert?" I asked no one in particular. "Where is my brother?"

"Tending to his wife," Sir Philip replied, riding up next to me. "He said we should go ahead."

I did not like this idea at all, but as I looked into the distance, I saw dust rising up from the road and a crowd of figures moving toward us.

"We ride at once!" I cried. "Lord Brian, lead the way. To Wallingford!"

Soon I heard not the sound of bells, but that of hooves upon the road, moving us farther from Westminster—farther from the goal. I turned to look behind me one last time at the shrinking form of Saint Edward's church, where I was meant to be crowned. How would I ever get there now? My heart was heavy, but I was far too afraid to give way to tears. All I could think of was escape. It was only once we had put a good five miles between us and the angry mob that I had two terrible thoughts. First, that I had left Adela. Second, that the Londoners were going to eat my food.

XV

Rouen, Normandy
June 1167

Oh, how my heart ached as I was forced to flee from my inheritance! Had I been thinking clearly, I might have observed then what all the chroniclers declare now: that I was too harsh with the Londoners and pushed them into the arms of my enemies. I could see nothing clearly then. My anger and impatience clouded everything. All I could think was, *Gain the crown. Then all will be well. Then you will see your sons again.* Everything that happened from the time of our victory at Lincoln to that awful morning when I was forced to ride with all haste away from a band of fishmongers and tailors had been steering me toward my doom, and yet I do not deny that I played some part in that sad affair. I had been taught to doubt those around me—to act upon my own will or suffer the consequences. I ask you, to what degree was I the mistress of my own doom? Are any of us truly free when passions seek to devour us?

Perhaps it would be easier to speak of what happened today than what has happened in years past, though I cannot say which touches me nearer. I crossed the river: not the Styx, but the Seine. I wished to speak with Rotrou, who has been archbishop of Rouen these two years after serving earlier in Evreux. I had met him a few times before, though I cannot say we knew each other well. I was to make his acquaintance far better this day.

Long had I avoided that journey, for within the walls of the cathedral lie the bones of my son. How different his death has been from any other! I was eager to visit the graves of my mother and forbears, but the graves of my sons are another matter entirely. True, I should be by their side. I should never cease to keep vigil, but I cannot.

My son Geoffrey's passing was less of a blow to me, for he was the image of his father. Spurning both me and the Almighty in life, my sorrow in his death was somewhat lessened. I felt as if I had already lost him long before, and I surely owe him no debt of visitation now given how far away he lies. Yet, my William was the very opposite: so pure, so full of love, the image of neither of his parents but my own mother. When he died, it crushed me, and I do not think I shall ever recover. Whenever I would look upon the cathedral, I could not help but think of him and say a prayer for his soul, but I feared to approach that place directly. The wound seemed too deep.

I had therefore hoped to claim the rights of title and old age to remain where I was and have Archbishop Rotrou come to me, but he was eager to welcome me back after such a long absence and besought me to come, promising to direct everything toward my comfort. He did not know the purpose for which I had requested the audience. If he had, he may have done differently.

Thanks to my own efforts, there is a bridge over the Seine, and this was the path we took to the meeting—myself and the few who accompanied me. The carriage stopped just to the west of the cathedral, in the open square occupied by blacksmiths, masons, and carpenters all working at their trades. The cathedral is to be made over in the same style as the abbey of Saint Denis, even as it seems half the churches in Christendom will be. I have nothing against improvement, except that it is often more expensive than necessary. I suppose then I do have something against improvement. When the horses can barely walk through on account of the piles of stone and wood planted here and there, one is bound to question how long such things will last.

The archbishop had requested that, for the sake of privacy, I meet him in the base of the new tower dedicated to Saint Romain. They say one day it will rise to the heavens, but at the present it hardly merits the name of tower. When I climbed out of the carriage, I was immediately met with the sound of metal upon metal, hammer upon wood, and the cries of voices high above to their fellows down below, bidding them load the next stone to be raised. The archbishop was standing just outside the entrance, a thin man with a gray beard, his golden cope shining in the midday sun. His garments appeared so heavy that he was surely sweating underneath them in the heat of summer.

"Hail, Empress Mathilda, and welcome again to the cathedral church of Our Lady of the Assumption!" he cried over the noise, bowing his head in obeisance. "I beg you to forgive our state of construction. Come now and I will show you what has been accomplished thus far."

It seemed to me that the main thing that had been accomplished was the destruction of a large portion of the west front. I have said there was an entrance, but in truth it was more of a large hole. The stone work above it, which in my youth held many statues of the saints, had been either partially or wholly removed. It was difficult to tell what of the original remained beneath the scaffolding. The great doors had been taken off their hinges to allow both materials and men to move more freely.

"My lord archbishop," I said, raising my voice as best I could to meet the din, "my hearing is not what it once was. Will we be able to talk inside the cathedral, or would it perhaps be better to meet elsewhere?"

"The baptistery is quiet," he assured me. "I will lead you there."

I took hold of the arm he offered and we made our way toward the entrance. A small wood roof had been thrown up in haste to block any falling stones, but I doubt it would have stopped more than a pebble. I felt much more at ease once we were inside.

"This way," the archbishop said, pointing to the room on our left.

We walked through the short passage that opened into the baptistery. Here the ceiling climbed a bit higher and the three outer walls each had two windows allowing the sunlight to stream down. The low arches were crowned with capitals on which vines and animals were carved. The font itself sat in the middle of this space, and somewhere above us could be heard the same workers I had so lately seen, still shouting at one another.

"What do you think?" the archbishop asked, a smile on his face.

Poor man! He clearly hoped to impress me, but I had seen Westminster Hall, Saint Peter's Basilica, and the cathedral of Aachen. It would have taken a great deal more to impress me.

"Very nice," I replied.

I sensed from the look on his face that this was not the answer he hoped for, and I aimed to change the subject.

"You do not mind if I sit, do you?" I asked, pointing to a bench against one of the walls. "My feet ache if I stand for too long at once."

"Not at all," he replied, guiding me toward my seat. He then began looking around from one direction to the next, and I reasoned he was searching for another place to sit so that he would neither crowd me nor stand while his superior sat.

"Please feel free to sit next to me," I told him, patting the empty space on the bench. "I will keep it a secret if you do."

He smiled and did as I proposed, though taking care to remain as close to the opposite end of the bench as possible.

"Now, to what do I owe this great honor, my lady?" he asked, folding his hands together on his lap.

"The honor is also mine. I should have come much sooner. Be certain that it is not any hatred of your person that has kept me away. You see, the last time I set foot in this place was more than a year ago."

"That would have been when the viscount of Dieppe was buried?" he asked, referring to my son William.

I cast my eyes down to the floor. "Yes."

"I am sorry for your loss," he said in a low voice. "You have known so many losses in your time."

"More than tongue can tell. Those in youth felt sharper, but now that I am ancient, the sum of them is a weight so great that had I not been brought low by misfortune, I should be driven into dust all the same."

"You are not so ancient, are you? I thought we were close in age."

I pulled my eyes back to him. "We are, I am certain, but years alone do not make one old. Dejection and suffering take their toll, but nothing creates wear as quickly as grief. We are among the last of our generation. Not only that, but we lag behind many of the next. Two sons have I lost, and as for my siblings, most of them were dead long ago and I see not the ones who are left. It is the curse of the aged: to linger on as phantoms without warmth of love, clinging to forms that decay."

"I too feel that pain. My brothers have long since gone the way of all flesh. My brother Roger—"

"I remember him! Or perhaps it is better to say, I remember about him. I thank God for your family, archbishop. You make a good name of Beaumont."

"Unlike my cousins?"

I could see that Archbishop Rotrou was not the type of person to avoid a difficult subject, for it was his cousins, Waleran and Roger Beaumont, who had committed themselves to the cause of the usurper throughout most of the war and were altogether contemptible persons. I was glad to see that his manner was in no way defensive: his arms were crossed, but he was smiling.

"There is no point pretending I loved the twins," I admitted. "The world knows our history well enough."

"Indeed, they merit your hatred."

"I do not hate anyone. I did in former days. Waleran, Stephen, the wolf of Ypres ..."

"The what?" he asked, leaning in as if he believed he could not have heard me correctly.

"Ah, forgive me. That was our name for William of Ypres back in the day. He too is now food for the maggots. I hated them then. I hate them no more. Perhaps I have no vigor left for hate."

He leaned back and nodded. "Time has healed your wounds."

"On the contrary, it does no good to hate when one is so close to death. My final hours must be reserved for sanctification."

Here he lowered his brows. "Are you close to death?"

I nodded sadly. "That is why I have come. Perhaps I do not look so very ill now, but I assure you I feel it. My lungs are torn apart. I have a cough that hangs upon me day and night. The disease consumes me. I may not last until autumn."

The mere mention of coughing caused me to do it again. I pulled out a cloth from my pocket to cover my mouth, and when I finished, I saw again the sign of blood that had become so frequent.

"Are you certain?" the archbishop asked. "Perhaps you may recover."

I sighed and placed the cloth back in my pocket.

"Oh, I am most certain. I have seen death in many forms. I have often been close to it myself. I know its face well enough when it comes knocking at my door, and this time I will be forced to let it in. One can only shut the door on death so many times."

"Then I am deeply saddened. You have been a true voice of reason as queen mother, a bringer of peace." His words were soft and slow, his eyes moist.

"There are words I never thought to hear a man say of me! No one accused me of creating peace in the former days."

The archbishop stroked his beard thoughtfully. "The former days were evil."

"All days are evil, and those of false peace most of all. But again to the point—Will you lead the Mass at my funeral?"

Here was a change in his mood. He sat up a bit straighter and folded his hands in his lap once again. "It would be a great honor, but not one I would cherish, for it comes at the expense of such a great loss. Do you wish to be buried with your ancestors in the cathedral?"

My mind was immediately carried back to a dark room in the palace not a mile away. I was in terrible pain, moving in and out of dreams. My breath was shallow and fast. Someone was asking me where I wished to be buried. I quickly broke out of the memory.

"That choice was put to me once before, and I say now what I said then: I will be buried at the abbey of Bec-Hellouin," I told him. "Will you attempt to change my mind?"

"Of course not!" he replied quickly.

"Then you are alone. Not only that, but I think you do poor service to your own church. Royal burials are a boon to any cathedral. I hope if some man comes to Normandy with a holy relic for sale, you will not defer so quickly."

I meant it as a jest, but his reply was entirely serious. "Those already dead give little thought to such things."

"Do they not? I doubt that Saint Martin enjoys being buried in such wealth as he rejected in life, yet there he lies in Tours, calling the pilgrims from near and far."

He chose not to draw me into debate on the matter, but said, "I will see to it that you are laid to rest at the abbey. It is the least service I can perform."

"And God bless you for it, but only he knows what will happen after we are both gone."

"You do not think they would move your bones!"

I could not help but laugh. "I know of bones that have traveled more often than myself and much farther."

Again, he chose not to laugh but kept his expression fixed. I suppose I had just informed him that I was to die and he did not want to give the impression that this caused him anything but grief.

"Well, be assured that I will do everything in my power to keep them where you desire," he told me. "Have you given any thought to a memorial?"

"I leave that to my son the king. We will see how much gold he is willing to spend on the woman who bore him and what epitaph he grants to the one who refused to surrender his inheritance."

"Do inform me if you have any desires as to the manner of service. I have no fear that Masses will be said for your soul for as long as Masses are said."

"I wonder if they will do any good."

These words seemed to have quite an effect on the archbishop and finally provoked a different response. He raised his brows and asked, "You doubt the Mass, my lady? I did not take you for such a … person."

"You were thinking 'such a heretic.'" He rushed to deny it, but I held up a hand to quiet him. "Have no fear! I do not doubt the Mass. I doubt myself."

"How so?"

For a moment, I allowed my eyes to wander around the room. My mind moved backward, or perhaps upward, crossing the span of the years until it came to a point in my youth. I was in Saint Edward's abbey church, looking upon the grave of the Confessor, clinging to the hand of my mother, whose veil was as a waterfall of silver from her head.

"He is dead, mother?" I asked.

"Yes, he is sleeping," she replied. "Sleeping until the great resurrection of souls at the end of days."

"Is he not in heaven?"

"Why yes, his soul is, but his body remains here."

A hundred candles had been lit for the late king, and their flames burned before my eyes. A glow filled the space as if from another world.

"Will I go to heaven, mother?" I whispered.

But my mother was no longer there. The candles had long since burned out. I was not in Westminster, but Rouen. I looked back at the man beside me. I closed my eyes and breathed deeply. Then I spoke.

"*Memento mori.* For as long as I can remember, those words have been at the center of my mind. 'Remember your death. Remember that you are dust.' From the first moment I knew anything, I knew that I would die. And I have almost died many times over! At times I was under threat from violence and at other times made to suffer in my body. Life has often led me to the contemplation of my own mortality, and yet I have never felt ready to be received into that other world. When my second son was born, I looked death more clearly in the face than at any other time. Not only that: I saw myself, and what I saw led me to fear. I was not ready to die then, not because I was young, but because I knew myself to be so tainted with iniquity that should I appear before the Almighty he would cast me from his presence. He would send me down to that depth from which no man returns, or at best I would be left to ascend the baleful mount for a thousand years in torment and agony. I cried to the Lord, 'Grant me the time to make good on repentance. Grant me all faith in believing!' I called upon every saint I knew by name and even those I did not, bidding them beseech the Lord on my behalf. Long I waited for an answer. I rose from my sick bed, but part of me remained there ever after, beseeching again and again, praying that when the time finally came for me to depart, I would do so in confidence. Well, here I stand about to fall, and still I am torn apart by doubt. Still my spirit trembles within me. I am no more ready to die than I was three decades ago. I must smile at men and say all is well. 'Be not troubled on my behalf. I go to a better world.' Yet my heart feels nothing of that assurance. I am wasting away— yes, I am failing. This is the end of my existence. I must enter the hereafter, but what will come hereafter? If only I could be given just once that quiet whisper of the Spirit telling me all is well, I would go in such peace as only the saints have known. But I am no saint. I am an empress."

I had made this speech with a real display of feeling, but the archbishop simply continued to stroke his beard, making no reply. Just when I began to feel offended by this lack of sympathy, he spoke at last.

"My lady, I do not want to seem impertinent. Do I have your leave to ask a rather personal question?"

"By all means. I doubt you can say anything that will wound me more than I have already suffered." That is the beauty of growing old, you see. There is little left to lose. The danger was entirely on the part of the archbishop, who might be surprised at what lay within me.

"What kind of man was your father?"

"The king? King Henry?" The question surprised me, and I wondered if I had mistaken his meaning.

"Yes, I believe it is common knowledge that he sired you," he replied with a smile.

"Over this matter a war was fought."

"Thanks be to God your son sits now upon the throne, but that is beside the point. I repeat, what kind of man was your father?"

I attempted to play his game. "Bold and proud, a keen administrator, a leader of men—"

"That is what the chroniclers tell me. I do not want to know what kind of man history says he was. I want to know what kind of man he was to you, or more precisely, what kind of father."

I am sorry to say that I was no longer enjoying the archbishop's presence as much as I had before. He had hit upon one of the few subjects that could still raise up the devil in me during my old age.

"I spent little time in his presence," I replied.

"Yet I suspect he is ever present in your life."

"Even so."

"Was he good to you?"

"He left me a kingdom, or at least he attempted as much."

"But did he leave you any reason to fear him?"

It was clear that the archbishop intended to make some sort of philosophical point. I knew him only a little and he was not the kind of person to whom I would normally have spoken such painful secrets. But again, I thought, *I am almost dead, my father is long dead, and my son is safe upon the throne ... or as safe as such a man can be. What do I have to lose?*

"My father was the kind of sovereign that everyone feared," I explained. "No sooner did he speak, no sooner did the decree part from his lips, than it was done. Such absolute power he wielded like the forces of nature, blowing this way and that. When I was fortunate enough to feel his pride ... but that was not common. No, I was more often caught in the tempest of his anger."

"Now we come to it," he said solemnly.

"Yes, I admit it," I said softly. "I feared him then. I fear him still, although his power over me has decreased. But why are you so eager to know? What does it matter to anyone what a woman thinks of her father, even if she be an empress and the daughter of a king?"

"It matters because we often look to our earthly fathers for an image of our Heavenly Father."

I shook my head. "I see what you are saying, but from a young age I knew that my father's behavior was not in line with the commands of God."

Archbishop Rotrou stood to his feet and began to pace thoughtfully, his hands clasped behind his back. *Now I've done it*, I thought, but even as I began to worry, he turned on the spot and addressed me.

"Let me try something else. Are you familiar with that verse which says, 'Perfect love casts out fear'?"

"Yes, it is in Saint John's first epistle."

"Your Highness' knowledge of scripture is excellent," he said, clearly attempting to flatter me. "Now, God Himself is love, the source of all true affection. His love is not a changing thing, but absolute. It leads us to praise. If we knew this love as a constant thing in our lives, I dare say we would fear nothing."

I began to see where he was leading me. "But I am afraid, so you suspect me of not knowing God's love."

He sat back down again, closer to me this time, gesturing with his hands as he spoke.

"Maybe you knew it at some time. Perhaps it sprang up in your soul like the flowers of spring only to wilt in summer. To any extent that you have not known that love, you have known fear, and I suspect that nothing has caused you to doubt the love of God more than the lack of love shown to you by your father."

I paused for a moment and considered. I had to admit that his words had merit. No one had asked me such things before, nor had they stopped to consider the effects my father's behavior might have had on the rest of my life. Indeed, I myself had done little to investigate these matters, perhaps because I sought to avoid my father at all costs, even in death. Yet, I knew the truth somewhere inside me. I had been taught not to trust from the start, and still I struggled.

"If this be true, then what am I to do?" I whispered, my eyes growing moist. "I cannot exorcise the memory of my father. He will always be with me, whether in heaven or in hell."

"Surely you do not think yourself bound for hell, my lady!"

I could no longer prevent a tear from falling. "You tell me. The Church teaches that if anyone dies in mortal sin, he or she will not enter heaven. What if I should die before seeing a priest? What if I only fool myself, and my heart does not truly repent of those sins I have committed?"

Here were the questions I had always been afraid to put to a priest. Fortunately, he did not respond harshly.

"You are afraid, madam. You are afraid because you do not see. You have not glimpsed the *visio beatifica*."

"To do so is my heart's desire," I whispered.

"Then you will, most certainly! I have spent my life in the Church, and I dare say I know its doctrines as well as any man in Normandy, but you must not think that those doctrines are only there to drive one to despair. We beseech men to confess so that they will know the weight of their sin. We seek to drive them to the cross of Christ! Upon that cross, a Savior hangs and bleeds. In him is love, not that we loved him, but that he loved us and gave himself up for us. That love draws us to heaven. It works in us the perfection God seeks, which we could never work in ourselves. Love speaks words of comfort to us. It bids us carry on and know that, in the words of the apostle, to live is Christ but to die is gain. Now you see through a glass dimly, but there face to face. When his countenance rests upon us, all fears are ended."

The archbishop was an old man, but he spoke with the passion of youth. His eyes seemed to gleam with a sudden fire as he asked me, "Do you think that the one who took upon himself the iniquity of the world is so lacking in mercy that he cannot cover your sins?"

"No, I would never—"

"Do you think that he who granted paradise to the thief upon a cross would deny it to you? Do you think the sacrifice of Christ too weak to extend grace even to the worst of sinners?"

"I do not!" I assured him, my heart pounding. "I have all faith in Christ, but none in myself!"

"Then you are firmly on the path to salvation, for one must begin by despairing of one's self. Despair is the path to hope, and hope does not disappoint us. You will reach heaven, my lady, not by anything you have done, but by the richness of his mercies, the grace given you that lends you life. You say confession is the teaching of the Church, and so it is, but grace is the heart of our confession. We are lost without it. It is grace which grants us the power to love God as we ought. We stand before him with empty hands, and he fills us to the point of overflowing."

I could not help but smile as I said, "You speak much as Anselm was wont to do."

"I deserve no comparison with that great man. I think you knew him."

"Yes, he was the guiding light of my youth. He told me once, 'Fear not, Lady Mathilda. We do not shudder before gods of wood. The Lord shed his own blood. It is accomplished—it is satisfied.'"

"And did you believe him?" he asked thoughtfully.

"I wanted to ... I still want to."

The archbishop nodded and patted my hand gently. "When you do come to death as we all must, think not upon your sins, but the love of Christ. Allow that love to seize your heart and raise you up to heaven, where love finds its source."

"Eternity ..." I whispered.

We continued in that manner for awhile longer, and our conversation did lend me some peace. At length, we were forced to cease. As we made to depart, I stopped and looked down the nave to where I knew my son was buried.

"Grant me leave, archbishop," I said quietly. "I wish to attend upon my son."

"Would you like me to go with you?" he asked.

I considered for a moment, then replied, "No, it is not far, and I do not fear to be alone. I have learned the secret power of stillness."

He let me go and I began making my way toward the altar, the rows of columns passing slowly on either side. The sounds of construction could still be heard, but I paid them no heed. I felt as if I was walking not through air but time itself.

I came to it at last: the *effigia* of white stone. It was not a bad likeness of him, though it was surely too short. There sat his beardless face staring up toward the heavens, his hands clasped in prayer. In marble, he was preserved, but below his form was surely given over to decay. Those very bones were formed within me. I carried them to Normandy to defend what was his by right. I carried my son through the cold winter air, our hearts beating as one. No longer did he have a heart to beat. He had passed behind the veil that blinds living men: the door by which we all must enter but none may return.

There were some candles burning nearby and more sitting in a basket, waiting to be lit. I reached out and took one in hand, then lifted it to meet the flame of another. I watched as the orange light crossed over from one wick to the next, joining them in the same fire. I then pulled my candle away and set it in one of the empty spaces, its flame dancing slightly.

Returning to the grave, I placed a hand upon the stone form of my son and knelt. Tears filled my eyes. The light of the candles seemed to bend amid that water. A single tear fell and landed on one of the stone tiles, reflecting the glow on its surface.

"My son," I whispered. "Oh, my son … It is almost over. It is almost done. You cannot return to me, so I will come to you." Lifting my eyes to heaven, I inquired, "What will remain of us here on earth? What will they say about us when we are gone?"

Are there any words in the tongues of men more loathsome than, "I have failed"? I had often felt grief on account of the conceits of others—found myself the play thing of powers beyond my control. I had known the torments of broken sleep, when one curses waking for fear of what the day may bring forth. Of such things, I was well aware, but I had seldom felt the piercing blow by my own hand directed.

And the origin of that calamity is readily apparent, for when I was but the challenger, my mind was for ever set upon the injustices done me by others, and rightly it should have been. But when I attained that for which I had fought, I found myself overwhelmed by a burden which no one can know until it is truly felt. Though I never enjoyed the sovereignty which the sons of Adam inherit from birth, I possessed just enough power that, when combined with my little experience, I was able to do myself great harm.

Had I been wrong to believe as I once did? Was there something within me that prevented me from reaching the heights of my fathers? For I had sighted the prize before me, but in that moment which matters most of all, I failed. There was my doom written out: the work of years banished like the morning dew in summer's heat.

These thoughts tormented me as we raced through Middlesex and Buckinghamshire, seeking the castle of Wallingford as if it were the only water in a desert land. We were forced to ride well north of the Thames to avoid the allies of the false queen who still held Windsor, finally stopping to rest in the valley just north of Uxbridge. Having ridden faster than anyone who might have brought us news, we endured a night of dreadful ignorance. I still thought of Adela, whom I had in my haste left behind. What had become of her? I feared I could not forgive myself if the Londoners had taken her prisoner. But what could they want with a poor maid? I prayed I would not have to find out. And to think that all my possessions had surely been pillaged! Would I ever see them again?

At first light, we moved into the hills, which would grant us better protection. There my horse suffered as a stray piece of metal pierced its foot and caused great pain with every stride. I left the poor thing with some farmer in the hope of returning one day. Alas, I never saw him again. I was forced to ride the rest of the way with Sir Drogo, until his horse could no longer bear the double weight and I began sharing with Sir Philip. The younger knight said barely two words in all those hours, and I reasoned he must be fearing greatly for Lady Adela, whom I believed he secretly cherished in his heart.

These delays and a new fall of rain caused our pace to slow, and we wandered in the forest for a good two or three days before it suddenly opened to reveal the River Thames once again, less than half as broad as it is when it reaches London. By that time, we were within a league of Wallingford, where we would have safety to lay our heads in relative peace. When the castle was finally in view, a magnificent fortress near the river bank, Lord Brian bid us tarry for a moment while he rode ahead to inform the household of our arrival. As it so happened, there was no need, for they had somehow received word ahead of time. Ours would not be a triumphal entry— clearly, all England knew of my humiliation.

I had only been to Wallingford Castle once before, and then very briefly. It was shortly after the new lord and lady took up residence, at a time when I was quite low in spirit. Ever since, I had made efforts to avoid the place, for in it I was sure to be met by unhappy memories. However, since the start of the war it had become something else: the place of greatest resistance against the usurper. Standing closest to London of all our castles, it had been made to feel the wrath of the false king, and yet it stood firm. Most faithful of servants was Brian fitz Count. So, although my second visit to Wallingford came at a time when my heart was again cast down, the sight of that place caused me to hope.

When I entered the courtyard still riding with Sir Philip, I was met with a most welcome sight: my brother Reginald, the earl of Cornwall, come out to greet us.

"Earl Reginald!" I cried. "I did not think to see you here so soon, but I am glad of it!"

"My lady," he said with a bow, then standing up straight and breaking into a smile, "We have been here for the better part of a day. What took you so long? Does it have something to do with you sharing a horse?"

"What sharp eyes you have," I replied in annoyance, for only a blind man could have missed it. "Come and help me down."

He did as he was commanded, and when my feet were safely placed upon the gravel, I asked him, "Have you heard anything of the Scottish king?"

"Actually, yes. He is fled to his earldom of Huntingdon until he receives word from Your Highness to congregate."

"Very good," I said, feeling a sense of relief. "Did you say someone else came with you?"

Reginald opened his mouth to answer but was interrupted by a voice calling out, "My lady! Empress Mathilda!"

Oh, what relief filled my heart as I turned to see Adela running out of the keep, bearing not a single scratch but rather a broad smile upon her face! So happy was I that I also ran to meet her, not caring what anyone might think. We embraced for a moment and then I said, "Adela, you cannot know what great joy fills my heart to see you alive! Did you come here with Earl Reginald?"

"Yes, he has taken such good care of me, you need not worry," she assured me. "As you know, I cannot ride well, so the earl offered to take me on his horse. Lady Wallingford has been exceedingly kind to me. Really, she is the best sort of person. But who else is with you?"

"Lord Brian you will have seen, and we have also Earl Robert and Lord Miles among our number, soon to be Earl Miles." I could see that these names had no real effect on her, so I added, "And of course, my knights accompanied me: Sir Drogo and Sir Philip and all the rest."

Here her eyes seemed to grow brighter. I stepped aside to reveal all the men behind me. I noted that her gaze moved straight to the knight with whom I had so lately ridden. Part of me wanted to say something, but I bid myself, *Leave it alone, Maud.* I did leave my maid to speak with the rest of them and entered the keep through the open door. The room into which I walked was the great hall, and rather great it was: larger than the standard for a castle of this type and filled with tapestries from Flanders. *Those must be a D'Oyly inheritance*, I reasoned. Of course, I had been in that room once before, but at the time my mind was far too caught up in my own displeasure to pay heed to such things.

There were no tables in the room at that hour. Instead, the floor was covered in thick straw on which we the visitors would sleep. Even as I stood there, a pair of servants were casting it here and there with their forks, to what purpose I was not entirely certain. One of them disturbed a mouse which soon felt the bottom of a boot.

"Empress Mathilda!" a voice called, and I turned to see the lady of the castle coming in through a side portal. She was dressed in a lovely blue gown, with a string of large pearls hanging from her neck. I strongly suspected that upon hearing I was come, she had put on some of the best things she owned. The effect was indeed grand, and though she must have been over sixty years old by that point, she showed little of her age. She was still quite comely as she had always been. Following behind her was Lord Brian, who stood quite a bit taller than his wife and apparently had been too busy commanding the servants and the grooms to remove his cloak or muddy boots. They both knelt on the straw before me, and I gestured for them to rise.

"Your Highness," the lady began, speaking before her husband as usual, "I wish we could welcome you on a happier occasion, but we are nevertheless greatly honored by your presence.

Oh, how I have sought it these many years! Too dark our home has been without your light to brighten it!"

"I am sorry it has taken so long for me to return," I said quietly. "I am also very sorry to impose upon you at such an hour when there are few provisions to be had."

"Not at all! Not at all!" she said with far more cheer than seemed right for the occasion. After all, she was receiving us after a hasty and shameful retreat. "What is ours is yours, as they say. I hope you will make your stay with us for at least two weeks!"

"Thank you, but I do not foresee that I will remain more than a day or two. I must make for Oxford and the house of your kin. They will be better able to host my court."

This answer clearly discouraged her. Her whole countenance seemed to droop. Well, I was not trying to make anyone sad, but the idea of spending two weeks in that place was rather more than I could bear, even if I had not just experienced one of the worst incidents of my entire life.

"Is that so?" she asked softly. "What a shame! I have grown rather fond of your girl, Adela."

I was attempting to think of what words of comfort I could offer when Lord Brian finally placed a hand on his wife's shoulder and said to her, "My dear, the empress has told us she must go to Oxford, and she is quite right. We do not have the space here." Then to me he said, "Fear not: you will not be forced to join the men on the floor. We have a guest chamber available, or if you prefer you can use our own rooms."

"That will not be necessary," I replied. "Show me this other place you speak of. I am certain it will do."

With that, Brian returned to the yard to give some instruction to the grooms and I was led by Lady Mathilda up a flight of stairs to the upper level of the keep, where a line of three doors stood before us. The only light was from a candle on the wall.

The lady removed it from its sconce and began walking down the passage, pointing to each door in turn.

"My lord's chamber, my chamber, and here," she said, pointing to the final door. "This will be your chamber for as long as you remain."

She turned the knob and opened the door to reveal a small room with a straw bed, a water basin, and a single chest. Some light entered through a window to the right, and on the floor were two deerskin rugs.

"I know it is not fit for a queen," she said sadly, setting the candle down upon the window sill, "but hopefully it will do for the present."

"Trust me, lady Wallingford, I have laid my head in far worse places," I assured her, my smile genuine.

"If you wish, I can have some books brought to you from my lord's collection," she continued, moving a step closer to me. "I know you are both so fond of reading."

There was something odd about the way she said this: a great weight seemed to hang upon the word both. She took another step closer and whispered.

"He is so committed to you, Lord Brian. Even when that villain Stephen was upon us like the chill in winter, he did not cease for one moment to defend this fortress—to promote your cause. I believe there is nothing he would not do for you if you required it."

I was beginning to feel uneasy about our conversation, for I wondered how much the lady of Wallingford knew about our common history. I chose my words carefully.

"I am indebted to you both for your faithful service on behalf of the kingdom."

There I had also used the word both, but for the lady and her husband, directing the matter away from myself. She smiled again, took my hand, and patted it with her own.

"Let us know if you need anything at all," she concluded, then left the room, shutting the door behind her.

I breathed deeply and fell upon the bed, clasping my hands together upon my forehead.

Two weeks? I'll be fortunate to survive a day here, I thought.

Flames. All around me, flames, falling from the sky and rising from the ground. I ran out into the darkness, to the outer reaches of my mind. So cold was the ground below me—ice, heat, wind, and a voice.

"Maud!" it called upon the air. "Come!"

I awoke with a scream, my body covered in sweat. It was the same dream I had experienced some weeks earlier—the same feeling of dread. But was it the Londoners I feared, or something else? Could it be Stephen? No, he was locked away in Bristol Castle. Surely it could not be. And yet I had seen it: I had seen Oxford on fire, only not quite the Oxford I knew in life. It was somehow different, as if fear itself had come alive and given a shape to that darkness, and everything about me was chaos.

Rising from my bed, I bent over the basin and threw some water on my face, rubbing my eyes as if to remove the traces of that apparition. I thought back over the past few days, from my joyous entry into Westminster to my most shameful of departures. Was I really so wrong to act as I did? No, it did not make sense. How had it gone from triumph to ruin so quickly? One day I was queen—the next, an exile from my own city.

I walked over to the window and stared out at the night sky. The stars looked down from on high, keeping watch over England. What did the saints make of our deeds? There were some who said they must be caught up in slumber, so full of evil were the days. It was as I stood there gazing out that I remembered the face of Bishop Henry at the feast. What anger was in his eyes! What a savage smile! Then he rose and departed without saying a word, just moments before the bells rang out.

"He knew they were coming," I concluded. "He knew it the whole time—probably even arranged it. No wonder, since he was spending all that time in the city, never deigning to come to my court. Arse!"

I was then forced to cease my speech for fear that I might wake the others. However, I could not calm my spirit. I had not failed. I had been betrayed by a man meant to be a spiritual guide for the kingdom—a man who scarcely deserved the name. I wondered where he had gone that day when he left the feast. Had he run up to some hill to enjoy the show? Had he fled immediately to the false queen to make his obeisance? Or had he perhaps ridden to Winchester to seize the last of the royal coin and build up the defenses of his fortress? Oh, of all the men born to women, Henry of Blois was surely among the worst! I could not decide whom I hated more: him or his brother.

"Lady Adela of Blois will have much to answer for on Judgment Day," I concluded.

I was far too upset to return to sleep at that moment, so I decided that I would see if the earl of Gloucester was awake to discuss our next moves, if indeed we had any moves worth making. Lady Mathilda had leant me one of her fur robes, and while I felt rather odd wearing anything that belonged to her, I could not wander about in only my under things. I therefore put the robe on over my simple tunic and tied it at the waist with the belt she had provided. Alas, the thing stopped well above my ankles, as its owner was none too tall. However, the trim of fox pelt was soft enough against my skin to make up for this. I was about to leave the room when I remembered my hair, which was hanging down.

"Oh, never mind it," I muttered, and made my departure.

The stone floor was cold under my bare feet as I made my way down the passage, the only light coming from the candle in its sconce some twenty feet ahead. I could hear the gentle hum of the wind outside, a kind of yearning call stretching across hill and plain. I held out my fingers and allowed them to run along the wall, moving over each bulge and crevice. Suddenly, I felt wood and recognized that I was standing outside the door Lady Mathilda had noted earlier as "my lord's chamber." I felt within myself a mix of fear and curiosity, or something very like those things. I placed my palm against the wood, lingering for the space of a few breaths. Then I heard the sound of low voices coming from the direction of the stair.

Moving to my right, I looked down the falling steps and saw a pair of figures seated there, lit only by the moonlight coming in through a window slit. They continued speaking softly as I moved down to their position. There I saw clearly that it was my brother and Lord Brian, both sitting on the stair, legs sprawled out and arms crossed. As they heard me, they looked up and bowed their heads in turn.

"Do neither of you lords sleep any more?" I inquired.

"I should ask you the same thing," Robert replied. "Starting at the drink early, are we?"

"Well, if I was, I would have good reason to," I told him, feeling rather annoyed, "but as it so happens, my sleep was poor."

"I am sorry to hear that," said Brian. "Would you prefer to sleep in my bed?"

This question was innocent enough, but it certainly led the mind to a thousand places less innocent, and I thanked God that my brother did not choose that moment to make some unseemly jest.

"It is not a lack of comfort that ails me, but those mares of the night, haunting my sleep like the demons they are," I complained.

"You mean your dreams?" my brother asked.

I took a seat on the steps just above them. "Yes, that's it. Well spotted."

My brother sighed, evidently feeling he did not deserve such a tone. "Because of our flight from the Londoners?"

"I think not. I have had this same dream before, when last I was at Oxford. Now it visits me again."

"The same dream?" Brian stated more than inquired. "I have the same dream often, but it is hardly worth noting. I keep looking for something I cannot find. You would think after all these years I might succeed for once."

"Well, not that anyone gives a damn, but I have a dream where I am in the middle of battle and have forgotten to wear anything!" Robert complained.

"You mean any armor?" asked Brian.

"No, anything as in anything: as naked as I came from my mother's womb."

"See, this is why I did not ask you," I said. "I knew it would be something of that sort."

"What are you implying?" my brother asked, his brow lowered.

"Peace! I only wish to return to the matter at hand. This dream of mine—I believe it is a herald of woe. I see the castle all in flame. I confess I am somewhat afraid to go there now."

"Are you serious?" inquired Robert. "It's only a dream. Take care that you do not let womanly fears stand in your way."

"My lady," Brian offered a bit more kindly, "I am sorry this dream has caused you to fear, but perhaps Earl Robert is right in this: dreams come and go with little sense of order. Despite what the chroniclers would have us believe, they may mean nothing at all."

"Perhaps ..." I muttered. "You will both tell me we must go to Oxford no matter what I have seen in my dream, and you are right. There is no point setting store by such things. But has anyone heard aught of Bishop Henry?"

"I assume he rode back to Winchester, since he did not come with us," Robert said, "or perhaps he rode north with some of our men."

"I think not," I commented. "I saw him get up and leave just before the bells sounded, as if he knew what was about to happen and wished to avoid it."

"He may have left for any number of reasons," said Robert.

"Oh, come now!" I chided him. "Do not tell me you do not have your own suspicions. None of us ever liked him very much. You will remember that he scolded me in a most vile manner a few days earlier, he never came to Westminster Palace, and then right before he left the feast, he looked at me oddly. That man knows something about our calamity: make no mistake."

"It is certainly possible," said Brian. "Indeed, more than possible. He was absent from Westminster more often than not, and he has always been a sly fellow. He forsook his own brother. I doubt not that he would forsake an empress if the time was right."

"By which you mean if it gave an advantage to himself," Robert seemed to snort as much as speak. "Yes, you are both right. I do not like it. I do not like it one bit."

"Robert, will you ride to Winchester?" I asked. "After we have settled in at Oxford, ride to Winchester and seek him out. Tell him the Empress Mathilda, lady of the English, demands to speak with him as his rightful sovereign. If he refuses to yield, we must assume the worst and consider him a foe."

My brother took hold of my hand and kissed it. "For you, my lady, I would ride there a hundred times."

"There is no need for that," I said, pulling my hand back as he let it go. "Once will pay for all."

I rose to leave but turned my head to offer one final word to my brother.

"Robert, is there still hope? Can we still take London?"

He remained quiet for a moment, the look on his face thoughtful, then said, "I do not deny that it will be difficult, and it may take far more time than we had hoped, but yes, it is possible. As I live and breathe, I will not rest until I see you crowned in Saint Edward's church."

"Let's hope we all continue to live and breathe ..." I muttered, then returned to what would be another awful period of sleep.

The dog days were near upon us as we made our way to Oxford through the thickets and high trees of that large forest that sits along the Thames. The ride could be made in a single morning and was best done as such, for in the eve great swarms of insects would foul the air, so one could not hope to pass through with flesh fully intact. Oh, the heat of those long days!

My captains and I were agreed that we must make a stand at Oxford Castle, not through strength of arms, but by calling all the lords and bishops to our side. Therefore, as soon as I made my residence again in the Tower of Saint George, I gave instruction to the clerks we had brought in from the city to begin writing letters to those earls who were not already with us—Devon, Pembroke, Essex, Norfolk, Warwick, and Guines—along with the bishops of Lincoln, London, Ely, and Saint David's. It would also be necessary to fetch Archbishop Theobald, but I meant to write that letter myself.

Then there was Bishop Henry of Winchester. I took great care in choosing the words I would send to him. When I had finished, I summoned Earl Robert to join me in the main hall of that tower, the same room I had used earlier in the year for receiving visitors. It was not so grandly arranged on this occasion, for the castellan had received no knowledge of my coming ahead of time. A single table with four simple chairs and a pair of seats by the hearth were all that the room could afford. I chose to sit by the fire, or perhaps I should say the lack of fire, for it was far too hot to light one. I sank into the chair with its cushions of plain cloth, looking down at the bound parchment in my hands. I turned it over a few times, for what reason I know not, considering how its words might be received.

The door on the far side of the room opened, but to my great surprise it was not Earl Robert who strode through. No, it was Drogo leading a party of four men who formed a line as they entered, removing their caps, placing hands upon the hilts of their swords, and bowing low. They were all still in riding cloaks, the dust of the road evident upon them, and it was only when they stood up straight again that I truly saw their faces and recognized two of them: Alexander de Bohun and Guy of Sablé, both from the land of Anjou. It took a moment for me to make sense of this, for though I knew the men of old, I had never thought to see them in England. Therefore, my mind at first was confusion, as when one sees a duck wandering through a cathedral. Though the existence of ducks is known to all, they are so little in the great houses of God that it would take one a moment to recognize, *This is indeed a duck walking among us.* Thus it was when I saw two men from the past suddenly in my presence.

"My lady, these lords were sent by the count of Anjou to attend upon Your Highness," Drogo explained, though he need not have done so. It was clear enough why they had come: to make sure my husband's will was done. He continued, "Alexander and Guy you know, and may I introduce Pagan of Clairvaux and Juhel of Mayenne." As he said this, the two men bowed again in turn. I was surprised to see that they did not bear the long hair formerly favored by the Angevin lords but were closely cropped on their heads.

"Excellent," I said, though my feelings were truly not so positive. "Welcome, good lords. I hope you bring us pleasant tidings."

I rose and walked toward the lone table in the room. Behind me, the men began whispering to one another. No doubt they were debating whether to follow me, as I had not summoned them. I was content to allow them to remain in that state of un-certainty for a moment. I took the seat at the head of the table and adjusted the bottom half of my gown, all without looking in their direction. Still, I could hear the whispering continue. I allowed my arms to rest on the table, folding my hands to-gether, and took a moment to examine the ceiling high above, from which a hundred candles were suspended in a procession of metal rings. I had watched the poor man who had to light them balanced upon his ladder, reaching out with his light upon a long metal pole and almost falling to the ground. *They ought to devise a better means of doing that,* I thought.

Finally, I looked across the room at the men, who were by that point simply staring at me, the mouth of poor Pagan de Clairvaux hanging somewhat open and all of them bent for-ward ever so slightly, waiting upon my command.

"Please join me," I said, pointing to the other chairs.

Relief washed across their faces immediately. I believe one or two of them exhaled rather loudly as they crossed the dis-tance between us. Soon they would recognize what I already knew: that there were more men than chairs. They would have to decide who was to sit closest to me, who farthest away, and who would have the humiliation of standing while the rest of us sat. Alexander de Bohun was quickest to the mark and took the chair on my right, but the other three halted within one pace of the table and began whispering again, gesturing with great feeling. I enjoyed this sight for just a moment, then chose to end their misery.

"*Seigneur de Mayenne,*" I called to the man closest to me, "have a seat on my left. *Seigneur de Sablé,* on the end, if you please, and *Seigneur de Clairvaux,* if you would be so kind as to stand next to Sir Drogo. Otherwise, you may bring over the chairs by the hearth."

Lord Pagan and Drogo looked at one another and evidently decided through that exchange of glances that going to fetch more chairs would make them seem less manly. They made a show of strength by remaining on their feet.

I turned to my right to address Alexander de Bohun, and saw that he was attempting to scratch his head through his cap. As soon as he noted my eyes upon him, he ceased this action and sat up straight, dropping his arms.

"My lord of Bohun, what news from the duchy of Normandy?" I asked.

He nodded his head and began, "Most excellent countess of Anjou and lady of the English peoples, we are sad to hear of the calamity in London town. When we landed at Arundel"— this last word he said with such stress on the beginning that his voice seemed to catch in his throat—"we thought to travel to you at London, but we were surprised, yes, surprised when we passed through Winchester to find the bishop there in his palace, and he told us the sad tale."

Up to this point, I had been wondering why these men had taken it upon themselves to come to me merely to recite the sad tidings of the past few weeks, but at the mention of Bishop Henry, I was suddenly caught up in his words. So, the snake had crawled back into his hole after all! Well, at least this meant Earl Robert was likely to find him at home. But as much as these first words seized my attention, I was utterly bound by what he said next.

"He received us there at the *château* Wolvesey"—this last word he said very much as if it was a wolf and a sea—"and let us rest on his fine beds of feather. Such a good man! But he said he had just spoken to *la reine*, ah, the other one."

"Bishop Henry has spoken with the false queen, Mathilda of Boulogne?" I asked, wanting to make sure I understood him correctly.

"I do not know why you say this is false. I speak truth," he replied.

I sighed in frustration. "No, I know you speak the truth. It is this woman Mathilda, who calls herself the queen, that I declare to be false. Her husband is no longer the king. But never mind that: tell me, when did Bishop Henry speak with her? What did they discuss? What was his mood upon relating these tidings?"

The man looked at me with a rather blank stare, scratching his head as if uncertain what to say. "*S'il vous plaît* ... forgive me, Your Highness," he stuttered. "My knowledge of the Norman tongue ... it is not the best. The bishop mentioned the land of Mortain which belongs to Prince Eustace."

"It most certainly does not!" I replied.

At this point, Alexander de Bohun looked across the table to his *compagnon*, his eyes crying for help. Lord Juhel leaned forward and offered, "The bishop told us of all that had happened in the past few weeks and that the false queen, as you say, wanted her son to be given the lands of his father, but I think you have already refused this, no?"

"Yes, that is correct," I assured him. "Did the bishop give any sign of which way he might be leaning? I fear he may have secretly changed sides—gone back to his brother."

"He said nothing about that to us, but if Earl Robert has gone to Winchester, perhaps he will find you an answer."

"Perhaps ..." I murmured. "But what of Count Geoffrey? How goes his progress in Normandy? He has not surrendered it all to Count Theobald, I hope."

The men were taken aback by this comment. They lowered their brows and all seemed eager to speak, save for Lord Alexander, who had removed his cap to begin scratching his scalp directly. He took to it with the ferocity of a dog upon a fox. The skin was pink from this effort and bleeding in places.

"My lord, what on earth is the matter?!" I asked. I then looked over to where poor Pagan of Clairvaux stood and saw him scratching his scalp as well. "What is wrong with all of you?!" I demanded. "Are you infested?"

"*Poux! Le poux!*" Lord Alexander complained. "*Sauvez-nous!*"

By instinct, I moved back in my seat. Indeed, I may have pushed the whole seat backward. "Which of you have the lice?" I demanded to know.

Sensing that our conversation had taken a turn for the worse, they all looked at one another, none of them wishing to speak.

"I've seen them all scratching their heads, my lady," said Drogo. "I'm sure they all have them: that is why they removed most of their hair."

"They ought to have bathed!" I cried, rising to my feet and stepping further from the table.

"My lady, please do not be angry!" Juhel de Mayenne begged. "To tell the truth, the evil things have entered the camp on the other side of the water. Count Geoffrey ordered that all the heads be shorn."

"And did that help?" Drogo asked, laughing.

"Clearly not, or Lord Alexander's skin would not be the color of a ripe apple," I concluded. "My lords, I demand that you remove yourselves from my presence and do not return until every louse has been banished from your heads. If you wish to make your thoughts known, send a letter."

Thoroughly ashamed, the four men quickly made to leave, their heads hung low, as if this might prevent the lice from escaping. I wasted no time.

"Drogo, have someone clean this whole room," I said, "and see to it that the Angevin lords are thrown in the Thames and scrubbed from head to toe. As for the clothes, burn them and give them new ones."

When Drogo did not immediately move but looked at me in a state of confusion, I asked, "Yes? Having thoughts, are we?"

"Forgive me. Do you actually want us to burn the clothes, or is that simply a manner of speaking?"

I sighed loudly and marched across the room toward the entrance to my own chamber. Once inside, I tore off my head covering and cast it far from me, then drew a new one from my lone chest and tied it on as tightly as I possibly could, hoping in vain it would keep the lice out. The mere mention of the things made me itch all over, and I ordered myself to be calm. It was only after I had done this that my mind returned to the subject to which my thoughts had been captive only a few moments before.

"Cousin Henry," I whispered, "one of us must fall, but it will not be me. No, it will not be me."

XVI

When the Angevin lords had been thoroughly cleansed of every last louse, I met with them again and heard of my husband's push through Normandy as far as the River Seine, where he remained camped with his men. Farther than that he would struggle to go without the support of either the archbishop of Rouen or King Louis of France. Even if Louis had been of a mind to turn over the duchy of Normandy to ourselves and our heirs, he was occupied by his battle with Pope Innocent and my cousin, Theobald of Blois, over a matrimonial dispute that plays no role in this tale. I will only say that given the ill fate of the French king's own marriage—his wife being the same Eleanor who would one day depart and marry my son—he should have known not to meddle in anything having to do with matrimony, that blessed estate not being his most natural disposition. I have never met him even in my old age, but those who have say he would be better suited to the monastery than the role he now commands. Sad are the dooms thrust upon men by birth! I of all people should know.

I inquired after my husband's dealings with the Beaumont twins, who had earlier pledged their loyalty to him within the duchy of Normandy, no doubt simply to safeguard their estates on that side of the Channel. Might they be made to pledge fealty to myself within the kingdom of England? Without a coronation in Westminster, this was less certain, and the ambassadors had no new information for me in this regard. Given how Waleran had abandoned Stephen on the field of battle when he owed every inch of his life to the false king, I had no great hopes that Waleran would remain true to me even if he did pledge as much. He had been a constant traitor since his youth.

The other devil who occupied my thoughts was Geoffrey de Mandeville, earl of Essex. To treat with Earl Geoffrey was to take on the entire family Vere. The first Aubrey de Vere had come to England some time after the great conquest and served as a chamberlain to my father. His son, also Aubrey, had likewise been a chamberlain to my father and Stephen. He had several children, three of whom concern us most directly: Aubrey, Rohese, and Juliana. The third Aubrey had become head of the family in May of that year following the death of his father. Rohese was the wife of Geoffrey de Mandeville, and Juliana was the wife of Hugh Bigod. Yes, that was the Hugh Bigod who lied to the old archbishop of Canterbury and claimed my father had chosen Stephen on his death bed. When all three of them offered their fealty together, I accepted it, but was filled with suspicion. I had not forgiven Hugh Bigod for his perjury, and I would not have trusted any of them to put a shoe on my horse.

Even so, I had no real choice in the matter. Alas, when did I ever have a choice in any matter? The die was cast for me ere I left the cradle, and it had brought me by a sequence of turns to the table with Earl Geoffrey of Essex, Aubrey de Vere, Hugh

Bigod, and the four lords sent by my husband. Truly, Fate is a cruel mistress!

There we were in the same room in Saint George Tower, perched high over the city of Oxford, the lone table now provided with enough seats for everyone. Earl Robert had gone, but my uncle the king of Scotland was among us once again after traveling north for a short time following the retreat from Westminster. I asked him to join our meeting, and I also asked Lord Brian of Wallingford, for I was badly in need of a friend in that hour: one whose calm presence might keep me from saying what I really thought about the Vere men.

Before the meeting began, I had spoken with Brian briefly in the corner of the room.

"I am not sure how I will make it through this conversation without calling Hugh Bigod out for the liar he is," I explained. "Setting aside that business where he attempted to steal Norwich Castle from the usurper—"

"The less said about it the better," Brian agreed.

"—he helped to plunge the kingdom into this miserable state in which it now stands. He shows a lack of faith to the truth as much as any lord, or indeed any lady, for they tell me his poor wife spends all her nights alone, if you take my meaning."

"I do take it, but you must know you can say none of this during our discussion."

I sighed. "Yes, I am keenly aware of that. I am constantly aware of all the situations in which I must not speak. That is why I need you to help me, Lord Brian."

"Oh? How so?" he asked.

"We must have some sign between us so that if you sense me about to tear into Hugh Bigod or any of the other members of the *familie* Vere—"

"As they no doubt would most justly deserve ..."

"Precisely. But I cannot say it. I need their loyalty to safeguard the crown."

"So, you want me to keep you from declaring Lord Hugh to be the liar that he is."

"By means of a sign, yes."

He smiled for a moment, no doubt devising some secret mischief in his mind. "And what would you like the sign to be?"

I sighed once again. "Well, it cannot be anything too overt or they will be on to our game."

He nodded solemnly. "I have somewhat of a reputation for studying matters of the law and trade. Perhaps I could say something that would excite no one's attention, such as, 'Have we sufficiently considered the matter of market days in Stortford? They are currently set for Tuesday and Friday, but I think perhaps we should switch the former to Wednesday, the better to promote trade with the neighboring village of Thorley.'"

"Where?"

"Exactly. I dare say, they will all remain mute."

I shook my head and laughed softly. "Your knowledge of this island never ceases to amaze me."

"So, this will be the sign, then?"

"Yes." Raising a finger, I added, "Use it wisely."

Brian smiled broadly. "This is a fun game. We should play it more often."

I rolled my eyes, and that was the end of the conversation.

So, there we all were half an hour later, sitting around the table, staring at one another. I was perched again at the head of the table, King David of Scotland at my right hand and Lord Brian of Wallingford on my left. Seated on the same side of the table as Brian were the four Angevin lords, who were meant to be supporting me in the discussion but in all honesty stood in for my husband as a separate party to the agreement. Across from them, sitting next to my uncle, were the three lords Vere—Geoffrey, Aubrey, and Hugh. For men who had lately fled from Westminster, they were dressed quite finely. It had been less than two weeks since that calamity, but they had clearly found a way to visit one or more of their estates and retrieve their finest apparel: red hose held up by gold bands, outer tunics of green and blue stitched with gold thread, and cloaks held in place by brooches, each of which bore the arms of their great house made from precious stones. As my own things had been left in the Palace of Westminster, I was wearing a rather simple white gown borrowed from the lady of the castle, although I did at least have my German royal crown on my head, for I had been wearing it at that lamentable feast. I mention all this only to make clear to you that while they were the ones asking me for favor and demesne, appearance alone might have led one to think that it was I who was in need of their help—which, in truth, I was.

"Very well, let us begin," I said. "The king of Scots and the lord of Wallingford are witnesses between us. I thank you, Earl Geoffrey, for arranging for your brothers in marriage to be with us today."

Even as I said this, my gaze traveled down the table to where Hugh Bigod sat, his face leaning against his right hand, the elbow below it sitting on the table. It was a most careless manner in which to appear before one's sovereign. He sniveled loudly, his nose evidently troubled by some defect in the air. There was a large wart on the end of that nose such that one could not look upon his face without being constantly aware of it. Earlier I had observed that he had several teeth missing and the rest were badly out of place, their color closer to brown than white. But none of this displeased me half as much as his poor character. Oh, how I wanted to tell him what I thought of him!

"King David, would you please read for us what has been promised to these men in gratitude for their loyalty?" I asked.

On the parchment before him were their demands, which had increased by the day. He recited, "The earldom of Essex is confirmed to Geoffrey de Mandeville. To Hugh Bigod, you will grant the earldom of Norfolk, and to Aubrey de Vere … no, this cannot be right."

The man in question interrupted, "The earldom of Cambridge, Your Highness. That is correct."

"No, you cannot have Cambridge," my uncle told him. "That lies within my domain. Cambridgeshire is part of the earldom of Huntingdon, which belongs to myself and my heirs." Here he shot me a glance as if to say, *You would never stand for this, would you?*

"I was promised the earldom of Cambridge along with the movables therein!" Aubrey de Vere protested.

"Lord Brian is most expert in the law," I said. Turning to him, I asked, "What say you? Is the whole of Cambridgeshire within the earldom of Huntingdon?"

"It is, my lady," he confirmed, "and thus to grant it anew would be to deprive the king of his due."

"I hope you are not intending to go back on your word to us," Earl Geoffrey said, an edge to his voice. "We discussed the matter: all three of us are to be earls."

I breathed in deeply and forced myself to smile. "And so, you all shall be!"

I turned again to Lord Brian and said in a low voice, "What earldom might I grant in the South?"

"There is this one, my lady," he replied. "Oxford has not yet been assigned."

"Does it not lie within the Beaumont lands?" I asked, truly surprised.

"No, it does not, and Stephen never granted it to anyone. You are free to do with it as you wish."

Here I paused, for what I very much wished to do was award that earldom to Brian himself. Without question, he was as worthy of an earldom as any of the other men I had appointed as such. His service had been just as faithful and even greater in substance. His birth was also nobler than most men in the kingdom, being the natural son of the duke of Brittany, although not born in wedlock, and his lands fell closest to Oxford. But Brian had never given the impression that he wanted an earldom, and for my own part, I could not decide if it would be more suspicious to award him such a prize or not award him anything. After considering for a moment, I concluded that I would have no choice but to grant the thing to another.

I once again faced Lord Aubrey and announced, "I shall create you earl of Oxford, my lord. What say you to that?"

He seemed to think upon it for a moment, then answered, "I say it is a fine solution, so long as you will swear to it and not change your mind."

"I do not intend to change my mind," I assured him, a bit offended that he would propose it. No, if anyone at that table was guilty of fickleness, it was surely Hugh Bigod, who after perjuring himself to allow the anointing of the usurper, had then reversed course not once but twice, and was now thinking to offer his loyalty to me, the same person whom he had first thought to keep off the throne by his lie. As changeable as the winds was Lord Bigod. I observed this but held my tongue.

"That is well. I am content," King David concluded. "Now, back to the matters before me. Earl Geoffrey is confirmed as sheriff and justiciar in Essex, and created the same in Middlesex, Hertfordshire, and the city of London. In addition to the Tower, he is to be granted the castle at Stortford, the better to defend against invasion from the north."

Here Lord Brian cut in. "That castle is in the possession of the bishop of London."

"What need has he of it? You cannot think to fix him as guard of the city," Earl Geoffrey complained.

"I am going to speak with the bishop about this," I said to Brian. "He will understand. Indeed, as it was I who so lately raised him to the position in which he now sits, I think he cannot object if I make this request of him. He has other houses."

I could see clearly from the look on Brian's face that he had less faith in our ability to appease the bishop than I did, but he nodded and did not press the subject further.

"And do not forget the new castles you promised me! You said I could build them as needed throughout Hertfordshire … to defend against any rebellion in the country," Earl Geoffrey said, the last part of his speech apparently added to make his demand seem less like what it was: an attempt to gain greater control over the citizens of London. Fortunately for him, the citizens of London were not in my favor at the time.

Here one of the Angevins, Juhel de Mayenne, finally raised his voice. "Is this wise, Your Highness? In Anjou, we do not allow lords to throw up fortresses wherever they please. He has the Tower of King William and many houses for his pleasure. I do not think Count Geoffrey would approve of this."

Not only Earl Geoffrey, but all the Vere lords glared across the table at him. I quickly tried to explain.

"The lands are not in our power as of yet. This is all dependent on Earl Geoffrey's ability to gain them through strength of arms. Given the situation we are in, with our forces cleft between England and Normandy, we must reward any lord who takes it upon himself to fight for our common cause. Should he gain the lands, he is welcome to build such fortresses as are necessary to hold them." I then added, "And I thank you for bringing up the will of Count Geoffrey, but he is not here. I have given him leave to bargain on that side of the Channel, for his presence there provides him with special knowledge. Even so, you must trust my judgment on this side."

"Is this your judgment, my lady," he asked, "or has Earl Geoffrey forced it upon you?"

He had stumbled upon a fair question. It was certainly true that I would have dealt with none of those men if I had a choice. But I was not about to accept a rebuke from a man I barely knew on that subject—one who had not been there in England suffering with us through each turn of Fortune's wheel, attempting to hold together a nobility more at odds than at any point since my grandfather's conquest.

"This is the business of governing," I assured him, though in my heart I also felt its injustice. "Now, King David, please continue."

My uncle leaned closer to the parchment, then held it farther away, attempting to find some angle that allowed him to read it. I had not wished to say anything, but I did not believe his vision was what it once had been. Finally, he arrived at an interpretation.

"It looks as if Earl Geoffrey wishes his son, Arnulf, to be made a baron. My lord, I was not aware that you had a son by that name," he said, looking to the man on his right.

I noted as he said this that Aubrey de Vere crossed his arms against his chest and looked in a most ill humor. I quickly leaned over and whispered in the king's ear.

"Arnulf is Earl Geoffrey's bastard son. I suspect Lord Aubrey does not approve of how his sister has been treated."

"Ah!" my uncle whispered in return. "Best to avoid the subject then," he added with a wink.

A good deal more was said about pounds *per annum*, the building of castles, and rights to this and that. We had almost finished when Earl Geoffrey interrupted to add another request.

"I beg you to add language in this charter pledging that neither you nor Count Geoffrey will make any agreement with the citizens of London without my consent."

I was taken aback by these words. Yes, I had made him justiciar over London, but though that gave him authority to act in my name, it did not allow him to prevent me from acting. I could not help but think of the agreement I had made with Bishop Henry of Winchester, which had clearly led him to believe that he would make all decisions about ecclesiastical matters. Now, Earl Geoffrey demanded such authority over the chief city in the kingdom. Would any of that kingdom be left for me to rule, or was it all to become the play thing of men in whom I placed little trust?

"Earl Geoffrey," I began, "while I have no intent of entering into a new accord with the Londoners at the present time, I do not see why I should be prevented from doing so in the future simply because it does not appeal to you. How then am I ever to hold you to account?"

The earl scoffed loudly and placed his fist upon the table, leaning down upon it as if to prevent the table from rising into the air.

"Do you not remember, my lady, that it was the Londoners who chased you away from the seat of power? I warned you about them! They cannot be trusted," he argued.

I laughed. "My lord, if the past few years have demonstrated anything to me, it is that I cannot trust most of the men in England at all, and the others I can only trust on holy days."

"I hope you are not including us in that company!" Hugh Bigod complained. "We are men of honor!"

The very devil had placed this temptation before me to say to Lord Hugh, *You have even less honor than you do teeth!* But I felt a light tap upon my left knee and turned to see Lord Brian, his eyes wide, clearly begging me not to say anything. I sighed and leaned back in my chair.

"The Londoners are my mortal enemies!" Earl Geoffrey declared. "You cannot think to join hands with both them and I."

"Them and me," Juhel de Mayenne said helpfully.

"What do you know?!" the earl bellowed. "I've eaten oranges more Norman than you!"

"My lords, calm yourselves!" King David cried.

"See, what no one is saying is it was the Londoners that caused this whole mess!" Hugh Bigod argued. "They were the ones who picked Stephen."

I stared at him, my breath coming quickly, my gaze so fierce I am amazed it did not burn holes in his face.

"Why, you—" I began, and God only knows what might have come next had Brian not interrupted me.

"Has anyone considered the matter of market days in Stortford?"

We all turned to look at him, and for one of the rare times in our acquaintance, I felt that Lord Brian of Wallingford looked rather nervous.

"I see in my notes here"—he pointed at the parchment in front of him, which I was certain bore no mention of the town in question—"that they hold them every Tuesday and Friday, but it seems to me that Wednesday would be more appropriate given the trade with Thorley."

"What's that about Thorley? I own that place!" Earl Geoffrey objected. "Why did you not speak to me about it first?!"

Brian had clearly not foreseen that his words would provoke such a response, but he dealt with it well.

"I only raise the matter to learn your desire," he said in a far more pleasant manner than the earl deserved. "Tell me your will and I shall see it done."

As quickly as he had grown angry, the earl seemed to lose interest. "Do whatever seems best to you. I care not," he replied, then waving a finger at both Brian and myself, "Just see to it that you consider my thoughts on these matters."

It was at this moment that the door on the far end of the room opened and Adela poked her head around it.

"My lady, forgive this interruption, but I have something you will want to see," she called across the room.

Happy to receive any excuse to leave that meeting, I rose from my place and walked over to where she stood. Even as I did so, she swung the door open all the way and revealed an ivory box that I recognized immediately: the treasury of all my most precious items. No, not my jewels, but the gifts from my sons, my grandmother's paternoster, and the amber moth, along with letters I had received over the years. I placed my hands over my mouth to mute a squeal of joy.

"How on earth did you get it?" I asked, running my fingers over the carved figures on the outside, caressing the signs of wear produced by years of travels.

"It was Sir Philip's idea," she said. "We sent an inquiry to the bishop of London bidding him inform us if he had any knowledge of this box. He was able to find the man who had seized it, a blacksmith whose shop lies on Cornhill. I believe he had one of his servants pay the man some small sum for it. I am sure he did not know what he possessed, nor how dear it was to Your Highness, or he would have demanded half the kingdom for it."

She handed the box to me and I took it gently, as if it were a newborn babe. Lifting the lid, I immediately saw lying on top the moth trapped in dark yellow stone. I held it up to the light which came in from the upper windows, turning it this way and that. The stone seemed to come alive with a sudden fire. Placing it back inside the box, I said, "I am truly in your debt, Adela. You cannot know how much this means to me."

"Oh, but I do," she told me, placing a hand on my arm. "I would have walked to the ends of the earth for it."

"Would you place it in my chamber, please?" I asked.

She nodded and took the treasure in hand, while I turned and walked back to my seat. I took up my place at the table once again, the' lords still caught up in some discussion regarding jurisdiction. I looked over at Lord Brian and saw that he was smiling at me. I smiled back.

Upon returning to Oxford, I had sought out the physician Grimbald, that old servant of my father. He was still living in the city, a true master of his craft. He would receive pupils from all parts of Britain and Normandy, as well as some from Ireland and Flanders. Once, I believe he had a young man who traveled all the way from Pisa. In the evening, he would take a seat in one of the taverns, and his students would crowd around him, pens in hand, ready to take down every word he spoke. Why? Because he was one of the few men in England who understood the science of the Moors, and surely the only one who spoke the language of that people. He revealed to them secrets of which Galen could only dream.

My request to speak with him was met by another letter in return.

Great Empress Mathilda —

Meet me in the meadow north of the city on Wednesday next. It lies along the river and was given over long ago for grazing. I have passed many a pleasant hour there. Come to me at dawn and we shall converse in private. I can be found next to the small orchard that lies on the eastern side.

Your true servant,
Grimbaldus

So, I rose early on that day, the tenth before the Kalends of August, as the monks were singing their prayers across the river. The cooler air of night still hung about us, even as the river was draped in mist, and every blade of grass bore the dew of morning. I mounted one of the horses I had taken to using: a female whom I called *Frija* after that old goddess of the Germans. Her coat was light gray with darker spots, and when she ran, she could keep pace with the fastest males. Perhaps that is why I liked her.

My usual habit was to ride with several of my knights, but as Grimbald had mentioned a private conversation, I rode with Drogo alone through the town and out the north gate, as was necessary to travel in that direction, for the river could not be forded next to the castle. When we were outside the walls and came to the vast stretch of grass that the physician had mentioned, I told my knight, "Wait here, if you would. The good doctor requested we speak in private."

He gazed across the meadow. All one could see were the forms of hundreds of sheep, both black and white, noses to the ground as they chewed on the green blades. The soft sound of bleating was the only one upon the air.

"I don't know, my lady," he concluded. "I hate to abandon you to ride alone, especially during a time of war. Just this month you had to flee for your life!"

"That was in Middlesex, Drogo: far from here. Do you foresee that the Londoners will come riding up the Thames in boats, passing Oxford Castle without being sighted by any of the watchers on the wall?"

"No, but I—"

"Do you imagine that there is someone waiting in this very meadow, crouching behind one of the sheep, just in case I happen to pass by? For surely no man could hope to hide anywhere else in this place without trees."

"My lady," he said, his frustration clearly showing, "I am sure you are correct that the chances of any assault upon your person are small, but I have committed my life to safeguarding yours. It is only natural that I should ask such questions. I have not forgotten what happened in Straßburg all those years ago. I failed in my duty, and I have never truly forgiven myself."

A chill passed over my heart as I remembered the night: the rough hands upon me, the foul breath and fouler words. I knew my knight was not at fault for what took place, and indeed the Lord in his mercy had spared me from anything worse. The threat to me in middle age was different than those I faced as a young woman, but I valued the words he spoke. One could never be too careful.

"And what do we know of this Grimbald, anyway?" Drogo asked. "How well can you really know anyone?"

There I felt able to provide an answer. "Sir Drogo, in an hour when I trust hardly anyone, I would gladly trust Master Grimbald with my life, even as I do you. He was a friend of my mother before me, and what's more, he is quite aged. I have nothing to fear from him."

Drogo nodded in acceptance of my words. "Very well, my lady, if you are certain. After all, I cannot command you. Even when you were a little girl, I could not make you follow my direction."

"What is this?!" I objected. "When has my behavior ever been less than pliant?" He opened his mouth to speak, but I raised a hand and commanded, "Do not answer. I assure you I jest."

With that, I tugged on the reins and bid my horse take me forward into the lush meadow. As we flew through the herd of sheep, none of whom seemed to pay us much heed, I could feel the beast below me breathing, her chest expanding and contracting as her legs boldly strode. I bid myself breathe as one with her, and for a moment I imagined that I was no longer Mathilda, lady of the English, but the horse beneath me, running freely across the plain. The rising sun had sent its rays piercing through the mist. I was no longer riding, but running over England, my hooves pounding upon the foundation of earth, under which the remnants of earlier times were long buried but might one day be revealed. I felt myself outside of ordinary time and caught up in something far greater: a time as unceasing as the earth, as firm as the mountains of stone, and yet new every morning. There were no cruel words here or commands against my person. There was no chain upon my freedom, but only the ancient voices of the island bidding me to be. And perhaps in that moment I was living more fully than ever before, or perhaps I had merely sensed the fullness I always had. All this I felt in the space of a few breaths.

I pulled myself back to the present as I saw clearly the lines of trees and in front of them a man clothed in a simple gray cloak, seated upon a rock. Quite how the rock had come to be there, I could not say. It seemed thoroughly out of place and must have been brought there from a nearby quarry. But what did it matter why the rock was there? What mattered was the man seated upon it, staring off into the distance, perhaps watching the sun's reflection upon the River Thames, or perhaps caught up in some memory. It was not until I was very close indeed that he turned and looked in my direction, a broad smile behind his long gray beard.

"Empress Mathilda," Grimbald called, "you do me great honor!"

He began to rise as if to help me down from my horse, but I bid him, "No, remain where you are. I do not want you going to any trouble on my account."

I alighted without difficulty and led the animal over to one of the closest trees, which to my delight was filled with green apples, not yet ready to be picked but things of beauty nevertheless: the promise of sweetness. I used the rope I had brought with me and tied my horse to the tree, then walked back toward the physician. Even as I did so, I suddenly heard a sound behind me that could not have come from the horse and spun around, my heart beating faster. I remembered Drogo's words of warning, and for just a moment feared that I had indeed walked into some kind of trap. But then I saw several rows down from me a pair of boys perched in one of the trees, yelling back and forth at one another and laughing. So merry were they, I doubt they were aware of my presence. What I had thought to be an object of fear was anything but, and yet it filled me with a sense of grief.

"Do not mind the children," Grimbald called to me. "Come and sit beside me."

I did as he commanded. The rock was even larger than it had appeared from afar, so there was no difficulty in finding room for two persons. The old physician looked at me, studying me closely.

"You do not greet me," he said. "I think you must be sad."

"Not sad, exactly," I replied softly. My eyes moved back to the boys in the apple tree. "They make me think of my sons— the sons I have not seen in so long."

"Forgive me. I could not hear you," he said, moving a bit closer.

"I said they bring my sons back to mind, those boys in the tree," I repeated more loudly.

"Ah! Those are the sons of the farmer. They let me sit here. I come quite often. They take me for an old fool, I am certain. It is good to meet those who think no more of me than I deserve. How old are your sons, my lady?"

"Henry, eight years old. Geoffrey, seven. William, four years … no, his birth date was yesterday! He is five now. So far … horribly far away from them I am."

"Perhaps it is not so far," Grimbald offered. "Distance is a strange thing, or perhaps it is better to say, there are different kinds of distance."

I very much suspected that he had something to add, so I did not speak. Instead, I watched as the sheep continued to feed across the meadow. It was not the time of year for lambs— surely most of them were weaned. When I was a little girl, I used to visit the animals that were kept out in the yard at Westminster, and their keeper would answer the endless questions I produced. "How many lambs does a ewe have each year? Can they run when they are first born? Which kind of sheep has the softest wool? How do you keep them from being eaten by wolves?" Oh, how I must have wearied him!

"I used to come here as a boy," the physician finally said, apparently thinking along the same line as myself. "Even then, the sheep were grazing. It is said this land was granted by King Alfred to serve as a pasture for all time."

"That must have been two hundred years ago, or perhaps more," I spoke in wonder.

"When I return here, I feel almost as if no time has passed," he explained, "as if I am still a boy, eager to climb a tree even as those lads behind us. Of course, the orchard was not here then. It must be about fifty years old." Here he leaned in and raised his thick brows. "In case you did not know, I am rather ancient."

"There is some kind of enchantment about this place," I agreed. "I felt it as I rode across the plain, though I could hardly put it into words. A kind of spiritual communion, perhaps."

I had been staring off into the distance as I said this, but now as I looked over at the doctor, I wondered if he thought I had taken leave of my senses. I had heard my own words, and they sounded rather odd. Enchantment? I doubted that the most excellent physician in England set much store by such things. However, he surprised me with his words.

"I do not doubt what you say. After all, you are a child of this county the same as myself. There are certain places on this earth—places that bear special significance for ourselves—that when we visit them, it is as if we are closer to those things we imagine: great moments of the past in time out of mind. Once when I was traveling with the king, your father, in the Duchy of Normandy, we happened across the seat of my ancestors. I had never before set foot in that place, yet I felt at once that I was home. 'Here is the place where it began,' I said to myself. A person can have more than one such place, but I suspect that this part of the country speaks to your soul, even as it does to mine. Something of you exists here and always will, never changing, always constant. Our natural lives are as the wind that blows through this grass, here one moment and gone the next, and yet we are also eternal."

"Is this why you called me out here?" I asked. "To speak about the past?"

"No, I thought perhaps you needed some encouragement," he replied, patting my hand lightly. I looked down at his own hand and saw the deep valleys formed by wrinkles, the hills of callouses brought on by years of labor. "These past few weeks—"

"Yes, quite," I said softly, my eyes now staring down at my feet.

"It is not an end," Grimbald assured me, withdrawing his hand. "That is, perhaps it is an end of one thing, but there will be other chances: new beginnings."

"That is what my brother says. He thinks we still have a chance. Indeed, the usurper remains in prison, and we control much of the country. The nobles are mostly faithful for the moment. But there is the matter of—"

"The bishop of Winchester. Yes, he is a sly fellow."

I looked back at him. "Did you guess that is who I meant, or did you hear it from someone?"

"There are rumors abroad," he muttered. "Bishop Henry never did learn the art of keeping his thoughts to himself."

"Perfect," I said with a sigh.

Here he patted my hand again. "Lady Mathilda, I held you the day you were born. I watched you wiggle in my arms, eager to move and take on the world. I had no doubt you were a warrior in the body of a woman."

"Are you sure you are not reading the book from back to front?" I asked. "That you are not seeing now in that child what you have seen in the adult?"

He laughed. "See, this is what I mean. You are more than a match for Henry of Blois."

"So, what must I do, then? Earl Robert has gone down to Winchester to command his presence in Oxford, but I suspect he will not come. When that happens, I will have to make one of two choices."

Grimbald shook his head. "Surrender is not a choice here. If you do not stand up to that man, you might as well hand him the crown."

"So, again I ask, what am I to do? Ride down to Winchester and knock on the door of Wolvesey Palace, demanding to be let in?"

He sat up straighter, taking on an air of authority. "You are to ride down to the royal palace in Winchester—the place that is yours by right of birth, not that thing he has built for himself on the river—and you are to summon him to yourself. And if he will not yield, then you will make him come."

"What ... lay siege to his palace?" I asked.

"Precisely. Break down the walls if you have to. Make him submit to your authority."

I could not help but scoff. "There are any number of bad things that could happen as a result of such actions."

"And what will happen if you do not act?"

I looked into his eyes even as he stared into mine. I knew he was right, but the situation was anything but simple. Throughout the war, sieges had not produced many favorable results. The castles of England were grown stronger since the time of the Conqueror. And Bishop Henry was no simple priest: he had a vast number of servants at his command, and I was certain he had been in communication with the false queen and could summon her and the wolf of Ypres at the sound of his whistle—perhaps even an angry mob of Londoners. Since returning to Winchester, the bishop would have strengthened his walls and brought in stores of food. Even if I called every noble I could muster to make war against him, how could I ensure that they would remain on my side and not run over to the false queen once they had the chance? Surely there was no way for me to ensure it, but Grimbald was right: I had no choice but to try. I could not allow any of my subjects to openly defy me, however great they might be. Every king must prove himself able to defend his crown, and if I was to be England's queen, I would have to do the same.

"It is strange to think that just a few months ago, I joined hands with Bishop Henry in the cathedral of Winchester," I said. "He received me with all honor. Now I am to lay siege to his palace, the very palace where I walked with him in his garden? Life is a strange thing."

"Life is strange, and these are even stranger days," he agreed.

Suddenly, I heard the distant sound of a bell. I looked in the direction from which it seemed to come, but the last remnants of mist clouded my eyes.

"It is the abbey of Godstow," the physician explained, "greeting the sun and bidding it cast its warmth upon the earth."

"The bells mark out the hours of our lives, heralding both birth and death," I spoke. "But what doom does this bell announce?"

"That is the thing about life," he said with a smile. "We never know if we are coming or going—if it is the beginning or the end. But a flame that burns as brightly as yours does not, I think, burn out easily."

On Friday of that week, there was a great gathering in the hall of Oxford Castle: not the one in the tower, but the separate building in the midst of the yard. Lord Miles of Gloucester bowed before me, and I officially created him earl of Hereford, though he had known he would receive it for some time. By that point, the archbishop of Canterbury had arrived, as well as a host of other lords and bishops. Our aim of making a show of strength had been achieved, but not an hour passed when I did not think of Earl Robert's journey to Winchester. What would Bishop Henry say, and of even greater import, what would he do?

The following day, brother Reginald requested my presence at an archery contest on the one patch of grass inside the castle walls, which was just below the keep. Now, entering such a contest with Earl Reginald of Cornwall was surely the height of folly, for he could shoot better than any man I had ever met. However, he assured me that it would be a friendly affair, including myself, Earl Miles, Lord Brian, and Sir Drogo. I agreed to join on the condition that Sir Philip would also be allowed to take part, for I had it in mind to speak with him and hoped this would give me an opportunity. The lord of the castle, Robert D'Oyly, had declined to shoot on account of his age, and his son was off riding.

So, there we were in the heat of midday, standing about with bows in hand, three targets set some thirty yards away, a pair of servants waiting off to the side to retrieve the arrows. Given that I seldom shot, I considered it a great act of faith on their part that they would stand within the same county as myself. Having no bow of my own, I was forced to choose between those in Lord Robert's keeping. I selected one made of yew and flax, only about four feet in length. This suited me better than the larger bows, which I found more difficult to control. I was a woman of average height: I did not need a weapon meant for giants. I stood there running my right hand over the bow while my left hand held it fast. I had seen many bows being carved, and something about it always filled me with a kind of awe.

"Your shot, Reginald!" Earl Miles called. "Show us how it's done!"

My brother preferred a crossbow for this sort of shooting and had an elegant weapon crafted in Senlis out of wood from the nearby forest. He raised it, his gaze fixed upon the target, then let the arrow fly. It landed very near the center, off by less than the length of a finger. There were calls of "Well done!" and much clapping of hands from the rest of us, but for his part, Reginald looked dismayed. Though he had hardly a care for most things in the world, he was never content with anything but perfection when it came to archery.

As Lord Brian stepped forward to make his best attempt, I walked over to where Sir Philip of Honfleur stood off to the side. This was, of course, the main reason I had asked my brother to summon him to our gathering, for I had never known Philip to take a particular interest in archery. As I approached, he was gazing off into the distance, apparently looking at nothing of consequence.

"Sir Philip!" I called, and he immediately looked in my direction. "You have no love for our sport, I think."

"You mistake me, my lady," he replied, with a quick bow of the head. "I was merely lost in thought."

"Much thought wearies the mind," I told him, planting my bow on the ground and folding my hands on top of it. "I myself try not to think more than a few times a day, the better to maintain my health."

I said this in a most solemn tone, without smiling. The knight turned his head slightly to the side, no doubt trying to decide if I spoke in jest. In the bright sun, his green eyes seemed to sparkle. Were I a young maid of lower standing, I do not doubt that I might have taken a liking to him even as Adela, though his conversation would have tired me rather quickly.

"Oh, come now, Sir Philip! I merely jest," I assured him.

A look of relief swept across his face. "Ah, I was not certain. I would hate to speak anything contrary to a royal lady, but I suspect you must have thoughts all the time that far exceed anything that passes through my own mind. Lady Adela says you read the great works of philosophy and theology."

"That is proof of nothing," I said with a smile, noting that he had mentioned Adela. "Anyone can stare at words on a page. Only the very wise can fully understand them. Indeed, there is nothing so dangerous as a man who understands half of some text. He is likely to put it to all sorts of terrible uses. Better to know nothing at all than to know half a thing, I say."

He nodded. "You speak good sense, my lady, and you give comfort to a person like myself who does not even pretend to know things. I would have you teach me, but I suspect your pains would be wasted."

"Speak not so! Do not drag yourself down without cause, in particular around those who sit above you. It may seem humble, but it does you no favors. There are many kinds of knowledge, and you excel in those that I need. That is why Sir Drogo first promoted your cause to me, and I always trust his judgment in such matters. But I do have some knowledge that may help you at this point in your life, if you would bid me share it."

"Of course, my lady!" he replied eagerly. "I would accept anything from you as a gift from the gods!"

He has never read about Pandora, I thought, but kept it to myself.

"Listen then to my words," I told him, allowing the bow to drop into one of my hands. *"Nulla est sincera voluptas, sollici-tumque aliquid laetis intervenit."*[24]

"What does that mean?" he asked, his eyes grown wide.

I looked back at the men who were shooting. Drogo had just hit the outer edge of the target, and Lord Brian was attempting to cheer him with a pat on the back.

"All our joys are tinged with sadness," I said softly. "It is the way of the world. This is what it means to live under sin's awful curse. We pour ourselves out into the works of our hands, only to have them snatched from us. We reach toward the heavens, only to be pulled crashing back to earth."

I looked at Philip again and saw his mouth hanging slightly open. "Do you mean to send me into despair?" he inquired.

"No, I mean to tell you this: you have only a few short days on this earth. They will be filled with miseries untold. If God has given you some gift, some possibility of joy, then why on earth do you not reach for it?"

"Because I will come crashing back down to earth ..." he seemed to ask as much as state, clearly uncertain what kind of response I desired.

"You might," I agreed, nodding my head, "or you might rise higher than you ever thought possible, seizing joy when you never thought to have it!"

"My lady," he said, his breath coming quicker, "I sense you are speaking of something, but I cannot think what."

I sighed, more for effect than out of true frustration. "Sir Philip, we are fighting a war that presses in on all sides. As my defender, your life is in danger every day. In a single moment, you may be pulled into the endless sleep of death!" I noted that his green eyes were grown large with concern. "This is not

---

24 Ovid, *Metamorphoses*, VII.453-4.

a moment for playing games! You stand here waiting to shoot, but I ask you, what do you love most in this world?! What would bring you the greatest joy?! If there is even a small chance that it is within your grasp, then why on earth do you fail to seize it?!"

My words came with great passion and I could see the effect they were having. Philip of Honfleur seemed to grow taller as each one poured out.

"Yes, my lady, I see what you mean!" he replied. "I am ready!"

"Are you certain?" I asked.

"Yes, I have never been more certain of anything! I know what I must do!"

"Good," I said simply. "Now go shoot."

"What?" he asked, suddenly all confusion.

"Go shoot. It is your turn," I repeated.

I pointed my bow in the direction I wished him to walk. The others were standing there staring at him, waiting for him to take his mark. He shook his head slightly, as if attempting to move his thoughts from the great excitement into which I had thrust them to the matter at hand, then made his way over.

As soon as his back was turned to me, I had to raise a hand to my mouth and look in the opposite direction to hide the laughter I had been withholding. I had planted the seed well and hoped it would soon grow and blossom. Even as I was lauding myself for a thing well done, I heard the voice of Lord Brian behind me.

"What are you smiling about?"

I whipped around, willing my face to look anything but happy.

"It is none of your concern," I replied.

"You are correct. I am not filled with concern, but curiosity."

"And in that curiosity, you must die."

He smiled. "Is it about Sir Philip?"

"Never you mind!" I commanded.

"Very well. Keep your secrets," he concluded. "And how does the empress fare today?"

"I've been better," I admitted. "This business with the bishop of Winchester hangs like a dark cloud over my thoughts."

"Is there anything more I can do to be of service?" he asked. "I cannot imagine what you have felt these past few weeks. I hope you have not suffered greatly."

I dared not admit how much I had suffered for a whole host of reasons. As it so happened, I did not have to reply at all, for I heard another voice cry, "Empress Mathilda! My lady!"

I turned and saw John fitz Gilbert approaching quickly, his black robe swaying in the wind.

"Yes, what's the news?" I inquired.

"Earl Robert has returned and waits to speak with you, and we have another visitor as well."

"What is the visitor's name?" I asked, most unhappy that he would leave things there.

"William, my lady. He is the lord of Elmley Castle."

"William de Beauchamp?" asked Brian. "The sheriff of Worcestershire?"

"The very one," he replied.

Brian and I looked at one another, evidently thinking the same thought: William de Beauchamp was a servant of Waleran of Meulan, that man raised so high by the usurper. Did he intend to forsake his master and join our side, or might he have come to announce that Waleran himself would defect?

"I do not know who to meet with first," I said quietly.

"Better make it Robert," Brian said. "Do you want me to come with you?"

"Yes, and let's bring Miles as well."

Having retrieved Earl Miles, we walked back to the Saint George Tower and climbed the stair until reaching the hall.

There we found Earl Robert of Gloucester laid back in one of the two seats by the hearth, his legs crossed and his own arms hanging over those of the chair, in his hand a cup no doubt filled with something strong.

"Since you come alone," I called while still walking toward him, "I take it our friend the bishop has turned traitor."

My brother replied with a grunt that did not seem to confirm or deny what I had said. Having reached his position, I took the chair opposite, while Miles and Brian stood nearby.

"I do not speak that language. You can reply in our own tongue, Latin, German, or if you must, the native speech of this island. I do not remember much of the latter, but I could make an attempt," I told him.

Robert simply smiled and took another drink from his cup. The three of us stared as he swallowed one, two, three times, then having emptied the thing, set it aside.

"What is that animal the ancient Greeks used to write about? The one that guarded the old city of Thebes?" he asked.

"The sphinx," Brian replied, "though it was not exactly an animal."

"Yes, that's the one!" Robert declared, pointing at him. "A sphinx. Bishop Henry is a sphinx."

"How so?" I asked. "I take it he has not grown the legs of a lion or the wings of an eagle."

"No, he is speaking in riddles," said Robert, "riddles that only an Oedipus could solve. I went down there as we discussed. Having inquired after the bishop and learned that he was in his great palace, I requested entrance and was granted it immediately. I was brought directly to the man himself, who was seated in a great chair the like of which I have never seen: carved and painted with figures, covered with fabric no doubt purchased from Venice or perhaps farther east, and so high off the ground that his feet did not fully touch the floor, but only his toes. I, on the other hand, was seated in a chair so low to the ground that my knees rose up, and although I am a whole head taller than the bishop, he was looking down on me."

"How very like him," I muttered. "And what riddles did he offer you? Truly, sphinx is the correct word for such a character."

"I will tell you, but I need more wine first," he said.

Robert pointed to a pitcher sitting on the ledge above the hearth. Earl Miles made to retrieve it, but Lord Brian, likely because he was lower in rank, put out a hand to stop him and reached for the pitcher himself. He was about to fill my brother's cup when Robert simply grabbed the whole thing out of his hand and gestured for him to return to his place. We all watched again as Robert raised the pitcher and drank from it directly—one, two, three swallows.

This is going to take all day, I thought, *and I am not in a patient mood.*

"Right, so there we were," my brother began, setting the pitcher on the floor. "I told him the purpose of my visit: that I was come to fetch him to Oxford to your royal court, for you had matters of great import to discuss with him. He gave no direct answer but smiled in that sly manner that is his wont.

"'Do you have any answer for my lady?' I asked.

"'I wonder that you have remained so close to the empress when she has treated you so poorly,' he said.

"'I remain close to her because she is my rightful sovereign even as she is yours,' I said.

"Again, he did not answer, but attempted to make common cause with me. 'Come, come, Earl Robert. You and I are not so different: we are each of us very near the crown, kept from it only by an accident of birth. But God makes happy accidents. It is no dishonor to be a lord of the Church.'

"You know how he is when he speaks this way. He condescends.

"'You have certainly made the most of your position,' I said, hoping to check his pride.

"Then he answered, 'I do what I must for the Lord I serve. Yes, there is a Lord even higher than the king of England.'

"'Or queen,' I offered.

"He skipped over this entirely and said, 'I wonder that the empress raises up these men left and right, men whose blood cannot compare to yours and mine, and makes them even as powerful as yourself. This is poor thanks for all you have done.'

"I saw clearly what he was doing. He had no doubt heard rumors that we had argued and wished to divide us and thereby conquer. Well, I refused to allow it!

"'I have by birth as much as any sovereign could give. What more could I hope to receive?' I asked him.

"He laughed—the kind of laugh that is not merry, but full of guile. 'One thing I have learned by observing the nobles of this land,' he said. 'There is always more.'

"We were making no progress. I very much suspected him of treachery, and I had no desire to play his game.

"'Why do you attempt to catch me out?' I asked. 'Do you seek some boon for yourself?'

"'Nothing that you could give me,' he said.

"'But perhaps something the lady of Boulogne could give you?' I pressed, hoping to get to the point.

"Here his countenance changed. He took up the defense, though I noted he did not deny speaking with her.

"'She cares for her son, my nephew, and why should she not? It is the natural act of a mother to love that which comes from her own flesh, even as it is natural that she should plead for her husband.'

"But I argued, 'The abandonment of one's sovereign is less natural.'

"Again, he would not acknowledge the point at hand: he would not admit to treachery, but neither would he deny it. Instead, he offered another riddle.

"'Earl Robert, are you a man or not?' he asked.

"And I asked him in return, 'What kind of question is that?'

"He said, 'A simple one. A necessary one.'

"To which I replied, 'Of course I am a man. What do you take yourself for?'

"Here he leaned in and almost whispered, 'Then you know as well as I … there is nothing natural about men being ruled by women.'

"I thought I had him in his treason then. I said, 'And yet you were ready to make my mistress your queen not so long ago.'

"'Who says I am not now?' he asked.

"'You yourself have said it,' I argued.

"But the sphinx replied, 'Such things are unnatural, but we may just as easily argue that war is unnatural.'

"'In my experience, I would say it comes as naturally to men as anything,' I told him.

"Here he showed his arrogance again. 'Men of the world, perhaps. I would not know.'

"I swear, someone give this man the martyrdom he craves that we may all be rid of him!

"I asked again, 'Will you come to my lady at Oxford or not?' and once more he did not give a straight answer.

"He said, 'She believes she has no need of me. I wonder that she should trouble herself to summon me.'

"So, I asked, 'Is that a no?'

"He then gave me the closest thing to an answer I was to receive, protesting that he was 'much occupied' at the present time. 'Tell my lady that I regret I cannot join her in Oxford, but

I should like very much to hear if she has had any change of mind regarding the inheritance of my nephew.'

"'You know she cannot abide that answer,' I told him.

"But he argued, 'Men can abide a great deal if necessity demands it. I myself am living proof.'

"That, I'm afraid, is the sum of what was said between us. I stayed one more night in town and sent word again the next morning in case he had one of his many changes of mind. It took several hours for me to receive the reply from some servant that, 'My master is at his prayers and cannot receive visitors, be they ever so high and mighty.'

"'At his prayers all day?' I asked, very much doubting this account.

"But the servant was made of the same stuff as his master. 'Yes. That is his way,' he assured me.

"And so, I decided to return, for I could see I was pressing at a door that had been bolted fast. That is the end of my tale."

The three of us—Earl Miles, Lord Brian, and myself—had remained mute as he spoke, as if bound by some spell. His report did not surprise me. I had long since assumed the worst when it came to my cousin. I also knew well enough the hatred many men held in their hearts for the female sex, especially as it concerned the exercise of power, so I did not cry in objection when he told of Bishop Henry's claim that it is unnatural for any woman to be raised above a man. Such a thought, I well knew, was common enough, and it was for that reason that I had always spoken of the inheritance of my sons as much as my own right to anything. But that those words should come from the lips of Henry of Blois was more than prejudice: it was proof that he had decided against me once and for all, and allied himself with the false queen. The irony of course being that she was just as much a woman as myself, but such ironies never seem to trouble those seeking power. That was the real reason I was rejected: I was not willing to be controlled by the bishop.

"Somebody say something," Robert finally pleaded.

"I did not want to speak before the empress," Miles said.

I sighed deeply and rubbed my forehead with both hands. "We must think this thing through to the end. The bishop openly defies me. I cannot simply overlook that, especially after what happened in Westminster. I cannot allow him that freedom, even if he is Henry of Blois."

"Oh, and there is something else," Robert interrupted. "All those men he excommunicated, the ones who had supported Stephen ... He has reversed their excommunications without granting the other bishops the courtesy of involving them. The dean was kind enough to tell me."

"What clearer sign could there be that he has changed sides?" asked Brian. "It was at the great council in Winchester that he first excommunicated them, the very place where he announced his allegiance to the empress. If he has gone back on one, he has gone back on the other. And we know he has formed an alliance with Mathilda of Boulogne. Why else would he be speaking to her and pleading on her behalf?"

"Right you are," Miles agreed. "He is lost to us, and truly, I would like to see how he explains this change of mind. He had to make the whole kingdom believe he was wrong to support Stephen, but it was not his fault. How does he intend to do that the second time around? Does he think anyone will fail to see through his wavering and judge it for what it really is: promotion of self?"

Lord Brian smiled and said, "I think you will find that such sound reason is in short supply in this kingdom."

"In every kingdom," I added. "There is no telling how many bishops and lords he may take with him into rebellion if we do not act. If he will not come to us, then we must go to him.

When we arrive, he will either accept a meeting or refuse. Then we will have to decide whether to attempt an arrest. If we do attempt it, we will have to overtake him in Wolvesey Palace. That is no small obstacle."

"There is another matter to consider, Your Highness," Miles offered. "He may be hoping to trap you. Perhaps such servants as he has are already well armed, and we do not know where the false queen makes her stay these days."

"Either London or Windsor," said Robert. "One is two days' march from Winchester, the other three days."

I shook my head. "That is only if we are fortunate. They could be even closer, hiding somewhere in the country."

"Our spies would know if a large force was on the move," he countered.

"Our spies, such as they are, did not warn us when the Londoners poured out of the gates," I argued. "Even if we do receive information, there is no way to know if it is correct. There are rumors abroad—rumors and falsehoods whispered in every ear. I do not think there is any way of knowing what we will face until we arrive."

"Then we must arrive with a large force," said Brian, "as large as we can gather at this time, and we must act quickly before Mathilda of Boulogne can call for more men from Flanders."

"If we arrive with a large force, Bishop Henry may take it as a declaration of war," noted Robert, quite rightly. He looked me firmly in the eyes. "Are you ready for that?"

"Few men are fully ready for war," I said quietly.

"Earl Miles, Lord Brian, myself," my brother began, pointing at each in turn, "we have fought in many battles. We have seen men cut down around us and heard their dying cries. We have plunged a blade into another man's flesh and felt it stick, then pulled it out again to see it covered in blood."

"Do you intend to scare me, brother?" I asked.

"Perhaps it would be better if you remained in Oxford," he said.

"But the whole point is to project royal authority. I cannot do that if I stay here," I argued. "I will not take part in the fighting, should it come to that."

Robert let out a sigh. "You fail to understand me. Should there be a battle, it is not likely to be fought out in some field. If we must lay siege to Wolvesey, it will be within the town itself, perhaps even inside the walls. The royal castle is so close, it might become part of the battle as well. If that happens, I cannot promise that you would be able to leave. The only way in or out is through the city itself. You may have no choice but to take part in the fighting."

"Well, brother, it is strange to hear you sing this tune. Is it not commonly taught that a sovereign ought to be with his men in battle, not leave them to fight alone?"

"It is not the same!" he proclaimed with real feeling.

"Why not?!" I cried. "Tell me, why is it not the same?"

"You know why," he replied, and I heard the words in my head, *Because you are a woman.*

I rose to my feet and said, "Be that as it may, I am going to Winchester. We are all going. We must wrestle the fox from his hole."

"But if we do seize the fortress and take him into custody, what then?" Brian asked. "Do you intend to lock him up?"

"When he sees that we are the stronger party, he will have no choice but to defer to whatever I command. He would never allow himself to rot away in some prison. It is in his nature to live well," I replied.

Earl Robert stood and said, "What I am trying to tell you is that much is uncertain in battle. I do believe we can overcome him, but it is possible that things could go the other way. It is possible that we could lose, and then the bishop, the false queen, and the wolf of Ypres will be more powerful than ever."

He was right, of course. I could see that. But I also knew we had an advantage that even such a defeat could not reverse.

"You forget, Earl Robert," I said. "We hold the winning card. We have Stephen as our prisoner. As long as we escape from Winchester alive, they cannot take control of the kingdom: not without someone to sit on the throne."

"They may put forward that brat Eustace," Miles argued.

"Archbishop Theobald would not crown Eustace," Brian assured him. "I have spoken with him from time to time. I think he understands quite clearly that either Stephen is the rightful king or he is not. If he is not the rightful king, then there is no reason to give the throne to Eustace. It must be given to the empress or Prince Henry. But if he is indeed the rightful king, then we all ought to be excommunicated. I note he has done nothing of the sort, so I doubt he would crown Eustace. Besides, no one in England wants that boy as king."

"It is decided, then," I said. "We make for Winchester, and perhaps I will work to gain the greater favor of the archbishop. Earl Robert, are you at peace with this decision?"

To my great relief, he nodded to affirm my words. "I am content. It is the right thing to do. I just wanted to be sure you recognize the danger that awaits. The greater earls are now on our side, but things can change quickly."

"This fight was always going to find me, whether I wanted it or not, and I can never know loyalty until it is tested," I said. "What point is there in delay? The faster we move, the less time our enemies will have to ready themselves."

Having reached an accord, we all made to return to the archery contest, the four of us walking in a line toward the steps. I was the first to descend, and when I did, I was met by another man coming up: a man I did not recognize, who pulled off his hat and bowed his head.

"Empress Mathilda, I am William de Beauchamp," he said, restoring his hat to its place. "I am come to swear fealty to you and may the devil Waleran rot in hell!"

With all my heart, I said to him, "Sir, I could not agree with you more."

XVII

When my sons were naught but babes, they would wake at all hours of the night, crying out for milk. However, with Henry, I did not feed him. His care was given over to the wet nurse, and he was ever on her teat in those early days.

It was not that I had forsaken him. Indeed, I spent as much time with him as I could, but it was not the custom in Anjou for great ladies to place a child upon the breast, nor was it the custom of the Normans. I simply did the only thing I knew, and in truth I was glad at first, for my body was able to recover from my painful labor. But over time, I came to feel a distance between myself and my son. Whenever something upset him, there was the wet nurse to comfort him, pulling out her breast and placing him upon it. I believe he came to look upon that woman as his mother, and I found that I did not care for it.

When my second son came, I swore to do things differently. I told the ladies around me that I would feed that child if it was the last thing I did, and they dared not oppose me. But then I became so ill immediately after the birth that my Geoffrey had to be fed by someone else, and when I finally tried to place him on my breast, there was no milk for him to drink. I had to give him back to a wet nurse.

William was my last birth and he came in the middle of a war. It was the worst time to try to nurse a child, but thanks be to God, I was able to do it. I awoke time and again, dragged that child to my body, and allowed him to suckle. Perhaps this is why, from the beginning, I felt closer to him than the other two. Even when he had been weaned, if he needed comfort, he did not go to a wet nurse or even to Adela: he came to me. He would curl up next to my body and stare into my eyes, his own full of tears.

"*Mama!*" he would call, and I knew he was full of fear, sadness, or both, even if he could not put it into words.

"Do not fear, my son," I would tell him, stroking his head with one hand and embracing him with the other. "Everything will end up right. You'll see!"

Such assurance did this give him that often he would fall asleep right there in my arms with nothing in the world to vex him, even as I was trembling inside and knew not whence our deliverance would come.

In the last days of July in the year of our Lord 1141, as we built up our strength to march on Winchester and bring justice to the door of Henry of Blois, I thought back on those moments and wondered who would hold me and promise it would all end up right. Once it had been my own mother, but I doubted anyone around me could fill such a role at that time. I had grown too old and too hard to believe such promises. I had seen far too much of the world.

No sooner had I decided to ride to Winchester, than we began gathering up every man and weapon we could muster. It was fortunate that many of the earls were already in attendance at Oxford, including the earl of Warwick, who had missed the ceremony for Earl Miles but arrived the following evening. As a member of the *familie* Beaumont, his presence was especially helpful, and combined with the defection of William de Beauchamp, I hoped it might cause even Waleran to bend the knee. After all, he and his twin brother had already done so in Normandy, and if the account of William de Beauchamp was to be believed, the earl of Worcester was bereft of strength and coin.

I spent as much time receiving the counsel of my captains as I could possibly spare. Although the fastest path to Winchester would have taken us past the fortress of Wallingford, we chose instead to go by way of Devizes Castle, which you may remember had fallen into our hands of late. I objected to this idea at first, for it was out of the way and would cost us at least a day of riding, if not more, but earls Robert and Miles were both keen to join forces with John Marshal, the castellan of Ludgershall, before reaching Winchester. He had sworn fealty to me by that time and would be able to meet us if we went that way. He knew both Wiltonshire and Hampshire as well as any man alive, and as the former marshal of the king's horses, he kept a great many animals that could be of use in battle, if it was to come to that.

I certainly hoped it would not come to that. The royal palace of Winchester had only one means of entry or departure, which was the front gate that led out into the city. One first had to enter the town and only then could one hope to enter the castle, unless of course one had a siege tower of extraordinary size. This meant that as long as one held the city, the royal palace was quite safe, but if the city was to fall, then anyone in the palace would be trapped without the ability to flee. Perhaps this was why there were two wells within the castle walls.

Our aim was to meet with Bishop Henry and cause him to see reason: not truly to change his heart, which no man could

hope to achieve, but to make him believe he was safer supporting my rule than not. If he would not submit, then we would
be forced to arrest him and place him in jail. Several possible
prisons had been proposed for the bishop's stay. Some favored
keeping him in the dungeon of the royal castle at Winchester, as
this would free us from having to transport him cross country, a
sure hazard with enemies on the road. I preferred Devizes, for
it lay farther from the supporters of the usurper. But perhaps
the best solution was put forward by Drogo, who said, "Throw
him in with his brother in Bristol Castle and let them bite each
other to death."

My uncle, King David, had not been with us that day of
the archery contest. He was seeing to some affairs in his own
lands, which could be reached in a single day's ride, be it ever
so long. We were therefore bound to wait for his return before
departing, not only because I required his men, but also because I craved his advice. He finally arrived on the following
Sunday, and happily he had with him a hundred knights at
his command, having gathered up all the men who had scattered from Westminster and then some. Perhaps of greatest
import, he brought along a man by the name of Thomas whose
origin was somewhat of a mystery: I suspected he was from the
Norman lands in Sicily. This Thomas—or Tommaso, as he was
known in his own tongue—was an expert in means of warfare,
in particular the construction of trebuchets.

"He has surely been in the pay of every lord under the sun,"
Robert told us. "In such cases, one is simply glad to have the
man on our side!"

The smiths in the castle worked from dawn until dusk crafting arrows, repairing armor, and forging new swords. Then
they continued into the night, their fires providing the only
light and the beating of their tools the only sound. There were
three cobblers in the city of Oxford at that time, and they were

all kept busy making new shoes to cover the feet of our knights and archers. Of course, we dearly hoped there would be no battle, for nothing is certain once an arrow is fired. My brother Reginald was, as we have seen, well known at the taverns, and he was able to induce more than one of the pupils to take on tasks that required the ability to write or draw, or simply two legs to run and two arms to carry. For my part, I spent many hours in the chapel or my own chamber praying with the paternoster of Margaret of Scotland in my hand, my fingers no doubt covered with callouses from the number of times I pushed one bead after another, chanting, "*Ave Maria, gratia plena, exaudi suppli-camentum meum! Ora pro me!*"[25]

On Monday, the fifth before the Kalends of August,[26] we set out from Oxford, a host of some five hundred persons. We were forced to travel without Earl Geoffrey of Essex and the other members of his family, for they had to return to their own estates to gather up their men. I was loath to part with them, for I trusted them most when they were directly within my sight, but I had no choice. We needed every man they could muster—that is every man who could hold a weapon in his hand—but most of all we needed their knights. As the knights were not in Oxford, they had to be fetched. And so, we set out without three persons whom I dearly desired to keep near my person.

The road from Oxford to Devizes is pleasant, coming as it does out of the wood and into the beginnings of the great plain around Salisbury. That is an ancient place, filled with strange hills and stones left by peoples long gone. Had we all been at our leisure, I might have made another attempt to visit the great *Stanhencg*, but it was necessary to keep to our business. To

---

25 "Hail Mary, full of grace, hear my supplication! Pray for me!"
26 July 28, 1141.

increase our speed, we had chosen for some of those on horse-back to ride ahead of the carts. Therefore, I, King David, Earl Robert, and several others came within the shadow of Devizes on the evening of the second day.

We were met there by John Marshal, who had come over from his castle of Ludgershall to meet us, taking the opportunity to make a survey of anything in the castle that might be of use to us in bringing Bishop Henry of Winchester into submission. He was a man of medium size, about the same age as me, and very polite. Once he had aided me in alighting from my horse, he held out his hand and said, "Good empress, you must be weary from your journey. Allow me to lead you to the upper chamber, where you may rest your head. It used to belong to Bishop Roger of Salisbury."

"Then I am certain it will be as grand as any in England!" I said cheerfully. "Bishop Henry took it for himself on my last visit and I have yet to lay eyes on the place."

The two of us walked through the hall and up the stair to the private quarter, where a passage led toward the room of which he had spoken. I was surprised when he opened the door to see there was yet another stair of wood to climb, but oh, what a sight to see when we had reached the destination! The chamber filled the entire upper portion of one of the castle towers, with the stone roof high above serving as its ceiling. There were three windows, each with a place to sit, and a bed covered in what I was sure must be silk, even as a canopy of silk hung above it. And the number of chests and candlesticks! The carpets purchased from the East with designs of flowers and vines bursting into life!

Now I see why my cousin kept this room for himself, I thought.

"How has this place been thus preserved?" I asked in wonder. "It does not look like it has been through a war, with men fighting over it time after time."

"Well, Stephen did not take any of it, because he hoped to use the place again, and his men were not able to take any of it with them when they surrendered the castle," he replied.

Even as he was speaking the words, Adela entered behind us with a basket of my things and gasped as she saw the riches with which the place was ornamented—the tapestry and marble wash basin.

"Heaven and earth! Just how rich was this bishop?" she asked.

"Far more than you or me," I assured her.

It was already growing dark, and there was not enough food for a full meal nor enough ladies for dancing. Therefore, the few dozen of us who had arrived early, along with another ten or so men who had come with John Marshal, all sat around the two long tables in the hall, eating some bread of millet and such meat as the butcher had on hand. Some of the men had pulled up the carrots growing out in the garden, but they were tiny things and hardly worth eating. There was no wine in the cellar of Devizes Castle, so we made do with what we had brought from Oxford. As I sat there next to Adela taking a drink, I said to her, "I think I have done very well."

"Very well at what, my lady?" she asked.

"Very well at keeping quiet."

She tipped her head slightly and lowered her brow. "I still don't know what you mean. Is this something about Bishop Henry?"

I turned to look at her directly. "All these long months, I have said nothing about your friendship with—"

"Oh, my lady, look!" she cried.

For a moment, I thought she was simply attempting to distract me from a discussion about Sir Philip of Honfleur, but I turned around and saw to my great surprise that my brother Robert and Lord Miles had just entered the room on either side of Waleran of Meulan, earl of Worcester, looking just as foul as I remembered him.

"Good lord," I murmured. "Am I really seeing this?"

"I think so, for I see it too," Adela replied.

I rose from the bench on which I had been seated and walked toward the three men, meeting them a short distance from those crowded around the tables. As I approached, Earl Robert, as if by instinct, reached over and grabbed the arm of Earl Waleran, and seeing what he had done, Lord Miles did the same with Waleran's other arm. I looked into the eyes of Waleran Beaumont: those eyes that had pierced me that day when he was a prisoner being led in chains. His face bore a new scar on his left cheek. *He could not have received that at the fighting in Lincoln, so quickly did he flee,* I thought. He had far less hair than the last time I had seen him, which was back before my father had died, but what he had left was grown quite long. His clothes were rather poor, his hands filthy: on the whole, he looked like a man who had been to hell and back, and perhaps he truly had been. Nevertheless, his conceit had not abandoned him along with his hair.

"Many leagues have I traveled to be here, lady of the English, for so I must call you," he spoke, or rather scoffed.

I smiled and told him, "I wonder that you took the trouble to do so if it was such tribulation."

"There is no need for that. I know when I am beaten," he said softly, "although in truth it is Count Geoffrey who places me in this position more than yourself."

"He approached the castle perhaps half an hour ago," Robert explained. "The guard questioned him, but he carried no weapon. He is come to make his submission."

"You have my man, I think," Waleran continued. "He has several things which are owed me, and he has scorned the House of Beaumont most perversely."

"You act as if he were your tailor," I said. "He is a lord in his own right, and he has freely offered his fealty to me as rightful sovereign."

"I will have it out with him," Waleran muttered.

"All in good time," said Robert. "First we must address the matter of your submission."

"Let go of me and you shall have your desire," Waleran answered.

Earl Robert nodded and both he and Miles relaxed their grips. I then looked on in awe as Waleran Beaumont—earl of Worcester, the man who had held the usurper in his hands—dropped down to one knee and, reaching out, took my right hand and kissed it. His eyes rose and met mine. His words came as if with a fire.

"God save Mathilda, queen of England."

By the next morning, Waleran of Meulan and William de Beauchamp had made an end of their quarrel, and as they performed a sufficient repentance for their rebellion—or as sufficient as I was likely to receive—I allowed them to proceed on to Normandy, where I hoped that Count Geoffrey would see to it that they behaved properly. Waleran never would have humbled himself before me unless he felt he had no choice. It was as good a sign as any that the war in Normandy was going well. How I treasured this good news in that tense hour!

We held at Devizes for one more day as the rest of our company arrived, then proceeded on through the Pewsey Vale at dawn the following morning. We set a pace as fast as could possibly be met, stopping only once at midday, and then for no more than half an hour. There was so much worth saying, and yet little was said. I had seldom ridden in such quiet. We pushed the carts almost to the point of breaking, and as the light of day began to fade, we saw the great trees of Collingbourne Wood rising before us and continued under their boughs toward the home of John Marshal: Ludgershall Castle.

Some time that night Drogo said to me, "I have been speaking with the men, my lady, and they cannot keep up this pace. We really must rest here another day at least before continuing."

"The spies of the enemy may have received word of our movement by now," I argued. "Every day we delay gives a greater advantage to Bishop Henry. The only hope we have of gaining his submission is to catch him at home and alone. If he is able to call for the false queen, then we will be in the middle of it."

"The middle of what?" Drogo asked with a keen smile.

"The middle of a battle, that's what!" I barked. "No, we cannot wait. I must speak with Earl Robert."

I did talk with my brother and the rest of the captains. We agreed that once again a lead party would set out the next morning and ride at speed to Winchester, while the rest would come after two days' rest and take two days to reach the destination. I only hoped that the castle of Winchester was full of food, or at least that the people of the town were willing to sell us some.

At day break, the chief persons among us—including King David, the archbishop, the earls, and the best of the knights—packed our things once again and rode into Hampshire, crossing the River Test by mid morning and moving south from Andover until, after another long day of riding, we arrived at the western gate of Winchester, city of kings. Those ancient walls first built by the Romans and made better in our own age stood to guard the castle, the cathedral … and the bishop.

"Let me be the one to approach first," Archbishop Theobald offered. "If Bishop Henry has heard of our coming and assembled everything for battle, then it is safest to put forth myself, for they are unlikely to shoot at me."

I was taken aback by this. Yes, the archbishop of Canterbury had been at my court and sworn loyalty to myself, but I would not have called us the best of friends. His manner was often dour. I could not pick out any real interest of his except theology—a noble pursuit, to be sure, but a man must also have a hobby. I never sensed that he had come to my side due to anything but necessity. Therefore, his willingness to place himself forward as our representative, in danger of life and limb, was extraordinary. Indeed, it was so extraordinary that for a moment I doubted his intention, but then I considered how deep was his feud with the legate, and I thought it impossible that they could be plotting together.

And so, we watched as he rode toward the gate. We were far enough away that we could not hear his conversation with the men above, but close enough that those guards could easily see the extent of our company and make a guess at our intent. I said nothing to those near me but bowed my head in prayer, beseeching my Creator, *Let them open the gates. Let them remain true.* I stayed that way long enough that my brother Reginald said to me, "My lady, are you well?"

I quickly opened my eyes and looked over at him. "As well as I can be for the moment. We will see what happens."

The archbishop had pulled his horse around and was riding back to our position. I breathed in quickly, bidding myself remain calm. The evening sky was clear and some birds were singing in the distance. There was no sense of dread over nature, and yet I thought in that moment how many a man and woman had met terrible ends under the bright sun, on days when most of creation rejoiced. He was approaching us quickly. Was he about to yell that we should flee? No, it seemed not.

"All is well!" the archbishop called. "They have welcomed us to approach, and then they will happily open the gate."

"I still say it could be a trap," Earl Miles said. "We should send others to the gate before the empress."

"Your concern does my heart good," I told him, "but if it is indeed a trap, we are in greater danger once we are inside the gates than when they are opening, and greater still when the doors have closed behind us. Nevertheless, we have with us a hundred men able to fight. I say we go together, seeking our greatest safety in numbers, and pray that they are less willing to fire on a woman than a band of knights riding alone. I have faith in those who have sworn to defend me."

I said this boldly, but in truth I did feel the sharp edge of fear within myself—the cold grip of terror. Nevertheless, I had made my choice, and we rode forward as conquerors. Closer and closer we came, until the walls towered over us, and I thought of my sons so far away. "Henry, Geoffrey, William …" I breathed their names. I longed to hold them again, and I feared that whatever lay behind the doors might separate us for ever. But it was for their sakes that I had to be strong, and I was thankful that at least some of those I loved were by my side.

When we were within a hundred feet of the gate, so close that anyone on the wall could have thrown a stone and hit us, we halted, even as the great doors began to open. Had I not just been there and seen this, only a few months earlier? Again, the doors groaned upon their hinges. A crack of light opened between them and grew ever larger. I strained to see what awaited us, but Drogo pulled his horse in front of mine and raised his shield. Lord Brian did the same, followed by Sir Philip and earls Reginald, Baldwin, and Robert. I turned to look at my uncle the king of Scotland, who was still next to me and raising his own shield.

"I hope you've said your prayers, niece," he told me, winking.

"I assure you, there is no saint who is not utterly tired of hearing from me," I replied, then called to those in front of me, "What's happening? Are we to fight, fly, or enter?"

"Enter!" Robert declared, and even as he said it, they began riding forward.

I followed them into life or death. I still could not see what lay ahead. We passed under the gate and on to the High Street, where I was very pleased indeed to find that there was no band of men with weapons in hand, but only a few people of the town cheering as we passed by, some peeking out of windows to see the purpose of the noise, then smiling and waving.

"We have done it," my uncle said. "We have surprised him."

"Nothing is certain yet," I replied, unwilling to let down my guard.

We did not continue to the town square, but quickly turned right down one of the side streets that led toward the entrance of the royal palace. There was still no sign of resistance, but I heard the sound of bells coming from the direction of the cathedral and Saint Mary's Abbey. I wellremembered how the bells had announced our doom at Westminster, and I naturally turned to look toward the noise, but my brother Robert called back, "It is the hour of Vespers. Be not afraid!"

Finally, we saw the inner castle wall breaking off from the main city wall, and before us the bridge that led up to the lone entrance. The fortress, inside which lay the palace, was perched on a slight hill, the better for its defense. There were a few men upon the walls, but they did not point their weapons at us. We rode up the bridge and reached the gate house.

"Open in the name of Empress Mathilda, lady of the English!" Lord Miles cried.

They moved immediately to fulfill this request, and within the space of a moment we had all entered the upper court of the royal palace of Winchester, the home of my earliest youth.

To my eternal delight, it stood ready to receive me not as an enemy, but as rightful sovereign. The great hall and royal rooms stood to the right, along with the chapel of Edward the Confessor, though it was hidden from view. To our immediate left were the stables, and before us the great armory, which we very much hoped was still well stocked. On the other side of the palace were the kitchen, brewery, and butcher. A gravel path led slightly down hill to our left, where I knew there to be further quarters for guests and the entrance to the lower yard that housed the keep and royal exchequer.

"Everything seems to be in order," Earl Robert said.

He alighted from his horse and the other men followed his lead. The grooms were coming forward from the stables to receive the animals, and as I turned to look back toward the great hall, I saw the steward of the palace, Roger fitz Herbert, coming forward with a great set of keys hanging from his belt. Drogo helped me to the ground and I rustled the bottom of my skirt in an attempt to remove as much of the dust as I could. When I raised my eyes once again, the steward was directly in front of me. He removed his cap and bowed.

"My lady, welcome again to Winchester! This is a pleasant surprise."

Thank God it is a surprise! I thought.

"Is this the entire company," he continued, "or will there be others coming?"

"Lord willing, there will be others in a few days," I answered. "Tell me, are the palace rooms ready to receive us, and do you have any food in your larder?"

"By chance, we just received a large delivery," he said. "Do you intend to remain for some time?"

"I do not yet know the answer to that question. I must speak with the bishop of this city," I replied. "His Highness the king of Scotland is with us as well."

"Oh, I did not see him there!" said Roger fitz Herbert, looking behind me and seeing for the first time my uncle, who had handed off his horse and was stepping forward. The steward bowed again and said, "My lord, King David! You are most welcome!"

"Yes, yes," my uncle replied. "Where is the cellar? It's been a long day."

Most of the men were then led into the hall, which was near the entrance to the cellar that held such wine as still remained there in time of war. I continued to walk with the steward toward the outer entrance to the royal rooms.

"As you will perhaps remember," he said, "we have four great rooms here and three smaller ones. The finest—the king and queen's chambers—will naturally go to yourself and the king of Scotland. To whom would you like to give the others? Have you brought any ladies with you? I did not see any."

"No. My only maid, Adela, is still at Ludgershall," I replied sadly. "She cannot ride at speed with the rest of us, so it is just me for the present time. But have no fear: I am perfectly able to dress myself and such."

"I was not in doubt," he assured me.

"Let us give the other rooms first to the earls of Gloucester and Hereford," I continued. "Then a room for the earl of Cornwall, and naturally one for the archbishop of Canterbury, though I hope he will soon be able to move into the episcopal palace. If he is indeed able to move there, we can place my personal guard in that room, Sir Drogo and Sir Philip and all the rest. Adela will reside with me when she arrives."

"That leaves one chamber here and the rest will be in the guest house or the hall," he said. "Perhaps one of the other earls?"

"Give it to the lord of Wallingford," I answered. "He is often in my counsel."

"As you wish," the steward replied.

We had worked our way through the lower passage, where the lesser rooms lay, and up the stair to the chambers for the king and queen. Of course, I was not yet a queen and I had no king of my own, but only a count who did not keep my company. Even if and when I was to bear the royal crown, I would never allow my husband to bear the title of king. I was happy, therefore, to give the king's chamber to another sovereign: the king of Scotland.

"My brother and I used to play on those stairs, I think," I said. "I seem to remember dropping balls down them to watch them bounce. I do not think the servants cared for it."

"I imagine not," Roger fitz Herbert said with a smile. "Here is the entrance to the queen's chamber."

"Yes, I remember. My mother was very fond of it."

"Ah, the late queen! My predecessor in this position told me great stories about her. I was here in the time of Queen Adeliza, and then Queen Mathilda." I think he must have seen the look on my face at this point, for he quickly added, "But I very much look forward to the day when we will have a Queen Mathilda indeed, and one who will rule with wisdom and justice!"

"You are too kind," I offered, and truly the poor man meant no ill.

He placed a key in the lock and turned it, then pulled the latch and swung the door open. Before me was the very room in which I had stayed earlier that year, but to me it would always be my mother's room. The tapestry she had cherished, which portrayed the virtues of faith, hope, and love, was still hanging next to the bed. The desk that had belonged to her, at which she spent so many hours writing to men of the Church and encouraging them in their work, sat by the lone window, and on it an hour candle was burning brightly. The window looked out over the roof of the great hall, beyond the castle wall, and out to the city of Winchester. I moved closer to it and gazed into the distance, where the cathedral stood painted in color by the setting sun. Just to the south was the abbey of Saint Mary, and then the great fortress of Wolvesey Palace, in which Henry of Blois resided at that very moment.

"There is parchment and ink in the drawer if you need to write," the steward said.

I looked back at him and replied, "Thank you. I will just need some quiet now."

"Of course," he said with a bow. "We look forward to receiving you for supper whenever you are ready."

When the door was closed behind him, I immediately moved to the desk and opened the drawer, in which I did find everything I would need to write a letter and seal it. I sat in the chair provided and began writing the words.

To Henry of Blois, bishop of Winchester, abbot of Glastonbury, and legate of His Holiness the Pope—Your rightful sovereign, the Empress Mathilda, bids you come at once to the palace of Winchester to discuss matters of state. We look forward to receiving you. MATHILDA IMPERATRIX

Looking at the letter again and feeling I needed to make a show of strength to bring his will into line, I scratched out the word "*IMPERATRIX*" and wrote instead, "*REGINA*." Then I folded the parchment, heated the wax over flame, and pulled out the seal I carried in a pouch on my person: the royal one that bore my image. I pressed it into the red wax, noting as I did how very like blood it appeared. There was my image stamped in it—a queen of blood. I hoped it was not a bad sign.

Within minutes, the letter was sent with a messenger to Wolvesey Palace. All that was left was to await the legate's reply.

I spent much of the next hour in my chamber—that is to say, the queen's chamber—examining its contents and attempting to keep my mind off what might happen. There was a single large chest pushed up against one of the walls, and I opened it to discover that it was filled with gowns, furs, and shoes that must have belonged to the false queen. They were very fine, bearing all the marks of Flemish skill. I had come with only the clothes I was wearing and would have to wait for Adela to bring a few more gowns later in the week, so finding such a treasure store was a great source of cheer. What was more, nothing I had borrowed from the Lady D'Oyly was as fine as what lay in the chest.

I raised up one gown the color, it seemed, of spring rain, with silver thread and tiny jewels sewn into it. The cuffs were ermine, the sash pure silk. I had seldom seen its equal. What I did not know was if it would fit me. I had never seen Mathilda of Boulogne as a grown woman and thus had no idea how her form compared to mine except that I guessed it was more pleasing to the eye in some way or another, or else I would not have heard her beauty praised so often.

I removed the gown of brown wool and linen veil that I had been wearing and laid them on the bed, keeping my under tunic upon my body, then with great care lifted the false queen's dress up over my head and pulled my arms through. I allowed the skirt to drop down and saw to my great content that it was almost exactly the right length. Perhaps an inch too short, but no one was likely to complain about that, and the arms were quite perfect. There was no mirror to be found, so I did not know how I looked in it, but I chose to believe I was quite handsome. It had been so long since I felt as much.

Returning to the chest, I found a head covering in the French style of the purest white. I put it in place to the best of my ability without the aid of a glass. The air was not at all cold, so I had no need of a fur, but I felt around and found a small ivory box, not unlike the one in which I kept my dearest possessions. I opened it and inside was a great gold chain hung with lapis lazuli. It must have cost as much as twenty horses.

"Why did she not take this with her?" I wondered aloud. However, I decided it did not matter and placed it over my head all the same, allowing it to fall upon my chest. It was not too heavy.

Suddenly, I heard a knocking at the door. I rose and opened it but saw no one there. I then recognized that the sound was coming from the opposite wall, where the tapestry was hanging. I pulled it back, and to my great surprise saw another door that led to the king's chamber. I turned the knob and pushed it open, still holding up the tapestry. I was soon greeted by the sight of my uncle looking back at me, arms crossed and his face looking rather impatient.

"Supper is made ready," he said.

"I am sorry. I did not know you all were waiting. Also, how long has this door been here?" I inquired.

"Since the place was built, I presume. Your father showed it to me many years ago." He then took a good look at me from head to toe and added, "Hold on … Were you wearing that when you arrived?"

"Of course not. I found it with the false queen's things."

"Ah! So, the finder becomes the keeper, eh?" Here he smiled at me in a rather devilish manner.

I sighed and pulled the door shut, allowing the tapestry to drop back into place. I then moved quickly to the other door and opened it. It was a good thing I was looking where I was going, for otherwise I would have run into Brian fitz Count, who happened to be passing by at that exact moment, looking down at some book he was reading. By instinct, my hand flew up to prevent a collision, and when he felt my touch, he looked up.

"I beg your pardon, my lady!" he said, shutting the book and bowing.

"No pardon is necessary," I assured him, my heart beating rather quickly from the surprise of almost running into him. "Are you going down as well?"

"Yes, I was actually coming up to ask the king if he had found you, but I see you must have received the message." He then smiled and said, "You look lovely."

I said my heart was beating quickly, but upon hearing these words, it increased still further in speed. *Is he saying that because he feels he must, or because he truly believes it?* I wondered. *Is he allowed to say that? Yes, of course, don't be silly, Maud. Don't get carried away.*

"Thank you," I replied simply, hoping very much that my face had not gone red.

He placed the book in his left hand, held up his right arm, and offered, "Allow me to lead you down to the hall."

I nodded and placed my arm around his. I was often led places by all sorts of men in exactly the same manner, so there was nothing out of sorts, and yet I was very aware of how close we were. Was he thinking about the same thing? I had given him a room just below mine, which was next to a room that had a secret entrance by my bed. It made sense to do so—he was one of my chief captains, and we were in Winchester upon urgent business. But suddenly I wondered if some part of me had arranged it for another purpose without my mind fully recognizing it. No, it could not be. I had not known about the secret door. Yet the sense of guilt within me was strong, for I knew I loved him.

I said nothing during our walk, and he must have read this sign, for as we began to descend the stair he said to me, "I am sure you are worried about Bishop Henry's response. Whatever happens, we will be with you."

"It is not that," I said quietly.

We had made it to the entrance to the hall. I could hear the sounds of revelry within, but without we were alone. We both dropped our arms, and he asked me, "What is it?"

The look on his face was earnest, beckoning me to share. I had always wondered if at some point I would have to address with him the situation between us, whatever that situation was. And looking into his eyes at that moment, I felt that perhaps the time had come. I could feel the heat rising within me, and my eyes were growing moist. Then there was the sound of someone else coming down the stair, and we both turned to look.

"Found them!" my uncle cried, holding up a pair of dice. "They were buried with the rest of my things. I told Earl Robert I would play with him."

Feeling rather glad for the interruption, I pulled the iron handle on the door and swung it open to reveal the great hall. The wood tresses high above were hung with cords from which metal stars hung in suspense over the feast below. There were two hearths—one on each side of the room—and twin fires lit up the space. Everywhere, men held goblets of wine and mead, some bent at tables and talking, some linking arms and dancing, some walking back to the barrel for more. I strode through all of this in a daze, attempting to pull my thoughts back to the matter at hand: we were waiting for a reply from Bishop Henry, or for him to show his face. Upon this, a great many things depended.

There was a dais at the far end of the room on which four chairs sat behind a high table. The archbishop of Canterbury was already seated in one and my brother Robert in another. My uncle and I made our way up and took the remaining seats. I leaned on the table and began rubbing my forehead with one hand as I stared down at my lap.

What is wrong with you, Maud? Control yourself! I chided within.

Attempting to remove such things from my mind, I turned to my left, where Earl Robert was seated. "Have we heard anything from Wolvesey?" I asked.

"Not yet," he replied, lifting his bowl of soup and drinking.

"I suppose it could take quite a while, but then again, it is not a long walk," I mused.

"Have some soup. You'll feel better," he proposed, pointing to the bowl in front of me.

I held the bowl with both hands and moved it slightly, allowing the liquid to swirl. I could just see my faint reflection in its depths.

"I am afraid I have no appetite," I said softly. "Perhaps the bishop has driven it out of me."

The sound of the great doors opening at the other end of the room caused me to break out of my trance. I looked up and saw that it was Drogo pulling them open with both his hands, striding through with authority and looking directly at me. He held up his right hand, in which was a folded piece of parchment. I stood immediately and waved for him to come closer. He avoided one or two men who had been too much at the drink and reached my position. My heart was once again pounding. By this point, my brother and the Scottish king had also risen to their feet. The letter was placed in my hand and I broke the seal, unfolding it to read. The men on either side of me glanced over my shoulders at the four words written in black ink.

"What does it say?" Drogo asked.

I looked up at him and recited: "I will prepare myself."

"What on earth does that mean?"

This excellent question was posed by Earl Baldwin of Devon, a man whose skill for cutting right to the point had always done my heart good.

I had retreated with my captains to the chapel of Edward the Confessor, which is attached to the royal rooms and great hall by the passage between them. The place was quite dark, as the windows no longer had light to let in, and we were forced to make do with the few candles that had been left on their stands for anyone who wished to pray in the middle of the night. I had great need of prayer in that moment, but even more I needed the counsel of the men who were with me. My brother, the earl of Gloucester, was pacing in circles round the room, passing behind each of the white stone columns in turn. Earl Miles was bent over the altar table, pressing his fists into it as if it had done him a great wrong. Reginald was still gnawing on a leg of meat, evidently without a care in the world. Brian was sitting back against one of the columns, arms folded, staring up at the ceiling, in what degree of frustration I could not make out. Sir Drogo and Sir Philip were faithfully guarding the door, John Marshal was standing back against a column and kicking it softly with his heel, and before me stood the earl of Devon, Baldwin de Redvers, the letter from Bishop Henry in his hand.

"What on earth does it mean?!" he repeated more fiercely. "Who sends a letter like this?"

"I can assure you, it is all too ordinary for the man in question," I told him, rubbing my arms for warmth, as the chapel had lost all the heat of the day. "Nothing delights him more than speaking in a manner that leaves others in the dark. He exalts in his own cleverness." Watching my brother continue his circuit round the room, I called, "Earl Robert, please cease your pacing and join us here."

He did as instructed, taking a seat next to Brian on the floor, but looking very much as if he still wanted to punch something or someone.

"Now, how do we interpret the meaning of this letter?" I asked. "He thinks he is clever, but I dare say we have minds in this room that can match him."

"It seems he intends to come over this evening and just needs to ready himself," Reginald offered, biting the last bit of meat off the bone.

"If that were the case, he would not have sent a letter. He would have just done whatever needed to be done and come," Brian told him. Then to me he said, "He is trying to buy time, either to decide whether to come or flee, or simply to get himself ready for battle. Either way, we should not wait. We should send men over to Wolvesey."

There was a great pounding on the door and Sir Philip turned around and called, "Who is it? Declare yourself!"

"The king of the Scots," came the reply.

The two knights nodded at each other and Philip opened the door, allowing my uncle to stride in and join us.

"I have just spoken with the steward to judge the mood of the people," he said, taking his stand beside me. "He is quite certain they will hold true to us. They have not forgotten the oaths they made in the spring. He says there is a growing anger within the walls against the conceit of the bishop. They were not happy that he raided the old castle in the middle of town for stone. He keeps adding to his fortress, and they feel rather like a people in prison."

"This is excellent news!" I declared, then hastily added, "Not that the bishop has behaved in such a manner, but that we have the people on our side. Such a change from London! And they control all the gates, or has the bishop bought the city guard?"

"They should be free from the bishop," said Robert. "King David, is there any word of the loyalties of the nuns?"

"Yes, I did inquire as to that, and he said they are rather sore that Bishop Henry sends so much money to his abbey at Glastonbury while ignoring their need for wood in the winter. It is said that at Christmas last year, they were collecting for the poor of the city, as is their wont, but when they knocked on the door of Wolvesey Palace, they were given a meager sum because the greater offering had been sent back to the abbot of Cluny for the adornment of his house."

"Lord uncle, you know that there are few things that please me more than a recitation of the vices of that man, but we have little time for such discussion," I told him. "Before you entered, I was about to send over some men to call upon the bishop. We are afraid he might fly."

"How would he do that?" the king asked. "His palace lies within the walls even as ours does, and the gates are closed after dark."

"There are few gates in creation that cannot be opened for the right price," Brian noted. "The Church would even open the gate of heaven for enough coin. We are wasting time! We must go now."

"It must be close to midnight!" my uncle objected. "He is not going anywhere until dawn, and if we go over there, what will we do? If he refuses to open the door to us, we do not yet have a force that is able to seize the place. They are stuck back at Ludgershall. You would make a declaration of war to no end."

"Well, I don't like any of this!" Miles called from the far end of the room, pounding the table and walking back in our direction.

"Your thoughts are noted," I assured him.

As the rest of the men brooded, I walked over to where Robert and Brian were seated and crouched down, meeting their eye level.

"The king makes a good point," I said softly. "We would be hard pressed to begin a siege tonight."

"We have enough men to keep him from leaving, which is all we need at the moment," Brian replied.

I turned my gaze to my brother, who was still in a sour mood. "Lord Brian says go, King David says stay. Miles and Reginald do not seem eager to cast their votes. What say you? It will fall to you to lead the battle, should it come to that."

Robert sighed deeply and leaned his head back against the pillar. "I think the danger in doing nothing is greater than the danger in acting."

"Very well," I said calmly, although I felt anything but calm. "Who will you take with you?"

"I will go," Brian offered, and Robert nodded in gratitude.

Standing once again, I called, "Earl Miles, Earl Reginald, Earl Baldwin—gather all your men and make for Wolvesey Palace to collect the bishop. Master John, you and the king will remain here to guard the palace. Sir Drogo, Sir Philip," I added, turning to face them, "I think you should stay as well."

"Very good," Drogo replied, and all at once the men made to leave the room and carry out my instruction ... all except King David, who stood there with a frown on his face.

I approached him slowly, and when I was within a single pace and it was only the two of us left in the room, I said, "I am sorry I did not take your advice. I just think if we wait until morning, we give him too much time."

"You must do what you feel is right. It is your kingdom," he replied.

"But you feel I have made the wrong decision," I whispered.

"Only time will tell, niece," he said, turning and walking toward the door. "Only time will tell!"

When he had shut the door behind him and I was all alone, I turned and looked back toward the altar. Having received counsel, it was time for me to pray. I dropped to the floor and bowed, offering up words my mother had taught me all those many years before.

> *"Nunc laudare debemus auctorem regni caelestis,*
> *Potentiam creatoris, et consilium illius,*

Facta Patris gloriae: quomodo ille,
Cum sit aeternus Deus, omnium miraculorum auctor
    exstitit;
Qui promo filiis hominum
Caelum pro culmine tecti
Dehinc terram custos humani generis
Omnipotens creavit."[27]

---

27   This is from the Latin translation by Bede. Common English translation: "We
    should honor the guardian of heaven, the might of the architect and his purpose,
    the work of the glorious Father: as he, the eternal God, brought all wonders
    into being; first he created for the children of men heaven as a roof, afterward
    appointed the middle earth for the lands of men, the almighty Lord."

XVIII

What dread the mighty Trojans must have felt when the Greeks came to their city and pulled before those great walls engines of fearful might, to rip down the stones that guarded Troy and set the very sky alight with fire. How Paris must have cursed his theft in those hours, for Achilles was at his door! I had read that tale as a girl and thanked God I was not caught in such an hour. It seemed far better to be the Greeks than the Trojans, for every beast knows that to be trapped without hope of escape is among the greatest terrors of this world.

The Greeks had thousands of men on their side: a number beyond reckoning. With an immense fleet they crossed the Aegean, but we had only a few dozen warriors to send to Wolvesey Palace. How fortunate then that they were among the best in England! There was no better captain than Earl Robert of Gloucester and no better shot than Earl Reginald of Cornwall. Not a quarter hour had passed after our debate in the chapel before they departed. I could not sleep but stood staring out the window in my chamber, looking in the direction of the bishop's lair. It was a distance of less than a mile, but in the darkness, I could see very little. High above, the moon cast its silver light upon the city, yet it was not enough to provide me with a knowledge of what was taking place. Nevertheless, I stared.

Two hours passed without any news, and it was plain that the bishop had not immediately yielded to their demands, or he would have been in my presence at the royal castle. No, instead I was forced to wait another hour until a single rider climbed the bridge up to the gate house and was allowed into the upper yard. As soon as I learned of it, I made my way outside and saw three men conversing together, one of them holding a torch. *That will be Roger fitz Herbert,* I thought, *but who are the others?* I continued to approach them, the cold air of night filling my lungs, even as the stars looked down upon us.

"What is it?" I called. "What news?"

They all turned, and as I grew closer, I saw in the fire's glow the faces of King David and Lord Brian.

"We rode to the gate, and they began shooting at us from the walls," Brian explained. He must have seen the concern on my face in that dim light, for he added, "No one was hurt. They could not have seen much at this hour. I think they meant only to send us a message, not harm our persons. We have left some men in position to prevent any escape, and Earl Robert has led the rest over to the abbey grounds to make ready for the siege."

I placed my head in my hands. This was exactly what we had all feared would happen, but no one had desired it. We were facing a battle with a man of the Church. It was Stephen's movement against the bishops that led the nobles to break ranks with him. Of course, the bishop of Winchester was in that moment rather more in violation of the law of the land than the bishop of Salisbury and his relatives had once been, refusing as he was to submit to any request of his sovereign. But I was wise enough at least to know how it would appear to many in England: that I was moving against the Church, acting with terrible arrogance, and so forth. The allegiance of so many great men to myself had been dearly bought and was by no means certain. Yet, in the end, it was not my choices that had led us to that point as much as the choices of Henry of Blois. As ever, I was trapped.

The king moved to embrace me. "Have courage, niece! Lord Brian has assured us that no one was harmed. The rebel priest cannot hide for ever."

Looking up, I asked, "Just how good is your man, Tommaso? We will need to build trebuchets and towers."

"There you may rest at ease. He is as good as they come," he replied.

"I am unlikely to rest at ease until this waking nightmare is over," I moaned. "The rest of the company is not here until Monday. Can we hold on until then?"

"I believe so," Brian answered, "and with the light of day may come hope. When we have cut down the trees and shaped them into towers, we will truly see the mind of the bishop and whether he is willing to pay the extreme price for this quarrel."

"We must keep a watch upon the city walls so that he does not get word out to Mathilda of Boulogne!" my uncle warned. "She has it in her to raise up a host that could cause us real trouble."

"Only if she buys it," I muttered. "Think you that she has such coin remaining?"

I looked from one man to another but received only empty stares. Not for the first time in my life, I bemoaned my lack of knowledge.

"Very well, gentlemen. Thank you for your service. I shall attempt to get some sleep," I said.

And so, I left them to their doom for that night, thankful that the dream I had been having—the one where I was trapped in a castle surrounded by flame—was certainly of Oxford and not Winchester.

The light of morning brought no great change in our situation as Earl Robert and his men took up their place in Saint Mary's Abbey. Although the sisters there bore little love in their hearts for the bishop, I knew they would be most unhappy to have their halls filled with men of war and themselves caught in the middle of a battle. I sent word to my brother that the nuns should be moved to a safer place, but some refused to leave, so dedicated were they to that house. Though many arrows were sent in their direction from Wolvesey Palace, this was no threat against those who stayed under the roof and within the walls.

One day, two days, three days passed. How happy I was on that Monday, the fourth day of August, when the men in the northern tower of the royal castle—that is, the one named for Saint Augustine of Canterbury—saw a great host approaching the west gate! It was the remainder of our company ready to join the fight. Finally, we would be able to mount a true siege and hopefully drive out the bishop, and what was even better, we had no reason to suppose that Henry of Blois had gotten word to his evil allies. There was no sign of the false queen or William of Ypres. I did worry that we had heard nothing from Geoffrey de Mandeville, the earl of Essex, but his lack of haste was perhaps understandable given that he had to collect quite a few men before setting out.

In addition to this, I was very glad to have Adela with me. She knew as well as anyone how to bring me good cheer. That very day, she proposed that we walk over to the stables to pet the horses. There is such a feeling of calm that one often gets around animals. They are not troubled by as many things as us. As long as they have food and quarters, a chance to stretch their legs and feel the sun upon their bodies, they are content. I was also happy to show Adela the garden that lay on the other side of the palace, next to the northern walls and the Saint Augustine Tower. They called it the Queen Mathilda Garden, after my father's mother, Mathilda of Flanders. However, it was Mathilda of Scotland who lived in my memories in that place, sitting by the fountain and walking beneath the trees. She would go there in the morning to read her book of hours, then again in the evening to pray with her rosary, the very one that I had come to possess.

As it was the only part of the castle grounds that had anything green growing in it, Adela and I took to spending our afternoons there. We would sit on the grass and read, each with our own book, perhaps with a pitcher of wine at hand. As I was filled with worry every hour, I read very little and drank rather more. When I would rise to ask after the latest news, she would touch my leg gently and say, "They will tell you when there is news, my lady." Then I would try once again to content myself and make it through a few lines of Saint Jerome before wondering again whether our towers were in place, if they were able to understand the words coming out of Tommaso's mouth, if anyone had approached the outer gates, and if anyone was dead or close to it.

The weather was pleasant that August: not too hot and mostly dry. It must have been the third or fourth day after Adela arrived that we were sitting in the garden and Archbishop Theobald of Canterbury approached from the palace. As the bishop of Winchester had refused to comply with our requests, it was not possible to move the archbishop to Wolvesey Palace, nor could he rest his head at Saint Mary's Abbey, for it was very near the siege. Hyde Abbey was outside the walls and had no guest quarters at that time. Yet, if he was tired of staying in the royal palace, he did not show it. I will also say that for a man of the Church not accustomed to war, he did not show the slightest sign of fear.

As the archbishop walked toward us, his bright green stole shining in the sunlight, I saw that he held a letter in his hand. I called out to him, "Archbishop Theobald, well met!"

"And the same to you, my lady!" he said, bowing his head. He then looked at Adela and added, "And you, Lady Adela—I trust you are having a pleasant morning."

"As pleasant as it could be when the days are evil," she replied with a smile.

The archbishop pointed to the volume in my hand and asked, "What are you reading?"

"Jerome," I answered. "And you?"

He raised up the letter and said, "From a kinsman of mine, a former sheriff of London."

"Oh! Does he say anything of the Londoners or the false queen?" Adela inquired. "If he knows we are here, they must as well."

My heart sank as she said this, for I knew it must be true. Of course, we could never have kept our presence in Winchester a secret for ever, but if there had been time for word to reach London and a letter to come back in the other direction, then we might have an army upon us at any moment.

"Have no fear!" the archbishop said. "He is not in London at the present, but away on business to the west. Actually, he is presently staying at Oxford."

I let out a sigh of relief even as Adela asked, "So what does he write about, then? Anything of interest?"

I had half a mind to chide her for prying into a private matter, but to my surprise, the archbishop did not mind. "He has a son studying in Paris. He wonders if I might put in a good word for him."

How had my maid hit upon a subject of conversation with this man when I so often could not? I decided to pursue it.

"Is he at the abbey of Saint Victor or the cathedral school?" I asked.

"The abbey, but if he has gone there to sit at the feet of the learned Hugh, he will be disappointed. Last I heard, he was near death."

"Oh, I am sorry to hear that!" I said. "He was an excellent theologian."

Archbishop Theobald smiled, and I rejoiced to have provoked such a response. He then looked down at the letter again. "I think I shall advise him to transfer to the cathedral school. There is a young man there—well, not so very young perhaps, but he is not yet a professor—whom I have heard much about from the archdeacon. They think he will become the equal of Hugh or perhaps even Bernard."

I scoffed. "That is high praise considering he has not yet taught any pupils. What is his name so I may note him when he becomes pope?"

"Petrus Lombardus," he replied.

There was a break in the conversation and I glanced over in the direction of the eastern wall. I could hear the distant hum of smiths at work in the city. *What is going on out there?* I wondered. *Perhaps I should climb up and look over the wall.* I set down the book I had been holding and rose to my feet, but Adela was not about to let me leave.

"What was the name of your relative?" she asked the archbishop. "If he is a former sheriff, we might know him."

"Becket," he answered. "Gilbert Becket."

"Yes, I think I did hear of him once," I said. "Excuse me. I am going to have a look from the wall."

"As you wish," the archbishop said with a nod.

"Go if you must, but you know you will only drive yourself mad with this constant need for news," my maid called after me.

I was growing weary of her warnings and may have rolled my eyes as I turned and walked in the direction of the eastern wall. When I arrived at the steps, I climbed them with great care, for the wind grew stronger the higher I rose and there was no rail to keep me from falling. I reached the summit and turned my head in both directions: toward the Saint Swithun Tower on the left and the Saint Oswald Tower on the right. There was only a single guard keeping watch on that portion of the wall, as it faced the High Street and not any of the sources of danger. Moving to my right, I walked south to the Saint Oswald Tower and passed through it, nodding to a pair of guards standing within. They bowed with spears in one hand and shields in the other. Coming out the other side, I saw several more men guarding the space next to the gate house. The wall was so high that only the tallest could see over it without some aid, and I was forced to stand upon a wood block provided for the purpose.

The wind was coming quite swiftly from the north, and the flags bearing the royal standard were tossed about. Directly to the east, I saw the cathedral standing proudly, the final resting place of the kings of old. The abbey buildings were not tall enough to be seen from a distance, but just to the south the bishop's palace was clear enough. Somewhere beyond was the River Itchen.

"What are you playing at, cousin?" I whispered. "Come out and show your face."

I had just determined that there was nothing to see and was about to step down from my perch when something caught my eye. A bright light, as a star fallen from heaven, flew up from

Wolvesey Palace and moved in the direction of the cathedral. I blinked, thinking I must be wrong, but then it happened again … and again, and again. The sky was filling up with tiny fires, all of them flying north from the palace, moving in the direction of the town.

"My God!" one of the guards cried, and I looked to my right where several of them were gathering. I could not see very well beneath their helms, but I gathered that their faces were painted with concern.

I looked back to the east, my own heart filling with dread as I suddenly saw smoke rising from the site where I knew Saint Mary's Abbey lay. And still the flames were falling from the sky, one after another, upon the abbey, the cathedral, and the center of the town. I could see fires starting on roofs and smoke rising to the heavens.

"No!" I cried. "Oh, please God, no!"

I watched in dismay as the fires continued to grow, and I began to hear a rising clamor of distant screams from the streets below. The wind was blowing hard. In my heart, I knew what it meant: the whole town would go up in flame. Winchester, the jewel of England, the home of so much history, the pride of Wessex, would be burned to the ground. In despair, I looked toward Wolvesey Palace and screamed, "Stop it! Stop it, now! Why?! Why are you doing this?!"

But it did not stop. The flames continued to fall, one after the other. I could not believe my cousin would do it—that he would stoop to such a level, setting his own city on fire, burning the homes and shops to the ground. What kind of Christian would do such a thing?

Then before me, I saw a sight I will never forget all my days. Winchester Cathedral, one of the chief churches in the kingdom, a sacred place of great majesty, began to burn. There was smoke coming from the roof. The wood beams were surely set alight. I put a hand to my mouth and wept. In great bitterness of spirit, I wept, and I looked up to the heavens, where the sun was still shining down happily, and I cried out to my God, "Is there no end to hate?!"

I might have stood there weeping for hours, but a voice within commanded me, *Go, Maud! Do something! It does no good to stand and weep!*

I listened to the voice. There was another stair nearer the gate, and I flew down it, lifting my skirt to move faster. Arriving in the main courtyard, I looked around for someone—anyone who might be able to help in some way—but there was no one there. They had all gone to watch, just as I had. I turned back in the direction I had just come, and even as I did, the gate opened before me and Earl Miles rode in, the shadow of death upon his face.

"Earl Miles!" I called, running up to him. "Earl Miles! The city!"

"Yes," he replied. "I just rode here from the nunnery."

"Earl Robert, King David, Earl Reginald—are they safe?" I asked, my eyes still filled with tears, and in my mind, I thought also of Lord Brian.

"They are not in danger at the moment," he told me, "but we all will be as the flames grow. It looks as if the fiery deluge has stopped, but the wind will carry on the work."

"Divert water from the River Itchen," I commanded, "from every well! We must save this place."

"There is not enough water nor enough men to save it," said Miles. "We cannot bring it in fast enough. We can perhaps attempt to save a few things, but the greater part of it will burn. There is no stopping that now."

I closed my eyes and breathed deeply. Every minute was precious. I would have to decide. The people of Winchester had supported me, and that was surely why they had received the bishop's wrath along with the rest of us. Some of them were likely to die and all their property was in danger. My men in the abbey were clearly a subject of concern, as were the nuns, but they were also surrounded by much green grass to the south and could perhaps make their escape more easily than those in town. Then there was the cathedral: the symbol of the city. Even more than the royal palace, it was the greatest source of pride. Without the cathedral, there would be no Winchester. Yes, it was a building, but a building into which the men and women of Winchester had poured their lives.

"The cathedral," I answered, opening my eyes. "We must try to save the cathedral. Send all our men to help. Only keep those you need for the siege."

Miles nodded and pulled his horse round to depart, the gate once again opening before him.

"And Miles," I called, "tell them to open the east and west gates!"

He simply nodded and rode through the gate and back down the bridge. Feeling very much as if someone had picked me up and shaken me as hard as they possibly could, then set me back down to stumble upon the earth, I began to walk back to the place whence I had come, making my way around the hall and into the garden. There I found the archbishop and Adela where I had left them, only they must have learned of what was happening, for Archbishop Theobald had knelt beside her on the grass and was embracing her as she cried. I might have stopped to marvel at this act of compassion from such a great man, but my mind was too occupied.

As I approached them, I could not think what to say. What can anyone say in such an hour? It takes the spirit some time to recover after a blow of that kind. I stood there, the three of us staring at one another, the grief in our eyes speaking better than our mouths ever could. Then suddenly Adela looked up and asked, "Is it snowing?"

The other two of us gazed at the sky in the same manner. There was indeed something in the air, falling gently, blowing about in the wind. The flakes spun and danced as they made their descent, landing softly upon the ground.

"It cannot be snow," the archbishop said softly. "It is far too warm."

I bent down and took some in my fingers, then allowed it to sift back to the ground. As fine as sand it was, gray and terrible.

"Ash," I whispered. "It's ash."

The fires of Winchester burned for the remainder of that day and into the evening. I found that I could do nothing except remain in the chapel and beseech the Almighty. Once or twice, I climbed back on top of the wall to look out, but it only worsened my despair. Everywhere, the orange glow of flames could be seen—that is, where it was not blocked by the thick smoke. The day had been clear, but no longer: the sky was taking on a gray color as the wood of the homes burned. The fire had at first been mostly on the eastern side of the town, which had been directly hit by the rain of flames, but as we all foresaw, it had spread to take in everything north of the High Street and was moving closer to the royal castle.

"Do not fear, empress," the steward had said. "We are safe behind these walls. The flames will not reach us."

"Do you think that is my only concern?" I asked. "Do you think that my heart is not breaking for those who are now trapped in the flames, whether young or old? Do you think I am not in agony for my own knights who are battling against the fire, striving to save what they can? I have every reason to fear."

The poor man did not speak to me after that. I continued to go on without either food or drink, washing the floor with my tears. I closed my eyes to block out the pain of the world. Alas, I saw no darkness there but rather the savage fire.

In my mind's eye, I took the form of a great moth, even as the one set in amber. I was soaring over the roofs of Winchester, rising upon the ill winds, their heat upon my wings. I looked down at the bishop's palace, where our enemies gazed in perverse wonder upon the work of their hands. I descended over the walls of the monastery and saw on the green a dozen sisters fallen to their knees, rocking back and forth, reciting the prayer of the rosary, begging mercy from above. Then before me rose the cathedral, its roof covered in flame. I passed through the western door and saw my own men running to and fro, carrying chests in which were held the bones of former kings. Sparks fell from the ceiling as if they were a shower of flame. Then I flew out one of the windows and saw the heart of the town. I heard the cries of mothers for their children, the barking of dogs without owners, the lamentation interminable.

At some point, I was so utterly spent that I fell into slumber. My dreams were even worse than my waking vision: full of souls crying out in distress, begging for deliverance. It was as if I had entered hell itself. Such sleep brings no rest. I do not know if it was a minute or an hour before I felt a hand on my shoulder and awoke with a gasp.

"Empress," a voice said softly. "My lady, are you well?"

I sat up and rubbed my eyes. My whole head ached from weeping, or perhaps it was because the tiles of that chapel were never meant to serve as a bed. Slowly, I began to remember the state of things before I had fallen asleep, and my heart sank. Then I looked at the face of the one who had woken me. It was marked with soot, but it was certainly that of Lord Brian. My vision still somewhat bleary, I reached out and touched his face, not unlike a blind man searching someone out. Then becoming more aware of what I was doing, I dropped my hand and buried my face against him.

"You are alive," I whispered.

"Yes, we are all alive," he said, patting me on the back.

I pulled back and wiped my eyes. "Tell me the news. Tell me everything."

He nodded and began his tale, still kneeling upon the floor. "This was clearly something the bishop had decided to do some time ago, for they had everything on hand. I was in the chapter house of the cathedral speaking with Earl Baldwin when I heard the cries of, 'Fire! Fire!' I ran outside and saw arrows of flame falling from the sky. Then what appeared to be a bundle of rope hit the roof of the building in front of me and rolled down it, landing in the gutter. It had been dipped in oil and set alight. More of these objects were hurled along with the arrows, and within a few minutes, all the abbey buildings were on fire: the refectory, the infirmary, the church.

"We worked very quickly to get everyone out. Some of the poor nuns had black spots on their habits, but none were seriously burned, for we acted with speed. Most had left town already, thank God! We moved them out on to the grass, and that was when we saw clearly that the cathedral roof was on fire along with much of the town. Earl Miles had already departed to speak with you, so we worked to save anything we could from the precious store of the abbey. In the end, I do not know how much was spared.

"When Miles returned, we took your instruction and directed our efforts to the cathedral. I was in there as we sought to remove the chests holding the bones of the kings. Dust was falling from the ceiling, and we knew that above it the wood beams were burning and the lead was melting. We set some thirty men upon the task of carrying the buckets of water up to the roof and back down to be filled again, but it was difficult work. The stair was not wide enough for two men to pass easily, so they often ran into each other and spilled the precious water. I have never felt so helpless in all my life. I stood outside looking up, begging the flames to cease. We knew if we did not hold back the fire, the stones below would crumble and the cathedral would be destroyed."

"What happened?" I interrupted. "Did you succeed?!"

Here he smiled, though still looking weary as he did so. "The roof is no longer on fire. The cathedral is saved."

I sighed in relief and clasped my hands. "Thank you, Lord, for sparing your great house!" I cried. "But what of the residents of the town? Were the gates opened for them?"

"Many have fled west of the city, where they will hope to take refuge, but some have refused to leave."

"Refused to leave?" I asked in confusion. "Why?"

"Because their whole lives are within these walls: their homes, their shops. Already, there are thieves about. They will stay to defend their possessions if they possibly can."

"They would be better off alive."

"Yes," he agreed, "but for many, to lose all they own would mean death in any case."

I nodded. "Of course, you are right. Is there anything we can do for them? Anything at all?"

"Not as of yet. We will receive supplies from Andover the day after next. We will send word for them to bring in more from the port of Bristol."

"Just make sure none of it ends up in Wolvesey Palace," I said. "Bishop Henry is wicked beyond what I had feared. Who ever heard of a bishop burning his own city out of spite? No, he will receive no provision. He has not destroyed us, and he will soon be forced to surrender."

"I am certainly not giving up, and neither are the rest of the men," he agreed, "but our situation has grown more dangerous as much of the food in the city is burning. We depend now on the flow of supplies from the West."

I nodded. "And how are you? Did you come alone, or are there others?"

"Several of us came back in the hope of getting a few hours' sleep. We have been hard at work all day. I swear, I have never felt so weary in all my years. Of course, I am not as young as I once was."

It was difficult for me to think of any of those persons with whom I had grown up as old, but I could not deny that he might be right. I myself had been on the earth almost forty years, and he and brother Robert had several years beyond that.

"I think war has a way of aging one quickly," I said. "I feel it has been a hundred years since I left Normandy and a thousand since I was queen of the Germans." I let out a sigh and then added, "Come. Let us join the others. It must still be the first watch of the night."

"It is," he confirmed.

"Perhaps we will find some drink worth having. I would take anything but poison at the present time."

I rose to my feet and he did the same. We began to walk back toward the door when I observed he was walking with some difficulty.

"Are you hurt?" I asked, pointing to the foot he seemed to favor.

"It's nothing," he replied. "I tripped at some point while I was running. It should be better within a few days' time."

"You must rest it!" I declared. "Stay here at the palace until you are healed."

"Thank you, but I cannot," he told me. "I cannot afford to rest at such a time as this."

Although I could command him to rest, I decided not to do so, as I knew it would hurt his pride more than any pain he was experiencing in his foot. In truth, I did need him in the midst of the battle, even as I needed my other captains.

"Very well," I said, "but lean on me until we are back with the others."

He laughed softly. "I am a good bit taller than you and far too great a burden."

"I am stronger than I look," I assured him. "Come now, it's only fair. You would do the same for me, and you have."

Now it was Lord Brian who recognized there was no point in argument. He put his arm around me and we moved forward. I believe he made very little effort to place his weight on my shoulders, but perhaps we spared his foot a little. And so, we walked together, even as the fires of Winchester lit up the night.

The next day, a heavenly rain swept through the country and put an end to what remained of the flames, and then there was just a mess of burnt wood and broken dreams. A small block of houses nearest the royal palace had been spared, but most everything else had felt the cruel hand of the fire. We did receive goods from the West and sent for far more, but it was not enough to meet the need. Of necessity, we gave food first to those who were fighting or staying in the royal castle, for Bishop Henry could not be allowed to win. Then what was left we handed out to the people. Though they were glad to receive it, I am certain they would have desired more. John Marshal had been placed in charge of the supply line, which passed through his own lands before reaching Andover.

A week passed and then another week, but still there was no sign of surrender from the bishop's palace. Many of the towers and trebuchets we had been creating under the direction of Tommaso were destroyed in the fire, so it was necessary to build new ones. Sadly, we had already felled most of the trees nearby and were forced to drag new ones from farther away. This was hard work that required many men, and we had few to spare. We therefore hoped that the bishop had little food left and would surrender in less time than it took us to craft the means to scale his walls.

Our efforts were also hampered by the constant fall of rain, which was strange for the month of August. The ground around the city had turned to mud, making it difficult to move the trees or anything else. Many of our carts were stuck coming in from Andover. What was even worse, a siege only meets with much gain if the enemy's supply of water is cut off, and thanks to the abundant rain, Bishop Henry and his men could receive as much of it as they liked from the sky. Therefore, the siege dragged on.

Toward the end of August, a rumor reached us from abroad that Bishop Henry of Winchester had been seen with his sister-in-law and Prince Eustace at Windsor. We did not know whether to believe it, for if true, it would mean that the bishop found some way to escape immediately after we had arrived in Winchester. The writing on the letter had certainly been in his hand, so I had no doubt that he had been there upon our arrival, and in any case, people had seen him at Mass in the cathedral on Sunday. We had our eyes on Wolvesey Palace every moment from that first evening, so he could not have left after that. The very thought that we had been laboring all month when he was not even in residence was enough to drive me mad. I chose to believe that the rumor was false, at least until we received further evidence.

There was another matter that troubled me exceedingly: the earl of Essex and his awful family were nowhere to be found. His delay had by that point reached beyond all reasonable explanation. I began to fear that he might have betrayed us after everything I had done for him. It was on account of him that I had angered the Londoners. To win his support, I had placed myself in the position that resulted in my expulsion from Westminster. I did not want to believe it, but what choice did I have? I knew him to be the worst sort of man. Such an action would be in line with his character, and he did seem like the kind of person whom the usurper and his wife naturally drew to themselves: men of little honor who could be tempted to anything with coin. I believe Geoffrey de Mandeville would have betrayed our Lord even as Judas Iscariot, only he would have found a way to extract ten times the price.

"Are they coming here, Robert?" I asked him one day. "Will they make war upon us?"

His countenance was grim. "We must hope that Wolvesey falls soon and we are free to make war in the open. If not ..." His voice trailed off, and I dared not ask him more.

I suppose I can offer no good explanation for what happened next except to say that we were intent to pressure the garrison at Wolvesey Palace for as long as we possibly could, and we still believed ourselves to be in a stronger position than the false queen. On the first day of September, the men on the city walls saw a large force approaching—far larger than we had feared. They quickly took position along the River Itchen, then moved across and assaulted our knights by the eastern wall of the city and wrapping around to the south. This was the corner where the bishop's palace lay, and we could guess at their aim well enough. But was the bishop himself within or without? We still did not know.

That very afternoon, I was sitting on my bed in the queen's chamber stitching a small figure that was to be added to a gown. It was a simple flower, of what color I cannot remember. Time after time, I placed the needle through the cloth, pulled it out the bottom, then pushed it back through. With each stroke, my inner strain increased. What were the false queen and the wolf of Ypres plotting to do? Part of me was glad to finally face them, but the greater part was filled with dread. I had told my brother I was ready to enter a battle, yet when it came to it, I found myself less brave than I had imagined.

The door opened and Adela walked through it. This caused me to jerk in surprise, and the needle pierced my finger.

"Ow!" I cried, putting pressure below the wound even as blood began to trickle out.

"I am sorry, my lady," Adela said. "I did not mean to cause you a fright."

"It is not you that fills me with fear, but those men outside the walls," I told her. "What news?"

"Sir Drogo has asked to lead some thirty of the knights out the south gate to push back the forces of the false queen."

I sighed and looked down at the fabric I had been stitching, on which three red drops had fallen. "How many are the enemy?"

"I do not know, my lady. They are out in the yard making ready to leave if you wish to speak with them."

I rose from the bed and grabbed a small cloth that was lying on the desk. I had been using it to clean the ink off my fingers, but it would now serve another purpose.

"I will speak with Sir Drogo. Let us go," I said.

The two of us walked together down the stair and through the passage, then out the door and into the light of the sun. The knights were all mustering, pulling out their horses from the stables and grabbing shields and spears from the armory. Amid that confusion, I sought out the tallest man among them and found him in discussion with Sir Philip of Honfleur. Both were clothed in shirts of mail that dropped down to their knees. The younger man saw me and nodded in my direction, at which point they both removed their helms and bowed.

"You go into battle," I said. "What is your object?"

"The men from Essex are pressing hard against us," Drogo replied. "We lost three men in action this morning and another ten suffered injury."

I made the sign of the cross and declared, "The Lord deliver their souls unto heaven! But you said Essex? Are these Earl Geoffrey's men, then?"

"I am afraid so," he answered. "They were wearing his colors, sure enough, and then we saw the earl himself on horseback along with his relative, Hugh Bigod. They were in command. We had for our part the earl of Cornwall, who felled several of them with his crossbow. That forced them to fall back for the moment, but they will return. They are trying to push farther around the western corner. We will lie in wait for them and make our stand."

"May the Lord be with you both," I said solemnly. "We must not allow them to place us under a full siege. They have blocked the flow of goods from the East, but we must keep ourselves open to the West."

"That is our chief aim," Sir Philip replied. He then looked at my companion. "Lady Adela, will you give me something of yours to take into battle that it may serve as a guard upon me?"

Her eyes grew large as he said this, and I believe she did not know quite how to reply.

"Do you have anything?" I asked. "Anything you could give him?"

She opened her mouth to speak, but no sound was produced. Instead, she reached under her veil and pulled out the pin that had been holding up her tresses. As her hair fell over her shoulders, she handed the object to him, and he accepted it as if it were a holy relic, kissing it and saying, "You have made me brave."

Drogo grunted and declared, "Enough of that. Let's get moving!"

The two of them put their helms back on and went to join the others. We watched as the gates opened and the host rode off to meet their doom. I placed my arm around Adela.

"That was a very kind thing you did, friend."

"I wonder that he did not ask you," she said softly.

"What do you mean?" I asked. "It is you he loves, not me. Besides, he cannot very well ask an empress for such a gift. It would not be proper."

She pulled back and looked at me, her face painted with surprise.

"I do not understand this expression of yours," I said.

"Loves … me? No, it cannot be."

"It can be and it is," I assured her. "I never see him around you but he looks drunk with desire."

She shook her head. "He is kind to me, but he is kind to everyone. All the ladies love him."

"But do you love him?" I asked, lowering my head slightly and gazing firmly into her eyes.

Looking sad indeed, she whispered, "Yes. Yes, I love him very much, but I am thankful simply to be his friend. Believe me: he is from a good family. He will marry well. I am of no use to him as a wife or anything else."

I shook my head. "Content yourself with this fiction if you wish. The day may come when you have reason to doubt it."

She made to object, but I raised a hand to stop her. I then turned and walked back to the palace, leaving her to consider my words alone.

The next two hours seemed an eternity as we waited for news of their pursuit. Adela went to the chapel of Saint Edward to pray and I was only too happy to join her. I prayed for the knights fighting south of the wall, and for Earl Robert and his men still in the remnants of the abbey. I prayed for John Marshal and his companions, striving to bring us the food we needed. I prayed for my sons so far away—that they would remain in good health and I would see them soon.

I was kneeling before the altar and next to my maid, hands clasped on top of the rail. I looked over at Adela. Her eyes were closed, her lips forming words without sound. I believe she prayed with no less passion than Christ in Gethsemane.

"Adela," I whispered. "Adela, are you well?"

She opened her eyes and turned to face me. There were tears in her eyes.

"I am afraid for him," she said. "Afraid for them all."

I placed a hand on hers. "I am sure we will hear something soon."

She wiped her eyes on her sleeve and said, "You told me once, a long time ago—you told me you were once in love with a knight."

I breathed deeply. This was not the direction I had foreseen the conversation taking, and I did not want to reveal much.

"Yes," I answered. "Yes, that is correct."

"But you were not allowed to marry him."

"No," I said softly.

"I am sorry," she told me quietly. "So very, very sorry."

I stood and placed my hand on her shoulder. "Come, Adela. Let us speak no more of such things but go out to hear the news."

For once, she did not put up a fight, but seemed as glad as me to seek out any piece of information.

A few minutes later, we were climbing the stair next to the gate house and mounting the wall. The guards were running this way and that.

"What is it?" I asked one of them, holding my maid's hand.

"They have returned," he said. "That is, some of them have returned."

Adela and I both looked at each other, the concern in one face matched by that in the other. I could hear someone calling, "Raise the gate! Raise it now!" She let go of my hand and raced back down the steps. I was right behind her, moving just as quickly. As we reached the ground, the doors were opening, and through them raced a far smaller company of knights than had set out. I counted only a dozen in comparison to the thirty I had seen that morning. Their shields bore the marks of battle and some of the horses appeared to have bloody gashes. One knight had lost his helm, and all of them were covered in mud. Then I looked back and saw coming in at the end a horse with two riders, one holding the reins and the other leaning back against him: it was sirs Drogo and Philip, the older man holding the younger.

Adela burst into tears as two of the other knights rushed over to pull Drogo's burden from the horse, at which point he himself alighted and sent the horse off with one of the grooms. Sir Philip was lain on the ground, and the men pulled off his helm. Adela ran to him and I followed, fearing very much what we were about to see. We both stood over him while the others worked to remove his mail. There was a cut on the left side of his head and blood had run over that portion of his face. His eyes were closed, and I could not tell if he was among the quick or the dead. His helm was lying in the dirt beside me and I lifted it up to examine it. There was a dent on the side where his wound was. It did not look like a weapon had pierced through, so the force of the blow had done the damage. I looked back down as the men pulled the mail shirt over Philip's head, and I could see that the lower part of his shirt was soaked with blood. With one swift movement, Drogo ripped the shirt in half and pulled it back, then began placing pressure on Philip's side where the bleeding continued.

"He was fighting hand to hand with the Flemings," Drogo explained. "One of them had a dagger. It appears that it made it through his mail in one or two places."

Adela could contain herself no longer. She knelt upon the ground next to Sir Philip, holding his face in her hands, her tears falling upon him.

"Is he ... alive?" she asked between sobs.

"Only just," said Drogo. "Had I not placed him upon my horse and dragged him back, I do not think he would have survived. As it is, he may not survive. He has lost much blood and taken a blow to the head."

"Oh, Philip!" she cried, wiping the sweat and blood from his face with her sleeve. "Philip, I love you! Return to us! Lord Almighty, bring him back! Let him live!"

Drogo and I looked at one another, the tears forming in our eyes as well. He gestured for one of the knights to take his place and then rose and stood next to me, even as Adela continued to stroke Philip's hair and the other knight said, "We must take him away from here. Is there a doctor anywhere?"

"Go fetch some wine," I told him. "The wounds must be cleaned as soon as the bleeding has stopped."

He nodded and ran off in the direction of the palace, where I very much hoped he would find something in the cellar.

"We could not hold back both the earl's men and the Flemings," Drogo told me. "Our retreat was hasty, and the gate closed only just in time to save us from another hail of arrows. My lady, we have been forced to fall back everywhere. They are placing the city under siege. There is nothing we can do to stop it. They have far more men than we thought possible."

Each word cut into me like a knife and filled me with dread. I bid myself to breathe deeply. *Do not give in to fear*, I commanded myself.

"You have fought with all your might—with your very lives," I said. "You have been faithful and brave. I could not have asked more. We must continue to hope. I will speak with Earl Robert and the Scottish king. Perhaps we can find some means to fight our way out of the siege. Is the west gate still open to us?"

"Only for the moment," he replied. "It could be closed within the hour."

Suddenly, the man lying on the ground coughed loudly and I looked down to see that his eyes had opened and were staring up at the face of Adela. Drogo and I both moved closer and bent over him, but his eyes were fixed upon my maid.

"Sir Philip," she said, smiling. "You are in the castle. I am here with you."

With his right hand, he reached under his bloody shift and pulled out the pouch that had been hanging around his neck. It too was stained red. He held it aloft, his hand shaking.

"Reach inside it," he told her in a very hoarse voice.

She did as he asked and pulled out the pin she had given him just a few hours earlier. Seeming to strain as he did so, he placed his hand around hers.

"It was you," he said. "When I was there on the field, when I felt the steel pierce my flesh, I could sense you with me, bidding me to live."

"I was praying for you," she replied through her tears, "praying that I could see you again. I never told you how dear you are to my heart."

He to grasp her hand in which the pin was held. "You gave me that," he said, meaning the pin. "Now will you give me your hand?"

Her face seemed to come alive with a heavenly glow, as if his love had returned her to some angelic form: had allowed her to become what she always truly was.

"Yes!" she cried. "Yes, of course I will!"

And then she kissed him, and I doubt I have ever seen joy between two people again as I saw that day, with one of them perched above the abyss of death and everything around us given over to ruin. It was a strange and magic thing, and if for only a moment, I rejoiced to live my days under the sun, where such things might still take place.

The great Ovid wrote, *"Res est solliciti plena timoris amor."*[28] Too true it was in that hour, when the love of Philip and Adela, so bright and shining, brought them nevertheless into deeper darkness, for the shadow of death has a power beyond all things to destroy our greatest visions. The life of Sir Philip of Honfleur hung in the balance upon a great thread of fate, even as the fortunes of us all were very much in question.

I had ordered that he be lain in the room in use by the earl of Gloucester, as my brother had been spending very little time there in any case. There was one physician remaining within the walls, and he was kept exceedingly busy in those days. We sent for him and he examined the two wounds on Philip's side. At one point, the knife had pierced the skin only to hit one of the lower ribs. Although painful, this wound did not place him in great danger. The other was farther down and rather deeper, an inch or more into the flesh and two inches across, the doctor guessed. He could not be certain if it had pierced the bowels. With great skill, he stitched both the wounds, but warned that the chance of infection was high.

"I do not know what strength this young man has left in him," the physician said, "but let us pray it is great, for he will need it all."

Oh, how I wished to have the aid of Grimbald in those hours! He knew more about herbal remedies than anyone I

---

28 Ovid, *Heroides*, I.12. "Love is the thing full of anxious fears."

had ever met. It was he who had halted the infection that almost killed me after the birth of my second son. As it was, we were forced to make do. Adela kept a constant watch by his bed, cleaning his wounds and changing his linens, holding his hand and reading to him even as he softly groaned.

Meanwhile, the battle continued to rage. King David and Earl Robert rode forth bravely, leading their men against the forces of the false queen. It was an absolute necessity to keep the west gate open and our supply route clear. No one had seen William of Ypres on the field, and we soon found out why: he had been sent to ambush our forces to the north and thereby cut off our last source of food. We were fighting on all fronts, keeping up the pressure on Wolvesey Castle, opposing the false queen's men outside the walls, and striving to save our connection to the West.

Many of our knights had been in action every day for over a month. I do not know how they found the will to carry on under such conditions. Our losses continually mounted, but by the mercy of God none of our captains succumbed to death. I was sure every day I would hear that Reginald had fallen off his horse and broken his neck, or Brian had taken an arrow to the chest, but the angels of the Lord did not allow their feet to slip. The cathedral had been turned into an infirmary, with men laid out on pallets throughout the nave. The monks from Hyde Abbey showed their great kindness by caring for them, along with the nuns who had remained.

There was a brief respite on the Lord's Day, the seventh before the Ides of September,[29] such that some of our captains were able to gather in the palace and hold counsel together. We met in the great hall, which had long since ceased being a place for feasts. Even I had moved to a single meal per day, with

---

29   September 7, 1141.

such morsels at other hours as could be provided. I felt I must lead the way in this, but oh, how this necessary fast worked upon my body and mind! It was more difficult to do everything, and especially to do it in anything like a pleasant manner. We were seated at one of the tables—King David along with the earls of Gloucester, Hereford, Cornwall, and Devon, then Lord Brian and Sir Drogo—and none of us were what you might call whole.

Brian's ankle no longer troubled him, but he had fallen off his horse when the beast took a fright and was left with many bruises. Robert's left hand was wrapped in cloth from a cut he had received. The king of Scotland could not bend over without wincing from the pain in his back. Earl Baldwin had acquired some disorder of the bowels and had to rush off every quarter hour to relieve himself. Despite these maladies, they were all able in some manner to fight. None of them had seen as much food as he would have liked.

"What is the situation in the city?" I asked no one in particular, leaning over the table with my hands clasped together against my lips.

They all looked far too tired to answer, but Earl Miles spoke up for the company. "Many of the homes are abandoned, as you know. Those who remain are without clean water. They collect it in pails from the sky, but we have now gone without rain these five days. The path to the river is fully blocked, and the wells are filthy from the fire and everything else. Many go without bread and have begun eating the rats, though they have few means for starting a fire. We would give them more food, but it is most needed for those in the infirmary and those who are fighting, and we have received nothing from the West since Thursday. There is sickness spreading fast, adding to the general misery. When we ride through the streets, we see men and even women crouched in corners, letting out one discharge or another. Everywhere, there is filth. My lady, we cannot go on like this much longer."

I closed my eyes and nodded. I knew what he said was true. For the past week, ever since the arrival of the false queen and her band of Flemings, we had only lost ground, not gained it. A hundred of our knights had passed on to the next world, and with them the man Tommaso, whose refusal to wear armor had done him no favors when an arrow hit him in the back. In the end, his knowledge had done us little good. John Marshal was standing for us bravely at Andover, trying with all his might to bring in the supplies from Bristol by way of Devizes and Ludgershall, but his situation grew more difficult by the day, or perhaps by the hour. The wolf of Ypres was pressing ever closer to the River Test. We had surrendered every man we could to that fight: any more and we would have to abandon the siege of the bishop's palace.

"Do we know when more food might arrive?" I asked Robert.

He sighed and rubbed his face with his hand. "Last I heard, there was to be some today, but given that we have not seen it ..." He did not finish his sentence but merely shrugged his shoulders.

I looked over to my uncle the king, who was seated to my left on the bench, twisting this way and that in an attempt to stretch his sore back and gain some relief from his pain.

"My lord, King David, you have fought in many battles," I said. "How long do you suppose we have before we must abandon this siege? It seems our enemy is close to surrounding us entirely."

"It is true that I have fought in several wars, but our present situation is somewhat new to me," he said, letting out a low grunt as he happened to stretch in a way that only added to his misery. "It is rare to have a double siege, one inner and one outer."

I had hoped he might say a bit more, but he declined, perhaps too tired to offer anything else. I turned again to Miles, who seemed in the best shape of anyone there.

"So, what say you, then, Earl Miles? One day? Two days? Less?"

"It all depends on if those supplies arrive," he offered. "I say we wait at least until the end of the day to give them a chance before making a decision. This break in the fighting should open a clear path."

"But we do not know if they have rested from fighting north of here," Earl Robert countered. "I think we must let up a bit on the siege of Wolvesey and send more men north to aid Lord John. We can fortify the nunnery at Wherwell. It is close to Andover."

"The abbey of Saint Mary already lies waste here in town, as does Hyde Abbey just outside the walls," said Brian, rubbing his side where I guessed a large bruise must be. "Is there no other way?"

I shared this concern, for when men spoke ill of us, there was nothing that so enraged them as any occasion on which we were seen to take advantage of the Church, even if the matter could not be avoided, and even if our opponents had shown far less respect for the Church than we had. As a woman who was already seen to be usurping the divine order by many in the land, I was always afraid of this charge. It gave an advantage to those, such as Henry of Blois, who sought to paint me as an enemy of the whole spiritual realm. Never mind that I had shown a great concern for the Church all my life. Never mind that my mother and grandmother were perhaps the two most pious ladies in the history of Britain, and I sought to follow them in all that I did. Even if it was Stephen and not I who had lied to bishops and dragged them from their homes in chains, I was seen to be the one allied with the devil.

"I too fear turning Wherwell into a castle," I said. "Surely there must be some other site we can use."

"No such site exists," Robert assured me, the anger growing in his voice. "I am sorry to offend the scruples of anyone here, but we are in the middle of a war. The normal rules do not apply. Bishop Henry was the one who set fire to the houses of God, not us. The only way to save the Church is to use it as a defense. We either make use of Wherwell, or we yield to the enemy. Those are our two choices. We have no others."

I rose from the bench and walked over to the other end of the room, in the direction of the dais. There was a window above through which the sun was streaming. I felt I could not muster the strength for anything, even tears. I had not slept soundly since arriving in Winchester. Although I was never on the field of battle with them, my spirit had accompanied my men every hour, supplications pouring out of me day and night. Every part of me was weary, and my heart most of all. But the sun fell upon my members, and that warmth provided me, if only for a moment, with the will to carry on.

"Do it, then," I said, turning back to face them all. "Do what you must. I hope we live to curse these days from afar."

With that, I walked past them all, offering up a few words of thanks for their service, and arrived at the doors that led toward the rest of the palace. I opened one of them and strode through, having every intent to return to my chamber and seek out some form of rest, when I saw Archbishop Theobald coming in from the door to my left.

"Good day, my lord archbishop, if indeed we can call it such," I said.

"I am afraid we may not be able to do so," he replied, and as I looked at his face carefully, I saw that his expression was even more solemn than usual.

"What is it?" I asked. "Did you hear something?"

He stepped closer to me, hands folded together, and said, "I am just on my way to the room where Sir Philip is lodging. It seems he is not in a good way."

How those words worked upon my spirit! I would not have thought my mood could sink any lower but sink it did. All I could say was, "Adela ..."

"Come with me," the archbishop said, beckoning with his hand. As we began to walk down the passage, side by side, he continued, "My lady, when this war began, I must admit I had no particular love in my heart for you or your party."

Yes, you made it quite clear, I thought, but said nothing.

"I respected you as was your due, but it has only been in these last days, as the fury of Fate has been released upon you, that I have recognized your true character."

We passed the first two chambers and were near our destination. "And what is my character?" I asked.

We had arrived at the door and he stopped in front of it, turning to look at me. "You are a survivor, and I dare say those around you are as well."

"Thank you, I think," I said. "Now, we really must be going in if he is as bad as you have led me to believe. He may not be long for this world."

The archbishop nodded and knocked on the door. Almost immediately, it was opened by Adela, whose face was red from crying.

"Thank you for coming, archbishop," she told him softly, "and my lady, I am so glad you have come as well."

I embraced her, and as I did so I was able to look behind her and see Sir Philip of Honfleur lying on the simple bed. He was covered with sweat and appeared to be shaking. *So, the fever has got to him then,* I thought. Beside him was a small table with a basin of water on top of it and a pile of bloody strips of cloth. I let go of my maid and stepped to the side so the archbishop could enter.

Archbishop Theobald took hold of a stool that sat in the corner and pulled it over by the bed. Sitting upon it, he took Philip's hand in his and said, "I understand that you wish me to recite the rites over you."

"No," he replied with some difficulty. "That is, yes ... and no."

The archbishop looked up at me, and I raised my hands to signal that I had no idea what he meant. He then turned to look back at Adela.

"I thought I was fetched to perform the rites. Do you wish me merely to pray over him?" he asked.

"Actually, lord archbishop, we were hoping that you would marry us," she said meekly, looking as unhappy at the mention of her own marriage as anyone I had ever seen.

"My dear," I began, moving toward her and placing my arm around her, "I know you love each other very much and desire to be joined in holy matrimony, but this is perhaps not the best time—"

"It is the only time!" Philip interrupted, rolling over to face us all. As he did this, he seemed to bite his lip and let out a groan. "The fever is building. I may only have a few hours. I want to know that when I am gone, my wife will have every provision she needs."

"This is most irregular," the archbishop commented. "Do neither of you have family who might have something to say about this?"

"Our parents are dead these many years," answered Adela, "and our siblings are far off."

"I have siblings in Normandy, but I see not why their will should matter," Philip said. "The Church does not require it."

"This is true, but it is best to consider the consequences of one's actions," explained the archbishop. "You have not thought about this very long."

"Some times it does not take long to know what is right," the knight replied.

Adela looked at me with wide eyes—beseeching, pleading. "My lady, it is only your censure that I fear. I do not care what the rest of the world may think, but you have given me everything I have, and I value your counsel above all. If you tell me we must not do it, then I will not."

I sighed, wanting very much to be free from the charge which my maid had just placed upon me. How was I to instruct them? Might he recover and regret his decision? Might she discover him to be rather less gallant than hoped? I was no seer. Given that they were both in my service, I could perhaps forbid them to wed or even force it, but this did not seem in keeping with my own principles. Was I not the one who had told Sir Philip to seize joy when he had the chance? Was I not the one who had encouraged Adela to open her heart to love again? They had taken me at my word. How could I let them down at the final hour?

"Archbishop Theobald," I said, "I agree that it is most irregular, but there is nothing regular about the situation in which we find ourselves. If they wish to marry and there is no impediment, then let it be so."

"May it be according to your wish," he replied.

The necessary business was done, and within the hour Sir Philip of Honfleur had taken a wife. We only hoped that the infection that plagued his body would not take his life.

XIX

A string may be pulled only so far, and then it breaks. Wood may be pressed only so hard before it snaps. A man may be tormented for only so long before he will confess both the deeds he has done and those he has not—anything to make the pain cease. So I am told, and so I have been led to believe by experience. Everything in creation has its limit.

Amid the burnt remains of Winchester, we were hard pressed against such a limit. We had received a small amount of food that day of the Sunday truce, but not enough to sustain us. The rain was a thing of the past and we were forced to rely on the wells. There were two within the royal castle: one in the lower yard by the keep, and one in the Queen Mathilda Garden that had been made into a fountain. It was the only drink that remained, and we went back to it day and night. Yet even those stores were reduced by the lack of rain soaking into the ground.

As for Sir Philip, his condition at least was improved. He had married in haste, believing himself to be on the way out, but the state of matrimony seemed to have granted him new life. His fever was gone within two days and his pain lessened. Adela was naturally full of gratitude for this change, as was I, but we could not enjoy it too much, for the possibility of death still hung over us all as the sword over Damocles.

We were approaching that day of the Exaltation of the Holy Rood when the Church celebrates the finding of the True Cross by Saint Helena, and I could not help feeling that I was come to my own Golgotha. What must our Lord have seen when he stared death in the face? When he cried out in agony, "My God, my God, why have you forsaken me?" When he told the Holy Apostles that sorrow had pushed him to the point of death? Yes, in those hours I thought less upon the triumph of Helena and more upon the passion of our Lord. Although he besought the Almighty Father, there was no deliverance in that hour: not until all had been accomplished. Only after he had been made to feel the depth of that darkness, when he had faced the final temptation, when he had been driven down into the very realm of the dead, was he allowed to rise. I shuddered to think what suffering might lie ahead for all of us there in Winchester, fighting every hour to survive.

From the north and west we had received word that our efforts at Wherwell were not going well. Although John Marshal and his men were making use of the abbey and fighting bravely to defend our supplies, the wolf of Ypres was closing in like a hawk upon the prey. At the same time, we were struggling as always to keep the west gate open. The men in Wolvesey Palace were not backing down, and we could only conclude that the bishop had stored up great piles of food before the siege began to allow them to continue so long under those conditions. Of course, we knew by that time that the bishop was no longer in his palace and had not been for some time. What a tragedy it had all become!

Upon the Ides of September,[30] I received a note from King David of Scotland, who had been leading his men out each day to face down the forces of the false queen around the north side of the city, near the remnants of Hyde Abbey. It was delivered to me while I sat at the desk in my chamber, a scrap of parchment without a seal, but marked by his hand in black ink perhaps left in the monastery.

A great host on the other side of the river. Likely the Londoners. We cannot hold them back for long. Retreat or be cut to pieces. Tell Robert: all may soon be lost.

I felt a great surge of fear moving upward from my belly, filling my chest and sending both my heart and lungs off at speed. It seized me and would not let me go. Even as the letter remained in my hand, it shook. "Lord, save us!" I prayed. "Lord, make haste to help us!"

I rose from my seat, but my legs felt as if they were made of lead. I forced myself forward—one step, two steps, three—until I reached the door. My legs began to respond more quickly as I moved into the passage, and soon I was running. *I must find a messenger*, I thought. *Someone, anyone, or we will all be dead.* As it so happened, the first person I found was the steward, Roger fitz Herbert, who was standing down by the door, speaking with one of the servants.

"Lord Roger!" I cried. "We are done for! The earl of Gloucester must be informed if we are to have any hope!"

I suppose many men might have chosen that moment to ask a question, for a great many questions begged to be asked. However, he had enough wisdom to sense that any such talk would only increase the despair of our situation.

---

30 September 13, 1141.

"Leave it with me," he said, holding out his hand and nodding.

I raced back up to my chamber and immediately began sorting through all the items in the room to determine what I could not afford to leave. I say sort, but truly I was throwing things this way and that, my mind rushing as fast as my body.

I cannot stay here. I must be gone, I told myself. *How did I allow it to get this far? Why did I not flee as soon as the battle began? What good has it done for me to remain here? And now I am trapped, just as Robert feared. There is nothing he can do to safeguard me now. You are a fool, Maud. A pitiful fool.*

There were letters half written sitting on the desk, all containing private information which I had no desire for the false queen to read. The idea of her placing her fingers on my things and casting her eyes over my words repulsed me, but there was no fire into which I could throw them. I grabbed a small satchel on the ground, in which my last delivery of letters had come. It could be tied around the chest with a cord and was the only means I had to carry anything on my person. Into the satchel went the letters, my precious book of hours, the items from my sons, the amber moth, the paternoster. The works of theology were too heavy and would have to remain. If my enemies did stop to read them, perhaps they would be led to remember the judgment that awaits the wicked. Sadly, the false queen would have her gowns again, but I threw her jewels into the satchel: it was possible that I would need to pay a bribe at some point, depending on how things went.

I placed a few more items in the bag, knowing full well that it would only do me good if I was able to escape, and if things were as desperate as my uncle believed, that was by no means certain. I walked over to the window and looked out, and it was only then that I recognized how late in the day it was. The sun was casting a crimson glow on the cathedral towers from the west. Even if Earl Robert was able to organize a retreat within the hour, it would soon be night. We would be riding in the dark with Flemish wolves hiding behind every tree.

"Stay and be eaten or flee and be eaten," I muttered. "I like not these choices."

I had made haste to ready myself for departure, only to have nothing to immediately do. I decided to walk down to the lower level and check on Philip and Adela. However, when I reached the chamber, they were gone. Yet another reason to fear! I left the room and walked down the passage to the outer door, entering the yard. There I was relieved to find the two of them standing in the last rays of the sun, Adela with her arm around her husband, helping him take a few steps.

"There you are!" I called, and they both turned to face me. "Have you heard the news?"

"Lord Roger told us the worst of it: that we may be forced to flee any moment," Adela said. "We were just walking over to the stables to check on Philip's horse."

"Do you intend to ride in your condition?" I asked him, filled with concern.

"I think I will be all right," he replied, showing something less than the confidence I would have preferred. "I have been walking more—doing more things. In any case, I have no choice. My wife and I will not be safe here if the city falls into the enemy's hands."

I was about to tell them that they would be better off staying, for I was the one the enemy wanted: I and the chief captains. The rules of warfare stated that two such persons should not be harmed following a battle. However, I remembered how Bishop Henry had been willing to set fire to the entire city, causing great harm to many persons who bore no fault in the quarrel. Then in my mind I suddenly had an image of a Flemish brute throwing himself on top of Adela and reveling in violent pleasures, and I found myself in agreement with Sir Philip.

"We will have to ride at great speed," I said. "We cannot take carriages or carts."

"I can do it," he assured me. "I will do it, for our lives depend on it. My wife will ride with me."

"That will slow you down a good deal," I warned, though I need not have done so. He was more than aware of how such things worked.

"What choice do we have?" asked Adela. "What other horse should bear me instead? I do not have your skill. I cannot ride like the men."

I simply nodded and assented to their wish, but I greatly feared what might take place in the coming hours.

I returned to the palace and spent the next hour in the chapel, adding prayer to prayer, rending the very air with my cries to the Almighty. Adela came to check on me once or twice, but there was naught she could do to help. The light of the sun was completely gone and our darkest hour had come when Roger fitz Herbert entered the chapel and knelt beside me.

"Great lady," he said softly, "your captains are all returned. They have done great deeds and sent the Londoners back over the river for the night, but they say you cannot remain long."

"Where are they?" I asked, feeling the pull of hope.

"In the hall, consuming the last of the bread."

"Thank you," I told him, rising from my place of lamentation and making my way out of the chapel. Soon I was entering the hall, which was filled with what I assumed to be the last of our knights, most of them having removed their armor and left it lying around the room with little sense of order. One line of shields at least was leaning against a wall, and the knights themselves were sitting at the tables, or in some cases lying on the tables or the floor. A black cat had somehow made its way in and was eating the crumbs that fell from their hands and mouths.

The final crumbs of the final crumbs, I thought.

There was no longer any form of order. The high table on the dais was being used by the lowest men, while I found my brothers and the king of Scotland seated on the floor in the corner behind them. I cannot remember ever seeing men so weary. It seemed to hang upon their shoulders, causing them to sag. There was little light in their eyes, and I knew it had been long indeed since they had bathed in anything but their own sweat.

"What happened?" I asked them all. "I received the letter from you, Uncle. I sent it on to Robert."

"Yes, it came to me as the sun was setting," Robert replied. "I knew there was no time to waste, so I gathered up all the men and we mounted the horses we have been keeping over in the abbey stables. We rode out the west gate and joined up with the Scots north of the city, then we clashed with the Londoners by the river."

"And you destroyed them?" I asked in wonder.

The Scottish king laughed. "Not destroyed, niece, though we did cut some of them down. As soon as they caught sight of the great lords of Scotland and England mounted on horseback, falling upon them like the hand of the Almighty, they turned and fled back across the Itchen. But they will be back tomorrow and in greater numbers."

"At least you have bought us some time," I said hopefully.

"There is no time to do anything but gather up your things," Reginald spoke, or rather grunted.

"Already done," I assured him.

"We leave at first light," said Robert. "The circle is about to close around us. We must break through it and make for Ludgershall, or perhaps even fall back to Devizes. The city is lost to us."

I nodded grimly, knowing his words to be true. "I am ready to depart at any hour."

"Well, you cannot go like that," he continued. "If they see a woman in a gown, they will know it is you straight away. See if one of the messengers can lend you his clothes."

"Lend? I doubt I will ever be able to return them," I muttered.

The king of Scotland turned to Robert and asked, "What if they are to fall upon us when we depart?"

"It should not happen if we leave early enough. They have been riding out after the watches of the night are long done," he replied.

"But if they do …" I prompted him.

"If they do surround us or block the northern road, then we must break off into different parties," Robert said. "If they seize us all together, the war is over. If they only seize some of us, we may live to fight another day, for we have the usurper still in Bristol."

I hated the idea of any of our company being taken prisoner, for I had no faith in our enemies to treat them well, but there were no good options left to us. As my uncle had written, it was retreat or be cut to pieces. Of course, there was always the possibility that we would be cut to pieces in the retreat, but that was the danger of war. We had all known it might happen. It was the reason I had failed to sleep properly for the past six weeks.

"Very well," I said quietly. "How will we arrange our break?"

"The chief captains—myself, King David, Earl Miles—must all scatter in separate directions from yourself and each other," Robert answered, pointing to each of us as he did so. "Beyond that, we will place a core of knights around your person. Choose men you are willing to trust with your life, for they may indeed have to lay them down. My knights and I will guard against any assault from behind. If we are fortunate, John Marshal and his men will be able to join us at Wherwell and we can ride on to Ludgershall. Do you approve?"

I said nothing but nodded my head solemnly. It all made sense, and yet it filled me with dread. I did not want any of those dear to me to have to lay down their lives or surrender their persons to the enemy. As for those I chose to keep near myself, they would receive great reward if ever I could give it to them.

"I will go with you, sister, if you wish it," Reginald said. "I can hit a Flemish knight from fifty yards away while both of us are on the move."

This seemed a great declaration, even for Reginald, but I was in no mood to argue. "I accept your service, Earl Reginald, and am glad to have your bow beside me," I replied.

"Who else?" Robert asked.

"Drogo," I said quietly.

"And who else?" he asked again.

Normally, I would have asked for Sir Philip, but given his condition, that was not possible. I did not know Earl Baldwin enough to trust him with my life, nor any of the other earls.

It was at that moment that Brian fitz Count walked up behind me and asked, "What have you all decided?"

"We are arranging the retreat," the king told him. "The empress was just considering who should ride closest to her. Earl Robert, Earl Miles, and I cannot, but Earl Reginald is happy to do so. Sir Drogo also, we think, will join her, but she needs at least one more."

Brian looked down at me and said, "Of course, I will be honored to ride with you, if you will have me."

"That's settled, then," Robert concluded, not waiting for me to respond. "Any greater party might attract too much attention, so if anything should happen to us all, I leave it to you men"—here he pointed at Earl Reginald and Lord Brian—"to get her first to Ludgershall, then to Devizes."

"We shall do so or die in the attempt," Brian assured him.

And so, the matter was ended, or perhaps I should say it was begun.

> *"Agnus Dei, qui tollis peccata mundi, miserere nobis.*
> *Agnus Dei, qui tollis peccata mundi, miserere nobis.*
> *Agnus Dei, qui tollis peccata mundi, dona nobis*
> *pacem."*[31]

Those words poured forth from my mouth in the early hours of the fourteenth day of September, the Feast of the Exaltation of the Holy Rood. I was kneeling in that chamber I had come to know all too well—the Queen's Chamber that would soon be used once again by a woman who did not deserve the title—holding before me an image of the cross carved out of ivory. On it, the Savior of the World hung in agony. That world had thought him fit only for a crown of thorns. Even so, humanity is apt to deny honor to those who deserve it.

I was clothed in the raiment of a messenger, even as Robert had instructed. I did not care for it at all. The breeches were tight around my hips and loose everywhere else. The tunic was thankfully supplied with two slits on either side to allow for easier movement, but it hung well past my knees. The boots were far too large, as was the cloak, though the latter mattered far less. I was at least able to hide my hair under the cap. I had placed the satchel over my head and wore it to the side, as I had seen so many messengers do. It would have been far better to wear something that might help defend me against arrows,

---

31 Translation: "Lamb of God, who takes away the sins of the world, have mercy upon us. / Lamb of God, who takes away the sins of the world, have mercy upon us. / Lamb of God, who takes away the sins of the world, grant us peace."

but my captains had feared that as I had no experience riding in armor, it would be a greater danger than help, and I agreed with them. Speed was my greatest ally.

I kissed the crucifix one final time and stood, placing the object on the desk and making a final attempt to pull the strings on my boots tighter. "Mother Mary and all the saints, pray for me," I whispered, placing a hand over my heart. Then I pulled the cap down a bit further on my head and departed that room for the final time.

I made my way down the stair, striving mightily not to trip in my overly large boots. Everyone else had already left the palace, and it was only Roger fitz Herbert who stood by the threshold of the outer door to wish me well. He took both my hands in his and said to me, "I wish you every blessing in the world, my lady ... my queen."

"Thank you, Lord Roger. You have been a good friend to us," I told him. "Look after the archbishop and those who are too wounded to ride."

"It was most noble of the archbishop to remain and plead on behalf of the others. I hope his great authority will cause your opponents to show mercy."

I regretted that I could grant the steward little but kind words. It had been my custom to offer a pouch of coins at the very least after receiving hospitality, but any money I possessed might be needed on the road. I therefore left him with only an uneasy smile and walked out into the yard.

The first light of dawn was just beginning to show itself in the eastern sky and many of the stars could still be seen. The air was quite cool, and I was glad to have the cloak, even if it was too big for me. Every horse that remained had been led from the stables and most of the men had already mounted their beasts. There would be no royal banners or trumpets to sound our departure. We aimed to draw as little attention as possible, but there would be a hundred and fifty of us. My captains were still on foot and conversing with one another as I approached them.

"Good morrow, gentlemen," I greeted them, though what was good about it I could not say.

"Is that you under there, my lady?" Miles asked. "I would not have known you."

"Good," I said, this time meaning it most truly. "Is everything ready?"

"Yes, and we have no time to waste," said Robert, placing his helm on his head. "Your horse has been made ready. I still question the choice of a mare."

"She will ride as fast as any of yours, and she knows me," I argued. "Faithful Frija. I feel safer with her than any other."

My uncle David put his arm around me and said, "You know, in Scotland, we have some women who like to wear men's clothes on occasion. At first, it seems rather odd, but after a few pints ..."

"That is why I am never going to Scotland!" declared Reginald. "Now, sister, I will be just up at the front when you are ready."

I nodded, and he departed along with the others, save for Earl Robert and Lord Brian. My brother placed his hands on my shoulders and said with great firmness, "If anything should happen to us before we reach Ludgershall, I want you to ride as hard as you can to the west—always to the west. You have your guardians at your side. Do not wait to see what happens. Do not try to help anyone else. Ride with all haste. Do not follow after the wife of Lot. Do not look back and face destruction."

There were tears in my eyes as I reached out and embraced him. Though he must have been weary beyond all weariness, he felt as solid as a rock: immovable in body and spirit.

"I have prayed for you, brother," I told him. "I have prayed for us all."

I pulled away and allowed him to leave, and then it was Lord Brian and I standing there alone. It was to him that I was able to admit, "I am afraid. So very afraid."

He pulled out a dagger that hung on his belt and handed it to me. "Keep this with you at all times. It is your last defense."

I nodded and pulled the satchel around my body to place the dagger inside. Even as I did so, he said my name. "Maud."

Surprised that he should use my birth name, I looked up immediately and said, "Yes?"

"I am with you when the sun rises, and I will be with you when it sets. I promise you that."

"Let us hope the place we are is not the great beyond," I concluded.

With that, we made all the final preparations. As I walked toward the front of the line, I saw Philip and Adela sitting high above me on his steed. Adela was wearing men's clothes, even as myself. I reached up and took her hand. "My dearest friend, know the love I bear for you in my heart. May the angels of heaven safeguard you."

"And you as well, my lady," she agreed.

I then said to Sir Philip, "Trust to your experience. You know what to do."

"We are behind you, my lady, now and always. I cannot thank you enough for all you have done for us," he replied.

I then continued walking up to where Frija stood near the front of the line. Drogo was waiting beside her, holding out his hand to help me up.

"Of all the rides you and I have taken, Empress Mathilda of England, this may be the one that tests us the most," he said, "but do not fear, for I am with you, now and always."

"The most faithful of servants, and though not of my blood, you are my brother," I assured him.

Soon I was sitting upon Frija, and not for the first time I was thankful that Drogo had taught me how to ride in the manner of men, for it would aid my escape. The horse's breath was clearly visible in the cool air of morning, spouting forth in bursts that danced upon the wind. The last stars were disappearing. When all the men were in place, Earl Reginald, who was just in front of me at the head of the column, unsheathed his sword and raised it to the heavens.

"Ride now for Ludgershall!" he cried. "Follow the sun to the West! For the Empress Mathilda and for England!"

He placed his weapon back in its sheath, and as he did so, the great doors opened before us, revealing the ramp down to the city streets. Frija's muscles grew tense, and with a slight tug on the reins, I propelled her into motion. Our company rode through the gate and out into the city of Winchester, and I observed as we did so that it was the first time I had been outside those walls in many weeks. As we arrived at the road, the sound of so many hooves upon stone was as thunder. Earl Reginald of Cornwall set the pace between the houses on either side, riding far quicker than one would normally do in such tight quarters. Somewhere far behind us Earl Robert of Gloucester and his knights were in the back.

Through our friends in the city, we had ensured that the west gate would open to us, but of what lay beyond it we were completely ignorant. As we reached the High Street and turned to the left, I glanced back over my right shoulder just in time to see the first rays of the sun rising to greet the day.

Lord God in heaven, I prayed, *let me see my sons again.*

Very soon, we had reached the gate and found some good fortune: it did open before us. The riders flooded through it and on to the western road, and as we did so, I began looking this way and that for any sign of our enemies. Before us lay a small wood in which we could hope to find safety, but for half a mile, we were entirely exposed. The knights were riding two and three deep around me, unwilling to give anyone a clear shot. For Frija at least, there was nothing to fear. She seemed to be enjoying her morning run. Little did she know how much I suffered.

We were very close to the wood and had seen no sign of the enemy. I felt a small sense of relief and said to Drogo, who was riding just beside me, "Perhaps Robert was right: they do not ride out until later."

"Yes, it looks as if they are—" he began to say, but stopped immediately as we both heard the change in the air as something flew past us.

"Raise shields!" Reginald called, and several of those behind us echoed his command. Immediately, all the men around me held up their shields, even as I began to hear arrows hitting wood.

Naturally, I was seized with fear, and I think Frija knew it, for she jerked a bit to the left. All the horses began making noise as the hail of arrows continued. Just in front of me, Brian yelled, "It's coming from the wood! They were waiting for us."

"Turn north!" Reginald commanded. "Every man, turn north!"

I pulled on the reins with all my strength, and Frija made the turn to the right, even as the rest of the horses did so. I could see hardly anything from my position though the light of day was beginning to stream down in earnest. I gathered that we were riding along the edge of the wood rather than entering it. To my left, a young knight riding on the outside of the formation was hit by an arrow and fell from his steed. The beast quickly turned to the right, toward the column. Those of us at the very front increased our speed still further and were able to remain together, but the horse cut in front of the rest of the company. I took a quick look behind me and saw them breaking off in all directions to avoid it.

"Keep riding, my lady!" Drogo besought me. "Don't worry about them!"

There were still a few arrows coming in our direction from behind the trees, though the worst of it had stopped. Reginald raised his hand for us to slow down, and within half a minute the others had caught up behind us—that is, those who had not been fallen. I dearly hoped that Philip and Adela were not among the dead. As the storm of arrows ceased completely, I felt the smallest sense of relief, only to hear Reginald call, "Riders from the east!"

Sure enough, as I turned to look to my right, I saw a large company riding across the plain. It was impossible to be sure of their number, but I do not doubt it was a few hundred: far more than we had.

"Fight or fly?!" Lord Brian asked.

"Fly!" commanded Reginald. "We must fly. Let the others stay and fight if they will. This will be the Londoners and the earl of Essex."

We moved back in the direction of the very wood from which we had just been assaulted. The others were increasing their pace, and I commanded my horse, "Faster, Frija! Faster!" I patted her hard on the side of her neck a few times, and she responded, matching the speed of those next to us. She neighed loudly, lifting her head briefly to the sky and back down again.

Within seconds, we were moving beneath the trees, following a narrow path likely carved by hunters who were not attempting to out run enemies. Tree roots rose up here and there, and in places the path was covered entirely by weeds. Poor Drogo was forced to duck many times to avoid low branches, yet we could not afford to let up the pace.

"How far to the Test?!" I cried.

"Five miles at least," Brian answered.

We continued for a while with nothing to trouble us but the memory of those we had left behind and the prospect of more difficulties ahead. The trees grew closer together and the shrubs multiplied many times over. I longed for the sight of the river. We were to cross at Stockbridge and hopefully put that natural barrier between ourselves and our enemies.

Then suddenly out of the darkness came one rider and then another twenty. They were falling upon us on both sides, swords drawn. All around me I heard shouting and the sound of metal upon metal and metal upon wood. Our line was breaking down quickly, and both Drogo and Brian were riding so close to me, shields held aloft, that I feared we would strike each other at any moment. In front of me, Reginald continued to press ahead.

"Don't look back!" Drogo told me. "Whatever you do, don't look back!"

My insides were churning, my heart racing as fast as Frija. With every breath, I feared to see the men beside me fall … but they did not. Their horses pressed on, stride after stride, even as mine did. Although I did not turn to look, I sensed there were fewer knights left behind us. I had no idea if King David or the earls were fighting on or had been forced to break off from the line. Then the great noise behind me grew more distant. There were no new riders appearing from behind the trees.

"Almost there!" Reginald called. "Only another mile or so to go!"

We had broken off from the small path and joined the main road that led to the bridge. This made for much easier riding, and our speed increased. Although I had been solemnly warned not to do so, I briefly looked behind and saw that only about half of the knights remained, but my brother's company was near the end of the line. I could recognize them by the red shirts they wore underneath their armor. I snapped my head forward again and continued to follow Earl Miles as if my life depended on it, for it truly did.

The road grew wider and wider—enough for four horses to easily move side by side—and at length my brother, the earl of Cornwall, cried, "I can see the bridge ahead. Almost there!"

"Ride strong, Frija!" I encouraged her. "Just a bit farther!"

She did not let me down. I felt her breath coming hard even as her hooves continued to hit the road quickly. Then I heard someone crying out from behind the trees in a language I could not understand.

I naturally turned toward the source of the noise and saw another team of archers in the trees ready to fire upon us. I ducked down, and even as I did so, I heard an arrow pass just above me. Ahead of us, there were more men racing out on foot on either side of the road. They did not have weapons drawn but were bending down to attend to something.

"They are raising a trap!" Drogo called to those behind us. "Beware the trap!"

We were able to pass the men just as they began lifting a sort of net that had been lain across the road ahead of our arrival. I heard screams behind us and knew the rest of our knights were coming up against it, either hitting the barrier or breaking off to the left or right, losing their seats or moving back toward the hail of arrows.

"Reginald!" I cried. "Earl Robert and his men will be lost!"

"Keep moving!" he called back in return. "Do not worry about them! Here is the bridge!"

Within seconds, we were crossing the river upon the stone bridge. It was not a far distance, but at that moment it seemed an eternity. Behind us, the archers fired a few more arrows, but as we moved farther away, it seemed they had no one planted on the other side of the river.

"Keep riding!" Reginald beseeched. "Don't look back! Never look back!"

As we made it to the opposite bank of the river, we were immediately pressed up against a marsh.

"It is the Danebury Downs," said Brian. "Try to find a good footing."

I attempted to do as he said, though I had little sense of how to do so. I was not accustomed to riding in such conditions. Fortunately, Frija did not need much direction. So light of foot was she, she made her way across that ground without trouble. Slowly, it began to rise and grow more solid. We moved through a small patch of trees and mounted a hill, even as I heard nothing at all behind us. It was only when we had reached the summit that Reginald held up his hand again and called, "Halt here for a moment! Perhaps some others will follow."

The sudden stop seemed to cause as much distress to Frija as anything else. I immediately pulled her round and looked back in the direction of the river. I had to raise my hand to block the sun from my view. I could just make out a small gray line that I knew to be the River Test, shining in the sun's reflection. There were only the three men with me: none were trailing behind.

"I cannot see anything," I said, my heart full of fear. "What happened to them all?!"

None of them spoke, and I sensed the answer. Earl Robert and his knights had fallen into the trap. They were either dead or taken captive. I looked back to the East, willing Earl Robert to come riding up the hill, wondering what on earth had happened to King David, Earl Miles, and my precious Adela.

"The sun is high in the sky," Drogo said. "It will be midday soon."

Has it really been so long? I thought. *It felt like no time at all. A single moment, and all is lost to us.*

"We have stayed here too long," Brian told Reginald. "We must press on to Wherwell and meet up with the others."

"Right you are," he concluded. "On we march!"

With a click of his tongue, he sent his horse back into motion and the other two started to follow, but I continued staring toward the East, my soul as empty as the great caverns of the deep. We had lost our army. It was scattered to the four winds. We were alone, we four: alone against the forces of the enemy and the will of nature.

"Robert …" I whispered, tears streaming down my cheeks. "Robert, my brother …"

"My lady!" Drogo called, pulling his horse back in my direction. "My lady, we cannot linger! To linger here is death."

I slowly turned my head to look at him, and I believe he saw in my eyes what I felt: that I was already under the shadow of death.

"Think of your sons, my lady," he said more calmly. "You must fight on for them. You must fight on for this kingdom."

With some great difficulty of spirit, I nodded and the four of us were off along the northern road. There was nothing and no one left to us. We had come to Golgotha.

With heavy hearts, we pressed north along the road that lay on the crest above the river. In truth, it was little more than a path, and surrounded on both sides by trees. We were to follow that road another three miles to Wherwell. It was an awful thing to go on and on, moving farther from the friends we had left behind, fearing the doom to which they had been sent. None of us spoke a word, for we could not, and indeed we dared not: there was no telling where the enemy might lie.

At length, we came upon a family making its way along the road. They had a small cart in which I guessed all their earthly goods were kept. The father pulled it behind him, while the mother walked along carrying a babe and two other children ran along at the back.

"Make way!" Brian called ahead to them.

They did so, and we moved around them quickly, continuing along the path. A minute or two later, we came upon more peasants, this time in a small party of ten or so.

"Move aside!" Earl Miles commanded, and we rode between them as they parted in each direction.

Then there was another man walking alone, and what appeared to be another family, and soon it became clear that we were caught in a mass movement of people.

"Exiles from Winchester," Drogo said to me. "They are moving to escape the battle."

"Is it a good sign that we are going in the same direction?" I asked.

"I hope so," he replied, giving another tug on the reins.

As the danger had seemingly decreased slightly, I began to recognize how sore my whole body was from directing Frija this way and that. My legs in particular ached, and on account of both that and my grief I wished very much to lay down and sleep for an entire week, but I was not to enjoy such a luxury.

When we had pressed along that road for perhaps a mile and a half, we suddenly began to see peasants moving in the opposite direction, looking as if they were in a rush.

"Now, this might be a bad sign," said Drogo.

Earl Miles held up his arm for us to stop as we came upon an old man carrying a great burden on his back—a sack of some sort that seemed to be quite heavy.

"You there!" Miles called to him. "Do you come from Wherwell?"

Seeing clearly that Miles was a great lord, the man bowed and then rose again with great difficulty, his load threatening to drag him back to the ground.

"Wherwell, yes," he said, his accent thick. "Church … fire. No go!"

"Are you saying the church is on fire?" Brian asked him.

The man looked upon him with a blank stare, tipping his head slightly. "Church … fire."

"Please allow me, gentlemen," I said, directing Frija in front of them so the man could see me clearly. I then addressed him in the native English tongue to the best of my ability.

"Is the abbey of Wherwell on fire?" I asked him.

"Yes!" he said, evidently pleased to hear something he understood fully. "The foreigners are there: the men from Flanders. They trapped all the knights inside and burned it."

"You mean the forces of the empress? Of Empress Mathilda?" I asked him.

"Yes, I saw it with my own eyes. Those terrible Flemings fell upon it this morning. The nuns were running for their lives. Some of them, I am sorry to say, were given as prizes to those brutes. I beg you, do not go there if you value your life! Only death waits for you."

"I am indebted to you for your counsel," I assured him.

I then turned back to my companions and addressed them in our own tongue. "The wolf of Ypres is in Wherwell and has destroyed our fortress there. John Marshal and his men will not be able to join us."

"These are sad tidings indeed!" said Miles. "That was our road to Ludgershall. I suppose we must find some other way."

"If this is true, then nothing in Hampshire will be out of their reach," noted Brian. "We must head toward Wiltonshire with all speed. Once they have finished burning the abbey, they may well come down this road, and I do not doubt that others will ride up from Stockbridge. The road is no longer safe for us. We must ride cross country."

And so, we began to move farther and farther west, cutting through farmers' fields and low brush. I did not doubt that we were moving away from the enemy, for it seemed we were moving away from everything on earth. By the middle of the afternoon, we came upon a major road which seemed to have been passed over by many carts.

"Hold here," Miles instructed, and we did as he asked.

"Where are we?" I asked. "Have we missed it? Have we missed Ludgershall?"

"This must be the road up from Salisbury," said Brian, "in which case we have not missed it, but we ought to turn north very soon."

"Can we not take this road, or would that be too great a danger?" I inquired further.

Miles turned his horse around to face me. "The road does not go toward Ludgershall, but back to Andover. We must continue past it until we reach the first ridge of hills, then make the turn. If we come upon the River Avon, we have gone too far."

None of us had eaten or drunk anything that day. This added to our grief and weariness as we continued to ride, mile after mile, league after league. We were not far past the road when the ground did begin to rise, and not for the first time I was amazed at how my captains could know the land so well. Of course, I had spent most of my life abroad, unlike Earl Miles, but even so, I do not think there was a blade of grass that grew in England without him knowing.

"Not long now," he assured us. "A few hours at most."

I placed my trust in his words. Poor Frija had had no more to eat or drink than the rest of us, and I could sense she was desperately tired. Our pace was nothing like it had been out of Winchester that morning. Could it have been that very morning? It seemed years in the past.

At last, we arrived at another road of some import, and unlike the one coming from Salisbury, this one was carrying many travelers, all moving in the same direction from east to west. Like the ones we had seen earlier in the day, they appeared to be peasants carrying most of what they owned, attempting to flee the fighting. We joined that great sojourn, passing person after person on foot, weaving this way and that to avoid them. Some raised their heads to look at us, but most continued staring down at the road, their feet treading through dirt and mud, their spirits no doubt broken, even as ours were. The trees grew thicker on either side, and every so often we saw people sitting underneath, some gathered around fires and others simply watching the world go by.

Suddenly, Brian called out, "Cart down ahead!"

Sure enough, there was not one cart turned over in the middle of the road, but two. It seemed they had run into one another and fallen over. Their owners, a peasant of some sort and a merchant, were yelling at each other with great passion, perhaps arguing over who was at fault. The much larger cart, which belonged to the merchant, was still attached to a poor horse that lay upon the ground, kicking and neighing.

"Pull off to the side," Miles said. "Here: there is a small camp of peasants."

Just below the road on the right there were indeed a dozen or so persons gathered around a fire pit, though there was no fire burning at that moment. At first, I was not sure we should join them, for we could not be certain of their loyalties. However, given that at least half their number were women or children, it seemed likely that we could best them if their intentions turned violent.

"We cannot hope to continue along the road until the mess is cleared," Miles told us. "We might as well take some rest for a few minutes."

Although I wished for rest with all my heart, I also knew that I would not truly rest until I was safe behind the walls of Ludgershall Castle. Nevertheless, I alighted from poor Frija and Drogo helped me tie her to a nearby tree. I then sat upon a tree trunk that had long since fallen to earth and grown hollow inside. I stretched my legs and arms, moving my wrists and ankles in small circles in an attempt to relieve the pain of the day. Drogo stood just beside me as Brian approached the exiles in their camp and Miles went to help clear the road. I could see that at the back of the camp, they had created a sort of tent from tree branches and animal skins, under which a young woman sat nursing her babe. There were a few pots and pans sitting on the ground along with some bags of different sizes and logs for the fire.

I closed my eyes for a moment and breathed in the late summer air. Then the thoughts began to flood in: Winchester had fallen into the hands of the enemy, my friends and defenders were left behind, the false queen had won the battle, and we would be fortunate to hold the West. And what of Sir Philip and his new wife? Would I ever see them alive again?

Oh, what bitter questions invaded my mind! The more I thought about these things, the more upset I became, until grief was piled upon grief. Although Stephen was still held in our custody, it seemed unlikely—indeed, profoundly unlikely—that we would be able to overcome the enemy after such a defeat. The crown that had been within my grasp only weeks earlier would probably never sit upon my head, and what was far worse, it would probably never sit upon the head of any of my sons.

Drogo sat beside me and placed a hand on my knee. "Have faith, my lady. All is not lost," he whispered, no doubt wishing to hide our business from the peasants, who sat only a few paces away. "We will be inside the castle soon. You will be safe."

"Can we say the same for Earl Robert? For Earl Miles? For King David?" I asked in despair. "I fear they are lost to us for ever."

"They knew the danger when they set out," he replied. "And in any case, they may not be lost. Perhaps they escaped even as we did. If they were taken captive, we may ransom them."

"With what money? We have nothing left."

"I think that—"

"Please!" I begged, raising a hand. "Say no more."

"Understood," he said quietly.

At about that time, Lord Brian returned from his conversation with the peasants and said, "They do not speak much of our tongue, but I gather they are exiles from Winchester. I do not believe they are a threat to us. They offered me some water and I am sure they would do the same for you."

"Well, at least there is still some kindness left in this world," I said, rising from my seat.

Just then, Earl Miles came walking back down the ridge toward us and called, "Brian! Drogo! We need you to help lift this cart."

The two men immediately went to join him and left me to address the peasants alone. I stepped toward them slowly, their eyes fixed upon me. Apart from the woman and her babe, the rest were sitting in a circle, with a few on large stones and others on logs or the ground itself. Their clothes were filthy and worn, with holes that exposed their skin to the air. Some were old and others young, but all looked as if they had been to hell and back, even as I had. Their eyes seemed emptied of life.

"Excuse me," I said, looking from one to the next, "may I have some water?"

One of the men stood up—perhaps forty years of age and not very tall. He then tapped the woman beside him on the shoulder and she stood as well. She wore a simple gray tunic tied at the waist and I observed that one of her shoes was broken open on the end, allowing her toes to be seen. The pair of them moved back toward the tent and retrieved the leather bottle in which they were keeping their water store.

"Get the cups," the man said to the woman in the English speech. I guessed that she must be his wife.

She bent over and began to look through a sack in which, by the sound of it, all their metal goods were kept. I could just hear her muttering in her own tongue. From the bits I was able to piece together, I guessed at what they were discussing.

"Why should we give them water?" she inquired, or rather complained. "They are men of the empress."

"My dear, the Lord commands us to give water and bread to anyone who asks," he told her.

She stood up, a metal cup in her hand. "Even when we're sitting here starving? Even when she's the reason for our misery?"

He sighed, shifting the bottle in his hands. "Even then."

It was clear that the two of them did not know I could understand their speech. Although they were not yelling, it was still loud enough for me to hear from several paces away.

As they began walking back to where I was standing, the woman said, "I swear, if I saw that empress, all high and mighty on her horse, riding about as if she were Jesus Christ—"

"You have never seen the empress and never will," he assured her.

They were within a single pace of me and smiled. How little did they know that I saw through those smiles! The husband removed the top of the bottle and poured some water into the cup that his wife was holding out. Despite my great thirst, I was beginning to wonder if I should accept it.

"I would tell her what's what, I would!" the woman continued. "All that blood on her hands. Your shop destroyed, our son dead—all because she cannot bear the thought of being second place to anyone. I would set her straight!"

The cup was filled and she held it out to me, a smile on her face once again. However, I was not smiling in return. No, I felt ill. Her words, offered up in complete ignorance, had sliced into me with the force of steel. She had named me an arrogant and ruthless killer. I knew I ought not reveal myself, but oh, how the anger burned within me! And perhaps because I was in such an hour of desperation, bearing the weight of grief upon my person, I challenged her, reaching back across the years to draw on my knowledge of the English tongue.

"Has pain made you brave, then? Have at it!" I bid.

The look on her face changed immediately. The smile disappeared, and instead she wrinkled her brow, drawing back the cup she had offered.

"Who are you?" she asked.

"Empress Mathilda, lady of the English, daughter of King Henry."

"Oh, please!" she cried with a laugh. "You're not the empress!"

Her husband grabbed her arm with his free hand, his manner quite fearful. "I think she might be, dear."

The woman looked first at him and then back at me, recognition slowly coming over her. "But … Why is she dressed like a man? And hiding off in the shadows? And since when do any of these noble types speak our tongue?!" she demanded to know.

"My mother was a Briton," I replied calmly. "I was born here. I belong to this island. Why should I not speak its tongue?"

The husband dropped down on one knee and laid the bottle aside, bowing his head in respect.

"We beg your pardon, Your Highness! Please, my wife is over tired and has forgotten her place."

The woman, on the other hand, did nothing but stare at me. "I thought the empress would be taller," she said.

Oh, what insolence! I could scarcely believe what I was seeing and hearing. Although it was true that I held few conversations with the common man, the ones in which I did take part were generally full of respect for my person. I had known great lords who would treat me with disdain, but nothing like this.

"I demand that you answer for your words!" I cried.

"Very well, then, I'll give you an answer," she said, dropping the cup on the ground and pointing at me. "You … are an awful excuse for a woman!"

I heard one or two gasps from her fellows at this comment and her husband was clearly struck with terror.

"Please, Ælfthryth! I beg you!" he pleaded, tugging on the bottom of her tunic.

She heeded him not, but continued to look me in the eye, venom spewing from her mouth. "You go around riding about, ordering men around, setting towns on fire—"

"I have certainly never set a town on fire!" I yelled, caring not who heard.

"Oh, really? Then what was all that mess back there?" she taunted.

"It was your bishop who set the town on fire, not me!"

"Yes, but it was your fault." Here she pointed at me again. "You brought it upon us, you did."

"It was the bishop who brought it upon you by turning traitor."

She let out a savage laugh. "You're one to talk about treachery! You abandon your husband, your children! You have no heart at all."

I could not think what had possessed her to say such things, but for myself I was filled with rage. It was all I could do not to throttle her then and there.

"How dare you!" I cried, my eyes filling with tears. "I did not abandon them! The crown of England belongs to myself and my sons. I am fighting to defend their rightful inheritance."

She rolled her eyes. "Oh, spare us! Do you think anyone but you nobles cares about that?"

This caught me very much off guard. Here was the question of greatest import in the kingdom, and she pretended as if it were a matter of no consequence. I wondered if she was truly mad. Her poor husband was by this point curled up on the ground, head in his hands.

"Well, you ought to care! You ought to care who rules your own kingdom," I replied.

"Don't tell me about oughts!" she yelled, placing her hands on her hips. "I don't care who wears that crown as long as I have food to eat and a roof over my head and I can pass the night in peace. We had that with the king, but ever since you came, it's been nothing but war. Our churches are burnt, our homes destroyed. We have naught to eat, and it's all your fault! You and your evil counselors! We do not want your war. Take it back, bloody queen!"

I do not know if it was because of her vicious words or the weakness I felt in my person, but for once in my life, I was struggling to come up with a biting reply. I had not feared to enter a fight in the past, but suddenly I was not so much afraid to challenge as utterly unable to do so.

"I am ... I am not what you think," I stammered, my face lined with tears. "If you only knew ..."

The woman stepped very close to me, scowling as if she could kill me with the force of it. "All I know is before you came, I had a home and a son. My husband could work. Now my son is dead and we have nowhere to lie our heads at night. I pray to God that we will survive since you certainly don't care about us. You don't care about anything but yourself! How many people like me do you talk to? None! If you did, you would know what I am telling you. None of us want this war. None of us want you. Go back to France or wherever you came from and live in one of your many castles and let us have peace again."

"I should have you hung," I whispered.

She scoffed loudly. "And end my miserable life? Fine, then, do it! Send me down to hell, but you'll be there with me soon enough. All you have will dissolve into dust. You are one sad page in a book that some day men will be happy to tear out and throw into the fire. I see it in your eyes: you know it's true. You have clung to power with those fingers of yours, wringing the life out of those around you, and for what? It won't last. It will slip from your grasp and you will be destroyed. I hope I live to see the day!"

Nothing. I could say nothing in reply. The force of her hate had robbed me of speech, and I knew naught in that moment but the pain of her words.

"I beg you, my lady, have mercy!" her husband cried, raising his head just enough to speak. "She is deep in grief from the death of our son. I should have cut out her tongue rather than have you suffer this. Please, if you only knew what it is like to lose a child, you would understand!"

I begged myself to breathe—just breathe. Bending down, I picked up the cup from the ground along with the bottle. I poured more water in it and took a drink, allowing the liquid to run down my throat, hoping that for just a moment it would contain the fire within me. Then I set them both down again and rose to look the woman in the eye as I addressed her husband.

"Mercy? You ask for mercy from this world? This world that has none to give? Even so, I grant it, but on your account only, for we were thirsty and you gave us something to drink. It is the Lord's mercy."

"I spit upon your mercy!" the woman cried. "I hate you!"

I could say nothing more, and indeed there was nothing more to say. I began to step backward, putting space between the two of us, until I was far enough away that I felt comfortable turning to walk back up the hill. I was shaking, perhaps inside myself or perhaps without: I cannot be certain. I hardly knew why I was continuing. I took the final steps up to the road, wiping the tears from my eyes. There I found that the road had been cleared and my companions were walking back to retrieve the horses.

"What was that about?" Brian asked. "I heard you speaking to them in their own tongue. Did they threaten you in some way?"

"It was nothing," I lied. "Come, let us leave this place and find the castle of Ludgershall. I will have no safety until we do so."

He nodded, and within minutes we were riding back along the road as the sun sank lower in the western sky.

XX

If my life was hanging upon a string, then Fate had stretched it as far as she dared. The break had been coming for some time. Ever since I had returned to England, my soul had not been well. No, ever since the usurper was brought to power! Or was it earlier still? I had borne the contempt of the world for so long that I was utterly empty of joy. I had seen my hopes crushed so often that I scarcely knew the purpose of my own existence.

Tighter and tighter, the thread was pulled, until that hour when I received the scorn of a simple woman: the one who ought not have hurt me at all hurt me most, for she called into question everything I was to England and everything England was to me. Since I had returned to that island, I had been driven on through struggle after struggle, always persevering by the knowledge that my cause was just. Whatever else had failed, my faith in the purpose of that fight had not ... until I stood defeated on the road to Ludgershall, seeing myself through new eyes and wondering if it meant anything at all.

As we rode the last stretch to the castle, I felt as if I was marching through the Valley of Hinnom, with the scorched remains of everything I was lying round about.[32] I said nothing and gave no sign to the others. We had sought out that fortress as a refuge from battle, but I knew well enough that the real demons would follow me inside. Those words continued to torment my mind.

You are an awful excuse for a woman. You abandoned your husband and your children. You have no heart at all.

We reached the gate of Ludgershall Castle. The door was opened to us, and we rode inside.

Bloody queen!

There were few men left to guard the place, as John Marshal had brought most of his knights with him to defend our supply chain to the east. As the last rays of the sun disappeared, we led our tired horses to food and water.

None of us want this war. None of us want you.

We entered the keep and my companions set about removing their armor. I laid my satchel on the floor, pulled off the cloak, and reached up to take hold of the cap.

All you have will dissolve into dust.

I turned away from the others so they could not see the new tears forming in my eyes. I removed the cap and set it on the floor next to the rest of my things. I hardly cared if my hair was on view. I leaned back against the stone wall and slowly sank down, new aches revealing themselves at every point. Farther and farther I slid until I was sitting upon the floor. I reached forward and began untying the laces on my boots. I heard the others discussing the possibility of finding some wine, but it

---

32   The Valley of Hinnom lies below the old city of Jerusalem and is also known by the related name Gehenna. The Jewish and Christian scriptures describe it as a cursed location of ancient child sacrifice and use it as a metaphor for a place of punishment or purging in the afterlife.

was as if I was not there—not fully, in any case. When I had finally freed my feet, I leaned my head back and closed my eyes. What did I feel? Only pain: a sea of pain.

The next thing I knew, I was waking out of sleep. I blinked my eyes and wondered, *Where am I?* I saw before me the round walls of the keep with only a few small windows high above that let in no light. There were two doors: one that led outside and one that hid the stair leading to the upper level. There was a pit in the middle of the room, and in it the men had built a fire. They were quietly gathered round it, passing a bottle between them.

Oh, my thighs! My legs! I suddenly thought.

With the recognition of that pain, I arrived fully in the moment and remembered all that had taken place: fire, ash, arrows, Frija running, trees, the river, the woman and her husband. The images moved across my mind in triumph over me.

"She's awake!" Drogo said, rising to his feet. "You must have been tired unto death, Your Highness."

"Yes," I said quietly, "I suppose I must have been."

"We heard from a messenger while you were asleep," Reginald explained. "Wherwell fell to the Flemings under William of Ypres. They will likely come this way tomorrow. It will be known that you escaped from Winchester, and as soon as they discover that none of them were able to seize you along the way, they will make for the West."

"Any word of the others?" I asked wearily.

"Nothing," Reginald said grimly, casting his gaze down at the flames.

Lord Brian had the bottle in his hand and took a drink, then handed it to Drogo, who consumed the final drops and threw the thing aside. It rolled until it joined another two bottles that had already been emptied.

"We must leave here as soon as dawn breaks," my brother continued. "We make for the castle of Devizes as Earl Robert instructed."

The mention of Robert's name filled me again with guilt. What had become of him? Was he still among the living? I thought back to that moment when the net was raised, catching most of our knights in the trap. What would have happened if they had raised it a few seconds sooner? None of us would have made it to Ludgershall. I could not decide if that was a blessing or a curse. We four had been spared, but for what? To stretch out our hopes a few more days? We had no captains and no way to speak with them. All that, and we were still not safe.

"We saved some food for you," Brian said, retrieving something that had apparently been sitting next to him, only I had not seen it on account of the shadows.

Am I hungry? Yes, I must be. I have not eaten all day, I reasoned.

I rose to my feet, feeling once again the effects of a day's hard ride. I walked toward them and took the food from Brian's hand, which turned out to be a small piece of bread and some cheese. It was not the meal of a queen and barely worthy of a peasant, so I wondered what they had eaten, knowing they must have saved me the best.

"Thank you," I told him, then sat down and began eating.

"And happily, we have one more of these for you," Drogo said with a smile, pulling another bottle from behind his back.

I could not think why he had kept it hidden until that moment, but I accepted it gladly, as it was the one thing that might remedy my pain in some small way. Only when I held it in my hand did I recognize that it had already been opened and there was a bit missing.

"Forgive me," my knight requested. "I did not know it was the last one and had already taken a drink. Do you not want to drink it now?"

Raising my fingers, I made the sign of the cross over him. "I pardon you, Sir Drogo," I recited, then raised the bottle to my mouth. I think I would have consumed it even if a dog had gone before me. Happily, it tasted good: just the right amount of sweetness. "Where is this from?" I asked, for it had nothing written on it.

"Yes, we could not discover that, not that any of us cared very much," Reginald explained. "I suppose it is a thing of mystery ... much like myself."

It was a small jest, but one offered without a smile on the part of the giver and without any laughs on the part of the receivers. We were all far past the point of humor.

"You should get some rest, my lady," Brian said. "We have a long ride ahead of us again tomorrow."

"I think I'll drink a while," I told him. "I had a bit of sleep, and I do not think I could go down again just yet. Are you all going to sleep?"

"If I can," replied Reginald, and Drogo also nodded.

"Then go ahead to the upper level, all of you, and leave me be down here. If there are beds, you can take them," I offered.

"No, we will save one for you," said Drogo. "It is only proper. I think there were two. Perhaps we can share one and give the other to you."

"Share a bed with you?" Reginald asked in wonder. "We'll be lucky if we get any space at all. Do they make beds for a man of your height?"

"Well, sort it out between the three of you, but I cannot share, so if I am to have a bed, you will have to make it work," I said, continuing to sip the wine.

Brian nodded to his fellows. "You two go ahead. I'll remain with the empress. I do not think she should be alone, even within the keep. I would like to think we could be certain of the loyalties of the guards, but these are uncertain times."

They both nodded in response and rose to leave. Soon it was only Brian and I sitting in stillness, staring into the flames. Though I said nothing, my mind was working fast. I was thinking of a ship: a ship that might carry me from Bristol back to Normandy to be with my sons. In Normandy, Count Geoffrey had enjoyed victories of late. Perhaps we could settle for that land. Ah, but the false queen would come across the water and fight us there, and the king of France would likely join her. No, it would not work. I took another drink.

I set the bottle on the floor beside me and buried my head against my knees. There were words buried deep within me—words that had been held there so long. In that darkest of hours, I opened my mouth to speak them.

"I failed," I whispered, raising my head again.

Brian broke out of his stupor and said, "What? No! If anyone failed, it was your captains."

Then suddenly, the gates of my soul opened and a flood of words came out. "I am not a child, Lord Brian. I understand far more than any of you think, and I know when I have failed. What's worse is I do not see how I could have succeeded. If I had listened to my uncle less, if I had been kinder to the Londoners, if I had given my first born child to Geoffrey Mandeville, what would any of it have mattered? It is me they hate! There is nothing that can be done. They hate me." I beat my hand upon the floor in anger. "Oh God! Why was I ever born?! I am a plague to those around me. But for my sons, I have produced nothing of value. I ought to be wandering upon the moor like some vagrant damned to hell! And yet I am here, sitting with you, adding misery to your misery."

He shook his head and said, "You speak without sense." Seeing I was about to object, he raised a hand and assured me, "No, I do not mean that you are a woman without sense, but merely that you have abandoned it in this moment. Yes, we had a defeat today, but it is not the end. This sort of thing happens in wars. You need not—"

"Brian, they took Robert!" I cried. "They took him, and I was such a bitch to him!"

"No, you must not say that!"

"Well, it's true," I said, shaking my head in anger at myself. "My closest ally, my brother, my friend. I doubted him, even though he never doubted me. Even though he is one of the few people on earth I can trust, I doubted him."

"He understands. We will get Earl Robert back, I swear to you."

He said these words intently, and in the strength of his gaze, I could almost believe it possible. But it was a fleeting moment, and I felt again that great pang of guilt and shame which weighed upon me more than any chains my enemies could create.

"Then let it be part of the surrender," I whispered.

"What?! No, no, no ..." he objected.

"I mean it! There's no point any more. The people hate me! They would rather have a tyrant and a foreigner to rule over them. If that is what I am up against, then there is no hope of final victory: not when our best captain is lost to us."

I raised the bottle again and began to drain it quickly.

"You are speaking out of weariness," he said with a sigh.

"I am perfectly serious!" I assured him, pounding the empty bottle down upon the floor in such a manner that it is a wonder it did not break. "I've had it! I shall return to Anjou and my boys, and we will live out our days in peace. Let the usurper have this kingdom. Much pain will it give him. I swear that I—"

"Be quiet!" he yelled.

This stopped me in my tracks. I had never thought to hear such words escape his mouth. I stared at him, breathing hard, filled with anger.

"Do ... you ... dare ... dishonor ... me?" I asked slowly, stressing each word.

"I would never dishonor you," he said with great determination, "but you have spoken in despair long enough. Now it is my turn to speak. What about those of us who have sacrificed for you for years? We believed in you and your claim. We longed to see the usurper thrown down. What about us? You say you want to go off and live in peace, but that is impossible. If you give up, we may all be hung by year's end!"

"Oh, don't be a fool!" I objected.

"I am telling you this thing is bigger than you," he continued, pointing at me. "Consider that before you make your decision."

"Well, how kind of you to admit that it is my decision, for you seem to want to make it for me!" I snapped.

"That is not what I meant and you know it!"

I was so full of frustration by that point that I said, "Perhaps it is better that we say nothing, since our conversation only makes things worse."

"Very well," he replied, turning back to face the fire, which by that point was down to embers.

A few minutes went by in which the only sound was the wind outside. My thoughts continued to spin as I stared at nothing in particular, tears beginning to fill my eyes. At length, I could no longer contain them. They fell freely down my cheeks. I ought to have kept my feelings in check, but I was far too weary to concern myself with that. It seemed to me that there was no hope left. My whole being was in pain, and my heart most of all.

"My lady! My lady! Maud!"

"I'm ... sorry," I whispered.

Brian crossed the space between us and crouched beside me, placing his hand on mine.

"Please, is there anything I can do?" he asked. "Can I some-how lessen your distress?"

I was crying too hard to offer a reply.

"This is my fault," he said in frustration. "This is all my fault."

"What are you … talking … about?" I said through my tears. "I was the … one who made a mess of things."

"No, it is my fault," he assured me. "I thought this was the only way. I thought in time you would be happy."

I had no idea what he meant, but that tends to happen when one is overly upset. I ceased crying long enough to utter, "What?"

He let go of my hand and dropped to his knees. He looked straight into my eyes with that piercing gaze: not judging, not degrading, but simply meeting me. My heart began to beat faster.

"When you first returned to Normandy," he said, "I fell in love with you immediately. I had never met a woman like you, and what a thing of beauty you were! Absolute perfection."

"I think you have mistaken me for someone else," I offered, but he would not be bowed.

"Of course, I wanted you for myself, but what an idea! It was impossible. That did not keep me from dreaming. Indeed, I dreamed about you almost every night. Then when I awoke, I seized any opportunity to speak with you, for I felt it was the most I could ever hope for. I would never be your husband. I couldn't even be your lover, though in my flesh I might have seized that opportunity as well. I was sick with desire. Then one day, a miracle: you told me you loved me. It took me by surprise. I chased after you. I kissed you."

"I remember. I was there."

"Yes, it was one of the greatest moments of my life."

"Mine as well. I think of it often."

This brought forth a smile, but he put it away quickly. "In any case, I wanted to keep my wits about me. Truly, I did. I knew you would certainly be married to some prince so and so, no matter what I did. I had moments of despair because of that. I hated the thought of you with anyone else, but especially someone who would attempt to put out the fire that resides within you. That was what attracted me, like a moth to the flame. I wanted to bask in your light."

As much as I enjoyed hearing these words, I felt a need to ask, "Forgive me, Brian, but is there a point to this? The past is even more painful than the present."

He nodded and continued his tale.

"When you said you wanted to marry me, I feared I had gone too far. I had created a desire in you that I could not fulfill. I had been reckless. I therefore felt a need to save you from certain pain. And so, I determined to speak with your father and take his wrath upon myself. I read every legal text and history I could find looking for something I could use, but my search was rather fruitless. It was only my great love for you that caused me to think there was even the smallest hope.

"I remember the day well. We were traveling by boat down the river: your father and me. I had requested to speak with him alone while the others sailed in their own boats. After some time had passed, I said, 'My lord, King Henry, you have given me all that I have, and I can never thank you enough.'

"Here he interrupted to agree with me.

"I then told him, 'I have no right to ask you this. None whatsoever. You will think me mad, but I care for your daughter. She is more precious to me than anything on this earth: even my own life.'

"That got his attention. He looked at me and said very directly, 'If she is with child, I'll kill you!'

"'No, my lord! I would never do such a thing!' I replied. 'I love her and you far too much to sin against you both in such a manner.'

"He then expressed his inability to see the problem.

"'My lord,' I explained, 'if I may be so bold, I request to have your daughter in marriage.'

"There was the anger I had foreseen. 'You overstep the bounds, boy!' he yelled. 'I can see that my benevolence has gone to your head! What makes you think you can ask such a thing?! You are not worthy of her!'

"'No one is more aware of it than me,' I replied.

"Then he struck me across the face and said, 'That is for thinking to steal my crown!'

"'My Lord,' I cried, when I had recovered from the blow, 'no such thought entered my mind! Empress Maud would be the ruler, not I.'

"'Blasphemy!' he declared. 'Pure blasphemy! No lord would allow his manhood to be so dishonored. It would be a great offense.'

"'How could I be offended to dwell for ever with the most perfect creature I have ever found?' I asked.

"Then he said … Forgive me. I hate to repeat it."

"No, please, Brian—tell me," I begged.

"Very well," he replied with a nod and continued. "He said, 'Maud? My Maud? Have you taken a good look at her, boy? She is as plain as the day is long and even more stubborn. She will not make anyone a good wife. Here your lie is exposed.'

"I objected and he struck me again.

"'You are going to marry the lady of Wallingford. That is my will. Stop troubling my daughter,' he commanded.

"Here I made a mistake. I said, 'But my lord, she also wishes to marry. We love each other. We have no desire to be separated ever again.'

"He replied, 'Then you may tell my daughter that if she continues to foster this desire, I will strip her of all her privileges. I will disown her and hand the crown to another.'

"I was so angry that I asked, 'And what if she doesn't care? What if we decide to leave this kingdom and seek marriage before God elsewhere?'

"His eyes were filled with fury. I truly feared that he might attempt to drown me in the water that instant, but he simply said, 'Then I shall have you both excommunicated and you will be consigned to hell.'

"Well, as you can imagine, I was seized with terror. The more I thought about it, the more I came to believe that you could never be happy in such a situation. Indeed, I had gone too far. The only way to save you from your father was to consent to marry Mathilda D'Oyly and never raise the subject again. Perhaps you could love someone else, I reasoned.

"For myself, I would have taken the chance of accepting the king's wrath, for I had read in the case of Judith of Flanders how she had her excommunication reversed by the Holy Father after she married against her father's wishes. Yet I said to myself, We would have a few happy weeks, but then she would regret her decision. She would mourn all she had lost. She would come to see me as the greatest curse upon her life. And what's more, the kingdom might fall into war. Only a smooth succession can ensure peace.

"So, I did the thing I hated to do: I joined hands with the lady of Wallingford and swore to be true to her for the remainder of our natural lives. I abhorred it, for I felt a great fraud. This poor woman I took to myself had no idea that my heart already belonged to another. She deserved someone who would adore her even as I did you, but I was in no position to offer that when I was utterly broken inside. The king made me promise never to speak of what happened—never to say anything that might renew your affection for me. I had to act as if I was cold and indifferent. It pained me deeply, but I thought at least you had a chance to be happy. Only, you never were happy.

"He married you to that fool of a husband. The crown was stolen from you. I hardly ever see you smile, Maud. I used to love that smile, but it is a thing of the past. The kingdom descended into war anyway. Part of me wonders, would it have been better if we defied the king? Yes, it would have been terrible at first, but we could have gone abroad and lived somewhat happily. My home of Brittany might have accepted us, or maybe the Empire. Our troubles might have been fewer. Perhaps we would have had children.

"All of that was taken from us because I made a choice to act when I should have asked you first. I thought I was sparing you from misery, but it seems I only ensured your misery. I have failed you, and for that I cannot forgive myself."

I had been listening quietly as he released this flood of words. I felt the strangest mix of pain and pleasure. I wanted to answer him: to declare everything I felt.

"Well, I beg your pardon, for you deserve far better," he said, bowing his head and placing a hand on his chest. "I said I would love you for ever, and I meant it. I love you even more today, if that were possible. Perhaps it isn't poss—"

"Brian," I interrupted.

"Yes?" he asked, his eyes wide, hanging upon my words.

"Brian … my love. There is nothing to forgive. What you have done for me … Your loyalty never fails. I am happy simply to know you. I love you. I love you more than—"

I was unable to finish. With the same boldness he had shown all those years before in the garden, he leaned forward and kissed me. For a moment, all I could think was how wonderful it was to feel again that thing I never thought I would feel again. It was bliss. Somewhere in my mind, a sense that what was happening was not strictly right began to form, but my will rose to block it.

He pulled back for a moment to wipe the tears from my eyes and stroke my hair. I whispered to him, "I love you," and we kissed again. My weariness, so great moments before, seemed completely gone.

Then he asked, "My love, what do you desire? I will do anything: pray for you, hold you, lie with you. What do you want? You are free to choose."

I could hardly believe it. Not that one of us had broken down. I had long suspected that might happen. What surprised me was that it was Brian.

Perhaps it was because of the two of us, I was more impulsive. Perhaps it was because some part of me always feared that I loved him more than he loved me. Perhaps it was because I thought him all that was good and noble, and myself the lost sheep. But as it turned out, he was the one who broke. He had not exactly asked for it, and yet his eyes were asking for it … if I agreed. There had been moments of decision scattered throughout my life, but none seemed as thoroughly in my own control as this one. The choice was laid before me: to act or not to act.

If I acted, I would certainly be happy. I would have what I ought to have enjoyed all those years before. It was mine by right, or it ought to have been. Yes, ought was a word that held a powerful sway over me.

My husband had bedded dozens of women since we joined hands—perhaps even hundreds. He had fathered other women's children. He was an adulterer of the worst kind, for he thought his adultery was nothing and cared not whom it hurt. No, he could hardly fault me for returning the favor just once. Everything within me longed to be joined to the man of my choosing and the one my heart desired. I was not afraid. I was determined.

Such pain had been building in me for months and years! I longed to release it in a single moment. In one act, I could not only place a seal upon our love for all time, but strike a blow against every man who had ever made himself my tyrant.

Even God Himself could hardly fault me for being a natural woman just once, I reasoned. If I was a sinner, perhaps He made me that way. Perhaps I was already damned and this hell of a life was the only heaven I would ever know. So, why not do it? Who would ever know? Even if God did hold it against me, I could hope to repay my debt in the life to come.

Yes, I had almost made up my mind. My spirit was groaning, sighing, pleading. It compelled me to action. *I need you, my love. You are my joy. Please, heal my pain. Be joined to me.* I could already hear the words inside my head. All I needed was the courage to speak them: to make the choice.

I was about to say it. I swear, my lips had already parted. Then something passed through my mind: a thought, or was it a feeling? I saw a glimpse of something. It was the face of my son—the face of young Henry. He was looking at me, beseeching.

Mother, please! Mother! Do I not love you also?

I gasped for breath. A terror struck my heart. I heard the words of Abbot Boson: *You must think in terms of a thousand years.* I heard the words of my mother: *Let us hold fast the confession of our faith, for He who promised is faithful.* And then my mind turned and saw the figure of Anselm as he had appeared to me that night when all was dark and I was upon the brink of death: *Rise.*

And suddenly I knew. If I did this thing, it would not only be a sin against God. It would be a sin against myself, my progeny, and England. If my actions were discovered, I would most certainly become the whore of Anjou, and of course, they would be discovered. How could they not be? I would face the censure of both God and man. I would be cast out.

Perhaps I could have accepted this doom for myself, but I feared my sons would never wear the crown. History would be written differently. My sin would be the unmaking of us all. This was not a choice between pleasure and pain. It was a choice between death and life.

In that moment, I saw myself for who I truly was: not simply a victim, but also a victor. We would win the war—not immediately, but we would win. My children would sit upon England's throne for a thousand years, or perhaps even more. I knew it. Somehow, I knew it. It was madness, and yet I knew it.

My choice was made—that is, if I ever had one. I loved Brian, and that would have to be enough. Indeed, it had always been enough. After all, none of us are truly free. Free to err, perhaps, but not free to have joy. Joy is a gift. It cannot be seized. It can only be accepted. That is what I learned that night.

And so, I replied, "Pray for me, Brian. Pray that I will withstand temptation, for I love you and I want … You know what I want, but I can't. I cannot do that to my sons. Oh God, I wish it was not so. For once I wish I was weak. But I am not weak: I am like my mother."

He smiled and said, "I know, and that is why I will always love you. Forgive me. I was wrong to even ask. Truly, I have sinned against you."

"Oh, Brian!" I said, half laughing. "We are standing on the banks of the River Styx, our bodies worn beyond measure, clinging to life. If ever there was a time when the phrase 'the spirit is willing, but the body is weak' applied, this is surely that time! There is nothing to forgive. I know you would never force me. I know who you are."

"And I you. You are the greatest woman I have ever met: the strongest, the most intelligent, with a beauty beyond all the maidens of the hour. That is truer today than any day before it."

"You make my choice harder," I said, shaking my head.

"I beg your pardon again. I shall be quiet."

"No, I pray you, speak. Your voice is the dearest sound to me on earth. However, it belongs to the lady of Wallingford. Do right by her. That is your penance."

"Of course. I care for her. Truly, I do. She is a good woman, but it does not help that she bears your name. The comparison is not fair to her. She deserves better than a man chained to a memory."

"Have you ever strayed from her before?"

"No! Thank God, I have not."

"Then she is luckier than most of the noble women in this kingdom. The times are evil, Lord Brian. We must see our faults, yes, but it does not do to obsess over them. Not when they rape and murder next door!"

"Fair enough," he said, rising to his feet. "Now, up to your room and rest, my queen. I have said far too much. We both need sleep."

"Indeed, for my very life depends on you all," I agreed.

Looking down at me, he swore, "I will not let you down. I promise."

I smiled. "You never have before, and thus I believe you."

I awoke the next morning in a rather better mood. Indeed, I felt revived, though more in mind than body. But it was not a kiss that had revived me, nor a declaration of love. It was the revelation I had in that moment when the future was laid before me: a future in which there was hope stretching into eternity. I saw my life in a new light and felt assured of my purpose. I knew the road ahead would be long and full of difficulty, but I believed that if I could only persevere, I would have the joy set before me, and that gave me the strength to continue. I cannot explain this except that it came from God Himself: not a vision, but a feeling by which I was revived.

The weight of injustice bore down upon me as the earth upon Atlas, and all my efforts to fight it seemed destined to fail. But in my heart, I spoke a word against it.

If the times be not just, then I must unite myself to a higher time. I must join my fate to England itself, and in that land that gave me birth, I shall be born anew. All that I am, I cast upon eternity in the hope of a crown beyond decay.

That was my purpose, and I had to see it done. I would need every bit of strength I could muster, for we were still in great danger. It was Drogo who shook me awake before the sun had risen. I looked up at his face hovering above my own.

"My lady, I am so sorry, but we must depart," he said.

I rubbed my eyes. "Your breath is not the most pleasant thing to wake to in this world, Sir Drogo."

"Part of my stratagem to keep the enemy at bay," he replied, pointing to his head.

No, it was not the best way to begin the day, but I knew it could have been far worse. At least I was not being awoken by the wolf of Ypres! The four of us mounted our horses again and set out with the first light. Our pace was not quite as fast as when we set out from Winchester, for no one could hope to maintain such speed for long. I still thought of our friends left behind, but I did not despair of them as I once had: at least not of my captains. They were men of the world who had been through many battles and I had faith that they would somehow make it out of the hands of the enemy. But I did feel great concern for Philip and Adela, for they could not hope to trade off their names in the same way as the king of Scotland. Sir Philip was also less than whole, and though I held Adela in great respect, she was not built for war. I gave them to the Lord in prayer, bidding him watch over them with all his saints and angels.

It was less than twenty miles to Devizes, so we had a good chance to reach it by midday, but we were hampered by our general weariness, and we had not seen a decent meal since August. As we cut through the Collingbourne Wood on our journey west, we saw nothing like the flood of persons from the day before. This was a blessing, for though we were moving into territory that had been more friendly to me since the conflict began, we were still only four and not fit to take on a force of any great size. Reginald would hold up a hand every so often after hearing a noise in the forest, and we would all stop to listen or spy out anyone hiding in the trees. Of course, one could argue that if there was a person hiding behind a tree with bow in hand, the best thing to do would be to keep moving and not make one's self an easy target. Fortunately, we never had to put our method to the test in such a manner.

Soon we were moving down into the Pewsey Vale, through which flows the River Avon. I had begun that ride feeling a bit less sore, but two hours upon a horse had placed me firmly in the place of hurt I had hoped to leave behind. Every stride Frija took was misery for my thighs. Not only that, but I had pain traveling up my spine into my neck. My poor shoulders were begging me not to ride another mile.

Finally, I called out, "Forgive me, gentlemen, but I must rest. I cannot go on like this."

"Not long until we reach the river," Brian called back. "Can you hold on for a few more minutes?"

I merely grunted as we continued past the fields of wheat. A pair of men in the distance were harvesting the summer crop. They were the first people we had seen for about an hour.

"There! There is the river," said Reginald. "Not long now."

I was riding behind Earl Reginald and Lord Brian with Drogo beside me. I could therefore see little ahead of us but trusted their word. We continued riding and I soon saw the river as well: not a large thing at that point. I was rejoicing in my soul that we were soon to put another barrier between us and the enemy when there was an immediate change of mood in the others. Without uttering a word, Reginald and Brian both raised their hands and looked back at us, my brother mouthing the word, "Stop!"

Drogo and I did as they commanded, then followed as they departed the road for the field to the left. We began riding through the wheat, which was no easy matter as any real path had long since disappeared. When we were a stone's throw away from the road, Reginald directed us to halt and we all alighted, myself with some difficulty. As soon as my feet were on the ground, my view was blocked. The plants stood as high as my shoulders, swaying lightly in the wind. I could see Drogo's head, but nothing of my other companions. Then I heard a noise to my left and looked to see Brian ducking down and pulling his horse behind him. Raising his hand, he held it palm down and gestured for me to crouch as well. I did as he said, fearing very much the reason for all these instructions.

As he pulled his horse a bit nearer, I whispered, "What's out there?"

"The bridge is destroyed," he said, even as I encouraged Frija to drop her head down. "That is, much of it still stands, but the portion nearest us lies in rubble. We cannot cross."

Feeling rather ill, I seized upon what seemed the happiest explanation. "Is it possible that it happened naturally? Bridges do fall from time to time."

"This was an old Roman bridge," he told me, shaking his head. "It had stood for a thousand years. Highly unlikely that it happened to founder just before we were set to cross it. Someone will have gone after the foundation."

I nodded sadly. "So, what are we to do?"

"Reginald is going to investigate," he explained. "Drogo and I are staying near you for safety."

"Thank you," I said.

It was the first time the two of us had spoken more than a few words since the night before, but it did not seem odd. Indeed, it was all those many conversations that had happened in the past few years that were painfully odd. With the subject finally raised and addressed, I no longer felt any fear: at least, no fear on account of what might happen with Brian. Our present situation in the field was causing me quite a bit of concern, but I bid myself remain calm.

Soon there was another parting of the wheat and Drogo came through, crouching next to me while holding the reins of his horse. There was a look of alarm on his face, and I asked him, "What is it, Drogo? What have you seen?"

"I watched Reginald walk down toward the river for about twenty paces, then I saw him raise his weapon and crouch below the wheat. He must have seen someone down there," he answered.

"Someone waiting for us to pass?" I wondered aloud. "But how could they have gotten here before us? I know we were not going at full speed, but no one leaving from Andover could have beaten us here."

"They will have been sent out a few days ago in case we were to attempt an escape to the West," Brian said. "This is the only crossing point for miles and it lies on the road from Ludgershall to Devizes. They likely destroyed the bridge knowing it would force us to halt, and now they hope to pick us off from their hiding place."

"God save us," I whispered.

The wind moved through the field, causing the wheat to sway. I could hear nothing of what was going on closer to the river. None of us wanted to speak much for fear of giving away our position. Suddenly, there was a noise close by as of something moving through the wheat. We all turned to look in that direction and saw a crow perched on top of one of the stalks, its weight bending the stem almost to the point of breaking. The bird looked down at us with its black eyes, its head tipped to one side.

"That can't be a good sign," Drogo whispered, releasing the hilt of his sword.

The crow looked up, gazing in the direction of the river. Then in an instant it rose into flight at the same moment that a crowd of its fellows could be seen rising up around us, letting out great cries and swarming in the air. Then there was another sound: the scream of a man in pain. Drogo immediately stood and looked over the wheat for the source of the noise, then dropped down just as quickly as an arrow flew over all our heads.

"An archer down by the river—he has seen me," the knight warned.

My two defenders looked at each other, seeming to speak only with their eyes. Lord Brian nodded his head in the direction from which the arrow had come, and they both drew their swords.

Looking at me, Brian said, "At my signal, we will all let go of our horses even as Sir Drogo and I move out to face the enemy. You must remain hidden. Stay low."

"What if there are too many of them?" I inquired, my heart pounding with fear. "What if you are all killed? What should I do?"

"Run a mile or two and find someone who might hide you," he said.

"Can we not all just hide?" I asked in desperation.

"No time!" Drogo whispered, and without another word, they let go of their horses and drew their swords, moving off into the wheat.

I did not want to part with Frija. It seemed that if I would be forced to flee, a horse would be more help than anything. However, I trusted in the word of my men. I let go of the reins, but she remained laying on the ground.

"Very well," I said. "This is where I must leave you, noble Frija. I owe you so much. May we meet again in this life or the next."

I began to crawl along the ground as quietly as I could, striving not to disturb the wheat any more than necessary. I was thankful that the wind was moving the plants a bit on its own.

I heard more cries in the direction of the river and the sound of swords striking each other. Still, I crawled across the damp earth, fallen pieces of wheat scratching my hands and face. When I had made it far enough that I did not fear Frija revealing my position, I pulled my satchel around and reached inside. Where was the dagger Brian had given me? I felt one thing after another, but none of them seemed to be it. Then high above the noise of the wind I heard someone yelling, "Find the bitch! Kill the bitch!" This was followed swiftly by a loud groan.

I felt as cold as ice inside as my hand finally fell upon the weapon. I pulled it out and worked to remove it from its leather case, but my fingers were not working as they normally did, so full of fear was I. *Please, Lord, please!* I prayed. Even as I did, there was another scream of pain closer to me than I would have preferred. I was finally able to remove the knife and clutched it in my hand, crouching low to the ground.

Show no mercy. Plunge it into them, I bid myself. *Do not be afraid of the blood. Do not think: just do.*

I could hear someone close to me, moving through the wheat. I crossed myself and turned to look upon the face of my enemy, hand gripping the dagger, ready to strike … but it was

Reginald, holding his crossbow in one hand and raising the other to stop me.

"It's me, your brother!" he said rather more loudly than I would have preferred.

I exhaled and lowered my weapon as he bent down beside me.

"I saw three of them, and three have fallen," he told me. "Lord Brian and Sir Drogo are searching about for any others, but I think the danger is passed for the moment." He looked at the knife in my hand. "You were ready to stab me with that, I do believe. I saw it in your eyes. You would have done it."

I placed the dagger back in its sheath but continued to hold it. "I decided, you see: this is not how my story ends, in a field far from home, being defiled by some brute and made carrion for crows. I refuse to accept it."

He nodded and said, "Very good, my lady," a smile upon his face.

After a few minutes had passed, Reginald stood and whistled for his companions, waving his arm back and forth.

Very soon, they had both joined us, neither of them hurt and Drogo pulling his horse.

"It was only the three," Brian said. "I saw the farmer and his son. For a shilling, they surrendered their tale. There were only ever three, they said. They arrived last Friday and hacked and dug until they took down part of the bridge. They had been lying in wait ever since. The peasants knew not why they were here and were far too afraid to question them."

"What now?" I asked. "What must we do? I left Frija somewhere back in that direction," I added, pointing for them to see.

"I do not believe we can take the horses over the river. Do you agree, Lord Brian?" Reginald asked.

"I do," he said. "We will have to leave them here and continue on foot."

This did not please me at all. Not only did I hate the idea of parting with perfectly good horses, but I did not think I had the strength to make it to Devizes on foot after all I had been through the past few weeks. I was already in great pain. Brian seemed to read my thoughts and assured me, "There is no other way. We cannot remain here after what has happened, and we cannot ford the river with the animals. We must swim across and continue on the other side. There is no time to waste."

I lowered my head slightly and said, "I cannot swim."

"No matter, you can hold on to me, Your Highness," Drogo offered. "I am strong enough in the water for both of us."

A few minutes later, after we had made a quick effort to remove all traces of the struggle—I refused to look upon the bodies of our fallen enemies—we were standing by the river's bank. Earl Reginald walked in first, followed by Lord Brian and myself next to Drogo. We all waded in until the water reached our shoulders, then the others began swimming as I clung to Drogo's waist. It was difficult going: the water was moving quickly, and although my knight had sworn that I was not too great a burden for him, I feared very much that we would be pulled down. The water was not at all warm to the touch, and once I was full under it felt unbearably cold. At one point, I did get caught in the water and swallowed some of it, causing me to cough and gasp for breath.

"Not far, my lady!" Drogo told me. "Just hold on!"

His arms and legs beat against me as he cut through the water. I was holding on to him with everything I had. Then one of my feet hit upon the river's bottom, followed by the other, and soon I was able to walk on my own again. Reginald and Brian had already reached the shore and were attempting to shake the water out of their clothes when Drogo latched on to the muddy bank with one hand and me with the other, pulling me forward until I too could grab it. Brian reached down and pulled me out, allowing Drogo to see to removing himself. I stood there with my arms pressed against my chest, breathing hard and feeling colder than death itself. I looked back across the river and saw Frija moving through the wheat, uncertain what to do without her mistress.

"Come, let us continue," Reginald said. "We must make it to Devizes before night is upon us."

Furlong after furlong we continued, setting one foot in front of the other. I did not fully know how I was carrying on. I simply imagined what I had seen the night before—the future of England, a line of kings and queens stretching on for generations upon generations, the figure of my son Henry—and allowed its power to push me ahead. We cut through the fields as often as not, for the road seemed full of new peril. To our left a line of hills stretched on for miles. On one of them, I saw the figure of a great horse, its white body standing out against the green.

"They were first cut out in ancient times," Reginald told us, "perhaps by the Romans, or perhaps even earlier. This whole part of the country is full of such traces of the past. It is the beating heart of England."

It was an odd moment for him to give a history lesson, but I was glad of it, for as the pain continued to course through my body, I felt connected to the land over which I ran. Here were the dead still speaking to us, as if they could reach out and touch us. I liked to think that if my ancient fathers did see me in my moment of need, they would pray to the Almighty on my behalf. I could almost hear them bidding me to press on and live to fight another day. I reached once again into the depths of my soul for the will to run a race worthy of remembrance.

To escape is to survive, I told myself. *Forget the pain! Fight on!*

By late afternoon, we were coming near the end of our water and had consumed all the bread. Reginald might have shot some game, but we had no time to stop and cook it. We ran across the face of England, or when I could no longer run, we walked. Every mile, I thought it would be my last, yet every mile, I found enough strength for just one more. Even the men of war beside me were letting up the pace. They had been fighting since the beginning of August, suffering blow after blow, and receiving little more food than myself. Drogo in particular was rather gaunt.

As we were moving down a small hill, my foot caught on a hidden stone—perhaps my too large boots were at fault—and I took a hard fall, rolling for a short way before ending up on my back, staring up at the sky in pain. The others gathered round, their faces full of concern. I looked at my hands, which were bloody and raw where they had hit the ground. Just raising them seemed a great effort, so I let them drop by my sides.

"How much farther, Reginald?" Brian asked, kneeling down and placing a hand on my shoulder.

"Two miles at most, I think," he said. "That is, if I have read the signs correctly."

I closed my eyes and began to mutter. "You all go on. I will lie here … and sleep. Sleep until the ending of the world …"

"Oh no, no, no!" cried Drogo, and before I could protest, he reached down and lifted me until I was standing, then bent down and said, "Climb on my back."

Reginald reached out to support me. I did not want to burden my knight once again, but I sensed that I was not going to make it to Devizes any other way. I made an effort to walk, placing weight on my right foot and then my left, which promptly gave up its hold on the earth. Both Reginald and Brian caught me and Drogo repeated, "With all due respect, I demand it, Your Highness! Climb on my back!"

Too weak to object, I leaned on his back and he rose up, placing one hand under each of my legs as if I were a young child. I placed my arms around his neck, holding on as tightly as I could, and we set off again.

With each step he took, I felt the rhythm of the earth passing beneath us. I leaned my head on his shoulder and looked at the sun painting the sky in shades of red and orange as it sank toward the ground. I closed my eyes and dreamed that I was in Bishop Roger's chamber inside the castle, perched high in the tower, with silk sheets wrapped around my body and colorful tapestries on the walls, a marble basin waiting for me to wash my weary hands. I dreamt of the Doge's palace in Venice, the smell of perfume in the air, the taste of spices. I dreamt that I was sailing down the Rhine, gazing up at the magnificent heights. I dreamt of the garden in Rouen when it was summer and all was in bloom, and the plants were bearing fruit that my sons were picking, their faces covered in juice but smiling wide, their laughter rising up to the sky. I dreamt of a courtyard with a fountain, and in that courtyard my mother stood extending her arms, beckoning me to be wrapped in her embrace and feel the warmth of love eternal.

And then it ended, or rather we stopped. I raised my head and saw that it had grown darker. The first stars were visible and the moon was rising in the sky, but then I turned and looked at what lay directly before us: the castle of Devizes.

"We made it," I whispered. "Drogo, we made it."

He was panting heavily, his shoulders rising and falling, too tired it seemed to say anything. I wiggled my toes and found there was some life in them.

"Let me down," I commanded him. "I can walk from here."

"As you wish," he replied, allowing my legs to drop as I let go of his neck. He immediately bent over and placed his hands on his knees. "The others have gone ahead to the gate. We will hold here for a moment," he said through gasps of breath.

They were as good as his word. Not a minute later, the two of them returned across the bridge and the field, dark figures in the growing gloom.

"Come, my lady," Reginald instructed. "Take my arm. Sir Drogo is utterly spent."

With the strength between us of perhaps one man of able body, we four strode forward toward the main gate of Devizes Castle, and I doubt if in the history of mankind there were ever four travelers happier to reach their destination. When we entered the hall, we were met by a band of servants. Two women offered me greetings of, "Good evening, empress. This way, empress," leading me away from my companions. I began to weep as I looked back at them, somehow in my weariness feeling as if I was about to be parted for ever from those who had saved my life.

"Where are they going?" I asked, half in a daze.

"To their own rooms, Your Highness," one of the women said. "We are taking you to the best one."

"I am so tired," I said weakly. "So very tired."

"We know. You have come so far," the other woman replied. "Let us place you on the bed and get you in some new clothes."

"The bishop's clothes?" I asked. "But he is dead. He cannot have many good ones."

I am sure the women were looking at each other and thinking, *What on earth is wrong with this woman?* All I can say in excuse is that very odd things happen to a person denied food and sleep for too long. At length, they dragged me up the stairs more than I climbed them, and we reached the round chamber I had so envied only two months earlier. Within moments, I felt the silk sheets upon my skin and warm water on my feet.

"Well, I have made it," I said with a smile. "I am finally in heaven."

I then drifted into sleep, departing at least for a few hours from the great cares of my life.

XXI

Rouen, Normandy
August 1167

"Weeping may abide in the evening, but joy comes in the morning."[33] So the great king once wrote when he was delivered from all his fears, but I know no such deliverance. I awake with fierce pain in my chest, as if the mare were still pressed against it. The skin that clings so tightly to my bones is drenched in sweat. I strain to breathe. I can feel the hand of death upon me. Much weeping have I endured in these final hours, but I must not surrender to despair. I will remember that joy which I have always pursued—the thing that has driven me on when naught is left within me but the faint remembrance of hope.

I always knew things would end. I have lived every day with that shadow of death upon me, some times darker than others.

---

33   Psalm 30:5.

But it never was the time, for there was work yet to be done. Now there is nothing left to do but make an end. My Henry rules over his empire, with enough sons that I dare say his line will continue in one form or another. I believed it in those most difficult hours. I believed that we would endure—that England would endure. And beyond that, I believed in something else: I believed in eternity.

A week ago, brother Lawrence wrote to my son and bid him make haste to Rouen. "The thread of your honored mother's life is fraying quickly," he wrote. "She is not long for this world. Come now. Brook no delay." And though my son has oft avoided my call in the past, he did not fail me in this my final hour. He set out with all speed, and very soon we received the message in return: "Ready yourselves for the arrival of the king."

My beloved son was come to see me one last time. I refused to be found upon my sick bed, so I bid Adela arrive early to help me with my preparations. With the first light of day, I heard a knock upon my door. I was already awake, having been raised out of sleep once again by fever. With some great effort, I rolled over and swung my legs down to the floor, placing a hand on the bed post for support.

"Wait one moment!" I called, looking around to see where I had left my veil. I finally spied it upon the small table that sat by the hearth: the one where Lawrence always sits to record my words. I pulled myself up, joints aching, and dragged my body to the table more than walked. Taking the veil in hand, I wrapped it once round my head and then over my mouth. Although the physicians cannot tell me with any certainty if I can pass my disease on to others, I have assumed it is possible and striven not to cough on anyone, including my friend.

"Enter," I muttered weakly, my voice catching in my throat.

I coughed several times, bending over and rubbing my chest. When I recovered my breath and looked up, I was surprised to see it was not Adela who had entered, but her husband, followed by their eldest son, Roger.

"Sir Philip!" I said in surprise. "I did not think to see you this morning."

Both men removed their caps and bowed, then the elder man said, "My lady, it has been far too long. I think it must be half a year since I have had the pleasure of seeing you, though my wife keeps me well informed of your condition."

"You may find that being in my presence is not the pleasure it once was," I replied, coughing again. I looked the younger man up and down. He had long since passed his father in height and seemed to combine the best of both his parents in terms of his appearance.

"How are your studies, young man?" I asked. "You were in Paris for quite some time. Have you decided if you will pursue the law or enter the Church? If the latter, I know several men who would be happy to aid you in your pursuit."

"Yes, my time in Paris was wonderful," he answered, smiling and turning over his cap in his hands, "but upon my return, I found something even more wonderful close to home. Her name is Joanna."

I laughed weakly and shook my head. "Another win for the law!"

"Just what this world needs: another lawyer!" Sir Philip said, rolling his eyes.

Ignoring his comment, I asked Roger, "And what does your mother say to this?"

"She approves very much of my decision. She wants us to wed as soon as possible."

"And produce a full brood, no doubt," his father added.

"I'm surprised she made no mention of this to me before now," I said to myself as much as them.

"It is not official yet. I have yet to gain the blessing of the lady's family," Roger replied.

I smiled. "Just make sure when you do enter the family way, if God sees fit to bless you with a daughter, you will name her—"

"Mathilda? Of course!" he said. "I am sure if I had any sisters, they would have received that name."

The voice of my friend sounded forth from the passage behind them. "But it was God's will that I should be one female only among all you males."

Her son and husband moved to the side to allow her to enter, and they were promptly greeted with some harsh words.

"Why are you just standing here talking?" she inquired, hands on her hips, looking from one man to the other. "I asked you to collect the empress' things and take them out to the carriage."

"Yes, mother," Roger replied, then turning to me he asked, "My lady, where is the chest I am meant to carry?"

I pointed to a corner of the room he had not yet observed, where the chest in question sat ready for its journey. He bent down and lifted it, then departed for the outer yard.

"I'll see to the horses. They looked as if they could use some water," Philip said, turning to leave.

"Wait!" I called, leading me to cough again. "Before you leave, Sir Philip, I thought I should tell both of you that I have had Lawrence include the story of how you came to wed in my account. We just finished writing it."

Adela smiled broadly, but Philip said, "I seem to remember we passed many months when she refused me her attention."

Here the look on my friend's face changed immediately and she objected, "I refused you nothing! I did not know your intent. If you had spoken up sooner—"

"How could I when we never had a moment alone?" he asked, laughing.

"Surely this is of no consequence," I argued. "The point is that you did finally come together, and you loved each other very much. I trust that has not changed, despite the passing of many years."

"Oh no!" Philip said, looking at his wife with love in his eyes. "Nothing will ever change that: not if the whole earth were destroyed and the heavens came crashing down."

Adela smiled, her face taking on that same glow I had seen many years before, and though she spoke not a word, it was clear she had the same thought.

A few minutes later, I was dressed and ready to depart. I used one hand to hold a cloth over my mouth while I clung to Sir Philip's arm with the other. When he had helped me into the carriage, I leaned back against a cushion that Adela had placed there for my comfort, worn out by the small effort. As we rode across the river to the royal palace, I felt every dip in the road as if it were a blow. I closed my eyes and drew the air in and out, in and out. *How many more times will I be able to do that?* I wondered.

Upon arriving at the palace, I was helped out of the carriage and past the garden of herbs into the outer portion of the garden where the roses grow. For just a moment, I felt myself transported to another time: days I have never forgotten, when I was young and walked among the trees with the vigor of youth in my breast. In the present, I sat upon a stone bench that had been there since the time of my grandfather, King William, and the others left me.

There were only a few clouds in the sky and the sun was shining brightly. Somewhere near, a bird was chirping—perhaps a robin. I glanced forward to the break in the hedge from which I foresaw that the king would stride forth. I thought back over the course of my life and his. Out of many dark hours, the light of his birth had broken. Against all odds, he came forth and survived to be seated upon the throne of his fathers. Three sons the Lord granted me, and only this one remains. He is everything to me.

Then I saw him turn the corner and walk through the break in the hedge, clothed in raiment fit for his office woven with gold thread, and a great chain about his neck. The royal crown shone brightly upon his head. I remembered when he came into the world naked and bloody. The midwives wrapped him in cloth to keep out the cold of the world. No one would mistake him for that child now.

He strode forth boldly and called, "Here I am, mother!"

"Do not come too close!" I begged, raising a hand. "I am ill." Even as I said this, I coughed into my cloth again.

"I know. That is why I have come," he said.

I lowered the cloth and asked, "Do you intend to work some miracle? To raise me up from my death bed? Oh, I am sure you would. You would bend the heavens to your will—you would halt the very tide if it suited you, exceeding even the deeds of Canute, but you cannot hold back death. You cannot keep me here."

"Will you not let me sit with you?" he inquired, his eyes beseeching me. "Please, I am not afraid."

You ought to be, I thought. *You have four sons, but none of them are ready to rule. You are not in the favor of the Church.*

Feeling that I could not deny him, I consented, "Very well, but I will cover my face. If you were to fall ill on my account, I would never forgive myself."

I pulled one side of my veil across my mouth and draped it over my opposite shoulder as he sat down to my left and placed his hand on mine. I remembered how I once held his tiny fingers, gazing upon them in wonder.

"So, what do the physicians say?" he inquired.

"I may live a month or perhaps two, but I shall not see another Christmas."

"So soon?!" he said in alarm. "You still had some strength at the beginning of this summer!"

I smiled weakly—wearily. "Strength is deceitful, my son. The disease was doing its work."

"They say you eat hardly anything. I wish you would take something. I wish you would fight."

"I would take more food if I had the appetite, but there is no fighting this, and anyway, I have grown weary of fighting. I have been at war all my life. I long for eternal peace. Therefore, let me say a few things to you. I beg you, hear me out."

He nodded. "Whatever you wish to say, I will hear it."

"First, I pray you do all you can to reconcile with Archbishop Thomas."

"Ha!" he cried. "He is a swine and a traitor!"

"I know what he is, but you must not cling to bitterness, my son. You must not allow the wound to fester. Find a way to make peace with the Church that your rule may flourish."

He bit his lower lip, exhaling loudly. "Very well, I will try. What else?"

"Reconcile with your wife. Put the other one away."

He removed his hand from mine. "Why? Why should I not enjoy the company of the woman I love rather than a woman who I begin to doubt has any heart at all?"

"Because you made a promise," I told him, working hard to draw the words forth from my lungs, "and I know what it is to be a woman whose husband fails to keep his promises."

"Eleanor does not deserve your compassion. She is no saint."

"No, but she is the mother of your children, so reconcile with her. Third, be a father to your sons."

"What do you mean by that?" he inquired, crossing his arms and scowling.

"I mean you give them land and titles, but nothing of yourself. Be a father to them now before they are grown and it is too late."

I only just got the words out before I coughed several times. When I had recovered, he spoke again.

"Here you go too far. I have done right by my sons. I have treated them the same as my father treated me—the way great lords have always treated their sons," he declared, as if this would impress me. "I am readying them for what lies ahead. I have seen to their every need."

"It is not only the body and the mind which have needs, but also the human soul," I said quietly.

"You mean I am not around them enough, but I note that you were absent for most of my childhood."

I nodded sadly. "That has pained me to no end. I pray you forgive me."

Here he shook his head. "No, you mistake me! You did what you had to do. Even so, I am doing what I have to do. A king must be on the move, seeing to his affairs everywhere. You know this."

My chest was aching, and I rubbed it again. I had no breath for a long argument. Stifling another cough, I said, "I simply ask you to set your mind to reconciliation."

"Because it is the Christian way?"

"Because these are the persons who have the power to destroy you. Therefore, heed my words."

With a sigh, he told me, "I will do my best, but I cannot control the actions of others, and I will become no man's vassal. If the archbishop refuses to abide by the laws of this land, then I cannot possibly reconcile with him."

"I simply wish my last words to you to be ones of pe—"

I could not continue. My lungs were caught in flame. I began coughing, gagging, struggling for breath. I held the cloth to my mouth and bid myself take in the air, then out, then in, then out. My son reached to take hold of me, patting me on the back.

"Mother!" he cried. "Should I send for help? Should I fetch a physician?"

The coughing ceased. I pulled the cloth away and saw the marks of blood. The life was being drained from me with each gasp. I placed the thing down on the bench once again.

"No ... no," I whispered. "There is no need for all that. It has passed. The moment has passed."

"How often does this happen?" he asked, continuing to rub my back.

"First it was once a week, then once a day ... now once an hour," I told him, placing the veil back over my mouth. "Each time I recover, but sooner or later I will not. One day my strength will utterly fail, and there will be no more breath in me. All that will be left is eternity."

There were tears in my eyes, but the far greater surprise was that there were tears in my son's eyes. It was not like him to cry, though he was of such a humor that he might have drawn tears from laughter. He wrapped me in his embrace, despite my warnings. I ought to have forbidden it, but he was my son, and I feared it was the last time I would ever be held by him. So, I let him do it, and I felt the warmth of human love: that most blessed gift upon this earth, the breaking in of eternity.

"I cannot tell you how much it grieves me to see you suffer like this," he said. "You have not merited such a miserable death."

"Have I not?" I asked, pulling back. "I hardly know what any of us merit. I suspect when time has run its course and the living and the dead are brought to judgment, we will be rather surprised to see who is seated at the Lord's right hand and who is sent down into the fiery hell. But I must abide that judgment. I am almost ready for it now. Only one thing remains."

"What—are you to take the veil?"

"No, I speak of the account I am writing for your daughter: the one you are sending off to the Saxons."

Yes, my son's daughter, the one named after me: Princess Mathilda, quiet and kind. Only eleven years old, she is to be sent any day to wed Duke Henry of Saxony and Bavaria. He is a man in middle age, already wed once but in need of children.

"I know you believe her too young to marry, but I thought you would approve of a match within the Empire," my son said.

"That shows how little you know both the Empire and me," I concluded, coughing once again. "Duke Henry is a Welf. They have been at odds with the House of Hohenstaufen since the time I was there. They are opposed to … my husband's … kin." Here I also coughed.

"But they are not your descendants, so why should you care?"

What a question! I could see he had much yet to learn, but it would not be from me.

"Because I remember, my son. Memory is a powerful thing that we cannot escape. But in any case, I worry very much about my dear young Mathilda being sent off to marry a far older man. It is a repeat of my own situation. I know your decision is final, but I seek to grant her all the help I can. That is why I am leaving her an account. I have made it up to the years of the war, but I do not know how much longer I can continue. Even so, I will try. Lawrence is helping me."

"Will you allow me to read this magnificent account before you send it off to my daughter?" he asked with a note of derision.

"Certainly not! It is not for your eyes, nor those of any man. It is for my daughters: first Mathilda, then any daughters after her, until one day, if God so chooses, it will come into the hands of women who live in a kinder age when justice at last is done, and they will use it well."

He furrowed his brow. "I do not follow."

"There is no need. Oh, my son!" I said, grabbing his hand. "When I am gone, do not remember me as I am now: lifeless and wasted. Remember me when I was at my best."

His eyes were lit by a sudden fire and he smiled. "Riding across the plains of England, with Uncle Reginald and Lord Brian at your side! All the chroniclers speak of your bravery."

"They give five words to my bravery and five hundred to my arrogance."

"Even so, you endured much and suffered much, for glory and for England!"

I smiled weakly and shook my head. "No, not for glory. I never cared about that. Nor even, I think, for England, or at least not for England as it was then."

"For what, then?"

I took another breath and raised my hand to hold his face. "For the England that will be. For you, my son. Everything I ever did, I did for you."

My brother had warned me that at certain times of year, the city of Gloucester suffers a deluge. He never spoke truer words! I arrived there in the middle of September under a hard rain the like of which I have seldom witnessed. I had been in such a poor state during my brief stay in Devizes that my guardians determined I could neither walk nor ride. In addition to a foot that had been injured, I was quickly falling ill with a malady of the lungs such as one often sees in winter time, but perhaps on account of my weakness, it struck me sooner. I could not possibly stay in Devizes: it was still too close to the false queen's

army. Having no true carriage, they placed me on a simple lit-
ter between two horses, and in that manner, I was brought all
the way to the royal town of Gloucester, one of the few places
we could be certain to find friends.

Oh, how it rained day and night! I lay in bed gazing at the
window on the opposite wall, where drop after drop struck it
and descended slowly, running down the glass to the stone below, and finally to the cold earth waiting to receive it.

The very saints weep over this defeat, I thought.

The ladies who were assigned to my care would not allow
me to leave the chamber. "You need a full month of sleep!" one
of them declared, and she was right. While I had been in the
middle of that retreat, my body and spirit had both risen up to
guide me. I was carried as if on some divine wind, with visions
of greatness placed before my eyes. But once I had ceased running, I felt more clearly the pain I had been carrying all along.
I was not without hope, but every hour was bitter. I preferred to
sleep if only to escape the thoughts that tormented me.

Earl Reginald and Lord Brian had departed as soon as they
could in the direction of Oxford, there to seek information
about our friends and the movements of the wolf of Ypres. Five
persons were of greatest interest to me. Earl Robert, naturally,
was chief in my thoughts. Was he among the dead or the living?
King David of Scotland was of no less import. What of Philip
and Adela? I feared for them every hour. And had Earl Miles
been able to slip through the enemy's net? I had so many questions in need of answers.

As the days went by, we began to receive them. The first answer arrived at our threshold shortly after Reginald and Brian
departed, with no horse and no armor left to him. It was Earl
Miles of Gloucester, who as it turned out had fled cross country on foot, abandoning everything that might slow him down.
He had fallen off his horse in the forest just before the trap

at Stockbridge. Seeing the enemy round about and knowing himself to be one of the chief persons they would seek for their prisoner, he turned and ran, making his way up to Wherwell by end of day. There he was able to discover the sad tale of what happened when William of Ypres came calling.

As you may remember, our men under John the Marshal had fortified the abbey there. They were surrounded by a host of Flemings, and the nuns who were unable to escape in time fell into their greedy hands. Those brutes had no respect for the holy vows the women had taken but saw only handfuls of flesh for their own pleasure, much as a hungry man looks upon a pound of meat. John Marshal stood bravely with his men in the church, refusing to surrender, for he knew that we were fleeing from Winchester that very day, and the longer he could force the wolf to remain in Wherwell, the better chance we would have of reaching safety. He remained where he was, even when the Flemings set fire to the church and the rest of the men fled the place, seeking to avoid a painful death. Lord John did not even flee when the lead of the roof melted and fell upon him. He remained there until the Flemings gave him up for dead, took their booty, and departed. It was only after they had gone that he stumbled out, covered in soot and having lost one of his eyes, his skin marked by the fire's hand. When I heard this story, I recognized that it was his bravery that had delayed the Flemings long enough for us to make it to Ludgershall without meeting them. I owed my life to John the Marshal.

Sadly, Miles could tell me nothing of the others—nothing of Earl Robert or King David, and nothing of the greater part of our men except to say that things must have gone badly. I therefore continued to watch and wait. When I was strong enough, I began walking each day to the abbey church of Saint Peter to say my prayers. There I was able to meet again with my confessor of former days, Abbot Gilbert. I spent many hours sitting and staring at the fire in the hall of the castle, thinking back to the happy hours I had once spent with my sons. I longed for nothing more than to see their faces.

About a week after I had arrived in Gloucester, by which point I had recovered from both injury and illness, I was sitting in the solar upon that same seat by the fire I had so often preferred before, the rain coming down outside as usual. I held my mother's paternoster in my hand, and as each new worry occupied my mind, I pushed the beads to the left with my thumb, giving those fears over to God. It was not any saintly instinct in myself that caused me to do this, but the knowledge that I had no control over anything. How could I keep such things within myself when I was not made to hold them? Desperation had pushed me into the arms of the Almighty.

The sparks flew up and danced as the flames cracked. I had one fur draped over my legs for warmth and another covering my shoulders. I pulled the latter closer to myself with my free hand, continuing to move the beads with the other. Then I heard the door open behind me and turned to see a sight that filled my heart with joy: my brother Robert, returned to me!

At least, I thought it was, so like him did the image appear. But then my eyes perceived the deception, for it was not my brother but my nephew William who stood before me. He looked just like his father had in his younger days, before the cares of this world had turned his hair gray and drawn lines upon his face.

"Empress Mathilda, dearest aunt!" he hailed me with a bow. "I bring news."

"Praise the Lord! Poor thing, you are wet from head to toe! Leave your things to dry by the fire and have a seat next to me."

He nodded and removed his cloak, gloves, and boots, setting them out before the hearth. He then grabbed a chair sitting by one of the two windows and carried it over, placing it near mine. As he sat, I observed that while it was his custom to shave his face, he had clearly not done so in many days. I took this to mean that he had been constantly on the move from place to place since the rout in Winchester.

"It does me good to see you, William," I said. "Now, let go your burden: tell me everything you know."

"I have been hither and thither across the south of England," he explained. "I spent time at Wallingford, where the good lady was kind enough to grant me hospitality, and also at the castle of Oxford. I learned the whole sad tale. Who would you like to know about first?"

"Your father," I told him, still clutching the beads in my right hand.

He breathed in deeply and began his tale. "Alive but a prisoner of the enemy. He fell into the trap at Stockbridge and was taken by the earl of Surrey and his men, who in turn handed him over to the false queen. He has been brought to Rochester Castle. I have sought out information as to his condition from any person who would take my money. From what I can gather, he is in no immediate danger. They respect him enough to treat him well. He is even free to roam about the town—under the close watch of the enemy, of course. I received one letter from him before I came this way in which he said that he is trying to make a deal with them for his release, but they will accept no one less than Stephen himself in return. My father is pressing them to at least agree to release all our prisoners in exchange for Stephen, but they feel they have the upper hand given their victory at Winchester, so they are refusing to part with any but the earl alone."

I had foreseen that they would require the usurper in exchange for my brother, and thus there was little pain at this news. I quickly absorbed it and moved on to further questions. "What other prisoners? Tell me of the king of Scotland."

"Escaped to the North. He was separated from the company long before Stockbridge, at the time we were set upon from the East. He made it back to his own lands through bribery, for I am told he fell into enemy hands more than once. Fortunately, those hands were greedy for coin."

I placed one palm over my heart and closed my eyes, offering up a brief prayer of thanks to God, then continued. "That at least is good news. Do you happen to know anything of Sir Philip of Honfleur? He was traveling with my lady Adela, his wife."

"Nothing, I'm afraid," he said sadly. "I had not heard anything of Earl Miles either until I arrived here and found him in residence. I saw Earl Reginald and Lord Brian when they arrived in Oxford. Brian was of a mind to return to Wallingford, for that is likely where the enemy will strike next."

"What has the enemy taken in terms of land?" I asked, afraid to know the answer.

"All of Hampshire, but not much beyond. I am sure they will press toward Devizes when they can, but it remains in our hands as of this moment. Our port at Wareham is still open as well, so we are in communication with Normandy."

I breathed deeply and nodded my head. "Honestly, this news you bring me is about as good as I could have hoped. It seems we have lost a battle only and not the entire war. I do not mean to say that I am not filled with concern for your father: not an hour passes that I do not grieve his thralldom and pray to God for his deliverance. You understand, I hope."

"I do, my lady," he said. "I too feared far worse. I knew nothing of your own fate until the lords who had been with you arrived from the West. None of us knew—we feared you had been killed. When we learned how you pressed on through danger and hardship, slipping out of the enemy's grasp, our spirits were raised ... I cannot tell you how much ... that is, how glad we were."

I made no reply but stared into the fire, my mind turning over every element of the struggle this way and that, attempting to find a way forward. Things were not as grim as I had feared, but there was no question that we had lost much strength since the beginning of summer. Then again, our strength may have never been as great as we thought.

"My lady," William said quietly, and I turned to look at him. "I know this defeat has placed you in a difficult position. If you deem it necessary, I can step in and oversee the family estates until the war is over. You have still Earl Miles, Earl Reginald, Lord Brian, and the king of Scotland."

"There is no question of that," I assured him.

"Count Geoffrey has met with victory in Normandy. Perhaps you could call him here for a time—"

"No!" I said firmly. "I will not leave your father to rot in jail."

"Some may ask why not," he replied, "when the cost of his release is so high and there are other captains in the world. As much as I long to see my father given his freedom, he knew the danger when he entered your service."

I leaned forward in my chair, allowing the fur to slide off my shoulders. "You ask why not. Very well, I will give you three reasons. First, because I cannot possibly win this war without him. No matter what anyone else says, I know there is no man in England who can match him in battle. Second, because when a lord pledges loyalty to me, placing his person in danger to uphold my rule, I pledge in return to do all in my power to see to his welfare and keep him from harm."

I had raised a finger as I recited each of these reasons, and now I lifted a third. "Lastly, because he is my brother and I love him. We have had our disagreements over the years. I have not always treated him as well as he deserved, and he has been too harsh with me at times. But through it all, he has stood by my side, and I am not about to leave him to some ghastly doom. I lost one brother to the sea. I will not lose another to my own selfishness."

He nodded and whispered, "So be it."

Immediately following my nephew's report, I took two actions. First, I drafted a letter and sent it to Rochester making clear my will that Count Stephen of Mortain be granted his freedom in exchange for the release of Earl Robert of Gloucester. They were the most bitter words I have ever written. Second, I announced my departure for Oxford, there to establish my court again. Although Gloucester was no doubt safer, lying farther away from the lands of the enemy, it was a more difficult site from which to organize my forces, such as they were at that point. Seated in the center of England, Oxford was the perfect place to draw men to my side and maintain some pressure on the friends of the usurper.

Knowing as I did that Stephen would attempt to make a show of authority as soon as possible following his release, I spoke with Earl Miles about the coming days and what turns the war might take. He was keen to strengthen our hold on the Thames Valley, beginning with Wallingford, progressing up river to Oxford, and continuing into the West. This seemed a good idea to me, so we traveled cross country and arrived at the castle of Oxford on the feast of Michaelmas.

The castellan himself, Lord Robert D'Oyly, was ill and could not greet us, so I was led to my chamber by his eldest natural son: Henry, a man of no more than twenty years. I had only the one chest for him to carry, and most of the items in it were borrowed. It was strange indeed to think that I, the daughter of a great king, was left with so few possessions in the world. When we reached the same chamber I always used in the Saint George Tower, he placed the chest down by the window and I sat upon the bed, my gaze wandering about the room. Everything seemed to be just as I had left it.

Standing up to his full height, which was not all that great, Henry asked, "Do you have a maid to help you put these things away?"

"I ought to have one, but she is sadly lost to me at present," I replied.

"The one who used to be with you?" he pressed further.

"Yes, the same. She and her husband fled from the battle at Winchester and I have not seen them since."

"The lady Adela, right? She is wed to Philip de Honfleur."

My interest suddenly high, I looked upon him intently and inquired, "How do you know that?"

"Because they are here," he explained. "They arrived the day before last. My father and I recognized them and allowed them to stay."

"What … how … God be praised!" I stammered, rising to my feet. "Can it really be so?!"

"Yes, I can go get her if you wish," Henry answered. "We would have sent word to you, but it seems you did us one better and arrived."

"Bring her here at once!" I cried, my face breaking into a broad smile. "Oh, such excellent news you have given me. I ought to kiss you!"

His brow furrowed slightly and I suspected he was thinking, *Please don't.* But of course, I had not really meant to do it. I was simply overcome with joy that my friend and her husband were safe, though I still had no knowledge of Philip's condition. After all, the last time I had seen him, he had only just escaped the grasp of death and his health was still very much in doubt.

Five minutes later, Adela entered the room. I was naturally glad to see her, but to this gladness was added my confusion at the sight of her apparel. She had on the simple dark tunic of a nun, tied around the waist with a cord, but she had no covering on her head at all. Rather, her hair was held up in braids.

"Oh, my lady, how good it is to see you again!" she declared, moving forward to embrace me.

I was only too happy to embrace her in return, but when we parted, I told her, "I confess myself perplexed."

"Why?" she asked, tipping her head to one side.

"Why are you wearing the garment of one of the sisters? Last I left you, you had gone in the opposite direction, though I see from your bare head you have not taken a veil, so perhaps Sir Philip has reason to hope."

"Oh, this!" Adela cried, lifting up her skirt ever so slightly and laughing. "It belonged to a brother, actually: a brother of Malmesbury."

"Malmesbury?! What on earth were you doing there?"

"We were making our way up from Salisbury," she replied, as if it made complete sense. "But I suppose you will want to know what we were doing in Salisbury."

"I think you had better tell me everything that has happened since that day we fled Winchester, for there is nothing of sense in your tale that I can find."

She nodded her head in agreement and we sat next to each other on the end of the bed.

"How is your Philip? Let us start there," I offered.

"Oh, very well! He has some pain at the site of his wound, of course, but the skin is mostly healed from where they stitched it."

"And no more sign of infection?" I asked, still feeling uneasy.

"Not since we left Winchester—a miracle of the Almighty."

"Excellent!" I declared, feeling a wave of relief. "Now, tell me how you were able to escape that day."

Here she sighed and closed her eyes for just a moment, no doubt looking back upon the hour of dread.

"We were in the wood," she whispered, lids still shut. "All around us was chaos. The enemy was falling upon us on all sides. The line was breaking apart. I clung to him so tightly." Here she grasped her shoulders in remembrance of the moment, opening her eyes. "I prayed to Saint Romain for deliverance. I saw a knight coming at us upon his horse, his sword aloft. Philip reached up and grabbed his arm, thrusting it back. It only threw the man off balance for a moment, but it was long enough for Philip to direct us off the path and deeper into the forest. We were moving fast, jerking this way and that, plowing through shrubs, ducking to avoid branches, receiving scrapes here and there.

"'We must get back to the others!' I cried in despair.

"'To go back is death,' he replied.

"'But the empress! She needs us!' I protested.

"He said nothing but continued to lead us farther away from the battle, flying beneath the trees until there was no sound but the leaves beneath our horse's hooves. I recognize now that we could not have helped you if we had remained."

"No, all who remained were taken prisoner, and in any case, your Philip was in no state to fight. It is a wonder that he was able to turn even one man back," I assured her.

"He did suffer some real pain as a result, for it was on the side where his wound is," she acknowledged. "We rode on and on for miles. I lost all sense of time. At some point, we crossed the river. We tried to use the sun to find our way, but neither of us knew the land well, having spent most of our lives in Normandy. Philip was certain that if we continued north, we would find the road to Ludgershall, and at length we did come across a road that seemed to be of great import, for it was wide and we could see the marks from carts that had passed by in either direction.

"'Those must have been our supplies on their way to Andover and Wherwell,' he said. 'If we go to the left, we will end up in Ludgershall.'

"It was growing late and the sun was low in the sky. We very much hoped we would make it before darkness fell—"

"But you said you were in Salisbury," I interrupted. "Did you take the wrong road?"

"Now we come to it," she said, nodding. "We thought we were moving northwest, but we were actually traveling southwest, so the road went on for longer than we thought possible without arriving at our destination. By the time the sun was setting, Philip sensed something was wrong, but at that point we needed a place to rest for the night, and our best chance of finding one was to continue along the road and hope we came across someone—anyone, really, who would take us in. And that is when we came upon it: Salisbury, or Sarum as some call it. There is an inn there on the High Street called The Rose. We had a few coins on us, and they suited for a night's stay.

"We were fortunate that the city had remained faithful to you. I still had on my man's clothes, so I cannot imagine what the keeper of the inn and his wife must have thought. The long day's ride had worn Philip down and it became clear that he needed a long rest before continuing, so given our lack of coin, I appealed to the lady of the house to let me cook and clean for them for a few days in exchange for our residence there. But when she heard that we were newly wed, she took real pity on us and let us continue on free of charge, feeding us three meals a day and providing hot water for us to bathe. She brought me all that I needed to clean my husband's wound. While I was there, I had a chance to see the cathedral. Is it not magnificent?"

"I wouldn't know. I have never been," I said bitterly.

"Oh, I am sorry. You have lived here so much longer, I assumed you must have been. In any case, after we had stayed there three days, Philip was much stronger and ready to move. They gave us a sackful of food for our journey and even repaired one of our horse's shoes. May the Lord bless them for their goodness to us! We knew by that point that you would have passed on to Devizes, so we rode north across the plain, staying to the west of the Avon. Many ancient stones lie along that way. We even saw the great henge! Have you seen it, my lady?"

I sighed, my bitterness increasing. "No, I have not, though I dearly wish to do so."

"Well, it is a wonder to behold. You really should visit some time," she continued happily, failing to observe my frustration. "We arrived at Devizes by midday and found that you had gone to the West with naught but Earl Reginald and Lord Brian for company."

"Drogo was with me as well."

"Ah! I am glad to hear it. We followed after you, arriving at the abbey of Malmesbury that evening. There we found such hospitality as I have seldom enjoyed in all my days." She gave me a knowing look and said, "Of course, you have always provided the very best for me, my lady, but I have usually been about the business of caring for the boys or caught up in the travails of war. The monks were kind enough to grant me the only clothing they had for me to wear, which was one of their habits. After some discussion, we decided that you must have reached Gloucester by that point and were in good care, so—I hope you will forgive me, my lady—when the monks offered us the chance to stay in one of their rooms for a time, we took it. We remained for a full week. They were able to see to Philip's health better than anyone else in the kingdom could have done, except perhaps your old friend, Grimbald. They offered us separate rooms but I was most eager to remain with my husband. Every day, the pain of his wound lessened and he recovered some of his former vigor. We took long walks through the gardens and saw the treasures of the library. We even met the chronicler, William! The sound of the choir in the church: it was divine! Simply being there was the best medicine for our souls. Mind you, we had not been able before then to … well, you can guess my meaning …"

I looked at her with wide eyes. "Do you mean to say that you enjoyed carnal pleasures in a house of God?"

"You make it sound as if we committed some sin!" she said, taken aback. "We are husband and wife. It is no shame for us to be in the married way."

"Yes, but …" I stammered, placing a hand on my forehead. "How can I put this? You were dressed as a monk, in a house of God …"

"No, no! We were in the guest house!" she objected. "And to be honest, my lady," she continued in a whisper, a look of pure mischief on her face, "neither of us was wearing anything."

Perhaps I ought to have laughed at this, but truth be told, I was feeling rather jealous that while I had been dragged cross country half dead, my friend had been on a love tour of England's finest sites before enjoying a week of married bliss such as I had never known. Therefore, I determined that I must scold her at least a little.

"But to do such things among the virginal! You taunt those who have vowed themselves to the Lord."

She dropped her chin just a little and looked up at me much as a guilty dog.

"Was it so very bad, my lady?"

I patted her on the head. "Fear not, Adela. At least someone is enjoying the pleasures of life during this war. I take it at some point you heard the news that I was gone to Oxford?"

"Indeed. We came to join your court again."

"Well, I am glad to have you both here. We are in a bad way: perhaps the worst since I came to England. I will need all the help I can get."

"You will always have it from me, Your Highness," she promised.

On the Nones of November, the feast day of saints Zacharias and Elizabeth, I made for the priory of Saint Frideswide that lies just off Aldate's Street. That is the house founded by the woman also called Frithuswith in the ancient English tongue, daughter of one of the kings of old. Having pledged her virginity to the Lord, she was pursued by Algar of Mercia for his bride. He followed her all the way to Oxford, where the Almighty struck his eyes and caused him to walk about blind. In celebration of her deliverance, she founded the house that now bears her name, and there her relics remain. Her story made me think of my own mother, who was pursued even into a nunnery by the great men of the land who desired to be bound with her royal blood.

I had heard that Earl Robert would soon be joining us, free from his prison in Rochester. The usurper had first been released in Bristol, leaving the false queen and his son as hostages in his place. Upon reaching Winchester, he would meet with my brother and complete the next part of the exchange.

"He will attempt to win over the earl with great promises," Miles had warned me. "I know Earl Robert is the most faithful of men that walk the face of the earth, but even so, I am ill at ease."

For myself, I had no such fear. Once I had reason to doubt my brother, but he remained true. There was naught of the traitor in him. I therefore went to the priory to pray not for my brother's loyalty, but his safety. As much as I trusted him,

I had no such faith in the usurper. Who could forget how he had betrayed the bishops after promising them they would not be harmed?

I was greeted at the western gate by the prior, one Robert of Cricklade, who led me into the abbey grounds. My few companions remained at the back of the nave as I walked with the prior past bay after bay of columns and arches, the sun peeking through each window in turn and setting the shadows to flight.

"The Chapel of Our Lady will suit for your devotion," he told me.

This was an interesting comment, for he seemed to give a great deal of consideration to my comfort, when in truth it was the only chapel in which women were permitted to pray. I said nothing but continued to walk just behind him, my prayer book and rosary clutched in my hands. When we had almost reached the altar, we turned just to the left and entered the Lady Chapel, which in truth was only a small space fulfilling that purpose until a larger one could be built. Here a hundred candles burned on each side, as if the very air were made of flame. The familiar chevron pattern, so beloved of all the Normans, could be seen in places above, and just below it was a large window of stained glass in which the Virgin sat clothed in purple robes, her holy son in her arms.

"I will leave you to your prayers," the prior said with a bow, his skirt flowing gently as he turned on the spot and left the way we had come.

I looked down at the book in my hands and the paternoster that had been to hell and back with me. I raised them to my lips and kissed them each in turn, then dropped to my knees upon the tiles, which formed a great mosaic interrupted every so often by images of lions and griffins. I did not see what these beasts had to do with Our Lady, but I gave the matter no further thought. I set my eyes upon the image before me and prayed.

Salve, Regina, Mater misericordiæ,
vita, dulcedo, et spes nostra, salve.
Ad te clamamus exsules filii Hevæ,
Ad te suspiramus, gementes et flentes
in hac lacrimarum valle.[34]

But my thoughts could not be kept in check. As much as I attempted to set them upon the Almighty and beg the prayers of the Virgin, I could not help but imagine what was taking place in Winchester. Perhaps they had already met, or perhaps it was happening that very hour: Stephen of Blois and Robert of Gloucester, in discussion together. Would it be at Wolvesey Palace or Winchester Castle? Surely nowhere else in the city would do, for Bishop Henry had burned it to the ground. Would the younger brother of Blois attempt to join the elder in that conversation? No doubt he would, but Robert would not allow it. After what the bishop had done—the lies and the deceit, the spilling of blood, the destruction of much that was good—he would avoid the bishop like the plague.

Even so, I imagined them: brother Robert and cousin Stephen, sitting alone by a hearth, perhaps savoring some wine the false queen was able to bring in from Flanders. Would my brother drink it or suspect it of carrying deadly poison? Yes, I could see it all. Stephen would speak first.

"Let us end it, you and me."

---

34 Common modern English translation: "O, holy Queen, Mother of Mercy, / Hail our life, our sweetness and our hope. / To thee do we cry, poor banished children of Eve; / To thee do we send up our sighs, mourning and weeping / in the vale of tears."

And Earl Robert, shaking his head, would reply, "We have not the power to end it."

"What do you require?" the villain would ask. "Up to half my kingdom, it is yours."

"It is not your kingdom to offer," my brother would assure him, and from there the conversation would continue.

"May I ask you a question, cousin?"

"If you must."

"Why do you keep company with that shrew? You have sacrificed so much, and I cannot think for what."

"I have not sacrificed that which matters most: honor, pride, justice, the rule of law," the earl would say.

"It seems to me that you have turned your back on all the traditions of this land to follow a lord who is no lord at all. You are the son of a great king and yet you seem to count it a thing of little value, showing no care for your manhood." Yes, the usurper would surely make such a reply. He was obsessed with this conception of his own sex.

Here Earl Robert would answer, "I think that you and I have very different ideas of what it means to be a man of honor. Which one of us has stayed true to the wishes of that king you call great? Which one of us is fighting to see his will done? Who has placed the good of the commonwealth ahead of his own?"

Stephen would attempt to change the subject. "You know what I think? I think this is not about the countess of Anjou at all. I know exactly when your rebellion began: on that day in the Tower, when I asked to swear the oath first on account of my birth. From that moment, you were my enemy. I admit my words were harsh. I should not have spoken them of a man as great as yourself. But how much am I to pay for one moment? You attempt to take back your honor in this pointless rebellion, but I wonder that you cannot see how it dishonors you to take commands from that woman—to be sent hither and thither according to her every desire. I heard how she treated you at Oxford: how she shamed you in front of all your men. If you had any doubt about her character before then, you must see now that she is a monstrous harpy from the pit of hell. She will stop at nothing until she has made every man her eunuch. Here I sit willing to crown you with honor. Say the word and I will not only restore to you everything you have lost but grant you far more. Cornwall and Devon are yours. Oxford is yours. What else do you require? You see how I am ready to compromise."

"I wonder that you are willing to do so," Robert might say.

The usurper would nod his head and admit, "There will be no peace in England or Normandy until you and I stand on the same side."

"Or one of us falls. If you are as strong as you pretend to be and I am such a fool, then cut me down on the field of battle. Make an end of my rebellion and save Oxford for yourself."

"I may yet have the chance if you will not submit, but I would rather have your loyalty, cousin. Will you give it?"

And here would be the moment: the moment that Earl Robert of Gloucester would make clear that he was a man who could not be bought, even by one who claims to be a king.

"That I cannot do, for I am bound by honor to the lady of the English, the Empress Mathilda whose hand I kissed that day in the Tower, or have you forgotten that part of the story? I am not so petty as to start a war over a single word of scorn, but I remember what came shortly after it. We both knelt and placed our hands upon the Holy Rood. We promised to defend the right of the empress and the heirs of her body with our own lives. You are the one who has broken faith, not me. You are the one in rebellion against the laws of this land and the will of God."

"How can God will a woman to rule? Have you not read the scriptures?"

I knew my cousin would respond in such a manner, for he had attempted to throw the scriptures at me. How might my brother answer him? Perhaps he would say, "I have read enough to see what happens to men who usurp a throne, assault the Church, and violate the laws of God."

"So, you will not be moved, then? You refuse to bring an end to this destruction?"

"I believe there are times when men cry, 'Peace, peace,' and yet there is no peace.[35] The only true peace comes with the restoration of justice, which you will be made to feel, Stephen, if there is any power in me to make you feel it. I will not betray my sister and my father's final wish. I am not that kind of man. What sort of man you are is plainly on display. As for me, I make for the West, and you will see me on the field of battle once more. As I got the better of you at Lincoln, so I will prove myself your better again."

Ah, an excellent answer! I liked to think my brother would give it. But Stephen would not see it as honor. He would see something pitiful.

"It pains me to see you brought so low," he would claim, though in truth he would be enjoying it.

Here a clever reply would be necessary from the earl. "The one upon the high ground must seem low indeed to him who has overturned all that is fair."

And that would be it. They would part with a few words in each direction.

"May God save England from your designs," Stephen would say, setting aside his empty cup and rising to leave.

---

35   Reference to Jeremiah 6:14 and 8:11.

My brother would smile—perhaps even laugh. "May God save England from those who have none of it in their souls."

Yes, it would proceed in such a manner. It must. Earl Robert could not be bought with all the jewels in Christendom. He would depart from Winchester with his head held high. It would take him a day or perhaps two to arrive. Even at that hour, he might be approaching the walls of Oxford.

My mind a bit more settled, I began again where I had ended. "*Ad te suspiramus, gementes et flentes in hac lacrimarum valle ...*"

I heard footsteps behind me. Thinking it must be one of the monks, I continued with my supplication, only to feel the touch of a hand on my right shoulder. At this, I raised my eyes and looked upon the face of my brother, Earl Robert of Gloucester.

"Robert ..." I whispered. "Brother of my flesh."

"Away with your mourning and weeping," he declared, "for nothing has been lost that cannot be restored."

I rose to my feet and wrapped my arms around him, burying my face in his chest. It was not perhaps the most proper thing for an empress to do, but it was altogether proper for a sister who had feared she would never see her brother again. He embraced me in turn, and as I pulled back to wipe a few tears of joy from my eyes, I saw from the light of the candles that his own eyes were rather moist.

"I have prayed for this every day," I whispered. "Robert, forgive me. Forgive me for it all."

"There is nothing to forgive," he assured me. "I had much time to think when I was locked away in that castle, and you know what I have decided?"

"No. What have you decided?" I asked, genuinely at a loss.

"It is time, Maud. It is time for young Henry to set foot in the kingdom of England. This is his inheritance. What say you?"

"I say ..." I began, but then paused. There was nothing in the world I longed for more than to see my son again, to place him upon England's throne, and to restore justice to the land. But I knew the great danger involved and I feared for him. I suppose some would have said that were the worst to happen and he was slain, I had two more sons who could take his place, but that is not how a mother thinks. I had been through so much to bring that boy into the world, and I loved him as my own flesh. What if he were to fall into the enemy's hands? What if he ended up in an early grave? My brother sensed my concern.

"As God is my witness, I will not allow a hair on his head to be harmed," he pledged. "I swear to you upon my very life. Do you trust me?"

I swallowed hard, bidding myself to have faith. Despite the danger, I believed in what I had seen: I believed in that future.

"Very well," I agreed. "Let him come, for he will be England's salvation."

XXII

There is a tale told by Bede that when King Edwin of
Northumbria was attempting to decide whether to become a follower of Jesus Christ, he had his own mortality impressed upon him by the following thought: that a sparrow
flying through a chamber in winter, though it be the hall of a
king feasting before a mighty fire, enjoys but a brief moment
away from the bitter cold.[36] As quickly as it is come, it departs.
Scarcely does it know the comfort of warmth before it is cast
again into darkness—and of what lies in that darkness, we can
never be certain, for the light falls only within, and without all
is mystery. Before we would wish it, we are pushed into that
land of the unknown. *Pulvis et umbra sumus.*[37]

In this life, we often lack certainty. Upon the mysteries of
the divine, the philosophers spend their days in contemplation, but there are lesser mysteries created by the passage of

---

36 Venerable Bede, *Historia Ecclesiastica Gentis Anglorum,* II.13.
37 Horace, *Odes,* IV.7.16. Translation: "We are dust and shadows."

time. As the scripture tells us, we ought not boast even of to-morrow, for we know not what it will bring forth.[38] Only in the final hour will we know fully as we are fully known.[39] And thus it was that I found myself, not for the first time or the last, in an hour of great mystery, awaiting a doom that held every possibility of evil. I clung tight to the hope granted me from on high.

We knew full well that after his release, Stephen would immediately attempt to project his authority in one manner or another. Bishop Henry would be forced to procure the support of the Church for his double reversal of allegiance. The usurper would no doubt show himself often in public to drive away any doubts about his state, and in time he would gather up every man at his command to march against us in the West. We hoped very much for the help of the king of Scots, but my letters to him were never answered. It seemed plain enough that he had no further desire to involve himself in the war for England—at least not until there was some change of fortune. I did not fault him too heavily, as he could not be away from his own kingdom for years at a time given how often the men in the hills launched rebellions. But it was still a blow and one I felt keenly. He was an experienced warrior and we needed as many of those as God would allow. He ought to have offered some reply.

That December, Bishop Henry called his great council at Westminster with the usurper in attendance. We had learned of it only a week in advance and immediately sought an expert in the law to appear on our behalf, for not only was the crown in question, but also the spiritual standing of me and all my supporters. We had heard a rumor that the bishop would seek to excommunicate anyone who refused to acknowledge

---

38 Proverbs 27:1.
39 Reference to 1 Corinthians 13:12.

Stephen as king, claiming the support of the Holy Father. We could not simply accept such an action, so we cast about looking for an ambassador whom we could send. Lord Brian of Wallingford was the best expert on the English law I had ever known, but he was also duty bound to hold his fortress against the enemy, and in any case, it seemed better to send a man of the Church to a council of the same.

Here we met with good fortune, for among the many students in Oxford was a young man named Peter who came from the town of Tattershall in Lincolnshire. He resided among the brothers at the priory of Saint Frideswide and would study the great works of canon law day and night. It was this Peter who we sent to Westminster to argue our case, and as the days of Advent passed by one after another, we waited upon his return even as that of our Lord.

It was perhaps the day before the Ides when I was informed that the council had ended and our delegate was returned to Oxford.[40] Although I was eager to hear his tale, I knew it would be best to do so in the presence of Earl Robert and Lord Brian. The former was out hunting near Woodstock and the latter still in his castle at Wallingford, so I sent messages to both to come to Oxford with all speed. The next morning, the three of us arrived at the chapter house of the priory, where we were due to meet Peter of Tattershall. It was a fairly new room and very fine, with three levels of columns and arches carved into the stone walls, all leading up to the vault, in the center of which was an image of Frideswide herself. The windows on the east wall let in the light of the rising sun, for which I was most glad, as there was no fire in the room and I was eager for any source of warmth. Four chairs had been placed in a circle, and while the last of these remained empty, the three of us sat mute, none

---

40   December 12, 1141.

foreseeing that the conversation we were about to have would be pleasant. After a minute or two of this, I decided to speak.

"How was your ride up?" I asked Lord Brian.

"Fine. Nothing to report," he replied simply.

I nodded and turned to stare out the windows on the far wall, where a few monks could be seen bringing in branches they had cut from the nearby wood to decorate the church for Christmas.

"It's good to see you both again," Brian suddenly added, calling our attention to himself. "We have not all been together since Winchester—and Robert, I have not seen you since your captivity."

My brother did not reply but merely grunted, rubbing his forehead. He did not seem eager to discuss the matter.

"How are your wives?" I offered, looking at Lord Brian but including them both in the question so as not to seem particular.

"We have been doing well. Thank you for asking," Brian replied. "Since I returned home, we have been able to spend some time together. We had a few discussions that I hope will benefit our marriage."

I was intensely curious as to what these discussions might have included, given that the time just before he returned home was when—well, I am sure you remember now as well as I did then. However, I said nothing. As it so happened, I did not have to, for Robert interrupted.

"Ugh! That sounds awful."

"What? Talking to my wife?" Brian asked with a smile.

"If a wife wants to have a long discussion with you, you can bet it is for one reason and one reason only: to scold you," Robert argued, rubbing his eyes.

"Am I correct to assume all is not well in your home?" I asked my brother.

"I am not in the good graces of Lady Mabel: yes, that is true," he answered. "She believes me to be some sort of villain." He said this with a clear tone of annoyance.

"Does she say why?" inquired Lord Brian.

I could only guess that she had somehow learned of his indiscretion, but I said nothing about it. At that very moment, the door opened and Peter of Tattershall strode in, a bundle of papers under his right arm.

"My lady, my lords," he offered, bowing to all three of us, "I am come with the report of what I witnessed at the council in Westminster."

I could feel a firm knot forming near my stomach. The brief conversation had distracted me for just a moment from my fear of what the usurper and his brother might announce. With the time of revelation upon me, I was filled with something close to dread. *Best to hear him out and have done with it,* I reasoned. I therefore pointed to the empty chair nearest the door and he sat in it, setting the papers on his lap.

Peter placed his hands palms down on the bundle. "These are all my personal notes in addition to three letters from the pen of Bishop Henry of Winchester, papal legate: one for each of you." He untied the cord that was holding them all together and raised up the first piece of parchment, which had been folded and sealed. "My lady, this is for you. It bears the seal of the bishop. It was not for me to break it and read what he has to say, but I am certain he will announce to you that the Church has decided against you and returned its allegiance to Stephen, for that is what happened."

I closed my eyes and nodded solemnly. "We foresaw no other outcome, and yet it grieves me," I said, opening my eyes again. "But tell me, am I excommunicated?"

"No, as it so happens," he told me. "That was the one thing I was able to ensure."

He rose to bring me the letter, but I said to him, "Never mind that. Just set it aside."

He nodded. "As you wish. Now, these two," he continued, raising up a letter in each hand, "are for your lordships. Again, I did not open them, but they will be the letters of excommunication against you."

My heart sank, and my brother objected, "But I thought you were able to keep them from doing that!"

"For the empress alone," he explained. "I suspect he thought it would look bad to excommunicate a woman and the daughter of the late king. He would show mercy to no one else."

"It would only be mercy if we did something wrong," Brian argued. "This entire thing is a great injustice. We have committed no crime against Holy Writ."

"Did you show him the letter I shared with you?" I asked the delegate. "The letter that Bishop Henry sent me when I was still in Normandy—where he begged me to come?"

Peter sighed heavily. "I did show it to him before the entire assembly. You must believe me, my lady—I did everything in my power to put forth your case. I made the argument in exactly the words we discussed beforehand. I mentioned the oaths made to you, the perjury of Hugh Bigod, and all the rest. I appealed to the legate's own words in your favor earlier this year. I looked in the eyes of all those lords of the Church who had sworn to uphold your authority and appealed to their sense of honor … but I'm afraid there was no honor to be had among them. The council was not held to do justice but to make official that which they had already agreed to in their hearts. Stephen was there, you see. He was there to make sure they all fell in line. He and his brother had them all … well …"

"By the ballocks," Robert offered helpfully.

"Your words, not mine," said Peter. "I thought when I showed him that letter and read it for everyone to hear, holding it up that they might see his mark made so boldly, the bishop would at least attempt to deny that he wrote the thing. But no, he did not deny it. He simply repeated the same things he had been saying: that you surrounded his city with a vast army—"

"False," Brian muttered.

"—that you were plotting to kill him—"

"Also false," added Robert.

"—and that you broke your oath to him to preserve the freedom of the Church."

"An evil trinity of falsehoods," I concluded.

The monk nodded sadly. "They knew as I read that letter—they all knew I was in the right. I could see it in their eyes that could not meet mine but moved straight to the ground. They knew it was hypocrisy, and yet they did it, every man of them. I am sorry to say so, my lady, but I believe many of them never wanted to see your rule. They do not believe in the very concept of a female sovereign, and for any of them that still held some scruples about the business, Pope Innocent was ready to free them from their doubts. You see, the legate had a letter of his own to display from the Holy Father which criticized him in no uncertain terms for failing to support his brother's rule."

"Could the letter have been a counterfeit?" Robert inquired a bit desperately. "He has never sent anything to us."

"I think not," Peter replied. "It is in line with Innocent's earlier decision to accept what he sees as a *fait accompli*."

"The pope does not know ... cannot know the situation here in England," Brian charged. "There has been no time or opportunity for us to send our own men to Rome. Bishop Henry is taking advantage of his role as legate to pour words of honey into the ear of his master. He will have told him there is no real dispute: that the English laws do not allow for a female ruler and the Church cannot abandon a sovereign it has anointed."

"Even so," the monk said, nodding his head slowly, "His Holiness has ruled on the matter, and the legate has induced his brother bishops to perform the excommunication. I am profoundly sorry. I made the case to the best of my ability, but they were in no mood to hear it."

"How many of us are excommunicated?" asked Brian.

"In theory, anyone who continues to support the empress, but in practice it will apply only to the greater lords: yourselves, Earl Miles, Earl Reginald, any bishops not at the council who refuse to bend the knee—"

"Anyone whose land they wish to steal or whose seat they wish to fill with their own ally," I concluded. "The same thing happened when I was in Germany. In such cases, excommunication is not about anything spiritual. It is an excuse for any man who so desires to deny the fealty he owes to his lord on the grounds that he need not obey a man in disobedience to God. What they cannot achieve by the power of the sword, they will attempt to do by the power of the staff."

"Well, any man who thinks to use this to rise up against me will be in for a nasty surprise!" Robert declared. "Excommunication means nothing where there is no man who has the power to wield it."

"But surely the bishops can wield it, if they wish to do so," said Peter. "They can deny you the sacrament."

Robert laughed softly. "Do not take this the wrong way, brother, but that is the least of my worries. A man who has shown himself to be corrupt and in violation of the will of God cannot think to wield any power over me in this life or the next."

The monk looked rather nervous, beginning to speak and then stopping.

"What is it, man?" my brother growled. "Out with it!"

"Bishop Henry is papal legate," replied Peter, his voice reaching an ever higher pitch. "His order of excommunication carries the authority of the Holy Father himself, even if it was the bishop who wrote the words. I think you cannot be aware of what you are saying—that is, the extent of what you are proposing. Are you saying that the Lord did not grant the keys to Peter and that Innocent is not his successor?"

"Who's to say? We have two or three popes at any one time," Robert answered with a shrug. "How can we really be sure which one of them is the true one?"

The monk crossed himself in earnest. "By such reasoning, the Church will fall and Christendom with it. The Vicar of Christ is revealed to the bishops of the Church by the Holy Spirit."

"And again, I ask you, which ones?!" Robert asked, or rather yelled at the poor man. "Every man who has ever claimed to be pope has had bishops to back him."

"Gentlemen, enough!" I cried. "This is beside the point." When they looked as if they were about to launch into argument again, I repeated, "Enough! You turn things around! I have more reason than any of you to doubt the justice of the Church and the authority of the bishops. I have not forgotten what happened when I was in the Empire—the deeds of Adalbert of Mainz—and I see with what intent toward evil Bishop Henry casts his spell now. I watched as he set fire to the treasures of Winchester, caring not whom he killed or maimed. I know with what kind of character I must deal. But as for the Holy Father, I do not believe in the Church because of him. I believe in him because I believe in the Church. And as for the Church itself, I do not believe in it because of what it says or does in any particular hour, but because it has its mandate from Christ and he is its foundation. Men may fail, but Christ does not. This decision of the council is unjust in the extreme, but it will not cause me to lose faith in the seat of Saint Peter or the Church it is sworn to uphold. Decisions can be reversed. Errors can be corrected. The Word of our Lord never fails. Now, the only question for us right now is, what must we do next?"

"Write to Count Geoffrey for aid, and soon," Brian offered. "He must cross the Channel and invade the Southeast of England, or at the very least invade Flanders and make an end of the false queen's wealth and supply of men."

"This is good sense," I declared, pointing to him. "Let us speak more of this and think no more on what happened at Westminster, for we cannot control the actions of evil men, but we can refuse to surrender in the face of those evil actions. We can fight back—fight for what we cherish."

"Very well. Should I leave all this with you, then?" Peter asked, lifting the papers.

"Yes, leave them with me," Brian answered.

The monk handed off his burden and made for the door, turning only to say, "I am so very sorry."

And then he shut the door and it was just the three of us, sitting quietly once again, wishing very much that we could make our own escape.

"*Vivat Rex! Vivat Regina!*"

So the cries rose up in Canterbury Cathedral, stretching to the vault high above. The king and queen sat upon their thrones, golden crowns on their heads—but they were no king and queen, no matter how loud the people shouted. I wonder if the usurper's lips trembled as he pledged to preserve peace, forbid robbery and all unrighteous things, and command justice and mercy in his judgments, when he himself had broken the peace, robbed my descendants of their inheritance, and perverted justice from beginning to end. Did Archbishop Theobald's hands quake as they placed the crown on his head again? I imagine they must have done so, for he had spent time with me, and in that time, it was clear he understood too much to feel at peace with such an outrage. Perhaps the archbishop was a prisoner of the usurper's threats. I do not doubt that it was so.

It was in the season of Advent that they were crowned again, with several earls in attendance but only Archbishop Theobald and Bishop Henry of Winchester to represent the Church. The choice of Canterbury was clearly made for two reasons: to reward the men of Kent who had supported the usurper so ardently on account of the trade with Flanders, and to make clear to the archbishop that those months he had spent at my court and the support he had offered me must be a thing of the past. It was a demonstration of the power of Bishop Henry, papal legate, who if he could not hold the throne of Canterbury would simply bend the one who sat upon it to his will.

Oh, how the false queen must have reveled in that moment! What a savage smile must have broken upon her crimson lips! The victory was hers and hers alone. Like her mother, she could not bear to be second to any woman, even the closest of kin. Unless all were worshipping her, she was not content. Those men who swore they would never bow to a female ruler knelt and kissed the hem of her robe for one glance of her eyes.

Once this farce of a coronation was completed, Stephen began assembling things for war. We could not know at that time exactly what he was doing, but it was clear enough that he would seek to strike against us at the first opportunity. Earl Robert and I agreed that we should travel to Devizes, from which we might gather any men who remained faithful to ourselves. Since the defeat at Winchester, we had all been thrown here and there as a ship in a tempest. It was time to restore order to our side and agree on a way forward.

In the days of Lent, we moved southwest again in the direction of Swindon and then on the second day continued to Devizes. There we were met by Earl Reginald and Lord Brian, who had received our message and arrived ahead of us. Earls Miles and Robert had of course come with me from Oxford, as had several of my own knights and those of my brother, not the least of which were sirs Drogo and Philip. It was a pleasure to see so many friendly faces again.

One advantage of the castle of Devizes over that in Oxford was that I was able to once again reside in the bed chamber that had belonged to Bishop Roger of Salisbury. Where else would I have been able to enjoy sleeping on silk? The only other place I had seen such a thing was at the Doge's palace in Venice many long years earlier. Adela and I went ahead of the men to see it. I opened the door and the two of us climbed the few stairs that led to that haven of delight. My eyes traveled quickly around the room: the chests were still in their place to my left, the carpets adorned the floor, and before me the great bed was covered in the glorious fabric. I do not know why it might have been otherwise. Perhaps I had been let down so many times I foresaw nothing else.

"God be praised!" I rejoiced.

Beside me, Adela was out of breath from climbing all the stairs. She put a hand on her hip and leaned back slightly, closing her eyes and exhaling.

"Well, if it's that bad, lie down on the bed for a moment," I offered.

Opening her eyes immediately, she objected, "Oh, but my lady, I couldn't! This bed is meant for royalty or something very close to it."

"And you are close to me," I assured her, gesturing with my hand for her to proceed.

She smiled and nodded, then took her place upon the thing very carefully, as if it might eat her alive if she showed it too little respect. For my part, I fell upon it like a pile of rocks, taking my place next to her. We both lay on our backs, gazing up at the silk canopy above us that was the color of wine and adorned with gold stars. At length, Adela sat up and turned around to look more closely at the tapestry that hung above the bed.

"Who are they?" she asked.

"In the tapestry? Those are the bishop and the king," I said. Sitting up myself, I pointed and explained, "The shorter man on the left: that is Bishop Roger of Salisbury. He holds the staff of his office in his right hand. The man on the right, the one with the crown who holds the royal orb, is my father."

"Hmm ... I did not think your father was that tall," she mused.

"Of course not. These things never tell the truth. That is ... I suppose they tell a version of the truth, but not the fullness thereof."

"And what is the book they are both holding?" Adela asked.

"The Holy Scripture, I presume."

I leaned a bit closer so that I could clearly read the words in Latin, and I could not help but laugh.

"What is it?!" my maid demanded as much as inquired. "What does it say?"

"*Ego sum christus Domini,*" I recited. "Meaning, 'I am the Lord's anointed one.'"

She glanced at me oddly and said, "I do not see why that should make you laugh."

"It's just rather arrogant, I suppose. He has put himself on the same level as the king. He is the head of the Church and the king is the head of state. They are both anointed by God."

She looked back at the tapestry. "But was he the head of the Church? He was not archbishop like Theobald or even papal legate like Bishop Henry."

"Oh, I am sure in his own mind he felt he controlled it all," I said. "He served as regent when the king was in Normandy. He was in charge of the money, and that is real power. The other bishops did whatever he told them to do. He was the richest man in the kingdom: just look at this room!"

"I do wonder that he spent so much to decorate a place where he only stayed part of the time," she said, looking around at all the ornaments.

"This was not his room," I explained. "Not really. It belonged to his concubine. When he visited, I suppose he stayed in this room with her, but other than that it was hers alone."

"So, she was the greatest treasure he kept here," Adela said with a smile. "That seems odd for a great man to share a room with any lady."

"For the sake of appearance, she likely had her things in one of the other chambers," I said. "Speaking of sharing rooms, do you wish for Sir Philip to join you in your room?"

She shook her head no. "It would not seem right when none of the other men have their wives with them."

"That was the kind of thinking that cost Uriah his life," I jested.[41]

"What are you implying?!" she asked in alarm. "Who was he? Did his wife kill him?"

---

41   The allusion is to the biblical story of King David and Bathsheba, the latter being the wife of Uriah. After secretly committing adultery with Bathsheba, the king learned that she was pregnant and therefore told her warrior husband to spend the night with her, hoping to hide the child's true parentage. Uriah objected that he could not enjoy pleasure with his wife while his fellow soldiers were fighting at the front. Still needing a way to cover up his action, the king instructed that Uriah should be abandoned on the field of battle so that he would be killed by the enemy.

"No—" I began, but was interrupted by some loud knocking on the door.

Adela began to rise, but I held out a hand to stop her. "You are weary. Stay here," I commanded.

I walked across the room and down the few stairs, opened the latch, and swung the door open to reveal Sir Drogo of Powheile with a large cup of what I assumed to be beer in his hand.

"William Paganel is here," he told me, not waiting to be bidden.

I drew upon the far reaches of my mind to retrieve this name and its meaning, then said, "Right, the castellan of Nottingham, Ralph's cousin. I suppose he must have heard we were gathering."

"Yes and no," Drogo explained. "He was concerned for his estate and began riding south to request more knights. He halted at Woodstock when he was caught from behind by a messenger riding in even greater haste. There he learned that not a day after his departure, the enemy had fallen upon his castle and seized it under the command of William Peverel."

"What?!" I cried. "Oh, no, no, no ..." I turned and hit my head softly upon the door frame twice, then allowed it to rest there.

"He chose to continue on his way rather than return, and he has followed just on our heels to Devizes," the knight continued solemnly.

I pounded my hand into the frame and let out a sigh. Drogo tapped me on the shoulder and I turned to see that he was holding out the cup. "I thought you might want this after hearing that news."

"How right you were," I replied, taking it gladly. "Are they all waiting below, then?"

"Yes, all the men are gathered. Earl Baldwin is here as well. He was out chasing a deer when you arrived."

"I should tell him to save his strength," I muttered, taking a drink of the beer. The stuff was bitter—more so than usual. I closed my eyes and shook my head back and forth as if it would remove the taste from my mouth.

"No good?" Drogo asked in concern. "Reginald said it was far superior to anything in Cornwall."

"That is not much of a recommendation," I muttered. "Next time, bring wine or nothing at all."

"There was no wine … but I understand," he said with a nod.

We walked together down the passage, taking a right turn toward the stair. My thoughts were as bitter as the beer.

So, Nottingham is now held for the usurper. Oxford is opposed on three sides. But which one will Stephen choose to make his advance? Too few men. We have too few men. I have no choice—I must appeal to Count Geoffrey. But will he come? Can he afford to?

The prospect of seeing my husband again was not one I cherished. I had no doubt that during our time apart, he had found his way into the arms of every *puterelle* in Normandy—which is to say he had been whoring as much as fighting. As we descended the steps, a view of the hall opened before me. The two great tables were there as before, and banners hung from the wood beams high above: some showing the Madonna and child, others a bishop's miter, and still others the crossed keys of Saint Peter. Although the man himself was three years in the grave, the legacy of Bishop Roger of Salisbury was alive and well.

The lords were all gathered at the end of one of the tables, where a map lay spread open. Earl Miles had his hand upon it and the attention of all, but when they became aware of my presence, every eye rose to meet me and each man bowed in turn.

"Empress Mathilda! Lady of the English! My lady!" they greeted me.

I acknowledged them all with a nod of the head and took my place across the table from Miles. Drogo stood to my right along with earls Baldwin, Robert, and Reginald. Lord Brian was directly to my left and my chamberlain, John fitz Gilbert, to the left of him. Across the table and next to Miles was John Marshal, and this last face was the one that caught my attention. I had not seen him since the ruinous incident at Wherwell in which he lost the sight of one eye in my service. The eye in question was covered with cloth, and his whole face bore the strange marks of fire here and there. A surge of guilt seized me and I swallowed hard, but the man smiled, as if attempting to free me from what I felt.

Oh, what so many have suffered on my behalf! I wailed inside. *I must press on for their sake. I must see this done.*

Breaking away from these thoughts, I looked down at the map but could not make out much as it was upside down.

"Here," Miles offered, turning the thing so I could see it properly.

Drawn upon the vellum in deep black ink were many castles. They were marked with names: York, Oxford, Dover, Bristol, Devizes, Gloucester, Nottingham, Lincoln, Arundel, Wallingford. Every major fortress in England was marked and among them the rivers ran like veins filled with dark blood. The map made no distinction based on size. Every castle looked the same, and a few of the names were faded from what I assumed had been years of use. Such a map as this was of great value. My eyes moved from the center—where Devizes and Oxford were marked—farther to the right, where I could clearly see Windsor, Westminster, and London. This was surely where the usurper was holding court at the moment, and it seemed so close: only a matter of inches from our place on the map. I knew that inches stood for many miles, but even so, I liked it not.

I had many questions, but began by saying, "Gentlemen, thank you for coming. There was a time not long ago when I feared I would never see your faces again."

Here I looked at John Marshal, and I knew that a hundred more such faces were stretched across England, if not a thousand. I thought of the woman who had charged me with causing her son's death—in what manner, I knew not. I could only be certain that many had suffered and not only myself. Still, the men before me were alive and ready to continue the fight.

"You defended me boldly in the face of great danger to life and limb," I continued, struggling not to allow my voice to break. "I owe everything I am to you all."

"The greatest praise must go to yourself and your companions!" Earl Baldwin declared. "Reginald, Brian, Drogo—you have performed a feat to rival any of Hercules."

"God knows that each of you performed great deeds, and my heart will be for ever thankful," I concluded. "Now, for the matter at hand—Where is William Paganel? I was promised that he would be here."

"And he meant to be, but sadly he had to step out for some necessary business," Miles explained. "It is just as well, for I do not know about you, my lady, but I think it better to keep the number of men at this meeting as low as possible."

I nodded. "Very wise."

Earl Robert cleared his throat and pointed to the city of London on the map.

"Here is where the usurper makes his abode at the moment, but we believe he will soon march to the North and hold his court at York. There is to be a tournament there."

"A tournament? In the middle of all this?!" Reginald asked with more than a note of scorn. "Would that our fortunes were good enough to have time and money for such pastimes!"

"Actually, our spies tell us he is going to put an end to it," Robert explained. "You know how these things tend to descend into petty quarrels, with men abandoning all manners of court and taking up their swords to kill."

"Robert and I have discussed the matter, and we are certain that Stephen hopes to safeguard his gain at Nottingham, promote his authority in the north of the kingdom, and gather an army to march upon us," said Miles.

"Where is the blow to fall hardest?" I asked. "Is it to be Oxford as we have long supposed?"

Miles nodded. "Most likely, though Wallingford is another possibility." Here he looked to Brian at my left and said, "That will happen if he decides to strike from the East, though at the moment it seems more likely that he will come from the North."

"If the war comes to Wallingford again, we will be ready," Brian assured us all. "We have not been idle. The defenses are improved. We had to procure some food from the neighboring lands, which will not make Bishop Henry happy as some of those estates belong to him, but I have given assurances to all who would hear them that if it is at all within my ability, I will pay them back."

"Good," I said. "We cannot afford to make too many enemies of the common folk, though I think Bishop Henry is lost to us for ever."

Robert reached forward and pointed to the fortress of Wareham at the bottom of the map. "We still hold the port at Wareham. That is our connection to Normandy. From there it is not a long voyage to Caen, though we think that Count Geoffrey is now farther to the south. His last letter was sent from Tinchebrai."

"We must send messengers now, as soon as possible," argued Brian. "We have a space of two or three months before he will begin his summer push. Ask him to delay it: to stay where he is for a year and send any men he can spare across the Channel. No one is likely to press against him in Normandy. Theobald is caught in a dispute with King Louis, and all the Flemings are over here fighting us. The Beaumonts have made peace. Count Geoffrey can afford to break for one season to save our efforts here in England."

"He may not see it that way," I muttered. "He has only ever shown interest in the fight for Normandy. He sees little of value in this island."

"Surely he must see value in his sons' inheritance!" Miles argued. "He will send men—you'll see."

I raised my brows but said nothing. It seemed to me unlikely that Earl Miles of Hereford, who had never met my husband, could guess his actions better than myself. However, I thought it wiser to let things lie.

"Very well. The messengers will depart at break of day, and with any luck they will return within the month along with five hundred knights," Robert declared. "Do you approve of this?" he asked me, though I did not see the point of the question when he had clearly made up his mind already.

"Yes, it is our only option," I agreed. "We have been stripped of men and materials here."

Even so, the matter was concluded, and at the break of dawn the next day, we sent five men to meet with the count, bearing a letter written by my own hand. From my window high in the tower, I watched them ride through the castle gate and out into the darkness.

"Geoffrey of Anjou, you have been good for very little," I whispered. "Now is your chance to make amends."

I could almost hear his voice in my head.

Finally, Lady England! Finally, you admit that you need me! he taunted. *Long have I sought this day when you acknowledge that it is*

not I that need you, but the other way around. Your father knew it was
mine to command, and now at last it is so.

As the feast of Easter came and went, we awaited the return
of the messengers. I remained in Devizes for the time being,
as it was closer to that coast from which we hoped our help
would come, and most of my captains stayed as well. However,
Brian returned to Wallingford to watch for any movement of
the enemy from that direction, and after meeting with William
Paganel and sadly informing him that I could offer no help at
the present, I sent him back to Oxford to guard against assault
from the North.

When the last trace of chill departed and the month of
May had almost arrived, we received news that very much
changed our fortunes, though it came not from Normandy but
the North: the usurper had fallen ill. The rumor was spread
abroad that he had released all the men he had gathered to
his service—the army with which he had intended to crush us.
He lay upon his sick bed in Northampton, with the false queen
at his side, and no man knew whether he would rise from it
again.

All at once, the plots of the past few months were set aside.
We no longer had to fear the sight of an army at the gate, but
we had very much to fear the decisions of lords and bishops.
If Stephen were to die, that would leave four chief contenders
for the throne. First was the only person who ever should have
held that throne: myself. Second were the two sons Stephen
had spawned that remained among the living: Eustace, who was
of the age to begin training for the knighthood, and William,
who was only just old enough to read and write. Last was the
man who many of the Norman lords had wanted on the throne
ever since the death of my father: Count Theobald of Blois and
Champagne, elder brother of the usurper.

For my part, I could not see why any of the other options would be preferrable to myself. Eustace was too young to lead an army, and this was the chief reason that men were said to be born to rule. He was no man yet, but only a boy. Theobald, on the other hand, was as usual consumed by his own business on the Continent, most especially his dispute with the king of France. Unlike his brothers, he was at peace with my husband and therefore with me. He also possessed the same disadvantage that had once hindered me: he was too far from England.

I could see it was more essential than ever that Count Geoffrey should reply to our message with a large host of knights, and with himself at the head of the line if possible. The false queen had it in her to gather up the Flemings again and descend on London to have her son crowned. Would she wait to move with her husband's funeral procession? Would she take the chance of laying him to rest before rising in defense of her son's claim? It seemed unlikely. A woman like her would not be drawn in by sentiment.

I feared we could not afford to wait for the men we sent to Normandy to return. We needed to move back into the Thames Valley as quickly as possible and press east toward Windsor and Westminster. However, my captains assured me that such an action would result in ruin. We were still too weak, they argued. We had lost Winchester and the whole Southeast was held against us. The only hope if we were to step into that hornet's nest was to wait for help from Normandy. As much as I did not want it to be true, I sensed it was wise counsel. They also assured me that men would be less inclined to fight for young Eustace than they were for his father, even though the lad was married to a French princess.

At such an hour, one tends to pray more than usual, and so I made regular use of the private chapel on the upper level of the keep, just across the hall from my own chamber.

There Bishop Roger of Salisbury must have spent many long hours upon his knees, confessing his multitude of sins to the Almighty. No doubt, I had many sins to confess as well, but it was not the mercy of the Lord I sought in that hour as much as his sovereign power over all creation. I held the beads of my mother and grandmother to my lips and kissed them, clutching them in my hands. Time and again, I prayed that it would not be Stephen's sons who inherited the throne, but my own. I prayed that justice would be restored to England and all made right.

It was during one of those hours I was in the chapel, with the light of only a few candles and the company of none alive, that the door opened behind me and I moved my gaze for just a moment from the crucifix upon the altar toward the face of whoever had disturbed my peace. Any annoyance I might have felt fled away as I saw that it was my maid, Adela. In the dim light, I perceived that something was troubling her. Not only had she entered without knocking, but her face seemed to be wet. I could only just see the gleam of light reflecting from her cheeks.

"What is it, friend?" I asked. "What has happened?"

"My ... lady ..." she sniffled. "May I speak to you in ... private?"

"Of course," I said, immediately rising up and walking past her to the door she had left open. I pulled it shut and moved again to where she stood, her head bent downward, one hand covering her face. I took hold of her by the shoulders. "Whatever is wrong, you know you may tell me. I will not reveal it."

Dropping her hand, she looked into my eyes and said, "Oh, my lady! I am ever so afraid. When I went to relieve myself just now, there was ..." She seemed unable to continue, burying her face in her hands and sobbing.

Not knowing what else to do, I embraced her, waiting for her to come to a point where she could speak again. In time, she did.

"There was blood," she said, finishing the thought. "Not much, but it was there. I do not know what to do."

"I would say bear it for a few days and then move on with your life, but I sense there is more at stake here," I explained. "Has it been some time since you had your usual ... time?"

"Not so very long. I missed one month," she told me, sniffing again but no longer shedding great tears. "I thought perhaps I was in the motherly way. Indeed, I sensed that I was. I even told Philip as much, but now I see the blood, and I fear I have ..."

She could not do it. The tears began to fall again and she clung to me.

"You fear you have lost a child," I said quietly.

"Yes," she whispered.

I patted her on the back, my heart beating with compassion for her. How many women had rejoiced in the knowledge that a child was to be born, only to be driven to the depths of despair by that terrible sign?

"It may not be the end," I assured her. "How much blood was there?"

She pulled back a bit and said, "Not so very much, I suppose. Does it make a difference?"

"I think it might. Back when I was pregnant with Geoffrey, the same thing happened. Fortunately, I had Grimbald there, and he told me it is common for women to pass a small amount of blood in the early months and then go on to give birth to a healthy babe. And though my own life was heavily in danger upon his birth, there was nothing wrong with Geoffrey. He is as healthy as they come."

"I am glad to hear you say it. Perhaps there was never any child. That would be a sadness for Philip. It is his great dream to be a father."

"Only time will tell," I concluded. "Wait a few days and see what happens."

She nodded in agreement and, placing one arm around her, I led her in the direction of the door.

"I believe you need to lie down on some silk!" I declared. "It always makes me feel a bit better."

"Promise you will not tell Philip? I do not want him to hear anything until all is certain," said Adela.

"Not a word," I swore.

Two lives seemed to hang in the balance that spring. I did not trust myself to pray about Stephen, for though in my flesh I desired his end, I knew I must leave the vengeance to God. Was it God's will for him to perish? I knew not, and so I simply prayed, "Your kingdom come, your will be done on earth as it is in heaven."[42] As for Adela's child, whom I believed to exist and for whom I prayed every hour, my heart was as much caught up in the matter as if it were my own.

It was not long before we had some hope in her case, for save for that one moment, she never again passed blood, and there was good reason to suspect that she was indeed with child, for she had the strange smells even as I once did. For this I was filled with gratitude, but I still feared the fate of the kingdom. We had heard no news of Stephen for good or ill and were left to assume that he remained unwell but among the living.

But where on earth were the delegates we had sent to Normandy? They ought to have returned within the month, but two months passed and there was no sign of them. We

---

42 Words from The Lord's Prayer appearing in Matthew 6:10.

wondered if their ship had been wrecked while crossing the Channel and more messengers were needed, or perhaps they had been seized by the enemy somewhere along the road. Could it simply be taking many weeks to gather up the force that Count Geoffrey would lead across the water? With no information, we were left to hope for the best and tried not to assume the worst.

Meanwhile, we were joined by others of our companions. William of Mohun, who had fought on our side at Winchester, arrived near the beginning of May. We had also with us William fitz Alan and Roger de Nonant, but I was most surprised in the three men who arrived next: Earl Ranulf of Chester, Earl Roger of Warwick, and Earl Hugh of Norfolk. I cannot say that my heart was filled with joy to see them, for each had done me some offense. Ranulf had turned against me for a time and only attempted to switch sides at Winchester after the fighting started. In the end, he was no help to us. Roger Beaumont, earl of Warwick, had been with us at Oxford and was meant to come to Winchester, but for reasons that were still not clear, he had never arrived, and the absence of his men was surely one cause of our defeat. Then there was Hugh Bigod, earl of Norfolk, whom I still believed to be a liar and who had made no effort at all to help us since I had given him and his worthless relatives everything they asked for and more. Although I had not been told as much, I suspected him of joining in the treachery of his kinsman, Geoffrey de Mandeville. Certainly, it was within his nature.

On Whitsun, the day on which the Spirit descended upon the apostles, the herald announced a rather different arrival: the messengers had returned from Normandy. I was informed of this while visiting the horses and quickly made my way back from the stables to the keep. I brushed the dust off the hem of my gown and bid a guard open the door, then strode into the hall with all haste, making my way through the crowd of men that had gathered with a hearty, "Make way!" At the sight of me, they parted as the Red Sea, and I saw at the center of the gathering three of the men we had sent to Normandy. The first was Ralph Bohun, who was not a member of that great family but a servant of the same who had risen to become a knight himself. The second was Thierry of Bayeux and the last was named Raymond, but other than that I forget everything about him.

"Do you return alone?" I asked all three of them.

Thierry was the first to answer: a man of medium height with golden hair. "Empress Mathilda," he said, bowing his head, "I regret to tell you that it is only the three of us at this time."

"At this time ..." I repeated in confusion. "Are there more following after you?"

"No, my lady," said Ralph, "but we do bring a message from the count of Anjou." One of his eyes had an odd twitch that seemed to give the lie to everything he said, but I chose to believe him.

"Give it to me immediately," I demanded, holding out my hand.

Ralph nodded and reached into the leather bag he wore over his shoulder, pulling out a sealed note. I quickly took it from his hand and called out, "Earl Robert! Where are you, Earl Robert?!"

"Here!" he called, stepping to the front of the crowd.

I beckoned him to come next to me and my eyes searched wildly for Earl Miles. I finally saw that he was standing just to my left, close enough for me to tug his sleeve and pull him close enough to read. With one of them on each side, I broke the seal and opened the piece of parchment, my fingers struggling to match the speed demanded by my will. On it were all the signs of my husband's hand, which I would never have mistaken: bold and on a slant, with stray marks here and there and great drops of ink, as if he had not taken the time to properly ready the pen before setting it to paper, but kept dipping it in haste.

"Let us read it together," I said, and all three of us bent closer.

The thing read as follows.

Empress Mathilda, countess of Anjou —

I, Geoffrey, write this in my own hand from the fortress of Argentan, where I make my stay. I have received today five men who claim they were sent by you, though I know nothing of them. They have with them a letter which seems to bear your mark. Of course, all the news here has been of the defeat at Winchester. How did this happen, wife? Men say you were rude to the bishop and defied the laws of the Church. Moreover, they say you all fled like a flock of hens before the fox, and now Stephen is free to sit upon the throne again. It is good that you are still alive, for our sons' sake. I tell you I have listened to everything these messengers have said, but I cannot deal with them. They propose that I come over to England with some of my men, and as there is war at present between Count Theobald and the king, I am somewhat in favor of this idea, but I cannot treat with these people. They know nothing of our ways here and I know nothing of them. Where is the earl of Gloucester? Send him over and I will treat with him. I so cherish his prudence and steadfast loyalty. He has a high mind and is always diligent. So, send him across the sea that I may speak with him, and I will do my best not to neglect his wishes. However, I regret to tell you that, should you send anyone else, it will be a vain labor. Therefore, send Earl Robert at the first opportunity. He must come this summer and we will discuss all these matters, but my son I will never suffer to be sent to England. He is precious to me and I must see to his welfare. I wonder that you should obsess so much over that island, which has little to offer in wealth or power, and leave me to fight for the land of your fathers alone, but I suppose I shall never understand you.

Signed this seventh day before the Kalends of May,
GEOFFREY, COUNT OF ANJOU

I had only just finished reading and barely had time to take in the meaning of the words when Miles barked, "What on earth did I just read?! Jesus, Mary, and Joseph!" Then he offered several curses too quiet for anyone but me to hear.

I could have said any of a hundred things against my husband in that moment, all of which would have been entirely correct and just, but knowing how many eyes were upon me, I did not want to give any sign of anger or disagreement. I looked over at my brother, who was still gazing at the page.

"Robert?" I asked quietly. "Are you finished?"

Looking up, he leaned close and whispered in my ear, "Bastard."

"He has the power now and he knows it," I whispered back. "This was always going to be the way."

I took a step forward and raised my voice. "Gentlemen, I have read the letter from my husband, the count of Anjou. He says he will consider joining the fight here, but only if he is able to meet with the earl of Gloucester there and plot the advance together." These words did not come close to capturing my true thoughts about the letter, nor the whole of what my husband had said. He had shown no personal concern for my welfare, had bought into the lies peddled by the usurper's party, and had done nothing to encourage me in a moment of grief. I noted it but said nothing.

"But why can they not make the preparations here?" asked Earl Baldwin.

"That …" I began, struggling and failing to come up with some explanation, "is a good question. I have no answer."

"So, no one's coming, then? We're as good as dead!" said the earl of Chester.

"I thank you not to make such a proclamation at the present," I chided him. "For all we know, it is Stephen who is good as dead. Last we heard, he was still ill in Northampton."

"Well, you have to send Earl Robert over there," he argued. "Those Angevin troops are our only hope."

I opened my mouth to reply but was interrupted.

"Earl Ranulf, was it not you who so lately sided with the usurper?!" my brother growled, stepping forward until he was only an arm's length from the earl of Chester's face. "And you, Earl Hugh," he continued, walking over to where the man stood. "Lord Bigod, was it not you who failed to answer the call when the empress was in danger at Winchester? And Earl Roger, where were you when the flames fell from the sky and the forces of the false queen swarmed around us? Where were you when I was lucky to escape with my life?!"

None of the three men could offer an answer. Each one had a look on his face that revealed shame, fear, or both.

"But how can we part with Earl Robert?" my brother Reginald asked. "How can we part with him when we just released Stephen in exchange for him? I was under the impression that we all believed we could not win without him."

Here Reginald looked at me, but I said nothing. I turned instead to my other brother, the earl of Gloucester, who was staring at me in return. I knew he must suspect as I did that the whole thing was a ploy by Count Geoffrey to gain the help of Earl Robert in bringing all of Normandy under his rule: Angevin rule. Those sweet words about Robert's character were nothing but deceit. We both remembered with what annoyance my husband had treated him in the early days of the war, seeing him as a rival of sorts. Count Geoffrey's intent was likely along two lines: to use the strength of Earl Robert to pacify Normandy, but also to have that strength submitted to his own command.

"Earl Robert," I said, "take a walk with me."

As the rest of the men looked on, most in confusion, the two of us made our way to a far corner of the hall where we could not be easily heard. I folded my arms, tucking the letter under one of them, and asked him, "Do you think if you go to Normandy, he will meet our request?"

"Hard to say," he replied, shaking his head. "He clearly wants my help in battle, likely in the western half of the duchy because that is where my own estates lie. If it is to last for the summer season, I will be gone quite some time. You will be left to fend for yourself."

"Do you think it likely that the usurper's party will mount an invasion of the West Country?" I asked.

He sighed, placing his hands on his hips, his whole manner speaking of frustration and perhaps even resignation. "We don't know what is happening with Stephen. If he is dying, my absence may make it more difficult for you to take the throne that is rightfully yours, but they are unlikely to strike against you for some time because they will be too caught up attempting to gain support for young Eustace. If Stephen recovers, he could set upon our cities, yes, but it will take a bit of time to gather up his forces again. So much depends on things we cannot know."

"And do you want to go?"

"Do I personally want to go? No. It's a waste of precious time. It makes little sense in relation to our broader efforts. However, I do believe that if I go, I might succeed in obtaining something that would help us very much indeed."

"If you refer to my son, you read as well as I did my husband's pledge that he would not allow him to be brought to England," I argued.

"I read it," he said, a sly smile on his face, "but the count has not yet seen all my powers of persuasion on display. If I offer to aid him for a time in exchange for transporting Prince Henry to this country, it will be worth it, for your authority will be immediately established in a way it has not been before. Until now, men have been asked to serve a woman whose male heirs their eyes have never seen: who are too young to fight in battle. But Henry is not so young any more. He is not a man, certainly, but he is almost as old as Eustace. If he can sign his name, he can sign charters. He can begin executing the duties of kingship in this land for all to see."

It seemed that my brother was proposing that the kingdom skip over my rule and move directly to that of my son, or at least make me no more than a regent while Henry came of age. I suppose I ought to have been more offended, but I was not. As much as I enjoyed the thought of being queen, chiefly for the greater sovereignty it would give me over my own life, I had always been driven by concern for my sons more than anything else. What was more, if my son came to England, he would be raised in the household of my brother rather than among the Angevins, and I saw much benefit in that. I would be able to see at least one of my children on occasion. I would not be so alone.

"Let us assume the worst possibility: that as soon as you leave, Stephen is healed and is able to quickly gather an army to march on our lands. How weak is our position?" I asked.

"We can strengthen the defenses along the Thames, starting with Wallingford," he explained. "They will come from the North or East. If from the North, then it is essential that Earl Roger holds the region around Warwick. He will be the first line of defense. If they come from the East, then Brian will certainly need to hold Wallingford, but we also require the help of Hugh Bigod. He must find it in himself to be true. And the earl of Chester, Ranulf—he must do his part as well. If all these men remain faithful, I suspect you can all hold on long enough for me to return, even if Stephen does recover. But it will depend on that in every way."

"I have only slightly more trust in them than I do in the French," I told him sadly. "Is there any way they can be induced to keep their word? I do not have any more lands or titles to offer them."

"A very neat way: I will take some of their own men with me as hostages."

I nodded. "Yes, I suppose that might do it, assuming they care about the welfare of their knights."

"They will if they hope to hold their own estates," he concluded. "I think that is what we must do. I will go to Normandy with the hostages. I will dance to Count Geoffrey's tune, but I will return as soon as possible with as many men as possible, and I will not let the count go until he agrees to relinquish Prince Henry. In the meantime, Earl Miles will lead the defense here along with Reginald and Lord Brian. They will see to it that the other earls keep their word and defend you against all dangers. You need only hold on for a few months at most. Look every day for my return. I will not leave you alone among the wolves, sister. I will make good on my word. You will see your son before the end of the year in this very castle, and we will all be safe."

I reached out and embraced him, caring not who saw, for he was my brother. I clung to him, my heart full of fear for what awaited, but I knew there was no other choice. He was right as usual.

"We cannot let them win, Robert," I whispered. "If they win, then this is what England becomes. This injustice is what

England will be for ever. I refuse to allow it. I love this kingdom too much."

"I know you do," he said, pulling back. "I swear to you, I will return. You will live to see justice restored. What is wrong can be made right. You'll see."

I placed my hands on either side of his face. "Even so, let it be, for you are blood of my blood and flesh of my flesh."

XXIII

My brother remained with us only until the Feast of the Nativity of Saint John, then made ready to leave the following morning. He took with him men from the households of the earls of Warwick, Chester, and Norfolk, and gave their masters stern warnings that were they to fail in their duties to me as their liege lady, they would never see their men again and would face the full wrath of Robert, earl of Gloucester upon his return. That would have been enough to scare most men into obedience, so we certainly hoped it would have the proper effect.

As the sun rose on the seventh before the Kalends of July, I put on a cloak and made my way out to the stables, where I suspected I would find Earl Robert readying his horse for the ride. As I made my way on the dirt path covered in bits of straw, passing stalls that were mostly empty, I came at last to the one where my brother's horse resided, a great white thing named Raphael. I remembered when Robert first gave it that name, for he said it was a beast fit for angels to ride.[43]

---

43 Raphael is the name of an angel who appears in the Book of Tobit.

I saw my brother stand up next to Raphael with a blanket in his arms, already clad in mail. He had evidently been crouched down until that moment, perhaps tending to the animal's shoes. As Robert placed the blanket on the animal's back and bent down again to retrieve the saddle, I asked him, "Could one of the grooms not have done this?"

My words caught his attention and he looked at me in surprise, holding the saddle in his arms.

"You're meant to still be asleep," he muttered.

"I was not about to let you go without wishing you well," I said quietly.

He turned his back to me and fitted the saddle in place, then fetched the stirrups and began looping them through the holes, fixing the buckles under the animal's chest.

"Normally, I am happy to leave this to another, but when I ride into battle, I prefer to do it myself and alone." Here he looked at me again, as if to make clear that I was interrupting his process. "It helps get my mind in a state for warfare."

"And do you consider a meeting with my husband to be a kind of battle?" I asked, smiling.

He did not answer, but continued moving around the horse, making sure everything was properly in place. There was a great deal of sighing, and I could not help but feel that something other than the journey ahead was troubling his mind.

"What is it, brother?" I asked. "You seem in a mood."

Letting out a grunt, he abandoned his task and stepped closer, the mail jingling with each step.

"First of all, I have a terrible itch that I cannot scratch!" he complained. "Second of all, I've had another letter from the lady of Bristol Castle."

"Your wife? What did she want? To send you her love, I hope."

"She sent anything but love," he replied, seeming almost to growl. "She considers me an enemy of the peace."

"Whatever for?"

"Because ..." he began, wrinkling his nose and scowling. "Because my son is not what he ought to be."

"Which one?"

"The eldest one. The one I put in charge of Wareham."

"William!" I cried in surprise. "He seemed to be doing fine when last I saw him."

My brother only scowled all the more and turned to face his horse, patting the thing on the head. "You don't have these problems, do you, boy?" he asked the animal.

"Robert, if there is something you wish to tell me, do so quickly," I advised.

He swung around and approached me again, hands on his hips, eyes pointed down at the ground.

"You might as well hear it in case the rumor spreads. Earlier this year, my wife received a letter from the owner of an inn down in Wareham. He says my son often comes by for a drink and has also rented a room on occasion—"

"Why would he need to rent a room if he ..." I began, but quickly recognized that something was happening there that would have been less than acceptable at the castle. "Oh ..." I whispered.

"Perhaps you have guessed the better part of it," my brother continued. "He would bring many women up there, though the word 'woman' is perhaps too kind in this case. The owner cared not, for it seems that the better part of his business comes from his ability to keep quiet about such matters. But one morning, William never came down from the room. He had been quite drunk the night before and neglected to pay his bill at the proper hour. When the man opened the door, he found the place a mess, things strewn everywhere, and in one place a puddle of vomit. But that was not the worst of it."

"It wasn't?" I asked in fear, my insides already churning from his description.

"No. You see, the owner found no woman there, though one had entered the evening before. Instead, he found my son, as naked as the day he was born, holding another man, also naked, the pair of them asleep, not even a sheet to cover their indignity."

I covered my mouth with my hands, a bit overcome by the words he had spoken. Certainly, I was aware that such things happened, but I had not thought to hear of it within my own family. This was rather foolish, given the many tales about my uncle William.[44]

"You will ask if it was some mistake—perhaps they were too drunk to know any better," my brother said, but shook his head. "There was no mistake. When he woke them, they confessed to the whole thing. It had been going on for some time. The whores, it seems, were simply part of the deception. One person would sneak out a window while another snuck in—that was the way of it. So, the owner wrote to my wife and demanded she pay him twenty pounds or he would let it be known abroad that our son is a sodomite. She then wrote to William and bid him give her the truth of the matter. He made no attempt to deny, having been caught so clearly in the act, although he begged for the mercy of a mother and apologized for the shame he had brought upon our house. We had no choice at that point but to pay the man in full. The money

---

44 King William II of England died unmarried and childless. There were rumors in the 12th century that he had homosexual relations. However, the evidence (or lack thereof) is such that modern historians have not reached a firm conclusion as to what sexual relationships, if any, he might have had with men or women.

would have been better spent on our defenses, but what were we to do?"

"I understand," I said simply. I had no idea what else to add. Whatever concerns I might have had for my nephew's spiritual state were, at that moment, overwhelmed by the fear of what might happen if it was rumored abroad that the earl of Gloucester's son was taking part in unnatural acts. It seemed strange to me, for I had never thought of William as anything but a kind soul. Yes, I felt somewhat sorry for him that he had fallen into such a trap, even if he did bring it on himself.

"Who was the man he was with?" I asked.

"Does it matter?! Now Mabel blames it on me!" Robert moaned. "I should have raised him better, she says. I didn't take him out hunting enough, didn't make a proper man out of him ... she goes on and on. She cannot bring herself to condemn her firstborn son, so she places the fault on me."

"But that's just silly. Surely he is full grown and can make his own decisions," I argued, "and we both know how stout William has been in battle. He is as good with a sword as most men, if not better. No one would think him weak or womanly."

My brother closed his eyes and shook his head back and forth as if to remove the very thought from his mind.

"Look, there's no need to discuss this further," I told him. "You paid the man. Hopefully he will keep his mouth shut. Put it out of your mind. You are about to set sail for Normandy. You must return with an army and my son. That is your task."

"Most assuredly," he agreed with a nod. "She bid me speak with William when I pass through Wareham and impress upon him who he is and what he owes to this family. I have no desire to even see him."

I placed my hand upon his arm. "He is still your son—that has not changed and never will. You must accept that he will have iniquities, but it does not erase all that he is."

"I suppose so," he said grimly, "but what was good for the Romans is no good for us.[45] Best be off now and get on with the business."

He tugged on Raphael's reins, leading him out of the stall and down the path. I walked along side them, my heart heavy.

"This is not how I wanted to part, Robert. I had in mind something more ... more ..."

"I think what you mean to say is something less unseemly," he offered.

"Something befitting the affection between a brother and sister," I offered in turn. "I do not mind saying that I have been having a hard time of it. My dreams are filled with terror."

"You and your dreams!" he cried, laughing. "What is it this time?"

"Same as always," I replied quietly, casting my head down. "I am in the castle of Oxford. There are flames all around—"

"Well, it's clear, isn't it? You are thinking of the fire in Winchester!" he interrupted, perhaps hoping to bring a quick end to the matter.

"But why would it be Oxford, then?" I asked in confusion. "And why should it be cold when fire is hot?"

I could tell my brother was annoyed, but he did give it a moment's thought at least before replying, "You had the dream once, and now because you ponder it so often, it is returning to you. Yes, that must be the answer!"

"Perhaps," I admitted.

"I have arranged everything for the city's defense. They are at work as we speak. There will be fortresses at Bampton and Radcot," he explained. "Oxford is surrounded on all sides by water or walls. It is as safe as any city in England, I dare say, save

---

45   In the ancient cultures of Greece and Rome, it was often acceptable for rich and powerful men to engage in sexual acts with younger, less powerful male partners.

perhaps for London itself. So, fear not! In any case, what good did fear ever do anyone if they had no choice but to proceed?"

"You make a fair point. So, this is it, then? This is how we part?"

"I'm afraid so," Robert replied, pausing for a moment.

We had made it out into the yard. The men were gathering with their horses. The carts were loaded with weapons of war.

"Keep a watch for my return," he said. "Remember what I promised: by the end of the year, in this very castle, you will see your son."

"Would that I had more faith in the promises of men," I bemoaned, "but yours are as good as they come. Stay safe. Be brave."

As soon as the company had departed for Normandy, I traveled back to Oxford along with all the lords I had gathered. We did not know how ill Stephen remained, so we could only hope that there would be no more fighting that summer and we would have a few weeks to arrange our defense. As Earl Robert had ordered, fortresses were erected at Bampton and Radcot in case any of Stephen's supporters in the West decided to attempt an approach from that direction. The old manor at Woodstock was made into a proper castle with a new wall and ditch. Of course, there was no time to build all of this in stone, so it had to be made from wood: a pity, for wood is not as strong. We had great faith in the castle of Wallingford thanks to Lord Brian's wise decision to improve the walls over the past year and increase the stock of food.

The city of Oxford itself had a good natural defense in the form of the River Thames and its branches. The whole land to the south was little more than a marsh, and the old sites to ford had mostly disappeared, though we did fear that the water level might be lower in late summer. We therefore hoped for the addition of autumn rains before any battle would take place. Stephen was likely to approach from the north, hence the fortress at Woodstock. The Beaumont Palace just north of the wall was not well made for battle, so we relied instead upon the city wall. We knew Stephen might also come up the Thames, but that would force him to go past Wallingford. The West Country gave us less concern on account of the many towns we held in that direction, but Earl Miles nevertheless oversaw the construction of a new wall on the western bank of the river just north of the castle and another to the south of the isle of Osney. This ensured that there would be no easy path through those waters. Though we hated to do so, we also destroyed the three bridges that were close by: the Grandpont south of the city, the smaller bridge right next to the castle, and the one that crossed the stream by the abbey. This made its inhabitants none too happy, as they would have to cross by boat in all directions, but any delay we could buy would be worth it. Should the enemy come from that direction, he would be blocked at every point by either a high wall or deep water.

We would have liked to do more with the summer sun, but that was the most we could accomplish in a month. What upset me most during this time was the lack of news. Formerly, we had received occasional pieces of information from London and the Southeast, but we had not enjoyed such a benefit since Whitsuntide, or perhaps even earlier. This caused me no little distress, but I attempted to set my mind upon other things: most especially my maid, Adela, whose belly was growing by the day. Her condition became public knowledge as August wore on, and it was her intent to travel west for a time of solitude before giving birth. However, there would soon be an end to any such thoughts of travel.

It began with a rumor that the false queen had set out from Dover to her home county of Flanders, no doubt to gather support for their efforts in the war. We knew she was unlikely to do so unless her husband had recovered his strength, so this was as good a sign as any that whatever had been ailing Stephen's body since Easter had finally departed. At this news, the earls of Chester, Norfolk, and Warwick departed for their own estates to the north and east. They would be the front line of defense against the enemy's advance, along with Lord Brian of Wallingford. This did nothing to set my mind at ease, for I remembered the words of my father that whoever stands upon the front line must be most steadfast in the defense of his lord. Save for Brian, who I was certain would lay down his life on my behalf, the others had already proven themselves unfaithful in an hour of need, or at least tardy to the point of uselessness. I could only hope that the hostages my brother had taken with him to Normandy would cause them to behave as they ought. Only earls Miles, Baldwin, and Reginald remained with me in Oxford, along with my household knights.

The stress of that hour was great indeed, such as I had seldom experienced in my life. We sensed that the enemy was at work, but where and to what end? And where on earth was Earl Robert?! For the second time in a year, I had sent a party to Normandy in all haste only to have it tarry for far too long. We were in desperate need of help that very moment, but there was nothing—not a word. I clung to my brother's promise, but I began to fear that something might have gone horribly wrong. After all, this was not the simple band of messengers we had sent in the spring: it was Earl Robert of Gloucester. If he did not return, it would not be due to any failing on his part but something thoroughly out of his control. Perhaps the ships had all been lost in a storm, or perhaps they had been set upon by enemies along the way. Who was to say?

"It has not been so very long, my lady," Drogo kept telling me. "Have faith. Earl Robert will return."

I wanted to believe it, but I felt the danger of that hour keenly, an ever present threat working upon the corners of my mind. Every time hope is beaten down, it becomes more difficult for it to rise again.

On the first day of September, I learned that the master of the castle, old Robert D'Oyly, was too ill to rise from his bed. The physician Grimbald, one of the few men in Oxford older than the lord, examined him and determined that it was no infection but simply the breaking down of his body. It was thought that he would not be long for this world, so I rose and made my way across the courtyard to where Lord D'Oyly had his abode. All that time I had been staying in the tower, he and his family were in the building across the way, beyond the keep. The residences there were larger than those in the tower and the adornment more wonderful, but they were not as safe as the Saint George Tower.

I approached the building of timber and daub with its two stories crowned by a roof of thatch, doing my best to avoid a crowd of pigs that were being herded by one of the servants. A single door covered in blue paint stood between me and the inside. I knocked upon it thrice and it was opened by Grimbald. His white beard had grown even longer by that point, and he was clad as ever in thick black robes.

"Empress Mathilda," he greeted me with a bow of the head, "have you come to look in on the patient?"

"If it will not trouble him," I said.

From underneath his beard, I perceived a smile. "When have you brought trouble upon any man, my lady?"

"Ha!" I cried rather too loudly, likely attracting the attention of those in the yard. More softly, I assured him, "A long line of men would take objection to those words, not the least of them being my husband."

"And your cousins, I think," he said with a wink. "Come in, then."

I crossed the threshold and followed him down a small passage. The smell of incense was strong—so strong that it made an assault upon the nose—and I guessed it must be some remedy meant to ward off ill humors. The scent of myrrh was so heavy that I could not determine what else, if anything, was included.

As if reading my thoughts, Grimbald whispered, "I had nothing to do with the smell. In my experience, these things do little to aid the body, though they may lend some comfort to the mind. If it makes the patient happy—" Here he threw up his hands. " *'iidha kan la yaduru, falaykun lilarab.*"[46]

We had reached the stair and he began climbing with some difficulty, clinging to the rail on the right. I placed a hand on his back to support him if needed.

"Master Grimbald, I note that you left behind our Norman tongue just now," I said, as we continued upward.

"Ah, I wondered when you did not say anything immediately," he called back to me.

"Is it the language of the Moors? I know you speak it, at least a little."

"In my day, I could read it as well as Mohammad himself, though an ambassador to your father's court once told me my accent was exceedingly poor. He could barely understand me. That is what comes from never hearing it spoken."

He had reached the top and I arrived next to him, moving my hand up to his shoulder as he caught his breath.

"The saying is from Abulcasis, the greatest physician that ever has been," he continued. "It struck my mind in that

---

46 اذا ناك ال نكيلف ، رضي ال برلب. Meaning roughly, "If it does no harm, let the lord have it."

moment. Perhaps I have not remembered it correctly. Anyway, here is the chamber!"

He turned to the left and opened the single door that was there. It seemed to whine as it swung open. At once, I was overwhelmed by the smell. I could not help myself: I raised a hand to my face and used my sleeve to cover my nose. The doctor leaned over and whispered in my ear, "There are advantages of growing ancient. None of the senses work as well as they used to." Here he pointed to his nose, and I had to suppress a laugh, for we were in the presence of a dying man.

Most of the contents of the room had been pushed to one side so the space around the bed was clear. This was no doubt to grant those attending upon their master a path from which to do so. The old man lay under what appeared to be several layers of bedding. On the very top was a large bear skin: so large that I could not make out much of anything under it, including Robert D'Oyly. The small window on the far wall let in just a trace of light, and on a table below it there was a censer from which the smoke of incense rose to the ceiling. It cast a cloud over the whole room.

The physician raised a finger to his lips, and as I neared the foot of the bed, I saw that Lord Robert was asleep. Only his head stuck out from underneath his covers. Though his eyes were closed, his breath did not seem to come easily and the wrinkles on his brow moved from time to time, as if he were having some frightful dream. Grimbald pushed back the bear skin to reveal the man's chest, opening the shirt slightly and placing his ear to the skin.

"What exactly is wrong with him?" I whispered.

"His heart is weak," the physician answered. "The beat is irregular."

He rose again to his full height and took three steps to where I stood.

"He will not survive this month," he informed me. "The castle will need a new keeper."

"Well, that is ill timing," I complained softly.

He nodded. "Indeed."

A few minutes later, I entered the yard again feeling rather grim. When Robert D'Oyly was transferred to the next life, the estate would need to be passed to an heir. The children of Lord Robert's late wife—the ones who shared a father with me—could not inherit. Instead, it would be the oldest legitimate son, Henry, who would become the next lord of Oxford Castle and Baron Hocknorton. *Very well*, I thought. *We must make ready for the ceremony. Perhaps next month, or is that too early?*

I busied my mind with these things until I was almost back to the tower, when I heard someone calling my name.

"Empress! Empress Mathilda!"

I immediately turned to look in the direction of the main gate, from which the sound had come. I saw that it was Earl Miles running toward me at full speed, his eyes as wild as an animal about to strike the killing blow.

"What is it, man?!" I cried.

He was moving so fast that he struggled to stop when reaching my position, his feet sliding on the dirt. He stretched out his hand and grabbed my shoulder to avoid a crash, rattling me from head to toe.

"We were wrong!" he informed me, panting heavily.

"About what?!" I demanded.

"He comes from neither North nor East." Here he backed up slightly and made a broad sweep with his arm toward his right and my left. "He comes from the West: Southwest, to be precise. He has taken back the port of Wareham. He proceeds north at this very hour toward our cities."

"But how?!" I cried. "How did he get down there so quickly?"

He shook his head, still breathing heavily. "I don't know. Our communication has been so poor. He must have learned that Earl Robert set out from there and hopes to make a charge at our lands."

With each word he spoke, I could feel the strain in my body increase. Fear piled on top of fear.

I inquired, "How do we know all this?"

"One of the monks of Malmesbury sent a message. I ran to your chambers to bring you word, but you were gone, and no one could say where. So, I've been running around outside for the past quarter hour—"

"I am sure you did everything you could to find me," I assured him, "but now that you have, let us waste no more words. Where are the other earls?"

"Within the tower, up in the hall."

I turned on the spot and walked to the door, where two guards stood in place as usual. With a single firm look, I induced one of them to open it and began ascending the stair with Earl Miles behind me. My thoughts raced.

He has taken the port where Robert is to return. He has cut off our one connection to Normandy, and now he moves north. How many are with him? Will he turn west toward Devon? No, surely not. What value is that to him? He is coming for me alone. Not Bristol or Gloucester— only Oxford. This is where he wins the war.

I entered the hall and saw earls Baldwin and Reginald both pacing the room in different directions, one with crossed arms and the other talking to himself hands and all. Drogo was sitting in one of the chairs by the hearth looking as if he had just lost all his money at dice. Upon noticing our entrance, Earl Baldwin cried, "He'll burn it all to the ground! I'll have nothing left!"

"Peace, sir!" I instructed. "We must try to be calm."

He lowered his brow and turned his head slightly to the side. "How can you tell me to be calm?! We've been caught napping, that's what. The enemy is at this very moment riding up to my castles to place them under siege, with my family inside!"

I nodded to show my concern for his plight. "I understand how you feel, but we must be reasonable—" I began.

"Are you calling me unreasonable?!" he barked.

"No, certainly not."

He threw up his hands in frustration and turned to address Reginald. "Tell her!" he commanded. "Tell her the way of things."

My brother looked at me earnestly and pleaded, "We must set out this very moment to defend our lands. We have no choice."

"No, no!" I objected. "You cannot leave now! Our numbers are already low. We must stand together or be picked off one by one."

"No, we must stop him before he presses any further!" cried Reginald. "I refuse to sit here and wait for my doom to arrive whenever it pleases Stephen. We must take the opportunity to surprise him before he is able to hold his position and cut us off from Earl Robert's return."

"The lords are correct," Miles offered. "We cannot let him destroy our castles one by one while we all sit here."

I looked from one man to the next, surprised to find them standing as one in this matter. Their instinct was completely the opposite of mine. Had my brother Robert not told us all to remain together? Had he not commanded that they stay and defend me? It seemed at the first sign their estates might be in danger, they were deserting me for a battle they were unlikely to win. Still, they were men of war and I was not. Perhaps I was wrong and it was better to strike out against Stephen rather than awaiting his arrival.

"Who is to defend Oxford if you are gone?" I asked desperately. "The other earls have already departed for their lands to the north and east."

"Call them back!" Reginald argued. "They are doing no good there."

Here Drogo entered the conversation. "Do you trust them to come when called? They did not do so before."

"Yes, listen to Drogo," I said, pointing at him.

"They will come. Earl Robert has their hostages," said Baldwin. He had walked up behind Drogo's chair and gripped the back of it firmly, as if it had done him an injury. "They would not leave their lands so easily to the enemy, and neither should we. When they hear the enemy is in the South, they will have no fear in advancing this far."

I shook my head and gestured with both hands. "Has the lesson of this war not been that it is better to remain inside one's castle and wait out the enemy rather than riding out into open battle? What do you hope to accomplish?! If Stephen has as many men at his command as we fear, you cannot hope to defeat him on the open plain without Earl Robert—without the rest of the earls."

"And yet we must try," Baldwin concluded, pounding his hand into the chair mere inches from Drogo's head. "Come, Reginald! We must be off!"

"I have not commanded you to leave!" I objected. "You are sworn to defend me, and while I mourn any loss of your possessions and danger to your dear ones, you must first fulfill your pledge to the crown. Reginald, my brother, do not show yourself faithless!"

Reginald stopped and turned toward me. The anger seemed to pour forth from his eyes, and he released each breath as a dragon about to spit fire. Then his words came: angry, bitter, unyielding.

"Three years, sister! Three years I have fought and bled for you, and for what? I have suffered the loss of much I hold dear, and in return I receive the world's derision. They mock me openly upon the streets of Exeter. I have paid the final ounce of my nobility to defend you, as has every man here! Who was it that fled with you across the plain of Wiltonshire and drew the life from those who sought yours? Who was it that abandoned all for your sake? How quickly you forget! Have you any notion of what this has done to my wife? Have you held her to your bosom as she wept upon her couch? Have you told her it would all be well in the end while fearing it was a lie? Well, I cannot do it—not any longer. By my blood and toil, I have earned the right to judge in this matter. The enemy moves against my home, so I will do what any man would do, or at least anyone worth the name of man. I will defend my own, for that is the very height of honor."

"And am I not your sister?" I whispered, my lips trembling, the force of his censure bearing down upon me.

"You know nothing of war," he muttered.

I glared at him. "I know that it is the height of dishonor to violate the orders of one's commander."

"And if Robert were here, we would do what he says, but he is not here," my brother replied.

Oh, how the anger boiled within me! I yelled at the top of my lungs, "I meant me! I am your lady! I forbid you to go!" I turned and looked at Miles. "You will not stand for this, will you? Tell them they cannot do this!"

"My lady, you are behaving wildly," he said, raising a hand. "I fear you are driven too much by the humors."

"The humors?!" I scoffed. "What on earth do you mean?!" I do believe I gave him such a look as to make clear that any further conversation along that line was likely to end with him in more than one piece.

"Forgive me. Think on it no longer," he offered. "I must go with them though. It is what Earl Robert would want. His estates are as much in danger as theirs."

"But he told you that what he wanted was for you all to stay with me!" I declared, pointing my finger at each of them in turn. "I am sorry for all you have lost and all you may yet lose. Truly, it cuts me to the quick. Had I not been a woman subject to constant judgment, I would have let you see how many tears I have shed for all who have suffered hardship on my behalf. I would have let the pain flow from me as the sacred river that runs into the sea, where it would be carried off until the ending of time. But this is the nature of war: it calls us to seek after a greater prize and endure the sacrifices of the moment in hope of a better future. Even as Virgil wrote, "*Durate, et vosmet rebus servate secundis.*" Your lack of faith appalls me!"

My words appeared to grieve Earl Miles, who looked as if he might break into tears, but there was no such response from the other two, who were making to leave. I shook my head, unable to comprehend how things had gone so badly.

"Forgive me again, my lady," Miles said quietly. "I know you are angry now, but I truly believe this is for the good of our cause and it is the best way we can defend you."

Drogo had apparently had enough. He rose to his feet and walked over to oppose the earl.

"How dare you!" he cried. "After everything she has done for you, how can you deny her the respect she is due?"

"It is because of my respect for the empress that I go to fight on her behalf!" Miles argued.

My knight was having none of it. "Ballocks! To disobey royal command is treason."

At this declaration, Miles' nostrils bulged and he was filled with a sudden fury.

"Call me traitor again and I will make you pay for it," he warned, raising a finger.

Drogo walked so close to him that were he not a good half foot taller, their noses might have touched. Instead, the knight looked down at him with a glare as deadly as Medusa's.[47]

"Traitor," he whispered.

Miles shoved him and raised a fist to strike. Drogo was too quick and met his hand, twisting Miles' arm until he cried out in pain and wrapping his own arm around Miles from behind, rendering him helpless.

"You are a knave and a devil!" Drogo cried.

"Please! Stop this!" I yelled, afraid to step too near. "Violence will not help us. Drogo, I command you to stop!"

The knight looked at me for a moment as if begging, *Please, let me kick him where he will never forget it.* I shook my head no. Finally, Drogo shoved the earl to the ground and stepped away panting. I waited as Miles recovered and rose to his feet, too thoroughly humbled to speak.

"Go then, Earl Miles," I said softly. "Go and do what must be done. As I cannot stand in your way, I will not attempt to, but this is a sad day when a queen is dishonored."

He bowed and quickly made for the door, shoulders drooping, carrying his shame with him. When he was certain the earl could not hear, Drogo complained, "You should have let me finish it."

"That would have been just by the code of honor, but we are far past any such consideration," I bemoaned. "There is no honor left in England, save perhaps in yourself and a few others."

---

47 Medusa is a figure in Greek mythology whose eyes turn anyone who looks upon them into stone.

The knight walked over and put a hand on my shoulder. "Whatever comes our way, Your Highness, you know I will remain by your side, even as I always have. The rest of them can go to hell."

I said nothing but closed my eyes and prayed to God that I was in the wrong and the earls could find and defeat the usurper. However, I had little hope in their venture, and though I had heard Drogo's words, I was feeling more than ever what I had sensed so often throughout my years: I was utterly alone.

The days that followed the exodus of my captains did nothing to shake me from the resolve I had carried at the start. While I lacked much knowledge of warfare and did not pretend otherwise, I knew something of my cousin and of men in general. Having suffered first a terrible humiliation and then an illness that brought him well-nigh down to the grave, he would have only one object in mind. And if he had indeed learned of Earl Robert's departure, which we had tried so hard to conceal, he would have felt there was no obstacle in his way which could not be easily overcome. He was not coming for Reginald or Miles— for the treasures of Bath or Bristol. He was closing in for the kill. He knew that I was in Oxford, and having allowed me to escape once, he would grant me no such luxury again. In my mind, I could still hear those words that had pierced the sky amid the field of wheat: *Kill the bitch!* He would not rest until it was done.

The actions of those men who were meant to serve me only helped him in this regard. What was more, the lords of the North were nowhere to be seen. I had sent messengers to the earls of Warwick, Chester, and Norfolk at the first opportunity, but received nothing in reply. I had foreseen it, and yet I hated to be right. I was left there in Oxford Castle with only my own knights and those of Robert D'Oyly.

I had hoped to send Adela away from the conflict, but I had no idea what place might be safe. Gloucester would have been a good choice if it were not in the direct line of Stephen's advance. Yes, anything to the south or west was too dangerous, and as for the North, I had every reason to doubt that those lords were on my side. The less said about the East the better. No, there was no safe place for her to lay her head. I considered at least sending her to an abbey, where she might hope to claim the benefit of sanctuary, but I remembered how Bishop Henry of Winchester had not feared to rain down fire upon the nuns of his own city. There was no reason to suppose that even sacred places would be free from harm. In the end, she begged me to let her stay at the castle, where she could have my company and that of her husband. What was more, she had the aid of Master Grimbald, who kindly offered to remain with us for as long as I wished.

The day before the Ides, the lord of the castle breathed his last. As we had no idea what was happening to the south of us and how quickly Stephen might be moving toward our position, I did not feel safe leaving the castle, so the funeral train proceeded to Osney without me. They buried him in the abbey next to his wife, but I doubted he would rest in peace: not with the enemy approaching.

About a week later, we finally received a report of Stephen's position. To my great dismay, he was said to be in Gloucestershire, not more than a day's ride from Oxford. The earls had either failed to discover his army or been defeated on the field of battle. Stephen had still to advance past the fortresses of Bampton, Radcot, and Cirencester, but it seemed likely that within a few days he would arrive at his object. As I had suspected, he had not put many of our castles under siege. He was coming for me alone.

By right, Henry D'Oyly ought to have taken over the defense of the castle, but he had little experience in battle, so

I exercised my authority as rightful queen to appoint Drogo in his stead. Henry was a young man and seemed glad to be relieved of such a duty. We had only about a hundred souls inside the castle. The walls were strong and the waters of the Thames safeguarded us to the west; to the east was the city with its own set of walls. With the few men we had, we set about digging more ditches. A message was sent throughout the town that all the people should flee to the North and seek refuge there. I did not want a repeat of what happened in Winchester. Those students who were of able body and felt inclined to do so joined our force. Most of them had little skill with weapons, so we assigned them to a team that would take water from the River Thames to fight any fires the enemy might set.

On the eighth day before the Kalends of October, a foul rain moved in and fell upon Oxford from dawn until dusk. The sky was as dark as ever I saw it at midday. Adela was heavy with child, and in the absence of the lord of the castle, I had instructed that she be allowed to rest in his former chamber, which still smelled of myrrh. I would sit by her side often as she lay on the bed, holding her hand and stroking her brow.

"So dark ... as if the world is about to end," she whispered, gazing out the window. "Have you heard anything from Lord Brian?"

"Nothing," I said sadly. "I sent him a letter, but I fear it went astray."

"Between here and Wallingford?" she asked, evidently struggling to believe it. "That is less than half a day's ride."

"Perhaps I choose to believe it went astray," I admitted.

I placed a hand on her belly, hoping to feel the child move. However, there was nothing save for the slow rise and fall that came with each of Adela's breaths.

"I fear for this child," said Adela. "Even if it escapes both the sword of the enemy and those illnesses that claim so many little ones, it will live in a world that grows darker by the day. It is entering life in the middle of a war, with violence on all sides. I admit I fear for it every hour."

I looked into her eyes, from which ran tears that trickled down her face.

"I too am afraid," I told her. "Earl Robert has gone to fetch my son, but what will happen if he is drowned at sea? What if he comes here and the enemy seizes him? Will we ever see the light again, or have we already tasted the last of joy?"

"Well ... have we?" she inquired earnestly.

I smiled and shook my head. "No. No, this is only the beginning. Weeping may last for the night, but joy comes with the morning."

She sat up a bit, leaning on her arm. "How can you be sure?"

"I have seen it: not all of it, but enough. The Lord will not abandon us to destruction. I believe it with all my heart. This life is a brief hour of our existence—one filled with sorrows untold—but it is not all that we are. The cares of these days drive us down into dust, but then we cast our eyes to the heavens, and though the darkness is thick around us and the last of hope is ended, we reach out to that light, and as it claims us for its own, we rise to eternity."

"Oh, my lady ..." she breathed, shaking her head. "When you say it, I believe it."

"There are such things as false visions—I am not yet free of doubt," I admitted, "but my flesh and my bones declare the truth of this. I choose that which drives me on: I choose faith."

Suddenly, I felt a sign of life beneath my hand. A hand or perhaps a foot had pushed out to meet me.

"Did you feel that?!" Adela cried in excitement.

"Yes," I replied, smiling for the first time in quite a while. "I feel and I believe that life will triumph over death, light over darkness. What was once so wrong will be made right, and this child will live to see the world made fair again. But first comes the test, for gold cannot be known until it has passed through fire."

Even as we were discussing these things, there was a knock at the door. Assuming it to be either Drogo or Philip, I called out, "Enter!"

The door swung open and it was indeed Philip, back from his work upon the walls. He had been checking them for any weaknesses: cracks, sinking earth, or loose stones.

"Ah, Sir Philip," I said, "how go our efforts?"

"Everything is ready," he replied, walking over and taking his wife's other hand. "The city is empty save for those who choose to fight with us and a small number who were simply unwilling to leave. A few Cistercians have been brought within the castle: brothers from the monastery at Thame."

"Whatever for?" I asked. "They are far safer there than here."

"They are among the students who have offered to help us," he explained. "I thought you permitted it."

Sighing, I replied, "Yes, I did, but if we let too many in, we will only run out of food all the sooner."

"That is the one thing I am less worried about. We should have enough food to last until the New Year," he assured me.

I wished very much that I had his confidence. Rising from the bed, I walked over to the window and gazed out at the dark sky: an ocean of gray without beginning or end, stretching from Oxford out over England. For just a moment, I thought of those beyond the dark clouds looking down on it all, safe now from the dread of this world. Oh, to reside in such bliss! But there is only one path to that land, and all men tread it in fear. Some things we must end before we are permitted to begin.

"Very well," I said quietly. "Go out and speak to the men. Tell them to shut the gates of the city to both friend and foe."

"Are you certain?" he asked.

I turned from that bleakness, my spirit on edge, but my fiber and marrow strong. I looked in his eyes and repeated, "Shut the gates."

The day after I spoke those words, an hour or so past sunrise, I was called over to the roof of the keep. It was a space not more than fifty feet across, with a pair of archers standing by each slit, one ready to fire through it and the other pointing his weapon over the wall. Drogo stood in the middle, barking out instructions. Like the rest of the men, he was clad in armor, ready for battle to begin at any moment.

Having climbed the stair and risen through the door, I took my place beside him and asked, "Are they here?"

He nodded. "They are within half a mile, just beyond the new wall. Look!"

He led me to a slit that faced due west and the pair of archers stepped aside to allow me to look through. There was still some mist over the river, but to the north of the island I could just see a band of men on the far side of the wall, their armor gleaming in the sun. Some of them were surely hidden behind the row of wood spikes.

I asked a question though I feared to know the answer. "How many, Drogo? How many are they?"

"We cannot be sure at this point. These may only be the first and others are to follow," he replied.

I stood to full height again and looked up into his eyes. "How many?"

He sighed and nodded. "Perhaps three or even up to five thousand—that is, if this is the entire force. As I said, there may be others."

This was perhaps fifty times as many men as we had. What was more, I had seen the distant figures of what appeared to be great weapons of war.

"They have trebuchets and may intend to fire upon us from the opposite bank," said Drogo, as if sensing my thoughts.

"Can they get a clear shot from behind that wall?" I asked, attempting to seize any bit of hope.

"I'm not sure. It depends on the skill of their engineers. They are certainly well out of our range, but we have only bows and arrows." He must have noted the look of concern on my face, for he quickly added, "They will not find it easy to cross the river. The rain yesterday helped. The water is high and the bank thick with mud. They dare not swim for it, and it will take them some time to build any sort of bridge."

"Like Alexander at Tyre," I muttered.[48]

"What?" my knight asked in confusion.

"Oh, never mind it. So, what now? Do we just wait for them to act?"

"We could offer terms if you wish," Drogo replied.

"Ha!" I scoffed. "And what terms would those be?"

"We will surrender the city if they allow you to leave in peace," he offered.

"And go where?"

"Perhaps Gloucester … anywhere but here."

I closed my eyes and raised my head slightly, listening to the distant sound of church bells disturbed by the wind and, if I was not wrong, the drums of war beating on the far shore.

"They will not offer such terms," I concluded, opening my eyes. "That is not why they are here. We have no choice: we must hold the fortress until help can arrive."

---

48   During their siege of the island city of Tyre in 322 B.C., the Greeks under the command of Alexander the Great built a causeway or mole over a shallow channel that allowed them to bring their forces near the city walls. This was surprising at the time, as Tyre was thought to be virtually impregnable on account of its location and defenses.

"I think that is the right decision," he agreed with a nod of the head. "We have to hope that some of the earls show up. We might just have enough time to get a messenger or two past the enemy."

I descended back down the stair into the interior of the keep, then walked out upon the main wall. There I found about a dozen men, some running back and forth with supplies, others looking intently to the south. I had to move out of the way as a boy came by with a basket full of rocks, carrying them in the direction of the castle gate. As I did so, I came very close to the edge from which there was a drop of thirty feet or more back down to the ground. I quickly moved in the other direction, clinging to the wall for a moment until I felt stable again. No sooner had I done so than I saw Philip of Honfleur come around the corner, moving with great haste and yelling instructions to the men, some of whom began abandoning their positions and racing down the closest flight of stairs.

"Sir Philip!" I cried, waving my arm back and forth. "Sir Philip, over here!"

He looked in my direction and recognition came over his face as he moved toward me.

"My lady! You should not be on the walls. Get back in the tower!"

Ignoring his demand, I asked, "Are there any messengers left that we may send to Lord Brian and the earls of the West?"

"Any man who can mount a horse is needed for battle now!" he declared. "It is too late for messages."

Behind him, I saw three more knights run down the stair, and I asked Philip, "Where are they going? The enemy is on the far side of the river."

"Not all of them," explained Philip. "We have just seen men crossing the river near the ruins of the Grandpont."

"What?! How?!" I demanded to know.

"They appear to be swimming along with their horses. It doesn't matter. We have no time to lose. Forgive me, my lady— I must go!"

As he turned and fled down to the lower level, I cried after him, "God be with you, Sir Philip!" There were only a few men left on the wall as I stepped up to look over it. I saw the River Thames stretching out like a gray thread, and off in the distance there did appear to be figures moving across it: a number far smaller than the main host, but one that might cause us real trouble if it succeeded in breaching the south gate of the city.

"Mary, Joseph, and all the saints ..." I whispered.

I raced to the chapel, my thoughts moving faster than my legs.

I thought Drogo said they would not try to cross—that it was too treacherous. And now they have done it with horses? This is all happening too fast. Too late to send messengers. We are done for! No, you must not believe that. We need not win. We need only wait—wait and endure.

Soon I was bowed before the altar, offering supplications to the Almighty, willing my prayers to make their way to the highest heaven. I knew that Drogo had matters in hand, so I placed my trust in my defenders and did my part on my knees. I could only hope that I would not end the battle on my knees.

Little did I know that at that very moment, the band of knights who cast themselves upon fortune and entered that river had succeeded in their task. They had made it to the other side and mounted their horses, even as our men stormed down Fish Street and out the south gate with Henry D'Oyly and Philip of Honfleur in the lead. My defenders were brave and filled with a righteous passion, but they knew not what they were about to face. Though the two forces were almost equal in number, the enemy had sent his best ahead. It was Stephen himself who led that pack, the wolf of Ypres by his side. With them were the greatest of the Flemings: men bred for war and far more at home on a field of battle than in a church of God.

As I continued to pray, the two bands of knights met in the field just south of the city wall. Those on our side fought hard, but they could not maintain the pace of the enemy. They were caught within a storm of Flemings swirling this way and that. Though they strove to maintain the line, one after another of them fell by the sword, with Stephen himself casting down two or three. Sir Philip would later tell me that he had a clear shot at William of Ypres but was pushed off line by one of his brother knights who was thrown from his horse. In the end, there was nothing to do but retreat.

About a quarter of their number having fallen, sirs Philip and Henry led those that remained back toward the south gate with the enemy on their heels. When they neared the wall, the archers on top began firing at the enemy, but the two companies of riders were so close that it became difficult to distinguish one from the other. Some of those archers feared to shoot, while at least one other hit a knight on our side rather than the enemy. The men guarding the gate had mere seconds to decide whether it was better to shut the thing and leave our knights to their doom or keep it open and surely let in some of our opponents. In the end, they chose to hold it open and hope that our men could create separation.

I had been at my prayers less than half an hour when I heard the shouting outside increase. I could not help myself: I ran out into the yard to see what was happening. Across the way, the gate of the castle was opening and I could hear the bridge dropping into place. Proper caution at this moment would have meant running into the keep and sealing the door, but I was not aware of everything that had happened. Like a fool, I walked closer to the gate to see which of our men would come through and thank them for their service on my behalf. It was only as I came very close that I heard the pace of hooves and recognized this was no easy return but a hasty retreat. As the horses began to burst through the opening, I cast myself out of the way to avoid being trampled.

Only about a dozen men had returned, and they all swung their beasts back round to see what was coming in after them. One of the knights was missing his helm and I saw that it was Henry D'Oyly, blood and dirt all over his face. He was looking around wildly and crying, "Herbert! Where is Herbert?!"

"He lost his mount!" another called to him. "See, there he is on foot!"

I walked forward just a bit so I could see through the gate, driven on by a powerful longing to know—one that seemed to heed no warning of danger. A single knight was stumbling over the bridge. His left leg was clearly injured, and he was reaching down to drag it with every other step.

"Help me! Please, help me!" he cried, falling upon the wood planks.

Suddenly, I saw behind him on the other side of the moat a party of men riding in pursuit, making for the bridge. I gasped in terror, but I think no one heard it on account of the tumult. As I looked on, one of the knights who had just entered the castle gave his horse a swift kick and sent it into motion. He flew down the bridge as fast as lightning, reached down, and grabbed Herbert by one arm. He then pulled the horse round while at the same moment lifting the wounded man halfway off the ground. Strain as he did, he seemed unable to pull him any higher. Looking up at the few men standing above the gate, the rider commanded, "Raise the bridge!"

Then very many things happened at once. The enemy knights made it almost to the bridge but were hit by a shower of arrows from our men on the wall, causing them to slow for just a moment to raise their shields. The knight carrying Herbert flew back down the bridge just as quickly as he had gone out, even as it began to lift. A few seconds later, they were safely inside the castle, but the bridge was moving slowly and I was stunned to see one of the enemy knights on the far bank leap and grab on to it. This led two of his fellows to do the same, and under this extra weight, the bridge was even slower to rise.

Lord Henry yelled up to the men above, "Fire on them! Send them down to hell!"

This they did immediately, loosing not only arrows but many of the rocks I had seen the boy carrying earlier. One man fell into the moat and then another, but the last held on as the bridge rose ever higher. He then let go and tumbled down the slope, landing in the space between the bridge and the port-cullis, which had already been lowered. As I heard the sound of the bridge finally being shut into place, I placed a hand on my chest and let out a great sigh of relief. The men above the gate were still firing upon the enemy across the moat as their fellows below made to bind the trespasser. However, my thoughts were with poor Herbert.

I raced over to the knights who were finally alighting, several of them moving back toward the gate to help with the prisoner. Sir Herbert was laid out on the ground clutching his leg. The knight who had rescued him was bent over him, speaking to him softly.

"Who are you, sir?" I inquired, coming up beside them.

As Herbert looked up at me in pain, the other knight removed his helm and I saw that it was Sir Philip.

"My lady! You must not be here!" he cried. "I told you to stay in the tower!"

"And so I did, until …" I began, but I could not continue. He was correct. I should not have taken such a chance. How could I explain it? I had been drawn as if by something not of this earth. I lowered my head in shame, for though I was an empress, I was afraid to look him in the eye.

Being the good man that he was, Philip did not press the matter further, but asked, "Where is Grimbald? This man needs care and quickly."

"Over there," I said, pointing toward the residence.

He nodded and requested, "Could you help me remove his armor, since the others are busy?"

"Of course," I agreed gladly.

Herbert was groaning with pain, his teeth clenched. "Get it off me!" he begged. "My leg! My leg!"

"Do the buckles on that side," Philip instructed.

The knight had great leather pads strapped over his mail on each leg. I reached down and began loosening each of the straps on one side, but I was not as expert as Philip, who ended up doing half my work for me. Having removed both pads, we then pulled from either side until the mail came off by his feet, leaving only the man's breeches beneath. I could see clearly where a weapon had pierced through them on the left leg, leaving the fabric covered in blood.

"Put some pressure on that while I work on the rest of his armor," Philip requested.

I took the long sleeve of my gown in hand and pressed it on top of the wound, holding it firm with all my might. This caused the man to scream, a terrible sound that seemed to twist my bowels. He stretched and twisted in pain, but I held firm. I closed my eyes and bid the moment pass quickly. I could feel the cloth beneath my hands growing wet with blood.

"Mother Mary, please … Mother Mary, please …" I uttered, for I could find no other words.

"Finally!" Philip cried, and I opened my eyes to see that he had removed the last of the man's armor. "We must carry him. Take his legs."

"And let go of the wound?" I asked.

"I cannot carry him alone. He is too heavy," Philip explained. "It was all I could do to pull him off the bridge."

I nodded and did as he said. Philip put one hand under each of the man's arms, even as I lifted his feet, wrapping them up in my arms. He was indeed heavy, so much so that I doubted I would be able to make it to the destination, but there was no time to object: Philip was already moving.

"Come on! Quickly!" he instructed.

I did my best to keep up as we crossed the yard. Behind me, I still heard shouts rising to the heavens and could only hope that we would have a short break before the next blow fell— whatever it might be.

"What happened?" I asked, attempting to distract myself from the heavy load.

"It was Stephen and his best men," Philip explained. "They were too much for us. We retreated back into the city, but some of them made it in after us and others were able to jam the gate. There will be more soon enough. The city is lost to us."

Were I not so out of breath from carrying that heavy load, I would have surely cried "Oh, no!" or something far worse.

We were within a hundred feet of the entrance when another of the castle guard ran up and offered, "Step aside, my lady. I can carry him."

I did not have to be told twice. The knight took my spot and I bent over, placing my hands on my knees and gasping for air. I lifted my right arm and examined the sleeve. Its pale blue color was largely changed to red. Much of my belly was also smeared with sad Herbert's blood and my skirt completely covered in mud.

"A bloody queen indeed," I muttered.

As I began walking back in the opposite direction, I struggled to control myself. The experience of the past few minutes had shaken something within me. There were more men above the gate, and as I grew closer, I could hear that they were yelling, perhaps to someone beyond the walls. Drawn again as if by a strange power, I began moving in that direction. Happily, I saw Drogo walking along the wall on his way to the gate and I called up to him.

"Sir Drogo, how do things stand?"

"They have raised a flag to treat," he called back.

This was a surprise. I knew they would never offer terms that did not involve my personal surrender, but I had not thought they would offer terms at all. I climbed the steps just beside the gate, and as I neared the top, Drogo lowered his hand to help me up.

"You look worse than the men who made the charge," he commented in wonder.

"Yes, thank you, Drogo," I said, though I meant something like the opposite.

The space above the gate was covered over top and behind to create a kind of tunnel, and under it some men were gathered, including Lord Henry and Sir Philip. They were gazing over the wall at whoever was planted on the other side of the moat. It was Lord Henry who was calling across to the enemy while the rest stood mute. He looked back in my direction and his eyes grew larger for a moment, but he then turned and resumed his efforts. When Philip saw me, he looked as if he might scold me again until Drogo said, "Let it be, Philip. They are no danger to her at the moment."

Henry called over, "I am the rightful lord of this castle, and my allegiance is to the Empress Mathilda. I therefore deny you entrance on the grounds that you have usurped the proper place reserved for her by God!"

I could not hear what the reply was, but I guessed it was something less than civil, for Henry replied, "I'll thank you not to call me that!"

I leaned over and whispered to Drogo, "Who is he speaking to?"

"Stephen," he answered. "He has come forward with three of his men under a flag of truce. The others are all hanging back."

Suddenly, Henry turned in my direction and said quietly, "My lady, they are asking to speak with you directly. Do you wish to do so?"

For a moment, I considered whether it would be less pleasant to speak with Stephen or simply let him get on with attempting to destroy the place. Unable to reach a firm conclusion, I asked Drogo, "Should I?"

"It is up to you. The only men near enough to shoot at us do not appear to have bows."

I nodded and stepped forward. The wall was high: too high for me to see over at that point. No sooner had I observed this than Sir Philip turned the basket that had been holding the rocks upside down and helped me to step on top of it. I could then see clearly over the wall and across the moat to where Stephen sat on a great brown horse next to his flag bearers, a force of some twenty or so men on horse behind him. He had a royal crown upon his head and his great sword hung in its sheath. I wondered if he might draw it and attempt to throw it at me. No, surely it was a distance too far.

"Good morning, cousin," I called over to him.

"I would offer the same to you, but it does not seem to be going well on your side," he said in return, laughing at his own jest.

"You have made an offer of parley, so by all means, make your thoughts known," I replied.

"You are trespassing on royal property," he charged. "What is more, you are guilty of treason against your rightful king. I let you go once. I will not do so again. We know that the earls have deserted you, even Earl Robert. You will not last long within those walls. Surrender now and I will show mercy to your friends and this city. Refuse, and you will all be made to feel my wrath. There is no escape, shrew. You are defeated."

"Your terms are not to my liking and I therefore refuse them," I said, feeling not a tenth as bold as my words sounded.

"I thought you might," he said with a smile, then turned around and yelled, "*Guy! Arnulf! Apportez le feu!*"[49]

Suddenly, a pair of Flemings stepped out from behind the building that lay closest to the moat. They were pushing a cart on which lay a pile of wood and a burning fire within a metal stove. Stephen alighted from his horse and walked over to grab one of the planks, which appeared to be part of a sign hastily pulled down and broken into pieces. He lowered it into the flames and waited for it to catch fire.

"I warned you once," he called back to me, staring into the flames. "I will warn you again: surrender now, or we will burn the entire town. Our army is already crossing the river at the nearest bridge. Soon you will be entirely surrounded and everything left alive in this city will die."

He pulled the piece of wood back out, its end lit by flame. I thought I could see the color black spreading lower, beginning to consume the wood.

"I do not have long. Would you have me throw this in the water or on top of this house?" Stephen asked, pointing to the building beside him.

Of course, I knew something Stephen did not know, though he ought to have guessed it by the absence of any souls in the streets: there was hardly anyone left in Oxford. The threat was to buildings alone and not persons.

"Make your choice!" he commanded.

---

49 Translation: "Bring the fire!" or "Bring on the fire!"

I looked up and saw the spires of the churches standing high above the sea of brown roofs, and the thought of that city's destruction struck me to the bone. It may have been a den of arrogant boasters, all full of obscure knowledge while lacking a good deal of that thing called good sense, but there was also something in it that appealed, and the people had shown loyalty to me—or at least what passed for loyalty in those days. How could I let their halls and books go up in flames? How could I suffer their sacred places to be defiled?

But then I thought of every step along the journey, across the Channel and down the Rhine, over the mountains and on the paths of the emperors of old, through pain and sorrow, want of food and want of human kindness, enduring abuse at every turn, yet choosing always to continue the fight. I thought of everything I had sacrificed for the sake of my progeny, having endured the worst of one age for the creation of another, and I knew as surely as I lived that I must press on, no matter the cost, for to surrender then would have been to count as nothing the price that had already been paid.

"Do what you must," I replied on behalf of the kingdom I loved and my descendants.

Immediately, he turned and threw the thing with all his might, not even pausing to grant me a glare. It landed directly on the thatch roof and the fire spread quickly. The enemies all let out a great cheer and began grabbing the other pieces of wood to carry on the work. However, if Stephen looked back to see the expression on my face, he did not receive his reward. I had already stepped down and begun walking in the direction of the Saint George Tower.

"My lady, what do you want us to do?!" Drogo called after me.

I turned back and said to him, "Pray, Drogo. Pray for rain and hold the gate."

XXIV

I was no longer dreaming. The flames that had haunted me so many nights, invading my slumber like some foul pestilence of Satan, had broken out into the world of day. The thing I feared had come to pass: Oxford was on fire.

It took the enemy quite a while to accomplish it, for all was still moist from the rain. We offered resistance where we could, but that did not amount to much. For most of a week the fires burned until the clouds burst forth again with streams of rain. Despite Stephen's best efforts, there were portions of the city that were barely touched by those flames, but the rows of houses and shops so close together fared poorly, their precious books going the way of all flesh. I am sorry to say that one of these contained several works by the monks of Lindisfarne in the time of Saint Cuthbert. Their value was beyond reckoning. *Omnis pulvis redit ad.*[50]

---

50   Translation: "All returns to dust." Reference to Genesis 3:19.

As I gazed out the window of my chamber at that sight that made my soul ache, I looked for men to blame, as I suppose anyone would in such an hour. Of course, the enemy was most at fault, but he would have never been gifted the opportunity were it not for the actions of my friends, who at that point were friends in name only. How I cursed the lot of them! Miles, Reginald, Baldwin—all had dismissed my words. Yet for all my grumbling against them, another figure rose to the fore of my mind, the real author of my distress: my husband, Count Geoffrey of Anjou.

It was Count Geoffrey who had refused from the beginning to aid my efforts in England, although he ought to have been my greatest defender. He had shared the bounty of his table with harlots and denied me even the scraps. At no point had his hatred of me been clearer than that very year when I had appealed to him for aid and been met with scorn.

A terrible thought struck me in those hours, for I had always assumed it was my husband's lack of regard for the kingdom of England in comparison with the duchy of Normandy that caused him to deny me help, but I wondered if the issue was in truth more personal: he was hoping the conflict would make an end of me and he could carry on with our sons, taking another wife and ruling over Anjou, Maine, and Normandy. One part of me denied it—surely even Count Geoffrey was not so evil as to offer his wife up as bait to the enemy—but another part reasoned that it was the best explanation for why he had pulled Earl Robert away in my hour of need and neglected to return him.

Such thoughts might have pulled me down into bitterness like one stuck in a bog, but as the enemy surrounded us on all sides and put his great weapons of war in place, I knew I could scarce afford one moment of despair. As long as my sons lived, there was hope for them. As long as there was a God, there was the promise of justice. Even were I to go down in defeat, it mattered how I did so. Indeed, what one does in such moments often matters most of all.

As we entered October, the enemy began to bombard us, not only with arrows, but also with great stones. The southern wall of the castle—the one nearest my own chamber—suffered damage, though it did not fall. One night, the trebuchets sent a few balls of fire over the walls. The young men who had offered themselves to carry water began running about, moving to wherever the flames sprung up. We knew not if it was the enemy's intent to singe us or simply send a chill of fear through our bones. The outer buildings within the castle walls were emptied of persons, and none too soon, for the stables were partly destroyed and one ball crashed through the roof of that chamber where Adela had been laying the night before, scorching everything nearby. I thanked God that I had besought her to move into the other bed chamber in the tower.

We hoped each day to see the earls arrive from the West or at least Lord Brian from Wallingford, but there was no sign of them. Could it be that Stephen was correct and they had no intention of riding to our aid? I longed for Earl Robert to return and put the fear of God back in them. It was my only chance of escape. The possibility that I would spend the rest of my life in some foul prison, even as my uncle Robert did after the battle of Tinchebrai, was becoming more real by the moment, but I could not allow myself to dwell on it.

As October bled into November, there was a break in the fighting for about a week. It was only then that I recognized how much fear had taken hold of me, for in my relief I seemed to shake, not so much in body as in spirit. I was more aware of the terror in that week of peace than I had been during the hours of war, perhaps because it was the first time I had been able to properly think or gain anything like a good night's sleep since Stephen arrived.

"Why have they ceased fighting?" I asked Drogo one evening, as we sat by the hearth in the Saint George Tower, warming ourselves against the growing cold. "What does it mean?"

"Perhaps our allies have appeared not far from here and drawn away their attention," Drogo offered, "or perhaps they are waiting for more supplies. They have made no offer of truce, so I would not count this as a surrender."

"No, of course not," I agreed. "I think the absence of arrows overhead has brought me greater concern than their presence. The threat seems worse than ever, as if it were the strange calm before the tempest strikes."

"All we can do is wait and see. Have faith, my lady. Earl Robert will come."

I closed my eyes and imagined what it would look like: my brother with his five hundred knights, along with Lord Brian and all the rest, riding up from the South, meeting the enemy outside the gates, lifting the siege, and saving us from a dreadful doom.

"What are you thinking of?" Drogo asked.

I opened my eyes again and told him, "As you well know, the emperor used to speak with great awe of his forefather, Otto. Many long years ago, the Magyars came pillaging from the East, as was their wont, and laid siege to the city of Augsburg. Ulrich was bishop at that time, and he took up the defense of the city, urging the men to hold the wall in the name of the Lord. He appealed to them with the words of scripture: 'Though I should walk through the valley of the shadow of death, I will fear no evil ...'[51] Time after time, the enemy charged the gate, but the men of Augsburg held firm. They were waiting for the arrival

---

51   Psalm 23:4.

of the king. Imagine the bishop riding out upon the plain, his robes flowing behind him and his staff held aloft: how he must have shone in the midday sun! And whatever he bound was bound, and whatever he loosed was loosed.[52] Just when all hope was lost, the host of *Germania* arrived ready for battle. They fell upon the Magyars and scattered them to the four winds. And as the sun set, the knights of God declared Otto to be their *Kaiser, imperator* of all that remains of the Rome of old and the new world which we continue to build. When I think of those men trapped within the walls of Augsburg, I tell myself that I too must wait upon salvation. The better part of courage and the entirety of faith is believing in a hope to be revealed."

"Yes, I remember hearing of the old emperor, though I—" Drogo began, but was interrupted by a wail coming from Adela's chamber just to our left.

"Oh no," I whispered, rising to my feet.

And then a chain of shouts broke the stillness of that night. "No, no, no!" she cried. "No, Jesus, no!"

I do not remember if it was me or Drogo who reached the door first, but we entered more or less together. There we found Adela standing in only her plain tunic for sleep, her hair completely loose, one hand pressed against her large belly and the other grabbing between her legs.

"It's too soon!" she yelled, her eyes wide with fear.

I looked down at the space below her, where there was a wet trail on the floor, though no sign of blood.

"I will fetch Grimbald immediately," Drogo said, not waiting for anyone's agreement.

He ran off in the direction of the stair and I was left to tend to my friend alone. I moved forward and held her lightly as the tale began to spill out of her.

---

52   Reference to Matthew 18:18, which in the traditional Christianity of the day was seen to refer to the powers of bishops in general and the pope in particular.

"I only got out of bed to reach the pot. When I bent over, I could feel it coming out of me."

"Your waters?" I asked, wanting to make sure I understood properly.

"There was nothing I could do … it just kept coming."

"You can let go now," I said, taking hold of her wrists gently and raising both her hands up to her chest. "If the child is coming, then it is coming. There is nothing we can do to stop it."

I helped her to the bed even as she wept. The moment she lay down and I pulled the cover over her, she let out a groan.

"What now?" I asked, wondering if I had pressed on her somewhere without knowing it.

"My womb …" she groaned, and I recognized that she was having labor pains. "Oh, it hurts! It hurts so much!"

"Try to remain calm," I said, stroking her forehead. "I will just step out and see where Drogo and Grimbald have got to."

"No, don't leave me!" she cried. "Please, don't leave me alone!"

I held one of her hands in both of mine and pressed it to my lips. "Believe me when I say to you that I will only be gone for the space of a moment. Children do not break forth in a moment. I will return if it takes everything I have."

With this she agreed, and I ran out into the hall and down the stair, following the same path Drogo had so lately taken. Although I had wished to hide it, I was sore afraid. I had almost died upon the birth of my second son, and he arrived at the proper hour. From all we could tell, Adela was still a month away from that date: perhaps even more. I could only guess that the stress of the siege had caused her labor to come early.

The two guards at the door nodded in respect as I entered the yard, looking around wildly. The ground was filled with holes and everything was turned to mud. The burnt remains of the outer buildings were stretched out before me, and a dead dog lay off to the right, its body covered in flies. The vesper light cast shadows everywhere, save for the fire pit, where a dozen or so of the men were gathered, their hoods pulled up against the cold of evening, none of them speaking a word. I did not see Drogo anywhere. Feeling rather desperate, I cried out, "Drogo! Drogo!" But there was no answer.

I had promised Adela I would only be gone a moment, so I returned as quickly as I had gone out, yelling to the guards as I went past, "If you set eyes on Master Grimbald, send him up immediately!" When I entered my maid's chamber again, I found her curled up and clutching her belly in pain. I bent over her and she took my hand gladly, pressing into it with such force that I almost regretted my decision to offer it. When the pain seemed to pass, she asked, "Where are they? Have they forgotten about me?"

"I am sure they have not forgotten, but I could not find them right away. Do you think you could stand?" The look on her face implied that she was not fond of this idea, so I offered, "It will help with the movement of the child. Your pain might be over sooner."

"But I do not want the child to come!" she wailed. "It may die!"

"You have no choice," I assured her. "The babe is coming. You must accept it. You have already lost your waters."

Poor thing—she was so scared, and I could not blame her. I remembered what it was like to give birth, and I knew I must be firm when she could not be. I helped her to her feet with some difficulty, for she was struck by another pain as she rose. I instructed her to place her hands on the bed.

"Now, when the next pain comes, bend into it," I told her. "I will check again to see if Grimbald is come."

No sooner had I entered the hall than I saw Grimbald rushing in my direction with the satchel in which he kept the tools of his trade. He was moving quite fast for a man of his age, and even in that moment of fear, I could not help but marvel.

"Thank God!" I cried.

"Don't thank him yet. We have a long way to go," he replied.

The good doctor knocked on Adela's door, and having heard some sort of reply in the form of a grunt, he entered and found her in the same place I had left her, swaying a bit on the spot.

"Lie down," he instructed. "I need to examine you."

As I helped Adela back on to the bed, for in her large state movement was difficult, she whispered, "Is he going to look down there?"

"He has to see how close you are," I explained.

"But he's ... a man. Isn't that wrong?"

"Well, he's not here for a good time. He's here to preserve the lives of you and your child," I assured her. "I have known him for many years. He helped me at Geoffrey's birth. You can trust him."

She nodded weakly. "Yes, I suppose you are right. But does he know about these things? I thought only midwives—"

"Grimbald has left no aspect of the human body unexamined, whether it be the male or female body," I explained. "He is unusual in that regard. It is why all the students come to him."

Here she nodded again in acceptance of my word and allowed me to push her back gently. Once she was lying down, Grimbald asked, "How often do the pains come?"

Even as the words left his mouth, Adela grunted again and grabbed my arm, pressing hard. Looking over at the physician, I replied on her behalf: "Often."

"And she has lost some of her water?"

"Yes," I answered. "Perhaps all of it."

"And this has happened in the past few minutes?"

I nodded and he turned his gaze back to Adela, who had recovered from the pain.

"I will need to feel you both inside and out to tell how close you are."

"I understand," she said.

After rising for a moment and washing his hands in the basin, Grimbald sat on the bed again and lifted her skirt with one hand, placing the other underneath.

"I beg your pardon," he said, and then I could tell from the look of pain on her face that his hand had entered her. Grimbald's eyes seemed to grow large in surprise, and as he pulled his hand back out again and dropped her skirt he said, "You are mostly open already. Let me feel your belly."

As he did so, Adela groaned once again, and Grimbald told me, "Oh, yes, I can feel the muscles contracting strongly. The good news is I believe the child's head is coming first. It would have been rather more difficult were that not the case. So, my dear, although it is somewhat unusual for a woman's first birth, I believe this child will come quickly. Empress Mathilda ..."

"Yes," I said, "what do you need?"

"Fetch whatever cloths you can find. As there are no other women in the castle and every man is needed upon the wall, it will be the three of us only bringing this child into the world."

The prospect of it filled me with dread, but I did as he commanded. I went immediately across the hall to my own chamber and began stripping the covers from the bed as fast as I could.

"Come off, stupid things!" I cried.

Then there was a flash of light, as if I had been visited by some heavenly apparition. Outside, the sound of a terrible crash. The floor shook and I clung to the nearest bed post. It was no longer Adela's screaming alone that I heard, but also shouts coming from outside. Forgetting my charge for a moment, I dropped everything and ran to the window. There I beheld a fearful sight: the walk just beyond the tower, the very place where I had once dumped my own piss on a pair of churls, had been struck directly. Some of the wall had crumbled, and on the ground far below was a stone covered in some sort of pitch or oil and burning brightly, not unlike the few we had seen before.

I gasped as I recognized there was a man pinned beneath it, struggling to break free. He must have been either standing on the wall when it hit or had such an ill fate as to be in its path on the ground level. I could only just make him out in the light of the fire, for the sky had grown completely dark. Soon a few of his fellows were running toward him, trying with great difficulty to move the stone, but as they did so they too became covered in the oil and one of them screamed and leapt backward as his shirt caught fire. My eyes were immediately drawn from this to the sky above, where another flash of light flew over the wall and on to the castle grounds, followed by another and another.

Lord have mercy! I prayed.

It seemed that the few fire stones the enemy had flung at us before were only a test and this was the true assault. Here was the reason we had enjoyed those days of peace: for the enemy to gather his strength for that one night. Evidently, Stephen was not patient enough to wait for us to starve.

Remembering Adela, I pulled my eyes away from the window, quickly gathered up what I could, and ran back to her room, not stopping to ask before opening the door. My friend was crouched on top of the bed, bent over on her hands and knees. Grimbald stood above her, rubbing her back as she cried out in pain. Noticing my arrival, the doctor asked, "Should we inform the lady's husband of her condition?"

"Perhaps now is not the best time," I said quietly, setting the covers on the floor. "Forgive me, Grimbald, but I must take leave of you both for another moment."

"Is something wrong?" Adela asked desperately. "Is Philip in trouble?"

"Don't worry—I just need to check on a few things," I replied as calmly as I could. "You're doing well. Keep breathing!"

"Wait!" she cried, even as I turned to leave.

I spun on the spot and asked, "What is it?"

"If you see Saint Ouen, can you bring him?" she begged, referring to her figure of the saint.

"Yes," I replied without thinking, though it was not the greatest concern on my mind at that moment.

Racing back across the hall and into my own room, I looked out the window once again and saw that things had grown worse. Fiery objects of different sizes were falling from the sky as the trebuchets continued their terrible work. I was amazed that they were able to fling so many of them in such a short space of time. Many of our men had crowded the wall just outside my window and were firing arrows back at the enemy. This was surely bad news, for it meant the enemy was pressing within range of the walls—perhaps just on the other side of the moat. I could see more clearly due to the fires that had sprung up here and there, and I could make out Drogo shouting commands to the others. As always, I knew him on account of his height.

I felt the whole tower shudder as it was hit by one of the huge stones. Running back into the hall, I looked around in every direction but saw no sign of damage to the roof or walls, which was a great relief. I was glad we had covered Adela's window with cloth a few nights before to help her sleep, but I knew she could not remain ignorant of the chaos around us for long: she must have felt the floor shake as much as anyone.

Moving back into my chamber, I dropped to the floor and reached under the bed to where I knew an oak box was hidden. I pulled it out by the handle: it was a heavy thing, but it slid along the floor easily enough. Having retrieved it, I opened the latch and lifted the lid to reveal a short sword and three daggers nestled on a bed of ermine. These belonged to the D'Oyly household: the former lord of the castle had shown them to me during one of my earlier stays.

"For if the worst should happen," he had said.

The sword must have belonged to a lad, for it was not the proper length for a full knight. Even so, I knew well enough that I could not match skill for skill with any man who was likely to break into the tower. Would anyone be able to break into the tower? It seemed a mad thought, guarded as we were by water and stone, but I reasoned it was better to be more careful than not. In the case of an intrusion, my only hope would be in surprise, so I decided to take one of the daggers instead of the sword. Looking from one to the next, I could not decide, so I simply chose the one nearest my right hand. Its hilt was covered in gold and it sat inside a leather sheath fastened to a belt. As I drew it and held it aloft, a new flash of light caught the writing upon the hilt, and I was able to quickly make it out.

"'*Omne solum forti patria*,'" I whispered, reading it aloud. "'Every land is a brave man's country?' No, that cannot be right. 'Everything a brave man does is for his country?'[53] They would have done better to borrow that line from Horace."[54]

In the end, my need for haste won out over my desire to understand the particulars of Latin, and I placed the knife back in its sheath. Feeling very much that I had no idea what I was

---

53 Either translation may be correct depending on the context.

54 "*Dulce et decorum est pro patria mori* ..." usually translated into English as, "It is sweet and fitting to die for one's country." From Horace's *Odes*, III.2.13.

doing, I wrapped the belt around my waist just above my hips. Unlike the sword, it must have been meant for a far larger person, so when I tied it there was quite a bit of the leather strap hanging down.

No matter, I thought.

I heard more shouting outside and moved back to the window, where I saw to my dismay that even as the rain of fire continued, three ladders had been pulled up against the wall: the enemy was apparently climbing toward us. I could not think how they had been able to bring the ladders across the water to the small bit of earth that surrounded the castle. They must have built some kind of bridge and put it in place while we were busy containing the fire. All our archers were now pointing their bows down over the top of the wall, directing their arrows to those attempting to scale the height.

One of the enemy knights made it to the top and stepped on to the walk. He was met immediately by the sword of Drogo, who with one swift stroke knocked him to the ground before he had a chance to land a blow. But there were others coming one by one, and within the space of a minute they went from being immediately thrown down to fighting back to back against the castle's defenders. Not an hour earlier, I had been sure that the enemy meant to starve us into surrender or wear us down by a thousand pricks of a needle. Now, it seemed he was making a bold attempt to end things immediately.

Has it all come to this? I wondered. *Do I die tonight? Does the castle fall?*

In that moment, I saw in my mind's eye the faces of my sons and wept to think that I might not see them again and everything I had fought for from the time I arrived in England might come to naught—every sacrifice I had made would be emptied of meaning. I pressed my hand against the glass as the tears fell from my eyes. I watched as one body and then another fell to the ground, wondering all the while if I would be next. I felt unable to keep looking and equally unable to break away, as if I were under some awful spell.

I could still make out Drogo in the middle of it all, lifting his shield to block one blow, then raising his sword to meet another. He pushed through two of Stephen's men, sending one falling to the ground and the other back over the wall and into the moat. He then dropped his sword and grabbed the hook keeping one of the ladders in place. Another knight was able to join him and the two of them succeeded in freeing the thing and pushing it away from the wall. Soon, another ladder was sent crashing down to earth, and my knights were working on the third. All of Stephen's men who had made it on to the wall seemed to have been killed or otherwise removed from action. We had met the threat of the moment, but I knew it was not the end. If they did not have more ladders, perhaps they had more fire to send our way.

The pause at least allowed me to remember my friend and run to her aid. Truly, I felt guilty for staying away, even if it was only for a few minutes. This time, Grimbald was crouched down below her, his hand again feeling underneath her skirt.

"Thank God you have returned!" he declared, then addressing Adela, he said, "My dear, you are fully open now. The time has come."

"So soon?" I asked in wonder.

"This child is determined to enter the world as quickly as possible," the doctor said, shaking his head. "But what is going on outside? Is the enemy pressing in?"

"Yes, but we have turned him back for the moment," I explained.

"Did you find Saint Ouen?!" Adela cried. "Please, I cannot go on without him!"

I confess that I had completely forgotten about her request. I looked around the room left and right, glancing her basket of things in one corner. Lifting the top off, I reached in and felt around for the ivory figure of the saint. Try as I might, I could not find him. Rising and returning to the bed, I placed a hand on her shoulder and said, "I am sorry, Adela. I don't know where he went, but you can still pray to him."

She let out a scream that seemed to be in response to my words, but in truth was brought on by the pain of labor.

"No time for discussion! The child is coming," Grimbald said.

Adela was curled up again in pain, her body writhing.

"We must get her back up," the physician said. "Come now, up, up!"

"What should I do?" I asked, the fear of the moment rising within me. "How can I help?"

Grimbald had gathered up the cloths and placed them just behind Adela, ready to receive the babe. He pulled his satchel up off the floor and drew from it several metal objects, laying them out on the bed. I was too scared to inquire about their purpose.

"Ah! Mother of God! Mother Mary!" Adela screamed. "I cannot do this! I cannot!"

I grabbed her face and pressed it against mine. "Just one more moment, Adela. Just one more moment and you will meet this child. Now, do exactly what the doctor says."

I reached down and braced both her shoulders so she would have something to press against, even as Grimbald instructed, "As soon as your muscles contract again, push!"

Adela looked up to heaven, her face and her hair covered in sweat. She took a deep breath and gritted her teeth, letting out a terrible groan.

"That's it!" he told her. "Push! Push!"

She strained for several seconds until Grimbald said, "All right now, take a breath." This she did, the air moving in and out of her nose heavily.

"Wonderful!" I assured her. "Just keep doing that!"

"I can't. I caaaa—" she wailed, even as her muscles seized again.

We continued like that for several minutes, Adela straining against the pain, and myself and Grimbald encouraging her to exert herself, until the doctor finally said, "Yes, the head is very close now! Push again!"

"Almost there," I said, attempting to cheer her, but she had entered some other world of pain where noise hardly seemed to reach. Her eyes were closed, and she was making such sounds as I had never heard escape her lips. Her whole body was shaking with pain, weariness, or both.

Adela sent up a cry to the heavens as if the torment of a lifetime were departing her body, and the ancient hands of Grimbald moved with the swiftness of a youth to gather up her child.

"Empress, come help me now!" he instructed.

I rushed down to the foot of the bed and took the child in my arms as he used the cloths to clean its ears, nose, mouth, and eyes. The babe was crying loudly.

"How does it look?" Adela asked, turning to see. She had fallen upon the bed in weariness but had just enough strength for this small motion.

"He looks very well," Grimbald assured her.

"A boy?" she inquired. "Is it a boy, then?"

I took a quick peek at the child's lower region and confirmed, "Yes, a very fine boy. I am so proud of you, friend!"

She smiled wearily, for although her heart must have been filled with joy, she was very weak from the effort. When the afterbirth had come away and the doctor and I had seen to them both, we laid Adela back against some pillows and lowered her son into her arms. For a moment, she simply stared at him, her face full of wonder, then she looked up and said to the two of us, "Thank you, both. What would I have done without you? You must be his godparents."

"It would be an honor," Grimbald replied, "although you may consider choosing someone a bit younger … and waiting to see what Sir Philip thinks about all of this."

"Yes, we must tell him he has a son if we can find him," I said. "I will go and send for him."

The physician raised a hand and said, "It would be better for you to stay with her and help her feed the child. It is a woman's work. Allow me to go."

"Do not leave the tower!" I ordered. "It is not safe. There should be at least two guards below. Send one of them out."

He deferred to my wish with a nod and departed, closing the door behind him.

By the light of a single candle, I helped Adela place the child upon her breast. It was fortunate indeed that he began feeding immediately and needed little help. He sucked for a minute or so until the lids of his eyes dropped all the way and he entered the land of sleep.

"If you had told me when I was a girl that I would end up giving birth in a castle, I would have thought you mad," Adela said with a smile, holding the boy to herself.

"You make it sound like the height of comfort, when in truth we are in the middle of a battle," I noted.

"Hopefully some day we will look back on all of that as a bad memory and this as the beginning of new life. We will only remember the good things."

"I hope so," I said, gently rubbing the child's head.

Suddenly, there was a noise out in the hall and my head swung round. I stared at the door with great intent, as if doing so would allow me to discern what was taking place beyond it.

"What's wrong?" Adela asked. "Did you hear something?"

I had indeed heard something, but had no idea what it was, so it seemed best not to alarm her. Turning back, I patted her on the shoulder and said, "The two of you seem to be doing well. I'll just step out for a moment if you permit it."

"Of course," she agreed.

I hated to leave her yet again, but nevertheless I rose from the bed and walked over to the door, opening it slowly. The hall appeared to be empty, so I entered, keeping a hand on the dagger at my hip. I moved along as quietly as possible, afraid to find the source of the noise. Then I saw a pair of figures in the shadow just beyond the hearth. There were two chairs in front of the fire as usual, and I quickly hid behind the nearest one and looked out from behind it, attempting to mute even the sound of my breathing.

One of them was Grimbald. He had fallen to the ground and was pressed against the wall, looking up at the other man whose back was to me: a knight in full mail holding the point of a sword to the physician's neck.

Who is that other man?! I wondered, my heart racing. *How did he get in here? Is he one of those who climbed the wall? I suppose he must be. Perhaps he hid in all the confusion. But how did he get past the guard? Could he have killed them both?*

All these questions quickly faded away as I recognized it did not matter how the trespasser had arrived or even who he was. All that mattered was that he had made it in and was threatening Grimbald's life. His very presence in that room meant that the castle's defenders were ignorant of his existence and would not be rushing to our aid. So strong was the beating of my heart, that I could hear it—could feel it in every part of my body. The dark figure of that knight was as an apparition come up from Hades to threaten all I loved.

I thought of Adela and her son in the room just behind me. I thought of poor Grimbald at the point of the enemy's sword. And I must admit I thought also of myself, for I was very much in fear for my life. I could have gone back into Adela's chamber and attempted to block the door, but that would have meant leaving Grimbald to his fate: a man who had been faithful to me since birth and whom I had come to love almost as a father. Surely I could not abandon him. My hand was pressed against the hilt of the dagger, ready to draw it, but what would I do with it that could match the strength of a knight?

In the stillness, I could just hear the trespasser speaking to Grimbald over the cracking of the fire and the distant roar from outside.

"I'll ask you again: where is she, old man?" he growled.

"And I have told you, I know not," Grimbald lied, the strain in his voice quite apparent.

"I know that's her chamber over there," the man said, nodding toward the room that was indeed mine. "Her things are there, but where is she?"

"You must accept my answer or send me out of this world. I can do naught else," he replied weakly.

And in that moment, Grimbald looked in my direction, and for the space of a second our eyes met. He made no sign, but I knew he saw me. I felt he was attempting to speak to me with those sad eyes. Perhaps he was telling me to fly and leave him to his fate, or perhaps he was simply bidding farewell to this life, bracing himself for the blade that would pierce his flesh and let flow his blood.

"You will pay the price for your deceit!" the knight cried, pulling his weapon back to strike.

And then I was flying—yes, I must have grown wings and flown the two or three paces to where they stood. As the man was covered in mail, I knew there was only one place my dagger was likely to do any good, and there could be not the smallest pause for doubt, or I would fail. It did not matter that I was about to attempt something I had never done before, nor that I lacked the necessary skill or strength. My only hope was in surprise, and I had to seize it. As if the very angels were carrying me, I hooked my left arm around the knight's neck, pulling him toward myself and away from the helpless Grimbald. His large form reeled, the sword in his hand swinging freely. With my right arm, I swung the dagger round his head and plunged it backward with all the strength I could muster—back toward the man's face, for it was the only thing not covered by mail. And then I felt something truly awful as the blade struck against bone and became caught. It sent a chill through my body from head to toe.

The next thing I knew, I was on my back upon the floor, the man's whole weight on top of me. I pushed him off myself and on to the floor, surprised that he made no effort to fight back. After all, I had lost my only weapon. But he did not rise—indeed, he did not move at all, and I saw that there was blood on the floor, much of it flowing from where the man lay face down, forming a pool upon the wood boards.

"Oh, good strike, my lady!" Grimbald declared, still lying against the wall.

"What happened?" I asked in confusion. "I thought I barely hit him."

"You went straight through his eye!" he informed me, coughing loudly.

I turned my fallen enemy over, and sure enough, Grimbald was correct. By some miracle, my blade had struck one of the few places where I could have made a fatal blow, even though I had swung mostly at random.

Lord, have mercy on me, I thought desperately. *I've just killed a man.*

A sense of deep guilt struck me as the recognition of what I had done swept over me. I gasped and clutched at my chest, weeping with such violence that my whole frame shook. I had never imagined that I would become a killer. My father, my brothers, and my friends had all ended the lives of other men in battle, but I had never thought of myself in that way, and I knew that for the rest of my days, I would have to carry the weight of the knowledge that my own hand had ended the life of someone else. It was just, and yet it was a great weight.

"My lady, you must not be ashamed!" Grimbald begged me. "You had no choice. He would have killed us all." He coughed once or twice, then added, "Breathe, my lady. Breathe deeply. Let it pass."

I did as he said, closing my eyes and allowing the sense of guilt to drain out of me with each healing breath. As I did, I felt a ministry from on high, and my heart became still as I was restored little by little. Sadly, my sense of relief was brief, for as I turned back to look at Grimbald I saw that he was clutching his side and his breath was coming with difficulty.

"Are you hurt? I didn't think he injured you," I said, my concern rising.

"He dealt me a blow before you arrived. That is why I could not rise to fight," he explained.

I bent over him and looked at where his hands were pressed tightly against the folds of black cloth.

"Let me take a look," I offered.

"No, there is nothing for it," he muttered, each word coming with difficulty.

"How can you know that if you won't even let me look?" I asked.

In the end, he seemed too weak to argue. He lifted his hands, which I saw were covered with blood, and I found the place where the enemy's sword had sliced through his clothes. Although the light was poor, I could see that his flesh had been pierced by the evil stroke. The blade had gone straight in and probably quite deep.

"He will have hit my bowels ... I am ... bleeding on the inside," Grimbald uttered with great difficulty. "My empress, there is nothing ... nothing you can do for me but pray."

"There must be something," I said through tears, looking into the great blue spheres of his eyes, still perfectly clear at his age. Shaking my head, I begged, "Tell me, Grimbald, what can I do? Is there nothing I can fetch that will aid you?"

He smiled ever so slightly. "I would say you should fetch a priest, but I suppose there is none at hand."

I pulled him up slightly, causing him to groan as I did so, and laid him back in my arms, not unlike I had done with Adela's son just moments before. Was I to see in such a short time the beginning of one life and the ending of two others? The doctor gazed up at my face, his breath coming in rough spurts and a terrible sound in his throat. I thought about all the things those eyes had seen in the years he had walked the face of the earth. He was Norman by birth and came across the Channel as a young man, speaking even with my grandfather before he died. How many times had he walked beside my father? He remembered so much of my mother. He had watched the Tower rise over London and was there for the first feast in Westminster Hall. He had traveled abroad, meeting with bishops and kings. I thought I remembered him telling me he had once set foot in Granada and walked the pilgrim way to Santiago de Compostela before taking a ship back to England. Oh, what changes he had seen in our kingdom, and how it must have pained him to depart in such an hour!

As if guessing my thoughts, he said, "I remember, my lady ... I remember the day of your birth. I held you, tiny thing. Now ..." He coughed again and finished, "Now you are holding me."

"Why must you leave?" I asked softly. "Why can you not live for ever?"

"Only God is for ever," he whispered.

I nodded my head and continued. "In the absence of a priest of the Church, I ask you, brother Grimbald, are you sorry for all your sins?"

"I repent and throw myself ... upon the mercy of Christ."

I made the sign of the cross over him, then bent down to kiss his forehead and told him, "*Ad Deo, frater.*"

A few minutes later, Drogo and Philip both came up the stair and found us there.

"It is over for now," Drogo told me. "The enemy has retreated from the moat. But what happened here?" he asked, looking in alarm from the body of the dead knight over to that of Grimbald, from which the life had fully ebbed.

"Not only the battle is over," I explained, "but also the life of our friend Grimbald. This trespasser assaulted him, and now they are both passed on."

Removing his helm and placing a hand over his heart, Drogo said softly, "I saw two guards fallen below, but I did not know ... I am sorry, my lady."

"Where is my wife?" Philip asked. "Is all well with her?"

"She is well, and so is your son," I assured him.

A smile broke over his face as he asked, "I have a son?! Truly?! But it is so early ... oh, never mind it! God be praised!"

"Go to her," I commanded him. "Go to them both."

As the younger knight ran over to join the other members of his family, Drogo knelt beside me and closed the lids of the doctor's eyes.

"Our store of grain is burned, but I do not think that was the point of all this. They were coming for you, my lady. They hoped to kill you. They threw everything at us in the hope that one or two would get through."

I wiped my tears on my sleeve. "We must find some place to lay him for the time being, until we can bury him properly. He was the best of us."

"Yes," Drogo agreed, "the best of us and of England—the best of those who tread the middle earth."

Thus ended the days of the physician Grimbald, who passed from this life on the night of fire as I held him in my arms. He was the last of another world, and in that cruel parting, I felt something of England and Normandy was lost, never to be restored until that day when the world itself is made new.

XXV

"The fiercest man cannot out run the mother keen to defend her sons."

How boldly I had spoken those words! At the beginning of the conflict, the very hour we received news of my father's death, even as Stephen was already making for London, I made that declaration. I had little idea in that moment of the cost I would be forced to pay. Was it not our Savior who bid us count the cost before setting out?[55] How harshly it was drained from me as blood from a beast!

Scripture tells us there is a time to give birth and a time to die.[56] Everything has both a beginning and an end. After the night of fire, I sensed that the end was nigh. Our store of food was all but gone, for the flames had consumed most of the grain. The walls were crumbling along with our fortunes. Perhaps a third of my defenders had perished, and we could

---

55 Reference to Luke 14:28.

56 Ecclesiastes 3:2.

not even afford them a proper burial, hemmed in as we were on all sides. We had heard naught of our allies abroad. And still I could feel the jerk when my knife struck bone, and the blood seeping from the body of Grimbald—they haunted me. The vision that gave life to my aching heart had been smothered and choked. In such a situation, there is only one proper thing to do: admit defeat and hope the enemy shows mercy.

Brian had told me it was not my decision alone to make, and he was right. Throughout the war, I had seen how much my friends were forced to bear my burden. I had watched as their estates were stripped from them and I could offer no recompense. I had seen them robbed of food and comfort, and worst of all I had seen them die. I could not escape the image of Grimbald as he looked at me that night: his eyes gazing into mine even as the enemy held him at the point of a sword. I had felt the heaving of his chest as he lay in my arms, consuming the final dregs of his life. He had died defending me, even as so many others had. Their sacrifices were the height of nobility, and in such a time as the one in which we then lived, it was a great comfort to see that there were a few men left on God's earth who were faithful.

It was because of this that I knew I had to end it. I could not go on fighting when the result was certain. They had given everything for me, and if I could by my own actions preserve life, then I had no choice: I must do it. And so, I made up my mind to surrender Oxford Castle to the usurper and face whatever mockery of justice he chose for me.

This was the sort of decision that required a day or two to accept before informing anyone of it, and as it so happened, the wheel of fortune had one last surprise for us. The air grew suddenly chill—more so than I could remember at the beginning of the Advent season. Indeed, it was so cold that all the pails we had left to collect water quickly turned to ice, and the moat around the castle began to freeze as well. This was a cause of some concern given that the enemy had already crossed it once without the aid of ice. Yet Stephen seemed in no mood to fight in that cold: the trebuchets ceased most of their work. Why waste good stones and spend your effort to defeat someone who is about to surrender, especially when you can sit by a fire wrapped in fur rather than watching the frost form on your armor?

Then it began to snow as I have never seen snow before: as if the Lord had been saving it up for ten years to drop it all at once. The piles began to form within and without the castle, and all our men who remained sought protection inside the few structures that stood, including the Tower of Saint George. Hoping for a few moments to myself as I considered the awful decision I would soon be forced to announce, I remained in my own chamber while the rest of them gathered in the hall outside. As I stood there gazing out the window, looking at the distant fires of the enemy camp stretching out between the wall and the river, the fall of snow somewhat blocking my view, I recognized that the one part of my dream that had been lacking had finally come to pass: it was bitterly cold. We had seen the fire and now we saw the snow. It had always been a prophecy of woe.

"Dreams are fearful things," I muttered.

I looked out into the vast darkness beyond. Somewhere in the distance, little more than ten miles away, was the fortress of Wallingford, seat of Brian fitz Count. What was he thinking at that very moment? Having seen his character prove true over so many years and at such great cost to himself, I was sure he had not forsaken me as so many others had. He would have been trying to help me by whatever means he could, but there was simply no way to get a message through, and neither was there any hope of defeating Stephen's army without the help of Earl Robert. Maybe he had tried to ride to my defense and the battle had taken place well outside the city, where we could not see. Perhaps Wallingford had also fallen and Brian was Stephen's prisoner. All this remained a mystery, but one thing I did know: he would be dreading the possibility of my death or captivity as much as I dreaded the same fate befalling him.

Not more than a two-hour ride on a good day, and yet the distance seems eternal, I thought.

I could almost see him standing at another window in Wallingford Castle, or perhaps out in a field somewhere, looking in my direction and wishing he could cross the span. There had always been a great distance between us, but this time it was a matter of life and death. I could feel his spirit churning inside him as his lips parted and he breathed my name.

Maud … Come, Maud.

No, that couldn't be right. My thoughts seemed to be trailing off as I stared into that strange darkness. Then I remembered: it was from my dream. Yes, of course! The cracking of the fire, the howling of the wind, the heat and the cold, and then the voice … it was Brian.

Come, Maud. Come!

For a moment, I allowed myself to dwell on those words—to turn them over in my mind and know their full force. I felt the beating of my heart through which my blood flowed. That was the blood I received from my fathers and passed on to my sons. Those were the sons for whom I ran the race that I might win the prize.

"In England, the land itself rises up to fight the enemy."

That was what I had declared to Bruno so many years before, and I was speaking those words again as I watched the falling snow. All at once, everything was clear. I knew what I must do.

I strode out into the hall, where a few of the knights were gathered around as Adela showed them her new son, Roger. What a sweet thing he was, and how he had persevered against all odds! His was a life worth defending. I saw Philip looking at them both with such love in his eyes, and just to the side Drogo was making odd expressions, attempting to make the child laugh, although he was surely too young to do so. I hated to pull either of them away from such an occasion of joy, but it was necessary.

"Sir Drogo! Sir Philip!" I called. "Come with me."

They followed me back into my own chamber and I shut the door behind us, then turned on the spot and looked from one man to the other, wondering how they would respond to what I was about to ask of them.

"What is it?" Philip inquired. "Is something wrong?"

"What a strange question to ask in our present situation," I noted. "Forgive me, good sirs. I will get to the point. The snow is falling and swiftly. The river is now frozen solid. I see this as an opportunity."

"We are in no position to strike at this point—" began Philip, but Drogo placed a hand on his shoulder to stop him.

"My lady, if you are considering what I think you are considering, the answer is yes. It is possible, but I cannot promise it will work."

"I would only need a few to go with me. Perhaps no more than five," I told him.

"The smaller the number, the better. Let it be three," Drogo said.

"What are you speaking of?" inquired Philip. "Are you seriously contemplating … that is, do you intend to flee?"

"Given our situation, I would say it is the best option available to me, and the one that is most favorable for all the rest in the castle," I explained. "Tell me, Drogo, is it a good idea or have I finally gone completely mad?"

"Had you not proposed it, I might have done so," he assured me. "It is difficult to see anything out there in the present conditions. Tracks would be quickly covered by the new snow, and as you note, the water no longer presents much of a barrier. Nature seems to be inviting us to attempt it."

"They have twenty men or so just across from the gate, ready to shoot from the upper floors of the houses," said Philip, "but I suppose there is always the postern. They will have men there too, but the light is less and there is some brush down by the river. I don't know—it still seems a difficult feat."

"I doubt my fate will be any worse out there than it will be if I remain here," I reasoned, though in truth I had some false sense of comfort within those walls, even if they were on the brink of falling down. Stepping into the unknown is always more difficult.

"Well, I think we should try it, and the sooner the better, for we do not know when the snow might stop and we will need this darkness to make it to Wallingford," said Drogo. "I assume that is your object?"

"Yes, the nearest house of a friend, though if Stephen has been able to seize it, we will not receive much of a welcome. Do I take it this means you are coming with me?"

"Of course. You know you need not ask," he replied with a bow of the head.

Looking toward Philip, I said, "You have just become a father. I think it best for you to remain—"

"Not a chance!" he objected. "I know I've been something less than certain about this whole enterprise, but you said it right: my lot is no worse out there, and in any case, I'd hate to tell my son that I didn't join you when you made your glorious flight from Oxford!"

"Yes, well, let's wait a bit before we put that story down in ink, shall we?" I muttered. "Drogo, you said three, and I am fine with that number. Who is to be the third?"

"Not Lord Henry—he'll be left to tend the castle."

"To surrender the castle," I corrected him. "Tomorrow morning, at the very stroke of dawn, everyone here will throw themselves upon Stephen's mercy and hope that he has some of it left."

"Why not Gerard?" Philip asked, pointing at Drogo as if to force the thought into his brain. "He is a native of the county and will know the land better than the rest of them."

"Good enough for me, good enough for Her Highness, I hope," Drogo concluded.

"Yes, good enough for me, but what should we take with us? And what should we wear?" I asked.

"As for the former, we'll take only a bit of water and food, along with our weapons, of course. Armor would only weigh us down, especially in those heaps of snow," said Drogo. "As for the latter, I think our friends the Cistercians might be able to help us there."

Once we set our minds to it, there was no delay. Within the hour, it was arranged. The Cistercians were kind enough to let us borrow their cloaks, which according to the rules of their order were made of plain wool without dye. They were not perfectly white, but very near it. For what I hoped would be a long journey on foot, I was gifted a pair of boots that the lady of the castle had once used for riding—that is, before she went the way of all flesh. Why they were still there at the castle and not given to someone less fortunate, I could only guess, but it was fair to say that in that hour, I myself was not especially fortunate. I gave the few letters and personal things I had to Adela for safe keeping, bidding her hide them in some way from the enemy when he entered the place, but I kept the amber moth and rosary in a leather pouch hung round my neck.

The last thing I prayed before leaving the Saint George Tower for the final time was, *Lord make me quick and sly as a fox, that I might escape the wolves.*

After giving one last embrace to Adela and kiss to little Roger, I walked out into the storm, for such it was: the wind was catching the snow in its arms, dropping it wherever it wished. This was to say nothing of the new snow falling from above. I could hardly see ten feet in front of my face and was not sure how we would find our way to Wallingford, but it seemed at least possible that the watchmen all about us would be blind to our movements. Not only that, but the sound of the wind would be loud enough to cover the crunch of snow beneath our feet.

I trod through the sea of white, which reached well up my calves. Truly, it resembled a sea, for its surface drifted this way and that with the wind, even as waves upon the ocean. Only the distant light of a few torches revealed it to my eyes, lending it a strange glow, as if there was something of fire about it after all. I made my way slowly to the postern gate that was near the base of the motte, dragging my feet more than walking. I was within two or three paces of them before I saw the three figures clad in garments of white, even as my own. Standing near the wall as they were, they blended well with the light hue of the stone and even lighter snow. Of course, Drogo was too tall for his borrowed garment, so I could see a bit of his brown boots below, but those would be mostly covered by the snow.

"Good evening, gentlemen!" I greeted them, attempting to show more confidence than I felt. I briefly considered making some jest about the lovely weather we were having but decided against it. After all, once we left the castle, we would be every moment in danger of being struck by an arrow, run through with a sword, or dragged away to some horrible jail. The hand of death was heavy upon us. There is a time to be comical and a time to hold one's tongue.

"Edmund up on the wall says most of their scouts have gone back to the camp, likely on account of the weather," Drogo reported, pulling the edges of his hood against both sides of his face to block the wind and snow. "He thinks there are one or two still keeping a watch on the river, and of course, they can call for more quickly enough."

"How far until we are past their line?" I asked.

"A mile—perhaps a bit less, perhaps a bit more," said the man I took to be Gerard.

"I don't think the two of you have ever been properly introduced. This is Gerard," Drogo explained helpfully, though a bit late. Underneath the man's hood, I guessed that he had brown hair and a beard to match, though it was difficult to make anything out in the shadows.

"My lady," Gerard said, bending at the waist, "it is a great honor to be chosen to accompany you."

"Yes, remember that if things should take a turn for the worse," I bid him. Looking from one of their faces to the next, I said, "I am thankful I can run this race beside you. If we escape to safety, our deeds this night will be remembered in the great history of this kingdom, but there is much work to be done."

Drogo nodded and said, "Let us discuss what happens when we walk through this door. I will go first in case the enemy has a clearer sight than we suppose and fires upon us immediately. Gerard here will come next, then you, my lady, then Philip last of all. We will make our way down to the river, then walk across the ice until it turns to the east, at which point we will move south over land as far as Abingdon. There, Gerard is sure we can gain some horses and ride the rest of the way to

Wallingford. With any luck, Lord Brian will be waiting to open the gate to us." Here he spoke to me directly. "Empress, despite your feat of late, I would caution you against attempting any use of your weapon should we be set upon by the enemy. Philip and I will deal with it. You must remain with Gerard, for he knows the land. If the two of us should fall, he can still lead you to safety. Do you understand?"

I nodded solemnly. The same dagger I had used to kill the trespasser was hanging at my waist again. I felt its weight against my hip and prayed to God I would not have to use it.

Philip breathed in deeply, and I watched as the air escaped his lungs, forming a brief cloud. "Is that it, then?" he asked. "Are we all set?"

Gerard and Drogo both nodded and I reached out my hand.

"Take it," I requested, and each man placed his hand upon mine. Together, they formed a knot of strength, warm against the chill of the night. "Now, sirs, let us give them something to remember us by."

With these necessities behind us, Drogo approached the postern door, which was no more than a metal grate about two thirds the height of a normal door. It had to be made small enough that no army could enter through it at speed. The thing whined as he opened it, then he ducked and moved through. Gerard stooped to follow him, and I was left standing before the entrance, unable to see anything in the darkness before me. I turned and looked one last time upon the inside of Oxford Castle, where I had been trapped for more than two months. I feared to leave it—to stride into the unknown.

On your way now, Maud, my mother's voice seemed to speak out of my memories. *The hour is come. We are with you.*

I placed a hand to my chest and felt the bulge where I knew her rosary was kept.

Stay with me, I begged her.

I took my first step through the gate, which was more of a tunnel on account of the thickness of the castle walls. I felt along the stone with the fingers of my right hand, both to keep my balance and to tell when I was on the other side. One step, two steps ... and then I was hit in the face with something. What was it?

"Watch out for the bulrushes," I could hear Drogo say nearby.

The dead stalks were heavy down by that part of the river. Somehow, I had forgotten. My eyes slowly adjusted, and I could barely see the two men standing among the plants in front of me. Then I heard noise behind me and knew that Philip had made it through.

We spoke no more but moved carefully down the slope until we came to the ice. It groaned slightly as I put my full weight on it, and for just a moment I was transported to the night that Robert and I had skated on the pond outside London. The sky was clear then and the stars danced above us as we spun—not like this night when the clouds and snow blocked the light of the moon.

We took great care moving across the ice, and every moment I was afraid I would fall and either injure myself or reveal us all to the enemy. I could hear the distant sounds of their horns and drums. I imagined they were sitting around their fires, drinking wine to celebrate the victory that was near. The four of us continued along the river, our tracks in the layer of snow quickly being brushed away by the wind. Oh, the cold of that night! There are corpses warmer than we were then. I feared my very skin would freeze as the snow hit my face again and again.

In the whistle of the wind, I could almost hear my brother William charging me, *Go, Maud! Press on!*

And so I did, ignoring the cold and the pain, setting aside the fear, bidding myself to be brave. We came to a place where the bank stuck out slightly and there was a patch of brush. Drogo moved toward it and ducked down, the three of us following him. We held there for a moment and caught our breath, then he told us, "I thought I saw something ... someone by the eastern bank. You all stay here. I'm going to have a look."

My hand moved by instinct toward the place where my dagger lay hidden beneath the cloak. As Drogo moved through the brush, a new surge of fear coursed through my veins. I lifted my eyes to the heavens, where the snow danced above me. Somewhere beyond, the cloud of witnesses was looking down on us: my mother, my brother, Father Anselm, Bruno, the emperor, Grimbald, all the lords of old. The apostles themselves looked down on us. The saints and angels were witnesses to our flight.

"Please ..." I whispered. "Be with me now." My words were lost on the wind, but I believed they understood me.

Then I heard voices, at first faint above the roar of the wind and then growing louder. A pair of voices entirely of earth were talking freely, laughing, moving up and down in pitch, but they were not speaking the Norman tongue. They belonged to two of Stephen's mercenaries.

"*Sainte Mère, il fait froid! Je déteste ce pays. Je ne sais pas comment les Anglais peuvent vivre ici,*" one of them spoke, his voice deep and powerful.

The other man with a higher voice replied, "*Je préférerais être ici avec vous plutôt que de rester avec la comtesse. Elle sera bientôt morte.*"

Two words stood out to me in particular: "*comtesse*" and "*morte.*" I did not know much of their speech, but I could discern well enough that they were pairing me, the countess, with death. I turned to Philip on my right and saw that he was holding a finger to his lips, even as he wrapped his other arm around me, either to provide comfort or warmth. Gerard did the same, and we continued to sit there, listening to the two men talk. They must have been within five yards of us, but we were well hidden beneath the bank and the branches of a small tree.

Go away, I thought. *Just go away!*

I wondered what Drogo was doing—if he was trapped somewhere, unable to make it back to our position without being discovered. After another minute or two of conversation, the voices finally began to move away, and only a few seconds later some snow fell from the bank to Gerard's left as something moved in the bushes, sending the frozen flakes this way and that. Then I saw arms, legs, and finally a head push out from the thicket, and Drogo rolled as much as stepped down to where we sat.

"They've gone off now. We should continue," he said quietly. "Up now! We must be quick."

The others helped me to my feet and we continued walking over the ice. Below us, there was the faint sound of cracking as our weight pressed down again and again. I breathed in the air and sent it back out, my insides screaming with the chill. No matter which way I was facing, the wind seemed to hit me in the face, and for just a moment I closed my eyes since it was almost too dark to see anyway.

Did I not tell you to always be vigilant? Bruno asked me, breaking into my thoughts. *Never let down your guard!*

And then through the rushing air, a new sound struck me: a voice crying in the darkness.

"*Là-bas! Angevins! Angevins!*"

I heard Philip behind me say, "Run!"

I could no longer take each step with care, praying the ice would hold me. I could not take time for anything.

"*Angevins! Angevins!*" the voice continued to cry, sending more of a chill through my body than any power of the air. It seemed to be following us at equal pace.

Forward we ran, our legs straining, our lungs heaving. I was no longer sure which direction we were going. I simply followed the figures of Gerard and Drogo, locking my eyes on their backs and pressing on stride after stride. I believe I would have followed them into the very fires of hell. There were others shouting now, calling to one another on the eastern bank, no doubt trying to determine how best to cut us off. They could not have seen more than a slight movement in the sea of white, but perhaps they guessed what we were about. In that moment, as in so many others, it was the voice of Anselm that came to my mind, as if I were sitting across the table from him again, waiting to receive the drops of gold that would fall from his lips.

Go now, child, he said to me. *Rise to eternity.*

Beneath the ice, the sacred river flowed: the very lifeblood of England. In that hour, it refused to let me fall. I was passing over it as Christ upon the sea. My feet pounded the ice, but they did not slip. I could feel its cold seeping into my toes, but there was also the heat as of a thing that is kindled. Yes, I myself was being kindled.

One mile until we were past the enemy camp: that is what they had told me. I had little sense of distance at that point, but it seemed as if the river was curving to the left, which was a good sign. No sooner had I thought as much than Gerard and Drogo both took a turn for the bank on our right.

Another voice pierced the night, calling, "*Arrête-les!*"

I heard no sound of arrows amid all that wind, but I saw one hit a tree and send down a shower of snow that landed on our heads as we raced to climb up the bank and into the wood. My feet lost their hold and I landed face down in a pile of the stuff. Immediately, strong hands reached to collect me and pull me up to the bank, and then I was running again, this time beneath the trees. I thought I could still hear shouts in the distance, but they were less near than they had been. Beneath the trees it was perfectly dark. I had to stumble after the sound of my knights, running into more than one branch as I did so.

We continued that way until all I heard was the crush of our boots upon the snow and the whip of our cloaks against the trees. The others had let up the pace a bit, for which I was thankful. Then we broke out into a glade of sorts, where I saw that the fall of snow had slowed, and somewhere between the clouds, the moon had succeeded in showing its face. Drogo signaled for us to stop and we all bent over, gasping for air.

"Is anyone hurt?" Philip asked, after we had taken a moment simply to breathe. "My lady, you took a hard fall back there," he said, placing a hand on my arm.

"Actually, I landed fully in snow: no damage done," I assured him. "Did we make it past them, then?"

"Yes, we must be a good mile beyond their camp now," said Gerard, "but we are by no means out of danger. The watch saw us and will inform their master, though I think we hold the advantage now. They will struggle to track us until day arrives."

"By which point we must be far from here," concluded Drogo. "Come, we have not a moment to waste! On to Abingdon, and after that, to Wallingford!"

And so, we pressed on through the starless night, across the hills and plains of Oxfordshire covered in snow, four companions alone against the host of the enemy, with the fate of England in our hands.

"Open up! Open in the name of the empress!"

Drogo struck his fist upon the door as the other three of us stood shivering in the cold, our whole bodies weary and our feet somehow both numb and in pain, clinging to the reins of the horses we had been loaned at the monastery of Abingdon.

We had made it the thirteen miles cross country and come upon Wallingford Castle without any hindrance beyond the weather. There we were relieved to find that it was not in a state of siege, but we still prayed that it would be a friend who answered the door and not a foe.

Drogo pounded again on the gate, looking up at the watch tower directly above our heads. We had seen the light of fires rising from the yard beyond and the dark figures of guards walking along the wall ahead of us. However, it was also the third watch of the night and not a time when visitors normally come calling, so the delay was not much of a surprise.

From the lone window overhead, a knight in full armor leaned his head out and called down, "The empress we know, but not you. There is a war on. State your name and your business!"

"I am Drogo of Powheile, knight in Her Highness' service these many years, here with the empress herself come from Oxford, who commands that the Lord Brian receive her and grant her protection," he replied.

"What? I thought you were monks," said the guard. "Is the empress really among you?"

I threw back my hood and stepped forward, keeping a hold on the reins of my horse. "Look upon my face and see that it is I, Mathilda, daughter of King Henry, lady of the English. We wore these clothes to make our escape, but if you admit us, you will see plainly enough that I am no man, but a woman and your rightful queen."

"My apologies, Your Highness," he told me, bowing his head. "One cannot be too careful in such times."

"Oh, I quite agree," I assured him. "Now, if you please, open the gate."

Within seconds, the double doors swung open to reveal the ditch that lay between us and the main gate of the castle. We waited for the bridge to lower and then led the horses forward, taking care not to slip as ice had formed on the wood boards. The portcullis ahead of us lifted in turn, and just inside the walls I could see a man standing there with a torch in his hand, ready to receive us, even as others began to crowd about. As we continued walking beneath the portcullis, I could see his features clearly, even as he walked toward me: it was Brian fitz Count.

His face seemed to glow—in the light of the fire, yes, but also with joy, or perhaps relief. He shook his head and smiled, and I found that I could not contain myself. I burst into tears of joy as I stepped fully within the walls and knew that I had succeeded in my aim. I was safe and among friends.

"You can hand me the reins, my lady. We will lead the horses to the stables," Philip said.

I did as he asked without even turning to look at him. I was still gazing at Brian, our eyes saying everything our words could not, and I knew that he had been dying every day since he heard that I was trapped.

As the others broke off, Brian began to say, "How ..." but stopped himself. "No, it does not matter. There will be time for that later."

"I hope many more years," I replied.

He held the torch to the side and wrapped his other arm around me. For just a moment, we both shed a few tears, even as the sounds of celebration broke out around us. My companions were being lauded for their feat.

Pulling back, Brian said to me, "You had better come in now. You've been out in the cold too long as it is." Wiping his eyes, he said, "Forgive me. I just didn't know if we would see you alive again."

"Well, now you see me, and I am very much alive ... I think." I laughed for the first time in what seemed like years. "That is, parts of me are alive, but other parts are rather frozen."

He directed me and the two of us began walking toward the keep, the snow crunching beneath our feet. One or two persons approached to speak with me, but Brian waved them off, for which I was thankful. After all, I had just come through one of the worst ordeals of my life. There would be time to greet them all later.

"You need food and then sleep," he told me, repeating my own thoughts, "but perhaps you ought to know a few things before that."

"Yes, tell me everything of our situation," I begged.

"Reginald is here, as is Miles, but Baldwin has gone off to Cirencester to meet up with Robert."

Well, there was some good news if ever I heard it! I suddenly felt less weary.

"Robert!" I cried. "Do you mean he is back in the country?"

"Yes, I am sorry you had not heard. He arrived about three weeks ago and seized Wareham, hoping that would pull Stephen away from Oxford. Sadly, it did not. He moved north and sent word ahead for us to join together and ride to your relief. Of course, the others came here to Wallingford as soon as they learned that Stephen was moving toward you. I gave them quite a scolding for abandoning you, and they were as repentant as any men I have ever seen, though you will be the final judge of that. We have made raids on the outer parts of Stephen's camp every few days, but he refuses to be drawn, and his host has grown larger as people keep arriving to take part in the pillaging. A few days ago, we saw from a distance the fire he was launching toward you, and we feared the worst. I pushed to move against him in open battle, despite the less than favorable odds, but then the weather changed and there was no chance of that."

We had almost reached the door, but he stopped and turned to face me, once again shaking his head in wonder and smiling broadly.

"But you are here now! How happy this makes me! Hope is born again, and that is not the best of it."

"Truly? It seems far better than anything I dreamed would happen," I replied. "But what is the best?"

He placed a hand on my arm and said, "Henry is come."

Oh, what blessed words! The very angels of heaven could not have spoken anything fairer. Could it really be so?

"My son?" I asked oddly, as if there could have been another Henry of interest to me.

"Yes. He is staying now at Devizes. He is quite safe for the moment, though we will want to move him to Bristol at some point so he can be under the care of Lady Mabel. Robert already has a fine tutor for him there, a Master Matthew—"

He could not finish, for I embraced him again. Breaking away, I said, "Oh, Brian! How can I ever thank you and Robert for everything you have done? May I see him? May I see my son?"

"As soon as you have recovered a bit and we are certain the road is safe, yes, I should think so. After all, you are the ruler here. You go where you wish. Now, let us enter quietly. Some of the men are sleeping."

He left the torch in a sconce by the door, and as we walked into the hall, we did our best not to step on any of those sprawled out on the straw, several of them using their cloaks as pillows while a few clutched their swords in sleep. Brian pointed toward the door to the side and we walked through it and up the stair. When we reached the top, the lady of the castle was standing there in her night robe with her hair in a simple braid, a candle in hand.

"Empress Mathilda, welcome again to Wallingford," she greeted me. "I had to see with my own eyes if you had truly been able to escape. What miracles the Lord still works among us!"

"I am most sorry to impose, and especially at such an hour!" I replied. "I will gladly accept any bed you have to offer, even if it be the floor."

"I'll lead you on from here," she explained, placing a hand on my shoulder.

Brian gave me one last smile and said, "Good night, then, or perhaps I should say good morning."

As soon as he had closed the door of his own chamber behind him, Lady Mathilda and I walked the short span that separated us from the guest room I had used before.

"We always keep it ready ... just in case," she told me.

Once inside, she set the candle down on the small table by the bed and said, "Here, let me help you out of those things."

"There is no need—" I began, but she interrupted me.

"No, please, it is the least I can do for my sovereign."

I ceased protesting and stood still as she untied the cord around my waist and helped me slip off the monk's robe. She saw the dagger and said, "I trust you did not have to use this much."

"Not much, but I did have to use it," I replied quietly.

She quickly changed the subject. "Fortunate that you had something the color of snow to wear!"

"Yes. I told them if I succeeded, I would build a new house for the Cistercians, and now I suppose I must do so."

She continued to help me out of each item of clothing until I was standing in nothing but my under things, and it was at that moment that she chose to say something that immediately set me on edge.

"There is something I think I must tell you," she reported without meeting my eyes, her hands busy folding the clothes.

The tone in her voice had changed from just a moment before, and I feared very much what she was about to say.

"Very well," I said, the words seeming to stick in my throat. "I will hear it."

She placed the clothes in a pile next to the bed and reached over to the lone chest by the wall, from which she retrieved a robe not unlike her own. She stood to her full height, which was not much, and looked at me directly.

"My lord told me … he told me what happened when you were at Ludgershall. He told me all that has passed between you."

Her words cut through me more surely than any weapon of the enemy. The joy of a few moments earlier drained from me entirely, and I almost wished I was still locked inside Oxford Castle, where at least I would be free of the conversation in which I found myself.

"I see," I whispered, feeling very much as if I might vomit.

"Yes," she replied simply.

There was a deep hurt in her eyes: a hurt that I had caused. Much as I wished to defend myself in that moment—there were several things I could have said that might have helped—I felt the frailty of it all. In her eyes, I saw that there was nothing I could say or do to make amends or erase everything that had happened. To defend myself would only add to her injury. So instead, I asked her the question I had wanted to ask for so many years: the question that gnawed at my soul.

"Do you hate me, then?" I inquired, my voice breaking as I did so. "I would not blame you if you did."

She did not reply immediately but stepped behind me and placed the robe over my shoulders. As I slid my arms into the sleeves, she finally said, "No, my lady. I do not hate you. Perhaps I should. I cannot tell you how it pained me to learn that all this time, my husband has cherished another in his heart." Here she stepped in front of me again, but did not meet my gaze, looking instead at the wall. "Of course, there was a part

762

of me that sensed it. I saw his devotion to you, but I thought it no more than what a knight owes his lady. Even as there were so many signs, I did not read them, because I had no reason to doubt my lord. And then when he told me everything ..." She turned to face me, her eyes deep wells of black and green. "I suppose I did try to hate you for a time, but I found that I could not."

I breathed in deeply, struggling not to cry. It seemed too good to be true that she could know how I felt about her husband and still look upon me favorably.

"You are one of the few persons on earth to experience such a difficulty," I assured her.

She sighed and sat down on the bed. "Yes, I think that is why I could not do it. The more I thought about it—and I thought upon it long, both day and night—I saw that you are the same as me: a woman subject to the cruelties of life. I never chose who I would marry either. I never chose much of anything, same as you. And I suppose when one man finally showed you kindness, you were drawn to him even as I or any other woman would be ... although I think it was something more for you. In another world, in another time, I am sure you and he would be together. You seem made for each other ... and yet he is my husband."

Again, I was taken aback by her words. They might have been true, but I would never have thought she would be so gracious in her response. I felt a need to inform her that I meant no harm.

"Lady Wallingford, it is my great wish that your marriage will be preserved in all joy, for I know he seeks to be a faithful husband to you," I said. As I did so, the words seemed almost crude to my ears, but she did not take them so.

"Oddly, I believe you. Perhaps I am a fool, but I think it would be wrong in some way for us to turn against each other.

Women must support one another." Here she added with great feeling, "You are not my enemy."

I sat beside her on the bed and said, "Neither do I see you as an enemy. Indeed, I have often observed that you are as good a woman as they come. I fell in love with Lord Brian before he was wed to you. As you say, it was my father who did this to us all. You deserve such a husband—truly, you do. I think you are a far better person than myself."

"Me? No, no!" she replied with a laugh, which I took to be a good sign. "They will never sing songs of me, but you are meant for something better. Your son will wear the crown. You will be an eternal queen, remembered throughout the ages."

I was utterly amazed. Not two minutes earlier, I had braced myself for an intensely painful conversation, but instead I felt as if the lady of Wallingford had freed me from years of shame. She had forgiven me—chosen to see the best in me. I had known injustice that hurt me on so many occasions, but here was an injustice that was a healing balm, as the divine mercy itself.

"Never mind that," I said, patting her hand. "You cannot know how it cheers my soul to know that you do not hate me. I have borne this guilt for so long."

"Then I bid you cast your burden away!" she besought me. "Whatever sins you have committed, they are forgiven. Far be it from me to put myself in the place of God. Now, you need to sleep a good long while. I will leave you be. One of the men will set some food outside your door for whenever you desire it."

As she rose to leave, I felt I should say something else, but found I could utter nothing at all. Once the door was closed behind her, I began crying in relief for the second time that night. I sensed that one chapter of my life—a chapter I had barely acknowledged, a guilt that hung upon me like the dog which bites the doe—had come to a close, and I had seen a strange kindness on earth that restored my faith in the kindness of heaven. When I had calmed down a bit, I pulled the covers over myself and whispered those words my mother had taught me as I fell into sleep.

> *"Nunc laudare debemus auctorem regni caelestis,*
> *potentiam creatoris, et consilium illius*
> *facta Patris gloriae: quomodo ille,*
> *cum sit aeternus Deus, omnium miraculorum auctor*
>   *exstitit;*
> *qui primo filiis hominum*
> *caelum pro culmine tecti*
> *dehinc terram custos humani generis*
> *omnipotens creavit."*[57]

The castle of Oxford was surrendered to the usurper within hours by Henry D'Oyly in exchange for the freedom of all within. They say when Stephen learned of my escape, he flew into a fury for quite some time. Although he gained a great fortress and an even greater city, that was not the point. He had come to Oxford with one object, and it had slipped through his grasp. I might have paid the last of my coin to see the look on his face when he received the news, but it was better perhaps that I should save it. After all, we were still in the middle of a war. I accepted instead the sight of Adela arriving at Wallingford with her infant son, the two of them falling into the waiting arms of a proud husband and father.

---

57 Modern English translation as follows: "Now we must honor the Guardian of heaven, / the might of the Architect, and his purpose, / the work of the Father of glory / as he, the eternal Lord, established the beginning of wonders; he first created for the children of men / heaven as a roof, the holy Creator / Then the Guardian of mankind, the eternal Lord, / afterwards appointed the middle earth, / the lands for men, the Lord Almighty."

I was also cheered to see earls Reginald and Miles on bent knee before me, begging my forgiveness for their lack of faith. They fully admitted their error of judgment and swore to never doubt my instincts again. I knew they could not live up to that promise, but I was in a gracious mood. Placing my two hands on each of their heads, I granted them pardon and found that in doing so, I felt more a queen than ever I did in Westminster. As the Holy Scripture tells us, it is the glory of a man to overlook an offense.[58]

These meetings cheered my heart, but there were two still to come: the ones I longed for most of all. We knew that Stephen would not sit idle for ever, but the good news was that Earl Robert of Gloucester had returned from Normandy with a large force of knights. He had evidently been pressed upon by Count Geoffrey as soon as he arrived to help take several castles in the western part of the duchy, thus ensuring our control there. This Robert did on the understanding that, in turn, the entire force would make for England when their efforts were complete. In the end, the castles were gained but Count Geoffrey still refused to come, releasing only his knights. To this, Earl Robert replied that the count was welcome to stay in his own lands as long as he allowed Prince Henry to travel. Thanks be to God, my husband agreed, and upon hearing the whole tale, I could not help but think that this result was better for everyone in the end.

On the day before Christmas, I bid farewell to my excellent hosts at Wallingford, and mounted the horse they so kindly loaned me for the journey to Devizes. This time, I was accompanied by a company of fifty men at arms, a great improvement from the last time I traveled to the same fortress. Sir Drogo was the leader of that company, and I suspect he too was glad not

---

58   Proverbs 19:11.

to be carrying me on his back as he was forced to do before. We pushed all the way to Marlborough, then stopped to rest for the night. Even as a child can barely sleep the eve before Christmas, I found it difficult to rest at the thought of seeing my son the next day.

At the rising of the sun, we set out again. It was slightly warmer, and the road was mostly clear. Even had it not been, I would have continued. Before the morning was over, the trees parted and we saw the great walls of Devizes. I could hear church bells ringing in honor of the birth of our Lord, and it seemed for just a moment that all was right with the world.

When we were within the walls, Drogo helped me down to the ground. I brushed a bit of dirt off my cloak, and as the others went to get drinks for themselves and their horses, I had a quiet moment where I felt free to confide.

"Thank you, Drogo. Thank you for staying by my side, not only in our flight from Oxford, but through all kinds of dangers. Of all the men I have ever known, you have been among the most faithful."

"And by your side I shall remain," he told me. "Now, it is Christmas Day. Let's go inside and see them all, shall we?"

"Wait," I said, holding out a hand to stop him.

"What is it?" he asked.

I swallowed hard, and admitted, "I'm a bit worried, actually—worried about how this will go. Have I built things up in my mind? Have I assumed too much?"

He cocked his head a bit to one side. "Come again?"

"It's just that—I haven't seen him in so long. What if he doesn't remember much about me? What if his father has poisoned him against me? What if I barely recognize him?"

Drogo nodded thoughtfully. "Those are fair questions, but let me ask you in return, what do you hope to accomplish through all these what's?"

Now it was my turn to say, "I'm not sure what you mean."

"Nothing is certain in life. The future is always a mystery," he explained. "That is why you have to live it. You have to take the chance. Walk in there: see and be seen. No matter what happens, you are his mother and he is your son. You are on this journey together. You are bound by God and nature."

"How right you are! Thank you," I said, feeling a bit better. "Happy Christmas, Drogo."

"Happy Christmas," he replied with a smile.

I entered the hall, which was decorated for the feast with boughs of green on the tables and ivy hanging from the beams above. I had requested that no one follow me in, wanting to see my brother and son in private. My heart leapt as I saw Robert striding forward to meet me, but Henry was not there. The two of us shared an embrace and he said to me, "From the very jaws of death you come to us, more alive than ever. Forgive my tardiness."

"From what I hear, you are not at fault for that," I replied, as he released me. "And what is this I hear about a shipwreck? One of the men was telling me on the way here."

His countenance dropped and he shook his head sadly. "Yes, we lost five ships on the way to Normandy. Horrible business. Many good men drowned."

"I'm so sorry," I said softly. "I'm so sorry for everything you have been through on my account."

"And I for everything you have been through on account of my delay!" he replied. "But we are both here now, safe and whole. With the New Year, we will strike against the usurper again, and this time we have something more powerful than any weapon on our side."

"You mean my son," I commented with a nod of the head. "Where is he? I long to see him."

"I do not doubt it. He is grown into a fine lad, sister. He has learned all the dukes of Normandy going back to our ancestor Rollo and all the kings of France."

"Has he now? We must see to it that he learns the kings of England as well."

"Yes, he will be down in just a moment. The cook was determined to give him a pudding to keep up his strength for the day."

I sighed. "I brought him no gift. What kind of mother am I?"

"I think seeing you will be gift enough," he assured me.

Even as he spoke these words, the door at the opposite end of the hall opened, and I saw him walking toward me: the son who had removed my dishonor. He was the boy I had prayed for, the child I had fought for, the son I stood ready every moment to die for. He was taller, yes, and also surer of himself. I could sense it in his manner as he moved toward me. He held himself as one meant to rule. I had left him a boy and he had become half a man, yet he was still my Henry—that much was certain. I could see myself in his features. Not only that, but I could see my mother. The hair was his father's, but the rest was the House of Wessex.

And then he smiled at me. He seemed happy to see me: eager, perhaps, to make my acquaintance again. I cherished the talks we would have and longed for the day when he would take up a sword and fight for the crown he was born to wear. But in that moment, all that mattered was that he lived and he was with me.

He stopped directly in front of me and said, "Here I am, mother."

I held his face in my hands, staring upon him in wonder. Then I pulled him to myself, burying my face in his red hair, treasuring the scent of him—the fullness of joy within my heart.

"My son," I whispered, kissing his head. "Oh, my son!"

To her royal highness, Mathilda, princess of England, daughter of King Henry —

I, Lawrence, archdeacon of Rouen, send greeting upon your arrival into the duchy of Normandy and the occasion of your transfer to the domain of the emperor for your marriage to the duke of Saxony and Bavaria. Such a great honor to be bestowed on one so young! May the Lord bless you and keep you all your days as you seek to reign in wisdom and virtue.

I must admit the sad occasion of this letter. You will no doubt have heard the news of the death of that great lady and your father's mother, the Empress Mathilda, whose company I have been privileged to keep for the last few years. She was tormented by a malady of the lungs, and on the fourth before the Ides of this month, she passed on to her eternal reward. I am certain you feel the grief of this as keenly as myself. It is a loss for both Normandy and England.

I first met the empress shortly after becoming archdeacon when we discussed our mutual respect for Hildegard von Bingen. She told me she knew the House of Bingen from her time in the empire, and from there was born one of the greatest friendships of my life. When she was not busy with her many duties of state, she would summon me to her home and we would sit in the garden drinking the fruit of the vine, which more often than not she purchased from the Palatinate. This surprised me given the fame of the Angevin vineyards.

Over time, our conversation moved from matters of theology to tales of her many adventures. I would beseech her for these stories, and seldom did her lips part without divulging something of great interest to me. However, I knew she had not told me all, for there were some subjects she avoided completely. I sensed that I was not enough in her confidence, which would have been a matter of no consequence except that she seemed haunted still by certain things in her past, and I believed that discussing them might do her some good. A prideful thought, to be sure, for I knew nothing then and still know little of the ways of royal ladies.

Then one day, we were sitting on the same bench as usual, enjoying the late warmth of summer, when she said to me, "Lawrence, I need your help."

My concern rose and I replied, "Whatever it is you need, Your Highness, I would be happy to aid you. Anything for the mother of my sovereign."

I was over eager, and she knew it. A smile lit up her face for a moment, then faded again.

"One day, Lawrence—one day, I am going to die, and when I do, I must leave some testament behind."

"If you are concerned for your estate, I would be happy to find you a lawyer," I told her.

With a wit such as she often showed, she replied, "A lawyer is the last thing I need. They only make things tedious, don't you agree?"

"If you say so," I offered, though I had known several fine men of the law in my day, and I was certain she had as well.

"What I need is a scribe," she explained, "someone to write down my thoughts. I have it in mind to leave behind a record of my deeds for the sake of my posterity. You see, I read the chroniclers, Lawrence. I know what they write about me. They say I am of the stock of tyrants and that such character lives strongly in me. Not only that, but they neglect so much of what I have done. If that is how I am to be remembered ... no, it cannot be! I must leave an account for my daughters, especially the young Mathilda. She should know about the woman whose name she bears."

That was how it began. I would arrive with parchment and ink, and for hours on end she would tell me the story. Day after day, week after week, and on into months and years I wrote it all down, even as her health declined and our meetings grew further apart. And of course, she was caught up often in the affair of Archbishop Thomas, which is sadly yet to be resolved. I fear for what may happen now that the empress is not here to temper him and your father, but trouble not yourself with these thoughts.

What I deliver to you now is the account I have recorded from her very own words: the chronicle of Mathilda, empress of the Romans, countess of Anjou, and rightful queen of England and duchess of Normandy. Such a great name and so many titles she bore, but to those she loved most and best, she often went by the name Maud, as you will see in her account. This is the story of her true self and not the one imposed on her by others. When she opened her mouth, such things would come out that I never thought to hear from one so august. More than once, I was astounded by what she told me and struggled to write it down, so in awe was I of what she chose to disclose. I had never known a noble lady to speak so freely, but then again, it was never meant for the entire world: only for you and the rest of her descendants.

My regret is that we were not able to complete the chronicle before her death. She pushed hard in the final days to recite the tale of the siege of Oxford, even as she could barely breathe. I begged her to take more rest, but she would hear nothing of it. Her mind was set that you should have this account, so we continued, even as her coughs produced blood. When she was finally relieved of her suffering, I counted it a great mercy, and I am sure you will understand why we were not able to tell how your father grew to become great and fought Stephen of Blois until the day he accepted him as his heir and declared that Henry of Anjou would become king of England upon his own death. The rest of that story, you well know: how your father was crowned in Westminster Abbey, uniting the old House of Wessex and the House of Normandy in his rule, even as Saint Edward the Confessor prophesied. He has built an empire for himself that is the envy of all Christendom, approaching in greatness even that of the Roman emperor himself. May his fame live for ever!

Perhaps it is proper that the account is not finished, for history is never finished. No man accomplishes all he sets out to do. As you make now for the lands to the east, treasure the tales of your great mother. Like her, you were born in England. That land was dearer to her than any on earth, although it wounded her deeply. The people forsook her for another, but she still loved the land, for she did not mistake the sentiments of the moment for the thing itself.

Her England is not merely a place, as if sacred ground was only ground. It is a feeling, or perhaps an enchantment. It is a thing that grips one, as the ancients might have said, in the bowels, but we are wont to say in the heart. Although I have never set foot there, I felt in the empress' stories that it was brought alive and I had experienced it more truly than any man living. Her England is the temple of some strange force—an idea that drives men on. One day the very earth must perish and the elements melt in extreme heat, but as long as there is an idea, as long as there is someone to remember, there will be an England. This is what it means to be eternal: to be joined to a higher time.

I watched them lower her coffin into the ground by the altar of Bec-Hellouin. The archbishop led the Mass, even as she had requested, but it was not his cathedral that she chose for her eternal rest. She remembered the words of the abbot Boson, who told her to think in terms of a thousand years. It was he who set eternity in her heart, and it was another son of that house, Anselm, who taught her what it was to rise. And so, she lies not in her beloved England, or even in the ancient resting place of her fathers, but the abbey to which she showed such charity in life and in which she hoped to rest in peace until the great resurrection.

As the stone slab was pulled over the vault and dropped into place, I could not hold back the tears that filled my eyes. She had shared her story with me, and in so doing, had made me a part of her even as she became a part of me. The grief I felt was powerful, and I do not know if it shall ever pass until we are united again on that last great day.

At times, the space between the living and the dead seems an eternal abyss. The new cut grave offers us no comfort. Once they walked among us, but no more. We imagine that we could draw them back—that when we return from our hours of grief, they may walk through the door as they always did before. But that is the stuff of mere desire, and as the cold earth swallows the remains of those we love, we sense in our hearts that it is an end indeed. There will be no drawing them back. Death is the most final of all things.

But then again, when we have returned to that life and grief which should have passed continues to gnaw at us as a dog upon a bone, when we have given up the dead to their fate, they whisper to us softly, not as ghosts but as voices of flame and ice more real than anything of this world. And we discover at last that there is no eternal abyss but only the thinnest of veils between this realm and the other—that time has bent back upon itself and every moment that ever was and ever will be touches every other moment. They are alive in us. We feel them in our bones, the marrow of all we are. The cloud of witnesses speaks.

To live a life is to walk the path toward death, the passing into heaven or hell, wrath or mercy. We give so little thought to that which matters most. The man who is not ready to die is ready for nothing at all. We search for meaning in the cold, dark days of winter, when life seems drained of its color and the demons close in around us. We pass the resting places of the dead and ask ourselves, for what purpose did they live? For what purpose was I myself created?

The shroud of death wraps up not only our carnal remains, but our words and actions. It threatens to take them all into the deep, down into earth beneath earth, never again to feel the warmth of the sun. Only what is eternal matters: the remnant preserved by God.

And when you come at last to that hour—perhaps you have suffered long and perhaps cruelly—you recognize that you are nothing more than the corpses that lie beneath us. You are nothing more, and yet nothing less. Once, they were only memories, but now they are your future. Your future is eternity. You attempt to make yourself brave. You have spent the final measure of your days.

The foundation of your life laid down, another will now build, and another upon that, until the great mass of humanity and the triumphs of the ages are crafted into a single dwelling: a great temple that for ever stands.

A sigh, a breath, and then it fades. Darkness gives way to light and the messengers of heaven. It is time and eternity. It is the universe entire.

It is England: her England.

THE FATES OF THE
CHARACTERS

Stephen of Blois

Nearly the entirety of his reign over England took place under the shadow of a civil war later generations would call The Anarchy. In the late 1140s, Empress Mathilda departed for Normandy and her eldest son, Henry, led the opposition to Stephen's rule. Known at that time as Henry fitz Empress, he became duke of Normandy and then greatly expanded the new Angevine Empire by marrying Eleanor of Aquitaine. Stephen took steps to promote his own son Eustace as heir to the throne, but the latter's death in 1153 led him to ultimately appoint Henry fitz Empress as his heir instead, bringing an end to the war. Stephen died the following year, his troubled reign proving to be a mere interruption in the passage of the crown by primogeniture.

Henry of Blois

The bishop of Winchester's power was substantially diminished in 1143 when Pope Innocent II died and Henry's legatine commission therefore expired. His subsequent efforts to have his bishopric raised to an archbishopric were unsuccessful. He played a more minor role in the controversies of later years and died at the age of seventy-five in the year 1171, outliving most of his contemporaries. The prominent black tomb in the choir of Winchester Cathedral, once believed to belong to King William II, is now widely thought to hold at least some of Bishop Henry's remains.

William of Ypres

The chief military commander in Stephen's camp during The Anarchy, William of Ypres became earl of Kent in all but name. He was unpopular with the English people on account of his foreign birth and poor treatment of several abbeys, most notably the burning of Wherwell. In the late 1140s, he lost his sight and could no longer participate in battle, dealing a major blow to Stephen's efforts and perhaps influencing him to reach an accord with the Angevine party. During the reign of Henry II, the Flemings were banished from England, and William of Ypres lived out the rest of his days in relative anonymity, dying in his homeland in 1165.

Geoffrey de Mandeville

Although Earl Geoffrey returned his allegiance to Stephen after the latter's release from captivity, the two quickly fell out. Geoffrey was arrested and forced to turn over two of his castles and his custody of the Tower of London. This led the earl to rebel against Stephen, using Ramsey Abbey and the Isle of Ely as his base. Stephen besieged him and Geoffrey died of an arrow wound in September 1144, by which point he was an excommunicate. As a result, he could not be buried in his chosen abbey, but his body was finally accepted by the Templars in London and buried at Temple Church. His effigy can still be seen there.

Robert of Gloucester

Earl Robert defeated Stephen one more time in open battle, leading the empress' forces to victory at the battle of Wilton in the summer of 1143. Stephen was not captured, but the victory was important in establishing the state of divided rule that would exist in England for the next decade and marked the first major success for the Angevine party in England since the Route of Winchester. Robert's death at his home castle of Bristol in 1147 may have influenced the empress' decision to leave England in 1148 and take up permanent residence in Rouen, allowing her son Henry to oversee the war for England.

Geoffrey of Anjou

On January 14, 1144, Count Geoffrey crossed the Seine and captured Rouen, the historic capital of the duchy of Normandy. He was named duke of Normandy that summer but struggled for the rest of his life with rebellions in his home territory of Anjou. In 1149, he and the empress jointly ceded the dukedom of Normandy to their son Henry. Two years later, the count became suddenly ill with a fever and died at the age of just thirty-eight. The dynasty of English kings descended from him would eventually be given the name Plantagenet, which was Count Geoffrey's nickname, quite possibly after a flower (*planta genista*) he used to wear.

Brian fitz Count

Not long after the empress' famous escape from Oxford, Brian fitz Count put together a legal defense of her right to the throne and sent it to Bishop Henry of Winchester. He saw off a siege of Wallingford Castle by Stephen in 1146, only to be besieged again in 1152. This time, he was relieved by Henry fitz Empress himself, who would become King Henry II shortly thereafter.

The castle of Wallingford never fell throughout the course of The Anarchy, and this was a major factor in the final victory of the Angevine party. Brian's death is not recorded but seems to have occurred in the early years of Henry II's reign. His wife Mathilda then became a nun at the abbey of Bec. Empress Mathilda and Henry II made grants to Reading Abbey in his honor, praising the loyal service and love he had shown them.

Miles of Gloucester
During a hunting excursion in December 1143, Miles was struck by an arrow that was intended for a deer and died. Several prominent English noblemen suffered this fate in the 12th century, including two sons of William the Conqueror: Prince Richard and King William II.

Drogo
Since his time in the Empire, Drogo had been friends with Saint Norbert, founder of the Premonstratensian order. After Mathilda returned to Normandy for good in 1148, she granted charters for the founding of the new Premonstratensian community of Notre-Dame de Silly. Having served the empress faithfully for many years and through many dangers, Drogo became a canon of this new house. A Drogo "of Powheile" is attested as having been the empress' chamberlain, and it has been the assumption of these novels that he was one and the same with the knight Drogo.

John Marshal
John would become the first hereditary lord marshal of England, passing the title down to his heirs. In 1152, he was besieged by Stephen at Newbury Castle. His young son William was offered to Stephen as a hostage, but when John

subsequently refused to surrender, Stephen threatened to kill the boy. However, John Marshal continued to hold the castle for the empress and Stephen ended up sparing William's life. This boy would go on to become the famous William Marshal, 1st Earl of Pembroke, regent for the young King Henry III and the man who helped defeat the French allied forces at the second battle of Lincoln, thus fending off a foreign invasion of England and ensuring that the empress' descendants would maintain the crown.

William of Malmesbury

His *Gesta Regum Anglorum* ("Deeds of the English Kings") was expanded to include the early years of The Anarchy. Intended to reflect the legacy of Bede's *Ecclesiastical History of the English People,* it is now considered one of the greatest medieval English chronicles and an important work in the evolution of history as a discipline.

Adeliza of Louvain

Despite the tensions that must have been raised when she hosted the Empress Mathilda without his permission, Adeliza and her second husband, William d'Aubigny, 1st Earl of Arundel, seem not to have experienced great conflict. They went on to have seven children, putting an end to any doubts about Adeliza's fertility. She entered the monastery of Affligem in Flanders in 1150 and died the following year, so it is possible that she knew her health was ill and chose to return to her homeland for her final days. The earldom of Arundel and possession of Arundel Castle was passed down to her descendants, transferring through marriage to the FitzAlan family and then the Howard family, also gaining the title duke of Norfolk. They remain among the highest-ranking members of the British aristocracy.

Theobald of Bec

When Pope Innocent II died in 1143, the legatine powers he had granted to Bishop Henry of Winchester expired. Archbishop Theobald traveled to Rome to meet the new pope, Celestine II, where he secured an agreement that the Church would not support any change in the matter of the English crown while the succession was still in dispute. The result was that Theobald refused to crown Stephen's son, Eustace, as heir to the throne in the French manner. In 1148, when Stephen forbade Theobald and several of the other bishops to attend a papal council in Rheims, the archbishop escaped on a boat with Abbot Gilbert Foliot and managed to attend anyway. Pope Eugene III sided strongly with these two men and against Stephen, placing England under an interdict. In 1150, Theobald was officially appointed papal legate for England. After repeated refusals to crown Eustace as Stephen's heir, resulting in the archbishop's exile on the Continent, Theobald was finally instrumental in the creation of the Treaty of Wallingford, which named Henry fitz Empress as heir to the throne. He crowned Henry and his wife Eleanor of Aquitaine as king and queen of England on December 19, 1154 in Westminster Abbey. Thomas Becket was a member of Theobald's household and he was instrumental in the beginning of that man's career. Theobald died in 1161 and was buried with his predecessors at Canterbury Cathedral.

Thomas Becket

On December 29, 1170, just over three years after the death of Empress Mathilda, Thomas Becket was murdered in Canterbury Cathedral by a group of knights. It remains unclear to what extent these knights were acting upon the desires of King Henry II. It was a public relations disaster for the king and he was eventually forced to go to Canterbury and do penance in 1174. Often unpopular in life, Becket was immediately regarded as a martyr of the Church, and his shrine became the greatest place of pilgrimage in medieval England.

Henry II

The latter years of his reign were marked by familial strife. His four surviving sons—Henry, Geoffrey, Richard, and John—frequently quarreled with one another over the matter of inheritance. In 1173, all but John rose in rebellion against their father with their mother's support. Although the sons were pardoned, Eleanor was kept in custody for the rest of her husband's reign. King Henry's sons rebelled further in the 1180s, and the so-called young king Henry, whom his father had made co-regent in 1180, died three years later. The death of Geoffrey in 1186 left only Richard and John to split the inheritance. When he learned that even his favorite son John had turned against him, Henry's spirit seems to have been sapped. He died in the city of Tours in 1189, having established one of the greatest empires in European history and secured the largest holdings on the Continent that England would ever possess.

Descendants of Henry II

Richard succeeded his father as king of England, but famously spent hardly any time in that land, joining the Third Crusade and engaging in many celebrated adventures. Popularly known as "the Lionheart," he ruled from 1189–99 but had no legitimate children. As a result, his brother John became king of England, and his rule was to be disastrous in many ways. Most of his inheritance on the Continent was lost to the French, and his poor relations with the English barons forced him to issue the Magna Carta ("Great Charter") in 1215. When John failed to uphold his promises in that document, the result was the First Barons' War in which the future Louis VIII of France invaded England. While fighting to defend his crown, John fell ill and died. The previously mentioned actions of William Marshal were instrumental in securing the throne for John's son, who became King Henry III. The severing of England from the duchies of Normandy and Aquitaine meant that future kings of England would spend nearly all their time on the island and the kingdom gradually developed a more uniquely English character. The Plantagenet dynasty survived until the Wars of the Roses in the 15th century, when the Tudors came to power. However, Henry Tudor was himself a descendant of Empress Mathilda, and every English sovereign since Henry II has been descended from the empress. Her descendants who did not hold the throne were also instrumental in shaping English history and culture, and by extension impacting much of our present world. I am conscious that, as a descendant of the empress, I would not exist had she not endured the hardships of her present state to reserve for me a better fate.

AFTERWORD

"You are not here to verify,
Instruct yourself, or inform curiosity
Or carry report.
You are here to kneel
Where prayer has been valid."
        – T.S. Eliot, "Little Gidding," *Four Quartets*

The sky was overcast as I made my way through the streets of Rouen, its gray hue seeming to blend with that of the cobblestones below. With my husband beside me, I was walking in one of the best-preserved medieval city centers in France. We passed the last remaining tower from the old city walls that endured a siege by King Henry V, he of Agincourt fame. The tower is now named after Joan of Arc, though she likely never set foot within. Indeed, the tourist industry of Rouen is betting big on the woman who was executed for heresy by her English captors in one of the most striking episodes of the Hundred Years' War. But I was not there to mourn Joan, nor simply to enjoy the rows of half-timbered buildings that have stood since those bloody days. I was there for more personal reasons.

If you go to visit *Notre-Dame de Paris*, you will see a vast plaza in front of it with room for legions of selfie-stick-wielding tourists. This is a product of Haussmannization: the 19th-century remaking of Paris that removed its narrow medieval alleys in favor of broad, tree-lined boulevards. Rouen, on the other hand, maintains its medieval street plan, and thus its cathedral seemed to rise up suddenly when I turned the last corner. The courtyard in front of its western entrance was so small that even when I stood at its utmost end, I struggled to get the full height of the towers in the frame of my camera. This was the view that so fascinated Claude Monet, and as I gazed upon the oddly mismatched towers and Gothic doors, it was hard not to imagine it all as a blur of yellows, pinks, and reds.

As we approached the entrance and stepped inside, I discovered what I might have guessed: the cathedral of Rouen has not enjoyed the same degree of renovation and adornment as that of Paris. (This was, coincidentally, a few days before *Notre-Dame de Paris* went up in flame.) But I was not there to see beautiful stained glass, which I had enjoyed in spades during my time in Paris. I was there in search of the resting place of a woman whose life was separated from mine by almost a millennium, but whose hold on my heart was as substantial as any historic figure not appearing in the Christian scriptures. I was there as a pilgrim.

I had studied a plan of the cathedral, researched its history, and even contacted the archdiocese ahead of time in my efforts to locate her resting place within those walls. I knew the current building was constructed almost entirely after her death. Given this fact and her royal status, I guessed that she must be buried near the altar, or perhaps in the more ancient crypt below. And so, I began to walk in the pattern I tend to take through every great church: down the right of the nave, back around the choir, then down the left of the nave in a counterclockwise motion, stopping to examine each chapel along the way.

I passed the modern effigies that mark the presence on site of the remains of Rollo, founder of the Norman dynasty, along with Richard the Lionheart and others. I saw the chapel that is now dedicated to Joan of Arc, the events of her strange and momentous life portrayed in stained glass. But it was not until I reached the north transept, my eyes desperately searching, that my husband drew my attention to a fabric sign into which was stitched the following:

> *Grande par sa naissance, plus grande par son marriage, plus grande encore par sa progéniture: ici repose la fille, la femme, le mère des Henri: MATHILDE.*

"Is that Mathilda?" he asked.

I looked on the wall above it and saw the same words carved in Latin. It was no tomb but a simple memorial. Yes, my search for the remains of Empress Mathilda of England had brought me not to an effigy or even a slab of marble, but a barely noticeable carving and a French translation added in 2017.

We had made a special day trip from Paris in large part to honor the woman whose life story I had nearly completed. (At the time, I was halfway through the manuscript of the book you now possess.) I had imagined what it would feel like to stand near her bones. I wondered how it would affect me emotionally—if I would have the kind of odd spiritual experience people sometimes enjoy in such locations of personal importance. But as I was faced with the disappointment of no tomb and nothing of real substance, I was utterly deflated. How could it be that this woman whose life helped shape the history of Europe and the fortunes of England was now mostly forgotten, with no one willing to pay for a proper memorial? I was not so much upset that my day had not gone as I hoped as I was upset that the world had let her down. After all, she did not want to be buried in Rouen. She was moved there from the abbey of Bec and at least some of her bones have been scattered.

"What does it mean?" my husband had asked me, as we looked at those words in French.

Although I can read little of that tongue and only slightly more of Latin, I knew well enough what it said, for I had seen it in several of the sources I consulted for my research.

"Great by birth, greater by marriage, greatest in her off-spring: here lies the daughter, wife, and mother of Henry," I recited.

Those words had always seemed hollow to me. They defined her identity by the men around her rather than anything she herself accomplished. Surely she was greatest in herself! But since I departed the cathedral that day, having felt the place so devoid of her spirit that I neglected to light a candle as I usually do to honor an ancestor, I have come to two important conclusions. First, I have offered her a memorial in the pages of *The Chronicle of Maud*, and one for which I paid a high price, pressing on through exhaustion, pain, rejection, and frustration, not to mention income I could have been making doing something else. Second, while her epitaph may have bothered me at first, I doubt it would have bothered Mathilda.

"Greatest in her offspring." That is what it reads. Having now finished my trilogy of novels, I see more clearly how everything Empress Mathilda did from the time she was a young woman until the day of her death was for the sake of her offspring. They were the dream she never let die: her greatest investment, her hope and purpose. Her offspring are not only the kings and queens that have come from her line, but thousands or even millions of people living today. They have shaped the fate of England and by extension the fates of us all. They are her legacy. Yes, *we* are her legacy, for her blood flows in our veins.

> "*There are other places*
> *Which also are the world's end, some at the sea jaws,*
> *Or over a dark lake, in a desert or a city*"
>   – Eliot, "Little Gidding"

It was my genetic link with Maud more than anything that motivated me to write about her and makes me feel a connection with her. That is a strange sentiment in an era when links of blood and our most basic genetics are being deemphasized in numerous ways. It seems elitist to take pride in one's royal ancestors—utterly at odds with the egalitarian spirit of our age. But I have many royal ancestors, and none of their stories compel me like Maud's. It is her perseverance in the face of tremendous obstacles that has always endeared her to me even more than her royal blood.

I began this project not knowing if I could finish a single chapter. I had no professional or academic training for this type of writing. It takes tremendous perseverance and unfailing enthusiasm to complete a project of this size, and I doubted whether I possessed those things. Very quickly, I realized that my vision for the story, as limited as it was in those early days, would require three novels rather than one. A wiser person might have called it quits at that point, but instead I plowed on, for it seemed I had something of that necessary enthusiasm after all.

From the time I first started writing in 2014 to the time I sit writing these words now (September 2021), I have developed significantly as a person and an author. I wrote about Empress Mathilda becoming a mother, and then I became a mother. I wrote about her visiting locations, and then I was able to visit a few of them. I began to find new threads that I wished to weave into the tapestry: things I had not imagined at the start, but perhaps they were always waiting to be found. By the time

I came to the end of *The Eternal Queen*, I was operating on a different narrative plane than when I sat at Peet's Coffee in Beavercreek, Ohio (now Winans Chocolates + Coffees) and typed those first words: "Many are the tales men tell about me. Many are the names by which I have been called."

The first lines of this book, in contrast, were written at my childhood home in Muskegon, Michigan as I visited for Thanksgiving in the year 2016. It was the first time I had added to the novels since the U.S. presidential election, and the tension in the country and within myself was palpable. In that hour, the first words of Maud that poured out of me came as a lament: "There is a darkness over the land now." I was inspired by Shakespeare's history plays throughout this project, specifically those that cover the Wars of the Roses. There was no question as I began this final novel that its Shakespearean twin was *Richard III*, another tale of a usurper seizing the English crown.

But Stephen of Blois is not Richard III (and certainly not Donald Trump!). It is true that, as the empress says in this book, "If one lives long enough, one begins to see men in the bodies of other men," but it is equally true that, in the words of Nick Carraway in *The Great Gatsby*, "You can't repeat the past." Those who do not learn from history may be destined to repeat it, but never in exactly the same way. After all, history is not a cycle of discrete events, but "a pattern of timeless moments."

I hit there upon one of the chief inspirations for *The Eternal Queen*—an element that was not consciously present in the first two novels but rose to seize me this time around, taking my thinking to another level entirely. I had chosen the titles for all three books in response to a request from Amazon to make them more obviously marketable. (The original working title was *Reckoning*.) I followed their advice and included a royal term in each case—empress, monarch, queen—but the word "eternal" was meant to reference the fact that though she was denied the title of queen in life, that honor is her due down to the present day. It was only later that I realized the whole book and indeed the whole series was about eternity as a concept and goal.

Unlike the first two novels, which I composed in relatively quick succession, *The Eternal Queen* went through many fits and starts as I took breaks to edit and promote its predecessors, as well as focusing on my theological writing. About halfway through the manuscript, I became pregnant with my son Thomas. I had great hopes of finishing the first draft before he was born, but I did not write another word until he was about three months old. Then I struggled to find opportunities to continue while he was sleeping ... assuming that I myself had enough energy to work. The world was in lockdown and there was no one I could rely on for childcare. In my exhaustion, I often wanted to nap rather than write, but as they say, I persisted.

> *"And what the dead had no speech for, when living,*
> *They can tell you, being dead: the communication*
> *Of the dead is tongued with fire beyond the language*
> *of the living."*
>
> – Eliot, "Little Gidding"

The long break from writing had a tremendous effect on the novel, for in those days of pregnancy and early months of motherhood, four things happened. First, my aunt died. I flew home to Michigan for the funeral: back to the place where it all began. I stood beside her grave and felt new life move inside me even as her body lay lifeless in a coffin. I took a flower from her casket and placed it on the nearby grave of my grandmother. Here I was doing what I had sought to do at the grave of Maud, only these were people I had known in the flesh, whose very forms had embraced me. I thought often about death after that.

Second, my theological study brought me to the work of the Canadian philosopher Charles Taylor. I had received his book *A Secular Age* as a gift and intended to read it for some time. Shortly after giving birth, it seemed like the worst time in the world to study philosophy, but when a respected friend encouraged me to read the thing, I felt I had no choice but to do so. As I sat up during the night nursing my son time and time again, I listened to the audiobook in thirty-minute chunks, and in it I heard about how we have transferred from a medieval way of thinking to a modern, secular mode of the same. Our very notion of time has changed and we are caught within an immanent frame, denied communion with the transcendent. Taylor is not fully pessimistic about these changes and suggests no remedy, for he is a philosopher and not a theologian. But in my heart, I felt a longing for something of that older world that I had encountered in so many books during my research.

Thirdly and rather extraordinarily, I read T.S. Eliot's poem "Little Gidding" for the first time. Literature aficionados may be shocked to learn that I, a purported author, had made it through undergraduate and graduate education and at the age of thirty-three had not yet read one of the greatest poems in the English language. In my defense, I had long since gone through *Prufrock* and determined that Eliot was a great writer. However, it was only when I read "Little Gidding," the last of his *Four Quartets*, that I realized he had achieved something transcendent. I was utterly captivated by it, and in those dark hours of the early morning, as my son suckled at my breast, I read the poem to him, and the words were like holy water issuing from a sacred spring.

All these things were floating around my mind, flowing like streams in search of confluence. It was with the addition of the fourth element that they came together. I had been anticipating the release of Hilary Mantel's *The Mirror and the Light* for years. Long ago, I had been so fascinated with the story of Thomas Cromwell that I thought perhaps I should write something about him. Then *Wolf Hall* and *Bring Up the Bodies* arrived, and I knew it was the definitive fictional treatment of the subject. I loved Mantel's third novel of this Cromwell trilogy as much as the first two, but I felt increasingly tense as I approached the final chapter, knowing that the ax would fall. I listened to the last pages at something like four o'clock in the morning, holding my sleeping son in my arms. The account of Cromwell's death moved me, but there was something missing as I heard those final lines.

He is far from England now, far from these islands, from the waters salt and fresh. He has vanished; he is the slippery stones underfoot, he is the last faint ripple in the wake of himself. He feels for an opening, blinded, looking for a door: tracking the light along the wall.[59]

Stunningly beautiful, entirely fitting within the novel, and yet there was something missing. Perhaps it was found in the quote from Petrarch that Mantel includes immediately afterward: "For you perhaps, if as I hope and wish you will live long after me, there will follow a better age. When the darkness is dispelled, our descendants will be able to walk back, into the pure radiance of the past."[60] Yes, that was something closer to the mark. The confluence was happening within me, and the words were about to spring forth.

---

59   Mantel, Hilary. *The Mirror and the Light*, Kindle version (New York: Henry Holt and Company, 2020), 753.

60   Petrarch, *Africa* IX, as quoted by Mantel in *The Mirror and the Light*.

My third novel included scenes I had dreamed about for years, replaying them again and again in my head. I knew the general path it would take, but even halfway through the manuscript, I had not yet settled on an ending. But in the early hours of that morning, after my son was once again sleeping in his crib, I opened a note on my iPhone and typed out the heart of Lawrence's letter that closes out this novel. At last, it all made sense. Time, Death, Fire, Eternity, England.

> *"We shall not cease from exploration*
> *And the end of all our exploring*
> *Will be to arrive where we started*
> *And know the place for the first time."*
> — T.S. Eliot, "Little Gidding"

I first set foot in England in January 2007. I arrived at Gatwick Airport exhausted and fell asleep on the coach. Then I awoke to a vision of Oxfordshire—sheep grazing peacefully on rolling hills of green—and soon I was within the heart of Oxford itself and gazing upon the dreaming spires. It was everything I had imagined … minus the Carphone Warehouse.

As fate would have it, *The Eternal Queen*'s climactic scene takes place in that same city. The very river I strode along on my way to and from meetings with my tutor, where I saw swans and coots laying their eggs in spring, was the sacred stream on which Empress Maud ran. I did not know it then—there was so much I did not know. I wish that I had the same opportunity now to walk those streets and place my hand in that water. Perhaps I would know the place for the first time.

I remember walking into Salisbury Cathedral and coming to the grave of the Hungerford family, knowing that the bones that lay beneath the floor bore a genetic link with mine. That was the first time I lit a candle for ancestors, simply wishing to honor their lives rather than accomplish anything spiritual. In that moment, I realized I was part of England and England was part of me. I had never thought of myself as anything other than American, but my identity grew. I was American, but I was not *merely* American. I was also English in some strange way, not by birth or enculturation, but by the common bonds of history and love.

When I returned to the United States after completing my graduate study at King's College London, I felt a kind of grief. There would be no more cathedrals in my daily life. Raised in American evangelicalism, I knew nothing of consecrated churches or sacred spaces. This older mysticism has been replaced in the evangelical mind by the mysticism of internal emotion. But there is such an amazing sense of the spiritual in a cathedral: the work of generations of Christians raised in glory to God, the site where prayers have been whispered for hundreds of years. I feel something in them that I do not feel elsewhere. There are sacred places still in this world, and yet the transcendent is also accessible anywhere. As Eliot says, there are other places at the world's end. The intersection of the timeless moment is England and nowhere, which is perhaps to say everywhere.

The battles Maud fought, I am fighting for justice and recognition. Like her, I operate in a world dominated by men and too often filled with misogyny. I never wanted these books to be obsessed with gender, portraying Maud simply as a proto-feminist. But the patterns of the past repeat, and even as I saw the tide of injustice rising in my own day, I could not avoid this stream of Maud's life which added to her own confluence. So many things come back round in the end, but never in exactly the same way.

Upon this winding road I have walked as a pilgrim, through the great cities of the world and fields known to none but their owners. Here in the American Midwest, I had my own little piece of England that I returned to every time I worked on these books. I have completed the task now and am ready to move on, but England will always remain in my heart, as will Empress Maud. There are other battles to fight and other stories to write. I carry the great figures of the past with me everywhere I go, and I look to them for strength. The cloud of witnesses speaks, and I must train myself to listen.

A Few Final Words

"If the times be not just ..." This novel does not promote quietism, but patient endurance. Maud fought against injustice but was ultimately limited by the times in which she lived. The answer then is not to fight without hope, but to fight as one who believes in eternity. The one who believes in eternity waits upon a salvation to be revealed. That is why the Christian faith has so often appealed to the marginalized, the oppressed, and the disadvantaged. I would not want anyone to conclude from this story that abuse should simply be tolerated, but the reality is that the abused often have no champion but God himself.

As in my previous novels in this series, all scripture quotations are based upon the Geneva Bible translation, with occasional changes of wording to fit the style of this book. Extensive measures have been taken to minimize the number of words with origins subsequent to 1500 A.D./C.E. Some instances have no doubt been overlooked, and I admit a including few words for which I could find no equivalents of appropriate vintage.

Writing about Empress Maud has been one of the great honors of my life and a true joy. Thank you for coming alongside me on the pilgrim road. I am forever grateful for the trust you have placed in me, giving of your valuable time to read the story I have to share.

I am especially grateful for my story editor Kristina McBride and my copy editor Mark Swift, who returned to work on this project after also helping me with *The Forsaken Monarch.* I am a better writer because of you both. Julie Whitmer fulfilled one of my long-time goals by creating a map to accompany this book. Dr. David Crouch was kind enough to help me confirm the presence of Lady Mabel, Countess of Gloucester in the party that landed at Arundel in 1139.

Thank you to friends and family who encouraged me, especially my husband Jai who supported my decision to write. A project like this requires the commitment of more than one person. I am exceedingly blessed to be in a situation where I can write something like this.

Thomas Jaideep, I have dedicated this book to you. This is your family history. When you are older, I hope you will read, enjoy, and learn from it. My story of writing these books is inseparable from my story of becoming a mother, even as your story is inseparable from that of Empress Maud and the rest of your ancestors. I love you, I am proud of you, and you bring me great joy.

May God be glorified in these novels and all the works of my hands and heart.

With gratitude,
Amy Mantravadi

www.ingramcontent.com/pod-product-compliance
Lightning Source LLC
Chambersburg PA
CBHW050116030726
47505CB00007B/1901